"From alte[r] ... the wildest ... characters [...] pelling."

"Koch still pulls the neat trick of quietly weaving in plot threads that go unrecognized until they start tying together—or snapping. This is a hyperspeed-paced addition to a series that shows no signs of slowing down." —*Publishers Weekly*

"Aliens, danger, and romance make this a fast-paced, wittily written sf romantic comedy." —*Library Journal*

"Gini Koch's Kitty Katt series is a great example of the lighter side of science fiction. Told with clever wit and non-stop pacing . . . it blends diplomacy, action and sense of humor into a memorable reading experience." —*Kirkus*

"The action is nonstop, the snark flies fast and furious. . . . Another fantastic addition to an imaginative series!" —Night Owl Sci-Fi (top pick)

"Ms. Koch has carved a unique niche for herself in the sci-fi-romance category with this series. My only hope is that it lasts for a very long time." —Fresh Fiction

"This delightful romp has many interesting twists and turns as it glances at racism, politics, and religion en route . . . will have fanciers of cinematic sf parodies referencing *Men in Black*, *Ghostbusters*, and *X-Men*." —*Booklist* (starred review)

"There's a reason why this series is so popular and it's because there's nothing else out there in the universe like it." —Under the Covers

D0249869

DAW Books Presents GINI KOCH's
Alien Novels:

TOUCHED BY AN ALIEN
ALIEN TANGO
ALIEN IN THE FAMILY
ALIEN PROLIFERATION
ALIEN DIPLOMACY
ALIEN VS. ALIEN
ALIEN IN THE HOUSE
ALIEN RESEARCH
ALIEN COLLECTIVE
UNIVERSAL ALIEN
ALIEN SEPARATION
ALIEN IN CHIEF
CAMP ALIEN
ALIEN NATION
ALIEN EDUCATION
ALIENS ABROAD
(coming soon from DAW)

ALIEN
EDUCATION

GINI KOCH

DAW BOOKS, INC.
DONALD A. WOLLHEIM, FOUNDER
375 Hudson Street, New York, NY 10014

ELIZABETH R. WOLLHEIM
SHEILA E. GILBERT
PUBLISHERS
www.dawbooks.com

First Printing, May 2017
1   2   3   4   5   6   7   8   9

To the memory of my father-in-law, Douglas Vernon Cook, who taught his boys how to be wonderful men, husbands, and fathers, and taught me what it was like to have a great dad in my life for the last thirty years. We'll always love and miss you, Dad.

ACKNOWLEDGMENTS

This book crawled over the finish line, last and late. Lots of reasons, the biggest one being that my father-in-law was diagnosed and lost a fast and furious battle with cancer when I needed to be finishing up the book. As Kitty knows, life, and death, happens, and you can't necessarily stop it. Or not let it stop you for a bit.

I couldn't have finished this book without the incredible support of Sheila Gilbert, the most amazing and patient editor in the world, Cherry Weiner, the most supportive and protective agent in the world, Lisa Dovichi, the most dedicated critique partner and best friend there's ever been, and Mary Fiore, still the best and fastest beta reader in the West and the best mum, too.

Continuous love and thanks to Alexis Nixon, Kayleigh Webb, and the other good folks at Penguin Random House and everyone at DAW Books, especially Josh Starr and Katie Hoffman, for being amazing 24/7. Same again to all my fans around the globe, my Hook Me Up! Gang, members of Team Gini new and old, all Alien Collective Members in Very Good Standing, Members of the Stampeding Herd, Twitter followers, Facebook fans and friends, Pinterest followers, the fabulous bookstores that support me, and all the wonderful fans who come to my various book signings and conference panels—you're all the best and I wouldn't want to do this without each and every one of you along for the ride. (Yeah, I say that every time. Because it's true every time.)

Special love and extra shout-outs to: my distance assistant, Colette Chmiel, my personal assistant, Joseph Gaxiola, and my inventory manager, Kathi Schreiber, for figuring out how to create calm out of my rampant chaos and being my rocks when I need strength and my goofballs when I need laughs—you're all wonderful and keep me going far more than you realize; Edward Pulley for continually allowing me to steal Joseph away all the time with good grace and being willing to talk about whatever pop culture thing strikes me for hours on end; Brad Jensen, for helping at the drop of a hat and acting like I'm the one doing you a favor for it; Rhonda Moore and Al Barrera for doing such a great job of helping me with social media in 2016; Missy Katano, Edward Pulley, Kathi Schreiber, and Frankie O'Connor for using their strong Google Fu to become Team Research, thereby saving me tons of time and finding cool things I never would on my own, thereby making my books and stories all the better for it; Museum of Robots for making such awesome licensed products of my works every time I turn around and being awesome people at the same time; Shawn Sumrall, Amy Thacker, Joseph Gaxiola, Colette Chmiel, Jan Robinson, Craig & Stephanie Dyer, Koleta Parsley, Christina Callahan, Lynn Crain, Mariann Asanuma, Edward Pulley, Archie Bays, Anne Taylor, Terry Smith, Carol Kuna, Richard Bolinski, Duncan & Andrea Rittschof, and Chrysta Stuckless for fun, lovely, and delicious gifts that make the long nights and deadline stress totally worth it; Shawn Sumrall and Joshua Tree Feeding Program, for providing amazing prizes for my big Evening Erotica event year after year; everyone who puts in sweat equity with me at cons, especially Joseph Gaxiola, Kathi Schreiber, Brad Jensen, and Duncan and Andrea Rittschof; Slice of SciFi and editor Summer Brooks for giving me things to review so I still get out of the Casa, into the world, and continue to experience popular culture; Javier de Leon for once again being there and Robert Palsma for once again ensuring that he could be; Robert Palsma and Jan Robinson for still liking everything I do; Chris "Delicious" Swanson for awesome concert experiences and the hilarity of the Thor's Hammer Story; Scott Johnson for still having the best little B&B in San Diego and being a calm, supportive friend when things were going sideways; Michele Sharik and Brianne Lucinda for going long distances, and coming home from long distances, to see the me all the time; Adrian & Lisa Payne, Duncan & Andrea Rittschof, Hal & Dee Astell, Richard Clayton, and Dori Lovers for always showing up and making every event all the better for your presence; Oliver & Blanca Bernal for being family we got to choose; Eric and Jennifer Olson, for being there; Dan & Emily "Amadhia" King for constant love angel music, baby; the Authors of the Stampeding Herd—Lisa Dovichi, Barb Tyler, Lynn Crain, Hal Astell, Terry Smith, Sue Martin, Teresa Cutler-Broyles, Phyllis Hemann, Rhondi Salsitz, and Celina Summers—once again, our competition and your support kept me going, and I remain proud to pound hooves with every one of you (psst, buy their books);

author Sharon Skinner for being my road warrior buddy (psst, buy her books); and last but not least, Mumsy and Daddy for stepping up when we hit the panic button and giving me some desperately needed peace of mind.

Last only because that's where you put the best, thanks to my daughter, Veronica, and my son-in-law, Kenny, for being awesome all the time, and my husband, Steve, who was hugely supportive of all my writer stress, angst, and pressure while going through an incredibly tough time himself—you remain the best husband, father, and son in the world and I'm ever grateful that you're mine.

IT'S NOT EASY SAVING THE WORLD. Or worlds. Or galaxy, when you get right down to it.

And yet, I and my nearest and dearest seem to have to do it all the time. Some people vacation in Gstaad. Some people hit the yacht club. Some go out for dinner and a movie. We get embroiled in life-and-death situations involving crazed megalomaniacs, slimy politicians, and aliens of all shapes and sizes.

Of course, this is all because I'm married to the Alien of Aliens. Not only is Jeff the hottest thing on two legs—or any number of legs, really, since now I know a lot of aliens with a wide range of limb configurations—but he's also a born leader. Literally.

The surprises never stop coming for us. First, we got to discover that Jeff was part of the Annocusal Royal Family from the Alpha Centauri solar system, which was shocking since no one had ever shared that with him. Then we got to discover that, because he'd refused the crown on Alpha Four to return home to Earth, Alpha Four had just declared him the King Regent of Earth and called it good, again without sharing that with anyone else, like Jeff. They were kind of bossy that way.

And sandwiched in between these exciting royal facts was the "fun" of Jeff getting shoved into a political career he never wanted and then, due to those crazed megalomaniacs and slimy pols, becoming the President of the United States. And doing a bang up job of it, too, if you didn't mind that the President was kicking butt a lot more than his predecessors had. Hey, we might have been shoved into political careers, but you couldn't prove that any of our enemies noticed or cared.

Of course, that made me both the First Lady and the Queen

Regent, and the less said about how unprepared I was and re-main for both of those positions, the better. However, it came in handy when a ton of aliens were fleeing to Earth for protection and asylum. And I definitely represented, since my view of de-corum is that it's best left to others while leaving the kicking of butt to me.

Some people might be upset if the majority of the galaxy seemed to think they were The One for every girl fight around. But, as Joan Jett & The Blackhearts sang so well, neither Earth nor I care about our "Bad Reputation" throughout the planetary systems. Earth is considered the scrappy, nasty, vicious under-dog you should never count out. And I'm apparently considered the go-to girl for any alien looking for someone to stare down whoever's bullying them.

So, bring on the galaxy! We're not afraid!

Well, um, okay. Earth and I are, admittedly, a little afraid. I mean, we're great at the fighting. But we're not so good at the playing nicely with others. And that appears to be what's now expected. Save the day, instantly turn into the poster person for your planet. And Earth, as a planet made up of a fractious spe-cies that's spent the majority of its entire existence trying to kill itself, is not, necessarily, going to represent well in Galactic Po-lite Society.

Jeff carries it off perfectly, though. Because he was born to it with all that royal family stuff going on, and apparently the Force is strong with him on this one. I don't. Because I was, as Motörhead so perfectly puts it, "Born to Raise Hell."

In other words, I'm an Earth Girl, but I'll never make it easy.

CHAPTER 1

"**IT'S ANOTHER GREAT DAY** on *Good Day USA!*" the perky morning show host shared enthusiastically. "In our first hour we focused on all the new alien races we've gotten to know over these past few months." The audience dutifully applauded. "This next hour is going to be even better, though, folks. We can't wait, because we're just so excited to announce our next special guest!" More audience applause.

Didn't share any of their enthusiasm, but then again, I was the opposite of a morning person and was still wondering why I was awake at this hour. Also could not remember the host's name, which was because, in part, I was never up to watch these shows and, in other part, I was never up because I wasn't a morning person and therefore wasn't sure I currently remembered my own name.

She was pretty and Hispanic and that was all I was getting, because my brain didn't want to do any work beyond what my eyes were sharing. Was fairly sure her name started with a K, since that appeared to be a morning show requirement. My name started with a K, too. Perhaps, in another part of the multiverse, I was a morning show anchor. Though I sincerely doubted it.

Her handsome male cohost, whose name was also escaping me, nodded equally enthusiastically. He was perky, too. Obnoxiously so. "This is a guest everyone wants, who we're really proud to have been able to bring to our viewers first, because we go out of our way to start your days right! Don't we, Kristie?"

Bingo, and starting with a K. Now if I could only remember his name. The dudes' names didn't seem to have a letter requirement. Managed to remember that he was a former baseball player, so there was that. He reminded me a lot of the late

Michael Gower—big, bald, black, and beautiful, with definite charisma. The audience was clapping again. Was pretty sure there was a sign somewhere telling them to do so.

"We sure do, Adam!" Kristie said, still sounding amazingly perky. Hurray for the requirement on these shows to use your fellow host's name at least once every ten minutes. "You all know her as the First Lady of the United States. Coming out right now, here's Code Name: First Lady, Katherine Katt-Martini!"

Yes, that was me and, barring my being really lucky, I wasn't asleep and this wasn't a nightmare, at least, not a sleeping one. There were a lot of hells that politics had put me into, but none worse than this—being a guest on a morning talk show.

As the audience clapped themselves into a frenzy and I was gently shoved forward toward the stage by my so-called friends, I once again asked myself and the greater cosmos why anyone had thought this was a good idea. And also who hadn't shared with Kristie and Adam that I never wanted anyone to refer to me as Code Name: First Lady. Whoever it was would be receiving a very nasty talking-to whenever I got out of here.

Wasn't walking forward with the right amount of enthusiasm, and I knew it, since the stage manager hissed, "Move it!" to me. So much for the idea that being the FLOTUS got you any respect backstage.

Either he'd heard the stage manager or he was used to some guests not being thrilled to be on the show, because Adam jumped up out of his seat, trotted over to me, and escorted me to mine, potentially earning my lifelong love and adoration. He settled me into my so-called chair that was a lot more like a barstool with a back. I wasn't tall, so it was a little awkward. Of course, Kristie wasn't that tall, either, and she was making it work.

"Missus Martini," she said, beaming and perky beyond belief, "thank you for joining us on *Good Day USA!*"

"Happy to be here," I totally lied. "And please, call me Kitty."

She and Adam exchanged thrilled glances. I sincerely doubted they were as excited as they looked. They were the top morning show in the country, and they hadn't gotten there by being dull to watch. And on the morning shows, reactions were Broadcast with a Capital B.

"Thank you . . . Kitty," Kristie said, sounding as thrilled and perky as she looked. "Gosh, we have so many questions for you, don't we, Adam?"

"We do!" Perk, perk, perk. These two were the King and Queen of Perkiness. "Kitty . . . gosh, I can't believe I get to speak to you so informally, Kristie and I have been prepping questions nonstop since you agreed to come onto *Good Day USA!*, and now that you're here, I'm so excited that I just can't remember half of them!"

Prayed that these two weren't going to expect me to provide both questions and answers, because, if so, this program was about to go way down in the ratings. But a response seemed expected. "Um, that's really sweet of you to say."

"Isn't she great, folks?" Kristie perked at the audience, as if I'd done an Oprah and just given everyone a car.

The audience applauded hysterically. There had to be a sign somewhere telling them to do so, but I couldn't spot it from my vantage point of trying not to look at anyone or anything while still appearing poised and confident. Was pretty sure I was failing at all of it.

"Kitty, what's it like to be a human and yet part of the American Centaurion population on Earth?" Adam asked, apparently having managed to remember at least one of his prepared questions. He'd traded perky for inquisitive. So at least there was that.

"It's great. The A-Cs are wonderful people."

"They're stronger and faster than us, aren't they?" Adam asked. "And better looking, too."

"Well, yes." The A-Cs had two hearts, which meant they could move so fast a human couldn't see them, and they were also super strong. I felt that hyperspeed was the better of the two, but I wasn't going to complain about the extra strength, either. They also had extremely fast healing and regeneration, which was a huge bonus for those in active and dangerous roles. And, as Adam had said, they were all, to a person, gorgeous, representing every skin tone on Earth and every body type, too, as long as the term "hardbody" was applied as well. "But I don't think you have anything to feel inadequate about, Adam."

This earned me wild applause from the audience and some women whooped their approval. Adam looked flattered and a little embarrassed. So, presumably I was doing okay. As long as they didn't ask if I had any A-C bells and whistles, we were good. Because I did, and no one wanted me talking about it.

Due to the mother-and-child feedback that had happened when I'd been pregnant with and given birth to our daughter,

Jamie, I'd reverse inherited the A-C super strength and hyper-speed. I'd also gotten a talent, and one that wasn't normal for A-Cs.

Talents didn't go to every A-C, but they got talents far more frequently than would seem statistically normal. Jeff was an empath—in fact, due to being given Surcenthumain, aka the Superpowers Drug, by some of our enemies, he was likely the strongest empath in the galaxy. Empaths felt emotions, everyone's emotions, all the time. They had ways to block the emotions, but still, they were walking lie-detectors, among other things.

Imageers had been more powerful before our enemies had introduced a virus that successfully muted their powers. Done, most likely, to prevent Jeff's cousin, Christopher White, from discovering who our late, great enemy, the Mastermind, had really been. Before that, though, imageers could not only manipulate any image but they could read them, too, the pictures making a copy of mind and soul as well as the body, at least as Christopher had explained it.

There were also dream and memory readers, but that talent was extremely rare. The third most common power, however, was also the one that got the least amount of respect—troubadours. This power was all in the voice, expressions, and body language. In other words, perfect for actors and politicians, which was why it was looked down upon by most of the A-C population. Of course, what most of that population hadn't realized was that it made troubadours incredibly powerful and totally stealth.

However, my talent was none of these. My talent was being Dr. Doolittle. Thankfully there wasn't supposed to be an animal segment on today's show, because the chances of me having a chat with said animal would be high. I couldn't help it—animals liked to talk to me.

"What's it like to be married to an A-C?" Kristie asked, bringing perky back.

Well, at least these were softball questions, so I had that going for me, though I'd have rather been listening to Justin Timberlake bringing "SexyBack." But what I wanted and what I got were not always one and the same.

Of course, had to make sure I censored my reply, because, as far as I was concerned, the number one best part of being married to my husband was Jeff's bedroom prowess and regenerative abilities, and I knew beyond a shadow of a doubt that no one wanted me sharing that with anyone, let alone the largest morning show viewership in the world.

"Wonderful. Jeff is a wonderful husband and father, just like he's a wonderful leader." I was using the word "wonderful" too much. But this wasn't my element and six in the morning really wasn't my time zone, and despite everything I was still having trouble focusing. "I'm always proud of him because he always does what's best for his people."

"Do you mean for American Centaurion, for Centaurion Division, for the American people, or for the world at large?" Kristie asked, sadly trading perky for this show's version of hard-hitting. "He *is* the King Regent of Earth for the Annocusal Royal Family, who control all of the Alpha Centauri system, isn't that right?"

"That's right. And I mean for all of them. Jeff's always been focused on protecting the people of Earth when he was in and then the head of Centaurion Division, even before he became a Representative, let alone the Vice President or President."

Managed not to say more about the whole King Regent thing, in part because that made me the Queen Regent and in other part because Jeff was working really hard to ensure that the Earth governments remained at least somewhat stable. It was a very interesting time to be on Earth, but I didn't want to share that with the cast, crew, and viewership of *Good Day USA!* if I could possibly help it.

"What's it like being Queen Regent?" Adam asked, destroying my hopes of the conversation going elsewhere.

"It's fine. I'm more focused on the duties of the Office of the First Lady and my family." Thanked Jeff's Chief of Staff, Rajnish Singh, for drilling that line into me. Of course, Raj had been the one who'd arranged this little shindig, so my mental thanks were only halfhearted. Raj was a troubadour, so to him, this wasn't a Stress Test of Horror, it was just a great way to keep Jeff's approval rating high.

Kristie and Adam both looked at me expectantly. Apparently more of a response was expected. "Um, sorry, but honestly, I'm a little nervous. This is my first time on TV."

This earned me huge belly laughs from Kristie, Adam, and the studio audience. "Oh, isn't our First Lady just a hoot and a half?" Adam asked the crowd.

I'd been told there were two large TV screens where the

audience could see them, and there was also a smaller one in front of the stage, where the hosts and guests could watch whatever footage the show was airing, so that actors would know for sure what scene from their latest movie or TV show was being touted and therefore react accordingly. Hadn't spotted this before, but Adam and Kristie stopped grinning like the Joker and Harley Quinn and both looked ahead and sort of down.

Followed their lead, found the screen, and saw that it had images on it. Images of me.

CHAPTER 2

THERE I WAS, in my pink linen suit, taking down what looked like a terrorist six years ago. The start of Operation Fugly and my new life, really.

"I'm just amazed you were so brave on the spot," Kristie said as everyone watched me slam my Mont Blanc pen into someone's back.

In real life that had been a superbeing, and I'd put the pen into the jellyfish-like thing on its back, between its wings, into what I later found out was a parasite, at least as far as Centaurion Division was concerned. I'd discovered what parasites really were during our last fun frolic with world- and galaxy-ending danger, but that wasn't important now. Ah, the good old days, when Christopher and the Imageering team were able to change images on the fly. Missed those days. A lot. I wouldn't be here right now if those days hadn't been taken away from us.

"I'm just amazed that anyone ever buys linen," was the only thing I could think of to say. "Seriously, I didn't sleep in that suit, it just looks like it."

This comment earned roars of laughter from the studio audience, Kristie, and Adam. Apparently my role was to keep it light and keep things funny. Go me.

The scene shifted. Now we got to see me giving the eulogy for Michael Gower at the end of Operation Infiltration, which I still considered our darkest day. This wasn't a funny moment, and I was relieved that no one was laughing. We didn't stay on this too long, thankfully. But what we moved to made me cringe inside.

Sure enough, there it was, the impetus for all the Code Name: First Lady crap. I was on a Harley, Jeff was in a helicopter, leaning out to grab me off said Harley. It looked like an action scene out of any movie you'd care to name.

"So," Kristie said, as the screen went blank and she turned back to me, "as we've seen, you've been on television a lot."

"Not intentionally."

Adam chuckled. "I need to ask the question that's foremost on everyone's minds, Kitty. When is Code Name: First Lady going to hit the screens?" Well, at least he wasn't asking me about being Queen Regent anymore.

Hoped I had a poker face firmly in place. "I really think that's a joke, not something that's seriously being considered by anyone." This was a lie, because, sadly, I knew it was something that was being heavily pursued by at least one Hollywood studio.

We'd managed to keep Code Name: First Lady from being created only by applying a great deal of political pressure and using the old "for the good of the nation" speech a lot. Didn't feel like going into that here, though.

Kristie shook her head. "We know it's not a joke. And, let's be honest—it's what the people want, to see a movie about all you and your husband have done to protect the world." At this, the studio audience started cheering. Tried not to hate them a little. Failed.

"Well, I honestly don't know that it would be that interesting."

Kristie and Adam both snorted, then turned toward the screen again. Managing to once again not wince, I turned toward it, too.

This time they had my "get it together, you jerks" speech from Operation Immigration going, when I was addressing the conclave of religious leaders and hadn't known I was going live to the world. On the plus side, I looked totally in charge. On the negative side, this was, admittedly, interesting. Chose not to ask why, if they had archival footage, anyone would want to see a dramatic reenactment, because I wasn't stupid and I knew why—it was fun.

We were treated to this for a while, then the picture changed again. This time, the video showed something recent. Very recent. As in, last week recent.

Jeff and I were sitting at the front of the General Assembly of the United Nations. Normally we wouldn't have been in there unless we were addressing the UN. And, in that case, we'd have been waiting in a nice antechamber until it was time to go on. However, due to the problems that a whole bunch of aliens unexpectedly arriving had created for Earth in general and us in particular, there we were. Operation Immigration continued to pay dividends in terms of putting me places I didn't want to be.

We were up front and center because the Secretary General had decided the U.S. would get the prime seats at that Assembly. We weren't in the official delegates' chairs, but were sitting behind America's delegation, where support staff normally hung out. The chairs were far less comfy than the ones the delegates had, but that wasn't the issue. No, the issue was that my Official First Lady Color of iced blue matched the fabric of these chairs perfectly. So perfectly that it looked like my disembodied head was floating near Jeff's shoulder, since I was in a long-sleeved dress, versus a suit, for this particular shindig.

The audience tittered, and I couldn't blame them. Would have made a comment, but the sound was going and people onscreen were talking.

"It is a historic day for our countries, our world, and our galaxy," the Secretary General of the United Nations said, sounding really excited. Wondered if he'd gotten his start on a morning show. "Not only are we inducting several new sovereign nations into our ranks, but we are also officially joining the greater galactic community as Earth and the Solaris System become a part of the Aligned Worlds of the Milky Way Galaxy."

This earned a lot of applause both onscreen and from my live studio audience.

"After much worldwide deliberation," the Secretary General went on, after the applause in the General Assembly had died down, "the United Nations has reached a unanimous decision on who will represent Earth's positions within the Union of Aligned Worlds. I am pleased and proud to announce that Katherine Katt-Martini has agreed to represent Earth and all of her interests!"

More wild applause from the screen and the studio as we watched me walk carefully up to the podium and start my address. At least I looked like a normal person again, since the carpet and walls were not matching my dress and making me fade away like the Invisible Woman.

Thankfully, the video feed stopped. "How exciting is it to be representing Earth in the way you are now?" Kristie asked.

"I'm happy to do my part for my country and my world."

"Did you have to campaign hard to get the position?" Adam asked.

"Um, no. Not really." Not at all. Actually, I'd done everything in my power to abdicate the responsibility. But when the majority of the world and religious leaders say, "you da girl," it's hard to say no. Not that I hadn't, but I'd been overruled. By everyone.

Kristie laughed. "I'm sure you didn't. I'd want Code Name: First Lady to represent us, too!" Chose not to respond, which sort of worked out. "So, can you tell us about the Reptilians? I understand one was the Matron of Honor for your wedding."

Managed not to blink at this sort of left turn. "Um, they're great?"

Kristie looked at her notes. "Oh, and you had a Feliniad and a Canus Majorian in your wedding as well?"

"Um, yes. Yes, I did. And a Free Woman."

"What I believe you call Amazons, is that right?"

"Yes. Um, they don't mind. It's kind of a compliment." At least, Queen Renata of the Free Women always seemed okay with being compared to Wonder Woman's kith and kin. And her daughters, Rahmi and Rhee, who'd been sent to stay with me in a sort of Boarding School for Those Who Will Be Kicking Butt way just before Jamie had turned one, were also just fine with being called Amazons.

"I'm sure they don't!" This woman's perkiness knew no bounds.

Morning people were not my people. I was only still upright because the chairs were designed to kind of hold you up without appearing to do so and because I'd hooked my heels over the top rung of the stool portion so I couldn't slide off. At least, I hoped I couldn't.

Might have been upright, might have been talking, might have been hella uncomfortable, but what I wasn't was really conscious. I'd been awake for at least three hours, but those were hours far earlier than I normally managed to drag out of bed, and I was running on a form of autopilot with my main focus being keeping my eyes open. Felt a yawn trying to claw its way out and clamped my jaw. Meaning I couldn't say anything.

My silence was noticed. "So," Adam asked, "what are they like?"

Yawn abated! Now I wasn't sure what we were talking about anymore. "Um, the Amazons? Or the Reptilians? Or the others?"

"Any of them or all of them!" Kristie said. "And all the other aliens you've met, too! You're living a life of such excitement!" Perk, perk, perk. This woman needed to tone down the perk or someone needed to smother her.

Pondered my reply. It was probably not a great idea to share that Reptilians were basically giant lizard people I called Iguanodons, that the Feliniads were Cat People, and that I called the Canus Majorians the Major Doggies. I might have been barely conscious, but some form of self-preservation was working. Went with my go-to answer whenever someone wanted to ask about the glamour and wonder that were alien life-forms.

"They're people. Just like us. I mean, they don't look like us, in that sense, but they're pretty much people."

"Well, the A-C's on Earth aren't all that much like us, now, are they?"

Did not like where this was going. "They're a lot more like us than not, honestly. There are differences, of course, but the people of Alpha Four of the Alpha Centauri System are more like us than not. More like us than the Reptilians, for example, at least in terms of external appearance."

"Speaking of their appearance, what's it like to be married to President Martini? Did you always know he was bound for greatness?" Kristie blinked her eyes. Wasn't sure if this was a coded message or what.

Would have liked to have known what the code was, because this was a boomerang question, since I'd thought we'd covered this already. Managed not to either say that my husband was the hottest thing on two legs or ask her why she thought talking about the President's Hotness Level was an okay question, but only because I'd had enough coffee in the greenroom which, as it turned out, was not actually green. Just barely enough, but enough.

Went with basically what I'd already said. "Well, Jeff's always been a leader, since before I knew him. So him advancing as he has wasn't at all surprising to me."

Kristie nodded and blinked her eyes. "What are the aliens like?"

"Um . . ." Looked to Adam for assistance. "Which ones? I kind of thought I'd answered that. I mean, I assume you guys have footage of the various different races that are on Earth. Sort of thing."

Adam looked worried. "Kristie, you asked that already, hon."

"What are the aliens like?" she asked again, still sounding perky. And she blinked again.

"Ah, maybe we should go to commercial?" Adam asked, looking around for some kind of direction.

Might have been tired, groggy, and unhappy to be here. Might have been potentially the least interesting FLOTUS interview of all time. But what I wasn't was stupid or all that forgetful.

"What! Are! The! Aliens! Like?" Kristie perked, eyes blinking like mad.

And I groaned, as I unhooked my heels from the rung on the chair and slid to my feet. "Seriously? Not again!" Then I tackled Kristie to the ground.

CHAPTER 3

IT WAS A TOSS-UP—whether she was an android or a Fem-Bot. My money was on Fem-Bot, but I never ruled out android. Or clone. Or some other fun combination. She was definitely stronger than I'd expect your average female morning host to be, even if she worked out.

"Clear the set," I shouted to Adam. "She's going to explode!"

Had to hand it to him, and perhaps it was the athletic training, but Adam didn't question. He leaped up and started shouting for people to evacuate.

Meanwhile, what I was going to consider the Kristie-Bot—until such time as android or clone was proven—and I were tussling. Strong though she was, she wasn't fighting all that hard or all that well—either she had a major glitch going or her whole purpose was to blow up around me. Which was par for my particular course.

But she wasn't blowing up.

Not that this was a bad thing. I mean, I didn't *want* her to blow me up, let alone Adam, the studio audience, the crew, or the set itself. But I'd now tackled this Fem-Bot on live television and something needed to happen.

While we rolled around on the floor, considered if this was, in fact, her robotic job—make me react and look horrifically bad to half of the population of the United States. If so, she was spot on and I'd fallen for it. Big time.

Meaning I had to prove this thing I was fighting wasn't a human. Ripping her head off seemed the easiest way, but I wasn't sure if I wanted that shown on national TV, either. And what if she was an android? Those had what looked like blood inside. And if she was a clone that would be even worse.

Noted that the studio audience hadn't left. Also noted that we were still being filmed, meaning the cameramen and the rest of the crew also hadn't left. Nice to see how seriously they took this. Of course, it probably looked like the First Lady had lost her mind, and lots of people enjoyed a chick fight, so them all sticking around made sense. Though not if the Kristie-Bot exploded. Then them all sticking around would just make a tragedy.

Adam was the only other person reacting in what I felt was the appropriate manner, not that anyone was paying attention to him or listening to his advice to clear the area. Of course, everyone was here to see or put on a show, and that was definitely what I was doing at the moment.

Before I could decide what to do, a man ran out from backstage. He was vaguely familiar, but I was pretty sure I'd never met him before. He was handsome in sort of George Clooney-ish way.

He spoke quietly to Adam, who nodded, then both men came over to me and the Kristie-Bot. The man I didn't know reached down and pulled me up and off of the Kristie-Bot and Adam helped her up. She wasn't blinking anymore. She was standing there smiling.

The man who pulled me up let go. Then he started clapping. "Isn't she *great* folks? Kitty, thank you, and Kristie, thanks for being such a good sport. Code Name: First Lady is going to be amazing, folks, and you've got that as a guarantee from me, Jürgen Cologne!"

The audience went wild, screaming and cheering. The Kristie-Bot took a bow. I managed to keep my jaw from dropping.

The reason he'd reminded me of George Clooney was because he was literally being billed as the "next" Clooney in looks and talent. He was also a quadruple threat—actor, writer, director, and producer. Well, at least I now knew who I was "fighting" in terms of Code Name: First Lady. Pity that this man tended to get his way, usually through charm, smarts, a really strong will, and greater-than-average perseverance.

Cologne went on. "Now you can see why we're trying so hard to make the First Lady star in her own movie. She's a natural!"

More wild cheering from the studio audience. Decided that I hated each and every one of them. Forever. Potentially not as much as I was going to hate Cologne, though.

"Back after these messages," Adam shouted over the din. And this time, the crew actually did as requested and stopped filming. Or at least, stopped the feed to the network.

"I believe I speak for Adam as well as myself when I ask what the hell is going on?" Realized the mics were turned off, too, for which I was exceedingly grateful. Figured Raj had something to do with that.

I'd directed this question to Cologne, but he'd turned away from me and motioned urgently toward the curtains the upcoming guests hid behind. My Secret Service and Field agent protective details raced out, along with my personal driver and bodyguard, Len Parker and Kyle Constantine. The five Field agents surrounded the Kristie-Bot while the Secret Service moved Adam away from her and nearer to me and Cologne. Len and Kyle flanked me.

Manfred, the troubadour who was the head of this detail, had a small Organic Validation Sensor in his hand and he ran it all around the Kristie-Bot. The OVS looked like the wands they used at airports and concerts to do polite searches for metal and other unsavory things. But the OVS had been created to help us identify who was a real living being and who was not.

Manfred was behind the Kristie-Bot, and he nodded to the other Field agents on the team. Daniel and Marcus, who were both empaths and, therefore, bigger than Joshua and Lucas, who were imageers, each grabbed one of the Kristie-Bot's arms. She didn't struggle. At all.

"Emotions," Daniel said.

Marcus nodded. "Plenty of them."

"So, she's an android, not a Fem-Bot?" Just wanted to be sure and all.

"I'm better," the Kristie-Bot said with a smirk.

"She's dangerous, whatever she is," Len growled softly.

"She's on the borderline," Manfred answered. "Could be human with a lot of surgeries, could be a clone, possibly an android that doesn't have as much internal inorganic as the first generations did. Unlikely to be a Fem-Bot—they rate higher on the nonorganic scale."

"Whatever she is, she's going to explode. I realize she hasn't yet, but I also realize that—"

"She was sent to discredit you," Cologne finished. "We figured that out backstage." He shot me a megawatt Hollywood smile. "That's why I came out." He looked at the Kristie-Bot.

"You have a choice. Try to self-destruct and we'll get rid of you. Or tell us who sent you and we'll help you."

She smirked again. "I'm the most popular morning host in the country, which means in the world. You can't do anything to me."

Manfred, meanwhile, had run the OVS over Adam. "Fully human," he said quietly to me. "Eighty-seven percent organic."

"I have a hip replacement," Adam said. "And I'm doing my best not to freak out, but we'll be back from commercial soon and I really wish someone would tell me what's actually going on."

The Kristie-Bot shrugged. "I don't plan to 'self-destruct,'" she made the air quotes sign, "at all. I plan to go back on the air and finish our show." She smiled sweetly at me. "And now we can discuss how the First Lady really wants to make her movie."

Looked at Cologne. "Is this some horrific, elaborate ruse to get me on board with the whole Code Name: First Lady thing?"

He shook his head. "No. I was coming on to try to convince you on-air to give the movie the green light."

"So, you were trying to, what, blackmail me to give the okay?"

Got another shot of the megawatt smile. "Oh, I wouldn't put it quite that way." His smile faded and he turned back the Kristie-Bot. "What's your game?"

She batted her eyelashes at him. "I want you to hire me."

We all stared at her.

"Back in thirty," someone called from offstage.

"Um, come again?" I asked, for everyone within ear- and eyeshot.

She rolled her eyes, then smiled at Cologne. "I want to be in Code Name: First Lady. As one of the stars."

CHAPTER 4

WITH THAT BOLD CAREER demand sitting on the air, the
Kristie-Bot turned and went back to her chair.

"Ten seconds," the dude called. "Adam, get to your seat!"

Adam shot me the "what now?" look. Didn't feel we had a
lot of choice. "Um, I guess, the show must go on. And all that."
Looked to Manfred. "Do the fast fade, gang."

My security teams unwillingly disappeared behind the curtains offstage—mostly because Raj ordered them to in no uncertain terms—while Adam, Cologne, and I scurried to our chairs.
We were seated just in time.

"And . . . we're back!" the Kristie-Bot exclaimed gleefully,
mics all live to the world again. "Folks, wasn't that just the most
exciting thing? Adam, I'm sorry we didn't let you in on what we
were doing. Jürgen wanted to have you show a normal person's
reaction to the First Lady's kind of action!"

Had to hand it to her, she was back in form as the Perkiest of
the Perky. And I was now completely wide awake, so decided to
count that as one for the win column since I doubted I was going
to get more tickie marks over there any time soon.

"Ah . . ." Adam seemed lost at sea. I was with him in the life-
boat that was probably leaking. "Yeah. That was . . . exciting."

Realized I had no idea if I was supposed to have been "in" on
the "fight scene" or if I was allowed to share that I'd been clueless. Decided that, as my unwilling public appearances went,
this was definitely going to go down as the worst of the worst.

Thankfully, Cologne spoke up before I could. "That's the
kind of action I like to bring to the movie screens." He started
talking about his movie career and, thankfully, Adam and the
Kristie-Bot let him. I didn't come up, so I sat there doing my

best to look interested while I listened with one ear for cues that I'd need to speak and focused on what the Kristie-Bot really might be.

She'd been around too long to be a new alien race we didn't know about, barring her being the sole survivor of her race, which seemed unlikely. So that meant the choices were pretty much only Made From Scratch Android, Willing Android, Fem-Bot, or Clone With Benefits. Unwilling Android was not a choice—the unwilling ones tended to have real problems discussing their lack of being fully human, to the point of normally self-destructing.

Speaking of unwilling, two of our Top Gun Navy Pilots, Joe Billings and Randy Muir, had been partially androidized, very much against their will. We'd saved them before the full process—thin wires being inserted into their heads and bodies via some advanced scientific and alien means—had finished. However, we couldn't remove the wires, and Joe and Randy were now both more like the *Six Million Dollar Man* than regular human dudes. This was the most recent method of android creation we knew about, though I never put it past our enemies to come up with new and improved ways to do evil. But if I had to bet, if Kristie was an android, she'd gone in for the New Wiring Method.

We did have androids made from real, living people who'd had most of their human innards removed and robotic insides put in. We had two of these still alive and working with us—Col. John Butler and former Vice Presidential nominee Cameron Maurer. In both cases, we'd barely managed to keep them from self-destructing when they'd realized what they were, but we'd been able to shut them down and remove their self-destruct mechanisms.

Charles Reynolds, who was my best friend since ninth grade and also now the Director of the CIA, felt there were probably more androids like this out there, and Chuckie was pretty much never wrong. But so far, we hadn't found them.

Of course, an androidized clone also wasn't out of the question. But before I could consider that, or any other possibilities, a question was tossed to me.

"Beg pardon?" I'd been able to tell it was a question for me, since everyone was looking at me. My ears had heard the sounds, but my brain hadn't comprehended the words those sounds made. "Could you repeat the question?"

The Kristie-Bot smirked at me. Decided she was staying the Kristie-Bot regardless of what she turned out to actually be inside because she really bugged me and I refused to choose another moniker for her therefore. "We want to know which one of Jürgen's movies is your favorite. If you can remember."

Well, lucky me. Jeff was big into old TV shows, so I was well versed in those, and I'd seen lots of movies when I'd been younger, of course. But, while we hit the occasional movie, we didn't get a lot of opportunity these days, and the White House theater was being used for alien- and space exploration-type things more than entertainment.

So I hadn't seen a lot of his movies, but I'd seen some. One in particular, and I'd loved it. Made very early in Cologne's career, but that might hopefully play in my favor. "I'm a big fan of *Revenge of the Broccoli*."

Cologne snorted a laugh. "I think that makes you that movie's one and only fan."

"Dude, it was hilarious. I mean, there was no budget, and the script was meant to be sort of dumb, but all of you were acting your fuzzy little hearts out and it's great for what it is. Satire at its finest. Sort of thing."

Cologne gave me what looked like a genuine smile. "It's nice to know that someone appreciated that movie. Makes all the negative reviews sting less."

"As I well know, everyone's a critic. As long as you're doing the best you can, for the right reasons, no one else's opinion should matter."

"And that's why you're currently the most popular First Lady we've had, potentially ever," Adam said.

"Huh?"

"Oh your poll numbers are very high," the Kristie-Bot said. "You must know that."

"I honestly don't pay attention to stuff like that." Mostly because I didn't want to start my days depressed, angry, or wanting to hide under the covers. Call me a worrywart. Or, rather, a realist.

Adam grinned. "Well, it's true. The people love you."

"And I love them right back." Risked my life enough to protect them, after all. I'd better feel some sort of love.

This earned me a big round of applause as we cut to another commercial. All this mental contemplation and verbal gymnastics had given me a headache. Wondered if I could score a Coke and some Advil, but doubted I'd get that lucky. The not-really-greenroom was only for when you weren't on camera.

Opened my mouth, but Adam beat me to the punch. "Again, I want to know, what the hell is going on?" Thankfully, again, the mics were off, so we weren't sharing this with the studio audience.

"I do, too," Cologne said, to the Kristie-Bot. "Why did you do what you did? Blackmail?"

She shrugged. "It was effective."

"She's not a human, at least not a full one," I reminded everyone.

She rolled her eyes. "Human, alien, android, Amazon, giant slug—ultimately, what's the difference?"

"Usually homicidal tendencies and really nasty attitudes."

The Kristie-Bot laughed. "That's what makes us kin, so to speak. Some of the aliens are pacifists, but humans aren't, and you know it." She flexed her shoulders. "Some of us can see the advantages of taking the next step in terms of evolution."

"Androids can't evolve." Of course, no sooner were the words out of my mouth than I realized they were wrong. Presuming that the Kristie-Bot was, in fact, an android, and also presuming she'd willingly become one in the past few months, then, depending on how you looked at it, she'd evolved. In fact, realistically, androids were evolving at a faster pace than any other life-form on the planet. "You can't reproduce."

She heaved a sigh. "Really?"

Again, realized I was wrong. Cloning meant that you could create a version of yourself, raise it, then shove wires into it and make it "better." And Stephanie Valentino was hiding out at one of Late Semi-Great Madman Herbert Gaultier's old production plants, and we were pretty sure she'd copied if not stolen all of the Mastermind's information. Plus, she was being helped by the same person who'd helped her great-grandfather become the First Mastermind. And this kind of thing was right up the Tinkerer's alley.

I saw the future, and it was looking very much like the end of the world as we might know it, only without Michael Stipe's comforting twang sharing that we should feel fine about it. At least, presumably, unless it was Cool Bands Week at *Good Day USA!*, which I was fairly sure it was not.

Forced myself not to ask for someone to spin R.E.M.'s Greatest Hits and instead focus on the horrifying matter at hand. "So, you're now an android and all jazzed about it?"

She smiled. "I see nothing wrong with looking young and beautiful forever."

"Don't you think that'll be, um, noticed? After a while, I mean."

The Kristie-Bot looked right at me. "No. Because, sooner than you think, there will be plenty of us. This is the greatest thing in the world. Better, faster, stronger, and never aging. Seriously, who wouldn't say yes to that?"

"Not enough people," I had to admit.

"Back in thirty," someone called.

"Why do you think this will make me want to cast you?" Cologne asked. "In anything, let alone Code Name: First Lady?"

She gave us all a hard, cold, smug smile. "If you don't, I'll tell everyone that the fight wasn't pretend, that you all forced me to act like it was for the movie, but that, in fact the First Lady is a homicidal maniac."

CHAPTER 5

"WHO WOULD BELIEVE THAT?" Adam asked, sounding completely sincere. Decided he was indeed earning my undying love. Sadly, however, knew he'd be in the vast minority.

Cologne and I looked at each other. Heaved a sigh. "Honestly? I'd bet on everyone, on this planet and any other you'd care to name."

"Back in ten," we were advised.

"Share that I've got a part in the movie," the Kristie-Bot said calmly, as she plastered her Perkiest of the Perky Smile back onto her no longer fully human face. "Or else it's the FLOTUS is a homicidal maniac for the win."

"Better her in the movie than me."

Cologne snorted a laugh as we and our mics came back on.

"Welcome back to *Good Day USA!*" the Kristie-Bot said, perk at eleven on the one-to-ten scale. "We're here with the reason for Code Name: First Lady, Katherine Katt-Martini, and the man who wants to bring her exciting story to the big screen, the utterly talented Jürgen Cologne!"

She looked at Adam, who managed to lurch back into standard formula. "We sure do! Kitty, Jürgen, what's the Code Name: First Lady timeline?"

"Ahh . . . that's not really up to me." Hey, when in doubt, go with the truth. None of this was my responsibility.

Jürgen shared the megawatt smile. "We're still getting the cast set."

Decided that the most likely way to salvage this horrible situation was to do what the Kristie-Bot wanted. I didn't like acquiescing to my enemies, and anyone blackmailing me was an enemy. However, that didn't matter at the moment. It was time to cowgirl up and take a big one for the team.

Shot the cameras a beaming smile. "Honestly, Jürgen, if you're looking for talented actors who are also attractive enough to portray A-Cs onscreen, I think you should consider Kristie and Adam both."

The Kristie-Bot looked pleased, Adam's jaw dropped, but Cologne shot me a look I wasn't expecting—he looked impressed. "Kitty, that's a great idea." He turned to the hosts. "So, Kristie, Adam, what do you say?"

"Oh my gosh! Jürgen, Kitty, that's such an exciting offer!" Had to hand it to the Kristie-Bot—she was selling that this was the first time the subject had come up. "If you really mean it, I'm totally in!"

"Ah . . . me, too," Adam managed. He shot me the WTH look.

Patted his knee. "Adam, I just feel like you're going to be perfect." And I wanted someone around who knew the real Kristie before and after her presumed android transition. Couldn't say why, but I'd learned to never argue with my gut. Turned to the audience. "Isn't that right, folks? Adam's totally handsome enough to play an A-C."

The audience shared its agreement, and again women whooped. Adam looked bashful and flattered, which made him even more attractive. Yeah, Adam was definitely the right guy to play either Michael Gower or his older brother, Paul, in the movie. That I was now somehow enthusiastically involved in the planning of this film was a nightmare I was choosing to actively ignore.

"I agree," Cologne said. "I think it's going to be a *Good Day USA!* when we start filming Code Name: First Lady!"

The audience cheered and the conversation turned to moviemaking and all that jazz. I didn't have a lot to add in here, but made sure I was paying attention, just in case. We didn't discuss the Kristie-Bot's Delicate Condition during the remaining commercial breaks because we all went into the audience to shake paws during these. No one seemed averse to touching me, no one seemed about to explode, and a few of the mainly female audience members even gave me Atta Girls. Chose to toss this into the win column, just 'cause.

Mercifully, the last hour of this three-hour marathon came to a close. We'd seen many clips from Cologne's movies, a few more clips of me being Action Chick, talked a little bit about my Second Best Lady Cause that had transitioned to be my FLOTUS Cause, then Cologne gave everyone in the audience free passes to his current movie release, so the show ended on a high note.

Ripped the mic off as soon as possible. "I want to share that the President will want to be speaking with the three of you in the most urgent way possible. Today, most likely." Hadn't heard from Jeff, or anyone else, since my phone wasn't allowed to be with me when I was "on," but I knew my husband was watching this fiasco and therefore was going to send out an Executive Order sooner as opposed to later.

Raj joined us. "Yes, he does." Sooner for the win. "Under the circumstances, we need you to come with us right now," he said to the Kristie-Bot. "Under heavy guard."

She shrugged. "Again, none of you need to panic. I'm not going to blow myself up. That's not why I got the treatment."

"What do you mean, the treatment?"

She rolled her eyes at me. "The treatment that made me the best version of myself possible."

"You know, did you ever actually watch *Death Becomes Her*? I ask because that movie had quite the moral."

"You mean the brilliant moral of don't turn into a zombie?" she snapped. "I'm not. I'm better. I don't need to worry."

"I'll bet," Cologne muttered under his breath. "I'm happy to do whatever the President wants," he said to Raj.

"Me, too," Adam added. "Will we go with Kristie or Kitty?"

"Neither," Raj said. "You gentlemen will be going straight to the President. The First Lady has a tight schedule, but she'll join you later in the morning." Raj looked at me. "The President won't be alone."

Meaning that Chuckie would be with him, and probably Alpha Team as well. At least, that was my hope.

Shocking me, though it shouldn't have, Joe and Randy arrived. "Hey Kitty," Joe said. "Len called us in. We're here to handle certain situations."

Randy took one of the Kristie-Bot's arms. "She won't give us any trouble. Guaranteed."

The Kristie-Bot seemed unfazed. "You two look great." She smirked at me. "They won't be aging, either."

"We might," Joe said calmly. "We were saved from completion."

She sniffed. "Whatever. You're alive and well and look great. You're excellent publicity."

Raj and I exchanged the "oh really?" look. "Just who's advertising what?" he asked.

"Doctor Rattoppare. And she's advertising her skills."

I was many things. A wife and mother. A former marketing manager. The former Head of Airborne for Centaurion Division. The former Head Diplomat for American Centaurion. The First Lady of the United States. The Queen Regent of Earth. But I was first and foremost two things—my mother's daughter and Megalomaniac Girl. Meaning it was time to flip on my cape and make the leaps that were why we were all alive and I'd been sent here to spend three hours in hell.

"Is the doctor's first name Stephanie?"

Stephanie was Jeff's niece, the eldest daughter of his eldest sister, who'd been married to Clarence Valentino, aka one of the main A-C traitors we'd dispatched, finally, during Operation Sherlock. Stephanie had turned to the Dark Side years ago, in no small part because of her father's influence. Only Clarence had been a follower, and Stephanie was definitely a leader. She'd also been one of the Mastermind's special girlfriends. And she'd betrayed him because some adages never went out of style. Stephanie was the poster girl for hell hathing no fury like a woman scorned.

"Yes. Her grandfather is also a doctor and a part of the practice."

Time to take another leap. This one was even easier. "Trevor Rattoppare?"

The Kristie-Bot nodded. "They're both geniuses."

Cologne snorted. "They're tinkers? And you felt safe having work done?"

Looked at him. "Why would you ask that?"

"The name translates to 'likes to tinker' in Italian."

Decided that, movie I didn't want made or not, Cologne had just moved himself onto the team. Trevor had taken the last name that fit what he did the best. Interesting that he'd chosen the name, though, because I'd nicknamed him the Tinkerer well after that alias would have been established.

But then again, this was my skill. There wasn't a crazed evil genius or wacked-out megalomaniac I couldn't find the love with. Nice to know that, once again, I was batting a thousand.

"Your last name means perfume to most of this country," the

Kristie-Bot replied. "Does that mean we should expect your fragrance line, or that you smell extra special?"

"Per some women, I do," Cologne said with a grin. "However, we're not discussing me."

"No, we're not. Where are the good doctors working?"

The Kristie-Bot smiled slowly. "If you can find them, you can get treatment. I'm sure you're going to need work soon to keep your husband from straying. Someone that handsome has women throwing themselves at him constantly. Someone that handsome and powerful? Everyone's willing to do whatever they need to in order to get his attention. And, let's face it—someone as willing to get into a fistfight as you are isn't going to stay reasonably pretty for too long."

Wanted to let my fists clench, but didn't want to give her the satisfaction. Due to my enhancement, I healed fast and pretty perfectly. All A-Cs did, after all. But that wasn't relevant to what she was insinuating. And, in some ways, she wasn't wrong.

Jeff was the classic—tall, with dark wavy hair, beautiful light brown eyes, a big and broad body that didn't quit, and the best smile going. And I knew many women, and some men, threw themselves at him all the time.

However, a good marriage wasn't built on jealousy and distrust, at least not on my side of things. Jeff was the King of Jealousy, which was rather flattering. Jeff could have had pretty much anyone, and he'd chosen me. I hadn't lacked for offers, and I'd chosen him. A-Cs professed that they mated for life, and from what I'd seen, this was actually true.

But none of that mattered in this situation, because my marriage to Jeff wasn't the issue. The Kristie-Bot was trying to antagonize me. And she had no real reason to do so. She was getting what she wanted, after all, and I'd helped sell that on live television. Meaning there was, as always, more going on. Not a surprise, but there was more going on with *her*, specifically.

Stephanie hated me, and this sounded a lot like what I'd expect from her. After all, the Mastermind had cheated on her, even though Stephanie was a Dazzler—my private name for female A-Cs. So far, I'd never met a Dazzler of any age who wasn't a total hottie. And yet the Mastermind had slept with plenty of other women, including those who weren't nearly as young and beautiful as Stephanie.

So, that meant that it was likely that the Kristie-Bot was either programmed to dig at me this way, or else Stephanie had asked her to do it. Either way, that meant that there was more to the Kristie-Bot situation than just an actress wanting to remain viable for as long as inhumanly possible.

"Keep her on ice until I'm able to be there," I said to Joe and Randy. "That's an order. No one questions her without my being present. Including the President and whoever's with him, and whoever thinks they're going to be questioning her before I get there."

"Yes, ma'am, Commander," Randy said, as he and Joe both hit attention. This was the flyboys' way of letting me know that they knew we were in an action situation, even if it didn't look like it. Wondered if the other three flyboys were nearby or if they were on standby at the White House. Didn't matter. They'd ensure that what I wanted happened.

"What threat do you actually think I represent?" the Kristie-Bot asked with a disparaging laugh.

"No idea." Stepped up so we were nose-to-nose. "But I can guarantee this—I'll find out, and I'll stop it, before you're able to hurt anyone or anything. That's a FLOTUS promise."

CHAPTER 6

WE FINISHED UP at the *Good Day USA!* studio with Joe and Randy and my A-C security detail taking the Kristie-Bot to a secured room in the underground part of the White House Complex, Raj taking Adam and Cologne directly to Jeff and whoever he was with, and Len, Kyle, and my Secret Service detail taking me to my next scheduled appointment.

This was all done via gates, which were A-C technology that allowed the movement of life-forms and/or goods by passing through what looked like airport metal detectors. The gates let you go thousands of miles in seconds, though the payoff, for me at least, was total nausea. They were able to send you from planet to planet, too. So far, I'd managed to avoid space travel in that way, for which my stomach was truly thankful.

But *Good Day USA!* filmed in New York and we all had to get back to D.C., so we used floater gates—less visible to the naked eye than the stationary ones, but no less nauseating—and were back in the nation's capital within seconds.

Meaning I was finally in a supposedly safe haven—the Offices of the First Lady—surrounded by my loyal staff who would never willingly turn themselves into androids. I sincerely hoped.

Of course, safe was a relative term. Safe from evil morning show hosts, Hollywood movers and shakers, and potential android attacks—probably yes. Safe from being force-fed information I was never going to remember when it mattered—definitely not. Because the next appointment on my schedule wasn't with the public. No, it was time for Kitty Goes to Diplomat School 2.0.

Team commiseration about my latest media fiasco had been

brief—everyone knew me well enough to know that I'd been dragged out of bed far too early today to have a lot of patience for being berated. Besides, berating would happen later, of that I was sure. Probably in the Large Situation Room, or the LSR. With many frowny faces staring at me. I was scheduled to be in there at eleven, after all.

"Okay, Kitty—which solar systems are our closest allies?" Vance Beaumont, my Chief of Staff, asked, once the Secret Service had left for more interesting locations and I was alone with my torturers. Vance was one of those people who always looked like he'd just stepped out of the pages of *GQ*, had been a Washington Insider for years, and was married to the head lobbyist for Big Tobacco, Guy Gadoire. We'd started off as enemies, but somehow, Washington had worked its special kind of magic, and Vance was now my Right Paw in the White House.

Chose not to contemplate if Vance would be all for never aging and instead tried to come up with the right answers. "Alpha Centauri, Sirius, Tau Ceti, and . . . um . . . hang on . . . I have this . . ."

"Sloths and lemurs and lots of Y's in their names," Colette Alexis, the troubadour who was my Press Secretary, whispered.

"Stop helping her," Vance said sternly.

"Someone has to. I don't know why you're leaping onto this without us even having a snack." The Green Room Breakfast had been long, long ago. "Um . . . Yggethnia?"

"Got it in sort of one," Vance said, sarcasm knob already at eight on the one-to-ten scale. "And I'm 'leaping in' because you're here late. We were supposed to have started at eight-thirty, and it's close to nine."

"That's me, totally prepared. And pardon me. Did you schedule in a surprise potentially android attack?"

"Great on your preparedness." Vance didn't make this sound great, but I was already used to that by now. "And no, we foolishly didn't plan for your usual life to hit during the morning show. Next time, we'll be more prepared. So, what do you do if a representative of Bajooram challenges a representative of Themnir's right to speak?"

"There will, please God, not be a next time. And I suppose saying 'The nice slugs have the floor' is out, right?"

This comment earned me a lot of different looks from my staff. Vance shot me a long-suffering look. Colette looked supportive. Len and Kyle were trying not to laugh. Abner

Schnekedy, who was my Chief Decorator and Floral Designer—
because I was doing my best to not waste taxpayer dollars—was
trying not to look pained.

As with Vance, I'd met Abner in the most miserable of my
D.C. experiences—the Washington Wife class. Abner was married to Lillian Culver, the top lobbyist for the defense industry
who'd wisely chosen to keep her maiden name for business. And
also as with Vance and Gadoire, I'd started out as enemies with
Abner and Culver and yet, somehow, they were also now hugely
loyal friends we relied on. Things like this never ceased to
amaze me.

"Kitty, it's not the Washington Wife class," Abner said, right
on cue, but as gently as he could manage.

"No. Frankly, it's worse. At least the Washington Wife class
had an ending time."

"Dear," Mrs. Nancy Maurer, who was my White House Social Secretary and the Head of the Graphics and Calligraphy
Office that I still wasn't sure why we needed in this day and age,
said with far more gentleness than Abner had managed, "perhaps you need to stop resisting this so very much. It might go
easier that way."

Cameron Maurer was her son. We'd saved her and then him
during Operation Defection Election, and that had, as was so
often our way, meant that the Maurers were now a part of our
extended family.

"That whole spoonful of sugar helping the medicine go down
stuff only works in Disney movies."

"Oh, look what's on TV!" Elizabeth Jackson exclaimed, in a
tone of voice that indicated she was totally doing this to save all
of us from this situation. This was but one reason I loved Lizzie
like a daughter.

Due to the overall way my life rolled, somehow I'd gotten a
teenager assigned as my ward, in a very Batman and Robin kind
of way. Thankfully she was a totally awesome kid. And she really did make a great Robin, in no small part because she'd been
adopted by the remaining member of Team Assassination and
one of my go-to men on Team Tough Guys, Benjamin Siler. He
and Lizzie were known as the Vrabel Family to the rest of the
world due to a variety of factors, Lizzie's parents having been
murderous traitors, Siler being a semiretired assassin, and our
myriad enemies only being three of those reasons.

Normally Lizzie wasn't hanging out in my office, the First

Lady Duties tending to be too boring in her, and my, view. However, I wasn't the only one being forced into schooling I wasn't excited about, and Lizzie was hanging out in the hopes of convincing me to keep her schooled in the American Centaurion Embassy instead of going to school outside of our particular confines.

She was turning up the heat on this one in part because the kids started school tomorrow. Why they were starting on a Wednesday instead of a Monday was beyond me, but Vance had said there were good reasons and I'd chosen to believe him.

Lizzie wasn't the only one not wanting to leave the Embassy School and Daycare setup. Even Mrs. Maurer's grandkids, Chance and Cassidy, didn't want to go to "regular" school anymore. Had no idea if Sidwell had some sort of bad Kid Underground rep the rest of us had missed, but never had I seen so many kids so unwilling to go school. Of course, maybe they were looking at me as their role model, meaning I might have to pretend to enjoy this learning a little more. Later. Right now, something on television called.

We all turned gratefully to the TV screen while Lizzie dutifully turned up the volume. "In an unprecedented move," the Serious Newscaster shared, "the United Nations has voted to include flags representing not only American Centaurion, but also New Themnir, Free Lyss, Nova Netu, and the Galactic Freehold."

True to expectations, the majority of the aliens who'd fled to Earth during Operation Immigration were sticking around. The Vrierst were looking at moving to Jupiter, but for the time being had declared their little patch of Siberia to be their new homeland, and Russia had nicely acquiesced to having Nova Netu be within their confines, separate but equal, just as the A-Cs were in the U.S. and elsewhere.

The Galactic Freehold was what we were calling all the ragtag remains of alien life that the Yggethnian Jewel of the Sky and the Faradawn Treeship had managed to rescue on their way out to our neck of the space boondocks, along with any aliens from stable planets who just wanted to hang out on Earth because they liked it here. These, like Free Lyss, were actually staying on American Centaurion and U.S. soil, nestled nicely in the Arizona and New Mexico deserts, with some overlap into Mexico, which that country, like Russia, had kindly allowed.

The Galactic Freehold had originally intended to stay in the

Middle East, but due to a couple of major factors, had moved to the U.S.

"The Intergalactic School opens this Wednesday," the Serious Newscaster went on, sharing one of the two big reasons the Galactic Freehold had chosen a different location. "President Martini will be on hand to greet the students for the inauguration of Earth's first school dedicated to educating all our new population from different worlds."

The Intergalactic School was situated pretty close to the Dulce Science Center in New Mexico. Despite its size, the A-Cs had built it in less than a week, because hyperspeed remained the coolest superpower ever. The school buildings went up three stories and were connected underground, where they went down six stories, which was the A-Cs taking one for the team by letting the kids see the sun now and again. A-Cs were, at their cores, burrowers. Most A-C Bases had one floor on ground level and the rest went down many stories. Some started below ground. They didn't look like gophers, but they sure acted like them.

The school was wider than the Science Center, at least as far as I could tell based on the video, though not nearly as dull and institutional-looking, which was nice, and despite being in the middle of the desert, the grounds had been turned into lovely desert-appropriate landscapes and such. I hadn't spent much time there—my kids weren't going to go there, I'd had plenty to do while it was being planned and built, and architecture wasn't my thing. I wasn't against it, and I could admire a cool building as much as the next girl, but my input wasn't needed. I'd given the "make sure it's as safe as the rest of our Bases" command and that was the extent of my involvement.

"I'd be willing to go there," Lizzie said. "So would the other kids."

"You're getting to go to the best school in, literally, the world," Vance replied. "You'd think all of you would appreciate that just a little bit more than you're managing."

"The alien kids will be interesting," Lizzie countered. "New worlds, new histories. We could help Kitty by learning all about them."

"I appreciate the support, don't think that I don't, but, right now, you're going to Sidwell as planned." Of course, Jeff was going to have to be at the Intergalactic School instead of being able to go with me to take our kids to Sidwell. Yet another "these jobs suck" moment for us. There were a lot of those included in the POTUS and FLOTUS gigs.

"However, one serious question remains," the Serious Newscaster went on. "Why are the children of the President not attending the Intergalactic School? The school American Centaurion has both created and is managing?"

CHAPTER 7

"**T**HEY'RE GOING TO SIDWELL because we don't want them murdered or kidnapped," Vance muttered. "And we want them educated in ways that ensure they know how to handle this planet."

The camera turned to the Serious Newscaster's coanchor, the Intent Chick. After this morning, I was just relieved neither one of them seemed perky. "Well, per what we've learned about the Intergalactic School, it's doubtful that human or even A-C children would get the education they need there. The school is focused on allowing all the alien races to learn about their own planets' histories. Some Earth history will be taught, along with present-day galactic politics, but it does make sense for the President's children to school in a normal American school."

"Wow, someone's on our side? How did *that* happen?"

"Not all media is against you, dear," Mrs. Maurer said, as the Serious Newscaster and Intent Chick chatted back and forth about Education In America. "Though I can see the advantage for the children to learn about the other planets in our galaxy as well. By the way, you have a message from King Raheem. He called while you were at *Good Day USA!* and did express that he wanted you to call back as soon as you had a moment."

"Why didn't anyone mention this earlier? I see no reason for my having kept Raheem waiting."

"Because you need to be prepped for your new role in the Galactic Council more than you need to exchange recipes with *Raheem*." Vance was up for covering jealousy duties if Jeff wasn't available, which was nice, in a weird way.

"Raheem is the King of Bahrain, one of our now-closest allies, a dear friend who helped us literally save the world and the

galaxy, he has his staff send his recipes directly to Chef and
Pierre and vice versa, and no amount of prepping is going to
matter."

"That's true, in a way," Abner said. "Remember how you told
me she handled the King when they first met? Washington Wife
Best in Class all the way with that."

"True," Vance said slowly. He gave me the hairy eyeball
look. "But you could only do that because you'd heard all the
information, even if you only pulled it up under extreme duress."

"Stop selling her short," Len said.

Kyle nodded. "Kitty can handle anything."

"Dudes, I appreciate your support. And Vance, you guys have
been barraging me, Jeff, Raj, Colette, Richard, and a host of
others with this information for months now, in preparation for
what the damned UN chose to make official this past week, despite my hoping to be overlooked as the Galactic Council Rep
O' Choice. I've heard the information. I'm sure it's lodged in my
brain somewhere. But unless I'm supposed to go be the principal at the Intergalactic School along with everything else on my
plate, I honestly think I've got all that I'm going to get."

"Isn't responding to foreign dignitaries part of your job as
First Lady?" Lizzie asked, radiating innocence.

"It is." Vance shot a glare at Lizzie. "As we all know you well
know."

"None of us fell for the Innocent Approach," I added. "Just
so you know, the person you should hone your Teenaged Con-
ning Skills on is my mother. If Mom falls for it, then you're
good to go."

"I was only trying to help and to point out that Kitty's first
duty is to the Office of the First Lady," Lizzie said virtuously.
"You try to help and they complain."

"Get used to it, that's how things tend to roll." Went to my
desk and picked up the phone. D.C. still believed in landlines
and I wasn't going to argue with that kind of protocol, mostly
because it meant everyone might stop trying to teach me things.
"Going to call Raheem now. Please bicker quietly amongst
yourselves."

This earned me resigned looks from Vance and Abner,
amused looks from Len and Kyle, and Atta Girl looks from Mrs.
Maurer, Colette, and Lizzie. Decided I'd stick with Girl Power
and ignore the dudes for a bit.

King Raheem of Bahrain had been our guest last month.

He'd stayed in the Lincoln Bedroom, though his entourage had bunked over at Blair House, where all foreign dignitaries went. Raheem and I chatted regularly, as well—going through much of Operation Immigration together had definitely bonded us. I even had him on speed dial on my cell phone as well as the White House landlines.

He answered right away. "Ah, Queen Katherine, thank you for returning my call. How are you?"

There were so many ways to answer that question. Went for the most comprehensive. "As well as can kind of be expected, King Raheem. And why are we being so formal? Is everything alright?" Maybe Raheem was in danger and was trying to pass a secret message.

"Yes, all is well, but I saw the television show and in case you were not alone or on speakerphone, I felt a formal greeting was best."

"Gotcha. Nope, no speaker, with my normal staff and, for me, this was, sadly, business as usual."

He chuckled. "I look forward to knowing what's going on when you're able to share it with me, Kitty. However, that's not why I called earlier."

"Okay, Raheem, and good to know. I have to debrief the President and such before I can share, but be sure that you're using that OVS we gave you liberally and constantly."

"Interesting. I will ensure that it's always about my person."

"Do. Trust me, do."

"I always trust you. Which is why I needed to speak with you. Wasim will be arriving shortly. While he can stay at our Embassy and we have procured an apartment for him staffed with retainers we can rely upon, I would like to request that he stay with you until he acclimates."

Ran this over in my mind a couple of times. "Wasim is coming here?" Had no idea who Wasim was. Could not, for the life of me, remember meeting anyone named Wasim. Not that this meant anything. I barely recognized A-Cs I'd known for years now, and the less said about my ability to name most of the Secret Service agents and White House staff the better. I could have met this Wasim many times, but if so, he hadn't registered.

"Yes. We have decided that it will be best for him to be schooled in America."

"Gosh, can't argue with that mindset." Raheem wasn't giving

me much here, other than the fact that Wasim was of school age, which meant anywhere from kindergarten to advanced college degrees.

"Exactly. And I believe it will be helpful for him to have a friend already." And now Raheem was giving me exactly nothing. Fantastic.

"Um, yes?"

"Yes. Your ward is, I believe, only a year younger. Wasim will have a car, so he will be able to drive them both to school."

My brain scrambled quickly. There was no way Siler was going to allow Lizzie to be driven to school by a teenaged boy. Jeff wouldn't, either. My parents would also put their feet down, Mom's foot in particular. And I also wasn't an idiot. Teenagers and cars were a dicey mix, particularly a teenaged driver who was just coming to America.

"Oh, um, frankly, no. The kids will take gates or they'll be driven in our really secure cars." This was a safe response. Lizzie, as my ward, was given the same security level as the rest of our family was—a tonnage.

Raheem chuckled. "Wasim's car will be as safe as yours, trust me. I would not allow my beloved grandson or any of his friends to be in danger, particularly your ward."

Finally, the clear statement of familial relationship. "I can't remember, is Wasim your eldest grandson?" I honestly had no idea, but eldest or youngest seemed like the best bets and Raheem wasn't really all that old, so went with what I hoped was the best guess.

"Yes, he is, and see? You remembered perfectly."

"Go team. When does he arrive?"

"His plane has landed, and Ambassadress Nejem and her retainers have retrieved him at the airport. If they may bring him right over, that would be best."

"Sure, absolutely. I'll be happy to see Wasim, and Mona and the others, too."

"Wonderful! I truly appreciate your allowing Wasim to be a part of your family."

"Um, happy to? Also, if he's sixteen, why did you rent an apartment for him? Shouldn't he stay at the Bahraini Embassy? For safety and supervision?"

"Wasim is a Prince of Bahrain and will comport himself properly."

Managed not to say that Wasim was actually a teenaged boy, and the idea of proper comportment and a teenaged prince with a car and a place of his own didn't mix. "Good to hear."

"Your ward will have no worries about Wasim doing anything inappropriate until such time as they are good, close friends, and only as the relationship progresses appropriately."

Opened my mouth but no words came out. Managed one sound. "Ahhhh . . ."

"Excellent. At any rate, I need to advise the Ambassadress that she is to bring Wasim to the White House, so I must end our call. Thank you again, Queen Katharine—the Kingdom of Bahrain appreciates the kindness of the Annocusal Regency."

And with that, he hung up.

CHAPTER 8

MY MOUTH WAS STILL HANGING OPEN. "What is it?" Lizzie asked, sounding worried.

Managed to slam my jaw shut. Hung up the phone. Then turned to face the rest of the room. Everyone was looking at me with worried expressions.

"Dear?" Mrs. Maurer asked. "What's wrong?"

"So many more things than were wrong only yesterday."

"That doesn't sound good," Colette said.

"Care to elaborate?" Abner asked. He had a point. Why not share the horror with everyone?

"Um . . . as I understand things, Raheem's sixteen-year-old grandson is about to arrive on our doorstep. He has a room at the Bahraini Embassy and also, apparently, an apartment somewhere in the city, but Raheem wants him to stay with us until he acclimates."

"Excuse me?" Kyle said.

"There's more. Wasim has his own car as well. And, I think he's registered at Sidwell. because Raheem insinuated that Wasim could drive Lizzie to school."

"The hell he will," Len snarled.

"How the hell did he get in there last-minute?" Vance asked. "I have the entire student body roster, as well as faculty and staff listings, and no one from Bahrain was on the lists."

"His grandfather wants him there? That's all I've got for you."

"Why would he want to?" Lizzie asked. "Either send this Wasim kid to Sidwell or have him drive me to school?"

"Oh, dear God," Abner said. "He's trying to arrange a royal wedding, isn't he?"

"I think so, yeah." Always nice to know that Abner was pretty much as smart as the rest of my staff and associates.

"Wedding with whom?" Lizzie asked. We all looked at her. "Oh, hells to the no! I'm not getting married to some spoiled rich kid I don't even know!"

"Prince," Vance corrected. "He'll be a prince. And if we insult this teenaged prince in any way, then the tenuous peace Kitty's managed to force the Middle East into will shatter, because there are still factions there looking for reasons to freak out."

That there were. Because the other reason the Galactic Freehold had chosen to live on American Centaurion land in the U.S. was that the most anti-alien lunatics on planet Earth, aka Club 51 True Believers, had somehow not only infiltrated the Middle East but had moved their entire base of operations there. They were instigating whatever hatred they could—be it religious, xenophobic, homophobic, misogynistic, racial, or anything else they could think of—and sadly they'd found fertile ground. Just as most of the people of Earth had banded together to be better than we'd been before and enter a brave new world of galactic interaction, the extremists had also made their own love connections, and Club 51 True Believers were still in action, albeit underground.

"Speaking of freaking out, I cannot even imagine Lizzie's father's reaction to this." Frankly, I could imagine it. Siler was a trained, expert assassin. The reaction was easy to extrapolate. "Let alone Jeff's." Jeff was hugely protective of Lizzie and he wasn't above Berserker Rage. "Or my dad's." My father would go into a protective lecture mode of epic proportions. "Though my mom's reaction will definitely, hands down, be the worst." Mom might kill Wasim with a look. Mom *could* kill Wasim with a look. Wondered how I was going to prevent Wasim from being murdered by the people Raheem had sent him to for protection while simultaneously keeping his mitts off of Lizzie.

"We'll handle him," Kyle said darkly. Len nodded his agreement. Both of them had put Lizzie firmly into the Little Sister Category. They might actually be higher up on the Threaten To Dismember Any Boy Who Looks At Lizzie food chain than Jeff.

"Probably not a good idea," Abner said worriedly, clearly sharing my "don't kill the kid" mindset.

"Your mom will handle it," Lizzie said, sounding relieved. She had her phone out and was texting like mad.

"Who are you talking to?"

"Nana Angela." Yeah, Lizzie got to call my parents by their Grandparent Names. "I figure it's better to tell her first, versus my dad."

"Wise choice?"

"I'm also letting Aunt Amy know." Amy Gaultier-White was one of my two best girlfriends from high school, and married to Christopher. Who, as I thought of it, was probably going to be right in line after those players previously named to terrorize any boy looking at Lizzie.

"Why?"

"She has insights. Like, she said not to tell Uncle Christopher yet."

"Oh, good to know." Tried not to let this hurt my feelings. Kids didn't always go to their mother with issues, and while I wasn't Lizzie's real mother, I was in that role. So what that she wanted insight from my mother and bestie, versus from me? Jamie probably would, too, as she got older. Did my best not to feel depressed. Failed.

Lizzie looked up at me and grinned. "You have insights, too. And, I'll want them. But I can tell that you're freaked out and Aunt Amy probably won't be. At least not as much. And if she is, I can't tell from her texts."

"I was just not prepared for this. You're just a kid. I mean, you're our eldest kid, but still. You haven't even started really dating yet." Because our lifestyles hadn't allowed for it. Felt bad and like a real failure as a surrogate parent of any kind.

She tossed her head. "Dating's fine when I want to do it, but right now, we've got way cooler things going on. Some rich prince isn't going to get to me. Remember, I'm the one who kicked butt at my last school. For all we know, I already kicked this kid's butt. But if I haven't, don't worry—I can and I will."

"Good to know."

"Besides," she said with a shrug, "he's probably not even cute."

"We can but hope," Abner muttered.

"You can't kick his butt," Vance said. "Unless he makes one single move on you that you don't want. Then, kill him, and we'll figure out what to do." Good to know that Vance had also moved himself onto the Lizzie Protection Squad.

Mrs. Maurer cleared her throat. Which got our attention. "I think you're all overreacting just a bit. We are talking about a young man who's been sent across the world, away from his family and friends, to go to a strange school in a strange country. I'm sure he's no more excited about his grandfather's matrimonial attempts than Elizabeth is. Perhaps if we greet him as what he truly is—an exchange student—things will go smoothly. Or more smoothly than currently being imagined."

Colette nodded. "I think killing him would be a last resort and by last I mean only if it turns out he's an evil android or similar. And even then, my recommendation wouldn't be to kill him." She looked at Lizzie. "Decide if you like him for him once you know him. But he *will* need a friend. It's frightening to come into a tight group and try to find your place. Having someone who's there to help you adapt is a wonderful thing. If it leads to romance, then it does. But friendship is, many times, far more important."

"But if he does anything inappropriate, breaking his arm isn't out of the question." Hey, that was advice Mom was going to give, because she'd given it to me, Amy, and our other bestie, Sheila, when we were in ninth grade. Might as well beat her to the punch on this one.

"That's what Nana Angela said." Lizzie waved her phone at me. "She said that she's proud that this is freaking you out."

"Um, excuse me?"

Heard the door open and turned to see my mother coming into the room. "I'm pleased that you're having maternal reactions, kitten, that's all."

"Thanks. I think."

"So sensitive."

"You tend to give me reasons. At least some of the time." Mom came over and gave me a hug. "Mom, thanks for getting here so fast." Hugged her back. Things were always a little bit calmer with Mom in the room, less than stellar feelings about my parenting skills notwithstanding.

"I was already on my way, kitten." She let go of me and hugged Lizzie. "The Office of the President wants to get your debrief sooner as opposed to later."

"That's nice, but they have to wait." Quickly explained what was going on in terms of Wasim's arrival.

Mom heaved a sigh. "Why am I not surprised? However, what I *am* surprised about is that weren't given the heads-up about this."

Had to agree. "Yeah, I haven't heard a peep from Mona, or from any of the Israelis, either."

"And Mossad didn't advise me," Mom added, sounding slightly pissed.

That she was taking messages from the LSR to me or that she expected Mossad to contact her wasn't because my mother was a meddling busybody who was shoving herself into all our affairs. Rather it was because she'd written the book on counterterrorism and was, as it had turned out, the head of the clandestine and very kick-butt Presidential Terrorism Control Unit. She'd been running the P.T.C.U. for far longer than I'd known about it, and far longer meant decades. She reported directly into the Office of the President, and had for at least three administrations before my husband had assumed office. Every other government agency that dealt in any form of security, CIA and FBI included, dotted-line reported into her as well.

My mother was also the only non-Israeli, non-Jew to ever be in the Mossad. And she was, from all I'd gathered and seen over these past few years, highly regarded by current and former Mossad agents and treated as the living legend you didn't mess with. She was treated like the woman who could kill you six ways from Sunday by everybody else.

The Israeli Diplomatic Mission had several Mossad agents on staff, and we were close friends with three of them, who were, in turn, close friends with Mona Nejem, the Bahraini Ambassadress, and her bodyguard, Khalid. That neither Oren, Jakob, nor Leah had contacted us about this new wrinkle in all of our lives was just as weird as the fact that Mona and Khalid hadn't.

The com came on. "Excuse me, Chief First Lady, but you have visitors requesting entrance." Walter Ward, who'd been the Head of Security when we were living in the American Centaurion Embassy, now had the same Eye in the Sky role at the White House. He technically reported up to Malcolm Buchanan, whom Jeff had appointed as the official Head of White House Security, but Buchanan was mostly hands-off with Walter, because Walter had proven himself far more often than the rest of us usually managed. He was also a slave to titles.

"Hey Walt, if it's Mona and her entourage, send them right in."

"Ah, it's not the Bahraini Ambassadress, Chief First Lady. Or anyone else that's on Mister Buchanan's Automatic Entry list."

"Malcolm has an automatic entry list?"

"He does. He said to tell you, when you asked, that it's a far shorter list than yours. However, the Bahraini, Israeli, and Romanian Diplomatic Missions are all on that list."

"Huh. We'll compare lists later, I guess." Pondered this and heaved a sigh. "Who is it that wants to see me who is also clearly *not* on Malcolm's Fast Pass list?"

"Someone who's also not on your list, Chief First Lady. Ansom Somerall is waiting for entry at the main guard station."

CHAPTER 9

ANSOM SOMERALL WAS the Chairman of the Board of Gaultier Enterprises. At one time he, Quinton Cross, and Janelle Gardiner had been a Gaultier triumvirate dead set against Amy's desire to take control of her late father's company and turn it away from evil.

But Cross had been felled by the Mastermind's supervirus during Operation Epidemic and, once her protector was dead, Somerall had turned on Gardiner. We'd found and saved her from becoming God alone knew what during Operation Madhouse. But not before Somerall and his new cronies had created a Fem-Bot version of her.

Gardiner was under Mom's protective custody and literally hiding away from the world. She was running her side of things both business and personal via Amy, of all people, but her life was pretty much one of being hidden nicely, which sucked. She wasn't our friend, but by now she wasn't exactly our enemy anymore, either.

Amy was, therefore, assigned a protective detail to rival my own whenever she ventured out of the Embassy. Our enemies had really done a lot to cramp our styles, and none of us liked it.

Somerall was also the leader of the "let's get Lizzie" team. Apparently the kids Lizzie had taught severe lessons to at her last School For Gifted Minors were all related to a lot of international movers and shakers, most of whom were friends or friendly with Somerall and the rest of those whom I called the Dealers of Death—those lobbyists who handled all the bad things and, therefore, the bad people who ran those bad things.

Somerall had tried to get me to give Lizzie up to them when she'd first arrived during Operation Epidemic, and hadn't given up hope despite having literally no success. Perseverance was a virtue, so he had at least one.

"So, I suppose we can't just shoot him and pretend we were confused about who he is?" I asked the room in general.

"No," Mom said regretfully, "that's not an option. Besides, we're still tracking down what's going on between him and the NSA."

We'd discovered a Fem-Bot Factory and more at an NSA black site during Operation Madhouse. Sadly, we hadn't been able to find the people who were really responsible. I mean, we knew that Somerall and Talia Lee, the chief lobbyist for the fire-arms people and Gardiner's former bestie, were behind it. We just didn't have concrete proof, or the name of who at the NSA had chosen to go to the Dark Side.

"Should we get Lizzie out of here?" Colette asked.

"I'm not afraid of him," Lizzie snarled.

"We won't let him touch you," Len told her.

"True on both counts, but that doesn't mean we shouldn't be cautious." Considered our options while Vance showed his phone to Mom. "Walt, what are the odds I can say that he doesn't have an appointment and so I'm not able to see him?"

"He's not alone, Chief First Lady. Talia Lee is with him." Think of the Devil and she appeared.

"Neither of them have an appointment with the First Lady," Mrs. Maurer said.

"Anyone else with them, Walt?"

"No. They were dropped off by a limousine. Technically they're on foot and have no way of leaving."

"They can always call for an Uber or a Lyft." Looked at Mom. "Your call."

She shrugged. "I'm here with you. Len and Kyle are already here, and Malcolm, John, and Benjamin will be here shortly. We can let these two in. Walter, just be sure they're frisked with extreme prejudice, and by that I mean I want them wanded with an OVS and sniffed by bomb dogs."

"Yes, ma'am, Director Katt. It's being done as we speak."

"Call in the K-9 Squad!"

"Already done, Chief First Lady, per Mister Reynolds' in-structions for situations like this."

"Good job, Walt. Let us know if anything else is going on."

"Will do." The com shut off.

"Who called Team Tough Guys in?" I asked the room in general.

"Me," Vance said.

"Which was someone following protocol for these kinds of situations," Mom said approvingly. "It's nice to see that we have some team members who are able to follow instructions." Len and Kyle both looked a little hurt. Mom noticed and rolled her eyes. "I see Kitty's sensitivity is rubbing off on you two. I realize you were both busy being protective of Lizzie. It's not a mark against your competence."

"Call Me Maybe" by Carly Rae Jepsen sounded before I could give a snappy comeback. That was my ringtone for Jeff, so I quickly dug my phone out of my purse. "Hey, sorry, I'm going to be late. Or, rather, not early for my scheduled time with all of you."

"I know, baby, Walter just advised us. Buchanan, Siler, and Wruck running out of the room was also a clue. Do you need me, Chuck, or Alpha Team, too?"

"Nah, Mom's here, the boys are here, and," the door opened and Team Tough Guys entered my chambers, "the dudes have arrived."

"Tell Mister Executive Chief we're on top of it," Buchanan said. He reminded me a lot of Jeff, in that he was big and broad and handsome for a human, though he had straight brown hair and blue eyes. He also had Dr. Strange powers, in that if Buchanan didn't want you to see him, then you didn't see him. I'd long ago given up trying to figure out how he did it and had just accepted that he could and that it was always to my benefit.

"Will do."

Jeff grunted. "Buchanan may know what he's doing, but does he always have to be so smug about it?"

"Yes, he does. They've all earned the right to be smug about their massive competence."

Siler grinned at me. "Tell Jeff that we're sorry we're making him look bad."

Lizzie's adoptive father was a hybrid—half human, half A-C. Of course, his A-C half was Ronald Yates, aka Jeff and Christopher's grandfather, aka the First Mastermind. Siler's mother was Madeleine Siler Cartwright, and she'd been an Evil Power Behind The Thrones in her own right. At least until our side had killed her right before she could kill me.

Siler's fab parents had done weird experiments on him before his uncle had rescued him. So while Siler looked like a normally attractive man who could be from pretty much anywhere, with olive skin and dark hair, he didn't age normally. He could also go chameleon, what he called blending, so that you couldn't really see him or anyone else he was touching for as long as he could hold the blend. This had helped him greatly in his uncle's profession of assassination. It helped us all now in any number of ways.

"I'm not stupid enough to share that, Nightcrawler." Technically I should be referring to Siler as Wolverine, but since I was officially the team's Wolverine With Boobs, I'd chosen to focus on his blending talent. So far, only Siler and one bird species from Alpha Four could blend, and only I had the Dr. Doolittle powers. We weren't sure if Siler and I were just special or if the talents were just so rare that we hadn't hit others with them. I voted for special, because I needed the occasional win to keep going.

Jeff grunted. "They're full of themselves, aren't they?"

"You'd be the one who'd know."

"True." He chuckled. "Wruck, on the other hand, remains humble. I like him best."

"I'll let John know. John, Jeff likes you best."

Wruck wasn't a human, hybrid, or A-C. He was an Anciannas, what we'd been calling Ancients for decades. They were the elder race that was in a war with the other elder race, the dinobirds named the Z'porrah. Their initial friendship and then war was what had basically caused most of the anguish and accomplishments in the galaxy.

Among their other qualities, the Anciannas were shapeshifters. Wruck tended to look and sound like a European, but could and did alter his looks and voice as needed. He rarely went into his natural form, though, which, considering all the Anciannas looked like Biblical versions of angels, was a good thing for the mental well-being of Earth's human population.

Buchanan and Siler both snorted, Len and Kyle looked a little crestfallen, but Wruck smiled at me. "I'm sure that the President likes all of us equally."

"I don't," Jeff said. "Though apparently I just hurt the jocks' feelings. Tell them I like them best, too."

"Jeff loves Len and Kyle, too. In fact, he's feeling the love for everyone. This is why he called. To share the love."

"I don't love your newest visitors," Jeff said while the room chuckled. "And I don't trust them at all. I think they're both wearing emotional overlays, by the way. Good ones. I doubt the other empaths can tell, but Christopher, Raj, and I have spent our copious free time testing my abilities against the various overlays we have in our possession, and I'm getting better at spotting high-quality fakes."

"Go team. The K-9 unit is supposed to be doing our bomb sniffing and, to show you that I'm on top of things, too, I know the dogs will tell me what they got as soon as I'm with them."

"Yeah, Walter shared that, too. Well, that the dogs and their handlers were on their way." Jeff heaved a sigh. "So, enough about the looming 'fun.' How are you doing after the show?"

"Exactly as well as can be expected." Pondered this. As the Super Empath, Jeff could normally feel me when I was halfway around the world from him, empathic blocks activated or not. "You can't tell? Are the suspected overlays affecting you?"

"No, they're not. I can tell, baby, but it's always considered polite to ask."

Snorted a laugh. "Yes, we've built our relationship on politeness and protocol."

He chuckled. "Point taken. Your two new additions seem helpful and I've read them both. No overlays or blockers."

"Good. And?"

"And Adam's thrilled and honored to be here, deeply confused and worried about what's going on, and ready to join the team protecting you. Cologne isn't awed at all, but he's pleased that he helped out, and he's deeply worried about what's going on with the new robotic whatever you discovered. I really want to get your intel, though, baby. And we want to question the new robotic you've found, too, though I'm quite clear that you've said we have to wait for you."

"Pardon me. That kind of questioning is in my wheelhouse, and you know it. Are you having this call in the Large Situation Room, by the way?"

"Nope. I went to the Executive Washroom. Because it's about the only place I can get any form of privacy. If I consider having Joseph and Rob in here with me to be private."

"Say hi to them for me."

"Oh, I will do." Jeff's sarcasm knob was heading for eight on the scale. "I'd tell you to blow Somerall and Lee off because we have bigger issues, but I've paid attention, and I'm figuring that this is their crazed opening gambit that they're doing in person for some reason, versus on the phone."

"We are so in sync sometimes it's almost scary. Yeah, that's exactly what I think this is. But, you know, who knows? Maybe they're just here to try to wrest Lizzie away from us."

At this Siler's expression went dark. Jeff growled. "Tell Siler I'm with him and that if they so much as look at Lizzie wrong he has Executive Permission to kill them both."

"Ah, I really don't think Mom wants us doing that. Not that I disagree with the sentiment or anything, but, trust me, we have more going on than Walter may have mentioned."

"He said something about the Bahrainis coming by."

Interesting. Then again, Walter only knew I'd expected whoever was coming to be Mona and her entourage, they were on Buchanan's Short Approval List, and he didn't know about Wasim, so he wouldn't have said more to Jeff or anyone else. And other stresses had outweighed Wasim's imminent arrival for me, meaning Jeff probably hadn't noticed that particular stress spike. Ergo, decided not to share the full details with Jeff just yet. Might as well surprise him as we'd already been surprised. It would be more fun that way.

"Yeah, Mona's on her way over."

"At least you'll get to have a nice visit with friends somewhere today, look at it that way."

"I will do. And let me just say that I'm not sure that I'm ready for all that today's throwing at us, but I'll do my best."

"Then it'll all work out, because your best always saves the day, baby."

"Thanks, I needed that. Truly."

We shared that we loved each other and I got off the phone just as the com came back on. "K-9, Secret Service, and A-C Security have all cleared Mister Somerall and Miz Lee for entry," Walter shared.

"Then have them brought in via the same extra-crispy guard, Walt."

"Absolutely, Chief First Lady. Your Secret Service and A-C Security details will take the handoff and will do the escort. K-9 squad will also escort. Com off."

"They'll be going at human official speeds, so presumably slowly. Which means we have a couple minutes. What's our determination on Lizzie's presence?" Figured I needed to ask again now that her adoptive father was in the room.

"As long as I'm approved to kill them if they look at her wrong, let them in," Siler said.

"Jeff absolutely gave you Executive Permission, but I think Mom wants them alive for the time being."

"I do. However, I think we're going to get more information if Lizzie's in the room than if she's not. Especially since your A-C Security detail is with the visitors."

"And Prince, Duke, and Riley will totes tell Kitty if anything's up, too," Lizzie added. Correctly.

"Imageers and empaths and top police dogs, oh my."

CHAPTER 10

DID A FAST COUNT in my head—we were about to have a lot of people join us in my office. My office wasn't set up to host a kegger. "Vance, I think we need to choose another location for this group tête-à-tête. Any suggestions?"

"If we want room to run in case of attack, the Kennedy Garden would be my pick." Vance's sarcasm meter went well past eleven.

"I like it. It gives us room and also advises them that we're not interested in hanging out. Though I must remind you that the last time I went out on the lawns during times of potential crisis my personal Fem-Bot showed up to share that Operation Madhouse was underway."

"For the number of people, the Garden lawn is, frankly, the most practical," Abner added. Mrs. Maurer and Colette nodded their agreement. The rest of the room didn't look as thrilled.

"It also leaves Missus Executive Chief open for sniper attack," Buchanan said. "So my vote is no. And since I'm the Head of White House Security and also since my real job is to do what the Director of the P.T.C.U. assigned me to do, which is to protect Missus Executive Chief, her children—which includes her ward—and, by extension, her husband, my vote wins. We stay inside."

Mom heaved a sigh. "Malcolm has a point. However, I don't see how we're safe crowded into this room with, literally, thirty or more people and dogs."

Buchanan rolled his eyes. "Fine. Far be it for me to actually do my job."

"Com on!"

"Yes, Chief First Lady?"

"Walt, do Malcolm a solid and put the shields up. Or at least up over the Kennedy Gardens. We're going to receive our unwanted guests there. Please also advise whoever's leading that particular tour group that this is where they should go. And anyone else who might need to know, probably starting with the President."

"We have a time window where I can engage shields over the entire complex. However, that window is no more than thirty minutes."

"Make it so, and we'll be fast." Looked around. "Time to link up and do the hyperspeed daisy chain, gang."

"No," Vance said sternly. "The First Lady does not race to meet with those not on her schedule. The First Lady does not race to meet those who *are* on her schedule, either, but absolutely not for unplanned, uninvited, and unwanted visitors. She will gracefully arrive, not out of breath, regardless of the fact that she's meeting visitors outside and there's a time limit."

"What Vance said," Abner added. "Kitty, this is the time for you to do some Washington Wife channeling and remember that you're the top female in the world. Make sure *they* remember that."

Took a deep breath and let it out slowly. "Points taken. So, let's saunter gracefully downstairs, shall we? Definitely taking the elevator."

Thankfully, I didn't need to quickly change clothes. Because of my stint on *Good Day USA!* I actually wasn't in what I considered one of my FLOTUS Uniform options—either a black skirt and suit jacket with an iced blue blouse with black pumps and light blue accessories, or an iced blue suit with a cream blouse and cream pumps and accessories. My "color" had been determined to be iced blue, so now everything I wore had to include the color somewhere. I'd used to really love the color blue. Now it made me feel trapped. And the less said about anyone being stupid enough to put me into a light color like cream or white the better.

Of course, the A-Cs loved black and white. Adored it, really. They always wore what I called the Armani Fatigues—black suits and ties with crisp white shirts for the men, black slim skirts and pumps with white oxfords for the women. I'd been sick of black and white. Once. Now I was sick of blue and cream, too. If this went on, I'd hate the entire color spectrum soon.

However, today I was dressed in a sleeveless black and iced blue dress that had managed to remain fairly clean, despite my tussle on the studio floor. This was because we had a designer on exclusive retainer, and Akiko was, by now, well used to what I and, therefore, the clothes she designed for me, got up to. All of my clothes were treated with stain retardant, and most of them were made so that when I got physical the clothes wouldn't rip.

So I looked presentable for both our uninvited guests and anyone who might be hanging around with a telephoto lens. Actively put this into the win column because that column was really bare.

Grabbed my purse and dropped my phone back into it. Most First Ladies didn't run around with their purses on the White House grounds, which only proved to me that they'd had far easier lives as the FLOTUS than I was scoring. I'd learned long ago not to let my purse and its contents out of my reach, and nothing that had happened since Operation Fugly had ever given me a reason to change this mindset.

Thusly armed with whatever my purse might have on hand, we headed off. Based on the fact that we were on the second floor and had chosen to discuss what we were doing, we reached the first floor as Walter shared that the visitors and their security entourage were already waiting for us at the gazebo in the garden.

"Shields are active now, Chief First Lady. Please remember that I'll have to turn them off in thirty minutes so that those coming to join you and the President will be allowed through."

"God forbid we don't have everyone we care about protected or anything."

"I'd prefer to leave the shields on twenty-four-seven, but the White House can't function that way," Walter said regretfully. "We also have standard food deliveries along with other necessities due to arrive around the same time. I will plan to turn the shields back on once all those are through."

"Don't bother," Vance said. "Barring Angela saying any different, we have to continue to have Jeff function as much like a normal President as possible. Re-election will go far easier that way."

"We hope and, my God, is it really time to consider that?"

"It's never not time," Abner said as we got into the elevator.

Well, most of us. Colette grabbed Len and Kyle while Siler took Wruck and Buchanan, and they all hypersped off.

Colette and the boys were waiting for us when the elevator opened, and we headed off to something I hoped would go better than my time on *Good Day USA!* had. Vance ensured that we did indeed saunter. Mom and Len were in the lead, with Vance and me right behind them. Lizzie was behind us with Colette, Abner and Mrs. Maurer behind them, and Kyle brought up the rear.

True to form, Team Tough Guys were nowhere to be seen. Whether that was because Siler was blending all three of them or they were working spread out from each other, stealth was each of their middle names. Which was fine. The less our enemies got eyes on the three of them, the better. Buchanan had lost memories and almost died more than once because the Mastermind had spotted who he was. The less anyone could see my secret weapons, the better.

Speaking of stealth and the bird species that could go chameleon, felt something feathered nudge against my leg. Didn't reach down to pet Bruno, because that would have given away that at least one Peregrine was with us, but it was nice to know he was there.

Peregrines were Alpha Four birds raised for thousands of years to protect the royal family. They were beautiful, resembling peacocks and peahens on steroids. Emperor Alexander, Jeff and Christopher's cousin, had sent a set of twelve mated pairs to celebrate Jamie's first birthday, and Bruno and Lola, the Head Birds of this flock, considered themselves my immediate family's official protectors.

Originally, we'd feared that the Peregrines weren't going to mate, but that concern was a thing of the past. We had Peregrines in the way other places had pigeons. Actually, we didn't have any pigeons at the White House or American Centaurion Embassy because the Peregrines and ocellars—fox-cats from Beta Eight that had come home with us after Operation Civil War—considered them delicacies. No one complained—pigeons tended to be stupid, nasty, flying poop bombs and, until such time as a pigeon decided to chat with me, were fair game for my intelligent pets who understood the concept of walkies and litter boxes.

Thusly surrounded by armed and feathered protectors, we arrived in a stately manner. I was only stately because Vance had my arm wrapped through his so that when I inevitably tripped he was there to steady me. Len being right in front of me blocked most of that, too. Go team.

Somerall and the woman I assumed was Talia Lee were indeed in the gazebo, the many security forces spread out around them, with Secret Service and A-C teams outside of the gazebo and the three D.C.P.D. officers and their dogs on the inside. If someone randomly took a picture it would probably look like we were visiting a nasty Third World dictator.

The K-9 dogs were at their version of attention, meaning they were sitting bolt upright, muzzles forward. Also meant no dog lovies for me right now, but sacrifices had to be made.

Somerall fancied himself a ladies' man and flashed me a wide smile I was fairly sure he thought made women weak-kneed. Didn't work on me or the women with me, but then again, we knew him. He was a little shorter than Jeff, so I put him at six-two. Mid-fifties but with a full head of silver hair, good build, average nice looks. Had to admit if I'd met him randomly in the supermarket I might find him charming.

"Missus Martini, how good of you to receive us. I can't tell you how much Talia and I appreciate your taking the time," Somerall said as my escort team fanned out behind me. He sounded totally sincere, though I was sure that he was being sarcastic on the inside. "And we understand the need for . . . precautions."

"I'm sure you do." Somerall was definitely one of the reasons we'd needed precautions for a long time, after all.

Somerall stepped forward, hand extended. Prince, my favorite of all the K-9 dogs, growled. The kind of growl that shared that Somerall was going to lose that hand if he didn't step right back into his approved position. Extra treats for Prince were definitely in his near future.

Not being an idiot, Somerall so stepped back and put his hand down. "What, ah, good dogs you have," Lee said, tone indicating she didn't like dogs and never would. To her credit, though, she neither tried to step forward nor offer her hand.

"D.C.P.D.'s finest. I'm sorry, we haven't met. Who are you?" I mean, I knew, but why be nice about this?

Wasn't sure what I'd been expecting Lee to look like, but I'd presumed she'd be of Asian descent. She wasn't. She had blonde hair, blue eyes, and a Southern accent. She was trim and attractive, and her Washington color appeared to be fuchsia. Or so I presumed, since she was in various complementary shades, and her pumps matched her suit.

Unlike Lillian Culver, whose color was red and who first looked attractive before you realized she was really all bones and angles, Lee was more rounded and soft. But I recognized the look in her eyes—it was the same Killer Instinct look that Culver had always had with me until we'd become friends.

"I'm so sorry," Somerall said, oozing regret. "For some reason I just assumed that you two would have met by now. This is Talia Lee, the head lobbyist for the firearms people. Talia, obviously you know who the First Lady is."

"Obviously," Lee said. It was official, she didn't care for me. Somehow, I'd find the will to go on.

"Pleasure," I lied. "Now that we've been officially introduced, why have you two barged in? Normally appointments are made and confirmed or, in your case, Ansom, you call me and make ludicrous threats. Just wanted the personal touch?"

"No, we actually have something we wanted to speak with you about." Somerall looked around. "Privately."

"Oh, the presence of these thirty or so other people is plenty private enough for me."

"You may not agree once we share what we've come to discuss," Lee said.

"Huh. The last time I got an offer like this it was someone sharing doctored dirty pictures of me and men who aren't my husband. Let's hear what you two have and see if it tops that." Wanted to say that I bet that it wouldn't, but refused to do so, because I was smart enough not to sell my enemies short.

Lee shrugged. "Have it your way. We know who was making robotic versions of you and Janelle Gardiner."

CHAPTER 11

TOOK ALL OF MY SELF-CONTROL, but I managed not to say that we knew it was Lee and Somerall. Instead, I shrugged. "Really? How interesting. Who?"

"A relative of your husband's," Somerall replied.

Well, that much was kind of true. Stephanie was definitely creating androids and such. However, while she might have been involved with the Fem-Bot project near the beginning of Operation Madhouse, by the time we'd discovered it, it seemed quite clear that Somerall, Lee, and the NSA were the ones in charge.

"Really? Who?"

"Christopher White." Somerall said this in a Ta-Da! kind of way.

Managed not to snort, but it took serious effort. "Thanks for your ridiculous intel. We're done here." Turned to leave.

"Wait," Lee said. "It's not the real one."

Well, that was different. Turned back around. "Beg pardon?"

"We know it's not really your husband's cousin," Lee said. "But he looks just like him."

"Christopher doesn't have a twin."

"No, he doesn't," Somerall agreed. "But he's got a doppelganger out there, and that person is creating robotic versions of you and poor Janelle. And God alone knows who else."

The Washington Wife class would counsel serene acceptance and assigning a task force to investigate these claims. But I was far better off as Megalomaniac Girl. Just hoped Mom wouldn't mind what I was about to say.

"Look, we point-blank know that the two of you were involved with all the Fem-Bot projects. Feel more than free to try to deny it, but we have proof." We didn't, but I knew Mom's expression wouldn't reveal that. Just hoped no one else's did. Also really hoped the empaths were ready to work. "I'm just curious as to why you're turning on your partners all of a sudden. Though that's kind of your 'thing,' isn't it? I mean, you both turned on 'poor Janelle' already. What's to stop you from turning on your NSA partner? Let alone your other partners?"

"We're not," Lee said. "We're coming to you for protection."

Let that one sit on the air for a few long moments. "Come again?"

"You're protecting *her*," Lee pointed to Lizzie. "If you'll protect a murderous teenager, why not us? It's clear that you'll protect those who give you something in return. We have things to give in return for protection."

Had to hand it to them—this was a new one.

"You have Janelle in protective custody," Somerall pointed out, possibly because I hadn't said anything. "And Amos Tobin, too. We want the same protection. Frankly, we have far more to offer you than either one of them does."

New and getting newer. Decided to follow the best sales advice out there and keep my trap shut. Because whenever the question was asked, the offer made, or the definitive statement given—or, in this case, the bizarre exposed to the light of day— she who spoke next lost.

Once again, hoped the rest of the team was on the same page as I was, because I wasn't planning to say another word.

Not that I had to. "Whatever Janelle and Amos know, we have more," Lee said. "Lots more."

They'd been given the once-over with an OVS, per Walter. So they weren't androids, Fem-Bots or, in Somerall's case, Man-Bots. They weren't likely to be clones. Jeff felt they were wearing emotional overlays and those hadn't been found during their search, but that just meant the overlays were internal somehow, either surgically inserted or merely swallowed, to come out naturally later, icky a thought as that was.

Continued to keep quiet, in part to see what they'd say next and in other part because I literally had no idea of what to say. However, they were now staring at me. Nervously. This wasn't a look I was familiar with from Somerall, and had to bet that it was rare for Lee, too. Clearly, I needed to make sounds.

"Um . . . yeah?"

"Yes," Lee said swiftly. "And we're taking a terrible risk being outside."

My brain nudged. "You were dropped off by whoever drove you here. You were outside getting searched for far longer than we've been out here."

"True," Somerall said. "However, we have powerful enemies."

Chose not to comment because, as far as I was concerned, Jeff and I were their enemies, and I could certainly agree that we were quite powerful. Most of it was power we hadn't wanted, but at least we didn't create fake versions of people in order to create world- and galaxy-threatening problems.

My brain nudged more. "This person who you say looks like Christopher, how long have you known him?"

"Not long," Lee replied. "Just a few months, really. We were introduced to him by a . . . mutual friend."

"Name names or, once again, we're done here." Pulled my phone out of my purse, though, and sent a text. I was tired of doing all the heavy lifting on this one.

Lee and Somerall didn't speak until I looked up from my phone. Apparently they were either waiting to see if I was going to say something else or they were being polite and waiting for my full attention. Decided I didn't care which it was and gave them the "I'm bored, impress me" look. It wasn't a look I used a lot, but I'd been a teenaged girl, so that look was still in my repertoire. Noted that Lizzie had the look on her face already.

Somerall sighed. "Gideon Cleary's former aide."

Gideon Cleary was the governor of Florida and had been a major political rival and enemy of ours and the late Vincent Armstrong's back when Armstrong and Jeff were running for President and VP. He'd been tight with the Mastermind's organization. However, events from Operations Bizarro World and Epidemic had made him see the light of the side of right, and he'd left the Mastermind's team and joined ours.

However, his aide was indeed someone we knew well—Stephanie Valentino.

My requested backup arrived now. Showing that Vance's instructions about not looking as if you were racing were listened to at all the levels, they walked over to us, though I knew they'd used hyperspeed to get here quickly.

Somerall and Lee looked shocked. "Ah, Mister President," Somerall managed. "So kind of you to join us."

"The Director of the CIA felt that we were needed here." Jeff smiled as he came over to me and gave me a peck on the cheek.

"Loved the text you sent Chuck," he whispered. "I need Superman and Batman."

"Hey, it worked," I whispered back.

Chuckie strode over to Somerall and Lee. "I realize you've been searched and declared clean. However, I don't believe that you are. So, why are you here? The real reason, not whatever line of crap you've been trying to hand the First Lady."

Lee rolled her eyes. "It's not a line we've been telling her. We'll tell you the same thing. The person in charge of the robotics project that has made copies of the First Lady and Janelle Gardiner is the exact double of the President's cousin."

Had a hold of Jeff's hand, and I squeezed it hard and did my best to send an emotional signal for him to relax. "We were just at the part where Ansom and Talia were sharing that they were introduced to Fake Christopher by Stephanie."

Jeff heaved a sigh. "Fabulous. So, why are you here and sharing this? We know the two of you are up to your armpits in all of that as well."

Somerall nodded. "Yes, we were. We aren't anymore. Things are . . . out of hand."

"Out of hand how?" Chuckie asked in his dangerous James Bond About To Kill Blofeld way.

"He's taking it to extremes," Lee said.

"Extremes. You mean you were just fine with creating a freaking army of Fem-Bots who looked just like me and sending them against us during an important peace summit at Camp David, but now, for some reason, you're getting dainty?"

"Yes," Lee snapped.

"Fem-Bots?" Somerall asked. "That's a good name for them. We just call them robots."

"I like to name things, sue me. You still haven't shared what Fake Christopher is doing."

"I'd also like to know where you got your emotional overlays from," Jeff said genially. "They're pretty good."

Both of them blinked. "Ah," Somerall said slowly, "we don't have emotional overlays on."

Heard Mom snort softly behind me. Yeah, I didn't buy it, either.

"Pull the other one, it has bells on." I could say this with confidence because Jeff was just that damned good, and if he said he'd been practicing spotting minute anomalies, then he was so spotting them coming from these two. Frankly, I'd expected better from both Somerall and Lee, and, based on Chuckie's expression, he had, too.

Lee shook her head. "No, Ansom's not lying. We don't have any kind of emotional blockers or overlays on. We're coming to you for help—we wanted to ensure that you were all clear that we're telling the truth."

"However," Jeff said, "your emotions are off. Just a little, but I can tell."

The two empaths on my team both nodded. "The President is correct," Daniel said in his cute South African accent. "There's something wrong with their emotions."

"They're more off than the Kristie-Bot was this morning," Marcus added in his cute Spanish accent. I really enjoyed having an international team, especially at times when I could relax a tad and enjoy it. This morning had not been one of those times but, for whatever reason, Somerall and Lee weren't stressing me out nearly as much as being on *Good Day USA!* had.

Jeff grunted. "And you wonder why I'm jealous all the time. I've read the Kristie-Bot," he said in a louder voice, "and she reads more correctly than you two do."

Lee and Somerall looked at each other. "Do you think he did something to us?" Lee asked, sounding worried.

Somerall shook his head. "I have no idea."

"Look, the Little Theater presentation is great," Chuckie said, sounding bored. "But you're both full of it. I recommend that we take them into custody, thereby removing everyone's favorite targets for assassination from public view, and then get back to the serious matters of state that we're all dealing with."

No sooner were the words out of his mouth than I heard Bruno's Peregrine Shriek of Warning, followed by another sound that was never a good one. Someone was shooting. At us.

CHAPTER 12

HYPERSPEED AND PEOPLE trained to work with super-fast beings meant that our teams leapt into action.

I spun and tackled Mom and Lizzie, who were thankfully next to each other. Jeff tackled me, and Len and Kyle covered all of us. Meanwhile, Chuckie pulled Somerall and Lee down, and the A-C Security team got the rest of my team down and covered. My Secret Service team covered Chuckie and our "guests" while Jeff's team encircled our group dog pile.

I could just see around Jeff's arm and through Len's legs. And what I saw were the three police dogs take off like bats out of hell.

The Secret Service started moving us all inside, shouting orders and so forth, while the K-9 officers ran after their dogs. Meaning three dudes I really liked and their respective dogs I loved were heading for the danger, instead of away from it.

As we got manhandled, noted that Bruno was now visible and he was flying in the lead. The dogs were following him. Followed their trajectory. They were heading toward the South Lawn.

My brain nudged, hard. Walter had the shielding up on the complex, and we weren't past the thirty-minute mark. Meaning whoever was shooting at us was inside the shield, as in, someone Walter thought was trustworthy.

Didn't have to take too long with the guessing. "It's the Fake Christopher," I said to Jeff. "And that means Bruno and the dogs, and the humans with the guns, will hesitate." And that probably meant they'd all die. Because the gunshots weren't stopping. Kicked off my pumps. "Mom, don't let anyone follow us, just in case."

"Oh, of course not." Mom's sarcasm knob went well past eleven.

Jeff nodded, tossed everyone off of us, grabbed my hand, and we took off after the K-9 squad.

We caught up to the officers fast. "You get them to safety," I said to Jeff, as I dropped his hand and kept running after the dogs.

Dogs tend to be faster than humans, so they were well ahead of their handlers. However, they weren't A-C dogs, and I caught up to them pretty quickly as they, and I, rounded a big tree that was surrounded by a lot of dense bushes to see exactly what I'd been expecting—someone who looked just like Christopher shooting a semiautomatic rifle.

Shorter and smaller than Jeff, though still well-muscled, with lighter brown hair and green eyes, but still incredibly handsome. Yep, looked just like Christopher. Only Christopher wasn't given to randomly shooting at anyone, let alone the people who had been shot at.

He saw me and stopped shooting. The dogs encircled him, growling that he smelled wrong, while Bruno hovered over his head, squawking the same. "I come in peace."

Stopped running. "Sure you do. That's why you're shooting."

He shrugged and tossed the rifle to me. Jeff caught it. "I hate when you do things like this," Jeff muttered to me. "Your mother has everyone under control, baby. Why do we have this gun now?" he asked our would-be assailant.

"I'm shooting blanks," Fake Christopher said.

"Huh." Jeff pulled out the rifle's magazine. "They're actually blanks."

"That's different. So, if you're here 'in peace,' why shoot at us, blanks or no?"

"I needed to get your attention, time was of the essence, and I wanted to talk to the two of you alone," he said as if this was obvious. Remembered that our enemies knew our playbook—it was obvious that Jeff and I would have been the ones to come first, security details or no. "The two who came to you are lying."

"Are they? What do you think they've told us?"

"That I'm evil and they're afraid of me."

Well, that was basically accurate. "And you're saying that you're not evil and no one should fear you?"

He shrugged. "I was. I figured out how to overcome the programming."

It was weird, having a conversation with someone who really looked and sounded exactly like Christopher. Only he didn't, in that sense, because Christopher was a glaring champion and, by now, would have hit us with at least one of his infamous Patented Glares. The Fake Christopher wasn't glaring. At all. He seemed close to expressionless. Time to take the Megalomaniac Girl Leap.

"You're a Man-Bot, aren't you?"

"I was, if by that you mean a robotic version of a male person."

"I do indeed. Why did you create Fem-Bots of me and Janelle Gardiner?"

"I didn't. I assisted, but the plan wasn't mine."

"How many of you are there?"

"I . . . don't know."

Jeff grunted. "That's not good. How did they get enough time with Christopher to copy him this exactly?"

"You have to ask? When he was shooting up Surcenthumain before Jamie was born. Honestly, I'm surprised that they didn't launch a Christopher-Bot strike well before this."

"They would have," the now-confirmed Christopher-Bot said. "But other plans had higher priority."

"Whose plans?" I asked. "The Mastermind's?"

He nodded. "And others had plans, too. The group has . . . splintered recently."

"Due to us killing off a bunch of the leaders, right?"

"Yes."

"So, you're seriously not here to exact revenge?"

He shook his head. "I told you, I overcame the programming."

"How?" Jeff asked flatly. "Androids doing that, I can see how they managed it. But you? You were never human to begin with."

"Not all androids were human to begin with," the Christopher-Bot pointed out.

"True enough, but the ones able to overcome their programming all were." Considered things. "You were supposed to be put in place once they'd kidnapped Amy and created her Fem-Bot, weren't you? Because there's no way her husband wouldn't notice that she was now an automaton."

"Yes."

"And then the two of you could self-destruct when you could take out the most of us and cause the most damage."

"Yes. The plan was that she would be at your Embassy and I'd be at the White House."

"Fantastic. Is that plan still active?"

"Not anymore. I overcame my programming. I keep on saying that, but I don't believe you understand what it means."

"We don't, in that sense."

"It means I'm now autonomous and can make my own decisions."

"That's great," Jeff said, sarcasm knob at eleven and heading for twelve. "If only we felt we could believe you."

"How many more of you are there?" I asked again, before the conversation went in a way that, at this moment, didn't matter. Hoped we'd get a better answer than we had before.

"I'm . . . not sure. There could be many, there might only be me." Well, it was sort of a better answer. Maybe if I asked three times all the Man-Bots would appear, just like it worked in *Beetlejuice*.

"Uh huh," Jeff said. "There could be a million more of you, but you're not sure? Right."

"We weren't made to . . . know anything more than our programming. I know what I was programmed for. It was a solo mission. There might be more like me, but if there are, I haven't seen them."

Jeff shrugged. "And we only have your word on that, for whatever that's worth. So, again, you're here to, what? Warn us against the humans who came to warn us against you?"

The Christopher-Bot blinked. "They aren't humans. Not anymore."

"They checked out as organic enough to pass as human," I pointed out.

He nodded. "Their bodies are all organic. Their brains no longer are." He nodded behind us. "Same as their brains."

Turned to see Joe and Randy behind us, clearly ready to tackle the Christopher-Bot if necessary.

"If it can be done with us," Randy said, "then it can be done with anyone."

"As we saw earlier this morning," Joe pointed out.

Jeff groaned. "Does it get any better than this?"

"Oh, just wait, I'm sure it will."

"Yes, it will," the Christopher-Bot said. "Because they're here to gather video of as many of you moving and talking as they can. So that the next generations of . . . Bots . . . will be able to move forward."

"Okay, so, let's say we believe you. Who's behind this if it's not you and it's not Ansom and Talia?" Sure, it was likely to be Stephanie and Trevor the Tinkerer. But it was extremely likely that we had other enemies out there we didn't know about, and one of them could have been in charge. One of them worked for the NSA, or at least had worked, of that I was sure.

"The same person who's been behind all of this from the creation of the first Bot."

My phone rang before I could ask who this person was and verify that Ronald Yates hadn't come back from the dead. Dug it out of my purse, which I'd wisely put cross-body before I'd left my office. "Walter, what's up?"

"Shields have to lower, Chief First Lady. We have deliveries at the gates as well as the Bahraini Diplomatic Mission."

Heaved a sigh. "Walt, did anyone alert you to what's just gone on?"

"Yes, and I have eyes on you and the President. But Director Katt said that things were under control, though she agreed that Lieutenant Billings and Captain Muir should go to cover you."

"Yeah, Joe and Randy are here with us."

"Yes, I see them, too. Everyone else is inside, per Director Katt's order. I'm sorry for letting the imposter in. I should have had him tested." Walter sounded ready to resign.

"Um, why would you have ever thought to have done that?"

"Because we know there are copies of you, Chief First Lady. I should have assumed that there are copies of everyone."

"Walt, we *all* should have thought of that. Stop berating yourself. This is how we learn. By the way, where is the real Christopher and when did you let this fake Christopher in?"

"I've confirmed that the real Primary is at Dulce." Primary was an Alpha Four term for a close relative to the Head Dude who was also in charge of protecting things, which fit Christopher pretty much exactly. "The imposter arrived just before I put the shields on. He arrived via a gate."

"Oh really? Do we know which gate he came from?" Walter had been one of the Security agents running the gates at the Science Center before I'd hired him on as our Head of Security during Operation Confusion, and if there was anyone who could get intel out of the gates system, it was him.

"Yes, I've backtracked it. He came in via a gate from Dulles International Airport."

"Huh. You mean the same airport it's likely that someone flying in from Bahrain would be landing at?"

"Yes."

"Interesting. Don't write the letter of resignation I can practically feel you composing in your head, Walt. If I had to resign every time I'd made a minor error I'd never have had my first career, let alone all the ones since joining Centaurion Division. And that's an order."

"Yes, ma'am, Chief First Lady." He sounded a little better, which was good. "Shields will be going down in less than two minutes."

"Gotcha." We hung up. "I'm glad that at least Mom trusts us to handle things with only *Six Million Dollar Man* backup." Joe and Randy were flanking us now and both grinned at me.

Jeff sighed and pointed to the roof of the White House. Where I saw a lot of snipers, including one whose stance I recognized—it was the stance of someone who'd spent a long time shooting people from rooftops. "I'm just wondering why they didn't shoot him," Jeff nodded toward the Christopher-Bot. "Siler in particular."

"They did shoot at me," the Christopher-Bot said. "Then they stopped when Kitty got near to me."

"Don't refer to me in a friendly manner, please. We aren't friends yet. But yeah, that makes sense. So, who's the person in charge of this Bot Initiative? And why Bots? They're so much less adaptable than androids."

"We're more disposable," the Christopher-Bot said calmly. "We're made faster and on an assembly line. Androids take more time, power, care, and have a higher rate of failure."

"So how is it you can overcome your programming, then?" Jeff asked.

"I don't know. I just know that I have."

"Or," I pointed out, "you could be programmed to think this, come here and talk to us, and then explode."

The Christopher-Bot seemed to consider this. "That's true. I don't feel that it's correct, but I can see how it could be."

"So, before that potentially happens, who's behind all of this?"

The Christopher-Bot opened his mouth as Bruno screamed another warning. And this time, I heard a different, but no less threatening, noise.

"Run!" Jeff bellowed, as he grabbed Prince and flung him under one arm, while Bruno dive-bombed his way down to me.

I got the bird tucked under my arm like a large, feathery football as Jeff grabbed my hand, Joe grabbed Duke, and Randy grabbed Riley, and we all headed off for the nearest building at top speed.

"You, too!" Jeff shouted to the Christopher-Bot over his shoulder.

But it was too late.

CHAPTER 13

LOOKED BACK TO SEE the incoming rocket slam into the Christopher-Bot. It exploded in a shower of parts as we reached the stately front columns. Was prepared for more rockets to launch, but there was nothing.

"What the literal hell?" Joe asked everyone and no one.

"The weirdness thickens, basically. So, any guesses for who just blew up our latest informant?"

"No," Randy said. "But if he was right and Somerall and Lee have wires in their brains, then they're inside with everyone else right now."

My phone rang again. Dropped Jeff's hand but kept a hold of Bruno while I got my phone again. "Yes, Walt?" The guys put the dogs down, presumably because German Shepherds were a lot heavier than Peregrines.

"Shields are back up." Walter sounded shaken.

"Did all the deliveries and Bahrainis get inside?"

"Yes, that's what took so long. I'm sorry, but they were all coming in when the rocket launched, and turning the shields on when people are coming in can be . . . dangerous. For them."

"We understand. None of this is your fault."

"But it is, because this is my job."

Handed the phone to Jeff. "Reassure our most loyal and efficient security dude that he's not allowed to quit his job." Jeff took the phone and started speaking to Walter. Meanwhile, I looked around. "Dudes, this is getting weirder by the minute, and by that I mean we're well past what the real flesh-and-blood Christopher likes to call Kitty Weird."

Joe nodded. "Want us to recover the parts?"

"I want someone to do that, but I'm worried that whoever

has the rocket launcher will just start shooting at you two next."

"That was a very well-aimed, limited strike," Randy said. "It wasn't aimed at any of us, just at the robot."

Jeff handed me my phone back. "Walter's feeling better. Which makes exactly one of us. Seriously, has any other administration been unable to go out onto the grounds without expecting gunfire and bombs, or is it just us?"

"Nope, you're pretty much winning that one, Jeff," Joe said cheerfully.

"But look at it this way," Randy added. "You're leading the pack again."

"Oh yes, that makes me feel so much better." Jeff ran his hand through his hair. "Now what?"

My phone rang again. Decided answering it was what was currently what. "Malcolm? What's up?"

"We have the mad bomber in custody. So to speak."

"Who's we and who's the mad bomber?"

"We is me and Wruck, since Siler's having a nostalgic moment on the White House rooftop. And you're just going to love who the mad bomber is."

"Breathless with anticipation."

"It's Christopher."

Let that sit on the air for a bit. "The real one or another fake one?"

"Another fake one, per the OVS that, thankfully, all of Security are required to carry on their persons at all times."

"Yeah, that was a good order we put into effect. So, um, is this Christopher saying anything?"

"Yes. He says that he wants to speak with you and warn you against the robot he just blew up, as well as against Somerall and Lee, who he feels are there to kill all of you. He also insists that he's become a real boy and has overcome his programming."

"Just like the one he blew up just said. Right before he was blown up, I mean."

"Really?"

"Really. And the blown up Christopher-Bot also said that Somerall and Lee aren't fully human in their brain parts anymore. Which might be true, since Jeff feels certain they've got emotional overlays going and they insist they know nothing of this."

"Wonderful. So, it's the usual party." Buchanan sounded like

he wanted to hit someone or something, but didn't feel he had
an appropriate target. I could relate.

"Apparently so. And here I thought the day couldn't get any
worse than my morning show stint."

"Oh, never think that, Missus Executive Chief. That's pretty
much you daring the universe, and we all know that the universe
loves to take your dares."

"Okay, point totally taken. By the way, the blown up
Christopher-Bot said that he was the only Christopher-Bot in
existence."

"Huh. This Christopher-Bot says that he had to destroy the
other one because that one was impersonating him."

"Interesting choice, to program in paranoia. I don't get why
whoever's in charge has chosen that as a thing, but apparently
that's how this particular group of robotic loons are rolling.
Lucky us."

"Truly. So, what would you like us to do with this still-living,
if we choose to call it that, Christopher-Bot?"

"Um, bring him in? Carefully. Since I'm sure there's another
one out there gunning for this one. For all we know, there could
be a phalanx of them, all waiting to kill each other one by one.
It's like we've fallen into a Russian nesting doll factory or something."

"Something like that, I'll give you. I'm not confident about
bringing him into the complex when we already have two suspected living bombs in there already."

Handed the phone to Jeff. "Once again, you get to make the
Executive Decision. Enjoy Malcolm sharing what's happening
where he's at." Decided Bruno was getting heavy and put him
down.

He nudged against me to reassure me that he didn't mind and
had appreciated our cuddling. Gave him a scritchy-scratch between his wings as I looked around and gave Joe and Randy the
fast recap while Buchanan brought Jeff up to speed and they
discussed how much foolhardier we wanted to be.

"So, um, dudes, your thoughts?" Prince, Duke, and Riley, not
to be outdone by a bird, clustered around me for petting, which
I gave them in abundance.

"I think we need to get inside," Joe said.

"And stop Somerall and Lee from either blowing up, filming
everyone, or potentially being assassinated," Randy said. "We

need to get them under protection if they're really not human anymore. Or if they're still fully human, come to think of it."

"Not that we'll know without a brain scan," Joe added with a bitter laugh.

"That's it. We need their brains examined. You two, get them to Tito right now, under heavy guard. Tell him to do a brain scan and see what we get."

"Doctor Hernandez might want to take them to Dulce," Joe said.

"He might, but he can probably scan them here. Let's do the initial scan with them still under our complete control. Then, if they're robotic in any way, we'll decide what we do with them."

"You think the Christopher robot was lying?" Randy asked.

"I think it's got a lot of potential, since there is indeed another Christopher-Bot and Malcolm and John have got him. Honestly, right now, I think everyone's lying to us—Somerall, Lee, the Christopher-Bots, and the Kristie-Bot or android or whatever she is. I think we're surrounded by liars and it's time we get to at least a semblance of the truth. If that's even possible, probable, or even potentially viable in the far, far future."

Jeff handed me my phone back. "Buchanan and I agree with Kitty. Let's get everyone examined and then figure out how much we panic."

My phone rang again. Managed not to complain. At least these were all people I knew and liked calling. "Lizzie, what's up?"

"Um, the Bahrainis are waiting for you and I think they're totes getting kind of offended. I don't know that they know what's going on and all that jazz and I think you need to get in here, fast."

"Mona knows how we roll. So does everyone else with her."

"Ah, not *everyone* else," Lizzie said, sounding worried. "That Wasim kid didn't come alone. He's got bodyguards. And they're kind of jerks."

"Fan-freaking-tastic. I will be right there." Hung up and heaved a sigh. "Okay, you guys do whatever and get someone we can trust to gather up the late Christopher-Bot's bits. I have to go be diplomatic."

Joe grinned. "We'll advise Walter that the explosions will continue."

CHAPTER 14

COULDN'T FIND MY SHOES, which was problematic. Bruno, Duke, Riley, and Prince couldn't find my shoes, either. Gave up and went inside the main building via the foyer to the Diplomatic Reception Room at hyperspeed because Lizzie hadn't made it sound like a casual saunter or regally swanning in was in order.

Everyone came with me, though Jeff stopped to order some of the Secret Service agents nearby to handle Blown Up Bot Cleanup Duty. Lucky them.

Found everyone other than my team clustered in here with my mother, who had a long-suffering look on her face and, thankfully, was also holding my shoes. "Your team is trying to salvage the Bahraini situation. Len and Kyle went with them for protection."

"Why didn't you go with them?"

Mom gave me the "really?" look as she handed me my pumps. "Because I might know them."

Pondered this as I put my shoes back on. "Ah. And you might not like them. Or vice versa. Got it." Wondered just who the hell Raheem had sent with his grandson. Considered who Mom sent with her grandchildren—people like Buchanan, Siler, Wruck, and several other P.T.C.U. tough guys and gals. Yeah, okay, perhaps having the Mossad Mamma showing up before the official introductions wasn't a wise move.

"Thanks for catching on so quickly." Mom heaved a sigh. "You'll want to take both of your security teams with you. You might want to take Jeff's along as well."

This was different. Mom rarely shoved the Secret Service at us, because she understood how we rolled and was in favor of it most of the time. Therefore, she wasn't suggesting this because of anything that had gone on so far.

"You think I need to show that I have more bodyguards than Prince Wasim, don't you?"

"Let's just say that I've dealt with more teenagers and foreign dignitaries than you have, so far, and leave it at that."

"Len and Kyle are impressive, you know."

Chuckie nodded. "They are, but I'm sure Angela's right, Kitty. In this instance, you're going to need more than Len and Kyle. I'd suggest that Jeff go with you, only I think that would also give the wrong impression."

"That we were too impressed and therefore Prince Wasim would feel that he could do anything because clearly we're thrilled he's here."

"Exactly." Chuckie managed a grin. "On the plus side your security teams will get to do something."

"You mean other than guard the two potential prisoners?" Jeff asked, nodding his head toward the Security Huddle that was around Somerall and Lee.

"Yeah. Joe and Randy can handle them. They're taking them to Tito anyway."

As I said this, the rest of the flyboys arrived. "We called in backup," Joe said.

"Because we're not stupid or trusting," Randy added.

Jerry Tucker, my favorite flyboy, winked at me. "I hear we're back to the usual insanity, Commander."

"Always, as near as I can tell."

"Not to worry," Matt Hughes said with a grin. "We know how to bust heads."

"Or not, if they're going to explode," Chip Walker added.

"You guys light up my life. Okay, let's have you take Ansom and Talia to Tito pronto. Do the brain scans and such. And let me know immediately what's going on."

"I'll go with them," Chuckie said. "I want to have Buchanan bring the robot they caught back, too, and we might as well have Tito and a science team take a look."

"Under heavy guard," Jeff said worriedly. "We don't need any more explosions today."

"Not that that means we won't get them," I said, as I leaned up and gave him a quick kiss. Then I motioned to my security teams and they broke away and came to me. "Anyone know where our Bahraini visitors actually are?"

"Yes, I got a text from Lizzie," Evalyne Green, the head of my Secret Service detail, shared. "They're in the Blue Room."

"I got one from her too," Phoebe Manning, the second-in-command of said detail who was, thankfully, no relation to the late, unlamented android Leslie Manning. Had a moment of nostalgia for Leslie and Bryce Taylor, an also unlamented android who'd been her brother, as it had turned out. Not everyone from the Washington Wife class had somehow become my friend. Or were still living. "She seems more than a little freaked out."

My brain nudged. There was something about Leslie and Bryce it wanted me to think about. But I had no idea of what or why. "Yeah, Lizzie called me. Apparently we have a situation that demands bodyguard one-upmanship."

"I just hope they don't object to being scanned with an OVS again," Evalyne said as we started off. We were only going a floor above where we were, but it was going to take forever at human normal based on the route we needed to take to get there. Which was fine with me—now wasn't the time to use up my hyperspeed reserves.

"Better them objecting and being proven to be human than us having more androids or robots running around," Phoebe countered.

My brain nudged—harder. Okay, apparently it was time to think about Leslie and Bryce, aka, The Original Made From Scratch Androids.

Well, sort of made from scratch. They'd been made from their original DNA, because they were the children of Evil Genius Extraordinaire, the late and, in this case, great Antony Marling. Marling's androids could pass for human, complete with emotions, until you cracked their outer shell, so to speak. Though we'd destroyed Leslie and Bryce during Operation Assassination, most of the first generation androids like these had been destroyed during Operation Destruction, though we knew we hadn't gotten them all.

Leslie and Bryce had been Marling's real children. Though he and his wife, Cybele, and her sister, Cartwright, had done experiments on them, presumably because Siler had been rescued by his uncle, so they needed new playthings.

Controlled a shudder. How any parent could do what these had done to their children was beyond me. The thought of someone hurting Jamie, Charlie, or Lizzie—or any other child—like this made me physically ill and mad as hell. However, currently, I didn't need rage. Forced my mind back to whatever weird conundrum it was trying to make me ferret out.

So, anything android related came from Marling's work, with a major assist on the goal by Amy's late father, Herbert Gaultier, who was the man behind all the horrible cloning crap. Leslie and Bryce weren't real people anymore by the time I'd met them, and Gaultier's cloning had definitely been involved.

But the Fem-Bots hadn't come from them. The Kitty-Bot, the first one that we now had under our control in Dulce, she'd been with Ronald Yates at the start of Operation Fugly. And Marling and Gaultier had never insinuated that they'd done anything on that project, and nothing we'd found in massive CIA, FBI, and Centaurion Division investigations had connected them to the Fem-Bots in any real way. They had, however, been connected to the late Secretary of State, Monica Strauss.

Pulled out my phone. Chuckie answered right away. "What's wrong?"

"Nothing. Yet. I just have a relevant question. Have we ever figured out who made the first Kitty-Bot, the one that was with Yates impersonating me way back when? The one Monica Strauss used as her prototype. You know, before I knew you and my mom were working in covert ops and all that jazz?"

"Wow, you're really never going to let that go, are you?"

"You've known me how long?"

"Almost forever, and yeah, you're not. I don't have a lot for you. While you'd think that it was created by Titan Security under Marling's leadership, we haven't found any proof of such. Same with Gaultier Enterprises."

"What about all of our robotics information?" We had a lot of it, after all. I'd been too busy with all the Galactic Learning to think about all the Bots out there recently, but clearly today was the day to start up again. "And whatever we've found from the Kitty-Bot?"

"Well, that's kind of interesting, but I'm not sure we have the time right now."

"Is it something you can share with me at the eleven o'clock meeting that I'm sure is, despite all that's gone on, still on the books?"

He laughed. "Yes, everyone there has the clearance."

"Super, then we'll make it so at that time. Don't forget."

"Like you're going to, you mean? No, I'll remember. By the

way, I think we're missing the obvious. The Tinkerer would make the most sense for the original robotics creation."

"Oh, you know, I'd thought of that earlier and forgotten it."

"Shocker."

"Careful, I know where you live."

"Yeah, speaking of that, Pierre let me know that we have a new tenant in the Cairo. Apparently it's a bigwig from the Middle East. The building management seems to be quite thrilled about it. We were advised because the new tenant's on the same floor as me, Nathalie, and Elaine."

Elaine Armstrong was the widow of the late President and now Jeff's Secretary of State. I'd liked her a lot when she'd been the First Lady, and I liked her more now, because now she was doing the same thing she'd always done—helping run the country wisely and with great care and empathy—but with a great deal more power and influence.

I'd met Nathalie Gagnon-Brewer via the Washington Wife Class, but she fell on the Vance and Abner side of the house—close now, but originally, we weren't all that friendly. We'd become friends with her and her husband, Rep. Edmund Brewer, during Operation Sherlock, only to have him murdered by the Mastermind's henchmen during Apprentice Tryouts.

Nathalie had taken her husband's slot in the House and had been appointed the Secretary of Transportation once Jeff was President. The Brewers had lived at the Cairo, and Nathalie had decided to stay because Edmund had loved the building. She'd convinced Elaine to move into the Cairo after Armstrong's death, and I'd followed suit and had Chuckie move in there, too. They were in what they all called the Widow and Widowers Wing. But at least they had each other. And now they had someone else.

Stopped walking. "Oh. Oh no. I have a horrible feeling I know who your new neighbor is."

Chuckie was quiet for a moment. "Oh, hell no! You think Raheem put his teenaged grandson up at my building? Why the hell would he do that?"

"Because he wants Wasim where he can be looked after and protected. And he knows that the Secretary of State, the Secretary of Transportation, *and*, probably most significantly, the Director of the CIA are all living there. Welcome to your new role—Assistant Bahraini Prince Babysitter."

Chuckie groaned. "This day just keeps on getting better and better."

"Yeah, just wait. I'm about to meet our royal visitor."

"I'll tell Walter to expect more explosions."

"That's what Joe said only a few minutes ago."

"Because you and Jeff wisely surround yourselves with smart people."

"I'm not sure if I should be flattered or offended. I think I'll go for both."

"See? I said you were wise."

CHAPTER 15

WE HUNG UP as my entourage and I reached the top of the Grand Staircase that took us up to the State Floor, where Lizzie had told Evalyne that Prince Wasim was waiting to be greeted. My office was, apparently, not up to snuff for meetings of this level.

We headed for the Blue Room, where the President greeted visitors he wasn't greeting at the steps of the White House. The significance of the location wasn't lost on me. Hopefully the significance of the President not being here would be impressed upon Wasim.

"Any suggestions?" I asked Evalyne as we neared the doorway.

"Please don't give anyone any reason to shoot a gun."

"That's it? That's your advice?"

"For you? Yes." She jerked her head at the four dudes on my Secret Service detail, who all headed into the room before us. She also spoke into her Matrix-style headset that all the Secret Service had. "Cyclone is joining Comet in the Blue section of the Crown. Is Cosmos still with Playboy?"

I was close enough to her, and my hearing had been enhanced enough, that I could hear the response from Joseph, the head of Jeff's detail. "Yes. Cosmos, Playboy, and entourage are all in the Big Cement Mixer." Meaning they were going back in the LSR. Okay, that was good. Hopefully. "Big Momma is with Cosmos." Meaning my mother. So all was good. Mom would handle anything Jeff and Chuckie couldn't.

Pity she wasn't willing to handle what I had to.

We stepped into the room. Like so many around here, it was an oval and decorated in Early American Stuffiness. And, true to its name, the dominant color was blue. If I didn't pay attention to the people in the room. Because the dominant clothing choice color was black.

This wasn't unusual, since I was so used to the Armani Fatigues. However, people wore other colors to the White House and I'd kind of gotten used to seeing some of them, other than my iced blue. But security personnel tended to be traditionalists, and the ones with the kid I presumed was Wasim were traditional to the core.

There were ten of them, and they were all in business suits that fit them far better than most of the suits our Secret Service were wearing, meaning they were undoubtedly paid a whole lot more. They were all also big, mean looking, and clearly armed. This was technically a protocol breach of the highest order, but presumably Walter had given the Bahrainis special dispensation.

My people were on one side of the room, the big security guys were around Wasim on the other side. And Mona, Khalid, Jakob, Oren, and Leah were sort of in the middle of the two. The way we'd entered the room put us across from Mona and her contingent.

Kyle was standing in front of Colette and Mrs. Maurer, Len was in front of Lizzie, Abner was behind her, and Vance was sort of out in front, just barely, standing between the boys. Khalid was next to Mona, with Mossad behind them, but in position to react without hitting Mona or Khalid if necessary.

Wasim's bodyguards had Wasim nearest to the front, with two bodyguards within arm's reach of him and the rest spread out behind these two in a circular formation. It gave them a pretty unobstructed view of the room.

The room was definitely set up in an antagonistic way, only we weren't the antagonists. Could see why Lizzie was doing her best to advise everyone to come in with guns, if not blazing, at least set to stun.

Stopped walking and my security teams spread out, Evalyne and Phoebe staying near me, while the others moved to points around the room. Manfred went behind my team, Daniel, Joshua, Lucas, and Marcus went behind Wasim's section, and my four male Secret Service agents were at each point in the oval, so to speak, meaning we had five security personnel behind Wasim's people. They didn't seem fazed.

As I stopped walking, Mona flashed me a smile. "Your Majesty, may I please introduce Prince Wasim of Bahrain?" She curtsied to me, then bowed toward Wasim, her hand outstretched toward him.

Noted how I'd been introduced, heaved an internal sigh, and went into Queen Katherine Mode. I bowed my head toward Wasim. "We're pleased to have you visit us."

Wasim bowed back. "I'm honored to meet Queen Katherine, whom my beloved grandfather, King Raheem of Bahrain, holds in the highest of esteem."

"And we hold King Raheem in the same esteem." Looked closely at the bodyguards. They reminded me a lot of Khalid in certain ways. "We are also happy to welcome members of the Bahraini Royal Army to the White House."

Every one of them looked surprised, then quickly wiped those expressions off their faces. Interesting. Raheem seemed to really enjoy tests. Wasn't sure who was being tested this time—me, Wasim, Mona, or the bodyguards. If I was a betting girl, and I was, my money would be on all of us.

The security team didn't do anything, though, including say "thank you." Clearly Lizzie hadn't overstated anything.

Looked back at Wasim. He was taller than Lizzie, but only just. Slender, with black hair worn in a rather shaggy style that did only a few rock stars favors. He had none of the teddy bear look his grandfather had. He was pretty cute, or would be if he had a better hairstyle and wasn't in totally geeky coke-bottle glasses that did nothing to enhance his features.

Though he was wearing clothing I knew to be both fashionable and extremely expensive, he didn't look comfortable in them and they, therefore, didn't look that great on him. He also didn't give off the spoiled rich kid air I'd been expecting. He did remind me of someone, though. Someone I'd known most of my life and someone Raheem knew, too. Another likely reason he'd been sent here.

"Your bodyguards are either deaf and mute, or else they don't understand the proper protocols when they're welcomed somewhere." Looked back at the security dudes. "Or else they're being rude on purpose. A course of action I don't recommend." Turned back to Wasim and raised an eyebrow.

He gave me a nervous smile. "I'm sure they don't want to appear presumptuous."

Looked at my Middle Eastern Contingent out of the corner of my eye. Mona had a pleasant look plastered on her face, Khalid was stone-faced but his eyes were narrowed, Jakob and Oren looked similar to Khalid. They were all looking at Wasim and his bodyguards.

But Leah was looking at me.

Turned my head just slightly toward her. Clearly she'd been waiting for this, because she put her thumb and forefinger up to her nostrils, in a way that looked like she was gently rubbing her nose. But it was also the way someone would do to hold their nostrils closed against a bad odor.

Took this to mean she felt that something was stinking here. Agreed.

Stepped forward and got right in front of the bodyguard I took to be the one in charge, based on him being the biggest and closest in proximity to Wasim. "I don't think that's actually the case, Wasim. Is it?" I asked the man I was looking up at.

He made eye contact with me and shrugged his massive shoulders. "You aren't *our* Queen." He got a lot of contempt into those four words.

Worked for me.

Because Akiko really understood how I rolled, this dress looked skintight but it had a lot of stretch. Which was good, since I slammed my knee up into Mr. Not My Queen's groin.

He hadn't been expecting it. Nor was he expecting my rising elbow strike to hit his chin as he buckled from my groin strike.

I'd done all this at hyperspeed, so the rest of them weren't expecting me to grab Mr. Not My Queen and toss him at the rest of them as hard as nonhumanly possible. They were all heading for me, and they all went down like bowling pins.

All but one. That one had been near to the back. He'd leapt forward and tackled Wasim and had the kid shielded entirely with his own body.

"Based on my human bowling expertise, I want us to start a White House Bowling League. You guys can fight over who gets me on their team."

"Noted, and the Secret Service team calls dibs," Evalyne said. Risked a fast look around the room. Yep, all the Secret Service agents, my A-C agents, Len and Kyle, and the Middle Eastern Contingent other than Mona had their guns drawn and aimed at the guards on the ground. So much for Evalyne's request. "If any of you make a move toward the Queen Regent we'll shoot you dead."

"What she said. The nine on the floor are to go back to Bahrain on the next flight out of town, to not pass go, to not collect any kinds of dollars, and to explain to King Raheem that they were too busy being disrespectful to me to protect Prince Wasim. The one who actually did his job can stay with my blessing."

The guards who were getting to their feet all looked at Mona. "What the Queen Regent says goes," Mona said. "You will return in dishonor. And we will ensure that the King knows of this before you've even left the White House grounds."

"Already done," Mrs. Maurer said. Mona and I both looked at her. She shrugged. "King Raheem is one of your dearest friends. I wanted to reassure him that his grandson had arrived safely. Then the bodyguards started acting aggressive. I shared that with him. He's not pleased," she said to the men who were now mostly standing again. "But he thanks Queen Katherine for spotting traitors he thought were loyal."

"We *are* loyal," Mr. Not My Queen said as he was helped up by two of the others. "But we're loyal to our royal family. Not you and yours."

"Pity. Because, as near as I can tell, your king doesn't feel that way."

"No, dear, he does not. King Raheem is disappointed. Very disappointed indeed. In a very medieval way, as near as I can interpret from his replies." Mrs. Maurer managed to make this threat sound almost sweet. I was impressed.

Looked around the room while I pondered this particular situation. "You know, I realize that this is a fancy-schmancy room. But my understanding is that it's *the* most redecorated room in the entire complex. I wonder if that's because people tend to get shot in here for being overly rude and immensely stupid?"

"Potentially," Evalyne replied as the nine bodyguards looked around, clearly determining who they could grab as a hostage or similar. "As the Queen Regent said, this room gets redecorated frequently. It's in the budget, so don't test us, because we're all ready to shoot you dead and take the thanks of your King for saving him from having to do this himself."

My pondering came to a conclusion. And that conclusion was that normal bodyguards didn't pull stunts like this. They were paid to do a job, and I knew for a fact their job hadn't been to disrespect me and piss me off. And yet the eight backing Mr. Not My Queen didn't seem even remotely surprised about this turn of events. The dude with Wasim, who was still covering the kid, was the only one who looked like he hadn't expected any of this to happen.

Looked back at Mr. Not My Queen. "You're a True Believer, aren't you?"

He jerked. Just a bit. The rest of them did, too. Other than the one still covering Wasim. His eyes widened. In horror, if I was any judge. "I have no idea what you're talking about," Mr. Not My Queen said.

Khalid went to the one good security dude and Wasim and moved them behind the Mossad agents. All their guns were still aimed at the other guards and I knew all four of them were ready to shoot to kill. It was nice to have protective friends.

"Sure you don't. Nancy, please let King Raheem know that his security forces have been infiltrated by Club Fifty-One True Believers. Manfred, I want A-C Field teams to be with King Raheem on the highest of alerts by the time Nancy's done texting. Mona, please have someone verify that your embassy is not also infiltrated. Com on!"

"Already on, My Queen Regent." Walter sounded like he'd been waiting all his life to use that title for me. Possibly he had. "Phoebe advised me that I should be listening in. William has already sent teams to Dulles to check on their security footage." William was Walter's older brother and the most powerful imageer after Christopher and the current Head of Imageering, Serene Dwyer. He was also in charge of Dulce Security, meaning he was the Head of Security for all of Centaurion Division. "I imagine we're going to find out very curious things."

"I imagine we are, too." My bet was on us finding footage of these guys meeting up with a Christopher-Bot, but I was willing to be surprised and discover they'd met up with other enemies of ours, either instead of or in addition to. Why limit our enemies, right?

"King Raheem is confirmed as being under Centaurion protection," Manfred said as the room filled with A-C Field Teams who disarmed the security forces.

"He said to thank you, dear," Mrs. Maurer confirmed. "He's also relieved that Wasim remains safe." She looked at Mossad. "He's grateful to you as well."

Oren nodded. "Tell him it's our honor to assist."

"He appreciates that," Mrs. Maurer said. "He also requests that Lieutenant Colonel Daba be in charge of choosing the new bodyguards."

The entire Middle Eastern Contingent looked surprised by

this. "Excuse me?" Khalid said politely. "I believe you've misunderstood. There is no Lieutenant Colonel here."

Mrs. Maurer waved her phone at him. "Yes, dear, there is.
You must not realize you've just had a promotion. Congratula-
tions. You're not a Major any longer."

Wasim's only real bodyguard quietly congratulated Khalid.
The rest of them just glared at him.

"What's your name and rank?" I asked the good bodyguard.

"Naveed Murad. I am a Captain."

"Good to meet you, Naveed. Nancy, please ensure that King
Raheem is aware that Captain Murad is a credit to his army.
Unlike nine others I'm not bothering to name."

Mr. Not My Queen shot me a snide look, then said something
very nasty to Khalid. He was using native tongue, not English,
but the universal translator that most of us were equipped with
worked just fine. I was impressed that I could now tell that he'd
spoken in Arabic even though I could understand the words.
Wondered if the translator chip or whatever was installed
adapted what you understood as you learned. Then realized that
it was A-C created and figured that yes, it was.

Went back over to Mr. Not My Queen. "You're going to regret being rude to someone I consider a good friend. Especially
because I understood every word you said and, contrary to what
you're hoping, Khalid is not going to be cursed with inconti-
nence while covered in boils with horrible creatures eating him
from the inside out. However, if that's what you're hoping for,
you'll be thrilled to know that I'm about to hand you over to the
CIA. They have a lot of really fun things they like to do to confirmed international terrorists. I'm sure they have a way to give
you boils all over."

He glared at me. "We are not terrorists. And you and your
threats don't frighten me, woman."

"Wow, you know, you're kind of lucky there are other people
here."

"So I can't hurt you?"

"This from the dude I used as a human bowling ball? No. So
I can't really hurt *you*. Permanently."

"I know what you are," he snarled quietly. "You will warp the
Prince's mind, make him *American*," he sneered.

"Oh, blah, blah, blah. We went through this a couple of
months ago. I might have bought that you actually were concerned for Wasim's welfare, but only Naveed actually performed

the job you're all supposed to be doing. So, pull the other one and all that jazz."

"You will take him away from the true God and you will destroy our people and our world."

"Surely you don't think you're more impressive than the many religious leaders I dealt with. Or are you that full of yourself that you're going against what, literally, every religious leader in the world is saying to do?"

"Not every leader. What is happening in our world is the End of Days, and you have helped to bring that about. And hell will rain down upon you and yours for this." He sounded extremely confident of this. Then again, every fanatic sounded confident. And I'd heard this, in one form or another, from our favorite homegrown fanatics for far too long.

"That's what the True Believers say," Naveed said. "All of them, regardless of what God they follow. They feel all who are trying to live within the new world order need to die."

"Harvey Gutermuth and Farley Pecker must be beside themselves with happiness." Mr. Not My Queen's eyes widened. Just a bit, but I was close to him and watching for it. "Len, could you please advise the Director of the CIA that we have a new set of terrorists, both in our possession, so to speak, and worldwide, please and thank you?"

"Already done," Len said.

Was going to say something more when Mr. Not My Queen's eyes, and the eyes of all the others in custody, opened quite wide.

So I had a fairly good guess for who was now standing behind me.

CHAPTER 16

TURNED AROUND TO SEE exactly who I'd expected, based on reactions and my assumptions—Christopher.

Proving that it was really him, he was shooting Patented Glare #1 at the entire room. "What the literal hell is going on?"

"Hold that question for just a mo'. Not that I'm unhappy to see you, but why are you here? As in, in this room and right now?"

"William told me I was needed back here." He eyed Mr. Not My Queen. "You think you know me, don't you?"

The Bad Bodyguards all sort of nodded. Refrained from mentioning how that would be a cool band name, and instead kept my focus on the matters at hand. That was me, always taking one for the team. "So, we found the footage from Dulles?"

"Yeah," Christopher said. "Mona, did you go anywhere before you came to the White House?"

"We drove by our embassy, to show Prince Wasim where it was. We also drove by the Cairo, where the Prince will have a residence. But we didn't stop. Essentially, we came directly here."

"We were in three cars," Jakob said. "But one of us," he indicated the three Mossad agents, "was in each car. Oren, Khalid, and I were the drivers, and we never broke off from each other."

"Good. We're already having the cars searched. They need to be strip-searched," he said to the Field agents as he pointed to the prisoners.

"Not that I'm arguing with this mindset, but why so?"

Christopher heaved a sigh. "Because 'I' gave them something at the airport. All of them." He looked around. "Other than those two." He pointed to Wasim and his lone good bodyguard. "They weren't around at the time, just these nine."

Naveed cocked his head. "The only time would have been when we used the bathroom. They came with us," he indicated the male portion of the Middle Eastern Contingent, "while the others supposedly gathered the Prince's luggage."

"And we used the ladies' facilities at the same time," Mona added, indicating herself and Leah.

"Oh, they gathered it, all right," Chuckie said as he joined us in the room. "Only you have bags I'm willing to bet never came over from Bahrain. Good call," he said to Christopher. "Lots of explosives in the bags. Even those that belong to the Prince."

"We traveled with nothing harmful," Wasim said, sounding freaked out. Couldn't blame him. "I have no idea what's going on."

"It's totes okay," Lizzie said. "Kitty'll handle it. You'll be fine."

Wasim didn't look reassured. Decided that the rest of that conversation didn't need to be heard by anyone who was a Club 51 True Believer. "Yes, I will. Speaking of which," turned to Mr. Not My Queen, "were you aware that you were taking instructions from a robot?"

He stared at me. "What lies are you trying to tell me? He's right here."

"No, he's the person the robot was created to impersonate. I'm just curious if you knew you were dealing with a robot or if you thought you were dealing with a traitor."

"Answering truthfully might make things easier for you," Chuckie said.

Mr. Not My Queen snorted. "Now that is a lie for certain. However, no, we met with a human. Him." He nodded at Christopher. "He is one of us."

Christopher rolled his eyes. "Chuck, let's get them locked up."

Mr. Not My Queen made eye contact with Christopher. "Mahdi."

Christopher stared at him. "What?"

The word didn't translate, so assumed it was a name.

"Mahdi," Mr. Not My Queen said with more emphasis.

"Means nothing to me," Christopher said.

"It's the name of the Imam who leads Islam's rapture, essentially," Chuckie said. Noted that the entire Middle Eastern Contingent, which now included Wasim and Naveed, nodded at this. "And it's also clearly a code word. You're either supposed to give the countersign or react."

"But, since Christopher's not the Man-Bot you're looking

for, you just get to move along right now. Can we get these creeps out of my house and into severe custody?"

"Yes," Chuckie said with a chuckle I knew was intentionally evil. A couple of the captured True Believer Bodyguards looked a little uncomfortable. Clearly they taught fascinating things at the Farm and other CIA training facilities. "We'll be taking them somewhere nice and horrible."

"Good. Not Guantanamo, though. I may want access to them."

"Oh, no. Guantanamo is far too public for where they're going." Chuckie nodded to the Field teams and the Bad Bodyguards were trooped out. "Be right back," he added to the rest of us, and he grabbed a spare A-C. They all zipped off at hyperspeed. Which was the first part of the punishment.

Hyperspeed was hard on humans. It made any human who experienced it barf at best. If you went too fast too long, you passed out. Or, rather, you used to. These days, any humans working with or around Centaurion Division didn't run that risk, because I hired extremely well.

During the madness that led up to my wedding, aka Operation Invasion, I'd found Tito Hernandez, who was going to medical school full-time, working three jobs, and, in his copious spare time, moving up in the ranks of Mixed Martial Arts. We'd taken him away from all that and, like in *Charlie's Angels*, he was now doing what he was really good at on a daily basis. And there wasn't a day we weren't grateful for his presence.

Tito was exceptionally awesome and, in addition to the OVS, had created Hyperspeed Dramamine, which let any normal human handle hyperspeed without any negative side effects. Originally, we'd had to take a daily pill. Now it was a monthly shot, though the pills were still available for new people being brought into the fold.

However, I knew the prisoners weren't getting the Hyperspeed Dramamine. And that was more than okay with me. Really hoped they had a lot in their stomachs to barf out, because I knew without asking that Chuckie had everyone going at the fastest hyperspeed they could manage.

Once they were gone, Christopher barked some orders to my A-C Security team, and he and the five of them did a hyperspeed check of the room. Unsurprisingly, they were done fast.

"Bugs," Manfred said as they all pooled what they'd found onto the table that stood in the middle of the room. It had a vase with lovely flowers in it that had, somehow, remained unscathed during all of this. Wasn't sure who was more relieved, me or Abner, but shoved this happily into the very sparse win column.

Only to have it snatched away. Christopher pulled the flowers out and dumped all the bugs into the water. On the plus side, Kyle took the flowers from him, divvied them up, and handed them to Mona and Mrs. Maurer.

"Ah, thank you?" Mona said. She was clearly trying not to laugh.

"Lovely thought, dear," Mrs. Maurer said, lips quirking.

"Maybe we can take the other flowers in the room for me, Leah, Kitty, Evalyne, and Phoebe," Lizzie said, in that teasing way little sisters have. "And guys like flowers, too, remember." Kyle gave her a very gentle punch in the arm, and she grinned. Wasim watched this closely. Really wondered what his sibling relationships were like.

It was clear that, by now, everyone was controlling their Inner Hyena, other than Abner, who looked like he was deciding between crying or freaking out but had wisely chosen resigned acceptance, Wasim, who was observing more than reacting, and Christopher, who apparently hadn't brought a sense of humor with him on this excursion or else was so focused he hadn't really realized what he'd done. Or how much those flowers had cost.

"Let's search the entire complex," Christopher said after all the bugs were in water.

Looked to Mona, who was politely holding her half bouquet, though away from her body so water didn't drip onto her clothes. "Did you all actually hit the entire complex?"

"No, and I don't recall anyone wandering off, either."

"They didn't," Naveed said. "If you want to bring me along, I can retrace our route."

Christopher nodded, then looked at me. "Does he get the pill?"

"Yes, he does. Wasim should probably have one, too."

"What pill?" Naveed asked suspiciously. "The Prince will ingest nothing."

"Well, while I appreciate your devotion to the cause, especially after all we've just gone through, I'll wager the Prince plans on ingesting food and drink while he's here, so there's that. Also, A-Cs move fast, as I know you know. If you want to spend your time barfing your guts out, then, by all means, refuse the pill. If, on the other hand, you'd like to not be ill all the time, especially in danger situations, take the pill." Looked at Wasim. "Your grandfather took the pill I gave him without complaint. Because he's very clear that he and we are on the same side."

"We all take it," Khalid said.

"Oh, I'm sure Major Murad is just being extra-cautious," Mrs. Maurer said. "And, after all that's happened, who can blame him?"

"Excuse me," Naveed said politely, "but, as I said, my rank is Captain."

She merrily waved her phone at him, and she'd been texting one-handed, since she, too, was holding onto her flowers. Clearly Mrs. Maurer was enjoying this particular action. "Oh, yes, I'm sorry. What with all that was going on, haven't had a moment to advise you that King Raheem has raised you in rank as well."

Naveed looked shocked. Wasim, however, looked pleased. Took that to mean that Wasim actually felt safe with Naveed, which was all for the good.

"So, what's it gonna be?" I asked, after Khalid had congratulated Naveed. "Barfing or risking taking our evil Western medicines for the win?"

Wasim strode over to me and put his hand out. "I will gladly take whatever Queen Katherine feels is right. My grandfather said you were to be given my utmost trust and respect."

Dug the pill bottle I always kept handy out of my purse and gave him one. Tossed the bottle to Naveed. Looked back into my purse. "I wonder if I have water bottles in here."

Sure enough, the Elves delivered and I handed a small water bottle to Wasim and tossed the other to Naveed. No one questioned, which was good, since my answer was both one most wouldn't believe and one I couldn't say anyway. Made a mental note to try to have a chat with the King of the Elves sooner as opposed to later, though.

"Is there anything you don't carry in there?" Christopher asked, as Wasim and Naveed took their medicine and Naveed returned the bottle of pills to me.

"Nope, and for that you should be grateful."

He shot me a smile versus a Patented Glare. "I'm always grateful you're here, Kitty." His expression went back to serious. "Let's retrace those steps right now, though. I want whatever else these people stashed here removed faster than fast."

With that, he and my A-C Security team zipped off, Manfred holding onto Naveed.

Turned back to Wasim. "So, welcome to Washington. This is, sadly, what we call a normal day."

Wasim blinked at me. Then he smiled, rather shyly. "It seems very exciting."

"Oh, you have no idea," I said as half the room snorted. "But, truly, it appears you're going to find out."

CHAPTER 17

CHRISTOPHER AND THE TEAM were back fast, with a lot more bugs to drop in the vase. "No bombs, thank God," he said once they were done.

"Nice to know Chuckie found all of those they'd brought in the luggage. But we had the bugs in here a while—that means whoever was listening on the other end knows what's going on. At least somewhat."

"That's why they're in water, not smashed. Serene prefers it that way."

"Whatever works. Speaking of which, why were you at Dulce earlier?"

"Tell you later." Christopher pulled his phone out and dialed. "Lots of bugs found. Yeah. Yeah. No, no bombs. Yes, I agree. You'll be back when? Great, see you then." He hung up.

"Who were you chatting with?"

"Chuck. The prisoners are exactly where you're probably thinking they are and they have the bombs secured. The prince's luggage is back and so is his," he nodded toward Naveed. "Under the circumstances, we don't want anyone else from Bahrain sent over."

I was thinking the prisoners were under the Pentagon, but could pick up enough of a clue not to say so out loud. "I agree."

A Field team I didn't recognize came in, dropped off the presumably now-safe luggage and took the vase, presumably to send it to Dulce for Serene to play with its contents at her leisure which, knowing Serene, would be immediately.

Looked at Mr. Watch. I had fifteen minutes before my 11 a.m. with Jeff and everyone else in the LSR, meaning before I had to do my jobs as Recap and Megalomaniac Girl. Giving me a whopping quarter of an hour to be motherly. "Okay! So, let's get Wasim and Naveed situated, shall we?"

"Perhaps Prince Wasim should stay at our embassy?" Mona asked. Couldn't blame her.

Nor, sadly, could I agree with her, because Raheem had been pretty damn clear and, after all of this, he wasn't wrong to want Wasim with me. "While the Prince is more than welcome to do so, I know his grandfather wanted him here with us for at least a little while."

"The Prince has his own apartments," Naveed reminded us.

"He does indeed. But, until such time as his grandfather feels comfortable, I think we'll have the two of you rough it in the Lincoln Bedroom."

Somehow or other, despite this place being huge, we'd run out of living space. Jeff and I were alone in the gigantic Presidential Suite because Jamie and Charlie were in the West and East bedrooms, respectively, and had refused to sleep in our rooms with us unless thunderstorms and such were happening. Therefore, we had Lizzie and our nanny, Colette's eldest sister Nadine, in the Queen's Bedroom. We'd turned the West Sitting Hall into a playroom and entertainment center for our family and all personnel that were living in the White House with us.

The Third Floor had been remodeled to handle all of our personnel, and we were at capacity, in no small part because the majority of our animals—Earth native and galactic-foreign exotic—had come with us and had to stay somewhere, since kennels were out of the question because I wanted my father to continue to speak to me. Of course, the animals all slept with Jamie, Charlie, and Lizzie. A few faithful ones slept with us, but most of the animals had abandoned me and Jeff for the kids.

The East Sitting Room was historic and we had to leave it alone. We actively utilized the President's Dining Room and connected kitchen. The Yellow Oval Room and the Treaty Room were both important enough that we kept them as they were. So I could put Wasim and Naveed in the Cosmetology Room—aka where Vance, Akiko, and Pierre desperately tried to work their magic on me when I had to do public appearances—or I could put them into the Lincoln Bedroom.

Normally, I'd have shoved them into rooms over at Blair House or the American Centaurion Embassy, which was where most alien visitors stayed. But these were not normal circumstances. And besides, I didn't plan on us having anyone else staying with us anyway.

Wasim brightened up a bit. "Grandfather says that's where he and Grandmother stayed when they visited. Grandmother is still using the vase and towel sets you gave her."

White House towels were a "thing." I hadn't known this the first time someone had asked me to get them a set, but had discovered they were highly coveted shortly thereafter. So, we'd contacted the vendor and Jeff had had a tonnage of towel sets made up, which we'd paid for ourselves, just as we would any other gift. We kept them on hand to give to people, and I'd never had such luck with presents in my life.

The vase had been chosen by Abner and filled with special arrangements every other day while the King and Queen were here. We'd also arranged to have the vase filled with flowers weekly once they'd gone home, seeing as hyperspeed and gates made that really easy to do.

"I'm glad she's enjoying them." I was. It was nice to know that we were making someone happy somewhere.

"We will stay here," Wasim told the Middle Eastern Contingent in a tone that I was pretty sure he was hoping sounded royal. It didn't. It sounded like a dorky kid trying to be tough. He was really going to have a rough time at an American school.

Why Raheem wanted him here, with me and Lizzie, registered. It wasn't just for the clearly hoped-for love connection. It was to have Wasim protected beyond what a bodyguard could do.

Naveed bowed his head. "As you command."

"As you wish," Mona said, also bowing her head. Knew her well enough to be pretty sure she was relieved and worried both.

"Thank you for your good service to our person," Wasim said, still trying to be Extremely Royal and still failing utterly.

Noted Lizzie out of the corner of my eye. She was studying Wasim, head cocked a bit to the right. She didn't look derisive, and I had a feeling she'd come to the same conclusion I had.

Colette's words from earlier came back. It was hard to come into any tight-knit group and acclimate easily. And while there were a ton of us, we were indeed tight. And Mrs. Maurer had compared him to an exchange student—far from home and all alone. Much more alone now, since we'd just taken away nine men he'd thought would die to protect him.

Didn't think about it. Went to Wasim and hugged him. "Welcome home. We're really glad to have you with us, Wasim."

He hugged me back and I felt his body sort of relax against mine. "Thank you, Your Highness."

"Kitty, hon. You call me Kitty unless we're impressing someone." Let him go and went to Naveed. "I'm not sure if you're a hugger or if, should I try to hug you, you'd freak out."

Naveed smiled at me. The first smile I'd seen on his face. Looked good on him. "I think that, today, a handshake is more than acceptable. Royalty don't . . . hug their retainers where we come from." He put his hand out.

Took his hand and shook it. Then pulled him in and hugged him anyway. "Our kind of royalty does, though. All the time."

He started laughing as I let go. "You are not conventional in any way, are you?"

"Nope, not even a little bit. And I also know that, in your culture, shaking my hand is pretty much about as scandalous as my hugging you."

Naveed grinned. "It is. King Raheem, however, shook your hand. And you hugged him when he arrived at the White House for his visit. Indicating both that times are changing and you're a very special person."

"Welcome to the team, Naveed. I think you're going to fit right in."

CHAPTER 18

WE HEADED UPSTAIRS and installed Wasim and Naveed in their quarters. The Elves had already been by and had rearranged the room—now there were two beds, and the look was a little more masculine.

Once their luggage was dropped off, I showed them the rest of this floor, including who was sleeping where, explained what we'd done with the West Sitting Hall, and explained how the fridge in the Family Kitchen worked.

Not that Wasim and Naveed had never seen a refrigerator before. But the way ours worked were definitely different.

As far as the A-Cs and the general public that was intimate enough with them to be in A-C-controlled housing knew, there was an Operations Team consisting of dedicated A-Cs who handled clothing, housing, food, and any other requirements for the rest of the A-C population. I'd started calling them the Elves pretty much from day one, because that was how it seemed to me—like a fairy tale.

Their work was achieved via a subatomic, spatiotemporal warp process, filtered through black hole technology causing a space-time shift with both a controlled event horizon and ergosphere that allowed safe transference of any and all materials, based on gate technology.

Supposedly.

The reality was that while almost everyone in the world believed this, there were a handful of us who knew differently— me, Paul Gower, and Richard White. And what we knew was that there was no Operations Team, no Elves, and while the science might indeed be as advertised or it might not, everything was achieved by one person snapping his fingers.

That person was Algar, who was the God in the Machine for the A-Cs, and had been for millennia. Because he wasn't human, A-C, or, frankly, from this universe. And, to make it even better, he was a criminal on the run. So to speak.

Algar was from the Black Hole Universe, and he was in trouble because he was a Free Will Fanatic of the highest order. I had no idea of how many universes and galaxies he'd wandered through after committing his initial crimes against what the Black Hole People believed should be done—saving the races from themselves—before I'd met him. But he was literally the most powerful being in our particular galaxy, and I'd met a lot of powerful beings by now.

Basically, he used the refrigerators and cupboards and hampers and such as portals. You wanted it? Ask at the portal, open the door, and there it was. Algar always delivered. While, at the same time, he ensured that thousands of people firmly believed he didn't exist but an entire team of A-Cs doing this work did. It was impressive, really.

Gower and White knew about Algar because they were the current and former Supreme Pontifexes of the A-Cs of Earth and he considered them needing to know. I knew because, for some reason, I appeared to be his favorite. Hundreds of years prior, whoever was the King of Alpha Four would have known Algar and what he could do. But as the bloodline had altered, and the mindset as well, Algar had chosen to align with Jeff's father, Alfred, though Alfred didn't know who Algar was or even that he existed, at least as far as I knew. So when Alfred had come to Earth, so had Algar.

Gladys Gower, the original Head of Security for Centaurion Division, had known about Algar. Whether that meant William, and possibly Walter, knew, I couldn't say. Because Algar was powerful enough to be able to prevent any of us from talking about him, and he shielded our minds and emotions as well, so no one else could read us thinking about him.

So, I still thought of the Operations Team as the Elves for the most part, because those words Algar allowed me to say. And besides, I liked making him work a little.

"You say what you want," I explained in front of the fridge. "For example, I'd like a Coke and a donut, please. Then you open the door." I so opened, to find a lot of Cokes and a pink box that held nice, fresh donuts in it.

Removed the box and put it on the table. Grabbed one of the

Cokes. "Anyone else want one, or would you prefer something else?"

Apparently Coke was the drink of choice or everyone was being polite, because everyone took a Coke, leaving the fridge bare. "Thank you," I said to the fridge. Then I closed the door. "Oh, could I please have a mostly green banana, too?" Opened the door, and there it was. "Thanks again, you're the best."

"Why do you thank the machine?" Wasim asked as we all munched our donuts.

"Because someone's doing the work. Bringing you whatever food you want, taking your dirty clothes, cleaning them, and putting them back. Giving you lovely new clothes to wear if you need them. Cleaning up after you. And when someone does something for you, no matter how big or how small, and no matter if you can see them do it or not, you say thank you."

Wasim nodded as I finished my donut and started in on my banana. It had been far too long since I'd eaten, and I knew without asking that Jeff wasn't going to adjourn us for lunch promptly at noon, especially based on the day we'd had so far.

Had Wasim and Naveed both give the old Talking To Inanimate Objects thing a try. They both asked for something that could only be found in the Middle East. And both of them got exactly what they'd wanted.

Once we'd finished our snacks and Cokes, I got another one for the long journey to the LSR. Then I had Vance take my team, including Lizzie, Len, Kyle, and the Middle Eastern Contingent, including Wasim and Naveed, downstairs for an early lunch. I mean, one Coke and one donut could have only possibly taken the edge off of their hunger. The addition of a banana had only barely taken the edge off of mine. Besides, I liked to keep Chef on his toes, and I was fairly certain that Jeff wouldn't want them eating with everyone in the LSR.

Once they were all headed off, it was time to mosey over to the LSR, with Christopher and my two Security teams in tow. I was going to be late. Found the will to go on and sipped my Coke.

"Think it's safe to have Lizzie and the new kid across the hall from each other?" Christopher asked.

"Yeah, because the teenagers are both sleeping with adult supervision. Otherwise? Hells to the no." Not that I thought that either one of them was thinking about hooking up with the other. At the moment.

He laughed. "Yeah. So, Chuck told me that we definitely have the robot in custody. The one Buchanan found."

"I prefer the term Man-Bot."

"I'm sure you do." This earned me Patented Glare #2. "However, we'll go with robot."

"Dude, you've known me how long? We'll be going with Man-Bot, thank you very much."

He sighed. "Fine. Whatever makes you happy. At any rate, Chuck's pretty sure that the *Man-Bot* that met up with the True Believers was the one that you and Jeff spoke with."

"Interestinger and more interestinger. And see? Using the term Man-Bot didn't kill you or anything."

He groaned. "The Kitty-isms, they burn."

Laughed. "You're doing them, too, now, you know."

"Don't remind me. Anyway, no one's gotten anything more about other Man-Bots from this one. So we have no idea how many more of them there are, just that they're all likely to look like me." He sounded down.

"Now you know how I felt and feel. Trust me, Amy doesn't want the robotic version of you. She wants the you that is the real you."

"It's not that. I know how they got me as the prototype. I basically handed myself to them on a silver platter, because I was shooting up with the wonder drug."

Took his hand and squeezed it. "Everyone has something they've gone through. You don't shoot Surcenthumain anymore and haven't for years. Do you still have cravings?"

"No. Honestly I haven't for a long time. But it doesn't matter. They had me where they wanted me. God alone knows what else they got from me."

"Yeah." My brain nudged. Tried to figure out why.

"I just wonder who else they've trapped in order to duplicate them."

My brain nudged, harder. "You know . . ."

"What?" Christopher asked after a few long moments. "I know that look. What connection did you just make?"

"Not sure. But here's the question I need to ask—how is it I have a Fem-Bot?"

"They made a Fem-Bot of you to kill your mother. We determined that before you'd been with us two full days."

"Yes, but that's not what I mean. I *mean*—how did they get me in the first place in order to gather the info to make the prototype? As in, how is it that the very first Fem-Bot was made in my complete likeness? She sounds like me, looks like me, moves pretty much like me. And yet, I was never in a situation where I was helpless and someone could have or would have been able to do whatever they did with you and Janelle Gardiner."

Christopher didn't answer—Evalyne did. "Someone within the P.T.C.U. got specs on you somehow. That's the only thing that makes sense. Or the CIA. But a government agency that worked with your mother seems the obvious answer."

"Yeah, I agree. So, here's the next big question. Can we assume that it was Leventhal Reid? Or do we have a sleeper enemy that's still out there?"

CHAPTER 19

WE REACHED THE LSR, which wasn't that far away because, unlike the Original Situation Room, it wasn't in the West Wing. No, it was back on the State Floor, the same floor as the Blue Room.

The OSR, as we now referred to it, held about two dozen people at maximum. However, we tended to roll with two dozen people at minimum. The Cabinet Room held a few more, but we still ended up having far more people involved than, apparently, any other Administration prior.

So, we'd had the Elves redo the State Dining room to make it function as the main meeting area that we could, at a moment's notice, use A-Cs to alter right back into a dining room. We were nothing if not adaptable.

Jeff still used the OSR for smaller meetings. Meaning he used it about once a month, max. Same with the Cabinet Room, used about once a week, usually late at night, with live-in White House personnel making up most of the attendance. And we occasionally had to use the OSR and the Cabinet Room for LSR overflow.

All this meant, however, that Christopher and I were very much making an entrance when we arrived.

In addition to Alpha Team and key Embassy staff, Jeff's full Cabinet, all the Joint Chiefs of Staff, which included my Uncle Mort who was now their Chairman, my mother and several P.T.C.U. agents, including Kevin Lewis who was her right-hand man, many Congresspeople who were considered intimates including Senator Donald McMillan, who was Arizona's senior senator and one of the few politicians we trusted fully, and a variety of staffers, human and A-C, none of whom I'd bothered to get to know yet because I was still working on remembering who all the Field agents were, were all in attendance.

However, there was one staffer in the room I knew really well—Caroline Chase, who was McMillan's go-to girl and my sorority roommate and bestie. She was sitting next to Amy, both of whom gave me little waves of welcome, and they were surrounded by our Friendly Lobbyist Faction, meaning Culver, Gadoire, and Thomas Kendrick and, these days, Prince Gustav Drax, late of Vatusus, and his royal retainers. Yep, we might need an even bigger room than this one soon.

Chuckie was back on-site, and he was sitting on one side of Jeff while Raj was on the other. Team Tough Guys were also in attendance, though they were on guard more than not. Felt bad for sending Len and Kyle off to eat—they enjoyed being a part of these big meetings far more than I did.

However, it had probably been a good plan since there were notably no chairs available for me and Christopher. Steeled myself for a lecture of epic proportions.

Jeff grinned at me. "No, that's not happening. Chairs are coming."

Sure enough, the Chief Usher, Antoinette Reilly, came into the room, with White House personnel carrying several chairs. Chose not to ask why we hadn't used A-Cs for this—there were times it was better to let the humans on staff do their jobs, and this was apparently one of them.

Antoinette was a competent, pleasant, black woman in her late thirties. Before we'd arrived on her scene, her life had been filled with handling normal emergencies and keeping things going so that, in essence, everyone saw the ducks floating on the lake and no one saw the hysterical paddling underwater.

All that changed the minute Jeff became President. Antoinette and I hadn't gotten off to the greatest start, but she'd been right there with me during Operation Immigration and had flipped to the side of Team Adrenaline Junkie.

She gave me an Atta Girl smile. "We'll get you through this so you can focus on the children and their first day of normal school tomorrow." Managed not to say that this would be its own form of stress and just smiled and nodded.

The chairs for me and Christopher and, apparently, Antoinette were added next to Jeff, with Christopher between him and Raj, me between him and Chuckie, and Antoinette behind Jeff. Which begged a question.

"Who just showed up to kick Antoinette out of her seat and take the ones reserved for me and Christopher?" I asked quietly.

"Mister Hollywood and your newest jock addition took your chairs," Jeff replied softly. Sure enough, I'd missed Cologne and Adam, who were sitting near Airborne. "We figured we'd add them in whenever you got here. Antoinette's seat, however . . ." He looked down the table at someone I realized I hadn't registered as being present, seeing as how there always seemed to be a million people in this room.

Of course, this was someone who I should have noticed, in no small part because he was in traditional Arab clothing. And in bigger part because he radiated authority tinged with menace.

Ali Baba Gadhavi—the head of the large and incredibly dangerous Indian Mob, Bahrain's sorta citizen, one of Interpol's Most Wanted, and the Mastermind's former benefactor—was in the house.

CHAPTER 20

GADHAVI AND I had met near the end of Operation Immigration. He'd allowed me to do what I needed to in order to save the world, and we'd parted on friendly terms, in no small part because my team had been able to show him that Cliff Goodman, aka the Mastermind, had been planning a takeover of Gadhavi's empire.

Being on good terms with Gadhavi was something I still counted as potentially the biggest line item for my win column. This wasn't a man to cross, to treat with any form of disrespect, or to even tease. This was a man who meant business in all the ways that phrase could be taken.

While Raheem reminded me of a teddy bear, Gadhavi reminded me of a grizzly—he could be cuddly, possibly, but only as long as you didn't forget that he could kill you with one swipe.

That he was here and no one was trying to arrest him, my mother in particular, said More Is Going On very clearly.

He stood as I noticed him, and gave me a very formal bow. "It is good to be in your presence again."

Stood as well and bowed in return. "And I in yours." Hoped this was the right response, but he didn't start growling, so figured I'd guessed correctly. "What brings your august presence to us?"

His lips quirked—he'd questioned whether I was using sarcasm on him the first time we'd met, and I had a feeling he still wasn't a hundred percent sure that I wasn't teasing him in some way. That he found it amusing was a relief.

"I have information for you that has granted me safe passage." He looked pointedly at Mom. "And my respect for you grants safe passage for those you hold dear."

"I appreciate that, truly. So, if we can stop being formal, since we're all here as friends, I have to assume that whatever news you have is so dramatic and high level that you couldn't trust a courier, telephone, Skype, or email to share it."

He nodded. "It is that. And all of those options can be . . . waylaid, tapped, destroyed, and so forth."

Wow. Whatever the hell Gadhavi had for me, it was gigantic. "I appreciate you bringing this news to me in person. Um, would you like to sit again, or should we both remain standing?"

He smiled and gestured that I should sit, which I did. He didn't, however. Instead, he turned to one of the many video screens we had in the room and nodded. To a couple of Field agents who were manning whatever audio-visual Gadhavi had either brought with him or requested.

"How did he get here?" I asked Jeff as softly as possible.

"Gate. Request went through the P.T.C.U."

"Huh." Then I stopped asking quiet questions, because what was on the screen was far too unsettling.

An older, balding man with apple cheeks and white hair that was puffy on the sides was in frame. As always when I first saw him, it was hard to believe this was the face of the most intolerant person potentially in the world. Farley Pecker was at a lectern, preaching. He was speaking in English and being translated into a variety of languages, including Arabic.

A tall man of average build and looks was behind Pecker, and it was clear they were both on a stage. This man was in a business suit and was far enough away from the camera that it didn't catch the crazy look I knew was in his eyes. Harvey Gutermuth was unlikely to have lost that look since the last time I'd seen him.

At first I thought it was Pecker's usual hate and intolerance speech. Only as we listened, realized that it was much worse. He'd dumped his false view of Christianity and wasn't even going for specifics in religion now. No, he was talking about the End of Days and how every alien was actually a demon of some kind.

The camera panned to the audience. If you ignored who was talking, it was quite the We Are The World Gathering. And the crowd was, to a person, really into the sermon. "Am I wrong in thinking that there are a ton of people here, and they're from all over?"

"No, you're correct—every country is represented," Gadhavi said.

"You're sure?" Jeff asked, as Pecker ripped apart all the religious leaders who'd "turned from God" in order to welcome the alien demons to our world. He named names, a lot of them. Not that any of the world's religious leaders were hiding, but Pecker was sharing them as a hit list.

"Yes."

"How in the world did they get all those people to wherever this is?" I asked. "I know how we do it, but even the most traitorous A-C that ever lived wouldn't have wanted this particular rally to be going on." Because Pecker was definitely saying that all the A-Cs were demons, and that the only good aliens were dead aliens. Even Ronald Yates wouldn't have encouraged this. I found it hard to believe anyone had gated these people to this gathering.

Gadhavi looked at me, as Pecker named me, Jeff, Chuckie, Mom, really most of the people in this room by name, suggesting that we all needed to die. "They have powerful friends in many places. Including here."

"Are those friends wealthy?"

"Money is power, so yes, they are."

"Do you know who here is funding this?" Jeff asked. Noted that no one besides the two of us was adding in. Possibly because I wasn't the only one who was thinking of Gadhavi as a grizzly bear.

"Yes, which is why I came personally."

"Why?" Chuckie asked mildly, instantly proving my assumption wrong.

"Because these enemies of yours are also my enemies. Listen to the rest, distasteful as it is."

Sure enough, Pecker was now talking about how gangsters and criminals were all supporting the alien demons and should, therefore, be overthrown and their wealth taken by the good and true people who were at this rally. He started naming names, and Gadhavi's was high on the list.

"He's named everyone on Interpol's Most Wanted," Chuckie said when Pecker paused to let his assembly cheer. "And on the U.S.'s as well."

"And others." Gadhavi shook his head. "There is infiltration everywhere from these so-called True Believers."

"That's for sure." Did a fast recap to explain why we had nine Bahraini bodyguards in the Pentagon's supermax prison. "But I don't understand how they infiltrated so quickly."

Gadhavi shrugged. "There are always those who cannot see that change is here. As you said to me when we first met, not everyone is adaptable. Fear, as I know you know, is a strong motivator."

"Who is it you suspected would intercept your message to Kitty?" Chuckie asked.

Gadhavi cocked his head. "You feel that I speak to her only?"

"I know you do," Chuckie said pleasantly. "It doesn't offend anyone here. We're used to it."

Gadhavi stared at Chuckie for a long moment. Then he nodded. "You're correct. I have a list of names of those we are certain are funding these True Believers. There is also a list of suspects who have not been cleared or condemned, and I have that as well."

Pecker was now listing world leaders. Pretty much anyone leading a country that had even sort of said that aliens were sort of okay was on this list. Even North Korea got a shout-out.

"You know, when someone's lumping the crazies in North Korea with everyone else as being part of the Evil Empire, it's confirmation you're dealing with lunatics of the highest order."

"True enough," Jeff said. He was going to say something else when Gadhavi put his hand up. Therefore, we all focused on the screen.

Pecker was now saying that Jeff had no right to be the King Regent, to be considered the King of Earth. "If we want a king," Pecker bellowed, "then let us have one we know is true in heart and mind, one who is not a demon, and one who does not consort with demons!"

The crowd cheered and Pecker went on. "If the aliens think they can force a king upon us, then *we* will force *our* king upon *them*, and we will ensure that this world runs red with their evil blood!"

More cheers. The crowd seemed unanimously behind Pecker. Whoever was filming was taking the entire crowd in. Wondered who'd infiltrated this mob and figured I could ask about that later.

"I know you revere the One True God! I know you love our world, the world that belongs to us, to humanity! And I know you will join with me and support the man who can lead us against these demons!"

Had to hand it to Pecker, he really had the old-time pulpit rhythms going. The crowd was fully revved up and ready to riot.

"I give you our noble leader, and the true king of this world— Harvey Gutermuth!"

The crowd went crazy while Gutermuth put his hands up in that way people have when they're supposedly telling the crowd to quiet down but really want them to go on clapping. Gadhavi nodded to the A-C running the AV and the videotape was paused. Then he turned back to me and Jeff.

"And now you see why I felt I had to bring this information to you personally."

Jeff nodded. "I do. And thank you. What do we need to do in order to get these lists of supporters from you? I'm not insinuating that you came here to bribe us, by the way. While I haven't been in politics all that long, I'm fully aware that there's always a price to pay for anything and everything."

"I enjoy working with intelligent people." Gadhavi smiled. "I have considered the offer your wife made to me and I would like to accept."

Jeff looked at me. "What offer?"

"Um . . . I think he means when I mentioned that the new galactic order was going to need businessmen like Mister Gadhavi. Minus the human trafficking, drugs, extortion, blackmail, and gambling."

"Oh, the gambling can stay," Chuckie said. "It can even be increased. We've discovered that many alien races really love it. The rest, though, yes, needs to stop."

Gadhavi shrugged. "I'm a businessman. I can see the advantages to stopping many of the pursuits you named. But that is my price to help you stop these madmen."

Most of the room perked up. "You'll be helping us?" Mom asked slowly.

Gadhavi nodded gravely. "Yes. If I am to move into the, ah, new galactic order, then I must do my part to protect that new order and my new business partners and so on."

"We can't condone murdering these people," Mom said regretfully. "Though it would make everyone else's lives so much easier."

Gadhavi started to laugh and looked back to me. "I see where your attitude comes from." He turned back to Mom. "It will be an honor to work with you, and I say that rarely."

Mom barked a laugh. "Well, I say this rarely, too, especially to someone with your history, but, welcome aboard. The Presidential Terrorism Control Unit welcomes their newest expert consultant with open arms."

CHAPTER 21

FORTUNATELY, everyone in the room was able to roll with these kinds of out-of-left-field punches. Much official congratulating happened, then Chuckie asked for the Lists of Evil Names.

Gadhavi gave it to me, which significance was lost on no one. "Huh. Interesting and unsurprising as well, but Senator Zachary Kramer and his 'lovely' wife Marcia are high up on this list."

Nathalie made a sound of disgust. "I cannot believe I used to be friends with that woman."

"Alliances shift," Chuckie replied with a small smile. "As you're well aware."

She nodded. "I am. Kitty, is anyone in this room on the list?"

It was a good question. We had people, those held over from Armstrong's administration mostly, that we weren't totally sure of. But none of them were here. "Unless they're using aliases, no." Felt the entire room relax.

"You're correct," Gadhavi said. "Before I came over I confirmed who was in attendance in this meeting. If one of those had been here, I would not be."

"Huh," Mom said. "I didn't get that request. Charles?"

"Nope, didn't come through the CIA, either. Vander, did you hear anything, either from your office or the FBI?"

Evander Horn was an attractive black man who'd joined up with us during Operation Infiltration. He'd been the Director of the FBI's Alien Affairs Division when Chuckie had been the head of the CIA's Extra-Terrestrial Division. Jeff had moved Horn to Secretary of Homeland Security once he was President. So it made sense that, should the FBI have learned something, their Director, Tom Curran, would have contacted Horn.

"Not a thing. Not through my agency or from Tom." Horn looked worried. "The question is, I think, who here is working privately with Mister Gadhavi?"

"I am." Siler shoved off the wall he was leaning against. "And if that shocks any of you, I'd like you all to remember what I spent most of my life doing for a living."

Gadhavi nodded. "Monsieur Meurtrier is well known to me."

Didn't know how many people in the room had a French language background other than me and Amy, but *meurtrier* was the French word for killer. So, the alias fit.

Several people shot suspicious looks in Siler's direction. "Then that's fine with me," I said, to forestall recriminations. "Nightcrawler always has his reasons, and they're always in line with what we want and need."

Siler shot me a quick smile. "Thanks. Mister Gadhavi felt that, under the circumstances, he had to ensure he was coming into a safe environment."

"Looking at this list, I can't blame him. Unsurprisingly, gang, Ansom Somerall, Talia Lee, and the rest of the Dealers of Death who aren't in the room with us are all on this list."

"War is good for most of them," McMillan pointed out.

"And we're clear that they're not our friends," Jeff said.

"Which is stupid," Gadhavi replied.

"I agree, and before anyone else chimes in, Mister Gadhavi didn't say that to be a supportive team player. He said it because he understands how Centaurion operates. Vance and I have discussed this more than once—it makes zero sense for these lobbyists to have ignored us."

"Not if they're virulently anti-alien," Culver said. "I have no idea if they are or not, but sometimes money doesn't matter as much as your beliefs."

"Or their clients are anti-alien," Gadhavi said.

Chuckie nodded. "Yes, most likely. However, until you gave us this list, we didn't have any proof of which ones were or weren't."

"Do we know now?" Jeff asked. "I don't recognize half the names on this list."

"And yet, you should," Gadhavi said. "They all deal with arms, international commerce, and other industries that would have enjoyed a strong relationship with Centaurion Division. But instead they are doing their best to create a faction bent only on your total destruction."

"Do you feel that we're going to win?" Uncle Mort asked. "Is that why you've joined with us?"

Gadhavi shrugged. "I cannot see the future. And I have no idea who will prevail." He smiled at me. "I just prefer to work with those I respect, who offer respect in return."

Gave him a pleasant smile in return, but I didn't buy it, not wholly. He was a survivor, but more than that, he didn't want to be destroyed by these fanatics. If he was stronger aligned with us, then so be it. He'd make us stronger, so it was, at least for now, a win-win.

"The respect is definitely mutual." Stood up again. "But, I have other things to catch everyone up on. Since Mister Gadhavi is now one of us, I think it's safe to include him in my several debriefs, most of which are robot related."

"There's more than two?" James Reader asked. He was the Head of Field and therefore the head of Alpha Team, the handsomest human I'd ever met, the former top international male model, and Gower's husband. He was also one of my two best guy friends in the world. "We know about the morning show debacle and you've told us about the Bahrainis. What else have we missed?"

"Um, there were Christopher-Bot attacks."

He flashed me the cover boy grin. "We do know a bit about those. They happened here."

"Yeah, but you haven't heard my thoughts."

Reader laughed. "Okay. It's not a normal day if you're not thinking aloud to an audience."

"I resent that. I can't deny it, but I do resent it. However, since you're not wrong, there's things that are really bothering me about what's going on. We'll tackle the most recent question, which only a few of us know about, first. Christopher and I think there's a mole in the P.T.C.U. or the CIA who got my specs so perfectly that they could create the original Fem-Bot in my likeness."

This caused consternation in the room, unsurprisingly. I mean, I was worried, and I knew Christopher was, too. Everyone looked concerned, and there was a quiet buzz with people quietly talking to their neighbors.

Other than Mom. Mom didn't look worried.

Mom looked amused.

CHAPTER 22

"WHAT'S SO FUNNY?" I asked my mother. Because I saw nothing funny about the "we have a mole" statement, from any angle.

Mom heaved a sigh. "Really?"

"Really, Mom. I mean, it's not a happy thought, but who else could have gotten me so well without my knowing it?"

Mom rolled her eyes. "I doubt you're going to be impressing your newest recruit—excuse me, business partner—all that much, but here we go. One of your best friends is the daughter of Herbert Gaultier. You and Amy have been friends since ninth grade. You were at her house all the time, including for sleepovers. Who do you think got your specs, easily?"

The room relaxed again, while I gave myself a gigantic "duh" on this one. "Ah. Gotcha. And that makes sense."

"Are you *sure* it was him?" Christopher asked. "I agree that it makes sense, but at the same time, assumptions about this could be deadly to us later."

"Pretty damn," Mom said. "It's the obvious choice."

"Doesn't mean it's the right one," Chuckie said. "Not that I'm arguing. But Kitty and Christopher do have a point—if it's possible that it wasn't Gaultier, then we need to determine who else it could possibly have been, as fast as possible."

"And if it was my deranged father, then why isn't there a Sheila-Bot?" Amy asked. "Or a Brian-Bot?" Serene's husband, Brian Dwyer, had been my most serious boyfriend in high school. "Brian was over all the time when he and Kitty were dating. Or even a Chuck-Bot? I mean, Chuck and I weren't close in high school, but he was over at our house more than once."

Saying Chuckie and Amy weren't friends in high school was the understatement of the century, but everyone let this pass. A lot had changed since I'd joined up with the gang from Alpha Four, and Chuckie and Amy now being friends wasn't the strangest thing that had happened by far.

Mom heaved the sigh of the long-suffering. "I'll speak slowly. There's an Amy-Bot that's been prepped, we know this." Everyone nodded. "The Kitty-Bot was rolled out first, though, because the plan was to kill me, and I can promise you that Ronald Yates wanted me dead years before any of you knew what he was really doing in his spare time."

"But that doesn't answer the Sheila-, Brian-, and Chuckie-Bots Question, Mom."

"You should never get up as early in the morning as you had to today. It's clearly affected your thought processes. Sheila has no value as a robot—she's not influential in any way. Brian is an astronaut, yes, but it wasn't a goal of his that anyone knew about when you were all in school, and without that, he's also noninfluential. Charles was not identified by anyone but the thankfully now-dead lunatic Cliff Goodman as a threat until such time as I suggested him to the then-Director of the CIA. They had plenty of time get the specs on Kitty and Amy. Why bother with the others? They weren't going to be used as weapons."

"I can buy it for Sheila and Brian," Jeff said. "But not Chuck. Someone that brilliant? Who was already on Cliff's hit list? I don't believe they'd have passed up their chance to make a robot version of him, too."

My brain decided to represent. "Yeah, but even if they'd wanted to, Chuckie grew like a foot between the end of high school and the start of college. Of the five of us we're talking about, he's the one that looks the most different from when we were teenagers. Even if they'd taken his measurements, they'd have been all wrong. And women tend to stop growing in their mid-teens. So, yeah, I'm caught up, Mom. And I'm so with you on never, ever doing a morning show again in my life, no offense meant to you, Adam."

"None taken. I think."

White cleared his throat. "However, Missus Martini, if you recall, we did have a room full of, ah, recreations that we found." He was referring to the Room of Hot Zombies that White, Chuckie, and I had encountered near the end of Operation Confusion. "And Charles was represented."

Chuckie nodded worriedly. "Richard's right. If they were able to create lifelike replicas of us, why not robots?"

Mom had managed to kick-start my brain. She was great that way. "Because that was a different project."

"Obviously," Chuckie said patiently. "But how does that negate the robot issue?"

"First off, all the zombies were made to match everyone as an adult and there were no females. Why go through all that zombie stuff if you already had a Chuckie-Bot lined up? I mean, every dude who mattered at the time was represented, and they were all made up of formerly living parts. They were ready to go and they were not robotic. That took time and effort. I think Gaultier and whoever else abandoned the Bot Initiative. The Kitty-Bot hadn't worked, so they stopped bothering."

Mom nodded. "Or Marling had made such strides with the androids that it made more sense to focus that way."

Managed not to say that it could simply have been because Christopher had killed Gaultier during Operation Confusion in order to save Amy and pretty much all of Jeff's family. And though LaRue DeMorte Gaultier was the real brains behind so many things, she was working on cloning, which was more effective than robots or zombies could ever be.

Reader was looking at something. "I'm sure that Angela's right about who created the initial Bot." He looked up. "Due to what's going on, I had the robotic schematics we confiscated from the late Eugene Montgomery sent over. The Gaultier logo is on this. It's hidden, but it's here. I think there are other logos here, too. It's like a Hirschfeld piece—the logos are part of this one particular design. I found the Gaultier one because I know what it looks like and figured it would be here."

"So, it's like a Hirschfeld caricature only we're looking for logos instead of the name Nina?"

"Pretty much. I have no guess for how many logos are included, but someone out there does, because they did the drawing."

"Let's see if we can find that artist," Jeff said. "And yes, I know it'll take effort. Put the freeloaders onto it."

"Hacker International will love the challenge, I'm sure. Okay, so this now begs the question I'd asked Chuckie earlier—do we know who created the first Kitty-Bot? Those plans would indicate it was Gaultier."

"Potentially," Reader replied. "Also potentially with a lot of help. Someones's going to have to decipher this drawing, but Jeff, if Stryker's team could have done it, they would have already."

"How *Da Vinci Code* of whomever. But Hacker International might have missed it because they're not focused on art, in that sense."

"Maybe." Reader didn't sound convinced.

"It wasn't Titan," Kendrick said, before anyone else could add in. "I've had our records thoroughly searched."

"But it could have been," Horn said. "We know that Cliff Goodman cleared out anything he wanted to once Marling and Titan were exposed. For all we know, Marling was the originator."

"It's likely, but what about YatesCorp?" I asked. "The Kitty-Bot was with Ronald Yates on her inaugural run, after all."

"We've had a harder time searching there," Chuckie said. "They have legit reasons to not allow us in—they haven't really been implicated in a provable way in anything untoward."

"Honestly, that's kind of shocking."

"I know. Believe me, I know. They're well protected."

"Well, while we have Amos Tobin being so helpful and all that, I think it's time to launch a full YatesCorp investigation." By helpful I meant under our protective control, albeit unwillingly. As with Amy being Gardiner's proxy at Gaultier, Christopher was Tobin's at YatesCorp, since we'd decided that it was in our best interests to enact the Yates Bloodline Clause. "And can't Christopher ask for some of this?"

"Only if we bring more people on board under the bloodline clause," Christopher replied. "No one's happy I'm there, and everyone's doing what they can to not do anything I want."

"Why now for the YatesCorp attention?" Amy asked. "I mean as opposed to focusing on that?" she nodded toward the video screen, which had been paused on a panning shot that included Gutermuth onstage along with another view of the rabid audience.

"Because Christopher's got robotic doubles out there, and he's Tobin's proxy. Maybe Tobin wants that stopped, or maybe someone else does. And because someone started the Bot Initiative and the first Bot we know about was the one created to look like me in order to kill my mother. Yates and your dad were close, since we're taking the idea that it was indeed your dad who got my specs. Someone made that first Bot. We really need to know who."

"While I'd love to say that it was Cliff Goodman, my money's still on the Tinkerer." Chuckie got Cliff's name out without snarling. Since we'd taken out the Mastermind during Operation Immigration, Chuckie had seemed to finally be back to normal. He could refer to Cliff without going into a rage or a migraine. His naturally calm, cool, and collected demeanor was back. And he no longer seemed infinitely sad.

Not that I thought that him finally getting to destroy Cliff had made the loss of his wife, Naomi Gower-Reynolds, hurt any less. But it now seemed easier for him to bear, and Jeff was no longer worried that Chuckie was going to do something horrifically drastic.

"He wouldn't have had to be in hiding at the time," Richard White said. "And he preferred to be in close proximity to my father."

"Meaning YatesCorp or one of its companies makes the most sense. Speaking of sense, have we ever compared the robot schematics we found via Eugene Montgomery against the shredded ones we found at Marion Villanova's apartment?"

"Yes," Chuckie said. "They're different. Stryker can give you the full details if you want them."

"I will, but not at this precise time." I was getting hungry and therefore wasn't feeling totally up to comparing diagrams of robotic versions of me and my friends while combing through the tiny differences in detail. Just call me a quitter.

"Kitty, are we thinking the Kitty-Bot was made by the same people or company or whatever as the Fem-Bots that attacked us at Camp David?" Tim Crawford asked. Tim was doing the job that was still my favorite of any I'd ever had—he was the Head of Airborne for Centaurion Division.

Tim and I tended to think a lot alike—it was why he was good in my old position. So I didn't answer off the cuff. And it was a good question, since those Fem-Bots had all looked just like me, too. But they'd been far deadlier than the Original Kitty-Bot. "What do you think, Tim?"

He grinned. "Always nice to have my opinion valued. I think we need to remember that your theory that Monica Strauss was being her own Mastermind is sound, and we all felt that there were two separate robotics programs going. That we've confirmed that the two sets of schematics we have are different seems to confirm that there are at least two potentially competing programs. I think we need to figure out whether or not the

Original Kitty-Bot is the same design as those we had to fight off while dodging lab-created superbeings."

"We shouldn't ignore the superbeings, either," I pointed out.

"We haven't been," Lorraine Billings said. She was one of my two best A-C girlfriends and she was married to Joe. "But events have kept us focused in other directions." Lorraine was blonde and buxom and, like all the Dazzlers, gorgeous.

"However, we do have teams assigned to the project," Claudia Muir added. She was my other A-C bestie and married to Randy. She was a willowy brunette who kept the Dazzler tradition of being totally hot going strong.

Lorraine and Claudia were also Captains on Alpha Team, and all the Dazzlers were mathematical, scientific, and medical geniuses, at least by human standards. So if the girls said they had a team on the supersoldier stuff, then I could probably stop worrying about that. For the moment.

"But to Tim's point," Lorraine said, "we should also look into whether the Kitty-Bot is the same as either the Montgomery schematics or the Villanova schematics, or if she's a different design from either of them."

"Excellent point. So, then, next question—has anyone at Dulce or within Hacker International chosen to break down and reverse engineer her?"

There was silence from those who would know if this was happening. Wondered if, stomach growling or no, I needed to get Hacker International onto video conference. Noted that Raj was on his phone and motioning to the A-Cs on A-V Duty and figured he was anticipating my request.

"Um, guys? Why so silent?"

"Ah, no," Chuckie said finally. "No one is willing to do that."

CHAPTER 23

L **ET THAT SIT ON** the air for a moment. "Why not?"

"John Butler and Cameron Maurer are both adamantly against it," Chuckie replied. "To the point of near self-destruction against it. I get the impression they feel that she's sentient." Claudia and Lorraine nodded emphatic agreement.

"But she isn't. Is she?"

"Can't say. My initial reaction is no. However, I haven't had time to do any in-depth examination and, as I said, our two fully sentient and in-control androids are quite against it. We might have a better idea if the currently intact Christopher-Bot lasts long enough for examination."

"Wow, you're Mister Sunshine."

"It's a gift. We do know that the Kitty-Bot is unclear on where or how she was made, and she has no idea who her creator is, either." He sighed. "I do understand why Butler and Maurer don't want her harmed or destroyed—there's something kind of . . . plaintive . . . about her."

"Yeah, I remember. She was very focused on her mission, which I see I'm going to need to remind everyone was to blow up the entire Administration, but she was more like a child than a machine."

Seemed like it was time for me to have a visit with my robotic twin. I'd make a note to fit that in somewhere. After I ensured the Wasim situation was truly handled, doubly ensured that Gadhavi was happy to be playing on the side of sort of law and order, figured out what was going on with Somerall, Lee, and the Christopher-Bot or Bots, interrogated the True Believer Bodyguards, determined how to stop the crazed End of Days Hatemongers, and got all the kids to school, potentially dragging their feet and screaming all the way. No biggie. I'd get to visiting my Robotwin on Thursday or something.

"So, currently, the Kitty-Bot is kind of a dead end."

Chuckie nodded. "For the moment, at least. Though we'll investigate ways to determine her schematics safely so we can do the comparisons we've been discussing."

"May I ask how you know if someone is a Bot or an android without cutting their body open?" Gadhavi asked politely.

"We use the Organic Validation Sensor," Serene, who was sitting between Reader and Tim, replied.

"What is that?" Gadhavi asked.

"I'll explain, and I'm going to anticipate your follow-on question—what do we do if we don't have an OVS available, as in, how do we tell if someone is an android or a Bot?" He nodded. Serene grinned and stood up. Took this as my opportunity to sit for a while.

Serene was younger than me and the girls, but she was Dazzler all the way. She was also, we'd discovered, White's very much younger half-sister, because Ronald Yates had really been focused on beating Wilt Chamberlain's conquest record. And she was scary talented.

Like Jeff and Christopher, she'd had Surcenthumain given to her. In her and Jeff's cases, it had been unknowingly and unwillingly. The Surcenthumain had made her crazy, but with it out of her system she was crazy like a fox.

In addition to being the strongest imageer we had after Christopher, she was an explosives genius, and she was also our top scientist in terms of the Bots and androids. She was the reason Cameron Maurer was still around to care about the Kitty-Bot.

However, the thing I found the coolest about Serene was that she was also a stealth troubadour. And because she was smarter than anyone gave her credit for, since she did Blonde Ditz really well, she'd created the stealth A-C CIA made up totally of troubadours.

Raj was her second-in-command, and Colette and her middle sister, Francine, who was also my FLOTUS Body Double, were also in the corps. Basically, if the person was a troubadour, I assumed they were in Serene's Special Forces first and chose to be surprised later if that wasn't the case.

I was one of the only ones who knew she was doing this, though we'd finally shared the information with Jeff and

Chuckie. Christopher knew because I'd had to tell him during Operation Immigration, White and Mom had figured it out all on their own, and one other person was in the know. However, no one else—not even Reader, Tim, or the girls—had been told about this, because Serene felt that secrets were better kept if they weren't shared.

"The OVS is made up of a variety of sensors that are tuned to every spectrum of organic life," Serene started. Realized with horror that she was literally going to give Gadhavi a lecture. Was more horrified to look at him and see him nodding in rapt attention. Did a fast room check. Either everyone was interested or they all knew how to fake it better than I did.

Serene continued on, explaining the intricacies of how the OVS did its magic. Gadhavi and others asked questions. Questions that indicated they were paying attention. The questions branched out into how we told the difference between Late Model and New Release Androids, the Bot levels, and more.

However, fascinated as the rest of the room appeared to be, I couldn't muster up the enthusiasm. My ears shut off. My brain asked if we could play a game on my phone. Told my ears to listen for clues that I might need to speak or stop the class by making a joke. My ears shared that neither seemed likely. My brain begged for sweet release.

Wanted to fantasize about sex with Jeff, since that was always a good way to keep myself happy and entertained, but he was freaking paying attention to what was going on, too, and I knew he'd pick up the lust spike. Totally took one for the team and tried to focus on the million other things I had to worry about.

Mercifully, my phone rang. Being the Worst First Lady in the World, I pulled it out of my purse. Not a number I knew, but it wasn't a blocked number, either. Decided to answer just in case it was, against all the odds, Aerosmith's manager calling to tell me that the band had so loved performing for Jeff's inauguration that they wanted to spend the weekend with us. And it was a fantastic excuse to get out of the room.

"Hello?" I said as softly as I could, as I kept a hold of my purse and slid out of my seat as unobtrusively as I could manage.

"Is this Missus Martini?" A woman's voice, indeterminate age.

"Yes. Who's this?" Used a little hyperspeed burst to get out the door and into the hallway. Breathed a sigh of relief. Away from the lecture and no longer disturbing the rest of the class.

"This is Charmaine Cordell. Do you always act like you're having phone sex when people call you?"

Well, that was a new opening gambit. Decided that, regardless of why she was calling, up to and including if she was managing Aerosmith, I didn't care for her. "No. I was in a meeting and hurried out of it to take your call. I have no idea who you are or why you're calling me. Are you always rude when you make phone calls?"

She sniffed. "I have no idea what you're insinuating. I'm the President of the Sidwell Friends School Parent Teacher Association."

Fantastic. Great way to get off to a terrible start. I was batting a thousand as usual. "Oh. Nice to meet you." Not really, but I'd learned enough by now not to share that.

"I'm sure it is. I wanted to let you know that, particularly since you have so many children coming into our school, you're in charge of our first bake sale."

"Excuse me?"

"Surely you've heard of the concept of bake sales?"

"Um, yes. I'm still stuck on your idea that one early-starters kindergartener and one high school freshman are 'many.' "

She heaved a dramatic sigh. "You have, at last count, well over a dozen. Jamie Katt-Martini, Patrick Dwyer, Ross Billings, Sean Muir, and Ezra Weisman, early-starters kindergarten. Jonathan Price the Second, first grade. Miriam Price, second grade. Rachel Lewis, third grade. Cassidy Maurer, fourth grade. Kimberly Martini and Raymond Lewis, fifth grade. Chance Maurer, sixth grade. Elizabeth Vrabel and Anthony Valentino, ninth grade. Claire Valentino, tenth grade. Sidney Valentino, eleventh grade. I've possibly missed some, but those are who are on my roster."

"Ah . . . you do realize they're not all 'my' children, right? I mean, I'm happy to claim them since they're all great, but they aren't my legal children. You're clear on that, right?"

The Price and Valentino kids were among Jeff's many nieces and nephews, and the rest were Embassy kids. The Embassy kids were all great. Kimmie had been my flower girl and I adored her. The jury was out on the rest of the Martini Clan

Kids, mostly because I had no idea how badly Stephanie had or hadn't turned her siblings and cousins against us. But I wasn't going to share that with Charmaine.

She sniffed again. "Yes. However, they're all enrolled through the White House. Ergo, they all fall under you, as the First Lady."

"Do they? I'm sure their parents wouldn't agree."

"I'm sure that we at the Sidwell Friends School Parent Teacher Association will leave that up to you and your myriad relatives who are all apparently using their connections to you to shove their children into the finest preparatory school in the country." Received another sniff.

Had no idea who'd come up with the plan for the Valentino and Price kids to go to school with regular humans instead of A-Cs or instead of hitting up the Intergalactic School, but I was pretty sure that Jeff hadn't been the one to do it. Any time something like this happened with his family, though, knew I needed to look no further than his parents for the likely culprits. Alfred and Lucinda were about to have some 'splaining to do.

Though why only Jeff's eldest and youngest sisters' kids were going to school with ours was a mystery, too. One I'd have to figure out after I could get off the phone with Ms. Prez of the PTA. Who was, frankly, pissing me off.

"I'm certain that you'll find that all of our children belong in Sidwell."

She sniffed *again*. She was starting to remind me of the kangaroo from *Horton Hears A Who*. "Never in our history have so many unqualified students been enrolled. And we have your husband's administration to thank for that."

Decided she was totally that bitchy kangaroo from *Horton Hears A Who* and also decided it was high time I chose to hate her. "So, other than to insult a group of young, talented, bright children, my family and friends, and my husband, why are you calling me again?"

"Because you haven't done one bit of fundraising for the school and, as I said, that means you're in charge of the first bake sale."

"Why?"

"Because we took a vote and you were chosen."

"I feel so lucky."

"You should. It's a great honor."

"I note that I wasn't included in this vote. How is that fair?"

"The vote was unanimous, so your one vote wouldn't have mattered."

"Well, that's all neat and tidy then."

"Isn't it? And, as I mentioned, you have the most children registered."

"Um, gotcha and whatever, not my thing and—and I realize this will shock you—I actually have running the country and representing us galactically to do. We'll happily *shove* whatever money you want at the PTA."

She sniffed. Again. No matter what this woman looked like in person, I was always going to see her as a supercilious kangaroo with opera glasses. "We don't allow our students' parents to merely toss money at them. No, we of the Sidwell Friends School Parent Teacher Association pride ourselves on the fact that we honestly fundraise to support the school and school activities."

"So, seriously, everyone going to this school comes from wealth in some way and you're saying that none of the parents donate? Pull the other one or however you say it at the Sidwell Friends School Parent Teacher Association."

"Oh, of course we expect the parents to donate as well."

"Of course you do."

"Your donation envelopes will be mailed to you."

"Excuse me? Donation envelopes? Is this like a monthly tithe or something?"

"Yes, very much like that. This is only for the Sidwell Friends School Parent Teacher Association, though. What you choose to donate directly to the school is, of course, up to you."

"Oh, of course. And how generous of you to tell us that we can donate as we see fit to the school. I'll just bet there's a dollar amount you've given us for the monthly PTA Tithe, though, isn't there?"

"Yes, because how else will you know what's needed or expected?"

"Oh, gosh, good point."

"However, we also expect the children to represent. The Annual First Week Bake Sale is a fine tradition that raises funds for the first quarter."

"You raise all the money you need for the first quarter of the school year from a *bake sale*?" Good lord. What kinds of baked goods were these people bringing? The winning entries from *Cake Wars*?

"Yes. And you're in charge of it."

"Lucky me. When is this historic annual event happening?"

"Wednesday."

"Wednesday what week?"

"This week. This Wednesday. As in, tomorrow, for the first day of school."

CHAPTER 24

WORDS, LITERALLY, FAILED ME. I was standing outside the LSR with my mouth hanging open.

"I'm glad to see that you're finally taking this seriously," Charmaine said, as if my silence on the other side of the phone indicated consent versus shock.

Forced myself to speak. "I have no idea of how to run a bake sale. My first biological child is the one entering early-starters kindergarten. She's been in our Embassy's daycare school all this time and we don't do bake sales to raise funds for that."

Charmaine stayed consistent and sniffed. "Of course you didn't. However, it's different out in the real world."

"Gosh, I can't wait to see that real world of which you speak. However, since I have no idea of what to do, when to do it, where to do it, and so forth, if you want this sucker to be a success or even just not a total disaster, you'd better plan on giving me more information and people to help me. Otherwise, I'm going to call the head of the Sidwell Friends School and ask if the bake sale can be moved back to a more convenient time for me." Like never.

"Oh, you'll have a team," Charmaine sneered. "We wouldn't let a novice such as yourself work unsupervised."

"Right. So it's all my responsibility but you'll all be telling me what to do and how to do it."

"In a sense. I've sent the list of other parents who will be available to assist you, along with suggested treats that your many children could consider making, to your office. I believe your social secretary has them."

"And if she doesn't?" Mrs. Maurer had certainly not mentioned this and, all things considered, it seemed unlikely she was waiting for later to share this news with me.

"Oh, it was delivered ten minutes ago. I have the confirmation."

So she'd waited until she knew the information had arrived before calling me. This woman's spirit animal was definitely that nasty kangaroo. And I was Horton, only I had no Whos to help me.

"How convenient. Anything else you want to share with me at the eleventh hour?"

"Only that, despite our expectations, we hope that you and your many children will represent our school well. I, frankly, have no real belief of such, having seen you in action, but perhaps not all of those children have been spoiled by your example yet."

"You're really good at making friends and influencing people, aren't you?"

"Yes, I am," she said, totally ignoring that my sarcasm knob had been turned to eleven. "I've been the President of the Sidwell Friends School Parent Teacher Association ever since my twins entered kindergarten. They're freshmen now, and since my tenure our organization has never had to worry about funds."

"I'll bet."

Keeping consistent, she sniffed again. "Since you seem to think you're involved in running the country, I look forward to seeing if you can run a bake sale. It should be instructive to see what happens." And with that, she hung up.

Stared at my phone, then decided I'd better log this woman's information in, so I'd know it was the Evil Kangaroo calling next time.

As I was doing this, the door opened and Jeff slipped out. He put his arm around me and hugged me. "Want to tell me about it?"

"Not really, but I think I'd better." Gave him the fast recap as I finished logging in the Evil Kangaroo's name and nickname. "So, now, on top of everything else, I have to manage this stupid bake sale and this horrible woman is already being cruel about children she's never met. Maybe the kids met her kids or something and that's why they don't want to go to this school."

Jeff kissed the top of my head. "The kids are just scared of change. You'll manage this just fine, baby. Like everything else."

"All my things don't go according to plan all that often, Jeff."

This earned me a nuzzle. "But most of them do, and it all works out in the end. You want me to come with you tomorrow?"

"Yes, but you can't. By the way, why are Sylvia and Marianne's kids going to Sidwell? And, for the other by the way, why aren't Elizabeth, Constance, or Lauren's kids in Sidwell, too?"

He sighed. "I honestly have no idea. I can check with my parents, but not right now."

"I hope they have a good answer."

"Me, too." Jeff hugged me again. I turned and buried my face in his chest and he rocked me for a bit. "It'll be fine, baby. I promise."

Looked up. "You know you can't promise that."

He smiled, slowly and sexily. "That's true. I *can* promise this, though." With that he bent and kissed me.

Like always, his lips and tongue owned mine and, also like always, I was grinding against him in short order. Jeff was the God of Kissing and his kiss did to me what it always did—washed any fear or stress away and reminded me of one of the many reasons it was great to be his woman.

He ended our kiss slowly but his eyes were still smoldering. "Later on, I'll show you the other things I can promise you."

"Mmm, wish you could do that right now. Pity we have the LSR packed with important people."

He sighed. "True. And Serene's winding down on her lecture, too."

"Do I need to go back in? Part of me says I do and the other part says that I have to figure out what's going on with this whole bake sale horror."

"We're running a country and have the eyes of the galaxy on us. I say that this is what you have staff for. I'd like you back in the LSR with me."

"No argument. Let me call Vance and have him represent."

Jeff hugged me again then went back inside. Could hear Serene indeed winding down on the Q&A. Quickly dialed and Vance answered right away. "Glad you called. First off, because they have lives they need to get back to, the Ambassadress and her entourage have left the Prince and his bodyguard in our care."

"Not that this was a surprise. Were things okay when they left?"

"Yes. Mossad said to call if you need them. The Ambassa-dress said the same. Khalid said what I assume was the same to Naveed. Everything is secure. Plus, we sent two A-C Field teams with them, just in case."

"Good thinking, thank you."

"It's what I'm here for. Next, we just got some interesting information sent to us."

"Is it about the bake sale I'm suddenly in charge of?"

"What? What the hell? No, it's something else."

Groaned. "Of course it is. Tell Nancy to look for something from Sidwell addressed to me. Open it. Read it. Save my day. Then tell me what else is going on."

"Hang on." Heard Vance talking to the rest of my team. It was clear that they were in back my office. Was also clear that Lizzie and Wasim were still with them. Which begged a question. "Oh, my God, are you kidding me?" Vance said as he returned to our call. "Who does this to any new school parent, let alone the First Lady?"

"Charmaine 'I've been the Prez of the PTA for Life' Cordell does, that's who."

"This is something we can handle," Vance said soothingly, having apparently realized that his agreeing with my freaking out probably wouldn't help.

"Yeah, I hope so, though I'm just betting that I have to be on-site running this thing, don't I?"

"Yes, you do. Think of it this way—you were going with them tomorrow anyway and the kids will like having you there."

Could remember being in school. Sure, the little kids might be thrilled I was there. The older ones, however, might prefer to not have a parental unit hanging about, particularly this early in the school year. "Maybe. But that reminds me. Evil Kangaroo listed a ton of kids. But Wasim wasn't on that list."

"I'll ask why you just called this woman the Evil Kangaroo later and reply to your concern now. I assume that she isn't clear that Wasim is part of your underage entourage. He's registered via the King of Bahrain, not the White House."

"Lucky Wasim, apparently."

"Yes, let's hope. At any rate, we'll get this handled in some way, determine what you have to do when, and ensure that your team is with you tomorrow so that everything will go smoothly. Between me, Antoinette, Nancy, Chef, and P-Chef it'll be fine. We'll also call in Pierre. We'll be good."

Perked up. "Pierre, Chef, and P-Chef can be involved?"

Chef was the Official White House Executive Chef and he was a culinary genius. However, the White House scored an additional chef, the Official White House Executive Pastry Chef, or P-Chef for short. Apparently I was the first person to give the pastry chef her own gangsta name, but she rolled with it, in part because, as the FLOTUS, I was the one who did the Executive Food Top Dawgs hiring and firing. There were advantages to this gig. They were few and far between, but they were there.

He snorted. "Yes, per some of the paperwork Nancy's reading through. The children have to help whoever's doing the main baking and such, but an adult can do the majority. And that might be fun for them in a *Sound of Music* kind of way. It'll make for a good photo op, no matter what. I'll ask Mister Joel Oliver if he's available and, if he's not, then hopefully Bruce Jenkins can cover."

Oliver was now considered the top investigative journalist in the world, though that hadn't always been the case. He'd been thought of as a crackpot because he was sharing that the A-Cs were here long before most of the world realized he was right. Jenkins, on the other hand, was nicknamed the Tastemaker and had been our adversary at the start—until he'd seen that Maurer had been turned into an android and had run to us for protection. Both men were now firmly on our side, which was nice, because the rest of the press wasn't.

"My mind boggles. Let's go for what you were going to tell me about. Maybe it's not worse than this. Or will require that I miss this bake sale extravaganza."

"No, you can't miss it. This is part of being a parent of a Sidwell student. Involvement is required. Not all the time, but often enough. The school is very understanding of the parents' responsibilities in the real world, but they do request this kind of support. The PTA is quite strong. We don't want you on their wrong side if at all possible."

"Too late, I'm sure, but okay. So, the other news?"

"Zachary and Marcia Kramer have invited you and Jeff to a party. Tomorrow night."

CHAPTER 25

"**A**WESOME. Send our regrets in the nicest way possible, versus the way I'd say it."

"Oh, it's better than just that," Vance said. "It's a fundraiser for the Sidwell Friends School."

Let that one sit on the air for a moment. "Seriously? They're doing an impromptu fundraiser? On a Wednesday?" Why was this Wednesday suddenly the Mid-Week Day of the Year?

"It's timed for the first day of Sidwell's classes."

"Wait a minute. They have kids?"

"They do. Remember, Marcia is Zachary's third wife. He has lots of kids."

"The country is so lucky."

Vance laughed. "They're not all bad. The four kids from his first marriage all seem pretty normal. The two eldest from his second marriage are in college. His youngest from his second wife is a senior at Sidwell, and the two kids he has with Marcia are in first and third grade."

"Ugh, so they'll be with our kids. Lucky us."

"Yes, but it does mean you have to attend this fundraiser. On the plus side, you won't be alone."

"Because the Secret Service will be with us in force?"

"Yes, but not what I meant. You won't be alone because I know who else is invited. They sent the guest list, as is required for any invitations going to the President or First Lady."

"It is?"

"Yes, so that you aren't thinking you're going to a fundraiser when you're actually going to a political rally."

"I'll ask for that distinction later. And since we *are* going to a fundraiser, whatevs. So, I'll bite, who's on the guest list that you think we'll care about?"

"All the rest of the Dealers of Death, for starters. Lillian and Guy are also invited, by the way, as is Thomas Kendrick."

"Really? No one's mentioned this."

"Abner and I got our spouses' invitations, and I sent Manfred to find Thomas's and it was waiting for him in his mailbox. All of ours and Thomas's invitations arrived today, right when yours did."

"Huh. So, does that mean they don't actually want us to show but want to say that they invited us?"

"Potentially. The other possibility is that they expect you to say no or try to get out of it and asked last-minute in order to forestall the excuses outcome."

"Either way, it's their usual classless approach. So, who else is on the list?"

"Well, your new best friend forever, Charmaine Cordell and her husband."

"I feel so lucky. Anyone else?"

"Yeah." He paused dramatically. "Doctor Rattoppare."

Snatched the expected gasp of shock away. It hadn't been a fun day so far and part of Vance's job was being the person I disappointed on a regular basis. "Huh. Which one, can you tell?"

"No, there's no first name listed."

"I'll bet there isn't. Look, does this scream 'trap' to you as much as it does to me?"

Vance was quiet for a moment. "Yes, frankly, it does. I mean, only because we know that Rattoppare is an enemy."

"Just like the Kramers are. And Charmaine the Evil Kangaroo is definitely high up on my New and Improved Enemies List. What are you going to do about it?"

"The easiest thing—I'm going to call Marcia and ask her if it's legit."

"Okay, keep me posted. I'm going back into the LSR to deal with the Bot Initiative and all the other fun we're having."

"Just another day in office."

"Dude, truer words and all that."

We hung up and I slunk back inside. Contemplated telling Jeff about the latest stress test in our immediate future, then decided to save it for when we had fewer people around.

The general conversation was centered around the Bots, androids, and such, as well as who could be behind them.

Interrupted. "Sorry, and this may have been covered while I was out of the room, but do we have anything definitive on Ansom Somerall and Talia Lee? As in, are their brains normal?"

"No word from Tito yet," Jeff said. "He's not done with his tests, but he'll join us the moment he is. And before you ask, yes, he still has the flyboys with him, as well as other protection."

Figured the other protection was Tito's wife, Rahmi. And possibly her younger sister, Rhee, too, since they weren't in the LSR. Come to think of it, we were missing others I'd have expected to be here. Hoped Abigail Gower and Mahin Sherazi were both with Tito and Team, too. Just in case.

"The Christopher-Bot is in a containment unit brought over by Dulce," Buchanan shared. "It's in the underground parking area, under heavy guard. We haven't had anyone examine him yet, though."

"Why not?"

"We wanted to see if he was telling the truth first," Chuckie said.

"Makes sense. Are we sure he hasn't self-destructed?"

"Yes," Raj replied. "We're monitoring. He's fine, insofar as a Man-Bot can be."

"Raj, your acceptance of the Man-Bot moniker has earned you a reprieve from my blaming you for forcing me to go on *Good Day USA!*, and for that you should be grateful."

He grinned at me. "I am. And the Kristie Android is also contained, similar chamber, same area. Both are being monitored."

"Good job, though I think Kristie-Bot fits her better and I insist that she be called that regardless of what she turns out to be. It has a better ring. But anyway, we seem like we're at that dreaded 'waiting for the answers' time. Meaning I think it's time for lunch."

Half the room chuckled, but no one argued. Good. I was starving and it was honestly lunchtime. Jeff didn't argue, so either he was hungry, too, or could tell that I needed to eat and was being a good husband. I'd take it, either way.

Because we were essentially in a giant dining room, the Elves were contacted and everyone trooped out while the room was switched over, which took about a minute.

Since we were rearranged for eating, went to Gadhavi and had him sit with me and Jeff. "I appreciate the honor," he said as he seated himself next to me. Mom sat on his other side. Pointedly. He smiled at her. "I appreciate the honor of your company as well."

"I always like to spend time with the new recruits." Mom's sarcasm meter was only at around six on the scale. Even she was being careful of our new grizzly bear friend.

"Me too." Hey, I wanted to represent.

Gadhavi chuckled as he turned to me. "I see your sense of humor remains intact. Tell me . . . is our mutual friend still . . . well?"

He was referring to Russell Kozlow, who was yet another Yates progeny and who, for a variety of reasons, had chosen house arrest in the American Centaurion Embassy Complex versus a life of excellent crime with Gadhavi as a G-Company crime boss. Most of the team felt that this was because Kozlow wasn't all that bright. Jeff and Chuckie felt it was because Kozlow was more afraid of me than Gadhavi. I felt, however, it was because I was the one person who hadn't made Kozlow feel like a loser. Plus, we had his mother and he wanted to see her and get back into her good graces.

"He's good, yes. Did you want to see him?"

"No. I just wanted to verify that he chose wisely."

"He did in the sense that he's with the person who loves him best in the world." Which was his mother, Chernobog the Ultimate, the best hacker in, literally, the world. And which also wasn't saying all that much in terms of the love, since she'd point-blank told me during Operation Immigration that she preferred me to him as a relative, even though we weren't related. Then again, my relationship with Chernobog was almost as complex as mine with her son. Or mine with most of the people in this room, if I got right down to it.

Food arrived courtesy of the White House serving staff and we all got down to the business of eating, with everyone making very mundane chitchat, versus discussing policy or Bots or whatever. Mom and Gadhavi chatted about people they knew in common, both those that they liked and those that they'd love to see dead. It was an interesting conversation to overhear, and one that made me really glad they both liked me.

Chef was keeping his reputation intact, and today's lunch was his usual stellar bounty of deliciousness. Did my best not to scarf my food, but it took effort. Asked for, and got, seconds because in my experience, it was not a given that I'd get dinner on time or at all right now.

As we were finishing up, Tito came into the room. Hoped he'd eaten already, because there wasn't much left and I'd snagged the last roll available within my reach and wasn't giving it up.

"Jeff," he said quietly, "I want to give you the results, but not in a large group."

"Who besides me, Kitty, and Chuck?" Jeff asked.

"Alpha Team, and that's all." Tito looked worried. Well, we already knew things were boding.

"What about Richard?" I asked. White was my partner when it came to butt-kicking, and I'd found that it was best to ensure that he knew what was going on as soon as possible.

Tito nodded. "Probably a good choice, yeah. But no one else."

Jeff motioned to those who were on Tito's Request List while he gave Raj and Fritz Hochberg, the Vice President, a couple of instructions. Meanwhile, I apologized to Gadhavi for having to leave.

He nodded. "You have much going on. I'm sure the rest of us can deal with that," he nodded toward the video screens that were still in the room and still paused on the crowd cheering for Pecker and Gutermuth, "while you deal with other issues."

"You handle the inhuman humans while we handle the human robots?" Looked at the screen again. There was something bugging me about the people in this image. Not all of them, just some of them. But I couldn't make out who or what was wrong, just that my brain felt that this image needed closer examination.

"Something like that." Gadhavi paused. "What do you see?"

"I'm . . . not sure. But please ensure that everyone pays attention to the crowd, our imageers in particular."

"I will do my best."

"What more could a girl want than the best from the head of G-Company?"

Gadhavi chuckled. "I imagine I will eventually find out."

CHAPTER 26

WALKED NEARER TO THE SCREEN and Gadhavi and Mom came with me, Gadhavi presumably to continue chatting, Mom presumably to keep me moving. "I imagine most of the room will be willing to let you lead on this situation," I told him. "Particularly since you brought the intel to us." Honestly had no idea how the room was going to react once those of us Tito wanted left, but assumed that the grizzly bear was going to get to lead as long as Mom didn't feel that she had to put a tranquilizer dart into him.

Gadhavi's countenance darkened. "There are G-Company troops at this rally."

"And they're allowed in?" Mom asked.

He shrugged. "I presume that if you make the right promises that these people will welcome you with their arms open."

Looked at the still image. Something was still bugging me about it. Pulled my phone out and took a picture of the picture. "Let me know the moment you guys figure out what's going on over there." Then I followed Tito and the others out of the LSR.

Once we were in the hallway Jeff put his arm around my shoulders. Happily put mine around his waist and relaxed for a nanosecond. He hugged me. "What's wrong?"

"You mean besides everything?" Showed him the picture on my phone. "I have no idea why this shot is bugging me, but it is."

He looked at it. "Other than the obvious hatred, I don't see anything. But I can try to read it with Christopher if you want."

"We'll do the Go Team Move later. Right now, those in the LSR will be working on this while we work on our Fabulous Robotic Boys and Girls."

"As to that," Tito said as we headed downstairs to the medical offices, "Claudia and Lorraine, what I'm going to say may make the two of you nervous, but I don't feel that Joe and Randy are in the same situation as either Ansom, Talia, or Kristie."

"You examined the Kristie-Bot?"

Tito nodded. "And the Christopher-Bot as well. As you can see, no one exploded on me."

"Is that going to continue, or are they just waiting for the President to make an appearance?" Chuckie asked.

"No idea. Rahmi, Rhee, and Airborne are with them all." Tito walked us past the medical offices and to the stairs that led down to the lower level of the complex. "I have each one in a separate containment unit, so if they explode, they'll only take themselves."

"Good, but why aren't we using hyperspeed to get there?" Reader asked.

"Because I want to talk to all of you first. Alone." Tito stopped while we were in the stairwell. Memory shared that Mom had done the same during Operation Epidemic, presumably because this area wasn't bugged and was out of sight of cameras and such. "The situation is . . . interesting."

"I'll bite," Tim said. "How interesting?"

"Serene's level of interesting," Tito said, shooting her a grin.

"What's going on with their brains?" she asked.

"Gray matter."

We all stared at Tito. "I thought we'd agreed that robots didn't have gray matter," White said finally.

"Most don't. These do. In differing forms, Ansom, Talia, and Kristie all have more wires in their brains than Joe and Randy do. The wires are enmeshed within their gray matter so completely that there's no way to remove the wires without making them brain-dead. And before anyone asks, the answer to the question of 'how did inserting the wires into Joe and Randy, let alone these others, not make these brain-dead' is a simple 'we have no idea.' The science is beyond what we have at Dulce, and none of the other aliens who we're friendly with have any idea, though the Vata feel that it could be based off of their anatomy, though in a very far-removed kind of way."

"You said that we couldn't have those wires removed from our husbands," Lorraine pointed out. "And not just from their brains."

Claudia nodded. "You told us you didn't want to remove their wiring because of the risk."

"It's not quite the same. The wiring is tied in with Joe and Randy's physical structures tightly enough that I feel it would be far too risky to remove. If something went wrong, we could try to remove it from them and have a hope of success, however, again because the Vata can see some similarities to themselves. The wiring in the gray matter of these three, though, is so dense that there's no doubt that it would mean the destruction of the entity to remove. It's as if there are two brains in there—the real one and the electronic one, and they're so tied together that they've become one."

Resisted making a *The Man With Two Brains* joke, but only because the situation was so serious and I had a feeling that no one would laugh, other than possibly Tim.

"You said 'entity,'" Jeff pointed out. "Does that mean you don't think they're human anymore?"

"Kristie definitely isn't," Tito replied. "I'll want Serene and her team to do a scan of all of these, by the way, because I didn't find any self-destruct mechanisms at all."

"Is that true for Ansom and Talia as well?" I asked.

"And for the reproductions of Christopher?" White asked. "If you've had time to inspect the remains of the first one."

"We have, and what was left was similar to the one we have in custody. The Christopher-Bot is the least human. Ansom and Talia are still human everywhere other than their heads. I can't say for sure if they're recording, as you were told they were, or not, by the way. My equipment doesn't show it if they are."

Serene nodded. "Mine will. If we choose to take them to Dulce."

"I'm not sure that we should," Tito said. "The Christopher-Bot is adamant that they're enemies."

"Huh. That's what the one he blew up said, too. Has he given you any better reason for robotic fratricide?" And if he hadn't, wondered if I'd get a better answer from him when we did the questioning.

"Only that the other Christopher-Bot was a danger to all of us and lying. Though this one insists he's self-aware and has overcome his programming, too."

Jeff groaned. "When, if ever, does it get easy?"

Chuckie clapped him on the back. "Welcome to the highest office in the land. Hope you're enjoying your stay."

"Not even a little bit." Jeff sighed. "So, what is Kristie if she's not a human?"

"The best version of a humanoid robot we have. Different from androids in almost every way."

"That would seem impossible," Chuckie pointed out.

Tito shook his head. "It should be, but it isn't. I think whoever did her work didn't do the work on the Christopher-Bot, though. The architecture is different."

"What about with Somerall and Lee?" Reader asked.

"Not enough data to be sure, but if I had to guess, I'd say that they came out of the same or a similar factory as the Christopher-Bot, not Kristie."

"Day spa." Everyone looked at me. Shrugged. "Kristie considers that she's had a 'treatment,' as if this was a better form of plastic surgery. Whoever's doing this, and we pretty much know it's Stephanie and the Tinkerer, then they're masked as being the next 'in' thing for the rich and famous, and they're selling their practice as a fancy day spa."

Now I had to resist making a *Zoolander* joke. I was totally taking more than one for the team. Allowed myself to feel virtuous.

"Meaning if we don't stop it, then half of Hollywood will be robotic before the end of the year," Chuckie said.

"There might not be a downside to that," Tito said. We all stared at him. He heaved a sigh. "This could honestly be the answer to disease and longevity."

"If there are no horrible side effects like self-destructing or becoming an evil-controlled automaton," I pointed out.

"And if you don't want to be involved in any form of natural childbirth," Tito added. "Kristie's reproductive functions are not going to be able to work like a normal human woman's would. We got to Joe and Randy in time, but if what was done to Kristie would be done to a man as well, then those functions would be destroyed."

"Again, that sounds like most of Hollywood's personal wet dream. And since we know that cloning is working, that's your reproductive answer. In some ways, that's not as gross as it sounds, by the way. Not that I am signing up for it, in case anyone was worried." Jeff in particular.

He grinned at me. "Good to know."

"Practice later," Chuckie said quickly. The rest of the group nodded. Haters.

"But you said that Ansom and Talia are still human," White mentioned, possibly to get the conversation off of our sex life.

"And that their brains are more like the Christopher-Bot's? Is that right?"

Tito nodded. "The Christopher-Bot has gray matter. I can't tell if it's human or some other animal, by the way, because all the tests so far are coming back with odd readings and we haven't had time to run more, but it's smaller than the gray matter in the other three. The wiring is just as tightly entwined, but there's more of it."

"Compensating for the smaller brain?" Managed not to make a *Young Frankenstein* joke now, though I desperately wanted to ask if the Christopher-Bot's brain had been taken from Abby Normal. Knew that would make Reader and Tim laugh, but again, no one seemed in the mood for levity right now.

"That makes the most sense," Tito said. "But again, I don't have the right equipment here to be sure."

"It sounds like it's time to take a look at the Kitty-Bot," Tim said. "Regardless of what Butler and Maurer want."

"Maybe look at John and Cameron, too, if they'll allow it," I suggested. "Though we know that those two are Marling creations. But I still think it's key to know who created the Kitty-Bot, since we're pretty sure she's the original."

"There's no way they created the Christopher-Bot too long before Jamie was born," Jeff said. "And I can agree that Butler and Maurer are Marling's work, because we've seen inside them and they masked as human perfectly."

"You know, in all the science fiction films and stories, androids were described more like the Kristie-Bot, and robots were more like our actual androids." Hey, it needed to be mentioned.

Chuckie shrugged. "Our reality is different. That can't shock you all that much."

"No. Though our Bots don't give off the same emotions as our androids, so I guess that tracks." Jerked. "Meaning that Marling had to have had an empath working with him. Maybe that was Ronald Yates, but maybe it wasn't."

"Granddad was dead well before we ever discovered that androids were around," Jeff said slowly. "So even if he'd been who Marling worked with originally, someone else would have had to be there as the test subject. Do you think it was Stephanie?"

"No, because I think she was testing the overlays and such, meaning that she was already 'dead' to the emotions from the androids. Frankly, Stephanie's dead to emotions pretty much totally, other than the misguided ones."

Reader groaned. "So we have another A-C traitor we need to find? And that means that traitor is still around because, as I remember, no one in the former Diplomatic Corps was talented in any way, so even though they were all traitors and they're all dead, they can't have helped with the empathic side."

"Though they were indeed traitors, you're correct, James, they weren't talented," White confirmed. "Pointedly, by the way. They claimed that talents weren't needed in those jobs. A way to discredit Theresa, I suppose."

"Or else they were hella talented and none of you knew it. Doreen has become a good Liar—what if they were troubadours or something and kept it hidden?"

Jeff ran his hand through his hair. "I don't know who we'd ask about that. My father, maybe?"

White shook his head. "Alfred wouldn't have hidden these people's talents from me, Jeffrey. Ever."

"I agree," Serene said. "We should ask Doreen and any of their remaining family members."

My brain nudged. But I wasn't sure why.

"But this probably means we need to look at the older generation of A-Cs," Claudia said, "because they were more likely to be swayed by Yates."

My brain nudged harder. "Um, why just the older generation? I'm thinking we need to look at yours right now."

Everyone stared at me. "Why?" Reader asked finally.

"Because when the entire Diplomatic Corps 'disappeared,' the only surviving family member I paid attention to was Doreen, because she was the only one I knew. But those people all had families, and, seeing as how you're all essentially related to each other back through the generations, big families most likely. We already know that we have human agents who were working for the former Diplomatic Corps who turned against Centaurion once we defeated their bosses. What if we have some of those bereaved family members, children in particular, who aren't as on board with us as Doreen is?"

"You mean," Tim said, "what if we've ignored a whole lot of A-Cs who view us not finding their parents as a betrayal and have therefore gone to the Dark Side, possibly years ago?"

CHAPTER 27

"YEAH, that's exactly what I mean. They could have turned like Stephanie did, when they were young, or after we all apparently forgot to keep on looking for their parents. I don't even know who they are. I realize this will shock everyone, but I never paid attention to who they were once the Poofs, ah, handled the removal of evidence."

At the mention of their species, heard a soft mewling from inside my purse and several little balls of fluffy fur appeared in my hands. The Poofs were alien animals. Most thought they were from Alpha Four, but I knew they were actually from the Black Hole Universe. Algar had brought the original two Poofs with him when he'd fled.

Poofs were androgynous, and the original story was that they mated whenever a Royal Wedding was on the horizon. Either our Poofs considered that every single royal in the galaxy counted, or else they were on a far different plan, because we had constant Poof Population Explosions. Considering that the Poofs were literally the cutest things ever—balls of fluffy fur with black button eyes, ears and paws mostly hidden by the fur, and adorable purrs—more Poofs was never an issue.

That the Poofs could and routinely did go Jeff-sized with giant, razor-sharp fangs when danger threatened just made them better in my book. The Poofs were carnivores and had ensured that the former Diplomatic Corps would never harm anyone again by eating them. After White and I, along with Naomi and Abigail and Melanie and Emily, Lorraine and Claudia's mothers, had killed them all first. But still, the Poofs had provided vitally important cleanup duty.

However, once Jeff and I been shoved into the roles of the

Head Diplomatic Couple and we'd confirmed that Doreen was with us and on our side, I honestly hadn't thought about anyone else who might have been wondering what had happened to their parents, siblings, or children. Felt bad. Not for the dead Diplomatic Corps, because they'd been the definition of traitorous evil. But still, even if your parent was a traitor that didn't always mean you didn't love them.

Nuzzled the Poofs, whom I loved unconditionally. Harlie, who was the Head Poof and ostensibly Jeff's, Poofikins, who was my Poof, and Murphy, who was Jeff's real Poof, all nuzzled me right back. Felt a tad better. The Poofs attached to whoever named them, and they were really lax on what they considered a name. My firm belief by now was that the Poofs chose who they wanted as their owner, then jumped at the first sound they found acceptable to answer to for their foreseeable future.

Lorraine was texting. "Tito, I know you wanted to keep this small, but now I think we need her." No sooner was she done speaking than Doreen Coleman-Weisman appeared, hyperspeed remaining awesome.

Doreen was now our Head Diplomat along with her human husband, Irving. Doreen had broken with her parents because they'd hated Irving and had wanted her to marry Jeff. Yeah, some things bonded you for life, and everything that had happened at Jeff's parents' house during Operation Drug Addict had definitely bonded me and Doreen.

We brought her up to speed on what was going on and our latest Worry Theory. She nodded slowly when we were done. "I think we have cause to be worried. I know everyone, of course, and I've continued the fiction that we're still searching for the missing people."

"Oh, go team." Thank God someone was on that particular ball.

Doreen grimaced. "Sort of. But realistically, your concern is the right one, Kitty. We haven't made any progress at all, because, of course, we can't, since they're all dead. But it's very clear that no one's really looking for these people anymore. No one's made any kind of official statement about them for years now, and if I didn't know what had happened, I'd be asking questions."

"So, who's asking what questions?" Jeff asked.

Doreen shook her head. "That's just it, Jeff. No one is. There were five other diplomatic couples when my parents were in charge. As far as I know, all their families have accepted the party line that they all disappeared due to enemy activity and we're hoping to find them alive and well. The first month or so after they 'disappeared,' sure. But other than a few questions in the first few months, no one's asked me if I know what's going on, and no one's come forward to anyone else that I know of, either."

"No one's spoken to me about it," Gower said slowly. "And as the Supreme Pontifex you'd think they would have. Richard, what about you? Maybe they wanted you instead of me, since I was brand new as Pontifex when this all happened."

White shook his head. "No one has approached me about this since right after the events in question. And I confess that I shirked my duties, since I'd retired as Supreme Pontifex, and didn't search anyone out for counsel, since I didn't want to try to lie to them. Which was why I didn't encourage you to reach out, either, Paul. Just because those twelve people were traitors doesn't mean that their families were."

"But it doesn't mean that they weren't," I said. "Stephanie being the prime Exhibit A that I'll always be bringing up. We already know that their human drivers and such were loyal to them, since those people did a fast fade from Centaurion Division so they could race off and join up with our still-living enemies."

"You think the humans believe that the Diplomatic Corps went missing?" Jeff asked.

"No," Chuckie replied before I could. "Humans are all too aware of what kind of treachery can happen."

"I doubt that every single family member believes what we've told them," Doreen said. "My family is smaller than the average, but my remaining relatives only believe that we're still searching for my parents because I've said that we are. They also don't talk to me about them much because they know we weren't speaking when they disappeared."

"How many of the other Diplomatic Corps children wanted to marry humans?" Wondered how many of them had moved to Caliente Base when I'd annexed it as our Refugee Camp way back when.

"About half," Doreen replied. "The others were already married within our community. Realistically, I don't think that we have anything to worry about from those who did marry hu-

mans. They're all much happier now than they were when we
were all living in the Embassy."

"What about those married into the community? Have we
done any investigations into any of them? Not to mention the
rest of their families." None of whom I knew. Realized I didn't
even remember the names of any of these people, other than
Doreen's parents. How I'd been the American Centaurion Ambassador without being fired was beyond me.

"The CIA wasn't given access," Chuckie said. "Until these
people fell off my radar."

"I apologize for that," White said.

"Me, too," Gower added.

Jeff ran his hand through his hair. "No, that's all on me. I'm
the one who was constantly putting walls up to keep Chuck out."

"Let's be honest," Reader said. "It was all of us."

"Not me." Hey, it was true.

Chuckie grinned at me. "True enough, on all of it, including
that Kitty was never the person trying to keep me out. However,
I should have remembered these people—they did try to kill all
of us, after all."

"And almost succeeded," Reader added.

"Yeah, but Richard and I saved the day, and yes, I like to
bring that up all the time, especially on days when nothing else
is going right. Besides, the people who tried to kill everyone, we
handled. And there was a lot going on. You're allowed to lose
focus just like the rest of us." I was in no way going to berate
anyone for forgetting about this, because I wasn't big on hypoc-
risy.

Chuckie shrugged. "I appreciate the support. But even if
we'd been allowed in it doesn't mean we'd have found much.
The intel we need would be far more likely to be found by an
insider." Noted that he pointedly didn't look at Serene when he
said this. No one else seemed to catch this. Wondered how long
we'd go before Serene had to let the rest of Alpha Team in on
the fact that she was running the A-C CIA without their knowledge or consent.

Gower looked troubled, though, but he wasn't speaking up,
which wasn't like him. "Paul, what do you think?"

He heaved a sigh. It was going around. "Honestly, Kitty? I
don't know. I don't want to start a witch hunt. We're all working
on supposition and conjecture. For all we know, the families of

the former Diplomatic Corps are all going on about their lives with no ill intents and the culprits we're looking for in terms of everything going on with androids and Bots and all the rest are Ronald Yates and the Tinkerer only. While we might have a traitor or traitors in our midst, there's no guarantee that we do."

Serene cleared her throat. "Actually, Paul, we definitely have traitors on the inside."

Okay, apparently Serene had decided that the time to share was now.

CHAPTER 28

"HOW DO YOU KNOW?" Tim asked. "I mean, you sound certain."

"I am." She heaved a sigh, which was apparently our team's Go-To Move of the Moment. "Chuck, your thoughts?"

"I think everyone here is trustworthy at the highest levels," he replied. "After all, everyone in the world knows my agency exists and yet we still manage to do what we have to do."

Reader's eyes narrowed. "Are you insinuating what I think you're insinuating?"

Decided now wasn't the time to pussyfoot. "Yes. Serene's running the A-C CIA, using our worldwide network of troubadours. I'm sure there are some empaths and imageers and just plain regular A-Cs in there, too, but it's mostly troubadours."

Reader, Tim, Lorraine, Claudia, Doreen, and Tito all had roughly the same reaction. They were quiet, looked pissed for a moment, appeared to think it through, then relaxed and nodded. "Makes sense," Reader said. "And you didn't tell me about this why?"

Serene smiled sweetly. "I didn't want to worry you."

"Or be told no," Tim said. "Let's face it, that was your first reaction, James. I know it was mine."

"Mine, too," Lorraine said. "Only, like James said, it makes sense."

"How long has Kitty known?" Claudia asked.

"My bet is longer than anyone not involved," Doreen said.

"True enough," Serene said with a laugh. "And she approved it."

After it was already in place, but why spoil the mood? "The uncles knew about it. And also approved it."

"Good enough for me," Tito said. The others nodded and they all relaxed fully.

The uncles were two Russian cousins, and they weren't related to me by blood—they'd literally chosen to consider me their beloved niece. They also weren't with us any longer, having sacrificed themselves to save me during Operation Epidemic. I still missed them, terribly at times. That I'd gotten so emotionally attached to the two best assassins in the business was just one of those ironies life enjoyed throwing at me.

Of course, they'd been attached to me, too, hence the sacrificing. It was because of them that we were all still alive, had Culver working willingly on our side, had joined Siler and therefore Lizzie into the fold, and had stopped any number of Bad Guy Plans du Jour. Sure, they'd been hired killers. But unlike so many we'd met, they had honor. They'd killed for money and to protect me and mine, but never for fun or enjoyment.

So far as we knew, no one else outside of our Inner Circle knew that the Dingo and his partner, aka Peter and Victor Kasperoff, were dead. Siler wanted it kept that way for as long as we could manage—the uncles had put a No Kill order onto me and mine, and as long as they were presumed alive, we were presumed a little safer. That the others had relaxed because Serene's secret organization had gotten The Uncle's Stamp of Approval was just a testament to how much we'd all come to rely on them and trust their judgment.

"Good to hear," Serene replied briskly to Tim's vote of confidence. "Because I'm certain the traitors are gearing up to make their moves. And we have more of them than any of you are going to like."

"You mean in addition to the people we were just talking about?" I asked Serene. She nodded.

Jeff ran his hand through his hair. "Which members of my family?" He sounded resigned. Couldn't blame him.

"Your brother-in-law, Francis Carruthers," Serene said. "And his three children. Your sister Constance is not a traitor, and she doesn't appear to know what's going on with her husband and kids."

"All three of them?" Gower asked. "You're sure?"

"Very." Serene grimaced. "Jeff, I told you I was looking into your family and I also told you we had issues there. This shouldn't be a total surprise."

"We knew that all of them other than Jonathan were suspect," I reminded him.

Shockingly, this didn't appear to make Jeff feel any better. "What proof do you have?" he asked.

"Francis is working at Gaultier Enterprises. He's an assistant to Ansom Somerall's assistant."

"Meaning Amy doesn't see him if she's in meetings but he can affect things," Chuckie said, as he rubbed the back of his neck. "Camilla didn't discover this when I had her in there."

"Because he was hired on once she'd left. Whether that means her cover was blown or just that he'd finally gotten into the company we haven't been able to determine. The kids are all interning at Gaultier as well. They're out of high school and, as near as we can tell, following in Stephanie's footsteps."

"No one goes to college in the A-C community?" Hey, as per usual, I hadn't paid a lot of attention to anything that didn't immediately concern me. I'd have beaten myself up for this, but apparently it was working for me.

"No," Claudia said. "By the time we're out of our version of high school, we normally have the same education as if we'd gone on for an undergraduate degree. The rest we do hands-on."

This begged a question. "So why are the Valentino and Price kids going to Sidwell, then? I'm not going to believe that they aren't as smart as the rest of the clan. And neither Alfred nor Lucinda, let alone Sylvia and Marianne, gave us the heads-up on that. I got to find out a little while ago during an unpleasant phone call with the president of the school's PTA."

"Marianne and Jonathan's children are the youngest," White said. "They want them to assimilate in with humans and felt that this was a good way to do so. At least, that's what my sister told me. I'm sorry, Jeffrey, but I thought she'd let you know."

"No, my mother likes to tell me things last, Uncle Richard. You should be used to that by now."

"Lucinda is correct," Serene said, presumably forestalling any further discussions about my in-laws and their odd little ways. "Those two have chosen to support Jeff, and in order to do that, they have to support his children, too. So, they're also there so that Marianne and Jonathan can cover for the two of you as needed."

"See?" I said encouragingly. "One sister set is fully A-okay."

"One out of five. Not great odds, baby."

"More than that," Serene said. "But not much more. Sylvia, as you know, is on your side. Her three youngest children are schooling at Sidwell for the same reason that the Price kids are there—to watch out for your kids."

"Do we believe that? I don't mean, is that Sylvia's intention, because I'm sure it is. I'm asking if we believe that Stephanie hasn't turned her brothers and sisters."

"The Clarence Clone is fully on your side," Serene said. "And believe me, that matters."

We'd found the clone of Clarence Valentino on Beta Eight, during Operation Civil War. He wasn't stupid, but he'd been made quickly and without a lot of strong memories implanted, making him rather simple. And also lonely. He'd ended up helping us, and we'd taken him home to his wife and children, who'd missed their husband and father.

The Clarence Clone, or TCC for short, was more like the man Sylvia had married, not like the one I'd gotten to know and loathe and, ultimately, kill. Despite being told the truth, all the Valentinos, other than Stephanie, had chosen to believe that it was their real father after a traumatic head injury and kidnapping, versus a clone. We'd decided it was kinder not to push it.

"Well, I would believe that more if their kids were younger." It was hard to buy that Stephanie hadn't told her siblings that we were responsible for their father's death.

Serene shook her head. "Sibling rivalry is a fascinating thing. Louise, who is their second child and who is already out of school, was always jealous of Stephanie's tight bond with Clarence. TCC has no bond like that with Stephanie. He knows she's his daughter and therefore he loves her, but she's not his special favorite—realistically, he barely knows her. So the other kids, Louise in particular, have gotten all his attention."

"That's good, but, I don't see how that swings them back to our side."

Claudia laughed. "Because you're an only child. Lorraine and I luck out—we work with our moms all the time."

"And sometimes that's a pain," Lorraine added with a grin. "But we do love it. But our brothers and sisters don't get that time. Our parents drop everything to help us because of the positions we're in, meaning we get more of their time. So there's jealousies."

"Every family has them," Gower said.

"Are our siblings cleared?" Claudia asked Serene.

Who nodded empathically. "Other than Jeff's family, all of Alpha Team's extended families are cleared."

Managed not to share that I'd had no idea that my two best A-C girlfriends had siblings. That was me, Ms. Totally Unaware, Uninterested, and, apparently, Self-Centered. Felt like crap, but shoved the emotion aside—needed to focus on the here and now. I'd have oodles of time to beat myself up later.

Both Lorraine and Claudia relaxed a bit. "Our parents go out of their ways to make sure everyone gets their attention," Claudia went on. "But that's because they're focused on doing the right thing. Clarence was focused on moving up in the ranks and he sacrificed his daughter into that cause."

"She went willingly. Trust me, it was willingly and probably eagerly."

"True enough," Serene agreed. "However, even if the idea of being traitors had sounded good to the others, they're now getting more of their father's attention—remember, TCC isn't working unless you need him for something, due to 'what he went through,' so they have him all the time. They're excited to be getting all his attention now, and as far as I know, they've cut ties with their eldest sister."

"If you say so." Wasn't convinced, but chose not to push it. I'd undoubtedly have plenty of time to keep an eye on the Valentino kids, since they were officially My Responsibility per The President of the PTA From Hell.

"I do. Louise also has more sway with her younger siblings because she's home and with them, and she's going to be a teacher's aide at Sidwell, for Early Kindergarten." Opened my mouth to express worry. Serene put her hand up. Closed my mouth. "I have vetted her, Kitty. Believe me. My son will be in that class, too."

Couldn't really argue with that, so I didn't. "So, what about the others?"

Serene grimaced. "Lauren and Elizabeth's older kids are definitely following Stephanie's path."

"Which ones specifically?" Jeff asked, sounding ill.

"Patricia, Bonnie, and Darius Guerra, and Lloyd and Laura Fontana. The younger ones, like their mothers, seem unaffected. So far at least. However, Stephanie's still considered part of the family, so if she shows up unexpectedly, literally none of your relatives are willing to let us know it until she's gone. Lauren and Elizabeth in particular."

Jeff groaned. "Does it get any worse?"

"It does," Serene said. "Because their husbands both work for YatesCorp."

CHAPTER 29

"JEFF, WHEN WILL YOU learn never to ask if it can get worse? Because it always can." My turn to heave a sigh. "So when did Nero Fontana and Oscar Guerra start at YatesCorp? Because Christopher hasn't mentioned seeing them."

Nero was married to Lauren and Oscar was married to Elizabeth, meaning that, as we'd been told years ago, Jeff's only brother-in-law who wasn't evil somewhere along the line was Jonathan. TCC didn't count in this particular equation.

"They've been there since the first Diplomatic Corps disappeared," Serene said grimly. "And Christopher wouldn't see them—he's barely been there long enough to know anyone, and they don't actually work closely with Amos Tobin. Plus, they've been hidden—they both appear for all intents and purposes to be working for a benign company. But it's a YatesCorp subsidiary and where they go daily is to YatesCorp HQ."

Chuckie grunted. "This isn't a surprise. I told you when you two were getting married—I've never met men more jealous of someone else's success than your brothers-in-law."

Jeff nodded. "Yeah, I guess I shouldn't be surprised." He sounded down, not that I could blame him.

White hugged him. "Jeffrey, my father is the reason they turned. We can only do our best. We can't make others do their best, however. That's up to them."

Gower chuckled. "Once the Pontifex, always the Pontifex. But Uncle Richard is right—this isn't your fault, Jeff."

"Or Christopher's," Chuckie added. "They resent him almost as much."

"What about the humans who were working for the Diplomatic Corps?" I asked Chuckie, in part to move us off of Jeff's family for a moment or two. "I'd swear you were hunting them down."

"Was and did. All are at Gaultier. Camilla traced them all there. They're all still there, too, as far as we know."

Camilla was that rarity of rarities in the A-C community—a natural-born Liar, with a capital L. She'd been assigned by Alfred to protect us once I'd gotten pregnant with Jamie, and she was a big part of the reason we were all still alive to talk about Operation Confusion.

If we needed someplace infiltrated, Camilla was the go-to girl, and these days she answered to Chuckie, Serene, Jeff, and Alfred. Probably my mom, too. And sometimes even me. But Alfred's vote was the deciding one.

She'd been pulled from Gaultier to investigate Titan and then Drax Enterprises, which had worked out in a weird way. She'd also married Rhee when Tito and Rahmi had finally been allowed to tie the knot at the end of Operation Immigration. I rarely knew where she was assigned, but right now, I had a really good guess.

"What job is Camilla doing at the Sidwell Friends School?" I asked Chuckie. "Or, more to the point, are you aware that that's where Alfred's assigned her?"

He grinned. "I'm well aware. Your mother, Alfred, Serene, and I discussed this the moment Camilla and Rhee were back from their honeymoon. She's not the only agent assigned to the school. There will be obvious security, stealth security, and Camilla. The kids will be safe."

"We can but hope. They need to add Wasim onto their protection duty. Nothing bad can happen to that kid, or else we're probably at war with the Middle East, lots of aliens hanging around or not."

"Which is already handled, since your assessment is correct." Chuckie rubbed the back of his neck. "Serene, how likely is it that those you've identified are taking action now?"

She shrugged. "We're not sure. Frankly, Stephanie's learned from others' mistakes, as far as I can tell."

"Lucky us. I think we need to get on our way to the Bot Interviews, though, because time's flying by and I have to gather baked goods or some such for tomorrow because I'm just that kind of lucky, and Jeff and I are probably going to have to go to a party tomorrow night as well, and generally this week is really testing my ability to handle stress."

"What party?" Jeff asked.

"A fundraiser for the Sidwell school. Invitations arrived just a little while ago. The event is being hosted by Zachary and Marcia Kramer and, to make it even better, all the Dealers of Death are invited. And a Doctor Rattoppare, meaning that either Stephanie or the Tinkerer, or both, or someone acting as their proxy, will be there. Just to keep it interesting. Vance is confirming that this is legit and not some sort of elaborate trap, by the way. And if it's legit we have to go, at least as far as Vance is concerned."

"Only if it's legit," Chuckie said. "I find it difficult to believe that they want the two of you at any kind of party for any good reasons."

"The Kramers' kids go to Sidwell, so, as much as I'm also hoping for the 'trap' idea to be the winner, I'm resigning myself to the likelihood that we're going to have to go. Guy and Vance, Lillian and Abner, and Thomas have all been invited, too. Maybe we can pull in Camilla to go as Thomas's date."

"Maybe we all just won't go and call it good," Jeff said. "Presidential order or similar."

"Let's see what Vance finds out." No sooner said than my phone beeped. Took a look. "Huh. Hang on." Sent a reply text, then dialed. "Vance, you're on speaker."

"Thanks for letting me know who's lurking in the stairwell with you. Okay, I spoke with Marcia. The party is legit but it wasn't her idea. Apparently, Charmaine Cordell strong-armed Marcia into this party just like she did to you with tomorrow's bake sale. Literally everyone who's invited was invited today."

"That's potentially social death," Doreen said. "It's rude and seems so presumptuous—plus people have plans. The Kramers are well-placed politically, but even the President would have trouble getting people to an event with approximately a day and a half's notice."

"Vance, how was Marcia taking this?"

"About as well as you're taking the bake sale. She knows Charmaine personally, since she has two sons and a stepson there. She loathes Charmaine as much as you do, and she's afraid of her, too. She didn't say that, but I know her and I can tell. Oh, and good call on the social death, Doreen. Marcia's panicking that no one's going to come and that it will be socially embarrassing for them."

"Which it would be." Heaved the biggest sigh yet. "I cannot believe I'm saying this, but Vance, please let Marcia know that the President and First Lady will absolutely be attending the party."

Everyone stared at me. "Really?" Jeff asked. "I mean, these people are our enemies."

"I know. I don't like them. However, barring Marcia being the best phone actress in the world, she and I have a common enemy now."

"She's not a great actress and she's not pretending," Vance said. "Trust me, I know when Marcia Kramer is trying to fake me out. She's not. She actually offered to trade with you and take the bake sale if you'd do the party. But while we were talking she forwarded that idea to Charmaine, who shot it down in a nasty way—Marcia sent me a screenshot of the text conversation. Charmaine has the vicious insult down to an art form."

"Stop sounding impressed."

"Didn't say I liked her. But she's good at what she does, it's why she's still the president of the PTA—no one wants to lose her effectiveness."

"Good lord, how much power does this woman have?"

"At Sidwell? Per Marcia, Charmaine is the most powerful parent there. If you get on her bad side, your children will experience social death in a variety of ways. And the less said about how she'll make the parents' lives miserable the better."

"And the teachers and administration don't do anything about that, about this woman affecting how the children are treated?" Jeff asked, sounding appalled. The A-Cs all looked appalled, too.

Chuckie, Reader, Tim, Tito, and I all exchanged the "Aliens Are So Cute" look. "Yeah," Chuckie said. "Half of it they don't see. Half of it they have to allow, since this woman is the president of the most important association within the school. I'm sure the bullying is well hidden, but I'm also sure it's there. Just like at every other school in existence. Other than, apparently, A-C schools. Where I wish I could have gone."

"You'd have loved it there, I'm sure, but I'm glad you were with me."

Chuckie grinned and Jeff grunted. "Let me get this straight. This woman is ordering around both a senator's wife and the First Lady of the United States, otherwise known as my wife? Who else is on her list?"

"Every parent of every child attending the school," Vance replied. "And, believe me, she's going to be taking notes on how Kitty and Marcia do with their respective events. It is a competition, though not with each other. You're going to be in competition with what Charmaine feels is the level of excellence she demands. And that's pretty much a direct quote from that text conversation I read."

"Um, I'm in competition for how well I run a bake sale?"

"Yep." Vance sounded grim. "Think of it as a hazing ritual that you don't want to fail."

We all looked at each other. Couldn't be positive the others felt that I had no chance of success, but since that was how I felt, figured they were with me on this one.

Chose to make the only suggestion that seemed logical. "Maybe I can send the Kitty-Bot in my place."

CHAPTER 30

"SPEAKING OF THAT," Vance said, "Ansom and Talia are also invited to this party."

We all stared at each other again. "Ah, are they allowed to go?" Jeff asked finally.

"That's not up to me," Vance said. "However, I'm going to bet that they were seen entering the White House grounds. They came in on foot, remember?"

"Meaning that there will be questions we don't want to answer if they don't show," Reader said. "I sense a trap."

"You know, that's exactly what Kitty and I thought," Vance said, almost cheerfully. He and Reader didn't get along all that well, so I wasn't sure where he was going with it. "So I'd suggest that Alpha Team go with the President, First Lady, and their Robotic Entourage, just to make sure they're safe and all that." Ah, that was where he was going. Heaved an internal sigh.

"Thank God you're here," Reader said, sarcasm knob at eight and rising. "Because that never would have occurred to any of us."

"Can Chuck come to this thing?" Tim asked quickly. "And, frankly, can we really go to this? I'm serious. If there's an approved guest list, I don't know what kind of entourage the President can bring."

"The President can bring anyone he so chooses," Vance said. "Frankly, right now, Marcia will welcome the entire White House Complex staff. She has no idea if anyone *other* than Jeff and Kitty are going to show."

"We'll handle it. We have a day to determine if Ansom and Talia are set to explode and if they're broadcasting anything we don't want broadcast."

"Which would be anything," Claudia said darkly. "But I'm with Kitty—let's get downstairs and do the Bot reviews."

"Vance, tell Marcia we'll do our best to bring others along with us, and that we'll prep them for making donations."

"She'll owe you big-time, Kitty, that's a good plan."

Wasn't doing it to get Marcia Kramer on my side—it was just going to be a lot easier to roll in with what seemed like fifty people if I'd told her that I was trying to bring an army of donors along. Thankfully, the A-Cs had plenty of cash, so we could handle the donations portion of these festivities.

"That's me, Miz Helpful. Besides, if I can have an I Hate Charmaine Buddy at Sidwell, I'll take them, regardless of who they are."

We got off the phone and chose to hyperspeed through the complex to get downstairs. As advertised, we had a pack of people on guard duty. In addition to the flyboys and the Princesses, Melanie and Emily were there, as were Abigail and Mahin.

"No change," Melanie said as soon as Tito was within earshot. She looked like Raquel Welch during her fur bikini days.

Emily was studying a tablet. "Not a lot of fluctuation between them, either." She resembled a young Sophia Loren.

Yeah, Lorraine and Claudia came by their Dazzler gorgeousness legitimately. So had Abigail, who, like her brother, had beautiful dark skin from her mother and had the double whammy of getting the gorgeous from both her A-C father and her human mother.

"We're here in case things change and/or fluctuate," Abigail said with a grin, indicating herself and Mahin. Abigail and Jerry had come out about their being an item near the end of Operation Immigration—facing the end of the world did tend to focus people on admitting attraction and sharing that with friends and family. So I was pretty sure that she was happy to be helping Jerry and the rest of the flyboys "guard."

"And we are here because the Great Tito requested it," Rahmi added. She might be married to Tito, but that hadn't stopped her hero worship of him. Whatever made a relationship work well was A-okay with me, of course.

Rhee nodded. "But so far, nothing has happened." She sounded disappointed. Not a surprise—the princesses were from Beta Twelve, where butt-kicking was a way of life.

By contrast to all the Dazzlers On Duty, Rahmi, Rhee, and Mahin merely looked normally attractive. Mahin was also a hybrid, being one of Ronald Yates' many illegitimate offspring. Her mother was Iranian, and since human genetics ruled for external on hybrids, Mahin naturally looked Middle Eastern. She wasn't ugly by any definition, but in a room full of Dazzlers, Mahin and I were not going to win any beauty contests.

Like Abigail, who was a textbook female hybrid in that she was talented above the norm, Mahin's power was earth-bending. If it had dirt in it or on it, she could move it. Unlike Abigail and, so far as we'd found, all the other female hybrids, though, Mahin's internal parts were far more human than A-C. She could handle hyperspeed without Tito's special Dramamine, but she couldn't run at hyperspeed herself. She had only one heart, and she wasn't super strong.

By comparison, I had more A-C skills than she did, but she made up for it by being dedicated to learning all the many ways to kick butt. She and Abigail had also learned to work their powers in tandem, which was helpful in many ways.

Had a thought. "Mahin, do you have any special baked goods recipes from your homeland that you've been craving?"

She stared at me for a moment. "Ah, no? I mean, I'm sure I could make something if it was necessary."

"Kitty just wants company tomorrow," Jeff said reassuringly. "She'll explain later."

Mahin nodded. "If you need me, my schedule will be clear. But, don't we need to deal with what's down here?"

"Oh, we do. I just hate letting good ideas slip away." Resolved to take Mahin with me to the bake sale—had a feeling I was going to need all the moral support I could get.

The flyboys were each stationed in front of five containers I recognized—the A-C's portable containment units. They were 10x10x10, with thick steel walls, a heavy-duty door that locked securely from the outside, and windows made of thick shatterproof glass or similar. They were also set up so that those on the outside could hear those on the inside.

The only containment units I'd seen had been set up as medical bays. These weren't. Each of them looked like what was in an empathic isolation chamber.

"Why are they in Sarcophagi From Hell?"

"They're not that bad," Jeff said comfortingly.

That he was comforting me was probably an irony I should have felt guilty about. After all, I didn't need to ever use an isolation chamber. But Jeff did. All the time. Because when his empathic synapses shut down, he needed an isolation room and regenerative fluids or he'd die. We wouldn't have made it past the first two days of knowing each other without the isolation chambers. But that didn't make them any less creepy to me.

These days, we had a lovely isolation room in our Presidential Suite, because the Elves had moved the one that had been in our suite at the Embassy into the White House. They were helpy helpers that way. Meaning it was more like an austere hotel or cozy hospital setup. Meaning I'd avoided looking at a real isolation chamber for quite some time. So this was a harsh reminder.

It was slightly less creepy to see three people I didn't care for hooked up to the wires and needles and such, all on the rotating metal bed that could go every which way but was usually at a gentle angle so heads were higher than feet, but the person wasn't fully horizontal. But only slightly less.

Seeing what looked exactly like Christopher in the fourth chamber was just a negative reminder of Operation Confusion, when we'd had to put him into isolation due to his Surcenthumain addiction. Not comforting to remind myself that this was merely his robotic double, since Christopher-Bot the Second's existence was discomforting no matter what.

Of course, the fifth room didn't have an occupant so much as a collection of remaining Christopher-Bot the First parts. I was underwhelmed to discover that it was no less creepy than seeing full bodies.

All four of the other rooms' "living" occupants seemed relaxed, however. "Tito, are they conscious?" Had to ask, because I truly couldn't tell if they were breathing, let alone awake.

"No. We put them into a form of suspended animation. In part to ensure that if they exploded because of it, they'd be contained."

"Good thinking," Serene said. She looked around at the ceiling and walls. "This area is pretty sturdy."

"I know where you're going with this," Reader said. "I'm not sure that it's a great idea for you to do your examinations here as opposed to Dulce."

Serene shrugged. "Here or there, the risks are the same."

"To the White House Complex they're not," Reader pointed out.

"The rooms are too heavy to move easily through a gate," she counter-pointed out. Rightly. While we had big stationary gates at the Crash Site Dome, where the main gate equipment was housed, and we could also create big floater gates, the things we took through those were mobile—people or vehicles. There was a reason the A-Cs built the containment chambers in pieces, and it was because each piece was hella heavy, even for beings with super strength. Sure, we could have a bunch of A-Cs shove a containment chamber through a gate, but it seemed like a lot of needless effort.

"I'm with Serene. If she can bring what she needs here, it'll be faster and easier for her to do the examinations."

"I could try to help," Mahin said uncertainly.

"Absolutely not," Reader said calmly. "And I don't want Abigail offering, either. That's a waste of your talents and energy for something that's not necessary. I'm sure we'll need you, and sooner than any of us would like, but not for this."

"I agree." Jeff sighed. "And our legacy can't be turning the White House to rubble because it was convenient."

"Our legacy happens to be having kept most of this town standing more than once." Just felt that I needed to point that out, particularly since Abigail and Naomi had been the main reasons all of D.C.'s historic buildings and museums were anything other than smoking piles of rubble.

Chuckie sighed. "Kitty's right. Jeff's right. James is right. Serene's right. Tito, what, in your medical opinion, as the person who's examined these four the closest, do you recommend?"

"Like I said, I couldn't find anything that looked like a self-destruct or any other kind of bomb. And I examined the entire bodies of all four of them, and all the exploded parts. I've made sure that I and my staff know what to look for, just in case."

"Literally there's nothing dangerous going on with any of these," Emily said. "Their readings indicate that nothing has changed since Doctor Hernandez put them under."

"We found nothing that looked like any sort of bomb," Melanie added. "And we do know what to look for. Serene's our expert, but Emily and I aren't chopped liver when it comes to this sort of work."

"The choice is yours, Jeff," Reader said. "You know my thoughts."

Before Jeff could reply, Jerry, who was looking into the room with the Christopher-Bot the First's remains, shouted. "You all need to see this!"

CHAPTER 31

NO ONE HESITATED—we all trotted over to Jerry's unit and looked inside. To see the various Bot parts disintegrating.

"What the literal hell?" Tito asked everyone and no one. "Is there a contaminate in the room?"

"No," Emily replied tensely. "Readings indicate that nothing's changed from when we left it."

Didn't stop to admire the view. Headed over to the unit that Hughes was covering, the one with the Christopher-Bot the Second. He was still intact. "Can we wake him up?"

Emily was next to me in an instant. "I think so. Doctor?"

"Go for it," Tito said tensely. "I have no idea if we care if he melts or not."

"I don't need to see a *Wizard of Oz* reenactment, so I'm hoping not. Oh, crap." Ran over to the Kristie-Bot's unit. She was still intact, too. Did a fast check on Somerall and Lee, then went back to the Christopher-Bot the Second. He was blinking and seemed to be breathing. "Um, is he breathing?"

"He imitates breathing," Melanie said. "So does the Kitty-Bot. In order to fool people, the robots need to appear to be human."

"He's not taking in air so much as appearing to take in air," Tito added. "Same with blinking. Neither this one nor the Kitty-Bot need to blink to keep their eyes moist but they do it. To not blink would alert everyone quickly that something's wrong with them."

"Versus the others who are blinking and breathing because they have to?" Chuckie asked, as he eyed Joe and Randy.

Joe nodded. "If I don't breathe I die, Chuck."

"And I can't not blink without my eyes watering," Randy added.

"It's the same with the other three," Tito confirmed.

"So, the Kristie-Bot could still be killed, right? If she breathes, she could breathe in a toxin."

Everyone looked at me. "That was out of the blue," Jeff said.

"Not really. Stephanie's selling this procedure as the longevity solution, but if you can still die from breathing in a toxin, or just too much pollution, then it doesn't work totally as advertised."

"Are you hoping to use that as a way to convince people not to have the procedure done?" Chuckie asked. "Or are you hoping to kill off the Kristie-Bot?"

"Not sure if that would dissuade anyone who wanted to stay young and beautiful forever, but we need to know how to fight these things. I'm not suggesting slaughter, but I think that it might be time to think like our enemies do."

"Offensively as opposed to defensively?" Gower asked. I nodded. He shook his head. "I'm not sure that we want to be anything like them, Kitty."

"The best defense is a good offense," Rhee said. Everyone looked at her. She shrugged. "I enjoy watching American football."

"My sister is correct, though," Rahmi added. "As is Kitty. Preparedness is key when dealing with your enemies."

"I don't believe Missus Martini wants us going forth to randomly murder these people, if we can call them that," White said. "However, I agree with her and the princesses—we need to think like our enemies, if we can, so we can be prepared to counter them. We may actually have a way to be prepared if we can identify all the weaknesses in the Kristie-Bot."

"Thank you for the support, girls, and what Richard said. And clearly that won't work on the Bots, so we need a lot of ideas."

"I don't want to die," the Christopher-Bot the Second said.

I'd forgotten that those inside the containment units could hear those outside of them. "Um, sorry, but you murdered your brother, or duplicate, or whatever you call each other. And now his parts have dissolved."

"Into a puddle of goo," Jerry shared, sounding grossed out. He was still at his post, just as the rest of the flyboys were, though everyone else was with me. "The puddle isn't moving, so there's that."

"Good, I don't want to star in a remake of *The Blob* any time soon. So, Christopher-Bot the Second, what have you got for us about your brother's melting situation?"

"We're made of a polymer that will dissolve if we're destroyed," he replied calmly, without complaining about his new moniker. There might be hope for him yet. "This is to ensure that no one can duplicate us." He sounded like he was in a big fishbowl, but that was the result of the way the containment units worked.

"That sounds like an A-C fail-safe to me."

White nodded. "I agree, Missus Martini. Meaning that Trevor had something to do with the creation of these Bots."

The Christopher-Bot the Second cocked his head, hard to do while strapped to a metal table, but he managed it. "I don't know that name."

"Doesn't mean he wasn't involved," Reader said. "However, I still want to know why you blew up your counterpart, when he was warning us of the exact same things that you are."

The Christopher-Bot the Second seemed to actually consider this question. "I don't know," he said slowly. "Perhaps we were programmed to distrust ourselves?"

"But you said you overcame your programming and are now self-aware," Jeff said, rather gently. "I don't think it can be both."

"Why can't it?" the Christopher-Bot the Second asked. "Humans have programming that they do and don't overcome."

"Wow, philosophy from a Bot. But he's actually right. There's plenty that humans, and A-Cs for that matter, and probably every other life-form out there, do automatically. There are things we actively work to overcome, but there are some things that are so ingrained we might not even realize that we were programmed to think or do them."

"I'm more interested in the idea that you're made out of something that melts if it's separated long enough," Tito said. "That seems dangerous for you. We had you dormant for a while—would you melt if we'd turned you 'off' or similar?"

"I don't know," the Christopher-Bot the Second said calmly. "I just know that if we're blown up we won't be able to be put back together again. We're not Humpty Dumpty."

Jerked. "What? Why did you use that example, Humpty Dumpty?"

"It's a common one that humans understand."

"Why do you care about that?" Claudia asked.

"Because it's not something a robot would normally be programmed with," Chuckie replied for me. "Nursery rhymes and how they'd relate to other situations aren't necessarily information you'd put into a robot."

"But you would into an android. At least, Antony Marling would have and very likely did. So, what does that mean? Is he a product of a Marling and Tinkerer matchup?"

"Does it matter?" Tim asked. "I mean that seriously. I feel like our big issue right now is what we do with Ansom Somerall and Talia Lee. As in, do we take them with us to that party tomorrow or do we not? And what do we do with them regardless of the party? They said they weren't aware that their brains had been tampered with, right? So, how did someone get them?"

"Oh. Wow. Um, I think that there's a really good chance that they were 'gotten' by all those people we were talking about earlier. As in, we have those traitorous A-Cs and all those humans who used to work for the former Diplomatic Corp all bustling about at Gaultier Enterprises and YatesCorp. What if they're who helped get these two onto the New Robotics Lifestyle?"

Everyone was quiet for a few long moments. "That seems sensible," the Christopher-Bot the Second said finally. "If I follow you."

"Nice to know the robots are programmed to speak Kitty," Reader said with a quick grin. "But, I think that idea makes a lot of sense."

"I think that begs another question," Chuckie said looking worried.

"Let me guess what that question is. Who else has been made into some form of a robot without their knowledge or consent? And I'm going to answer that question myself. We don't know but it could be a whole lot of people."

"Commander! You need to see this!" Jerry shouted before anyone else could chime in on my Prediction O' Doom. We all ran back to his containment unit.

To see the goo remains of the Christopher-Bot the First forming into something. Something that looked like a big fist. "I specifically said I did *not* want to star in a remake of *The Blob*! Why is that crap turning into a fist?"

The Christopher Blob answered me before anyone else could. It started slamming itself at the door handle inside the room.

"Ah, is that going to be able to break through?" Tim asked.

"I can't feel anything from it," Jeff said. "It's got no emotions."

"If it has emotions, trust me, they're set to Rage Against The Machine, so let's be glad you can't feel them." Noted that the door handle seemed to be failing. "And it's hella strong, whatever it is. Anyone have any guesses for how to destroy that?"

Rahmi and Rhee produced their battle staffs. I still had no idea how they carried them, because one moment they appeared weaponless and the next they had their staffs. Decided not to care. Beta Twelve battle staffs had what really seemed like a big laser on one end and were sort of weighted like a javelin. They also worked better for women than men.

"We will stop it," Rahmi said grimly, as she stepped in front of Tito and activated her staff. The laser end glowed.

"It will not reach anyone else," Rhee added as she went next to her sister, staff already activated. They were definitely in First Line of Defense Mode. Alpha Team lined up behind them, with Abigail and Mahin behind them, while Chuckie, Tito, Melanie, and Emily pulled Jeff back. White stepped in front of him, a move that was totally in character for White and would mean that, should anything happen, Jeff would toss everyone off him to protect his uncle.

Raced back to the Christopher-Bot the Second. "Your counterpart that you blew up has first melted, then formed into a blob of goo, and now those that goo has formed into a sort of fist that's breaking down the containment room door. It's about to attack us. Any idea of what we can do to stop it?"

"It's coming for me," he said, sounding mildly worried. "We are enemies, remember?"

"He didn't even know you existed, and I don't know what you're both made out of, but it's certainly not anything normal." Or potentially from this planet. "Not sugar, spice, or anything nice, I can say that."

"That's females. Males are made of snips and snails and puppy dog tails."

"Commander," Hughes called, before I could ask about the Christopher-Bot the Second's nursery rhyme programming. "What do you want us doing?"

"Guarding your posts!" Like we wanted any of these others to get the chance to escape?

"Let me out, so I can fight," the Christopher-Bot the Second said.

Pondered this. Sure, maybe he was telling the truth. And then again, maybe this was an elaborate ruse to get us to let him out so he could kill us all. Had no bet either way, because there were so many other options.

Heard the others shout and spun around. The Christopher Fist has broken the door down and Rahmi and Rhee were going to town on it. It was, however, dodging them. Heard Chuckie shouting that no one should shoot a gun, meaning that the battle staffs were it. Saw Rahmi hit the thing. It seemed to take damage, but then reformed into what looked like a net. It tried to catch Rhee, but she managed to jump out of the way.

"Commander," Joe shouted, "that looks like one of the nets from the NSA black site!"

It did indeed. We'd been able to destroy those, but we'd used Drax weaponry to do it. "Poofs Assemble!"

All the Poofs of those people here—and by now, everyone we cared about had a Poof, and some had more than one—appeared in front of me, looking up adoringly. I enjoyed the Sea of Animal Love for a moment. "Poofies, Kitty has a situation. I don't think this enemy is one you can eat. I'm not even sure if you can fight it." Then I put on my Recap Girl Cape while keeping my Dr. Doolittle Hat on, and told them, fast, what was happening. "So, if you can bring us some weapons from Gustav Drax's helicarrier, I think Kitty can save everyone."

Harlie mewed, bounced up and down, and mewed again. Then all the Poofs disappeared.

Meanwhile, the net was dodging any and all attempts by the princesses to hit it, while it simultaneously seemed to be trying to get to Jeff. At least, it was heading for him and the clutch of people around him, despite said clutch moving Jeff and the princesses and Alpha Team attempting to knock the net down.

Thankfully, the Poofs were back quickly, Poof powers being awesome. Seeing as Poofs were actually Black Hole Universe animals, they had special abilities, one of which was to be able to "eat" a thing and then hack it back up when it was needed. Which they did now. Well, they'd already "eaten," so what they were doing now was hacking.

We had a full set of Drax weapons hacked up. The weapons

didn't even have Poof Spit on them, because Poofs were the greatest. Drax was pretty great, too, and truly what he'd first advertised himself to be—a weapons creation genius. Grabbed the laser gun Harlie had deposited at my feet. "Aww, I think I used this model to kill fuglies at Camp David. What good Poofies you all are."

With that, I looked up at the net that was now flying too high for the battle staffs to hit, and was also flying directly for my husband, and took aim.

CHAPTER 32

MY MOTHER HAD spent a lot of time teaching me how to shoot accurately and fast when I'd first joined up with Centaurion Division, and my life since then had given me tons of practice. I probably still wasn't as good as Mom, who was the Annie Oakley of Covert and Clandestine Ops, but I was damned close.

Hit the net several times and brought it down. Hit it on the way down, as did the flyboys, each of whom now also had a Drax laser weapon. Once it was down I shouted to them to remain at their posts, then ran to the remains of the net on the ground and shot the hell out of it until there was literally nothing left.

"I don't know how we sweep up debris of this nature and cleanse the area, but however we do it, or think we do it, it needs to be done now."

"On it," Lorraine said. She and Claudia zipped off.

"Nice shootin', Tex," Chuckie said.

"Nice thinking on calling in the Poofs," Reader added, as the girls returned with what looked like industrial-strength cleaners and went to town, their mothers helping them.

"Ah, I think you all want to see this," Walker called before anyone else could chime in on my ability to save the day. He was guarding the Kristie-Bot.

Cleanup done because of hyperspeed, we all trotted over, Jerry included since he had nothing left to guard, everyone else picking up a Drax weapon of choice on the way, because why should the flyboys and I be the only ones having any fun?

So, we all got to share in the fun news that the Kristie-Bot was awake and wriggling out of her straps. "Who woke her up?" Tito asked.

"No one," Emily replied, looking at her tablet. "She's done this on her own."

"That should be impossible," Melanie said, as she shifted her gun into the low-on-the-hip mode of firing.

"No, that blob thing was impossible. This is just our usual luck."

But a blob that turned into a capture net did indicate that the Christopher-Bots had come from the same NSA black site where we'd found Janelle Gardiner and the part of my team that had been captured during Operation Madhouse.

We watched the Kristie-Bot get loose enough to remove the straps. She then pulled all the various needles and such out. Then she stepped off of the metal bed. Waited for her to morph into something or start pounding on the door. She did neither. "What do you people think you're doing? You can't keep me out of Code Name: First Lady, you know."

"Wow, that's what you're leading with? Trust me, babe, you've got a part in the Movie From Hell. We were keeping you sedated or similar so nothing bad could happen to you or to anyone else." I mean, that was what I assumed Tito's overall goal had been.

"We can't let her out," Tito said softly. "If she can overcome what she just did, she could be highly dangerous."

"More dangerous than that blob-net thing?" Tim muttered.

"My girl handled it," Jeff said proudly. "Like she always does." Felt all warm and fuzzy, but didn't let it make me cocky.

But before I could chime in on this latest wrinkle in the linen of our lives, my phone rang. Sighed, pulled it out of my purse, and answered. "Kitty, you totes need to hurry up."

"Lizzie, what's going wrong now?"

"Nothing. But P-Chef's ready to start the prep for baking, and per the rules you have to be with us when we're making stuff for tomorrow's bake sale."

"Seriously?"

"Yeppers."

Contemplated suggesting that all the kids lie and say I was there, but that was definitely too big an entry into the Worst Mother in the World Awards to be even suggested aloud. "Um, can you guys start without me?"

"Not really. Chef says that he wants to ensure that you know what's being served and all that stuff. P-Chef agrees. So does everyone else."

"Of course they do."

"Go on," Jeff said. "We can handle this."

Managed not to say that they couldn't have handled the net without me, but let it slide. "Okay, I'll be there, soon. And 'there' is the White House kitchens, right?"

"No," Lizzie said patiently. "We're baking, so we're with P-Chef. Where else would we be?"

"Oh, the way my life goes, you could all be on Mars. See you soon." Hung up and heaved a sigh. "Are you sure you don't want me around for this?"

"*I* want you around for this," the Kristie-Bot said. "I don't trust any of these people, but at least I know you're trustworthy."

"Um, how in the world would you know that?"

"Your reputation."

"Yeah, I don't believe that, honestly. Are you supposed to explode and just don't want me to miss out or something?" Or morph or grow three times her size, or whatever. Really, after the Christopher Blob, I wasn't ruling anything out.

She rolled her eyes. "Look, I get it. Most people who do stuff like I've done, they're doing it to take over the world. I'm not. I'm just at the most attractive I'll ever be, and I want to be famous. Not just morning show famous, but whole world famous. And then I want to be whole galaxy famous. And the only way I'm going to get to do that is by first having the procedure, which I've done, and then starring in the most anticipated movie in years, which I now will do, thanks to you and Jürgen."

"What movie is that?" I asked politely.

"Really? Code Name: First Lady. I want to be in that and I want to be an important character. I don't want to be killed off in the first reel."

Jeff grunted. "I can't believe I'm saying this, but I've spent enough time reading her now. Her emotions aren't clear in the way fully organic beings are, or the way the androids' emotions are. However, I've figured out where the differences are and how they feel. She's telling the truth."

"What are the differences?" Chuckie asked.

Jeff shook his head. "I can't explain them to anyone who's not an empath. But I *can* explain it to the rest of our empaths. With a little practice everyone should be both able to spot a Bot and also able to read them properly."

"See?" the Kristie-Bot said smugly. "I'm helping already."

We all stared at her. "Um, am I interpreting you correctly?" I asked finally. "You want to be on the team?"

"Of course. I know that I'll have to have a good working relationship with you as well as Jürgen. You're my golden ticket. Meaning I need to be helpful, or your people will just have me have a convenient 'accident' before I can say you're a homicidal maniac."

"That's the best idea so far," Chuckie said cheerfully.

"We'll have Adam around to let us know if she's off," I said. "And we did agree to cast her on national television this morning."

"It's in my best interests to help you, not hurt you," the Kristie-Bot said.

"Tell me how to find Doctor Rattoppare."

She stared at me. "Why? I don't want her to reverse the process."

Hoped the others weren't being too obvious in their expressions, but reflection in the window we were all staring into said that several jaws had dropped. "Excuse me, but she can reverse it?"

The Kristie-Bot nodded. "Yes. It's in the agreement."

"What agreement?"

"The one you sign when you agree to become a patient."

"Huh. Would you happen to have a copy of that agreement somewhere we could see it?"

She shrugged. "Sure. It's at my house."

Reader was on his phone. "We need you, right now. Yeah. Underground garage."

As he hung up Christopher appeared. "I didn't bother to share that I was leaving the LSR. I don't think anyone will care—they're really focused on the stuff with Gadhavi, Pecker, and Gutermuth. What's going on?"

"We need to you to fetch something," Reader said. He nodded to the Kristie-Bot. "Tell him how to get to your home and where the agreement is."

While she did, Reader called in my A-C Security team. "They already know what's going on," he said to me with a grin, after he told them what they were doing.

The Kristie-Bot finished and Christopher nodded. "Back in a flash." My five guys linked up, Christopher grabbed Manfred, and they disappeared.

"If anything happens to them," Jeff said to the Kristie-Bot, "you will meet with a very public and very unfortunate accident from which you will not recover."

She rolled her eyes at him. "You just confirmed that I'm not lying."

Jeff shrugged. "Yes. I'm just confirming what I'll do to you if I've somehow read you wrong."

"I appreciate the concern, as do the other guys," Christopher said as the six of them reappeared and everyone, even the Kristie-Bot, jumped. He grinned. "Nice to keep you guys on your toes." While the Poofs politely hacked up weapons for Christopher and my A-C security dudes, he handed a large manila envelope to Chuckie.

Who read its contents, grunted, then handed said contents to Reader. Who read them, grunted, then handed them off to Tim. Who shared with others, so all the A-C women crowded around him and read over his shoulder.

Chose to not bother and just go to the source. "Chuckie, what's the good word?"

"I can't believe I'm saying this, but it's actually possible that Stephanie's trying to go legit. In the most radical way possible, but still, potentially legit. There are portions that deal with reproduction—the patient has to guarantee that they're of age and either have had all the kids they want or don't plan to have any more. There are portions that deal with reactions to the procedure and so forth. And more. That contract reads as comprehensive and totally legal."

"It did to me, too," Reader confirmed. "And, yeah, if a patient wants to have the procedure reversed, they can do so."

"There's a time limit," the Kristie-Bot shared. "After a few years, the wiring will become integral to every part of your body and then it's irreversible. But I really doubt that it's going to be an issue."

"Could be," Tito said. "If something goes wrong."

"Things go wrong with human bodies all the time," she replied. Accurately. "But this will keep my body safe from the most dangerous thing that it faces—aging."

"There's not a lot of proof that it works long-term, though," I pointed out.

"That's not true. The elder Doctor Rattoppare has had the procedure done. Years ago. He looks great and has been completely healthy since the procedure."

Once again, we all stared at the Kristie-Bot. "You've met him? The elder doctor?"

"Yes. Of course. They're in practice together. Grandfather

and granddaughter. It's really kind of sweet. Though, I wouldn't necessarily say they're sweet people. But they clearly care about each other. And they do excellent work."

"If we showed you pictures of them, would you be able to recognize them?" White asked.

"Of course."

"And you'd do that?" Jeff asked.

"Yes. I want to be in the movie. I get that it means I have to be on your side. I mean, it's stupid to oppose a popular sitting President. And besides, galactic famous, remember? I'm not going to achieve that by working against you. Well, not in a positive way. I don't want to be a famous villain. I want to be the biggest star in the world."

"She means it," Jeff said. He sounded shocked.

I wasn't. "You know, I'll take it."

"Come again?" Christopher asked.

"Look, I get the motivation. It's not mine, but I understand it. Hollywood is cutthroat. Our Kristie-Bot has found a way to put herself ahead of the pack. Sure, she blackmailed me and Jürgen to get a part in a movie, but, in the grand scheme of things, that's all she did. People have done far worse for the same goal. Frankly, far worse for a lesser goal. And, as we've already outlined, that blackmail can be so easily circumvented that we can literally laugh about it. It's just refreshing to have someone actually tell us what their Take Over The World Plan is and have it not include mass deaths and massive destruction."

"You think we should trust her?" Tim asked.

"I don't feel angry or threatening or anything," Abigail said. This was important, since part of her talent was being a reverse empath—if someone was feeling sad, it would make Abigail feel sad, and so on.

She and Naomi had worked as a team, and when they'd saved D.C. from the Z'porrah attack during Operation Destruction, they'd burned those powers out. To get her powers back, Naomi had taken so much Surcenthumain that she'd gotten her powers back and then some. As far as the rest of the world knew, she'd died. As far as I knew, she'd become a superconsciousness that was forbidden to come back to Earth and let anyone who knew her know she was "alive." This Earth and these people on it. But Naomi was representing all through the multiverse, and she was protecting all of us as best she could without getting caught. Including those of us in this particular universe.

Abigail had been able to create shields with Naomi, among other things. Now she did it with Mahin because I knew Naomi had given Abigail back her powers, and then some, when we were on Beta Eight. Whether Abigail realized how she'd gotten her powers back, her sister's powers, and extra boosts of power, I'd chosen not to ask.

"So Jeff's right," Chuckie said, "and the Kristie-Bot is being truthful?"

"Thanks for the vote of confidence," Jeff muttered.

"There's more," Abigail went on. "I've focused on the Kristie-Bot. I'm kind of excited, kind of impatient, feeling hopeful and optimistic. I'm annoyed in a way, but it's because I'm looking forward to being a part of this team. I know I'm going to achieve all my goals. And those goals feel very . . . starry."

"Starry?" Reader asked.

"Like I'm swirling and dancing and smiling for photographers. Greeting dignitaries all over the place and on other planets. Living large." Abigail shrugged. "I gotta say, I think she's legit."

Considered options. "Fine. You know what? Why not? Let's plan to have the Kristie-Bot and Adam do a human interest piece. Tomorrow. At the Sidwell Friends School First Day of School Bake Sale."

CHAPTER 33

THIS TIME EVERYONE stared at me. "Ah," Jeff said finally, "while I can say that her emotions show that she's telling the truth and even sort of seems on our side, and Abigail certainly seems convinced, I don't think it's a great idea to have her around our children and all the other children, either."

"That could be the plan," Chuckie said.

Reader snorted. "Really? Who in their right or even wrong mind would think that Kitty would suggest this? Who would possibly have known about the bake sale and that Kitty was going to be put in charge of it earlier than today? Not that I'm wild about this idea, but I can see the advantages. If they're forcing Kitty to do this, let's make it a good showing for the First Lady."

"I can see so many ways this can go wrong," Chuckie muttered. "So many I could just spend the rest of the day listing them."

"I want to examine her immediately," Serene said. "Risks of explosions or not. If she truly has no self-destruct mechanism and also isn't broadcasting back to anyone, then we need to know and clear her. Before she goes to school with Kitty."

"I'm all for it," the Kristie-Bot said. "Clear me, because I think that will be a great story. By the way, someone needs to call our producer. By now they have to be wondering what's going on with me and Adam. Normally we'd be prepping tomorrow's show."

"And you are, go team. Once Serene clears you, we can share the plan with Adam and you two can call in and get whatever you need. Understanding that our people will be vetting everything and everyone." That was me, predicting the happy outcomes—that the Kristie-Bot would be cleared, that *Good Day USA!* would be able to leap into action, that everyone from that show was going to be on the side of, if not right, then at least not Team Evil, and that things would work out just fine. Really hoped the cosmos wasn't going to get a good laugh about my optimism, but chose not to make any bets about it.

She nodded. "That's how it's always done. Oh my God, this is going to be fantastic!"

"Total excitement," Abigail said softly to me. "But I think you want more people along."

"I already planned to drag Mahin with me. Thanks for volunteering, Abby."

She grinned. "Happy to help. So, does that mean Mahin and I need to go with you to the kitchens where the kids are really impatiently waiting for you?"

Jeff grunted. "Incredibly impatiently. And their feelings are starting to get hurt."

"Pardon me for thinking this needed my attention."

Jeff kissed my cheek. "It did, but get going. We'll make Serene happy and have her do all the tests on everyone."

"Remember that the Christopher-Bot the Second is probably made from the same thing as the First and Not Lamented Goo was. Meaning he can morph into things. So Serene, if you test him, too, I want Christopher and the flyboys in there with these weapons set to nuke." Managed not to make a *Josie and the Pussycats* comparison statement, but it took effort. "And let me know if we make any breakthroughs. And remember that we need to clear Ansom and Talia for that fundraiser tomorrow night. And be sure, if we can be, that they can't morph, too."

"Got it all," Chuckie said. "We'll handle it. Get going. Make something edible."

I snorted as I, Abigail, and Mahin handed our laser guns to Jerry. "Dude, my plan is that I'm going to ask the Elves for a gigantic batch of Lucinda's brownies and call it good."

With that, Abigail grabbed me and Mahin and we headed for the massive kitchens.

Chef's domain was the large kitchen on the ground floor of the White House Residence. Technically, Chef was also supposed to hang out in the Family Kitchen on the second floor, where our family lived. But the Elves had taken the contract on that kitchen, so Chef made most of the food and the Elves got it to us. This kept Chef where he was happy and us from having to explain things we didn't want to.

P-Chef, however, was relegated to a room in the sub-basement level. The White House had a lot of levels that most people didn't see, didn't know about, or didn't think about. Other than A-C bases and such, I'd rarely been in a building that went down as much as this one did.

We arrived in P-Chef's Pastry Palace to find her, Chef, Vance, Mrs. Maurer, all the kids on Charmaine's list, and Pierre. Pierre was the Embassy's Concierge Majordomo and he was the most competent man on the planet. Pierre's presence ensured that everything would be alright.

Of course, my daughter being here was a big positive, too. Picked Jamie up and gave her a big hug and kiss. "Are you ready to get baking for the first day of school?" Part of me couldn't believe that she was ready for school—she wasn't even five yet. None of the kids in her class were. But Sidwell had the Early Kindergarten class for children who were advanced, and all of our hybrid children certainly were.

Jamie hugged me back. "We're all ready now, Mommy. Lizzie says we have to go to make sure that Wasim has friends!"

Wasim was indeed here, as was Naveed. Wasim looked like he wasn't sure if he should be happy or embarrassed. Naveed, however, shot an approving look in Lizzie's direction.

"Where's Charlie?" I asked as I put Jamie down. "And Nadine? And the majority of your security detail?" The only Secret Service agent I could spot in here was Keith, who'd joined up with my side of things during Operation Madhouse. He was a big dude, had adapted very well to how I rolled, and was therefore the Secret Service agent who headed up the kids' security team.

"Still at the Embassy," Lizzie answered. "Denise wouldn't let Charlie come over. So they stayed there and Jamie came over with Keith. They coordinated with your team."

"Miss Denise says that Charlie needs to stay with her and not get into the flour and stuff," Jamie shared. "I think she just misses us already and wants to keep him with her while we're all over here."

Had a feeling Jamie was right, and not just because she was talented far above the norm. Denise Lewis ran the Embassy School and Daycare and her kids were among those heading to Sidwell tomorrow.

Kevin Lewis was a former pro football player, big, black, and gorgeous, with great teeth, a great smile, and bags of charisma. Denise was blonde and fair, but equally gorgeous with the same great teeth, great smile, and charisma. Raymond and Rachel were beautiful blends of their parents, and they'd both inherited the teeth, smiles, and charisma. Like Reader, the Lewis family was representing in the Humans Can Be As Hot As Aliens Competition.

Raymond had been our oldest kid until Lizzie had come onto our scene, and he still acted like the leader. The very serious, very concerned leader who had to protect his troops at all costs. "I'm worried that they want us doing this the first day," he said. "It seems like a lot."

To my knowledge the Lewis kids weren't psychic, but it was truly as if Raymond had read my mind. However, my job as the adult was to take that very accurate worry away from him, where it didn't belong, and hog it all to myself.

Bent down and hugged him. "I know. But you know what? I think we're all more than up to the task. We'll show them that American Centaurion kids know how to do this just like everybody else."

"What do you think?" Jamie asked Rachel.

Who definitely pondered before she replied. Noted that all the kids, Lizzie included, were giving Rachel their full attention. Wasim saw this and did likewise. Jamie had told me and Jeff that she felt that Rachel was usually right about her pronouncements. I'd put this down to Rachel being the eldest girl in daycare, but the way all the kids were acting, Raymond included, did make me wonder.

"I think it's going to be hard at first," Rachel said slowly. "But in the end it'll be okay."

Everyone relaxed. Myself included.

"First things first, darlings," Pierre said briskly, before anyone else could share their prophecies. He started handing things out to everyone. "Aprons on. I believe we have the correct sizes for everyone, but if your size is wrong, just let me know and we'll get it fixed in a jiff."

The Elves had delivered again, and not only did we all have aprons, but we all had personalized aprons. And not the cutesy kind. We had full on Chef- and P-Chef-level aprons, each with everyone's first name stitched in Presidential Gold over the left breast.

Bruce Jenkins was here, too, with one photographer, introduced as Dion Callan France. He looked a little taller than Christopher, but still under six feet. He was slender and had a small build, medium brown hair, a smattering of freckles, and a shy smile. He was cute in a kind of Leonardo DiCaprio When He Was Young way.

"It's an honor to meet you," Dion said as we shook paws. "I'll do my best to get great photos of all of you."

"Are everyone's parents on board with that?" I asked Jenkins and Pierre.

They both nodded. "All the waivers have been signed," Jenkins said. "We're good. We'll be with you tomorrow, as will Joel. And we'll be sure that this is done right, Kitty. You know that."

Hugged him. "I do. Thank you." Thought about this. "He's allowing you to call him Joel, not Mister Joel Oliver?"

Jenkins grinned. "Professional courtesy. I'm literally the only peer allowed that privilege. He'd give it to you if you really wanted it."

"Nah. I like the MJO I'm used to—quirky."

Pierre handed me a scrunchie. "Let's get that beautiful hair up, shall we?" He then bustled about and either offered hair ties or did the tying, depending, to the rest of the girls, big and little. Our boys didn't have long hair, seeing as that wasn't an A-C thing in any way, shape, or form, but Wasim's hair was longish, especially around his eyes. Not to worry, though, because Pierre had a male headband for him. "Just like all the football players wear, or what we call soccer players, dearest."

Wasim smiled as he put on his headband. "I love football. And I know you call it soccer here."

P-Chef beamed at us. "Okay, let's get going and make the best baked goods your new school has ever seen!"

The kids cheered and we got rolling. While P-Chef got the kids started doing various things like making and rolling out dough, whisking eggs, and the like, Chef and I went over things, and he agreed that Lucinda's brownies would be winners. "Only she refuses to share the recipe." He sounded as frustrated as I felt.

"No worries. We can ask the Elves for some."

"No, dear, you can't," Mrs. Maurer said. "The rules are quite clear."

Heaved a sigh. "Then we don't get to bring the guaranteed best-seller with us. We'll have to make do."

"You can always request them for later," Chef said.

"Nah. We'll eat whatever P-Chef says isn't good enough to go over."

P-Chef winked at me. "Or what's too good."

"I like where your head's at."

Made do for several hours. Had to admit that even though baking wasn't my thing—nothing in a kitchen was ever going to be my thing, after all—this was fun. By far the most fun I'd had all day. And the kids were loving it.

After a couple of hours, Jenkins and Dion had more than enough in terms of photos, at least until the finished products were all done. So, since they both had personalized aprons, too, they also helped out. Jenkins was clearly doing this for journalistic purposes, because he was spending his time with Chef and P-Chef. But Dion seemed like he was really enjoying it. He and Pierre were talking fashion and celebrities while rolling out piecrusts.

Mahin and Naveed seemed to be getting along as well. Which was nice, because Wasim wasn't the only one here away from family, friends, and what was comfortable and familiar. They were speaking in Arabic and had chosen to work on pies together. Wasn't sure if this meant anything or not, but if nothing else it had to be nice for both of them to have an adult from their region to talk to.

As an icebreaker and get-to-know-you event went, this was also great for Wasim, because Naveed was occupied by Mahin so Wasim actually got to do things without his bodyguard hovering. Chef and P-Chef were covering the hovering portion, with strong Hover Assists from Pierre and Vance, but that was different. By the first hour Wasim was helping the littler kids, and by the second hour they were talking to and teasing him as if he'd lived with us for his entire life. And he was eating it up.

"Do you have a lot of younger brothers and sisters?" I asked him when he and I were together on the cookie icing team.

He nodded. "Eleven."

"Wow. That's a big family."

"It is. And . . . I miss them already." He swallowed, then looked over at me. "I'm glad there are so many other children here. It's less . . . lonely."

Nudged against him, because our hands were too busy and covered with icing for me to hug him. "You can stay here as long as you want, you know. I'm sure the idea of your own cool bachelor pad sounds great, but if you want to stick around, we're happy to have you."

"You really mean that, don't you?" He sounded a little surprised.

"Yeah, I do. You seem like a cool kid, you're fitting in well with all the other kids, your grandfather is one of my besties—why wouldn't I want you to stay here if you like it?"

"Because," he said in a low voice, "Grandfather wants me to, uh . . ." He stopped speaking, blushing furiously.

"Fall in love with Lizzie?" I said just as softly. He nodded. "Dude, we all figured that out before you even set foot on American soil. But you know what? Like I told her, friendship is more important. And in this country, you're both too young to worry about it. So far, we all really like you."

"You barely know me. What if . . . what if I do things you don't like?"

"You mean like every person on the planet?" I laughed. "I'm sure you'll do things we disapprove of, and I'm sure you'll have bad days just like everyone else. I'm sure that we'll do things you don't like, too. But family deals with it and moves on. So, consider yourself all-in."

He grinned. "Consider myself part of the furniture?"

My turn to grin. "You know the music from *Oliver!*? I do like you."

"I love Disney movies. All of them. Even the poorer ones."

"What are your thoughts on the comics?"

He hesitated, took a deep breath, and let it out in a rush. "I think Deadpool is hilarious, but please don't let my family know I read it."

"Wasim? I truly believe this is the beginning of a beautiful familial relationship."

CHAPTER 34

WE WERE FINALLY DONE with all the baking and such in time for dinner, albeit a later dinner for most of the kids. But they'd been having so much fun that none of the adults had had the heart to make them stop early.

Considering how the day had started, the afternoon and early evening had been pretty darned good. Jenkins felt that he had a great human interest piece on us, Dion was happy with the pictures he'd taken, plans were confirmed for the First Day of School Extravaganza, and the kids all seemed excited to be going. Maybe Charmaine wasn't an Evil Kangaroo and just knew how to get a lot of kids invested in their new school. Maybe.

Vance and Pierre escorted Jenkins and Dion out, I sent Jeff a text, and he met up with us outside of P-Chef's domain.

He picked Jamie up and twirled her while giving her hugs and kisses. Then he put her down and hugged all the rest of the kids, starting with Lizzie and going down in descending age order. Then he turned to Wasim. "I hear you're our newest addition."

"Yes, sir, I'm honored that you've allowed me to stay here." Wasim put out his hand.

Jeff chuckled, took his hand, then pulled the kid in for a hug. "We hug family here, son." They did the manly back patting thing, and Jeff let go. But I could tell Wasim felt better.

Which was good. Had no idea how demonstrative his family normally was, but he was going to have to get used to a lot of Public Displays of Affection from all of us.

Jeff shook Naveed's hand, picked Jamie up and handed her to me, put one arm around me and Jamie and one around Lizzie, then we all headed upstairs. The rest of the adults, other than

Chef and P-Chef, helped us wrangle all the kids, who were all more interested in the desserts they'd made than the healthy dinners waiting for them.

We'd already planned for all of the kids and their parents to have dinner together the night before the first day of school, so we rolled up to our private dining room across the hall from our bedroom.

All the parents and guardians who hadn't been baking were there already other than Serene, Joe, and Randy, who were still on Bot Duty. Noted that their sons all looked a little disappointed and felt a pang—Jamie and Charlie probably felt this way a lot, because it seemed like Jeff and I were always being pulled in a million different directions. Having to bake like crazy suddenly seemed like the best possible use of my afternoon ever.

Abigail and Mahin tried to excuse themselves, as did Naveed. But the kids were having none of it. They'd baked together, and that meant everyone who'd walked upstairs was staying. Fortunately, this room was good-sized and we had the space.

Jamie got out of my arms so she could hang onto Mahin with one hand and Abigail with the other. I was fine with that, because Denise and Kevin were here and they'd brought Charlie. My son was ten months old and basically adorable. But he still wasn't talking. For human children this wasn't slow at all. However, for A-Cs, and by his older sister's measure, Charlie was way behind.

By the measure of the other hybrid boys, all of whom were over four but still under five, he was behind. Ezra was the youngest of our "first wave" of Embassy kids, and he was heading to Early-Starters Kindergarten because, frankly, all of these kids were advanced, mentally and physically, and Ezra was no exception. Jamie was leading the pack, but Serene's son, Patrick, wasn't far behind, and Lorraine and Claudia's sons, Ross and Sean, weren't slackers, either. I could see why A-Cs finished their college-level schooling by the time they were eighteen—it was a kindness to humans that A-Cs tended to school separately, not the other way around.

Except when it came to my son. Continued to try not to worry about him, but it was difficult. In Bizarro World, Cosmic Moi had had three kids—two boys and Jamie. The Jamie there was at least borderline autistic, though much of that was because she was seeing into all the other universes where she existed. And she existed in a lot. But I didn't know what Charlie might be seeing, if he was autistic, if there was a developmental problem no one had identified, or if he was just fine and would catch up.

Then again, when it came to telekinesis, Charlie was number one with a bullet. And he proved it the moment I saw him, because he grinned his father's grin and lifted me into the air. High up in the air. Up to the ceiling up in the air.

Fortunately, Jeff was there, because while Charlie was great with the lifting, for the heavier items, like a full-grown woman such as myself, he wasn't always sticking the landings. Sure enough, he lost control and I dropped like a stone.

Right into Jeff's arms. "It's nice of our son to keep on giving us these nostalgic moments," Jeff said as he hugged me, hearts pounding. "At least I didn't really have to run to catch you this time."

"Go team." Checked out Wasim and Naveed. Their mouths were both hanging open. "Welcome to our world."

Was going to go over to Denise but Jamie stopped me. "Wait, Mommy."

"For what, sweetie?"

Denise smiled at me. "For this." She looked at Jamie. "Ready?"

Jamie nodded. "Mommy, I wanted to wait until you and Daddy were both with us. Miss Denise and I have something exciting to tell you! And show you!"

With that, Denise put Charlie down. As soon as his feet hit the floor, she let go.

"Mommy, Daddy . . . Charlie *walked* today!" Jamie sounded exceptionally proud, as if she'd trained him to do it. Possibly she had.

He'd been waiting for her cue, that was for sure, because the moment she stopped speaking he walked right to me and put his arms up.

Picked him up and gave him a hug. "Wow! Look at you!" Felt a huge wave of relief. He wasn't as behind as I'd feared. Gave him another hug. "Mommy's missed you tons, and I'm so disappointed Daddy and I didn't see your first steps, but I'm so happy that your sister did. But, Charlie sweetie, I'd really appreciate you not lifting me up unless it's really necessary. If Daddy hadn't been here Mommy could have gotten hurt. Though I love you no matter what, my little man."

He grinned at me again, definitely his father's grin, without looking even remotely remorseful. Had a feeling it was because he wasn't the least bit repentant. Also noticed something. "Um . . ."

"Do you see what I see?" Jeff asked.

"Um . . . yeah . . ."

Charlie grinned even wider. "I love you, Mommy. I love you, too, Daddy."

Jeff and I gaped. In addition to Charlie speaking and, apparently, walking, he had a full set of teeth. "Um . . . when did Charlie's teeth come in?"

"Oh," Jamie said nonchalantly, "today. I didn't want Charlie's teeth to hurt you, Daddy. So I made sure that he didn't hurt so you couldn't feel it."

A-C teeth tended to come in all at once. Considering that Jamie's teething experience had been so hard on Jeff empathically that he and I had had to go down to his parents' home in Florida to allow him to get through it, I couldn't blame Jamie for not wanting Charlie's teething to hurt her father. But this was beyond anything I'd expected.

For Jamie, "all at once" had meant weeks of teething agony. Apparently for Charlie "all at once" meant a couple of hours of Jamie doing whatever she'd done.

"Um, sweetie, did you, um, make Charlie's teeth wait and come in all at one time?"

Jamie nodded. "I've been practicing."

The room got quiet. "Practicing on who, sweetie?" I asked carefully.

Jamie gave me her "Mommy, you see but you do not *observe*" look. "My friends." She said this as if it was obvious. Probably was, if we'd been paying attention, which, based on the expressions on the faces of the adults, none of us had been.

Looked at the four hybrid boys. Come to think of it, their teeth had come in with a lot less pain than Jamie's. In fact, I couldn't remember if Jeff had been affected by the boys' teething or not, but if he had been, it had been mild enough that he hadn't mentioned it.

"Ezra only had teething issues for a week," Doreen said slowly. "And I remember thinking that Ross and Sean had had an easier time than Jamie, and that Patrick's teething had been even easier . . ."

"Jamie-Kat, are you sure that you didn't hurt yourself in order to help the others?" Jeff asked worriedly.

"I'm sure, Daddy," she replied cheerfully. "I know to be careful."

"She has a great career in dentistry ahead of her if she wants it," Denise said with a little laugh. "I was there with them both this morning. Jamie told me what she was doing, she didn't overstrain herself, and Charlie didn't suffer at all. I'd have contacted you immediately if it had been different. And I'd have called you both over to see Charlie's teeth and then have him walk for you but, well, you were a little busy."

"That's putting it mildly. When did he start talking?"

Denise shrugged. "Just now. You two got his first, well, sentences." She grinned and hugged me and Charlie both. "I told you he'd catch up."

"With a vengeance, apparently."

"I made Mister Keith promise not to tell you," Jamie said, looking up at him.

Keith nodded, looking slightly worried. "It seemed like the right thing to do."

Jeff laughed as he took Charlie from me and hugged and kissed him. "Yeah, it was."

Chuckie arrived. "You wanted me, Jeff?"

"Yeah. Charlie, let's show your Uncle Chuck what you did today."

Jeff put Charlie down and he trotted right over to Chuckie, and put his arms up. "I love you, Uncle Chuckie."

Chuckie gaped for a moment, then laughed and picked Charlie up. "I love you, too, kiddo." He examined Charlie's mouth. "All the teeth, too?"

Jamie shared her Magical Manipulation of her brother's developmental stages. Chuckie asked serious questions, which she answered more than Denise did. Chuckie seemed pleased with all that Jamie had done. "I'm so proud of you," he said seriously. "That was very well done and exceptional even for you, Jamie."

She straightened up and preened. "Thank you, Uncle Chuckie. I'm glad you're not mad at me." Realized we hadn't given her the Atta Girls that she not only deserved but clearly wanted. Felt like I was, again, winning The Worst Mother in the World Award.

He chucked her under her chin. "I promise, no one's mad at you. You're just amazing and it throws the rest of us sometimes. And parents worry the most. Your mother and father are just as proud of you as I am—they're still adjusting to what's happened, that's all."

"Chuck," Jeff said, "not that we're not thrilled about the rest of this, but Charlie also lifted, then dropped, Kitty."

Chuckie gave Charlie a stern look. "You know you're not

supposed to be doing anything dangerous like that. You'd feel very badly if your mommy got hurt."

"Hmmm, why do I get the feeling that you and Jamie and Charlie have had conversations Jeff and I are unaware of?"

He shrugged. "Because we have. I got in touch with Boz on Beta Eight, thanks to Emperor Alexander and King Benny. Boz agrees that the waterfruit you, Christopher, and I ate is why Charlie's telekinetic and why Amy didn't mutate like you did. The waterfruit fixed Christopher's issues, at least some of them. And it enhanced things in you, Kitty, which you then passed on."

"Enhanced what?"

This time everyone gave me the "really?" look. Chuckie sighed. "This question from the girl who talks to the animals?"

"Oh. OH! Yeah, I guess that's a form of telepathy, isn't it?"

"Yes, Missus Martini," White said, coming into the room with Christopher, Amy, and Baby Becky in tow. "So I believe we may be able to expect telepathic talents from Charlie as well. Jeffrey tells us that our young man here has things to share with the family."

Chuckie put Charlie down and he did a repeat, walking far more than toddling over to each one of them, telling them he loved them, showing off his new choppers, and then moving on to the next. He did this with every adult.

"Why isn't Charlie talking to the other kids?" Jeff asked quietly.

"Oh, he's talked to us plenty, Daddy," Jamie said casually. "We all talk to each other in our minds already."

At this everyone looked stunned and at each other, though Chuckie looked like this had confirmed his suspicions. I, however, looked at Lizzie. "Are they talking to you, too?"

She shook her head. "Not in the same way as they talk to each other. I think it's a hybrid thing, honestly. I mean, Jamie can reach me if she really needs to, and so can the other kids, but it takes a lot more concentration."

Looked at Raymond and Rachel. "But you two, no problems?"

Raymond nodded and looked guilty. Rachel didn't. She stood up tall. "Yes. And we can talk to Cassidy and Chase, too." The Maurer kids looked like Raymond—guilty.

Pondered why. "You know, it's not like it's a bad thing that you can do this."

Cassidy, who was a year older than Raymond nodded. "We

know. It's harder for Lizzie because she's already gone
through . . . through . . ." He looked to Denise.

"Puberty," she supplied. "And before anyone asks, no, I
didn't know, but I've suspected."

Turned to Chuckie. "Okay, none of them ate the waterfruit.
So, what's your theory now?"

He walked over to Jamie and picked her up. She hugged him.
Then he handed her to me. "There's a reason why," he said
calmly. "I know you know. Stop pretending that you don't. She's
exceptional. The most exceptional of a race of amazingly exceptional people, with DNA combined in from another exceptional
person."

"That's sweet and all, but, seriously, it can't just be Jamie."

"It's not." Chuckie heaved a sigh and rubbed the back of his
neck. "I think you need to consider how evolution on this and all
the Alpha Centauri planets happened. And I mean really think
about it."

CHAPTER 35

"WHAT ARE YOU SAYING?" Jeff asked in a low voice.

My brain decided to join the party and do some heavy lifting. The Anciannas had meddled on this planet. A lot. And Wruck had told me when he and I had first met that his people looked like us—all of us. I'd seen him and others in their natural forms—they did look like all of humanity in one.

"We've got Anciannas blood in us, somewhere. Not all of us, but some of us. Chuckie and me, for sure."

"You for sure," Chuckie said. "Me, I don't know."

"Your intellect would indicate it."

"Maybe. But even so, it's traces. Various things would bring a recessive trait to the fore, and some powers are created by high stress situations. I think it's why hybrid females are always so powerful, even when their sire isn't Ronald Yates."

"So, what, you think Erika Gower also has Anciannas blood in her?"

"I do." Chuckie shrugged. "They were here. We know it."

"Kitty said the Ancients were the Bible's version of angels," Lorraine said. "And we've seen them and they definitely fit the descriptions."

"We know some of them stayed and lived on Beta Twelve—it's why the Amazons are shapeshifters, after all. Who's to say that more of them didn't hang around? I mean, the Z'porrah and Anciannas that came here at the end of Operation Immigration were hanging out in that solar system that had intelligent life forming. It sounds more like their MO than not."

"So . . . we all have alien blood in us?" Brian asked, managing not to clutch Patrick to him, but only just. "Chuck, is that what you're saying?"

"Probably not all of us," Chuckie said soothingly. "But a lot. I think it's safe to say that the races that had large population numbers in the Middle East and Africa during Biblical times would have the most likelihood. Kitty's Jewish, Erika Gower is African-American . . ." He looked over at Mahin. "It might be why you don't have double-hearts, even though you're a hybrid."

She nodded. "That makes a certain amount of sense."

"So, how much of this is theory?" Jeff asked.

Chuckie shrugged. "A lot of it. However, the waterfruit? That's confirmed. Boz and the other Katyhopper Matriarchs all feel that it's affected me, Kitty, and Christopher. In positive ways, only, so there's that."

"If it protected Amy and Becky, then I'm great with it," Christopher said.

"So, what do we do with this information?" Jeff asked.

Chuckie shot him a small smile. "Eat your dinner." We all stared at him and he laughed. "This changes literally nothing. It's the same thing as discovering you share genetics with Abraham, Mohammed, Jesus, or some guy in the middle of nowhere that no one's ever heard of. It doesn't change who anyone is as a person. At all."

"Ah, okay," Jeff said, sounding dazed and suspicious both. "Chuck, we have room for you. Why don't you eat with us?"

Chuckie looked vaguely uncomfortable. "Jeff, is that a Presidential request, or just a friend request?"

Jeff opened his mouth, cocked his head, then shut his mouth. He shook his head. "Friend request only. If you already have plans, don't let us keep you from them."

Chuckie gave Jeff a half smile. "Thanks. I appreciate it. I do have plans for tonight."

Jeff clapped him on the shoulder. "Good. And I mean that. I'll see you tomorrow."

Chuckie nodded then gave me a kiss on the cheek. "Relax," he said quietly. "And talk to Wruck alone when you get a chance."

Gave him a fast hug, then he sauntered off. Chose not to ask why Jeff had acted like he had. I'd ask later, in the hopes that it was because Chuckie had a date, versus a covert mission.

The room was set up with four tables of eight. Normally the Whites would have been seated with us, but under the circumstances, we had Siler, Lizzie, Wasim, and Naveed with us instead. Since Charlie was still in a high chair, we were able to have Mahin at our table, too.

Dinner conversation managed to stagger back onto the topic of the first day at a new school versus all the things Charlie was doing, Jamie had done, and the kids were all capable of. Everyone seemed much happier discussing Sidwell and all the positives it offered.

Dinner was Chef's standard triumph of deliciousness, but I had so many things racing around in my mind I barely noticed my food. I mean, oh sure, I had seconds of almost everything, but still, I wasn't really focused on the food.

Let Jamie, Lizzie, and Wasim do most of the talking, meaning the girls chattered to their fathers, telling them all about what they'd done, and Wasim added in when one of them gave him his cue to talk, which was usually them looking at him expectantly.

Serene, Joe, and Randy joined us as we were getting dessert. The three of them kissed their spouses, picked up their boys, and wolfed down their dinners with the kids on their laps. The kids all looked happy again, so maybe quality time did matter as much as quantity. To top it off, Charlie did them a solid and waited until they'd caught up to everyone else to show them his new achievements.

Desperately wanted to know what was going on with our Bot Initiative, but had the sense to not ask about it with all the kids here. Tried not to wonder or worry if they were able to read our minds, because I had a feeling that they could.

Jamie, who was sitting between me and Lizzie, patted my hand. "It's okay, Mommy," she said quietly. "Fairy Godfather ACE has rules."

ACE was a Physic-Psycho Barrier that worked like a sentient net that the fine folks on Alpha Four had created then put around Earth when they'd banished our A-Cs here. But they'd included their talents in ACE's creation, and the empathic part of him had gotten attached to Earth and its inhabitants, so when ACE had become self-aware it had also become attached to Earth and its inhabitants. I'd been the one to communicate with ACE and channel it into Gower. And once I'd put Alexander on the throne of Alpha Four, he'd released ACE from bondage. But ACE had stayed with us.

ACE had also helped Naomi, Abigail, and Serene when they were young and their powers had manifested and terrified them.

It had helped me when I'd almost died in childbirth. It had helped the others giving birth to hybrid children. ACE was our loving observer and we were, as I'd put it way back when, ACE's penguins—the flock it watched over and cared about and loved, while trying not to interfere too much, so as to not affect and change us.

But there were a lot of powerful beings out there, including other superconsciousnesses. We'd been visited by some of these, acting like the Superconsciousness Police, during Operation Defection Election. They'd sort of taken ACE away from us. But once Naomi had become a superconsciousness herself, she'd rescued ACE. But ACE had to make compromises.

ACE's compromise was that it would share mind space with someone on Earth who was not powerful. And so ACE joined with Jamie. Because, as a child, she had no power in this world. That she was probably the most powerful person on our planet— at least until we'd gotten an influx of a tonnage of different aliens—hadn't figured into the equation. Basically, ACE had managed to find the Superconsciousness Loophole and had exploited it for all of our benefit.

Over time ACE had joined dead astronauts and then dead people we cared about into its collective consciousness. ACE wasn't really male or female, but most of the time we referred to ACE as male, probably because he'd started out inside of men.

Sometimes Jamie argued with ACE, but apparently not all the time. "Okay, that's good, Jamie-Kat. Fairy Godfather ACE has been around a lot longer than you have. You need to listen to him."

"Oh, I do, Mommy. Unless he's wrong. Then I don't."

Shoved away the fear these casual statements of hers gave me. "You know, Fairy Godfather ACE has a lot to teach you, Jamie-Kat. You don't know everything yet, even though I'm sure sometimes it seems like you do."

She nodded. "He does. And I know I still have things to learn, Mommy. Don't worry." And with that she turned to Lizzie and started talking about the cookies they'd made.

When ACE was in Gower I'd chatted with him all the time. Now, I had to wait until Jamie was asleep—because I wasn't going to discuss terrible people trying to kill us or any other huge issues with my little girl being awake and aware, and this way ACE could keep our conversations from her. This new way of communicating was also best if I was asleep, too, which made getting coherent questions out somewhat problematic. However, clearly I needed to have a chat with ACE sooner as opposed to later.

Charlie was between me and Jeff so I couldn't share what was going on. However, in addition to being the most powerful empath in the world, due to his Surcenthumain Boost, he could pretty much read my mind. He'd been working at doing this with Jamie, Chuckie, and a few others.

Dawned on me that every A-C talent was a form of telepathy. I'd sort of always known that, but hadn't given it a lot of focus or thought. However, if Jeff had developed stronger telepathy due to Surcenthumain and I had due to the Beta Eight waterfruit, that Charlie was telekinetic and Jamie and the other kids were doing mental connecting wasn't all that surprising.

"We really are the X-Men." Hadn't meant to say that aloud, but, as per my usual, my mouth had engaged without my brain's permission.

Jeff laughed. "I thought we were the Justice League."

True. I did think of Jeff as Superman, Christopher as the Flash, and Chuckie as Batman. And in Bizarro World I'd been Wonder Woman. "I guess we're kind of both. And we already have our sidekicks." After all, Lizzie felt that Siler was Mr. Dash and she was Quick Girl. As long as Wasim wasn't as crazy as Deadpool, he had a really good shot of fitting in perfectly.

Jeff reached over and squeezed my hand. "It'll be fine, baby. Whatever happens, we'll handle it. Just like always."

"Things just seem a little more . . . out there . . . than normal."

Jeff grinned. "Or, as we call it, routine."

CHAPTER 36

DINNER OVER, everyone took their children and headed home, which meant the Embassy, the Dulce Science Center, or NASA Base. Gates might make me sick, but they were pretty awesome, all things considered.

Nadine came and took Jamie and Charlie off for baths and such. She also escorted Wasim and Naveed down the hall to their room, in part, I was sure, because Nadine wanted to be sure that the teenaged boy was in his room before the teenaged girl got into hers.

Because Lizzie was my ward and we literally didn't have the space to add on a family suite—and because the Elves had made it clear that they wanted Lizzie living with me—Siler still slept at the Embassy. So, they said their goodbyes and he left with the other Embassy families. And because she was a teenager and she wanted to and I wasn't up to ordering her off to bed at the late hour of 7:30 p.m., Lizzie stayed in the dining room with us.

Serene sent Brian and Patrick ahead and took the time to brief me, Jeff, and, because she was here, Lizzie before she left. "I found nothing that indicates explosives at all in any of them. The Christopher-Bot does have an on and off switch, similar to the ones on Cameron Maurer and John Butler."

"In his ear canal?" Hey, that's how we'd stopped them from blowing up.

"No, that's the kill switch for the self-destruct, and that only works on Marling-made androids, Kitty, you know that. The on/off switch is inside the body cavity."

"Sue me for not remembering, and now I no longer want to know."

Serene laughed. "I figured. At any rate, none of the four are going to explode, unless the explosives are so minute that they can't be found with our equipment. Which is unlikely. Possible, because what isn't, but unlikely."

"What about the Christopher-Bot the Second melting and reforming?"

She grimaced. "That I don't know. There's nothing left of the goo for us to examine, and I'm concerned about taking a sample, based on what happened when the first one was blown apart. I think they're probably made of some sort of semicrystalline material combined with whatever would give them a successful human appearance."

Serene kept on talking, giving us a lecture on materials that could melt in the way the Christopher-Bot Parts had. My ears chose to shut off. Jeff and Lizzie appeared to be paying rapt attention. Either they were interested or were really good at faking it.

"So," Serene concluded, "without being able to dismember the intact Christopher-Bot, I'm not sure that we can tell. I'd have better luck with our equipment in Dulce, but before any of you say it, yes, that might be the plan, to get him inside the Science Center. So we're keeping him here in the containment unit."

"Has he shown any interest in trying to break out like the Goo of Horror did?"

"Not as yet, but we have a lot of guards down there, since we're keeping all four of them down there. And yes, they each have a bed and such now."

"Go team." Actively chose not to ask if any of them needed to use the bathroom anymore, because I decided that I really didn't want to know, one way or the other.

"What about the claim that Somerall and Lee were transmitting data?" Jeff asked.

Serene shook her head. "If they are, it's via a process we can't detect. I'm not willing to say definitively that they aren't, but I feel about ninety percent confident that they don't have the ability."

"They could just use their phones," Lizzie said offhandedly. She was looking at hers and texting. Actively chose not to ask her who she was talking to but it took effort.

We all stared at her. "What?" Jeff asked finally.

"I totes get it, that Christopher-Bot thing told you that those other two were broadcasting stuff. But the Bots don't sound, well, as smart as regular people or the androids, and anyone can broadcast with a smartphone."

Serene pulled her phone out and started texting at hyper-speed. "I'll have everyone searched for cell phones and similar. Anything found will be confiscated and checked."

"We didn't look for that?" I asked. "Not that it occurred to me, let me mention."

"I didn't," Serene said. "And Tito was focused on the medical side. So, no, we let that ball drop. I'm sorry."

"It happens," Jeff said. "Let's find out if we've been compromised or not before anyone falls on a sword."

Serene's phone beeped. "Huh. Yes, Kristie has a phone but she wasn't doing anything with it. In fact, she has quite a number of missed calls and unanswered texts, all from the people she works with."

"One down."

She nodded as more messages came in. "Both Ansom and Talia have phones and they were indeed recording," she growled.

"Recording, not sending?" I asked.

"Correct. There's no sign that what they recorded was sent."

"Damn."

This earned me shocked looks from Jeff and Serene. Lizzie was still involved with her phone. "Why are you disappointed?" Jeff asked. "Did we want them sharing what we're doing?"

"No, but now we don't know who they were going to send that information to. Meaning that we can't trust anything they tell us."

"They could have been doing the recording to have blackmail on you, not to send to anyone else," Lizzie said, still texting someone.

Gave up on being a non-helicopter-sorta-mom. "Who are you talking to?"

She looked up at me and grinned. "My dad. I was telling him he should have stuck around, so he asked me to tell him what you guys were talking about. He has a theory, by the way."

We waited. "Are you planning to share what that is?" I asked finally.

"Oh, sure. Totes wasn't sure if you cared."

"Don't give me teenaged attitude. It's the wrong day for it."

She laughed. "I wasn't. I'm just still talking to my dad. Anyway, he thinks that, if they're really unaware that their brains have been altered, then they might be being mind-controlled. He's got a theory on who's doing that."

"Who?" I asked.

She shook her head. "He won't tell me. He says he wants to be sure first."

Jeff ran his hand through his hair. "Is there a reason he didn't want to come back and share this in person?"

Lizzie nodded. "Yeppers. He's getting Mister Buchanan and Mister Wruck and they're going to handle it."

Jeff groaned. "I don't want people being randomly assassinated."

"He said that's not what they're doing. He just is sure that you guys are going to tell him that his theory is wrong. So he wants to verify it first. He'll tell you if they have to kill someone."

"That's not true. Malcolm will override any suggestion to let us know and Team Tough Guys will just handle it."

Lizzie shrugged and put her phone away. "My dad said you'd say that. But we're on radio silence now. His team is rolling."

"It never ends," Jeff muttered.

"It'll be fine," Serene said. "Go have some relaxed family time, Jeff. You need it."

"You do, too," he countered.

She smiled. "Which is why I'm going home right now." With that she hugged all of us and trotted off.

The three of us headed down the hall to do the Nightly Rituals. Lizzie had been included in them since the day after Operation Immigration because Charlie and Jamie both wanted her there, and who were we to argue? Our routine was Charlie first, then Jamie, so we did the Rituals twice. So far none of us minded.

The three of us sang songs in pretty good harmony, each of us told each kid a story, we sang another song, then hugs and kisses all around, petting for the various and sundry animals— Earth native and alien—that were snoozing with each kid, then it was time to turn out the lights.

It was only 8:30 by now, and Lizzie was in no way ready for bed, so the three of us went into our big suite and hung out, while Nadine did the nanny "make sure the kids are really asleep" thing.

"Who do you think my dad's after?" Lizzie asked the moment we were sitting down—me and Jeff on the couch and her in one of our fancy yet comfy armchairs—sipping Cokes, in her and my case, and water in Jeff's, and she'd pulled her phone out. Though she only had it on the arm of her chair, and she wasn't using it. One for the Teenaged Win Column.

"I have no idea," Jeff said. "I also don't know if I hope he's right or wrong."

Took a long drink of my Coke and pondered. "It's like with Hamlin, I think. Nightcrawler thinks he knows who's behind this, but he doesn't think we'll believe him. So he's going to find the proof first." Which begged the question of whom Siler suspected.

"That was a long, drawn-out process." Jeff sounded worried.

"Yeah, but Team Tough Guys is very aware, and with John with them, they should be okay."

"Wruck isn't invincible," Jeff reminded me.

"I know. But I'm not as worried as I could be. It's clearly not Stephanie. If it was, he'd have just told us that."

"I agree," Lizzie said. "I don't think he thinks it's a friend. He didn't say that you guys would be upset. He just didn't think you'd believe his theory."

"Meaning he thinks it's someone we think it couldn't be . . ." My brain nudged. Cliff had hidden as the Mastermind for far too long because of two things, one in particular—The Red Herring Gambit was a good one and worked nine times out of ten. We were Exhibit A for that, after all.

Meaning it was really damned likely that we'd screwed up. Big time.

CHAPTER 37

"WHAT?" JEFF ASKED. "I know that look. What connection did you make?"

"Is Chuckie on a mission, on a date, or just tired?"

"Huh?" Jeff stared at me. "Not that I think it's relevant to
what we're talking about or what I asked you, but he's on a date.
Why? God, you don't think Siler suspects Chuck, do you?"

"No, not at all. I just wanted him here when I shared my
theory."

Jeff shot me a look that reminded me of when he'd been
ready to kill Chuckie over jealousy. "So, I'm suddenly not good
enough or smart enough?"

Resisted the urge to roll my eyes and patted his hand instead.
"No. I just enjoy sharing this with others who enjoy making the
mental leaps with me."

"When have I not mentally leaped with you? When have I
not supported your theories?" Jeff sounded truly hurt, and I felt
bad.

"I'm really not trying to hurt your feelings. I just . . ."

"She wants someone who isn't going to be a Yes Man here,"
Lizzie said. "I'm too young and you just said it, Jeff—you'll
always support her theories. So, you want James or Nana Angela, Kitty?"

"Um . . ."

They both looked at me. "What?" Jeff asked. "You feel incredibly conflicted right now. You don't suspect your mother, do
you?" He sounded mildly horrified.

"Oh my God, of course not. However . . ."

"You think your mother will be upset with you?" Now Jeff
sounded shocked.

"No, Mom rarely gets upset with me, even when I screw up or we all miss something obvious that, at the same time, isn't obvious."

"I'm not following you now, baby. At all."

Refrained from mentioning that this was why I'd wanted Chuckie here. Jeff was smart and brave and all the wonderful things, but he didn't think like me. And even though he tried hard and got better at it every day, Chuckie and Reader and Tim still got me faster. But I didn't want Reader or Tim, in no small part because I knew they were with their spouses having actual quality time.

Or rather, I assumed they were. Realized I had no idea where Reader, Tim, and the rest of Airborne actually were. Or Tito, Gower, Rahmi, or Rhee for that matter. Perhaps they were all still with our Bots, meaning I could indeed grab them. Though another big meeting of a million people didn't sound like a great plan—it sounded like we'd never get to bed and that would delay me and Jeff from having sex. Not only was sex with Jeff still number one with a bullet on my Best Things To Do Always And Often List, but after the day I'd had, I really wanted sexy times with my husband. A room full of people didn't say "getting to bed early." It said "not getting any sleep for all the crummy reasons."

"I know, Jeff. And I also know I'm pussyfooting. I just . . . I want to be sure that what I'm thinking is really what I'm thinking. Because it'll affect everyone, Mom in particular."

"You don't suspect your *father*?" Jeff was back to horrified.

"Oh my God, no. No, I don't. This has literally nothing to do with Dad. At least as far as I know or can guess."

"Oh!" Lizzie sat up straight. "You're worried that your theory is going to make Nana Angela look bad, aren't you?"

"Yeah, I think my theory might indeed do that." And I didn't ever want to make my mom look bad, especially not to her boss, who happened to be my husband.

Jeff shook his head. "The only person who can hire or fire your mother is me, baby. And even if she's screwed up somehow, which I doubt, we all make mistakes, even Angela. Whatever it is, it's not going to affect her standing with me, or her position as the Head of the P.T.C.U. Tell me what you think. I'll do my best to play Devil's Advocate."

"Okay, and yeah, I doubt what I'm thinking would make you want to fire Mom, but I think it'll affect her confidence. A little, anyway. But . . . anyhow . . . what if Cliff's not the only one who's read *Ten Little Indians*?"

Jeff stared at me. "And suddenly I take back all the jealousy and wish Chuck was here. What in God's name do you mean?"

"You read. It's one of Agatha Christie's best, also entitled *And Then There Were None*." Jeff still looked blank. "It's the classic case of someone faking their death only to turn out to be the murderer."

"Who's faking death?" Jeff sounded totally lost.

"Sorry, this is why I wanted a human. Or Raj. Someone versed in pop culture. But we'll muddle through because that's how we roll. The biggest reason we didn't suspect Cliff of being the Mastermind was two things—Chuckie trusted him so we all trusted him."

"You especially," Lizzie said. "That's what Mister Buchanan says. If you'd suspected Cliff, then others would have. But he'd fooled Chuck, and that meant that if Chuck trusted him, you trusted him, and everyone else followed your lead."

"Other than Malcolm, and yes, succinctly put. The second reason I trusted Cliff, though, was that his car had exploded during Operation Sherlock, making us think he was a target, too."

"Oh." Jeff seemed to be catching up. "That's what you mean by red herring, got it. And that really did work, because even when Cliff did something odd, it was so simple to point to that incident and feel confident that the Mastermind was trying to kill him, too. I think I'm with you now. So, you think someone else is doing that to us? Who? And who has the motivation as well as the means?"

"Well, what I think Nightcrawler thinks is that it's the person we think we saved and are protecting—Janelle Gardiner."

Good thing I wasn't waiting for gasps of surprise or anything, because I didn't get them. Lizzie looked longingly at her phone, but didn't use it, meaning Siler had definitely given her the Radio Silence order and she was obeying it. Because she was a good kid.

Jeff's eyes narrowed. "So, you think Janelle, what, faked her own capture?"

"Sure, why not? We've been looking for the Big Boss in the NSA and Mom hasn't found them. What if there isn't one there, but just a flunky or an assistant or whatever who answers to Janelle and so is flying under Mom's radar? As in, what if

Janelle moved from Quinton Cross's supposed protection to the protection of someone at the NSA? Or vice versa?"

"It would fit," Lizzie said. "Supposedly Talia Lee was her best friend, right?"

"Right. And Somerall thinks he's a ladies' man. What if she let him think he'd gotten her to be his latest conquest, and she fooled him?" Memory nudged. "And that would also fit for Ansom and Talia being on their 'Lizzie is a dangerous girl' kick. Remember when Talia called me during Operation Madhouse? She was trying to foist the blame for the Bots onto Thomas Kendrick."

"Yes, but I'm still not seeing how Janelle is the one in charge," Jeff said. "Why was she in a cell at that NSA black site, then? And why did she give the other two up?"

"In the cell? They realized we were coming. Ansom and Talia split, Janelle put herself into that cell and made us think we were saving her. Then she's under P.T.C.U. custody—she probably thought she'd go under the NSA, but even so, Mom hasn't restricted her all that much, because she's viewed as a victim we need to protect, not a bad guy. Based on what they've been maneuvering, my guess is that this was always their plan—make us think Janelle needs our protection and therefore move her into the safety of our custody and out of our minds as a potential Mastermind, for want of a better term."

"Why give up her coconspirators, though?" Jeff asked again. "Why make us suspect them?"

"We already suspected them and they know it. And she could give them up, so to speak, because we had only her word and literally no proof. She could do that, with or without their knowledge and blessing, because her word with zero evidence isn't enough for a trial, let alone anything else."

Jeff grunted. "I hate to do this, but you were right—we need Chuck here." He pulled his phone out and dialed. "Hey, sorry. Are you guys done eating? Dessert, too? Good. Yeah, of course something's come up. Why would any of us get to enjoy a night out? Yeah. Yeah. Of course bring her along, she'll have insights, I'm sure. Yes, definitely call for a gate. Floater, right to our living room. Because I don't think we want to wait for public transportation and it's nicer to come out via the floater than into the bathroom and I'm trying to salvage the tiniest part of your evening for you. Oh, you're welcome." He hung up with a sigh. "I hate doing this to myself, let alone others."

"Maybe his date will be impressed with how vital he is to the running of the country."

Jeff snorted. "She already knows."

As he said this, saw the shimmering that meant a floater gate was forming. Then Chuckie stepped through, holding his date's hand. I stared. And realized that who this was shouldn't have surprised me all that much.

CHAPTER 38

"SO, CHARLES TELLS ME that we have the usual madness going on," Nathalie Gagnon-Brewer said as the gate disappeared.

"We do," Jeff replied. "Ah, would you two like a nightcap?"

They both stared at him. "You don't drink," Chuckie pointed out, sounding confused.

"Because it will kill you," Nathalie added. She shot me a worried look. "Is Jeff alright?"

"He is, he just feels bad that we've interrupted your date and he's trying to be folksy. He's addicted to old TV shows, remember? They do the nightcap thing a lot in those old shows."

Chuckie grinned. "Thanks, Jeff, I appreciate it. And I'm good. Nat, do you want anything?"

Nat. He was calling her Nat. He'd given Naomi and Abigail nicknames, too, Abigail most likely because he was giving one to her sister and didn't want to leave Abigail out.

Felt all warm and fuzzy—he was better. He'd moved past the grief of losing Naomi and Cliff's betrayal, he was dating, and he really liked her, because the only other women he'd given a nickname to were his late wife and her sister.

"I'm good, too," she said as she sat down next to me, while Chuckie took the armchair next to Lizzie and across from Jeff. "We had a lovely dinner, and I'm too full to add anything else in right now."

They shot each other a fond glance, then both turned to Jeff. "So, what threat to national or international or galactic security is going on?" Chuckie asked.

Jeff looked at me. Took a deep breath and did my Recap Girl

job and caught them up to speed on what we were thinking and what Team Tough Guys might actually be doing.

Chuckie grimaced when I was done. "I can't believe we fell for it twice."

"You didn't," Nathalie said. "It's the same ploy but the setup is completely different. Anyone would have believed as we did—that Janelle was a victim, not the perpetrator."

"That's why the Janelle-Bot was in her house—she'd left it there to protect things." Though said Bot had destroyed a lot of the furniture while trying to kill me, Len, Kyle, and Bruno. Then again, it wasn't hard to order new stuff from Amazon, Bot or not.

"No beating yourself up," Jeff said to Chuckie. "We've had enough of that and Nathalie is right—this was well-played by our enemy. If this theory of Kitty's is correct, that is."

"It fits," Chuckie said. "Frankly, it fits better than Somerall and Lee turning on her. What they could hope to gain by doing that seems far less than what she can gain by doing this."

"And them blaming the Christopher-Bot, too. Maybe that's why he's saying that they're enemies, because he knows they're trying to make him the fall guy."

"He's a robot," Jeff said. "He might have overcome his programming as advertised. However, I think it's just as likely that he was programmed to say and do what he has in order to make you think that you've flipped him to our side, baby."

"That has merit," Chuckie said. "It's her playbook for sure, and we know our enemies know it and are doing their best to use it against us. However, one thing—Somerall and Lee said that 'he' was taking things to extremes. They might have meant the Christopher-Bot, but they might have meant someone else."

"So, there's also a dude involved. It's not a shock. For all we know, Quinton Cross had been a part of this as well and they replaced him with someone else when he died from Cliff's so-called Alien Flu."

"That Amos Tobin guy's going to be pretty jealous if that's the case," Lizzie said. "He tried to find her, find Janelle, didn't he?"

The four of us stared at each other. "Oh dear," Nathalie said finally. "Could all of that have been planned merely to get Tobin captured in such a way as to put him also into protective custody with Janelle?"

"I hate being played. Yes, it definitely could have been. We need to call my mom." Who hated being played even more than I did.

"No," Chuckie said. "We need to call Buchanan."

"What if they're in the middle of something and the ring alerts the bad guys that they're there and they get shot?" Hey, I'd seen this enough on TV, it was a legit concern.

Chuckie shook his head at me. "You got up *way* too early today. Their phones will all be muted." He pulled his out and sent a text.

"Now what?"

"Now we wait, Miz Impatience."

Didn't take long for Chuckie's phone to ring. "Eagle Pest Control, how may we help you? No, we specialize in rats and rat infestations. You're welcome." He hung up.

"Wow, I love hearing spy talk. What did you actually tell each other?"

"Buchanan asked me if we take care of bugs and annoying insects."

Waited. "That's it? Dude, I want to know what the sign and countersign were and all that jazz."

"Eagle is for Jeff or the White House or whatever," Lizzie said as if she was reciting something for an oral test. "Pest Control means we have an enemy situation. Mister Buchanan checked to see if we were being bugged, spied on, or if it was something else small-time. Chuck mentioned rats because that's what these people are, and also rats are a lot more dangerous and they're smart. Mister Buchanan said that you weren't what he was looking for but that he'd keep you in mind in case things changed, right?" she asked Chuckie.

"Right. Did your father teach you this?"

She nodded. "And the uncles. So, that means that they'll break off and come right to you. If he'd said he'd keep you in mind it would mean that they weren't stopping their mission."

"The uncles never taught me this." Felt a little jealous.

"They said they didn't need to," Lizzie said. "Besides, you totes always figure it out, Kitty."

"She does," Jeff said, rather proudly. Felt better.

The air shimmered again and this time Siler, Buchanan, and Wruck stepped through. Donned my Recap Girl cape yet again and brought them up to speed. "So, Nightcrawler, our big question of the day is—is Janelle Gardiner who you suspected or is it someone else?"

"I suspected her and Amos Tobin, so we're in sync." He perched on the arm of Lizzie's chair. She leaned her chin on his knee. It was a very cute father daughter scene. Resisted the urge to take a picture and instead finished my Coke.

"Go team. And, next up, I don't know how we tell my mother, but we clearly need to."

"I'll do it, Missus Executive Chief," Buchanan said. "She'll take it better coming from me than from you or Reynolds."

"Are they in secured locations or do they have more freedom than will be good for us?" Jeff asked, Commander Voice on Full. "Because I don't like the idea of traitors this good at faking everyone out being given the run of any federal building."

"They're not hanging out at CIA Headquarters. Um, are they?"

Chuckie managed a laugh. "No. Nor at the NSA, FBI, or Homeland Security, either."

"They're both in safe houses," Buchanan said. "With full-time P.T.C.U. and A-C guards." He grimaced. "But they're not all that restricted. Everything they do or say or send electronically is monitored, of course. But if they're talking in codes, then no one's spotted it."

"You wouldn't spot it if the codes relate to their legitimate jobs and businesses. I mean, Mom has them sequestered more for their safety than for the fact that we know they're shady. She's allowed them to work, because Janelle runs her stuff through Amy and Tobin runs his through Christopher. Oh, no freaking way!"

It was clear from everyone else's expressions that they'd all made the leap just like me.

"They're using Amy and Christopher to send their messages, meaning they can say anything because those two are above suspicion." Nathalie sounded as angry as I felt.

"They can't say just anything," Chuckie said, "because those conversations are taped and observed. But they can certainly say or write things that seem innocuous which Amy and Christopher will then share with the people who can decipher the innocuous into action."

Jeff groaned. "This job, it gets easy when?"

"Never," Chuckie said. "But you're good at it, so there's that."

"I don't feel good at it." He looked to Buchanan. "What do we do?"

"You? The three of you, and I mean you, Mister Executive Chief, Missus Executive Chief, and Miss Action Jackson are going to go to bed. It's the first day of two important schools tomorrow and everyone needs to get a good night's sleep. The Secretary of Transportation will also not be doing anything other than finishing her evening out with the Director of the CIA, who will also not be taking an active role."

Chuckie opened his mouth. Put up my paw. He shut his mouth. The One True FLOTUS Power in action. "Malcolm's right. This is a job for stealth, and you're now the face of the CIA."

Chuckie sighed. "You're right. I want regular updates. Not the sugarcoated kind you're planning to give to the President, either."

"Not a problem," Siler said. "We'll talk to Angela first and coordinate with both of you."

"At least let Commander Reader know what's going on," Jeff said.

"No," Buchanan said calmly. "This isn't an American Centaurion issue. This is a United States covert ops issue. This is what we do. Let us do our jobs, for once, without you. Any other questions or demands we'll override?"

"Yeah." Looked at Wruck. "What do you think about all this, John?"

He shook his head. "I'm along for muscle and backup. Benjamin and Malcolm are running this show."

Really wanted to ask him about our genetic makeup, but had the feeling that this really wasn't the time. Chuckie caught my eye and gave me a sign indicating that he wanted me to stay quiet. Knew what he wanted me to shut up about. Oh well, I'd just ask Wruck about Ancient Earth History another time. When he and the others weren't, you know, trying to identify a couple of traitorous murderers and all that.

Jeff heaved a sigh. "Fine. Please take all precautions. My wife frets quite a bit if one of you is missing or gets hurt."

Siler laughed. "We appreciate the concern." He patted Lizzie on her back and she straightened up.

"You sure I can't come with?" she asked. "It would be really instructive."

"Not tonight," Siler said. "And I want you in bed before ten."

She heaved a dramatic sigh. "Life's not fair."

"Nope," Jeff said. "Get used to it."

"Truer words and all that," Buchanan said. "We'll see ourselves out via the gate in your bathroom."

The number one thing on my Aliens Are Weird List was that almost every gate they had was in a bathroom. This made a lot of sense in terms of airports, train stations, bus stations, and the like, but less in terms of normal households. And yet, more residences had gates in the bathrooms than anywhere else, though basements were the number two location of choice. I'd given up asking why a long time ago and had merely accepted that the A-Cs really liked to find a theme and stick with it.

They nodded to us, then Team Tough Guys strolled off to our bathroom. They still managed to look cool while doing it, which was a skill, really.

"What do we do about Ansom and Talia going to Marcia's party tomorrow night?"

Chuckie shook his head. "No idea. Let's see what those three find out and what your mother wants done. You all really need to focus on all the school-related activities." He stood up. "And we should get going. You're not the only one with an early day tomorrow."

Jeff nodded. "You're with me at the Intergalactic School, right Chuck?"

"I am, and Alpha Team will be, too, along with half the Secret Service." He grinned at me. "And yet I'm still more worried about what Kitty will get up to at Sidwell."

"Hilarious. Not that you're wrong, of course."

Nathalie gave me a hug. "Tomorrow will be wonderful. Just be yourself."

Hugged her back. "Let's hope you're right."

Chuckie came over and offered her his hand. She took it and he helped her up. "We'll see you tomorrow, bright and early, Mister President," he said with a grin. "Kitty, enjoy your day at the school with the kids."

"I'll do my best. You two enjoy the rest of your evening."

"You want me to calibrate the gate for you?" Jeff asked.

Chuckie shook his head. "We'll leave through the gate in the Secret Service office."

"Wow, the one that's not in a bathroom? Look at you, all fancy."

Chuckie laughed. "That's us."

Jeff got up and escorted them to our door. Once they were gone he looked over his shoulder at us. "You two want more sodas while you discuss this romantic turn of events?"

"That seems totes like profiling to me," Lizzie said.

"Not that you're wrong," I added.

Jeff laughed. "Be right back. Don't start the gossip without me."

CHAPTER 39

JEFF CAME BACK with Cherry Cokes for all three of us and we did indeed discuss the Chuckie and Nathalie matchup for a while. We all agreed that they were both good enough for the other, felt that the match had good potential, and speculated about how long they'd been dating.

Well, Lizzie and I speculated, and Jeff confirmed or denied. "Why didn't you tell me he was finally dating again?" I asked, once we'd finished with that game.

He shrugged. "I didn't want to get your hopes up. Frankly, he hasn't wanted to get his hopes up either, and neither has she. They've both been very tentative, and it's been a very slow start. Thank Elaine for this, by the way."

"Because she had Nathalie move into the Cairo? In which case, we should thank Pierre, too, because he's who put Chuckie there."

Jeff chuckled. "Nope. Elaine played matchmaker. The three of them eat together a lot since they work together and live in the same building and on the same floor. Elaine started a dinner round robin, then once she was sure they were clicking, she 'felt ill' or 'was exhausted' when dinner was at either Chuck's place or Nathalie's. It gave them a safe way to test the waters. They haven't been dating all that long, really."

"He likes her. A lot."

Jeff nodded. "He does. She likes him a lot, too. So, if all goes well, two people who deserve to be happy again will be."

Lizzie sighed a happy sigh. "I just love it when this stuff happens. The uncles weren't big on the romance side of things, and my dad refuses to date."

"Why?" Hey, I was curious.

She shook her head. "He says it's because he's too different and that having me as his daughter gives him all the family he needs. But I don't believe it." Her voice dropped. "I think he has a lost love or something and he's still pining."

"Interesting take." Frankly, had a feeling Siler was telling Lizzie the truth. He aged so slowly that it could make a long-term relationship difficult. And the Assassination Lifestyle didn't lend itself to romantic entanglements. "But that just means you get all his attention."

She smiled. "It does, so I don't mind." Despite two Cokes and far too much sugar during the afternoon, she yawned. Widely.

Jeff grunted. "Time for bed, young lady."

"Awww, do I have to?" But she didn't sound like she wanted us to give in.

"Yes," Jeff said firmly. "As everyone's said, tomorrow's a big day."

We escorted Lizzie to her room—in part because Wasim was here, in part because neither one of us put it past her to go after Team Tough Guys to help out or observe, and in part because while she might complain about our being overprotective, actually Lizzie liked it a lot.

Hugged her and gave her kisses on her forehead, handed her off to Nadine, who was already ready for bed and confirmed that Jamie and Charlie were fast asleep, and Jeff and I headed back to our room.

"At last we're alone," Jeff said as we closed the door.

Leaned against him. "Today has been so . . . long."

He hugged me. "It has. You were up so early, how're you holding up?"

"Honestly? I'm ready for bed."

"I have no complaint about that whatsoever," Jeff purred.

Perked right up. "Yeah. It's been a *long* day."

Jeff grinned. "Let's make it longer." And with that, he bent and kissed me.

As per usual, Jeff's mouth and tongue owned mine and, also as per usual, in short order I was grinding against him.

Jeff had me up in his arms in a moment and I wrapped my legs around him and we did one of the things we did best—got our clothes off while ravaging each other.

Because we were in the White House and didn't want to ruin things that were priceless or merely just old, I didn't kick my

shoes off with abandon and Jeff didn't toss our clothes all over
the place. We managed a nice trail of stuff all the way to the bed.
I was proud of us, with the tiny part of my mind not consumed
with Jeff's mouth, hands, and what was my favorite body part of
his, which was a very tiny part of my mind indeed. In direct
contrast to that body part of Jeff's, which was in no way tiny.

We were naked and in bed and the day was totally looking
up. In the past, prior to Jamie's arrival, we'd have taken hours on
foreplay. Sometimes we were still able to, but two children and
a teenaged ward, and Jeff being in the highest office in the land,
plus my Galactic Representative Responsibilities, meant that
foreplay was limited so we wouldn't get caught midway through
because some lunatic was trying to blow us up or one of our
children had a bad dream.

So, Jeff merely spent a few minutes nipping, licking, and
otherwise arousing my neck, which was my main erogenous
zone. Once I was practically screaming due to arousal, he moved
down to my breasts.

He'd taken me over the edge this way our first night together,
and he had a record he was quite proud of to maintain. So my
breasts always got the special time they deserved and enjoyed.
He sucked, nipped, and stroked, while I gasped.

"What did you bake for me?" he purred into the spot on my
chest between my breasts.

"Oh . . . oh God . . . Jeff . . . ahhh . . ." I was rarely able to be
coherent when he had me going, and almost never felt it was
worth the effort to try.

He sucked my right nipple. "What was that?"

"Gahhhh . . ."

Now for my left nipple. "Come again?"

"Oh . . . yes . . . *please*." The last word said in a wail that
turned into a yowl of happiness as he stroked my nipples with
his thumb and little finger, slid his tongue back up to my neck
and his other hand around to the small of my back and I went
over the edge.

"Mmm, that's what I like," he purred against my neck. Then
he reared up and I saw that he had my favorite look of his in the
world on his face—his Jungle Cat About To Eat Me Look.
"Ready for more, baby?" he asked in a half-purr, half-growl that
made my hips buck.

"Always." Hey, I was clear that there were times to make sure
I spoke up.

He grinned a very wicked grin, then pounced on my neck again, ravaging the spot that turned me into a puddle. Then he worked his way down to my breasts, shared some love with them, then trailed his tongue down to my navel.

He traced my navel for a bit, while I whimpered and thrust my hips at him. He enjoyed making me work for it and wait for it, and if he didn't deliver so spectacularly I'd have been miffed. But Jeff was always worth the wait.

Sure enough, he finally took his talented tongue down between my legs and the real wailing began. As he stroked me inside and out, conversation—beyond wailing his name and yowling in cat-in-heat-speak—was out of the question. Coherent thought was pretty much out of the picture, too, as Jeff treated me to a variety of ways that his tongue, lips, and teeth could arouse me. There were quite a lot of ways, and he proved his dedication by always trying to find more of them.

Finally, as he gently rubbed me between his teeth, I flipped over the edge. Grabbed his head, wrapped my legs around him, and thrust like a crazy person while I screamed his name.

Fantastic orgasm finally done, let my legs drop and he nipped the inside of my thighs, causing my hips to buck yet again, then his tongue stroked my body all the way up to my neck. As he kissed me he slid inside me, and the real fun began.

Wrapped my legs around his back and used my heels to shove his butt, aka his Perfect Thrusters, toward me. Jeff ended our kiss then started to do what I wanted—ratchet it up to eleven on the sexy scale.

We thrust wildly against each other until I was sailing away again without being able to even pause between seeing the edge of climax and tumbling over it.

My legs dropped, and Jeff straightened up and flipped them up to his shoulders. "Mmm, you want more, baby?"

"Oh . . . God . . . yes . . ."

He chuckled. "Good. Because I'm not done with you."

In this position it was hard for me to move much, but that wasn't an issue. As he thrust into me, Jeff's hand snaked around my thigh and he started playing with me, stroking me between two of his fingers, pleasuring me inside and out.

Didn't take long for my eyes to start to roll back into my head as another orgasm hit, this one so intense that I couldn't do anything other than gasp.

Jeff let my legs fall halfway, hooked his arms under my

thighs, and ratcheted me back up to the edge, with slow, steady strokes that became faster and faster. Finally, we were back to wild and as he roared his release, it triggered me again and our bodies shook in time together.

Finally, our bodies slowed, and he let my legs down, slid out of me, lay down, and pulled me on top of him. Snuggled my face into his neck. "That was fantastic."

He kissed my head. "Glad you thought so. It's always fantastic with you for me, baby."

"You say the nicest things. And do the nicest things, too."

He chuckled. "You up for more or just want to sleep so you're rested for tomorrow?"

My turn to rear up and look at him. "You have to ask? I think nothing will get me prepared for tomorrow better than spending more time doing this with you."

Jeff smiled. "You really are the perfect woman." Then he pulled me to him and kissed me for a long time.

CHAPTER 40

SUPER SEXY TIMES DONE, after we did it four more times, I was finally happy, fulfilled, and relaxed enough to fall asleep, my head on Jeff's chest, his arms wrapped around me.

My last thought before drifting off with my face snuggled into the hair on his chest was that it would be awesome if whoever did me a solid and shared some intel with me in my dreams.

Sometimes, you should be careful what you ask for.

I started dreaming immediately. Vivid dreams in living color. But they were chaotic and didn't make sense. Thought I saw Michael Gower and his Poof Fuzzball. Then I saw Gladys Gower. Then a weird hazy thing that might have been Naomi or could have been Sandy the Superconsciousness I'd gotten to know and even sort of like during Operation Defection Election. Mephistopheles, the giant red faun fugly of my nightmares, was around, too. And more.

Things I didn't recognize, things I did, people who looked familiar, people who didn't, places I didn't recall, places I did— my dream was crowded, like an overstuffed cornucopia of the galaxy spilling out people, places, and things to share with me. Sharing what was the big question.

Every person or being or thing with a mouth was talking at me. Not to me, since I couldn't make out anything coherent, but definitely at me.

Managed to share in my dream that I hadn't wanted to talk to everyone who'd ever died, anywhere, ever. This helped a little bit. In a weird way.

Most of those with mouths moved to the sides and settled in like a chorus. And, as they all sang the chorus of "Listen Like

Thieves" by INXS in a sort of operatic style, I realized they were a Greek chorus. Wondered if Chef had put something in my food.

However, at least this meant that most of the talking at me stopped. As long as I could ignore the chorus, I was good.

As the chorus did their best to ensure that I couldn't ignore them and shifted to "Bohemian Rhapsody" by Queen, the full song, no less, albeit softly, someone I didn't know stepped forward. "You've asked for guidance," he said. He was balding, average looking, and I figured around fifty. I'd never met him before, though there was a tiny inkling of memory that said I might have seen him somewhere before, in passing.

"If possible, yes."

There was a crowd of people and creatures behind him. Definitely spotted Michael, Gladys, Fuzzball, and Wayne Ward, who was Walter and William's middle brother. He'd been one of the empaths murdered horribly during Operation Confusion by Gaultier and his set of megalomaniacal geniuses. Started to have an idea of what I was talking to. Also started to get worried.

The Spokesman nodded. "We're here to help, but there are rules."

"Yeah, I know. Straight-out answers are forbidden, actual advice is forbidden, actual warnings are forbidden, crazy clues that make no sense but will seem sensible and even prophetic the moment the thing you're warning me about happens but not a moment before are totally A-okay."

"Pretty much, yes."

"You're human?"

"I was."

Looked around, particularly at the chorus. Mephistopheles was in the chorus. He waved cheerfully to me as they hit the high falsetto notes in the song.

"Is the song a clue?"

"Everything's a clue," the Spokesman said.

Groaned. "There are times I wonder why I ask for help."

"We wonder, too."

"Oh, not the old wheeze that I'll always manage to prevail. That sounds great but reality says that there's a whole lot of times I've only just managed to prevail by the hair on my chinny-chin-chin."

"Nursery rhymes and fairy tales are helpful," the Spokesman said, essentially unhelpfully.

"Is that a clue about the Christopher-Bot the Second? Because if so, not getting it."

"Why not? You think right."

So it *was* a clue. And right now, what I thought was that I was definitely talking to ACE. Only not so much to ACE, but to all those who'd died who he'd chosen to bring into his collective consciousness.

"Is Terry here?" Christopher's late mother had implanted part of her consciousness into Jeff when he'd been a little boy. In turn, he'd implanted it into me. And she'd helped me, as much as she could. But ACE had taken that trace of Terry away.

"She is not able to assist in this matter."

"Why not?"

The Spokesperson shrugged. "She has no information that can help you right now."

Based on the chorus lined up, that would make her the only one. Searched the crowd. Definitely didn't see Terry. Saw a lot of others I knew, but not her. Meaning ACE was keeping her away from me for whatever reason. Possibly Terry not being around was a clue. Possibly it was just the price the Superconsciousness Police were extracting for this particular visitation. But, one way or another, I had to work with who was actually here, so to speak.

Considered this. The Gowers, Wayne, and Fuzzball made sense, and I'd already known they were in ACE's Collective Consciousness Menagerie. Mephistopheles made sense, in that weird, fugly way my life liked to roll. Presumed some of these were dead astronauts. In fact, if I was a betting girl, and I was, the Spokesman was probably one of these, most likely the highest-ranking person and so the one doing the talking. And that made sense.

All the people that didn't look like any people I'd met—and by now, I'd met people who were giant Cthulhu monsters and human-sized slugs and tiny cockroach-rat things and everything you could think of in between—did not make sense.

"Um, why are there so many of you? And by that I mean so many I wouldn't recognize?"

The Spokesperson seemed thrown by this question. Go me. "Ah, we've traveled quite a lot."

ACE had definitely gone walkabout, or into Superconsciousness Custody, or both, or something I couldn't comprehend, and he'd been gone from Earth for months. Only a few of us knew that, but I was one of those few.

"So, you've gone all over the galaxy now?"

"Not to all of it," the Spokesman said. "But much of it."

Looked around again. "Why did you join all these people in?"

"They were good people who died too soon."

Looked right at Mephistopheles. "Pull the other one and all that jazz."

Mephistopheles grinned at me. Always kind of nice in a horrible way. My dreams were awesome like that. He also gave me a thumbs-up, which considering his digits were like clawed fingers, also fit the nice in a horrible way theme so near and dear to my dreaming heart.

"Some are joined in because they can help you, you specifically, and to lose their knowledge would be a dangerous thing."

Thought on that, and thought hard. There were a lot of people here, more than I could count and, realistically, more than I could see. Terry was actively absent and I'd asked for her and been turned down. But that was because what she knew wasn't what I needed to know. Ergo, it was time to roll the dice again and see if I got a seven or snake eyes.

"Is Antony Marling here and, if he is, can I please speak with him?"

Expected to wake up. But I didn't. Or if I did, I was awake surrounded by people now singing "Sorry Sorry" by Rooney. They now had musical accompaniment. It was impressive in that Gonna Need Therapy When I Wake Up way.

The chorus of this song was "sorry sorry for making your life a living hell." And, as a trim, unexceptional-looking man somewhere in his sixties walked up, realized that everyone probably had their own theme song. Well, at least the Tunes Of My Nightmare would be a good compilation album.

"Hello, Missus Martini. Looking lovely as always. You remain *tres belle, mademoiselle*."

Yep, that was Marling's flirty catchphrase all right. Reminded myself that in Bizarro World, Marling had been a good guy—the top doctor in the world for autism, also focused on curing dread diseases and such. Meaning there was a good part of Marling, and that might have been why ACE joined him in. I'd seen the good part of Mephistopheles, after all, at least in my dreams.

"Good to see you, I think. We have a situation that, as all our situations go, is out of control. Can you tell me about the robots, or Bots as we call them, versus your androids?"

The chorus finished the song and were quiet. Presumably this was the speaking-only part of the program.

"I can, but your people will find all the information they need. However, you have far more to fear from the cyborgs than you do from my androids or her robots."

"Cyborgs? That's a new one."

"Yes. It's what we call those who've had the advanced wire insertion treatment. To differentiate them, since they are indeed different from my androids and her robots."

He'd said "her robots" twice, indicating that I was missing a key clue. "Who was the originator of the robots? I think Janelle Gardiner has taken that initiative over, and I think she took over from the late and, at least in my case, unlamented Secretary of State, Monica Strauss. But was someone in charge of them first?"

He nodded. "We didn't agree on the androids. She felt that they were inelegant."

"Oh my God, how? I mean that seriously. Your androids have fooled the strongest empath in the galaxy. They're nasty and unpleasant but can be kind and loving, just like humans. You might have tried to kill everyone I love and steal my baby girl, but you were an artist, dude, a true genius. How can anyone call your androids inelegant?"

He smiled, a real smile. "Thank you." He looked over to Mephistopheles. "I see what you mean." Then he turned back to me. "You meant that, truly. We were nothing but enemies, and yet you find a way to compliment me honestly."

Shrugged. "Dude, I see no advantage in pretending that someone who is a freaking genius is less than that. No one's touched the hem of your creation garment, at least as far as I know. Well, actually, not quite true. Stephanie and the Tinkerer are doing terrifying work with inserting robotic wires into humans, which I guess I should start calling cyborgs?" He nodded. "I need a flowchart for all of this." Now he laughed. "But those cyborgs aren't masking *as* humans like your androids still can and do."

"You flatter me, but I appreciate it. They are following her design, not mine, though they've made vast improvements."

"The design—is it the same one that we found after Eugene Montgomery was killed?"

"Originally, yes. However, viewpoints diverged. One side wanted fully robotic creatures wearing skin suits, so to speak. The other wanted real humans mechanized."

"Of course they did. So, who diverged with whom on this? Was it another she?"

He nodded. "He enjoyed the competition."

"He is Ronald Yates?"

"Yes."

"Naturally. Okay, so who are the 'she's,' the women who headed up these projects?"

He shook his head at me. "You truly have to ask?"

The chorus burst into song again, this one "Don't Wanna Think About You" by Simple Plan. Definitely a clue.

So, gave it the old pondering go. Perhaps it was because I was asleep, or the song, or whatever, but my results were limited. "I can only come up with two—Madeleine Cartwright and LaRue DeMorte Gaultier."

"Why would you need more than those?" Marling asked.

"Wow. So, taking that line, Cartwright was your sister-in-law and she was all about the big supersoldiers, and while she didn't approve of you making your children into androids, she sure approved doing experiments on her son, so it's not her who felt your stuff was inelegant. But since LaRue was and, if there's a nasty afterlife where the evilest go, still is a royal bitch and a traitor so many times over I've lost count, I'm guessing that it was her."

"Good insights."

"But she was focused on cloning."

"You don't see how the two projects would intersect?"

I'd already considered this when I was awake. "Giving myself the 'duh' on that one. I mean, why would only some of our enemies think like that? And why limit yourself, right?" He nodded. "But, once LaRue started, Cartwright got involved, didn't she? I mean, it also makes sense—she'd have had full access to Strauss and she was good at spotting talent."

"Yes."

"And, LaRue and the Tinkerer would have had the old 'aliens hiding on Earth pretending to be humans' thing to bond over. So, the insertion method is LaRue's, and I can see that it's kind of elegant in its way. And the full on Build A Robot President method is what Cartwright fooled around with in her spare time. And both were assisted by Herbert "Build A Zombie Army From Murdered A-C Parts" Gaultier."

"What else?"

"Oh good, there's more. Gimme a mo." Considered what else I knew. "The first robot was the Kitty-Bot. She, even more than the Christopher-Bots, is definitely a robot with limited programming, but that's because she was the first. The Kitty-Bot Army was far more advanced. As was the Janelle Gardiner Bot. But none of those follow along the plans that we found, at least not completely."

"You're sure?"

"No, because no one will let us reverse engineer the Kitty-Bot because our two saved androids think she's a person."

"So?"

"So . . . what?"

"Exactly."

Stared at him. "So . . . it doesn't matter? Because we have the plans and Strauss is dead. But Janelle is carrying on her evil work. Most likely with an assist from Marion Villanova and Evan the Limo Driver who now works for Zachary Kramer, meaning the Kramers are in with the Gaultier and YatesCorp team, since Amos Tobin is also involved. And therefore they're not working with Stephanie and the Tinkerer."

Stephanie's lab had been right near to, but hidden from, the NSA black site where the Fem-Bot Armies were being created. Meaning she'd known about them but they hadn't known about her. But then, why was a Dr. Rattoppare invited to their party?

"See? You didn't need my help."

"I hate it, just *hate it*, when someone with the answers says that to me. I did need the help, because I didn't get to most of this on my own and even if I had gotten to all of it, confirmation from the Folks in the Know is always nice. But, you're telling me that people turning into robots and robots saying they've become real boys isn't a problem?"

"It's not your *biggest* problem."

"Fantastic. So, can the Christopher-Bot the Second, or could the now-melted first one, for that matter, actually overcome their programming and become self-aware? In case you somehow don't know, which I doubt, his gray matter is about half the size of a human brain."

"Size doesn't matter as much as capacity."

"So he could overcome his programming?"

"Anyone with a functioning brain can overcome their programming."

"But is his brain functional? And by that, I mean, are any of the people who have the wires in their brains truly their own people, or are they all being controlled by someone else?"

Prayed that this answer would be a good one, since it affected

Joe and Randy. I didn't care if the Kristie-Bot wasn't her own woman, but if Joe and Randy were being controlled, I didn't want to contemplate what they'd do about it, because I had a good guess and it didn't predict a happy outcome.

"You'll find that most people are being controlled by someone else, wires in their brains or not. It's who's at the controls, and who those people choose to allow to be at their controls, that matters."

"I love philosophy. It's so useless right now, but still, it was a fun class. In college. Let me rephrase. Are any of the people with wires in their brains going to go haywire—see what I did there?—and go nuts and start attacking their friends and relatives and such and try to take over the world or similar?"

"Ask what you really want," someone I was pretty sure was Gladys Gower, shouted from the chorus. "Muir and Billings are safe—you got to them in time."

This earned said shouter a glare from the Spokesman and a chuckle from Marling. "Some of us are more willing to break the rules than others," Marling said.

"Your daughter included," the Spokesman added.

Definitely a clue. Or a warning. "Yeah, about that . . . how many rules did Jamie break to protect Jeff from Charlie's teething and such?"

Marling shrugged. "A few."

The Spokesperson looked stern. "She skirts the line quite a lot."

"She gets results," Marling replied. "She only does it for life and-death situations."

"So, Jeff could have died from Charlie's teething pain?"

They both looked at me. "You had to go to Florida to prevent his agony," the Spokesman said. Waited for him to add "duh," but apparently he was showing restraint. "And that was before your husband had one of the most stressful jobs on the planet."

"Gotcha. So, the major things you all don't get in trouble for?"

They both looked uncomfortable. "Not so far," Marling admitted.

So, there was a time limit or a level of unapproved activity that would create awareness of what we were doing out here. Had a horrible feeling it was going to tie in with Algar's being discovered hiding in plain sight in some way, because losing both ACE and Algar at the same time was the definition of Earth's, and possibly the galaxy's, Armageddon. "Um, good?"

"Yes," the Spokesman said. "Very. Your daughter understands much for one so young. But even so, she must be taught
what is right and what is not."

"That sounds like a rhyme."

"Does that make it wrong?"

"No, just makes me want to know why we're all Doctor Se-
uss and Lewis Carroll all of a sudden."

"Much is said about adult things in nursery rhymes. But not
everyone bothers to listen."

"True enough." Got the impression we were done with this
topic. Time to move on to my next worry. "What about Ansom
Somerall and Talia Lee? Are they trustworthy?"

Marling snorted. "You already know the answer to that question, regardless of wiring."

Meaning hells to the no. Not a surprise.

"You have very little time with us left," the Spokesman said.
"Choose your question carefully."

Question. Meaning I had only one left. Didn't count on them
letting me get away with asking several questions without pause.

"What is the greatest threat to me and those I care about the
most right now?"

There was a buzzing sound of everyone talking at once. The
Greek Chorus joined in as well. Everyone seemed to be talking
amongst themselves, but finally it stopped and everyone nodded.

"We have reached consensus," the Spokesperson said. "And
we tell you that flying pests are always a problem."

And with that, the chorus started singing, "So Long-Farewell-
Goodbye" by Big Bad Voodoo Daddy, and everything faded out
of view.

CHAPTER 41

WOKE RIGHT UP. "Well, that was actually kind of helpful in a totally unhelpful way."

"Whazzat?" Jeff asked as he rolled over, then went back to snoring softly.

Decided it was time to be conscious while asking questions. Got out of bed, pulled on my nightclothes, which were the A-C standard issue of white t-shirt top and blue pajama bottoms, and pulled the covers up over Jeff. Then trotted to our ginormous closet, put on my lovely Official Presidential Robe in dark blue, and sat down in front of our hamper.

"I just had the weirdest dream and you're literally the only person I can talk to about it."

Normally Algar liked to play coy and not show up until I'd begged a lot or was about to give up. Not tonight. I blinked and there he was, a rakish, handsome dwarf with tousled dark, wavy hair, and eyes far too green to be from Earth.

"I saw. Interesting display."

"So, you can see what ACE and the others are doing?"

He nodded. "ACE has found a very clever way to get around the limitations put upon him. It's impressive, really."

"Go team. So, do you agree that the Bots aren't my biggest worry and that the cyborgs are?" Wondered if that meant I now had to call Kristie the Kristie-Borg or Seven of Nine. Nah. She was too damn perky for a cooler name. And she'd blackmailed me and Cologne. Kristie-Bot all the way. Besides, I couldn't just tell everyone that she was a cyborg because the explanation for how I'd come up with that name was one I couldn't really share.

"Yes and no. Your biggest worries are coming."

"Oh, joy. Any chance you're not going to pussyfoot around and instead be clear with what you're telling me?"

"No, you know the rules."

"I hate the rules."

"That's one of the things I like best about you."

"Good to know. I have no idea what I should focus on."

He shrugged. "That's pretty much how you've lived your life. You roll along and handle what comes as it comes. It's a rarer trait than you'd think, but it's a large part of why you're successful. Little to nothing throws you."

"I feel all warm and fuzzy. Still unclear on how to protect my loved ones, the world, and the galaxy, but still, warm and fuzzy. Of course, I was kind of hoping you could help me decipher the so-far useless clue that flying pests are an issue. Should I be expecting a plague of locusts or something?"

Algar chuckled. "In a sense."

Managed not to roll my eyes. "That's it?"

He shrugged. "You asked some good questions."

Resisted the urge to scream. "Thanks. I don't feel like I got good answers."

"I'm sure you don't. But that doesn't mean the answers were wrong."

"Thanks for that. So, let me ask these good questions of you—what are Janelle Gardiner and Amos Tobin planning?"

"That isn't a question you asked when you were asleep."

Resisted the urge to bang my head against the hamper. "Could you, perhaps, do me a solid and actually, I don't know, impart information that I will both need and am unlikely to figure out until it's too late? I won't be able to have my music playing."

For the first time, Algar looked slightly concerned. "Why not?"

"Um, because I'm not allowed to be in my Happy Place tomorrow. I'll be at a stupid bake sale and it will be a huge photo op and all that jazz, and the First Lady is supposed to be focused on the fundraising and the kids, not on listening to Aerosmith."

"Well . . ." He seemed lost, like this was something that had never occurred to him to be possible.

"And then, if there's time, I'll get to zip over and wave at the Intergalactic School's opening, and, again, I'm not supposed to be focused on anything other than the joys of learning and ensuring that Jeff gets to leave on time."

"I see . . ." Still lost at nonmusical sea without an iPod.

"And after that, Jeff and I and you and ACE alone knows who else are going to the Kramer's so that we can partake in yet another fundraiser and, yet again, I will be prevented from listening to music."

"Are you done ranting?"

"No. So, while I always find my various playlists soothing," and helpful, since I was about 99.99 percent positive most of them were being created by Algar these days, but I was smart enough not to say that aloud, "I will be tuneless for most of tomorrow. And, because tomorrow is going to be a busy day with my and everyone else's children potentially in whatever crossfire might happen, I'd really love an assist on this one."

"Does the school have a radio station?" Asked as if this was the total solve for all my problems. Of course, in Algar's mind, maybe it was.

"Really? How would I know? All the kids that fall under the Evil Kangaroo's umbrella of 'mine' are going there tomorrow for the first time. They could have elephants or not have bathrooms— I truly have no idea."

"Evil Kangaroo?"

Explained my *Horton Hears A Who* analogy, which amused Algar to no end. Go team. "At any rate, let's get back to the matters at hand. Who do I have to watch out for the most between Stephanie and the Tinkerer, Janelle Gardiner and Amos Tobin, the Christopher-Bot the Second, Ansom and Talia, or a player to be named later?"

"It's always the person you're not suspecting that can hurt you the most."

"Gosh, thanks for that. We could have used *that* hint back when we were still thinking Cliff Goodman was a great guy."

"The situation is similar. Not the same, but similar."

"Aha. The Kramers, then? Are they who we need to watch out for?"

Algar sighed. "You need to watch out for everyone and everything, as always. But don't worry. When you need it most, and if you pay attention, you'll find a guide."

"Thank you, Raiden. Am I heading into the wastes of Outland where you cannot travel, are you just trying to be obscure, or do you just want to do a *Mortal Kombat* movie marathon and this is your way of suggesting it?"

He laughed. "I suppose that's for me to know and you to find out." And with that, he snapped his fingers and disappeared.

"No *Mortal Kombat* marathon for you," I muttered. "Not with clues like those, mister."

Sat in the closet for a little while more. Not that I was expecting Algar to return but because the clues I'd gotten seemed so vague that I really wanted to see if I could make connections.

All I got was that we had the Bots that fell under Gardiner and probably Tobin, and the *Death Becomes Her* group of cyborgs under Stephanie and the Tinkerer. None of these seemed like flying pests.

The bake sale was set to be outside, so maybe the big warning was that we were going to attract flies and mosquitos? While that could be challenging, it didn't seem worth all the warnings.

Then again, we did have Wasim with us, and the oncoming big issues with the Club 51 True Believers World Tour. Didn't see flying pests being an active worry there, but maybe that's what the Powers That Be considered all the anti-alien/anti-everyone people to be. I certainly felt they were annoying pests, and that was putting it mildly.

Decided I wasn't going to get anywhere with all of this, so headed back to bed to get a few more hours of sleep before my Day In Hell began. Wasn't sure if I was hoping for dreams or not, but other than feeling like Terry was just somewhere I couldn't see her, I dreamed nothing concrete. Why I was feeling that it was Terry instead of anyone else was beyond me, let alone whether it was a clue or just my own subconscious at work.

Woke to the peppy sounds of "Can't Stop the Feeling!" by Justin Timberlake. Listened to the full song, since I figured this was likely to be the nicest part of my day.

Was wrong, since Jeff and I showered together and I got to enjoy a few mind-blowing orgasms in one of our favorite spots to do the deed. So that was nice and quite refreshing. Almost felt ready to face the Evil Kangaroo. Almost.

While we got the kids ready for school, gathered up all the various baked goods, ensured my now-vast entourage was prepped, and verified that Naveed was given Secret Service access and a team of agents to help him protect Wasim, tried to run over my dreams and such in my mind. But this was a big day for the kids and all of the parents, too, so I ultimately gave up and hoped that I'd figure it out on the fly.

Denise was practically out of kids to watch at the moment,

so she came over to the White House with Becky so they could spend the day with Nadine and Charlie. Had to figure it was good for him—maybe with the two of them focused solely on just the two youngest kids he might not get away with lifting everything he could spot. Hey, a girl could dream.

Gave him lots of hugs and kisses. "You be good for Mommy, Daddy, Jamie-Kat, and Lizzie, my little man. We're counting on you to behave for Nadine and Miss Denise while it's just you, Becky, and them."

Charlie grinned at me. "Yes, Mommy."

Hugged him tighter. "Thanks for taking one worry off of Mommy's mind."

He hugged me back. "Aunt Terry says it'll be okay, but you have to listen like a thief," he whispered.

Reared back and stared at him. "Um . . ."

He gave me a really innocent look, turned away, and reached for Jeff. Who apparently hadn't picked up any of this, including what I had to figure was my loud emotional reaction.

Jeff took Charlie and gave him an airplane ride. Charlie seemed once again like any little kid with his father. Eyed Jamie and Becky. Neither one of them seemed to be actively extending any kind of talent, but then again, Becky was so young that she could be doing whatever and I'd have a hard time telling. And Jamie had gotten very good at faking me and Jeff out when she was using talent and didn't want us to know, and she'd been training the other talented kids, at least insofar as I'd been able to determine. Sidwell had no idea what it was in for.

Heaved an internal sigh about the excitement that was my daily life. Reminded myself that Jeff's mother and sisters had been worried that I couldn't handle our talented children, especially if Jeff wasn't around. Well, it was time to pull up the Big Girl Panties and represent in the Efficient Mother category.

The Secret Service had decided that security concerns meant we were taking a gate over, because Sidwell had allowed American Centaurion to install gates at the school. With the number of kids we had attending, if we drove our big, burly, black SUVs it would look like a freaking parade every morning and afternoon, and the school wanted that even less than we did. Meaning we all met up at the Secret Service offices on the ground floor.

Because we had so many going over, it was decided that Len and Kyle and any other security personnel who weren't going to be staying at Sidwell would remain here and join me at the

Intergalactic School, meaning only Evalyne and Phoebe from my Secret Service team and my Field security team were going with me, and most of the Field security was going to stay at Sidwell to guard the kids.

Even so, we had a ton of adults and a whole lot of kids in black pants or skirts, white shirts, and dove gray sweaters. Considered if Vance had chosen Sidwell simply for the uniforms, because the only thing that wasn't like what the adults wore was that the school uniforms weren't made by Armani.

Ready with all of our baby ducks in a row, and several rows of big ducks, we started through the gate, with Manfred going first and Devon Jones, the P.T.C.U. agent I'd requested to be mine forever during Operation Madhouse, going through right behind him.

Manfred and Devon shared that they were unscathed at the school, so started through, with the gates calibrated so each kid could go through with an adult. Siler and Lizzie went through first, while Jeff hugged and kissed me and Jamie. "You two have fun. Jamie-Kat, remember that you need to not try to show up all the normal kids."

"I know, Daddy. Lizzie told us to try to fit in the first week until we have the lay of the land. Then we'll figure out what needs fixing."

Jeff and I exchanged the "God Help Us" look. "Ah, right." He kissed her again, then hugged and kissed me, though rather chastely considering the number of people that were around. "Hang in there, baby. It'll go fine and you'll make all of us proud."

"God, I hope you're right. I'll do my best to get to the Intergalactic School before the end of the morning."

He nodded. "I'll have someone advise you if you're needed earlier so that the First Lady can get back to her work."

"Yeah, I doubt the Evil Kangaroo is going to go for that, but hope likes to spring eternal and all that jazz." Gave Jeff one last kiss, took a deep breath and let it out slowly, steeled myself for the gate, then took Jamie's hand. Managed not to squeeze her hand too hard as we stepped through the horrible gate and exited into what I truly wasn't expecting.

CHAPTER 42

"UM, ARE WE IN A BROOM CLOSET?"

It sure looked like a broom closet. There were brooms, cleaning supplies, a sink, and metal racks holding other supplies. It was roomy, for a broom closet, but as gate locations went, it wasn't all that much better than a bathroom.

Devon was there, waiting for us, and he moved us away from the gate, which was near the sink, so that Keith could step through. "Yes, this is a broom closet. It's also on the floor of the school where the administration is, and where, therefore, children, parents, and teachers rarely are."

"Every school I went to had a very active administration section."

"This one does, too. However, this broom closet is in the area that's the least trafficked. We chose this location for obvious reasons, therefore. And you three need to move on out, so that the rest of the group can come through."

Keith opened the door, went through first, then nodded to me and Jamie. The coast was apparently clear, so we stepped through the doorway.

Looked around. Looked like every other school administration area I'd ever seen. Boring hallways with lots of doors, some open, some shut, all with those little windows so near and dear to school builders' hearts.

Manfred was up ahead, but Siler and Lizzie were waiting for us. So was a plump, attractive black woman I took to be the principal, since she was dressed in a nice gray suit, looked to be somewhere in middle age, and had an air of authority.

There was a slender Asian man behind her who was in a

black suit. Possibly the assistant principal. Possibly the principal's secretary. Possibly a parent.

Realized I had no idea who was who around here because I hadn't paid one bit of attention to any of this—for all I knew, this woman was the school nurse and the man was the janitor and we'd invaded his broom closet. Gave myself another Terrible Mother Award.

Before I had to engage these people, Wasim and Naveed came out. Naveed looked fine but Wasim looked rather green. "You okay?" I asked him quietly.

"That gate transfer was rather horrible."

It was always nice to find someone, anyone, else who didn't enjoy the gates. Put my arm around his shoulders. "Yeah, I hate them, too. They've never been easy for me."

"Do they bother everyone?"

"No, we're just lucky. Doctor Hernandez has created several things that he'd hoped would work on me to handle it, but so far, nothing has. However, once we're back at the White House we'll ask him to see what he's got. Just because nothing's worked for me doesn't mean it won't work for you."

He nodded. "I'm willing to try anything safe and legal."

"Well, Doctor Hernandez would never give you anything dangerous."

"I know my medical records have already been sent to him, so I'll plan to check in after school."

Was about to take one for the team and head us over to Lizzie and the people I didn't know but should have, but fortunately Vance came out of the broom closet and hustled us over. Paws were shaken and I was introduced to Mrs. Miranda Paster, who was indeed the principal, and Mr. Hiroki Yamaguchi, who was the assistant principal. Felt amazed at my prescience, but didn't let my having guessed right go to my head.

We exchanged the usual pleasantries but I didn't have to interact too much, because the rest of our kids and their parental escorts were exiting the Stealth Broom Closet and were being introduced in turn. Was not at all disappointed by this.

Vance had and kept the lead in this situation, since he'd been the one to enroll all of our children into the school. Apparently he and Mrs. Paster had created quite the friendship, because it was clear she was happy to see him.

"With all those from American Centaurion, we'll have just about twelve hundred students, which is large for us," Mrs.

Paster said as she led us downstairs. Wondered if she was counting our phalanx of security in those numbers, but managed not
to ask. Hey, I was keeping it low-key.

"The camera crews are already here," Yamaguchi said. So
much for that low-key idea. "We have them set up where you'll
be running the bake sale."

"Oh. Good."

He gave me an encouraging smile. "We truly appreciate your
willingness to get involved so quickly and with such a big un-
dertaking. This kind of publicity is very good for the school."

Had the choice to respond or run. Earning at least one small
Good Mother Point, I did neither. Instead, I merely smiled and
kept hold of Jamie's hand. I had to escort my little girl into her
classroom, and not even the Evil Kangaroo was going to prevent
that.

We trooped down three flights of stairs and were now on
ground level, where we were greeted by a small cadre of women,
most of whom looked tense. One in particular did not. She was
a little taller than me, had her blonde hair done in an up-do, was
wearing a linen sheath dress without a wrinkle on it, low-heeled
pumps, and a whole lot of pearls. Knew without asking that this
was my new nemesis.

She gave us all a tight smile. "Ah, the new arrivals are here
to fill our classrooms full to bursting."

Mrs. Paster gave her a polite look. "Missus Cordell, this is
Missus Katt-Martini, otherwise known as the First Lady of the
United States. Madam First Lady, may I introduce Missus Char-
maine Cordell, the President of the PTA."

"We've met on the phone." Looked at the women behind the
Evil Kangaroo. They all seemed nervous and uncomfortable.
Time to channel what I could of the Washington Wife class. "I'll
be with all of you to handle bake sale things after I ensure that
all the children are settled. Until then, my Chief of Staff and my
other assistants can handle whatever it is you need."

Vance went to the other ladies and started discussing bake
sale needs. Abigail and Mahin followed, as did those lucky security agents who were carrying our various foodstuffs. All
these women seemed just fine with this.

But, naturally, the Evil Kangaroo sniffed and her eyes narrowed. "I think you need—"

"I don't care what you think," I interrupted sweetly. "My
daughter, my ward, and the other children in my care come

first." Nodded at the nearest Secret Service agent, who happened to be Keith.

He took the hint, and started barking official-sounding orders. None of the other agents argued, though Phoebe winked at me as she moved Charmaine and the other women out of our way.

Mrs. Paster led us on to the various classrooms. Fortunately, we'd arrived early, because the campus was a huge triangle that took up twenty acres, at least according to Yamaguchi, who was providing the color commentary. Each school set was in its own buildings and areas, so Lizzie and Wasim were separated from the other kids in the upper school building near the athletics areas, just as the middle school kids were in what I'd foolishly thought was "all" of the school—a wood-clad building with a lot of ecological bells and whistles.

Lizzie and Wasim were definitely sticking close together, and Devon broke off with them and shadowed Lizzie just as Naveed was doing for Wasim. The kids hugged me and Lizzie hugged Siler, waved to the others, then went into their building. Sent Marcus and Lucas along with them, just in case.

The middle school kids did the same—hugged their parental unit, waved, and went into their cool Save The Planet building shadowed by their Secret Service or Field agent of what I presumed was Mom's choice.

Once these kids were done, Siler escorted Mrs. Maurer back to wherever the heck Vance was, and Kevin, who'd been the Lewis parent chosen for the first day, nodded to me and went toward the side drive that allowed school vehicles to get from one main street to the other, as well as to the parking lot and parking garage, more easily. There was a big, black, SUV waiting for him. He got in, but the car didn't move. So, he was now on P.T.C.U. duty, meaning the car's driver was probably Buchanan and that Siler would likely be in there shortly if he wasn't already. Worked for me.

The littlest kids were in a complex of buildings that had once been hospices, which were the farthest from where we'd entered the complex. The only part of this gigantic city triangle that wasn't part of Sidwell was a post office. Manfred pointed it out to me. "That's where you'll come in, gate-wise, if you're coming to this part of the campus."

"Nice to know the post office is also representing. Are there gates in every post office?"

He chuckled. "No, and you know this because if there were, no mail would ever be late."

Early-starters kindergarten was in a nice room painted in pastel colors. It reminded me a lot of the school we had at the Embassy. The temptation to ask why we were shoving our children out of the safety of our cocoon was strong, but I kept my mouth shut. There were reasons, I'd heard them all, and they were all valid.

Got hugs from all the kids and kisses from Jamie, then the little ones bounded in to meet their teacher, Miss Lisa, who was young and pretty, with a cute short haircut and what appeared to be a great deal of energy. She'd need it.

Louise Valentino was here, too. She ran over and hugged me and all the other women, then hugged all the kids. Jamie took her hand, looked up at me, and smiled. "We'll be fine, Mommy. Louise is here." Decided to accept that Jamie was right and did my best to relax.

Wanted to stick around, and I knew Lorraine, Serene, Claudia, and Doreen did, too. However, all of us had jobs to get back to and I had the Bake Sale From Hell to manage. Besides, the kids were focused on the other kids in class, Miss Lisa, and Louise. So far, so good. For them. For us, we were all kind of down when we left them under Keith, Daniel, and Joshua's watchful eyes.

Manfred took us to said post office so the other gals could gate it home easily and I could see where this gate was. Shocking absolutely no one, it was in the post office's public bathroom. What actually surprised me was that the women's had a gate as well as the men's.

"My legacy."

Doreen snorted a laugh. "True enough. Hang in there. Call me if you need more backup."

"That goes double for Alpha Team," Serene said, as Lorraine and Claudia nodded.

"Just figure out what we're going to do at the fundraiser party tonight and we'll call it good. It's a bake sale and I have help. I mean, what could go wrong, really?"

We all stared at each other. "The mind boggles," Lorraine said finally.

"Yeah," Claudia added. "We're on your speed dial. Thankfully."

With that my friends stepped through the gate. Heaved a sigh as I turned to Evalyne and Phoebe. "What do you guys think?"

Evalyne grimaced. "In the relatively short time we've known you, what I've really learned is to expect anything and everything."

Phoebe shrugged. "And we also expect that, whatever happens, you'll roll with it. And so will we. So, let's go get this bake sale done so that we can all go visit the Intergalactic School."

"You think things will be calm there?" I mean, we could hope, right?

"No," Evalyne said flatly. "I think that if something's going to go wrong, it's going to be there. Which is why I want you there sooner as opposed to later."

CHAPTER 43

THIS WAS A NEW ATTITUDE. "You're okay with me getting into the action, whatever it happens to be, now?"

"Yep," Phoebe said cheerfully as Manfred called Vance to find out where they were. "We've decided that it's in our best interest to listen to Keith. His view is that you're the commander and we're just here to follow orders."

"Who are you and what have you done to Pheebs and Ev?"

They both grinned. "We've learned that if you can't beat 'em," Evalyne said, "then you join 'em. Now, let's go sell some baked goods and get out of here."

We found the bake sale set up near to the upper school buildings, closer to the Wisconsin Avenue side. We were on and near lots of grass, a couple of concrete paths, and a circular driveway. Tables were set up and laden with foodstuffs. There were men and women both manning sections, and everyone had cashboxes as well as swipes on their cell phones. We looked like a small county fair. So far, so very prepped. Maybe this wouldn't be bad after all.

Adam and the Kristie-Bot were here now with several Field teams. Press was additionally represented as promised, with Oliver, Jennings, and Dion all there, and Oliver and Dion both had cameras. Oliver was alone, presumably because the *Good Day USA!* team was already set up and filming.

Well, alone if you didn't count the African grey parrot on his shoulder. Good old Bellie—my avian nemesis and true competition for Jeff's love—was here. My luck cup was running over. She looked at me, I looked at her, and we both looked away. Yeah, she hated me, too.

Last but not least, my personal section of the K-9 squad was in attendance as promised. Gave Prince, Duke, and Riley pets, which earned me several horrified looks from the parent helpers, presumably because they didn't want me to contaminate the food. Received a wipe from Mrs. Maurer, cleaned my paws in a very obvious manner, tossed the wipe into a garbage can, saw the parent helpers relax. So far, so very good.

Met everyone helping. Stopped trying to remember who was who by the second person because this was the biggest bake sale I'd ever seen and there were at least thirty parents here if there were two. Instead, thanked them profusely for their help. Everyone seemed happy to be there, though I saw many of their eyes dart toward Charmaine, who was hovering in the background. Clearly Vance hadn't exaggerated this woman's power in any way.

Marcia Kramer was here, too, looking stressed out of her mind. Decided to go all in on the Washington Wife Experience and gave her a hug. Noted that this was noted by everyone. "Why are you here?" I asked her quietly. "Don't you have to prep for the party tonight?"

"I do, but I wanted to support you in this." She gave me a weak smile. "Friends need to stick together."

"True enough." Friends? Vance had possibly not overstated how grateful Marcia was that I'd confirmed our attendance at tonight's fundraiser. Meaning she'd hate me forever if I didn't show, not that I planned to miss it. Not with Dr. Rattoppare on the guest list.

Charmaine came over once I was done meeting everyone. "Now, the bake sale will run all day or until we're out of food."

"That's great, but I have an engagement, so I won't be able to stay here all day." She was getting me until noon. After that, I was heading to the Intergalactic School and the Evil Kangaroo would just have to sniff at herself.

Charmaine drew in breath for a mighty sniff, but she didn't get to release it because Abigail interjected. "That's why we're here," she indicated herself and Mahin. "We're the Cultural Attachés for the American Centaurion Diplomatic Mission and we'll take over when the First Lady has to go on to her next appointment of state."

Charmaine released the sniff slowly. "It's highly irregular."

"So is making the First Lady run a bake sale on the first day of school," Abigail replied. "And yet, we're managing." With that she took my arm, turned us around and headed us over to the American Centaurion Food Fest section.

"What are you getting?" I asked her softly.

"She's a supercilious bitch, that's what I'm getting. So I'll give that right back to her. I think it's the only thing she respects."

Mahin looked around. "I'm confused. Who will be buying the baked goods?"

"Kids at the school, teachers, administrators. I assume, at least." Had no idea, really. Vance and Mrs. Maurer were in conversation with the women who'd been behind Charmaine when we'd arrived, and they were too intent and too far away to bother.

"So, we're raising funds by selling things to the people who already pay to go here and to those who earn their livings here?"

"Um, yes?"

She shook her head. "That seems so . . . circular and insulated."

"Well, it's not like you want strangers wandering onto the campus of an extremely private school," I pointed out.

Abigail jerked. "Or, you do." She nodded toward the circular drive where a couple of tour busses were pulling in. A city bus stopped in front of us and let out a lot of people, most of whom headed for us. Cars pulled into the circular drive and dropped people off.

Mahin nudged me. "They're coming in from other directions."

Sure enough, people who were not schoolchildren and didn't look like teachers or administrators were heading for us. Vance saw this, broke off, and came over. "The good news is, this is standard. They advise everyone they know and advertise the bake sale. The bad news is that they've been advertising that everyone can meet the First Lady and buy something baked by her and her children."

"Oh my God." Did it get worse than this? Refused to ask aloud, since the chances were that it could and would.

"Game faces, people," Charmaine barked. Everyone jerked to attention, my people included. "Let's get that money and give these people something to remember!"

The first people came over to our tables, from one of the busses. A tour group that was up from Florida and had added on the bake sale as a stop. Most of them were retired, all of them were nice. Shook a lot of paws, but we sold a lot of food, too. *Good Day USA!* used this as their first major interview opportunity, and everyone was pleasant and, per Adam, we got good footage.

Was far too busy to take a lot of stock of the situation, but on the rare occasions I got to look around things were going amazingly well. We were even more like a little county fair or farmers market now that we had a ton of people. Our security teams and the K-9 officers and dogs were patrolling, so no one was able to sneak onto the campus to perpetrate evil, and no one seemed to be trying to create issues. Our media representatives were entertaining themselves by interviewing a ton of people who seemed more than happy to be on camera. Even Bellie was behaving herself. Thanked the various Powers That Be and went back to work.

Within the first hour I'd relaxed and started to enjoy this. Sure, it had been sprung upon me in a ridiculous way, but maybe that was how Charmaine got everyone into the swing of things. After all, we had a ton of help, money was flowing in, baked goods were flowing out, people were leaving happy, and this was probably going to be my best media outing ever. I had a long line of those who wanted to meet me, but I remained behind my table—if you wanted to meet the FLOTUS, then you bought a cookie, that was my current motto.

Not everyone wanted to meet me, which was more than fine. Some people hung around, but most didn't. They got their delicious baked goods, saw the FLOTUS or didn't bother, gave an interview or didn't, and headed off.

School had started at eight-thirty and the bake sale at nine. By ten we'd run out of a few things, so tables were consolidated, but that went smoothly and we still had plenty. Running like clockwork. The first tour busses were long gone and new ones were in.

Eleven rolled around quickly. There had been no time to be bored, which was nice. I'd have preferred to have been doing all of this in a t-shirt, jeans, and my Converse, but I was in my Casual FLOTUS Warmer Weather Uniform of a sleeveless dress that was iced blue with black blocking along the sides and low-heeled black pumps.

As with the dress I'd been in the day before, Akiko had ensured this one was from her First Lady Activewear Collection, though I felt its color pattern did more to enhance my curves than yesterday's dress. That was me, paying attention to the superficial things so many seemed to care about so much. My feet kind of hurt, but otherwise I was comfortable and this was going better than I could have imagined in my wildest dreams.

More table consolidation and the upper school kids came out to get goodies as a tour bus left and two more took its place. Lizzie and Wasim were still together, which was good. They were also with kids I recognized—Anthony, Claire, and Sidney Valentino. The five of them didn't look adversarial, so that was one for the win column.

They wandered the tables, presumably to not look like they needed to race over to us like babies. Which was fine, because the other kids seemed to be doing the same thing. Every table was busy but, based on adult reactions, no one's kids had headed to them first. Figured this was both normal teenaged behavior and would be in stark contrast to when the littler kids arrived. At least, I hoped so.

Tried to spot which one was Marcia's stepson and which belonged to Charmaine, but couldn't do it. Considering Charmaine's were supposed to be twins and in Lizzie's class, I should have been able to pick them out, but I didn't see any obvious candidates.

The kids were on a bake sale break. Per what Vance and Mrs. Maurer had gleaned, the high school kids got first dibs. The middle school would get their chance at noon, and then the lower school kids would get their turn. This was to prevent the littlest ones from making themselves sick and so that the older kids could help with the next level of consolidation. Per those whom my team had spoken to, the schedule worked.

A whistle blew, three quick bursts, and the teenagers began wandering over to what I assumed were their family members. I figured the kid who looked nothing like Marcia but who was helping her and seemed comfortable with her was her stepson. Still couldn't spot Charmaine's twins. Or Charmaine. Figured things were going well and she was either off somewhere sulking or congratulating herself. Worked for me.

The tour busses had been served and were driving off and the kids were starting their assigned "move these things to that table and put this other table away" duties when Lizzie, Wasim, and the Valentino kids finally graced us with their presences. Wasn't sure if they were just being slow or hadn't realized what the three-whistle signal indicated. Actively chose to believe they hadn't been clear.

"Well," Lizzie said as they joined us, "this all just stinks."

CHAPTER 44

STEELED MYSELF FOR whatever was coming. "What happened?"

"We still have a lot left," Lizzie replied, sounding disappointed. "I thought ours would sell out first."

Managed not to share that she'd practically given me a heart attack. She was a teenaged girl and, for the first time since I'd known her, truly in a teenaged environment. And, therefore, she was acting like a teenager—overly dramatic. Go figure. Had a feeling Mom was suddenly snickering for no reason, karma being a bitch and all that.

"It's alright," Wasim said reassuringly. "For what we brought over, I believe more than half is gone."

"Most of ours are gone," Sidney said rather smugly. At seventeen he was the eldest of "our" kids. "We brought Grandmother Lucinda's brownies."

Now I managed not to share that I hadn't realized they'd brought Lucinda's brownies. We had six tables assigned to us, so my missing something was understandable. But still, I could have used a snack. If I grabbed a brownie now, it would be too obvious. And I'd probably have to pay extra for it, too.

"We helped her make them, Aunt Kitty," Claire, the sixteen-year-old, said quickly, possibly interpreting my silence for disapproval. "We didn't break the rules."

"And we had the younger cousins help, too," Anthony said. "So everyone was involved." He was Lizzie's age, fifteen, and so in her class here.

"I'm sure you guys were as obedient to the rules as we were, and I'm frankly amazed that any of Lucinda's brownies were left after the first five minutes of the sale." I was. They were the best brownies in, at minimum, two solar systems. And now these kids had the recipe. And I didn't. Actively had to choose not to be bitter.

"Yeah, me too," Anthony said as he shot a little glance toward Lizzie. "Though I think it would have been cool to have gotten to bake with P-Chef."

"It was," Lizzie replied. "You guys will have to come over and hang out. Chef and P-Chef are totes cool with it." She sounded sincere. Hoped this meant that things were going well. They'd only been together a few hours, after all, and presumably at least some of that had been spent learning.

"That would be great!" Anthony sounded as if his career goal was to win *Master Chef*. Didn't buy it. Claire didn't either, if I took her rolling her eyes and wandering over to Abigail to be a clue, which I did. Apparently a few hours was all it took for some. Then again, Lizzie was a pretty awesome girl.

Wasim gave Anthony a look I'd seen a lot when I was younger. I'd never registered it for what it was, but I'd sure seen it. Took all of my self-control to not take a picture and send it to Chuckie, but I refrained. "As Lizzie said, it was very cool. It's an honor to have gotten to work with Queen Katharine's chefs."

"Our grandmother is a great cook and baker," Anthony said, returning fire.

"She is," Sidney said, as if his word on the subject was final. "Liz, which ones did you make? I want to be sure we buy yours."

This earned Sidney the same look from Wasim that Anthony had received and a matching one from Anthony himself. Sidney merely gave them both the smug smile of an older boy who's confident that he's got the edge in terms of a younger girl's interest.

Lizzie, however, seemed utterly oblivious to all of this, even though only the day before we'd been discussing that Raheem had sent Wasim out to make a love connection with her. Then again, at her age, I'd been oblivious to a lot of this, too, even with clear hints. Frankly, I'd been oblivious to a lot of this when I was already a great big grown-up girl with even clearer hints. Some of us focused on different things.

Lizzie didn't react either positively or negatively to Sidney's shortening of her nickname, she just cheerfully pointed out which treats she'd made that she was most proud of while Sidney and Anthony started to stack their individual purchases of far more baked goods than either one of them was likely to eat in a year.

Wasim, meanwhile, seemed forgotten and more than a little frustrated and forlorn. Yeah, I'd missed this look a lot growing up, but others confirmed that it had been present. I had no idea if any of these boys were good enough to date Lizzie, or if she had any interest in any of them beyond being friends. However, I liked Wasim and he deserved a fighting chance.

Pulled my purse out from under the table where I'd stored it and looked inside. Had a ton of Poofs On Board. Not an issue. Also not what I needed at this precise time. "Some special treat only available in the Middle East and definitely not for sale here that Lizzie will really enjoy, please and thank you," I whispered to my purse. Reached in and came out with a neatly wrapped napkin containing a pastry that looked like a small, weird Twinkie. But it didn't smell or feel like a Twinkie. It smelled amazing and felt like a kind of cookie.

Nudged Wasim and handed it to him. "Just found this," I said quietly. "I think P-Chef sent it along specially for you."

He brightened up as he saw it. "Lizzie, try this!"

She turned and took the offered treat. "What is it?"

"Ma'amoul. It's a specialty from my part of the world."

She took a nibble, then a bigger bite. "That's totes delish. What is it and what's in it?"

Wasim was suddenly standing tall. "*My* grandmother says it's a kind of shortbread cookie and they come with different fillings."

"This tastes like the filling is fig. It's awesome."

"The fig-filled ones are my favorites," Wasim said, sounding happy and relieved. "I'm pleased you enjoy them, too."

Lizzie finished the ma'amoul. "That was great. What was inside yours?"

"I gave the only one we had to you. I hoped you'd like it like . . . I do."

Lizzie stared at him for a moment, then she blushed, just a little, and smiled. "You're the best, Wasim, thank you. But that means we totes need to get P-Chef to make more of those. Do you have the recipe?"

"I do," Wasim said confidently. I doubted he did, but was quite certain that Algar had used the recipe Wasim had grown up eating and that Raheem's family had made for generations, meaning we could get the recipe without issue or delay.

"Good plan," I said before Wasim could add that P-Chef had made this. Lizzie would follow that up and it would be a lot easier if she didn't. "While I'd love to let you guys eat everything, why don't you figure out what we need you to do to help? I'm pretty sure Mahin has that knowledge."

Congratulated myself on my for once deft handling of a teenaged romantic situation as Mahin shared what we'd sold and told the kids what to do to help her and Abigail rearrange our stuff for the next waves. Was about to ask what I should be doing when I finally spotted Charmaine.

She was near the circular drive, surrounded by a group of people I hadn't seen before. They all looked like they were parents, though some of them could have been staff and faculty. I could barely remember who I'd met already, of course, so I might have met all of them already. But I didn't think so.

Wondered if these were parents who were coming in for the next shift. But looking around at the expressions of those parental helpers who were also looking Charmaine's way gave the impression that these others weren't around to help out.

And apparently I wasn't either, because it was once again time for me to give *Good Day USA!* some of my uninterrupted attention. At least if I took the Kristie-Bot's waving at me to get my attention to be a clue, and since she and Adam were heading toward me in a determined manner, with their crew in tow, I did.

"Kitty, is this a good time?" Adam asked me when the person who'd been buying things at our table moved on.

"There's never a good time, or, if the cameras are rolling, all of our times are good. Take your pick."

He laughed. "Okay. Well, we want to spend a few minutes discussing why you chose to put your kids in Sidwell."

Uh oh. I hadn't made that decision—Vance had. Vance had made a lot of my decisions because he was, frankly, far more qualified for the FLOTUS job than I was. My strengths lay in kicking butt, playing chicken with intergalactic terrorists, and staring down religious leaders.

Managed not to look around frantically, but it took effort. Instead, stretched and took a casual glance about. "Honestly, that's a fast answer—because it's a great school." Per Vance.

Even though a couple more tour busses were pulling up, things looked calm, so I could see why they wanted to the interview right now. Melville and Prince were walking the perimeter in front of us, near Wisconsin Avenue. Other security was around, Evalyne, Phoebe, Naveed, Manfred in particular. People were milling about and wandering the tables, but this was the least busy we'd been since we'd started.

"Well then," the Kristie-Bot said, "what else do you suggest we chat about? We talked about why you're doing this bake sale already."

"Believe me, I remember." That had been the most uninteresting conversation in recent memory. The only saving grace had been that, in addition to the kids, Vance had forbidden all press to interact with, film, or take pictures of Charmaine, meaning she hadn't had any moments in the spotlight. It was a small, mean-spirited victory, but I was all about taking it.

"We could do a comparison between Sidwell and the Intergalactic School," Adam suggested.

"A positive one for both schools, of course," the Kristie-Bot added. "We're not here to do smear pieces."

"I appreciate that, but we can't do a comparison of anything until I get *to* the Intergalactic School, which will be this afternoon."

Realized what I'd said right as the Kristie-Bot jumped on it. "Oh, that's a great idea! We'll let you keep on doing what you're doing so well here and get prepped for another interview at the other school. What a scoop!"

She pulled her crew away a few feet, presumably to get all set up to go to New Mexico. She also waved a couple of men over who looked vaguely familiar. Was pretty sure I'd seen them at the *Good Day USA!* studio but wasn't prepared to swear to it.

"Kill me now," I said to no one in particular.

"If you insist."

CHAPTER 45

LOOKED UP AT ADAM. "Promise?"

He shook his head with a grin. "Nah, I was lying."

"But if you killed me now, then I wouldn't have to do all the rest of the stuff that *Good Day USA!* wants me to do and I wouldn't have to worry about Code Name: First Lady, either."

"Sorry not sorry," Adam said, "but you have to live. However, I am sorry about Kristie jumping on that opening I'm sure you didn't mean to give her."

"I didn't, believe me." Noted that the *Good Day USA!* cameraman had said camera trained on us. "Um, Adam? Why is that dude filming us?"

"Huh. No idea. Unless . . ." His voice trailed off and his eyes narrowed.

"Unless what?"

He heaved a sigh. "I don't need this, and you need it less than I do. They may be trying to get footage that will insinuate that you and I are, ah, friendly."

"Wow, that old wheeze? It's been tried on me before."

"It's been tried on me before, too," Adam said grimly. "It's the reason my wife divorced me. And I think you may have spotted who ruined my marriage, which was information I didn't have before. Excuse me." He headed over to where the rest of the *Good Day USA!* people were and started speaking to the cameraman in a way that I was pretty sure was threatening, since Adam was much larger and, from what I could tell, hella pissed.

Oliver and Bellie took the opportunity to join me. It was nice to see a friendly face I knew I could trust. The less said about the beakface on his shoulder, though, the better. "How goes it, Madam First Lady?"

"Oh, you know, just living the FLOTUS dream and all that."

"Floaty! Floaty!"

"Thanks for that, Bellie. So, MJO, do you want to do an interview here, too, or am I able to miss out?"

"Well, if *Good Day USA!* gets to have you, I believe I should do my best to also get a scoop."

"Wow. A scoop. About what?"

"Whatever you'd like to share. We are, of course, not focused on the children at all."

"I'll let the irony of us doing this at their school pass. Somehow *Good Day USA!* is going with me to the Intergalactic School later."

"I'm sure it will be fine."

"I'm not. So, I have many things I'd like to tell you, none of which I can share here."

He nodded. "I've exchanged communications with several people. And have reached out to my various sources. Bruce has done so as well. And we'll be accompanying you to the Intergalactic School and the fundraiser tonight, as well, so even if our compatriots from *Good Day USA!* are there, you won't be alone."

"You guys are the best. Bummer that I know you're going to bring Bellie along."

"Oh, now, you and she just got off to a bad start. Miss Bellie is quite a lady and I'm sure that, if you give her a chance, you'll love her just as you do all your other animals."

Doubted it, but now wasn't the time to say that aloud, in part because I could see Charmaine on the horizon. She was rolling with the same bunch of women and couple of guys I'd already spotted.

Oliver took Bellie off his shoulder and put her onto his hand. He spoke softly to her, while she looked at me in her evil bird way. "Floaty!"

"I think she'd like you to hold her," Oliver suggested.

"Are you kidding?"

Jenkins and Dion joined us. "You know," Dion said cheerfully, "a shot of you and Mister Joel Oliver's gorgeous bird would make a wonderful picture."

"Dion! Dion! Bellie likes Dion!"

"I see Bellie's drawn another man into her web of avian deceit."

"Dion's right," Jenkins said. "And Bellie's quite sweet and tame as well as beautiful." He stroked her head and she leaned into it, making a soft noise that almost sounded like purring. She'd definitely learned new tricks.

The kids clustered around us, and not just mine—many of the kids who were out here had gathered to watch the show. "That bird is parkour," one of them said. Couldn't identify the speaker. Could identify that one of the kids had music playing—if I concentrated I could just hear it. Matchbox Twenty's "She's So Mean." Refrained from asking whoever to turn it up, but it took effort.

"Totally," Claire agreed.

"Parkour is the French semi-sport of running acrobatically around cities and leaping tall buildings with a few impressive bounds," I shared. "I kind of thought everyone attending Sidwell would know that."

Claire rolled her eyes at me. "Oh, Aunt Kitty, I love you but you are *so* old."

Didn't know which was more shocking—Claire saying she loved me or that I was now ancient. Chose to show my range and be floored by both.

"It means hardcore," Lizzie said to me in a low voice. "Sorry, I'll try to catch you up on what the young folks are saying these days so you're not embarrassed."

Managed not to say that she probably needed to bring me up to speed on music, too, since I didn't think the kids were listening to Matchbox Twenty these days, but managed to refrain. Also refrained from sharing that the only embarrassing thing was that I was now surrounded and everyone seemed to think I should be holding the stupid parrot.

Caved to peer pressure. "Fine, let's see if Bellie leaves me with any part of my hand." Reached out slowly and carefully, prepared to pull my hand back at any moment. However, and unlike every other time I'd tried to be nice to this bird, she allowed me to pet her head. "She does have soft, lovely feathers."

Bellie preened. "Bellie likes Floaty."

Heard the kids start to giggle. Actively chose to ignore them. Was too busy being shocked by Bellie's sudden affinity for not trying to kill me.

"Why don't you hold her?" Oliver suggested, as he moved Bellie from his hand to mine. Shocking me to my core, Bellie didn't instantly try to shred my hand. Instead, she closed her claws carefully so that she was holding on but not painfully.

Stroked her head with my other hand. She did the whole lean into it and imitate purring thing. Had to admit it, it was kind of cool. "Wow, you're right. Bellie's being awesome." Gently ran my hand down her back and gave her a gentle scritchy-scratch between her wings, where I did it on all the Peregrines.

Bellie opened her beak, stuck her tongue out, and bobbed her head from side to side, while making a stuttering sound, kind of like odd laughter. She looked hella cute and the kids ate it up.

"She likes that," Oliver said. "That's her way of showing that she's enjoying something—her way of giggling."

Noted that the *Good Day USA!* team was filming this. Well, Dion couldn't be the only one who'd thought it would make a great photo op. Might as well give them a show. "Does she like her tummy rubbed?"

"She does."

Stopped the scritchy-scratching and stroked her tummy. Bellie did more of her bird giggle while extending her wings. She was definitely the center of attention, but she was being great and, frankly, when she was like this, I could see why every man who'd owned her had fallen madly in love with her. Antony Marling had loved her more than his children. Jeff hadn't, thankfully, but I was still glad I'd shoved her off on Oliver before Jeff had to choose between her and me, in part because I still wasn't sure who he'd pick if push came to shove.

Speaking of shoving, several people did. Charmaine and her entourage, to be exact. They shoved past whoever was on the perimeter and got right up next to me. Took a closer look at the entourage—had definitely not met any of them and none of them had been working the bake sale. That boded in a familiar way.

"What's going on here?" Charmaine asked imperiously. "And what is that *thing* doing around food?"

I might not have been Bellie's biggest fan, but she certainly wasn't worthy of this kind of disdain. And anything the Evil Kangaroo wanted to degrade was instantly going to earn my defense. Stopped petting Bellie's tummy, moved her closer to my chest, and started stroking her head. Just in case Charmaine had any ideas about hitting at the bird.

"This is a highly trained, extremely intelligent, beautifully plumed African grey parrot, with a vocabulary and comprehension level that surpasses many humans. Her full name is Rybel-leclies, but her nickname is Bellie. To her friends. You can call her Princess, however." The only one around here who was getting the Queen title was me, thank you very much.

Charmaine stayed true to form and sniffed. A big one this time. Several of those with her did as well. Great. The Evil Kangaroo had indeed brought in her reinforcements. "So you have a filthy bird around the food we're selling and you seem to believe that it's fine because she's with you?"

"Actually, she's with Mister Joel Oliver, but yes, it's fine. She's well trained. She only poops on people she doesn't like." Waited for Bellie to poop on me. She didn't. Didn't have time to marvel, but planned to do so later. Heard the faint music change to "Fair Fight" by The Fray. Had to figure out which kid was listening to what, for this age group, was oldies music. I liked his or her choices.

"Get rid of her," Charmaine snarled. "Now."

"Or . . . what, exactly? This bird has helped save the world more than once. What have you done?"

Charmaine drew herself up to her full height. "I am the President of the Sidwell Friends School Parent Teacher Association and you would do well to remember that." The men and women in her entourage nodded.

This group reminded me of *Heathers*. Well, high school and *Heathers*. And *Mean Girls*. Basically, Charmaine was the Big Woman on Campus here. Maybe she'd been like this in high school, maybe she hadn't and was living out the dream now. But either way, she felt that she was the one running things, and based on the expressions of the people behind her, they did, too. Frankly, based on everyone's reactions to her and what Marcia had told Vance, possibly everyone here thought Charmaine was all that and an extra-large bag of sniff-chips.

I probably should have backed down. Only, that wasn't how I rolled. And, regardless of anything else, if I hadn't backed down before a king and the entire religious community of the world, I sure as hell wasn't going to back down to the President of the PTA.

"And you would do well to remember that you don't intimidate me. At all."

"Just because you're the FLOTUS, don't think that impresses anyone here." Charmaine's nostrils flared. Had no idea whether that meant she was going to go for a Gold Medal Sniff, turn on her heel and stalk off, share that the hand that rocked the bake sale ruled the world, or try to slap me. Her expression was hard to read. But I never got a chance to find out.

"Bellie loves Floaty!" Bellie shrieked. Then she flew off my hand, right at Charmaine's face.

CHAPTER 46

AS OFTEN HAPPENED during times of shock and intense crisis, everything suddenly started moving in slow motion.

Charmaine screamed and waved her arms around. Bellie shrieked her new battle cry of "Floaty! Floaty! Floaty!" and flew around Charmaine's head. The people with Charmaine started flailing at Bellie, who merely flailed right back. She was far better at it than they were.

But this meant that Oliver, Jenkins, and Dion got involved, to get people away from the bird. People around us started shouting. Another bird screamed and this scream I recognized— Bruno had come along in stealth mode, which was his job, after all, but he was stealth no longer. He rose up to defend Bellie, meaning there was now a giant Peregrine flapping around the people with Charmaine.

Naturally, all this activated the rest of my security teams. Including the canine one. Especially the canine one.

Heard Prince barking and, because I had that keen Dr. Doolittle talent of mine, I could tell that he was informing Duke and Riley that I was under attack. Heard Melville, Moe, and Curly all shout—it was clear the dogs had all jerked out of their handlers' holds, because I could make out what the men were shouting, which was for the dogs to get back under control. As if.

Of course, this meant that all three dogs were going to be barreling in, ready to bite down hard and read the perps their rights later. And my security teams were right behind them, similar intent plastered on all their faces.

Prince was coming from the street side and Duke and Riley from behind and to the side. But no matter which direction they were coming from, people and tables were in the way. The dogs didn't care—they were trained, they were on a mission from God, and they were big and strong. The people got out of the way, most of them of their own volition. The tables couldn't.

Tables flipped over and baked goods, cashboxes, cash, and change went flying. People started screaming and running, some away, some toward the action. Bellie was still squawking but had risen above the fray. She remained the luckiest bird in existence. Bruno landed on my shoulder, the better to observe the fight and protect me at the same time.

Somehow, while this was all going on around me, I was in my own little Cone of Safety. Knew it wouldn't last, but appreciated it nonetheless.

Time snapped back for me as I got body slammed by someone infiltrating said Cone of Safety. That'd teach me for noticing something positive and being grateful for it. Managed to stay on my feet and Bruno remained on my shoulder, though he shrieked a death cry at the poor woman who'd been knocked over by Riley.

The three dogs were able to get in position around me, creating a Dog Protection Barrier. This was great and all, but we had kids here and I had no idea where they were or if they were safe. Sure, they were teenagers, but they were still kids. And five of them were "mine," two in particular.

Looked around for Lizzie and Wasim, not to mention the Valentino kids, which meant I got to see the table with pies on it flip due to the Secret Service tossing it out of their way. This in turn meant I had a prime view of said pies slamming into people's faces—including Mahin, Naveed, and Mrs. Paster.

Cupcakes were sailing through the air, cookies were flying, what I thought might be the last of Lucinda's brownies sailed into the crowd, landing on the *Good Day USA!* team. Perhaps in a form of cosmic retribution for the pies, the Secret Service were hit with several cakes. We had a full on Pastry Riot going. Had the feeling that was going to be the headline, too.

Some of the kids were freaking out. Others had chosen to channel Bluto from *Animal House* and turn this into a food fight. Interestingly enough, only Charmaine and her entourage of Mean Adults were trying to grab the money, now that they weren't dealing with Bellie and Bruno. Then again, couldn't really fault them for it—there was a lot of money flying around, and all of it had been earned.

Managed to spot my kids. Lizzie and the Valentino kids had Wasim surrounded in a protective circle. He didn't look happy about this, but since Naveed was covered in pie and had three overturned tables and about fifty people between himself and his charge, this was a good thing.

Somehow, with all this commotion and chaos I could still hear faint music. Had no idea who had said music on them, but the song was now "The Ballroom Blitz" by Sweet. There was no way in the world a teenager of today was listening to Sweet. Not that they weren't great, but this same kid would have had to also love Matchbox Twenty and The Fray, and I wasn't buying it. I'd been and remained musically omnivorous, and I liked music from every era. Sweet's era had been over thirty years ago, and most kids didn't want to like the same music as their parents.

Meaning that some kid was on the Algar Channel for me, because this scene was pretty much acting out the song lyrics and Algar liked his little jokes.

Spun around to try to find the kid with the music. Which was a good thing, as I was able to duck just in time to have a cupcake thrown with intent sail over my head. Risked a look to see who it'd hit. Evalyne now had a cupcake on her chest and a seriously pissed expression.

Looked back to spot the thrower and saw two kids, a boy and a girl. The boy was on the shorter side and heavy. The girl was taller and thinner, but with a sturdy build. They both had dark curly hair, dark eyes, olive skin, and their features were similar. They looked related and about the same age, and about the same age as Lizzie. They were throwing food at anyone and everyone, but mostly toward Lizzie's group and me and the animals. They were throwing far less at Charmaine and her entourage. And they were laughing, the kind of nasty laugh that the mean kids use when they're tormenting the weaker kids.

Figured I'd spotted Charmaine's twins and Lizzie's new nemeses. And that meant it was time to get more involved. "Bruno, my bird, I think I need to have a talk with those kids."

Bruno lifted off from my shoulder and headed for them. As he did that, I stood up and Bellie dove down and landed on my other shoulder. "Bellie loves Floaty!"

"I'm so glad. Let's help Bruno," I said to Prince.

The dogs allowed me out of the Dog Protection Barrier and we headed for the kids I was prepared to swear, as we got closer, were Charmaine's twins. They looked nothing like her other than the shape of their eyes and their expressions, but I figured that was probably enough.

The girl threw a cupcake right at me while the boy threw one at Bruno. But Bruno was a guard bird and he dodged it easily and I was a jock and I wasn't panicked. Caught the cupcake and dropped it on the ground. "Stop it. Right now."

"Why should we?" the boy asked.

"Because your mother's not going to like it when I tell her you two are who started the food fight and are keeping it going."

The girl smirked at me. "She won't believe you. She knows we'd never do something like that."

"I'll bet. Prince? Share our views on this."

The dog trotted up to them and growled. The deep, dog growl that said that dogs were just wolves who'd chosen to play nicely with humans, and that the humans who were getting growled at were about to lose their play nicely privileges.

Both kids stopped smirking. "He's going to kill us!" the girl shrieked.

This might have been effective under normal circumstances. But when people are screaming and running and things are utterly chaotic, no one's paying much attention to a faked out teenaged scream.

Shrugged. "Only if you throw food at anyone again, me in particular." Both of them dropped the cupcakes they were holding. "Nice to see you're smarter than you look."

Somehow, the music was still audible. Had to find the kid who was playing this music. The song now was "Calm & Collapsed" by the Exies. Algar was once again giving me a hint for what to do, as if getting things calmed down wasn't my desired outcome.

Realized that what I hadn't seen around were any A-Cs. Sure, I had Daniel and Joshua with Jamie, but Lucas and Marcus had been assigned to Lizzie and Wasim, and Manfred had been with me. And yet, I didn't see any of them moving at hyperspeed or even human speed. Couldn't look for them, though, until I'd calmed things down here.

The music changed to "Pride" by Saliva. Pondered this for a moment, then went with the only thing I could think of. "Look, you two have a choice. You can continue to be jerks, or you can actually act like campus leaders. If you act like jerks, I'll ensure that I have a camera crew following you around to capture your every jerkish move. If you actually act like campus leaders, however, that camera crew will want to interview you about how you helped get this situation under control."

They looked at each other. "Okay," the girl said slowly. "What do you want us to do?"

"Not that we're saying yes to it," the boy added.

"Of course I wouldn't expect Charmaine's kids to do anything for an altruistic reason."

Shockingly, they both jerked. "We're nothing like our mother," the girl hissed.

"At all," the boy added.

"Really? I'm not seeing any dissimilarities at the moment."

"Fine." The girl tossed her head. "We'll show you. Seth, you get the others to stop throwing and get the tables set back up."

"What will you do, Shelby?" Seth asked suspiciously.

"I'm going to lead adults over to safety." She pointed to the circular driveway. It had grass in the center, and people were there. Realized that the A-Cs had been pulling people out of the chaos and putting them there, but that meant they had to keep them there. So Marcus and Lucas were on crowd control and Manfred and Abigail were bringing people over. However, they were having to do it at human speeds because the last thing we needed was people throwing up and apparently they'd figured that out.

"Great plan. Seth, go to that group of kids first." Pointed to Lizzie's team. "They'll help you. If, you know, you ask for their help instead of ordering them to help. And Riley, you go with him." The dog wuffed—he was clear on his role.

The twins stared at me for a long moment. "Got it," Seth said. He trotted off, Riley at his side, stopping at each teenager they came to. They stopped whatever they were doing and started to help.

Meanwhile, Shelby and I split up, with Duke going with her and Prince sticking with me. One by one we grabbed people and told them to calm down. This rarely worked on the first go, but since the food wasn't flying anymore, it was easier to point out that it had *only* been food flying.

In less time than I'd have thought, the teenagers were all working together to calm down the adults, and everyone was moved off to the circular drive area. The only injuries were minor and all related to panic, not food, other than the few people who'd slipped and fallen. Oh, sure, everyone was covered with baked goods, but once the A-Cs didn't have to do crowd protection duty, they were able to collect the money and cashboxes using hyperspeed.

Was about to congratulate myself on a job well done, in that sense, when I looked toward the street.

There were news vans on the street. Lots and lots of news vans.

CHAPTER 47

"SO," READER SAID as we sat in the Original Situation Room and watched the footage on every TV screen, "want to tell us what happened?" It looked far worse than it had while it had been happening. The only saving grace was that Jeff was already at the Intergalactic School and so wasn't sharing this experience with us.

"It wasn't Kitty's fault!" Lizzie said. She, like Wasim and the Valentino kids, was pretty much covered in pastries. We hadn't had time to change clothes.

"It's never Kitty's fault," Tim said. "We're all aware of that. You all look delicious, by the way."

"Thanks for that."

"The birds are going to be a bigger problem," Claudia said. We were watching Charmaine's moment in the news sun.

"That woman set killer birds on me!" Charmaine screamed into the camera. The camera zoomed to me, standing with Bellie on my shoulder and Bruno in my arms. The birds looked amazingly calm and had no food on them anywhere. Same could not be said of me, but still, I was one of the cleaner ones in view.

The camera swung back to Charmaine. "She tried to kill me!" she shrieked. One of her entourage nudged her and she got herself under control. "The First Lady is a menace to our school, and I can only assume that all the children in her care will be as well. They have no place here at Sidwell. She insisted on being involved despite our concerns about the increased security risk if she attended, but she wouldn't be stopped. And now look at what's happened!"

"That is a total lie!" Charmaine was really lucky I hadn't

heard her say this live at the scene. As it was, I still wanted to go find her and pummel her to death.

"We know," Vance said soothingly, while he nursed a black eye.

"You seem unhurt," a male reporter said to Charmaine. "By either birds or the First Lady."

"Whoever that man is, I want to send him a fruit basket."

"By the grace of God," Charmaine replied with a mighty sniff. "Those birds are killers."

"I think we're going to have to put the birds into quarantine or something," Lorraine said.

"No, you're not," Adam said strongly. "*Good Day USA!* is the only team with any footage of the birds in action, and we've already destroyed that portion."

The Kristie-Bot nodded. "We don't want to do anything to jeopardize Code Name: First Lady."

No one replied to this, mostly because we were now watching the interview with Mrs. Paster. She looked like she'd been an extra in the pie scene from *The Great Race*. "This is highly unusual for our school, however, mishaps do happen. I'd like to reassure all those with loved ones at Sidwell that we are just fine. There was no real damage done, we have only a few minor injuries that have already been attended to, and while the upper school has been excused and sent home, the middle school and lower school were unaffected and are still on campus. Safely on campus."

"Missus Paster gets a fruit basket, too. A big one."

"Is it true that it was the Washington P.D.'s K-9 squad that started the skirmish?" a female reporter asked her.

"I really have no idea," Mrs. Paster said, taking a big one for the team. Was pretty sure she'd been in position to see the dogs knock everyone out of their way.

"You are so lucky," Melville muttered to Prince.

Prince whined, lay down, and put his head on his paws. Duke and Riley did likewise.

"Did this happen because the First Lady insisted on being involved, as we heard from another witness?" the reporter asked.

"To my knowledge, the First Lady was asked to take part. We do have our parents and guardians as involved as possible."

Mrs. Paster was giving calm, noninflammatory information. Which meant that, naturally, the camera feed went to someone else. We now had a group of students. "That was totally parkour!" one of the boys said.

"This was the best first day of school ever!" a girl shared.

The teenagers were all for the food fight, so that was good. The cameras stayed on them for a while. Other stations had more Charmaine, parent helpers, more kids. The parents weren't nearly as thrilled as the kids, but for the most part, I wasn't getting all the blame. The security teams were, however, which wasn't good.

"Was there a reason that Bellie started this?" Reader asked me, as he gave the parrot an icy look.

Bellie had decided that we were now the best of besties and was still on my shoulder. Oliver hadn't argued, possibly because he, Jenkins, and Dion looked as covered with pastries as Mrs. Paster. Reader hadn't allowed any of us to clean up once Manfred had called for a floater gate and gotten all of us out of there.

"Charmaine was insulting me and looked about to attack. I think Bellie thought she was protecting me."

"And just what were you all doing while this was going on?" he asked Manfred, Marcus, and Lucas, his Commander Tone on Full. His gaze went to include Evalyne and Phoebe, too, and all the other security staff standing against the walls, K-9 officers included. They all looked like they'd been mud wrestling where the mud was made of frosting. The cleaning staff was going to have their work cut out for them in this room.

"Trying to control the situation," Manfred said. "Unsuccessfully."

"That's not true," I interjected. "It all happened really fast, and everyone did what they could."

Reader turned back to the screens. "What they could. Really. I'm looking at people trained to stop superbeings or bullets, trained to handle terrorist and hostage situations, trained to keep it together and keep people safe. And yet what I see them doing is being unable to power through a barrage of baked goods in order to get to the First Lady and cover her."

"The dogs made it through, and Bruno was on the case."

This earned me Reader's Death Glare. "Ah, yes. Bruno. From what we've managed to gather from your various descriptions of the event, it was Bruno appearing out of nowhere that caused the panic."

"No," Oliver said. "It was Bellie. I take full responsibility for all of this. And I'm willing to go on record and meet the press, so to speak, and declare that."

One of the stations had a replay of the action. The only

saving grace we had was that the news vans hadn't been there at
the start, so the video feeds had started sometime after the birds
had settled down. However, it still looked like the Carnival of
the Ridiculous, with a lot of panicked people slipping, sliding,
and running, and a lot of teenagers throwing food. Some adults
were throwing food, too.

"Hey, freeze that."

Tim had the controller, since Raj was with Jeff, and he dutifully hit pause. "Why?"

"I want us to zoom in on the adults who are throwing food. I
think they're part of Charmaine's gang."

Tim rewound the footage a bit and we all took a closer look.
Sure enough, once my back was turned, all of Charmaine's people were tossing food around.

"That's interesting," Tim said slowly. "It's as if they wanted
to make this worse."

"I think they did," Serene said. "Look at their expressions.
They look sly."

"Like they're happy this is happening," Lorraine added.

"Why would they want that?" Claudia asked.

"To discredit Kitty," Lizzie said. She looked around.
"Where's my dad?"

"Your father, Kevin, Wruck, and Buchanan are still on-site,"
Reader said. "They're the reason the news vans were delayed.
But once this broke out, they couldn't hold the news crews off
any longer."

"Go Team Tough Guys. But who tipped them off that things
were going on? I mean more than a successful bake sale, which is
what we were having right up until Charmaine started in on me."

"Hmm," White, who was sitting next to me, said.

We all waited. "Hmm what, Richard?" I asked finally.

"It's no secret that you're close to the K-9 squad. Prince was
on camera saving Jeffrey's life during the national convention
after all. I don't believe it would be a stretch to think that Charmaine was trying to incite an animal reaction. I believe that she
just got the one she wasn't expecting."

"You mean you think she was trying to get the dogs to attack?" Abigail asked. "Why?"

"To cause havoc," Naveed said. "Frankly, that no one was
truly hurt is amazing."

"We focused on that," Marcus said. "Because Lucas and I at
least are fully aware that the First Lady can take care of herself."

Lucas nodded. "We used hyperspeed to get to those about to be truly harmed and to get them out of the way. There were only four of us," he nodded at Abigail, who managed a grin, "and it was a different kind of chaos than we're used to, so it took us more time."

"It's harder to spot who's in danger when there isn't a giant monster or a madman with a gun," Manfred added.

"So, Richard, what you're saying is that Charmaine was trying to bait me in order to get the dogs to get involved? Why?"

"I'd say it's a simple answer," Reader replied before White could. "To shove you and the kids out of the school."

"But why would they want to do that, dear?" Mrs. Maurer asked. She looked almost as pristine as when we'd gone over, because Manfred had gotten her to safety first, under the very correct idea that this was what I'd have wanted. "Having the White House children is an honor that the school cherishes. It's why the principal and vice principal have been so supportive and unwilling to blame you or the rest of us."

Looked at White, who nodded, then at Reader. "You want my guess?"

"Always, girlfriend." He grinned at my expression. "Yes, I'm mad at all of you, but no, not in a long-term way. So, what's your theory?"

"I think Charmaine and her crew are up to something they don't want us discovering. And that means they're up to something with major ramifications."

"Makes sense." Reader nodded. "Like espionage."

CHAPTER 48

"SO WHAT ARE WE LOOKING FOR?" Lizzie asked.

"You?" Reader said. "Nothing. The five of you are going to get cleaned up and then be ready to help get the younger kids and bring them safely back here. Period."

"Aww, but we can help," Lizzie protested.

"If it's okay, Lizzie and Wasim could come to the Intergalactic School with me. Potentially to give us a good story, versus a bad one." And also potentially to check it out. I was pretty much now on the side of Lizzie's idea of sending all our kids there—it had to be safer than having them where the Evil Kangaroo held sway.

"If you insist," Reader said with a sigh.

"Why not the rest of us?" Claire asked.

"Because your older sister's there, and I think James is right—we need you guys to help with the younger kids. Besides, I actually do want you doing something at the school."

The Valentino kids perked up. "What?" Sidney asked.

"I want you befriending Seth and Shelby Cordell."

They all stared at me. "They're jerks," Anthony said finally. "They're in class with me and Lizzie. We hate them already and it's only been a couple of hours."

"And they aren't necessarily in on their mother's plans. I got through to them by saying that they were just like her. The moment they heard that, they stopped egging on all the food fighting and instead started helping out."

Claire and Sidney looked at each other. "We have experience with it," Sidney said finally.

"He means Stephanie," Claire explained, presumably because she felt we were all too old to catch on. "And Sidney's right—we do have the experience to be able to spot if they're doing what their mother wants or not."

"Why didn't you guys turn?" Lizzie asked.

It was a good question, and one we all wanted to hear, so none of the adults interjected.

Claire shrugged. "Stephanie was always our father's favorite. But, even when we tried to do things he wanted, he didn't care about us in the same way."

"Until after the accident," Anthony said. "Now he loves all of us and doesn't want us to do things to hurt the rest of our family. He's a lot better." His siblings nodded.

"But we were around him and our sister before he was hurt, and we know what they'd do," Sidney continued. "How they'd pass signs to each other, what Stephanie acted like when she was on a mission or whatever for our father, stuff like that."

"I'm sure this will be different," Claire said, "but we should still be able to figure it out."

"Making friends with them is going to be the hard part," Anthony muttered.

Lizzie nodded. "Word."

"Use Wasim." They all stared at me. Heaved a sigh. "Wasim is a Bahraini prince. Use that, the status that comes from hanging out with royalty. It may not work, but if it does, use it."

Wasim nodded. "I would be amenable if it was for a good cause, and this is."

"Great. Then it's settled."

Reader's turn to heave a sigh. "I can only imagine Jeff's reaction to this plan."

"Don't tell him and then we won't have to worry about it. Okay, kids, unless any of you have more intel, you all need to get cleaned up and ready for the rest of our fun-filled afternoon."

"Oh, Kitty, I won't need to see Doctor Hernandez after all," Wasim said.

"Oh? Was your second gate trip okay?"

"Yes, because I listened to music during the gate transfer from the school. It helped tremendously."

Stared at him. I'd been with Centaurion for over six years and I listened to music as often as I could, and yet this had literally never occurred to me. "Um, what?"

"Music. I listened to music." He pulled his phone and earbuds out of his pocket. "Music?"

"Yes, I know what music is. Did you check that it was safe to do before you did that?"

"No. Why would I?"

He was a prince and had spent all his life as a prince. Had no idea how he'd turned out as normally as he had, but that he'd acted in a royal way and just done whatever he'd wanted to wasn't a surprise, really. That he didn't do whatever he wanted to all the time was the shocker.

"Um, because it could have been dangerous."

"If it was, I would assume that I'd have been warned of such."

"We do tend to tell humans what to do to avoid being killed," White pointed out. "I'm not clear on why you're reprimanding Prince Wasim."

"True enough and I'm not really reprimanding. I just didn't realize we could use electronics going through the gates."

This earned me the entire room's "duh" look. "Ah, Kitty?" Tim said. "We send cars, tanks, jets, and weapons through gates. Almost all of them are turned on and have electrical systems."

"I have no idea where you got that idea," Reader added. "I mean that seriously."

"Me either, but I'm going to choose to blame Christopher for it, because he's not here. So, um, kids, carry on. And, thanks for the tip, Wasim. Your news is possibly the best news I've had all day. If only all the news we got was that good and positive."

Wasim beamed. "I'm happy I could help."

"Me, too. Now, go get ready to help some more, all of you." The teenagers left the room far happier than when they'd entered it. One small one for the win column.

"As for the rest of you . . ." Reader heaved a sigh. "I want to stay angry, but I can't. Field actually read the situation right and took the correct course of action. Secret Service did their best. I don't blame the human K-9 officers for what happened." Received the hairy eyeball look. "Because I know that the person who could have contained all the animals didn't."

"Oh my God, seriously? It happened fast, James. You didn't even see the start but it was calm one moment and chaos the next. The dogs and the birds all settled down the moment I could collect myself, and once settled, they didn't act up again. Unlike the humans."

"I hate to say it, because I don't want you to snarl at me, but I'm with Kitty," Tim said. "Especially since we have footage showing those people throwing food. Those were strategic tosses, too. Did you notice that almost all of them were aimed at security personnel?"

The room had not so noticed, so we re-ran the footage again, including the footage from *Good Day USA!*, which we had on hand, though it wasn't being broadcast.

The *Good Day USA!* footage was the hardest to see, since the cameraman was being pelted by food and, from all I could tell, still arguing with Adam. However, because of that, their camera was trained on me, and the footage started earlier than anyone else's. True to what they'd said, the footage began after the bird attack. Bellie and Bruno were both up in the air and the dogs were heading in.

In the video my attention wasn't on Charmaine any longer, and the moment I turned away, she nodded her head at some of her people. They moved out from their Entourage Huddle and began to toss things around. A couple of them gathered the money, but they also threw the cashboxes again. And everything they were tossing was at the policemen or other identifiable security, and at their backs. Most of those things they tossed hit.

"My God, who took the hits with those cashboxes?" I asked.

"All of us," Evalyne said. "Though I have to say that some of those cookies hurt worse."

"All security get cleaned up and then see Doctor Hernandez immediately," Reader said. "Field agents as well."

That team shuffled out of the room and we were no longer crowded. We continued to watch the feed. "They're not stealing the money," Claudia said. "They're picking it up, but it's clear that they're not pocketing it. Why?"

"They aren't doing this to steal the bake sale funds," Serene replied. "And if they're gathering the money, then it's a good cover for why they're milling around and low to the ground."

"Harder to spot them when they're low," Lorraine pointed out. "I didn't see this on any of the other coverage."

"Do you think they figured on media coverage?" Tim asked.

"Yes," Oliver said emphatically. "They'd been advertising the bake sale and that the First Lady was going to be there."

My brain nudged. "Wait. How far in advance was this thing being promoted?"

"Three weeks," Jenkins replied.

"When was my presence promised?"

"One week ago," he said. "The first two weeks it was a stay

tuned for our special parental guest, after that, it was come see the First Lady. Though they didn't use your name or title. The wording was 'top woman in the country' which is clearly you."

"I'm flattered. However, Charmaine told me I had to do this yesterday."

"And we had no knowledge of this event at all," Vance said. "And we should have."

Mrs. Maurer looked pissed. "We received nothing prior to the phone call you received from this Charmaine person."

"I thought our people scoured the media for things like this."

"They do," Vance said. "Both our team and Jeff's team and, as far as I know, the CIA and FBI scan as well."

"This isn't advertised in the papers," Oliver said. "It's a very word of mouth kind of thing. The bake sales are quite popular, since everyone tries to outdo everyone else and the student body is filled with movers and shakers. Hence why busloads of tourists arrived. It's a regular event."

"They do two every quarter," Dion added.

"Can't wait. So, why did all our teams miss this? Frankly, MJO, why didn't you warn me?"

He looked surprised. "It was a bake sale at your daughter's new school. Not only did it seem benign, but I truly thought you'd already been advised and had agreed to help out. Why else would *Good Day USA!* have been along?"

Why else indeed? I hadn't had time to fill Oliver in on everything, and I had no idea what he did or didn't know right now. However, as everyone on Alpha Team loved to tell me, this wasn't my job.

"Okay, so while everyone else has fun figuring out who knew what when and so on, I and the press are going to get cleaned up and head over to our next stop."

Everyone stared at me. "Really?" Serene asked finally.

"Really. You guys figure it out, do whatever we have to in order to ensure that we're all at the Kramer's fundraiser tonight, and let me know if I need to make a statement other than 'I want to be left alone.' I'm heading over to the Intergalactic School where, to my knowledge, the idea of a bake sale has never been forwarded."

And with that, I headed off for my rooms and the shower, the press corps trailing after me like journalistic ducks in a ragged row.

CHAPTER 49

CLEANED, DRESSED, and pressed, we were all ready to go in less than an hour. I chose wisdom over propriety and was in jeans, my Converse, and an Aerosmith t-shirt. The bake sale might not have erupted into real life *Cake Wars* if I'd had my boys on my chest.

The press corps was assembled with the teenagers at the Secret Service offices. Per my text update from Vance, White was there, riding herd on the young'uns and the others, the K-9 squad was staying on-site and would escort the Valentino kids to Sidwell and back, along with the rest of the security teams that had been with me at the school, and security at the Intergalactic School had been warned that I'd be there soon.

On my way downstairs I ran into Gadhavi. Chose not to ask why the Grizzly Bear of G Company was wandering the White House halls freely. Right now, I'd take a grizzly and all of G-Company over the PTA.

"We studied that picture," he said by way of hello. "We found nothing."

Pulled my phone out of my purse and looked at the shot I'd taken. As I did, realized that my iPod was plugged into my portable speakers. I never left it that way. Checked my iPod out. It was on a Listen Like Thieves playlist that, before today, I hadn't had.

So that was how he'd done it. Not via a person, but via my purse. It made sense and was something that would be totally believable if discovered. Moved the iPod and speakers up to the top. Why miss out on any clues Algar might toss my way? Sure the ones at Sidwell hadn't helped much, but why risk it?

Looked at the picture. As Gadhavi had said earlier, not a lot there other than hate. But I'd seen something. "I need to look at this on a bigger screen."

He nodded. "The picture is still up in the meeting room."

We went there together, him expressing sadness for my horrible experience and me trying to play it down with limited success. By the time we were there, he was pledging to replace any and all funds the bake sale had lost or should have made as his donation and I was ready to ask him to roll with me to the Intergalactic School. Refrained, but only just.

We were alone in the LSR, which made me feel very tiny. Didn't feel alone, though—Gadhavi had a presence that definitely filled a room.

We stared at the blowup of the image that had bothered me. Looked at the groups individually. It was easy to spot who was from what region because people were clumped together.

Had to figure that what my subconscious had spotted was on the periphery, so that's where I focused. It took a few minutes, but finally worked my way to the upper right corner. And there they were.

Hit speed dial and he answered on the first ring. "I saw the spectacle."

"I'm sure you did. Are you with Jeff?"

"No. I'm in my offices. Working. As I'm supposed to. No school visits or food fights for me."

"Blah, blah, blah. Do you remember the guys that were assigned to be my drivers and bodyguards?"

"You mean Len and Kyle? Yes, I remember them. I hired them. They're with Jeff, though, if you're worried."

"I wasn't because I figured they were doing something helpful somewhere. And I wasn't hit on the head, Chuckie, so yeah, I remember Len and Kyle. I'm talking about the guys before them, the ones I hated."

"You hated all of them. That's why I had Len and Kyle put in place. But no, I don't really remember them—I didn't work with them, you did. And that was at a time when your husband was doing his best to keep us far apart."

"Wow, did I interrupt an afternoon delight thing with you and Nathalie?"

He laughed. "No. I'm just not sure what you're calling about."

"The picture of the True Believers rally, the shot that bothered me. I think I know why I was bugged by the picture."

"I'm breathless with antici . . . pation."

"I knew I loved you. But I kind of thought you'd make the leap. I think I'm seeing some of them in this shot."

"You're sure?" There was no playfulness, boredom, or exasperation in his tone now. "How sure?"

"Not a hundred percent. I didn't hang with these guys too long and it was years ago. But I think I see them."

"Call Reader in, immediately. He'll know them. I'll be there in a moment."

Hung up and sent Reader a text. Alpha Team zipped into the room. Explained what I thought I'd seen and they all looked at the picture.

"I think you're right," Reader said slowly, as Chuckie joined us. "Those look like the drivers who we were pretty sure helped kill our agents when we all first got to D.C."

"Aged several years," Tim added. "Just like the rest of us."

"Oh, Operation Assassination was just full of fun, wasn't it?" Gadhavi chuckled. "Interesting name."

"Only Kitty calls them that," Chuckie said. "The rest of us just call them what they were—the latest in a long line of attempts to overthrow world governments and enslave sentient races."

"He's even more fun at parties."

This earned me chuckles from the room, even Chuckie himself. "However, these fall under our Centaurion's Most Wanted file."

"You have a wanted file just for American Centaurion?" Truly, I learned something new every day.

"The CIA has a wanted file for everyone," Gadhavi said.

"He's not wrong," Chuckie replied. "I only see two of them here, though."

"That doesn't mean there weren't more. They're at the edge of the shot, but the room looks like it goes on farther than the camera shows."

"They worked with aliens, though," Tim said. "Why hate them now?"

"Because the aliens they liked disappeared." As in, were the former Diplomatic Corps and were dead. "And we haven't done anything to find them. All of those men disappeared and went to our enemies. We shouldn't be surprised that some or all of them are here."

"I'll bump this list up to higher priority," Chuckie said. "It helps to know where they were."

"Are," Gadhavi said. "This rally has not broken up. It's being called a seminar, and they're there for several days."

Reader grimaced. "That means Alpha Team needs to get over there. Which means we can't be with Jeff and Kitty. I mean, I'd love to think that we'll catch these guys and be able to bring them in this afternoon, but I've learned things rarely go that smoothly."

"You'll need to coordinate with my agency, too," Chuckie said. "Meaning I'll need to assign resources. Though I should be able to make the fundraiser tonight."

"I will go as well," Gadhavi said.

"Thank you, that would be great." Hey, he had money and he was already offering to make donations. Had no idea if he had kids, but if he did, perhaps he wanted them to school at Food Fight Central. Stranger things and all that.

"Don't count on the rest of us," Serene said. "And we want the Pontifexes, both current and former, staying in the States, too."

Realized that Gower wasn't here. I mean, White wasn't here, either, but he'd been in the OSR. Gower hadn't. Chose to believe that it had taken me this long to notice Gower's absence because I was still shaken from the bake sale debacle. That was my story and I was sticking with it. "Where's Paul?"

"With Jeff," Serene replied. "Blessing the school."

"Wish he'd come with me to Sidwell, then."

"I don't," Reader said with a laugh. "But I don't like the idea of you going to your next stops without me."

"I will accompany the First Lady," Gadhavi said calmly. "No harm will befall her."

Could tell that the others wanted to argue. However, no one did. Yeah, Gadhavi had that effect on everyone.

"Good," Chuckie said finally. "And thank you."

Gadhavi gave Chuckie a formal bow of the head. "And I thank you for your hospitality and assistance in helping me to move into our brave new world together."

No one seemed to have a good comeback to this, so checked Mr. Watch as a way of smoothly moving us on. "Okay, I think we're late to get to the school, which is pretty much the story of my life. James, just keep us posted, but I agree that this is a job for Alpha Team. Chuckie, let me know if you're not making the fundraiser tonight, otherwise I'll see you here so we can all go over together."

"Sounds good. I'll coordinate through Vance if that plan needs to change in any way."

"Gotcha. Oh, James, before I forget—any movement on the robotics logo conundrum?"

"Yes, since we have more to go on now. We've found what looks like a variety of initials all tied together. We're still untangling it, but the assumption is that anyone who worked on it added their initials or logo design in. Titan Security and Yates-Corp logos are there, for certain, which makes sense. But, as with the Gaultier logo, those are well hidden."

"So it's the usual suspects," Tim said. "Nothing new, nothing exciting, either."

"Look for something that indicates LaRue or Madeleine Cartwright. Or even Monica Strauss. One or all of them were involved with what Eugene got, I think."

"I won't ask where your guess is coming from, other than the obvious," Reader said. "No idea if we can spot what LaRue's signature would be."

"Ask John." Jerked. "Oh. You know what? Ask John to look at the whole thing. There's a really good chance that whatever the writing is could be in the Anciannas alphabet."

"Good idea." Reader grinned. "See? This is yet another reason I wish we were rolling with you."

Hugged him. "Me, too. But for right now, we can't. So you do your thing and I'll do mine and together we'll save the world."

"Just like always."

"Or," Tim added, "as we call it, routine."

Gadhavi offered me his arm as we all chuckled. "Are you ready, Madam First Lady?"

"For whatever they throw at us, Mister Gadhavi the Honorable."

He grinned. "You are the only person I know who doesn't fear being their full self around me."

Chuckie snorted. "That's because she likes to live on the edge. The rest of us like living." He nodded to Gadhavi. "Don't hesitate to contact me or Angela immediately if you feel there's real danger. You, more than many others, I trust to make an objective decision about your and Kitty's welfare."

Gadhavi smiled. "Despite what you just said, you, too, are also your full self around me. So you, too, must enjoy living on the edge." He shook his head. "Clifford lied to me about all of you. It has been simple to prove. And because of his disloyalty and your help in stopping him, and all of your help, I promise you that you can all be yourselves around me. I am, as they say, now on your team, and teammates help each other and are allowed to be relaxed with each other."

Managed not to shout Go Team Grizzly but it took a lot of effort. Instead I stepped forward, arm in arm with a grizzly bear who'd chosen to sheath his claws. And they said politics was boring.

CHAPTER 50

GADHAVI AND I joined the others without incident, which, for the past day and a half, was something of a miracle.

Wasim and Naveed both eyed Gadhavi, who gave Wasim an extremely formal bow. "Your Highness, it is an honor to accompany you and Queen Katherine."

Wasim seemed shocked, but he lurched into Royal Action and bowed his head in return. "We appreciate your assistance."

"Kids, you ready?" I asked the Valentinos before any more bowing or protocol could be perpetrated.

"Prepped and enthused," Claire said.

Anthony shot a look at Lizzie. "You sure you don't want me to help at the Intergalactic School, Aunt Kitty? Wasim might be a better choice to go back to Sidwell."

"I'm sure," I said firmly. Wasim was not going to be out of my sight. He'd been here less than two days and had already seen more action than he'd probably experienced in his entire lifetime.

"You're always trying to get out of work," Sidney said. "Not today, little man."

"I'm not a little man anymore," Anthony muttered.

"The youngest always gets the brunt of the teasing," Gadhavi said. "But never fear. The youngest many times will use that and become the most powerful."

Decided I'd table asking Gadhavi where he fell in his family's birth order for a less stressful time. "Great. Where is our loyal press corps?"

"Already there," Vance said. "We figured it would be better to let them go ahead and get set up. Plus, from what we've heard, it's been extremely quiet and without incident over there, so it's a good opportunity for some positive press."

"Where's Bellie?"

"In your offices, with Nancy, who is staying on-site with the rest of your team, most of whom never want to leave the White House complex again, just in case."

"Good on Bellie's location and the team's decision to take a breather. You're staying here, too."

He shook his head. "I don't think that's a good idea."

"I think I need someone here who can handle the negative press that's likely frothing at our gates. Colette is great, but this is going to require a human with your kind of skills and you know it. Besides, you need to take care of that shiner you acquired."

Vance sighed. "If you insist." He brightened up. "But since you won't be here, the White House should be quiet, so that's nice."

"Hater. Anyway, I'm seriously going to be looking to see if we should transfer the kids to the Intergalactic School. If this first day was any indication, we're really not wanted at Sidwell."

"Missus Paster contacted me about that," Vance said. "She's worried that you'll want to pull all the kids and spent time stressing that Sidwell is normally not a hotbed of people rioting over baked goods. She definitely doesn't want you to leave the school."

"Give it a chance," Wasim said quietly. "The first impression isn't always the right one."

"Did you like it there?"

He shrugged. "No more or less than I've liked any new school. No more or less than I liked my first hours here. But if I'd judged America on my first hours I would be running home to Bahrain the moment you weren't looking."

Gadhavi nodded. "The Prince speaks wisely. And I will guarantee his safety, as well as your ward's. At either school."

Chose not to question this, or point out that no one could guarantee that, head of G-Company or not. Instead, did one last look around. "Not that I mind that they're likely taking a breather, but where's my Secret Service and Field security teams?"

"Other than Manfred, still prepping to go over to Sidwell with the Valentinos," Vance replied. "You'll fall under Jeff's protection details the moment you're there, and Len and Kyle are there as well, so you should be fine. Manfred will be here momentarily to handle the Kitty wrangling."

"And I'll be along as well, Missus Martini," White said.

"Sounds good." Pulled my earbuds out, plugged them into my phone so I could get calls if need be, and put them in my ears. "Hey, the smartest guy in *this* room suggested trying music to make a gate transfer easier on my stomach," I said to the "really?" looks I was getting. Wasim looked flattered. "This is my first opportunity to test if it works for me."

Went to my music. Sure enough, there was a Listen Like Thieves playlist here, too. Hit play and was rewarded with "Ready For Action" by The Crystal Method. Tunes going, almost everyone here that needed to be, dressed for success. Slid my phone into my back pocket and I was good to go.

True to Vance's promise, Manfred arrived now. He had a quick word with the Secret Service and Vance, then he stepped through the gate. I followed.

Wasim was on to something. While the trip was still nauseating, it wasn't nearly as bad with music going. Hoped Algar would create a Gates Playlist for me, but didn't count on it.

Stepped out not into a bathroom nor a broom closet nor a creepy basement. Managed not to faint from the shock. Looked like we were in a normal-sized, well-lit room that had only non-cloaked gates in it. Reminded me a little bit of the Dome but done in miniature, so to speak.

Len and Kyle were waiting for us. "We let you out of our sight for ten minutes and see what happens?" Kyle said with a grin.

"Hilarious. True, of course."

"You okay, Kitty?" Len asked. "And Lizzie?" he added as she stepped through.

"Yeah, we are."

"Totes okay." Lizzie looked around. "Where are we?"

"This is the North American Gate Room," Len said. "Each continent has its own room."

"Bet Antarctica's is the smallest."

"No," Kyle said. "We have an expectation of more alien races coming, many of which will need a frigid environment."

"More learning. Goody."

Naveed was the next to exit, then Wasim came through, earbuds in. Unlike me, he took them out and put them in his pocket. "Mister Gadhavi needed to take a call from Mister Reader. He and Mister White will be along shortly."

"Gotcha. We'll wait."

"Why is Mister Gadhavi coming along?" Len asked.

"Because he wants to." I mean, there was no other answer, really.

"I see." Len and Kyle exchanged the "we're screwed" look.

"He's coming to protect Queen Katherine," Wasim said.

Was about to ask Wasim why he was Queening me when I'd told him not to unless we weren't alone. Then again, with Gadhavi around, technically it wasn't "just family." Well, until Gadhavi moved himself into the Embassy's Zoo section to be closer to Kozlow and get to know Chernobog. The way things were going, I expected to be calling him Cousin Ali Baba within a month. Not that this was a bad thing, and so much better than calling him Enemy Mine.

Of course, Wasim might be trying to pass the boys a clue, the clue likely being "remind Gadhavi that Kitty has power, too." In which case, Wasim was right on.

My music changed to "Opportunities (Let's Make Lots of Money)" by the Pet Shop Boys, and Gadhavi stepped through the gate. Nice to know that Algar felt Gadhavi was helping us out for more than altruistic reasons.

"Is everything okay?" I asked Gadhavi as White came through the gate.

"Yes. Commander Reader needed me to smooth certain paths for his team. It's done, and he asked that I tell you not to worry."

"That admonition has never worked in the history of the world, but I'm sure something will come by to distract me and so make it seem like it worked."

"Which is victory, in that sense," Gadhavi said.

"Good point." Turned to the boys. "So, where's Jeff?"

"We have no idea," Len said cheerfully as they headed for the door. "We haven't seen him for hours."

CHAPTER 51

"UM, EXCUSE ME?"

Kyle grinned as he opened the door. "We're not here to protect Jeff, Kitty. That's the Secret Service's job. We're here to handle you."

"I resent that."

"Don't," White said, as Manfred went out ahead of us. "The boys haven't been here all that long."

"They're obviously yanking your chain, Kitty," Lizzie said as she breezed past me and headed after Manfred, White following her.

"Everyone's a critic."

Gadhavi offered me his arm again. "I look forward to seeing this campus now that it's completed."

Took his arm. "Lead on, Macduff."

All the gate rooms exited into a security setup very much like the one at the Dome. We were verified as being us, walked through an actual metal detector that detected many things in addition to metal, were given badges that identified us as guests, and handed a map. The A-Cs thought of everything.

Of course, this place was huge and not everyone had hyperspeed. Maps were a wise choice. The badges were color coded to identify whether the wearer was a student, teacher, faculty, parent or guardian, other family member, press, non-teaching or administrative staff, important dignitary, or security.

Len, Kyle, Manfred, and Naveed received red badges indicating they were security. The rest of us scored the dignitary color of purple. It was thrilling to have a different color on, even if it was just a small plastic rectangle, though my music changed to Shania Twain's "That Don't Impress Me Much," so clearly Algar merely found this to be a waste of time. Hater.

The gate rooms were, keeping to the A-C's burrowing roots, on the bottom floor of the underground section, meaning we had a lot of levels to get through. And all of them were packed. Apparently we'd arrived during break between class periods.

Of course, within fifty feet of leaving the gate room I was lost. Mazes were not my thing. Figured Chuckie had already memorized the layout from studying the architectural plans for five minutes, but for me, places like this were super mazes and I was super lost in them.

"We should have asked for a guide."

"Oh," Kyle said. "We thought you'd want to see everything first."

"Isn't that what a guide does? Takes you to the stuff you want to see and all that?"

White chuckled. "I know the layout, Missus Martini, never fear. And I know where Jeffrey is—but he did suggest you tour the school before you join up with him, Rajnish, and Paul."

White took point and the rest of us stuck close to him. Fortunately, Gadhavi had been given the Hyperspeed Dramamine because the school was huge. We used the slow form of hyperspeed—which always sounded like an oxymoron but wasn't—to get through it, but even the slower speed was hard on humans. Also fortunately, my three Middle Eastern men didn't object to holding hands with others, though Gadhavi made sure he was holding my hand and Wasim made even surer that he was holding Lizzie's.

I'd been intimately involved in the alien incursion we'd had less than three months ago, and I'd been around a lot of the new aliens now housing on Earth. However, I'd been with adults, and only a handful of them at any one time. There were a lot more than a handful here.

We zipped through spacious hallways that kept to the A-C theme of really nice hospital/austere luxury hotel with a lot of educational and One Galaxy Together! signs, posters, and artwork all over. There were potentially more of these than there were classrooms and auditoriums, and there were a tonnage of those.

Apparently One Galaxy Together! was the Intergalactic School's theme, since there were IGS: OGT and IGS/1GT logos on every kid somewhere, whether on their clothing, school supplies, backpacks, or all of the above, on the students who were really going all out for school spirit. The A-Cs seemed to have missed the whole mascot idea somewhere along the line, but slogans worked almost as well. My music switched to "Be True To Your School" by the Beach Boys, forcing me to control the Inner Hyena. Apparently Algar was as amused by the rampant school spirit as I was.

These happy propaganda hallways were filled with young people who looked like humanoid giant slugs, minotaurs, and honeybees, tree-people, sloths, lemurs, cloud-like manta rays all wearing some weird pod necklace, neon turtles, butterfly-fish, rat-sized cockroaches, and more besides. Along with a lot of A-Cs and other "pass for human" aliens like the Vata and those from Alphas Five and Six, we had other Alpha Centauri inhabitants represented, so we had humanoid cats, dogs, lizards, and a wide variety of Mustelidae including otters, skunks, and ferrets. Many of them were wearing caps with IGS on them.

There were adult versions of all of these and then some. "This reminds me of every spaceport, space bar, or space town scene in any science fiction movie you'd care to name."

"Isn't it wonderful?" White asked. "Peace on Earth, goodwill toward everyone."

"We have tentative peace that could end at any moment and, as you know, there are many with no goodwill toward anyone in this school, yourselves included," Gadhavi pointed out.

"I know," White said. "But this gives me hope. The future looks much brighter than it has."

"Let's hope it stays that way." Didn't want to be the voice of doom, but I was far too used to things blowing up in our faces to let ten minutes at the shiny new school make me let my guard down.

"This place looks so cool," Lizzie said wistfully.

Wasim didn't reply—he was too busy looking around at everyone and everything. "Amazing."

Heaved an internal sigh. I'd prefer them all to be here, too, where I knew we had A-C Security and Field agents every fifty feet. Of course, I'd also prefer to be here, full-time, rather than FLOTUSing around D.C. But duty called and not just for me and Jeff. Not for the first time I recognized the sacrifices families made for one person's ambition. Of course, Jeff hadn't wanted any of this, but that kind of made it worse—none of us truly wanted to be here, we just knew we needed to be and so did what we had to in order to protect and serve as many people as we could.

We reached ground level and stepped outside. It wasn't even noon here, which was easy to see without consulting Mr. Watch because the sun wasn't directly overhead. It was warm, much warmer than D.C., and I heaved a happy sigh.

"You like the heat?" Gadhavi asked.

"I'm a desert rat, so yeah, I do."

He chuckled. "We truly have much in common."

As my music changed to "Space Cowboy (Yippie-Yi-Yay)" by *NSYNC, I was saved from having to give any reply to this by the arrival of some people who were actually Space Turtles—my favorite Turleens flew over and landed in front of us.

Turleens looked like a cross between turtles and Jiminy Cricket, with small shells on their backs that doubled as their space cocoons. They were about three feet high, came in green and yellow neon shades, and had two long fingers and one long opposable thumb at the end of their hands and two long toes on their feet. They weren't as adorable as some of our alien friends, but they were definitely up there on the cuteness scale.

"Muddy, Dew, Mossy! I didn't know you guys would be here!"

Muddy Cabbage, Dew Lakes, and Mossy Bark—as their names translated into English—were high-ranking officers in the Turleen Air Force, which should have been called the Turleen Space Force but wasn't. Why ask why, right? At any rate, they'd helped us save the day in a variety of ways during Operation Immigration, and I liked them a lot.

Muddy was their leader, and he gave me a bow. Dew was next in command, and she saluted. Mossy was the third-highest ranker, but he neither bowed nor hugged. Instead he and I did an intricate hand and elbow slap thing we'd created once we'd saved the world. Mossy and I had started out kind of as frenemies because we were, according to everyone, a lot alike. We were best pals now, hence the gangsta style greeting.

"We're here to make sure that, when trouble appears, you have backup," Mossy said.

"Not that we expect trouble," Dew added hastily.

Mossy snorted. "I expect it. I guarantee that Kitty expects it, too."

"We saw what happened during the bake sale," Muddy shared. "I believe we should have gone there with you. We might have been able to keep things under better control."

"Speaking of trouble. And you might possibly have been able to calm it down. Or else the press would be having a field day about evil Space Turtles attacking in support of our evil parrot. Or worse."

"Things happen for a reason," Gadhavi said. "Have there been issues here?"

"No," Muddy said. "We have our people patrolling the exterior areas, assisted by some of the others who can fly and survive in this heat. The Vrierst can only assist if the need is extreme."

"How can they even go to school here?" I asked.

"Cooling pods," White replied, explaining those pod neck laces I'd seen. "NASA Base worked with the Vrierst to create them for all who will be here."

"They're working well," Dew confirmed. "But there's no reason to push them to their limits, either the cooling pods or the Vrierst themselves. We Turleens are fine covering for them."

"Space Turtles for the win. So, where is my husband? I sincerely thought that he'd be here, do a photo op, and leave. I realize that was a foolish thought, now that the real size of this place has hit me."

"It hasn't," White said. "We've only covered a fifth of it."

"It's laid out like a combination of Dulce and the Pentagon," Len said.

"Meaning Kitty will be lost here forever," Kyle added. "Don't worry, Len and I will be memorizing the layouts. Director Reynolds has already given us blueprints and the assignment."

"The propaganda here is impressive."

My music changed to Elton John's "Sweet Painted Lady" as the boys coughed. "You did assign her that job, and the others took it on with gusto," Len said.

"Who?" Thought about it. And the song. "Oh. Wow. Meriel, Rhonda, and Jane are in charge of this?" They were three hookers who'd gotten inadvertently involved with us at the start of Operation Immigration and had, basically, never left.

"Yes," Kyle said. "They are now the school's promotion and advertising department. Yes, we all know that means propaganda—Meriel reminds anyone within earshot of it daily."

"And they aren't the only ones," Len said. "Mickey and Garfield are working here, too. They're the heads of maintenance and janitorial."

Those two were bums who'd also been swept up by us when

crazed lunatics had blown up the D.C. precinct where they were in holding cells. That left two more that I now figured were around somewhere. "What about Bud and Cujo? And why isn't the Operations Team handling maintenance and janitorial?"

"Because this is a group school, not just an A-C location, and people need jobs," Kyle replied. "And those kids are helping out, but they're back in school now."

"Senior year," Len added. "They're talking to Director Reynolds about joining the CIA once they graduate."

"Sounds familiar." That was, after all, what had happened when I'd met Len and Kyle the first time. Bud and Cujo were on Florida State's football team, just as Len and Kyle had been on USC's. Per the boys, though, Trojans were better assistants than Seminoles.

"Anyway, they're not here right now," Kyle said. "Though they want to be included in anything they can be, so if we do something big where they can attend, they'll want to."

"Got it. Okay, so, again, where are my husband, his Chief of Staff, our Supreme Pontifex, and all of what's become our personal press corps?"

"Oh," Muddy said, seemingly surprised that I didn't know. "On the roof."

CHAPTER 52

SO MANY QUESTIONS came to me, but they all boiled down to one. "Why?"

"Best view," Mossy said. "I'm sure there are other reasons, but to save you time, they're all going to be long-winded excuses to avoid admitting the fact that it's the best view and therefore the best place to take pictures of a very photogenic set of people."

It was also the best place to put someone for a sniper to be able to shoot them. Didn't say this aloud, but was kind of surprised no one else seemed concerned. Then again, we were in the middle of the desert, next door to Dulce, and Dulce had ground-to-air missiles. They didn't use them often, but they had them.

"Succinctly put, and this is but one reason why Mossy and I are bonded forever. Can we get up to Jeff and the others right away, or do I need to see more of the gigantic compound?"

"We can go there," White said. "Jeffrey just wanted you to see some of it."

"As much as you could take, would be my guess," Lizzie said.

"You don't know us."

She snorted. "Right. I suppose Wasim and I have to go with you to the top?"

"Yes, you do. You can wander around after we've seen the great view and all that."

"It's more than just a great view," White said, as we broke down and took an elevator to the roof. Why we'd dragged ourselves up six floors but were swooshing up the last three was beyond me, but perhaps our small group was tired. It had been a long couple of days for everyone, after all, and we weren't close to it being over yet.

We exited onto the roof as my music changed to KT Tunstall's "Suddenly I See," and it was clear White hadn't been wrong. "Wow. Did we get whoever designed the Burj Khalifa to do this area?"

There was a beautiful wooden walkway that went through the middle of the roof, all the way around as far as I could tell. There were benches scattered about, some with shade, some without. On either side of the walkway there were planters and plots of land, all of which appeared to be being used to grow food and flowers, at least those that could survive in a desert atmosphere and climate. There were small metal fences, just delicate bars, really, that protected the plants and such without blocking them from view or making it difficult for someone to work in those areas. And about every hundred feet there were small wooden pathways that let you go to either the inner or outer sides.

The outer part of the roof had what looked like a jogging path. And, to keep said joggers from falling off the roof, there was a ten-foot wall made out of some kind of glass that went around the perimeter. Presumed it was bulletproof, but didn't think this was the right time to ask. The inner side of the roof had seven-foot glass walls and another path that presumably was either for jogging, walking, or looking down into the vast interior courtyard.

And there was definitely a view. From the outer path on this side you could see the Dulce Science Center, which looked like nothing much since that was its form of camouflage and only one story was aboveground. But you also had a great view of the natural desert, as well as the mountains in the distance.

The interior courtyard had a lot going on—ramadas where I presumed students ate or worked or just hung out, baseball field and football field with an impressive track around it, both complete with bleachers, basketball, volleyball, and tennis courts, several different pools, small buildings scattered about, and lots of young trees.

The complex was so large that I literally couldn't see the sides far from us. As Len had said, it was pentagon shaped, and I wasn't sure but had a feeling it was several times larger than the one in D.C. Hoped there was a really good evacuation plan in place that was more detailed than "find a A-C and hold on tight."

All lighting was solar, and there were both low lights and high ones, so that you'd be able to be up here safely at night. Everything fit just so and it all looked beautiful.

The feeling that I was looking at the City of the Future was strong, especially since there were so many different kinds of people down below. This also all reminded of more than the Burj Khalifa—it was also like the top of the All Seeing Mountain on Beta Eight. Presumed Algar had had his hand in the design in some way. Tears for Fears' "Me and My Big Ideas" came on. Yep, Algar had been involved.

"And we can't go here why?" Lizzie asked, sounding more sad than mouthy.

Heaved a sigh. "There are issues wherever someone goes, you know that. No place is perfect."

"This place looks it, though." Couldn't argue with her point of view.

We moved from the interior view back onto the main walkway. "Where are the others from here?"

"There are several small stages up here," White said. "They're at the nearest one to where we are."

We kept on walking, marveling at anything new, and shortly we arrived at our destination. The stage backed up against the outer wall, and there was a lovely mountain vista behind it, which was clearly why this was the chosen spot for it. Figured the other stages and such would be set up with similarly pretty background views.

Jeff was holding court with more than just our friendly press corps as "The Show" by Lenka came on. There were a lot of reporters and such here. Reminded me a lot of the press briefing room at the White House. Gower was seated onstage, and Joseph and Rob, Jeff's number one and number two Secret Service agents, were standing at either side, ready to leap if they had to, looking impressive and not the least bit bored otherwise. Representatives from every race that was schooling here, including human, were sort of grouped around the stage where the press could see them.

Raj met us as we got within range. "Kitty, how are you feeling?"

"Normal. Why?"

"Expect to get hit with questions about the bake sale. Are you up to replying?"

"Yes. A mishap sent some food flying and some kids and

others in attendance gave in to the urge to have a food fight. No one sustained anything other than minor injuries and things are back to normal."

"Nice spin." He didn't sound impressed.

"Fine. What do you want me to say?"

"I want you to deflect as much as possible. Positive comparisons to this school and Sidwell wherever possible."

Lizzie snorted. "Sidwell's fine, but this? This is like the Taj Mahal of school campuses. There is no comparison."

Raj gave her a polite smile. "I'm sure you'll want to support your own school."

"What own school? Wasim and I were there, like, two hours before all hell broke loose. It was fine. This looks totes better."

"I have to agree," Wasim said. "I believe if my Grandfather had seen this in person, I would be attending the Intergalactic School."

I didn't, but then again, I felt confident I knew the real reasons Raheem wanted Wasim with us. However, if we transferred Lizzie to the IGS, then Wasim would transfer as well, of that I was also confident.

However, having had time to think about it a little, I didn't want to transfer them here. It was indeed great, and sure it was only a gate away, but if Lizzie went here, then all the kids would want to go here, too. I didn't want the kids that far from me on a daily basis, Jamie in particular. If I could have been a room mom every day, then maybe. As the FLOTUS, it was bad enough that the kids were going to be schooling outside the Embassy. Schooling outside of the city, let alone the region, was that much worse and far more dangerous. Gates could fail, after all, and then my little girl and my bigger little girl and all the other school-aged kids I loved would be stranded across the country.

More than that, though, I didn't want all of us to give up, just because we'd had one kind of crappy experience. It would set a bad precedent for us and for what others thought of us. Sidwell might not be for our kids, or it might be the greatest place in the world for them. But two hours for the eldest and one day for the littler kids wasn't enough time to be able to tell.

"We have to give it a chance, all of us, before we throw in the towel. First days anywhere are hard. First days with a lot of scrutiny are harder. But Vance chose Sidwell for you guys for a reason. Let's give it a little time before we start whining."

Lizzie heaved a dramatic sigh. "Oh, as you command."

Wasim nodded. "I agree with Queen Katherine. I was not raised to give up."

"Then positive comparisons," Raj said. "If you're asked. If not, happy smiles any time Sidwell is mentioned."

The kids nodded. "Will do," Lizzie replied. "We can follow orders. When we have to."

Raj led us through the press. The others sat in the first row in seats clearly reserved for us, but I got to get right up onstage. Jeff stopped speaking and helped me up, giving me a kiss on the cheek. "You okay, baby?" he asked softly. Proving again why he was the greatest husband in the world, he didn't ask me to take my earbuds out and pay attention to the press briefing.

Kissed his cheek in return. "Yes, and all the kids are fine. I'm glad I'm here with you now, though. But sorry I'm not dressed for success." I was literally the only person here wearing casual clothes who was over the age of eighteen or whatever ages the various aliens considered to be school age. Frankly, Wasim was better dressed than me.

Jeff squeezed my hand and didn't let it go. "You always look great, Kitty, no matter what you're wearing."

"How are you doing? There are a tonnage of people here."

"My blocks are on high and I'm wearing a prototype—a reverse emotional blocker, so that, if it's on, I can block any and all emotions."

"Wow. What will the Science Center and NASA Base think of next?"

He grinned. "Per Serene, reverse engineering is where it's at." His expression went to serious. "But I can't even feel you, baby, or the kids when it's on. So if you get into trouble, you need to scream."

"Hey, I haven't been in trouble for at least an hour now."

He grinned again. "Could be a record."

Jeff kept hold of my hand, which made me feel happier than I had for most of this day, and we headed back to the front of the stage. Did get to see that the view from the stage was even better, because we were a bit higher.

Took a moment to admire said view. But as I started to turn back toward the front of the stage, my music changed to Joe Jackson's "Look Sharp."

Paused and looked around more closely. There were definitely flying aliens about—mostly Turleens, but I recognized a few others I'd met by now that had flight ability. None of them looked threatening. Well, none looked threatening toward the school. They were looking out, not in, and anyone on the outside might indeed feel threatened.

Checked out the mountains. Didn't see much of anything. Let my gaze travel down the mountain to the desert far away, then come closer. There was a lot of area to cover—even though the school complex was huge, it was dwarfed by the vast desert around it. Saw nothing untoward.

The grounds outside of the complex had all been done in what I considered upscale desert landscaping. So there were native trees, river rocks, cacti, and other flora and such that made it look like a desert botanical garden on the outside. But all that foliage gave someone room to hide. So I examined it as carefully as I could from over three stories up. And yet, still saw nothing untoward.

Was about to decide that Algar's clue had been about my choosing not to wear my FLOTUS Fatigues to this particular shindig, when the music changed to "In Dust We Trust" by The Chemical Brothers and my eye caught movement. There was a lot of dust on the horizon. More than a lone vehicle would create. More than a lone tank would create.

And there were no reasons for any vehicles to be out here. At least, no good reasons.

CHAPTER 53

THERE WERE NOT a lot of actual roads in or around the Science Center. Because of the gates and A-C hyperspeed, there wasn't a lot of need. There were a couple of really small, basically dirt roads that were used now and again, but in the past the vehicles that were housed in the motor pool area were used to get agents to superbeing formations that happened randomly in the desert. Mostly so they could transport a lot of weapons and carry back the dead or wounded. And most of those went through a gate to get to their location.

These days, with our superbeing formations down to about one a year, there was almost no reason to be driving in or out of the Science Center. And, since the IGS had all those nifty gates, too, just as little reason for someone to be driving in to the school.

Tugged on Jeff's hand. "I need your attention on something other than the press." He turned as requested and I pointed out the dust. "That doesn't look like a forming dust devil, and haboobs don't look anything like that, either. That's dust from either a lot of people, animals, or vehicles, emphasis on the phrase 'a lot,' and I think they're heading for the school, not the Science Center."

Jeff turned around. "Folks, we need to belay the rest of this for a short while. Raj, could you please escort our guests to the Visitor's Lounge for this part of the complex?"

Raj nodded and used his troubadour power to make everyone hearing him think that heading to the lounge was the greatest idea in the world. Well, almost everyone. Those who had come with me weren't leaving, and neither were those on Team Private Press Corps.

Raj called in A-C escorts, all of whom I recognized as being troubadours. Oh, sure, I couldn't have told anyone their names, but at least I had their talents down, which was something. Raj then had a quiet conversation with Adam, who nodded, and ordered the rest of his crew to leave. They didn't. Raj did some more talking and called in more troubadours. The crew agreed to leave. Raj held on to their camera. The troubadours took everyone who was going away to, hopefully, safety. Raj gave the cameras to some other troubadours, with the admonition to keep them under said troubadours' control.

Those remaining joined us onstage, Team Press Corps included. "What's wrong?" Raj asked as soon as the last guests were out of sight. "And let me say that there had better be something wrong because we need the good press this school is providing."

Pointed to the dust. "Something's wrong, likely bad news. Muddy, can you get your people who are on patrol to share what they see?"

He nodded, looked at Dew, who also nodded, then the two of them took flight. Mossy stayed with us. "I'm assuming it's an attack of some kind," he said. "And as for why our people haven't alerted anyone yet, my guess is that whatever's creating that dust looks benign."

"So not a tank, then."

"Could be a tank," Mossy said. "I'm just saying that if it *is* a tank, it's disguised as something innocuous."

"Based on wartime experience," Oliver said, "that dust looks far away, but it's quite visible. I'd expect to find out that we have several large vehicles or an inordinate number of people either on motorcycles or horses coming our way. Runners wouldn't stir up as much dust as we're seeing."

"I agree," Naveed said. "Based on the same kinds of experiences."

General consensus was that Mossy, Oliver, and Naveed were probably right, and since no one had binoculars and Jeff didn't want anyone else going out there, just in case, we'd have to wait to find out. Considered seeing if I could snag binoculars out of my purse, but there was just no way Jeff would believe I'd brought a pair along with me, so I refrained.

"Wonderful. Do we have any aliens who can't go through the gates who might be coming in a vehicle?" Hey, it was possible. Improbable, but possible.

"No," Gower replied, keeping our record of rarely if ever scoring the improbable consistent. "They're all more technologically advanced than we are on Earth, particularly as it relates to their own anatomies and abilities. All those issues were solved before the school opened. All our gates can now safely transport any kind of matter, even matter nothing like that found in the Solaris or Alpha Centauri systems."

"I thought we'd already used the gates for all of our aliens during Operation Immigration."

"No, we used them for several of the races and were fortunate that their anatomy and physiology was close enough to what we have in our two solar systems that nothing untoward happened. Basically, we were lucky, and no one wanted to trust in luck alone again."

We were at a school, but I chose not to ask any more questions about this. That last answer threatened to make my head hurt, and without Chuckie around to do Kitty Translations, didn't feel up to the task on my own, not after the last day and a half I'd had. Sex with Jeff seemed so very long ago.

Dew finally returned with a report as my music changed to "Danger Danger" by Hello Hollywood. "It's seven big, black busses. Muddy has stayed outside to command forces if needed."

Jeff and I looked at each other. "You're absolutely sure we're not bussing students in?"

He shook his head. "Not to my knowledge."

"Absolutely not," Gower said. "Security on the school is set up to prevent unauthorized people coming in. The only entry is via the gates system. Dew, was there writing on the busses?"

"Not that any have seen. The windows are black, too. The windshields are not, but they're also tinted enough that it's difficult to see who's driving."

"I grew up in pretty much the sunniest place around, and that level of tint sounds illegal. Meaning I think we should assume whatever's coming isn't our friend." Besides, Algar seemed sure. "Um . . . do we have an evacuation plan?"

"We do," Raj said. "But just about the worst thing in the world would be for us to have to evacuate the school on the first day."

"Worse than a bake sale food fight on the first day of school?" Lizzie asked.

"Much," Raj, White, Jeff, and Gower said in unison. Chose not to pay attention to the unison thing. I'd made a promise during Operation Immigration to ignore normal people talking in unison if I never again had to hear clones or the like doing so, and I was keeping that puppy.

Double-checked that Dion wasn't taking pictures. He wasn't. He looked too worried to use his camera as anything other than a blunt instrument. Shared that sentiment. He was huddled close to Jenkins who was, in turn, huddled next to Oliver. Surreptitiously checked out Adam and the Kristie-Bot. They looked worried, too, and had both moved closer to Joseph and Rob, who were doing their best to look impassive and not totally succeeding. Frankly, everyone had an expression of concern of some level on their faces.

"What kind of defenses does the school have?" I hadn't noted any on the blueprints, but that was the same as my saying that I didn't remember the names of all the A-C Field agents I'd worked with over the years—absolutely no surprise and proof of nothing.

"Dulce is next door," Raj replied.

"Uh huh. What else?" There was silence. "Hold on. There are no other defenses? Seriously? And Chuckie, let alone my mother, approved that?" Wondered if I was going to have to call Tom Curran and ask him to get the FBI to give the others some lectures on preparedness.

"No, we have other precautions," White said. "Such as shielding. Which I believe someone should probably put into place."

"Do we want to pull in any patrols first?" I asked.

"All but the Turleens, yes," Mossy said. "Our people are prepared. The others are helping in terms of surveillance, but I believe that we would prefer that they not be involved in fighting."

Dew leapt into the air. Shortly we had a stream of flying aliens zooming into the courtyard. Dew returned. "Only Turleens remain, and all are prepared for battle."

Jeff nodded and Raj pulled out his phone, stepped away, and started talking at hyperspeed. Saw the shimmer that indicated shielding was up. Hoped it would be enough for whatever was coming.

"There are things that can get through your shields," Mossy said, instantly dashing those hopes. "There are things that can get through anything."

"Wish we had a way of seeing anything." The busses were still far away. "I mean, if they're here to cause problems, Dulce could just blow them up."

Len was looking at his phone. Was about to ask if he could hold off on trying to get the high score on Bejeweled for a bit when he grunted. "The astronomy department has telescopes. They're mobile, too, since the classes are expected to come up to the roof at certain points in the school year."

Raj, who had just finished his call, also grunted, then made another.

"Where did you find that information?" Hey, no one here seemed to know about it.

"On our internal website, only A-C bases and select others have access."

"Set up by Chernobog," Kyle added. "Approved by Director Reynolds."

Len grinned at my expression. "No one's bothered to tell you about it because we all knew you'd only care when it mattered."

"You don't know me."

Everyone other than Adam, the Kristie-Bot, and Dion snorted. Gave it no more than one more day around me before those three would start snorting, too. "What She Came For" by Franz Ferdinand came onto my airwaves. And that did raise a point.

Looked at the Kristie-Bot. "Did you do this?"

"Do what?" She seemed genuinely confused.

"Trigger whatever or whoever's coming."

She rolled her eyes. "How many times will I have to say it before it gets through? You are how I become galaxy famous. There's nothing I want to do to harm you, or anyone else associated with you. Bad for you means bad for the Code Name: First Lady franchise."

Some A-Cs came up with seven small telescopes. They got them set up in a couple of seconds, then we took a look at what was coming, with some people taking turns. But not me. I held on to my telescope because it was time to toss on my Megalomaniac Girl cape, and Megalomaniac Girl did not give the eyepiece to anyone else.

The busses were as advertised, only, in addition to the window tinting, they were double-deckers, meaning there were a lot more of whoever or whatever inside. My guess was that each bus was holding between eighty to a hundred people. If there were people inside, that was.

"That tint is absolutely illegal. Meaning these aren't tourists. I'm with Mossy—those busses are likely a form of tank."

"We need to be sure before we bomb the hell out of them, though," Jeff said. "Because I don't want us killing innocent people just because their charter company skirts traffic laws."

"So, while we watch and they, thankfully, are doing nothing, are you serious that the only way in or out is via the gates?" "Ready To Go" by Guards came on. Was pretty sure it wasn't us Algar felt were ready.

"No," Kyle said before anyone else could answer. "That's the only way that's advertised and the only way students, faculty, visitors and such are supposed to get in or out. Officially. But there are exits because there have to be in case of gate malfunctions."

"Walter insisted," Len added. "As did several others, Director Reynolds, your mother, and Jeff included." Len was crystal clear about how little Jeff and I enjoyed the use of titles as applied to ourselves, which was only one of his sterling qualities.

Not a surprise that Walter had been consulted and put his foot down about this both. Walter had been intimately involved when our enemies had overtaken the Science Center to destroy us during Operation Infiltration. He knew full well that the gates could be compromised.

"Dulce is only half a mile away," Kyle went on. "So the expectation is that if full evacuation is necessary, everyone could get there quickly and safely, even on the hottest days."

Chose not to comment. Barring Brian having been involved in the architectural designs and these discussions, there was no one working with us who'd had to run in the Arizona desert heat for extended periods other than me. Meaning I should have been consulted about this so-called evacuation plan but wasn't. Now wasn't the time to complain about that, though. Now was the time to figure out if that plan could work.

Could it be done? Sure. Half a mile wasn't all that much. If you were in shape and had no disabilities. If you weren't or did, then fifty feet could be too much. Could all the many aliens do it? A-Cs, sure. The rest? Unlikely. A-Cs were from a hot planet and had two hearts. The aliens from outside the Alpha Centauri system weren't all equipped to handle the heat, let alone the distance, and not just the Vrierst. The idea of the Themnir moving fast at any time was hilarious, and while desert sand wasn't the same as salt, doubted that people who were giant slugs would do well sliding over it. And the less said about how the Faradawn would fare the better—willow trees and similar didn't really thrive in desert climates unless they had a ton of water and were protected from the elements.

"Are there tunnels that are connecting the school to the Science Center?" Hoped the answer was in the affirmative, because if the answer was no, my ban on getting pissed was over.

"Yes," Len said. Redemption. "But only two." And back to mostly pissed.

"They're big," Kyle added. "But it will still take a while to evacuate if there are no A-Cs who can assist with speed. Only those from the Alpha Centauri system seem to have hyperspeed. At least as we understand it."

"Fan-freaking-tastic. Seriously, how did Chuckie approve this? Or Mom? Or Walter? Because I see so many things I wouldn't have approved." So much for shutting up.

"We have the gates," Jeff said patiently. "We have the Science Center which is, for us, literally right next door. We have Home Base on ready alert and monitoring the school, just like the Science Center is. We have Field agents assigned to the school, more than are assigned to any other location, including the White House. We have shielding. We have security of all races, including human, represented."

Gadhavi cleared his throat. Realized he'd been utterly silent since we'd arrived at the stage. Wondered why, but that question was definitely for another time. "I believe Queen Katherine's concerns are quite valid. With very little planning G-Company could overtake and control this entire complex with ease. Despite all you've just said."

Then again, maybe he'd been quiet because he was planning a coup, for real or just to keep in practice. "In everyone's defense, the A-Cs are hella fast and they're trained in how to evacuate." God alone knew we'd had to do it often enough.

"And if you have traitors—and we have confirmed that you do—then they already know what you can do, what you are likely to rely on in case of emergencies, what you do not suspect, and so on. I strongly urge that you contact whoever has those missiles and have them sent into these busses. Apologize for a mistake later. If a mistake it will be, which I doubt."

My music changed to "Listen to What the Man Said" by Paul McCartney & Wings. Algar couldn't be clearer. And I agreed with him.

But before I or anyone else could do what Gadhavi suggested or argue about it one way or the other, the busses came to a halt, about a quarter of a mile away, pulling up next to each other in a kind of breakfront formation, not that this really worked in this particular setting. It wasn't as if they couldn't be hit from any direction or as if someone couldn't get around them with ease. Which made this formation sort of unsettling, especially based on what Gadhavi had just said.

The doors opened and people got out. Lots of people. Lots of people I recognized. Well, one person I recognized, duplicated what looked like well over six hundred times.

"Oh crap. It's a new Fem-Bot Army. Only our enemies have expanded their range."

They all, every last one of them, looked like Lizzie.

CHAPTER 54

"**WELL, NOW WE KNOW,** officially and fully, why Ansom Somerall and company wanted to get their paws on Lizzie."

"Why do they look like me?" Lizzie asked in a low, horrified voice. "*How* do they look like me?"

Stepped away from my telescope, pulled her away from hers, and hugged her tightly, ensuring my purse wasn't between us. She clutched me back even more tightly. She was shaking and I was pretty sure she was close to tears. Couldn't blame her.

"I agree," Jeff said, sounding furious and protective. "How?"

Thought about what I knew of Lizzie's past. "Your parents were Russian spies who were doing all they could to undermine the U.S. and destroy all aliens. They were willing to kill you when you didn't roll with them. And they were already hooked in with Harvey Gutermuth. To me, that says that your parents join the multitude of horrible people we know about who were willing to do terrible things to their children for their own gain or warped ideals. They gave whoever your specs so that they could create a new you if you did exactly what they hoped you wouldn't—stand up to them against their evil."

"How did they get Lizzie as she is now?" Len asked, sounding every bit as angry and protective as Jeff.

"They got pictures of her at her old school. They've gotten pictures of her as our ward. They've sent in things to film us like they did before. Pick an option, any of them work and more besides. Bottom line, that isn't important right now. Frankly, why they're right here, right now doesn't matter, either. Figuring out how to stop this particular Fem-Bot battalion is what counts."

"What do we do?" Lizzie asked, voice shaking.

Considered what I knew of Lizzie's present, or, rather,

Lizzie's life once she'd met Siler. Kissed the top of her head. "It's time for Quick Girl to help Superman and Megalomaniac Girl defeat the evil robot army."

She took a deep, shaky breath, let it out, then looked up at me and nodded. "Quick Girl reporting for action." Fear was gone, replaced with determination.

"That's my girl." Kissed her forehead, let her go, and turned to the others as my music changed to "Come Together" by the Beatles. Clearly Algar and I were of one mind. "Jeff, guaranteed we need Christopher here. Team Tough Guys, too, if they're available, but Christopher for certain. If he can't get in through the shielding, have him go to the Science Center, which should shield immediately after he arrives." You could get out reasonably easily through the A-C shield, but to get in required the shields to drop, which didn't feel like a wise choice right now.

Jeff was on his phone, barking orders, immediately. "What about Alpha Team?" Gower asked, while Jeff went back to doing what he did best outside of the bedroom—managing personnel in a crisis and leading the troops.

"They're dealing with our favorite hatemongers, and that means they're in the Middle East."

Gadhavi nodded. "From what Commander Reader and I discussed, they will not be able to be contacted for quite some time."

"Meaning they're going on a covert ops mission or similar, which is no surprise. Paul, it would be great if they were here, but I think we have to roll without them."

"I've advised Director Reynolds," Kyle said. "He's remaining in D.C. to ensure that if we need more support than the Science Center can provide that nothing mucks up the works."

"Good. Is he advising my mother?"

"Yes, already done. Same thing. She's staying in D.C. and has P.T.C.U. agents all over Sidwell, just in case. She's ready to send in a strike team or teams if we need them."

The Turleens were in a defensive formation, but nearer to the school than to the busses. Having worked with them in a danger situation before, I could attest to the fact that they were hard to hit and canny as hell. If we were going to have some kind of battle, I was happy the Turleens were here and on our side.

Jeff got off the phone. "We can't risk taking down the shields right now. Christopher, Buchanan, Siler, Wruck, Kevin, and the flyboys are over at the Science Center. Abigail and Mahin went to Sidwell, just in case this is a ploy to have us distracted so someone can grab Jamie. We're going to send missiles at those busses and those Fem-Bots as soon as I give the order, and then the others can mop up."

My music changed to "Stop Drop and Roll" by the Squirrel Nut Zippers. "Wait!"

Everyone stared at me. "Why?" Jeff asked. "Isn't this exactly what you wanted us to do?"

Tried to figure out Algar's clue, and I had to do it fast, since saying "my song says to stop" would only earn me a lot of problems, potentially including an extended stay in a mental hospital. My music switched again, this time to ZZ Top's "Waitin' for the Bus." Looked at the busses. "There's something wrong. They're lined up too neatly, the Fem-Bots aren't doing anything, there's zero aggression going on from their side. Something's wrong and I think that means they want us to fire first. So, just . . . don't fire yet."

Everyone started to talk at me. Other than Mossy. He shook his head, grabbed my hand, and leapt up into the air. As we rose up, he flipped me onto his shell and then pulled his head and limbs inside as the Turleens did when they were flying. "Hang on," he called to me. He had to shout since everyone else was yelling at us and Jeff was bellowing for me to get down. Hoped White and Gower would get him calmed down—we didn't want to have to replace all the glass this soon.

Dug into my purse. "Goggles, goggles, my kingdom for goggles." My hand hit a pair and I pulled them out. "You're the best, thank you so much." Got the goggles on as we breached the shield. Flipped myself onto Mossy's shell in the way I'd learned to do during Operation Immigration—as if I was riding a sports bike.

Mossy flew us past the other Turleens and to the busses. Couldn't speak for him, but I was keeping a very sharp lookout for projectiles and the like.

But nothing came at us.

"I don't see any weapons," Mossy said. As always, wasn't sure how I could hear any Turleen when they were inside their shell and I was on their back, but I could and that was all that mattered.

"Me either." My music changed to "Look Away" by Hootie & the Blowfish. Considered this. "Let's do a fast perimeter sweep."

Mossy didn't reply, but we zoomed off. The school was

gigantic—big enough to house at least half of the aliens that had come to Earth, maybe all of them. Sure, it was supposed to be for education, but the A-Cs were big on fail-safes.

We did a full sweep at top speed. When we got back to where we'd started, the busses and Fem-Bots were still in their weird Mexican standoff position. "Let's check the Science Center."

We did. Spotted nothing untoward, but did note that the busses and Fem-Bots were plenty close to the Science Center. Closer to the school, yes, but still, facing both buildings, in that sense. And therefore able to spot people leaving one building to get to the other.

"What now?" Mossy asked.

"Slow it down and let's check the school's perimeter again."

We went back to where we'd started—everything was the same and no one was making a move. My phone rang. Happily, my earbuds allowed me to answer almost hands-free. "Turleen Airways, where you're never fully dressed without a smile and a shell. How may we assist you today?"

Jeff sighed. "Why? That's the only question I'm asking. Why are you two out there, flying around like you're having a fun afternoon jaunt?"

"Because this screams setup, and it also screams trap, and there aren't enough Turleens around to carry Gadhavi with us."

"Why would you want him and not me?" Jeff sounded a little hurt.

"Because you're the most important man in the country if not the world. And I'd take Gadhavi because this particular weird standoff is probably bothering him like it's bothering me and Mossy."

"Yeah, it is. Hang on. What?" Heard voices in the background. "Your newest boyfriend says that this reminds him strongly of the Trojan Horse. He says to search carefully."

"Will do. Keep the trigger fingers on the missiles, just don't send them until I say, okay?"

"When have I argued with your command decisions?"

"Wow, do we have the time? Though, honestly, probably not as often as I've argued with yours."

"Thanks for making my point. Be careful, baby. I don't care about bad press. I care about you getting hurt or worse."

"Right back atcha, Jeff. Now, hang up. I need to concentrate and, despite how easy I make it look, riding a Turleen is a little challenging."

"You make it look great, and sexy, too," Jeff purred. His sexy purr. Yeah, I was definitely coming back safe and sound if I had anything to say about it.

"I'm always grateful you know what motivates me." He laughed and hung up. My music came back on, but now "Seek & Destroy" by Metallica was on. Not that I'd needed the hint, but still, confirmation was always nice.

Mossy and I had been flying along the wall where Jeff and the others were, and keeping low—not so low that someone could grab us, but low enough that we could see the ground and groundcover easily.

This close, there was a lot more than I'd been able to note from above. Lots of various forms of desert and river rock, all done in what I was fairly sure were Feng Shui patterns. Many cacti. Lots of small bushes. Many palo verde trees and others in the same family. Desert wild flowers. And no one and nothing of note otherwise.

The building was a bit different from human buildings. The outer walls of the ground floor had no windows at all. The next two levels were all dark tinted glass, and whoever had gotten the tinting job for those busses had also scored the contract for the Intergalactic School, because the tint was easily as dark if not darker. Had no idea if it was as dark on the inside, since I hadn't gone through anything in the upper levels other than an elevator and the roof.

However, what there were on the first floor were doors. They looked sturdy and like they locked from the inside, which was good. No visible locks I could spot, and no door handles, which was also good. But there were plenty of them. Tried to count but gave up and went with "lots" as my definitive number. None looked disturbed or like someone had tried to bash in, but we were too high up for me to tell if someone had tried to pull the doors open from the outside via unconventional means.

The side was long. I was fairly sure it was a mile if it was an inch. Flying on Mossy made it a lot easier to traverse and much faster than any method save hyperspeed, but anyone in shape and with the ability to run distance would have no issues running around the outside of this beast. And Field agents were required to be able to run fifty miles without issue. So the size wasn't a concern, in that sense.

But by the time we turned the corner for the next side I could barely see the busses. Meaning that anything could be going on and unless every single person was alerted, it was likely that no one would even notice. No one on the first floor could see out and no one on the second and third floors or the roof would have reason to look down. And even if they did, in a building this huge, Security wouldn't sound an all-hands alarm unless they knew for sure there was a full-facility problem.

Considered this. We'd had a lot of airborne beings patrolling. But we'd pulled them in the moment the busses had been spotted, and all the Turleens had gone to that side. So the only people guarding the other four sides of the behemoth were now gone. Gadhavi was right—this was starting to smell like the biggest bait and switch around.

"We need to be prepared to find someone or a small group of someones trying to break in," I told Mossy. "I'm betting they'll be on the next side, by the way."

"Why? The side, I mean. I agree with you on the fact that our enemies have focused us all on what looks like the threat in front of us and I expect to find out the real threat is behind us."

"I'm just spitballing here, but the side farthest from where we all were would be my guess. And they'd know because the press was filming, meaning they could just look at the view behind Jeff and determine which side of the building he was on."

"Why would we have missed them before?"

Had been considering this. "We were higher up, going a lot faster, and they know to look for patrols. We don't know to look where they are. There are a lot of hiding places—most of the foliage was put in as mature plants. Makes it prettier but gives many more hiding places."

We found no one on this side. Rounded the next corner. Nothing nearby. We continued on. And were rewarded about halfway along this side. If rewarded was the right word. Because it was hard to feel like spotting one of the doors slightly ajar was one for the win column.

Mossy landed and we went to investigate. The door opened easily. The outside had a couple of circular markings on it. The inner doors had had a long bar lock, had being the operative word. The bar was shattered. "I think they used a strong suction device, like you'd use to hold a heavy glass window, to pull this door open."

"They?"

"Could be more than one, yeah. But the Bots are strong. So could just be one." My music changed to "Problem Girl" by Rob Thomas. "Figure it's just one, though."

"One would be harder to spot," Mossy agreed. "Think this was left open for others to use?"

"Certain of it, yeah. I mean, there are hundreds of Lizzie-Bots out there. It would be safe to assume that some could get past us."

"Will they need to even bother is the question." Mossy pointed to the words on the inside of the door we'd just opened.

Emergency Exit—Operations Section.

CHAPTER 55

WE STEPPED INSIDE. No one was there, which wasn't a surprise. Assumed whoever had broken in had moved into position the moment the aerial support left the area. Fem-Bots were fast as well as strong, and this one would have been coming from the direction of one of the tiny towns on the main highway that was more of a place to get gas than anything else. It was far away, but not for a well-made robot. And one person running wouldn't raise much dust.

We were in a short hallway. Went to the opposite door. Opened it carefully—there was a lot of equipment in there. Saw no people, but then again, we weren't far in and, based on what I could see ahead, we were in the back of this room.

"What now?" Mossy asked softly. "If we're assuming that it's another Fem-Bot that looks like Lizzie, then all she would have to do is slip out of this room and she'd have the run of the entire complex."

"She won't be wearing a badge."

"So what? She's your ward. All she has to say is that she got separated from you and lost her badge somehow. They'll give her another one and send her on her way."

"To do God knows what, yeah." My music changed to "A Girl Like You" by The Smithereens. "Or, it could be worse. The Fem-Bot could be one that looks like me."

Mossy and I exchanged the "we're so screwed" look. "We need to alert the others," he said.

"And tell them what? We're infiltrated but we're going to have to evacuate a two-square-mile complex and then see if we can spot the robot imitating me? By the time we do that, whatever the Bot Army has planned will be put into action and likely completed."

"Well, I'm out of ideas." Mossy looked around. "How is it that no alarms have gone off? An emergency exit was ripped open from the outside. Shouldn't something have triggered?"

"Yeah, it should have." Checked the area nearest these others doors. "There. It's an emergency box. All they'd have to do was find it and shut it off. Done quickly enough, it would appear to be a glitch and potentially be ignored, if it was even noticed."

We used hyperspeed to check the entire room. No one and nothing looked amiss, not that I was a great judge of that one way or the other. Looked through the far door—it opened up to a main walkway. We closed the door and looked at each other. "Time to call Jeff, isn't it?"

"Past time." Mossy definitely had a sarcasm knob.

Hit Jeff's speed dial. "Yes, yes, you were right."

"I was right about what?" Jeff asked.

"Oh, probably a lot of things." Told him about what we'd found and what we suspected.

"I'm releasing the missiles," he said when I was done with one of my shorter Recap Girl updates. "So hang on." Heard him give the go order. "Okay, Kitty, you two—"

But before Jeff could tell me anything else, heard a lot of shouting and a couple screams and then a big explosion. The phone went dead.

"Hurry! Something's wrong!" We ran outside, I jumped on Mossy's back, and we raced off, this time at top speed. Was really glad I hadn't bothered to take the goggles off when we were inside.

As we sped around the next corner I could see the Science Center in the distance. Therefore, I could see a bomb explode just above it, having, I was pretty sure, just hit the shield. "What the hell? Did those busses look weaponized to you?"

"No idea, we didn't search them closely."

Around the next corner. Fortunately, we were flying low—a missile zoomed over our heads with what looked like most if not all of the Turleens on patrol following right after. "The busses have missile launchers?" My music turned back on, this time playing "Reflection" by Tool.

We reached the side we'd started at in time to watch a missile head from Dulce right for the busses, bounce off of something we couldn't see, and ricochet back toward the school. It hit, near to where we were, and the force knocked Mossy to the ground.

Scrambled to my feet and was relieved to see Mossy do the same. "Why are they still firing?" he shouted as another missile fired from Dulce.

"No idea." Knew how to find out, though. Pulled out my phone and hit his number on speed dial.

"Madam First Lady, we're a little busy," William said.

"Dude, you're busy blowing up our own buildings. What gives?"

"We were told to fire seven missiles, one for each bus. We programmed two to fire at once, then the rest of them to fire ten seconds apart. But I can't stop them—the first two were aimed at the busses on the outer ends. Those bounced back and one hit the school's shield, but the other ricocheted into us. Our shield held, but we felt shockwaves. We're offline and can't stop anything. We'll be back online quickly once the missiles are done firing, but we have two more to go."

No sooner mentioned than another fired. This one ricocheted back into the Science Center. "William . . . I think that missile just took out the shielding on the Science Center." Looked at the school. We were very close to it. Ran over and touched the wall. "And it's already down on the School, at least in the area where I am." Which was where the busses were.

"Then you have five seconds before the last missile launches."

Didn't stop to question or tell Mossy what I was doing. Just took off at the fastest hyperspeed I could manage and headed for the busses. It was easy enough to get through the Lizzie-Bot Battalion—they weren't paying any attention to me. Instead they'd split into two groups. One heading for the school, the other for the Science Center.

Reached the busses. Didn't try to go in between them—this close I could see the faint shimmer of whatever was being used to reflect the missiles back. Instead, ran around toward the left-most bus, turned when I saw where the shimmer stopped, then ran inside. I had about two seconds to find the off switch. Pity I had no idea where it was.

"I need a bomb!" Reached into my purse. There was a bomb, right on top. Slammed it onto the driver's seat, hit the button, and ran like hell out of the bus. Slammed into Mossy. Grabbed him and kept running.

Heard the explosion. Then heard another, bigger one. Kept

going until I was sure we were out of range, then turned around. The bus I'd been in had blown up. Couldn't tell if that had created a chain reaction or not, but the other busses were blown up as well and I saw no missile heading anywhere else.

Got a look at the Lizzie-Bots. Most of them were at the buildings, and they were climbing up the walls. Not like a person would, but like a spider would, or, rather, like a creepy Bot manifestation of a spider would—upper arms and thighs going straight out from the bodies, knees and elbows bent, hands and feet flat against the wall, head tilted back so that it was straight up in a position that no human would want to hold for long.

Time to make another call. Thankfully he answered. "Kitty, are you okay?"

"Yeah, Len, so far. Is Jeff alright? Our call went dead."

"Joseph and Rob tackled him when the missile was heading straight for us. He lost his hold on his phone and then I think it got trampled while the rest of us were running away. But Jeff's fine. None of us are hurt."

"Yet. The Lizzie-Bots are heading for everyone. But it's worse. I think there's a Kitty-Bot of some kind loose inside the school. I need you to find it and destroy it before it does any more damage."

"We can't leave Jeff here."

"You can and you will. This is a job for you guys—you know I'm outside. No one else does. Take Manfred and Kyle and get going."

"I don't think the three of us can defeat a Bot with the weapons we have."

"Then take Naveed, Joseph, and Rob with you, too. Take whoever other than Lizzie, Wasim, Paul, and Jeff. If you see a Kitty or a Lizzie, kill them without hesitation. That's a direct order. The flyboys would follow that order—will you?"

With that I hung up. Called Christopher. "Where are you?" he asked without preamble.

"Outside, where I think you and Team Tough Guys need to be. The Lizzie-Bots are going to overrun the Science Center and the school. We need the Flash. And get the flyboys into the air shooting every Bot they can find. There are hundreds of them."

"The Bots can't get inside."

"Yes, they can. I'd thought they'd brought a suction tool with them, but I think they have suction cups on their hands and feet. It's how they're climbing like creepy spiders right now. We have at least one inside and, crap! Gotta go. Do what I said!" Hung up and grabbed Mossy. "We have to get to that open door."

He turned back into a Turleen Pod, I jumped on, and we raced off, zooming around the corners at top speed. This would have been totally fun if we weren't in a life-and-death situation. Which was, basically, my statement for most of the things that had happened to me since meeting my first alien. Good thing said first alien was both the hottest thing on two legs and confirmed to be unharmed.

Reached the open door just before a set of Lizzie-Bots got there, made sure none were inside that I could see, and slammed the door shut. And now it was the fun of hand-to-hand combat against things that appeared to be quadruple-jointed and I knew to be hella strong and close to impossible to destroy without a rocket launcher. Which I didn't have. Could ask my purse for it, but that seemed iffy, and Mossy would absolutely notice.

"Get out of our way," they all said in unison. Yep, regular people unison would never really bother me again.

"Nope." Saw an explosion in the distance. Sincerely hoped the Turleens had brought the missile down before it hit anything or anyone. Then I was swarmed by Lizzie-Bots and was too busy fighting to pay attention to too much else.

CHAPTER 56

MOSSY AND I did our best to keep our backs to the door—protection for us and it kept the Lizzie-Bots out. For now.

But these Bots didn't fight as I was used to. They didn't fight like Lizzie fought, either. They were jerky and smooth at the same time and I wasn't getting their rhythm. Even though I was actually moving far faster than the Bots were, I wasn't connecting with them, but they were certainly managing to hit me.

My music changed to Lou Bega's "Mambo No. 5" and before I could even question why I actually started moving to the beat because it was so darned peppy that I couldn't help it. And dodged several hits. Listened to the lyrics—jumped, ducked, stepped right or left when the song said and, voila, missed more hits.

Chose not to ask why. Clearly the Bots were programmed to fight in a kind of double syncopated rhythm, which pretty much no human or A-C would normally do and, as the song rolled into repeat, realized it was also a lot like the beats when you were riding a horse.

Mossy saw that I was having results and he imitated my movements. It was like we were in a competitive dance and fight competition. Dancing with the Killer Bots. If you didn't get a good score from the judges you'd be destroyed by the Bots. Maybe it would catch on.

The Bots weren't programmed to switch it up, or else they didn't realize we were fighting them more successfully than we should be able to. Of course, we were mostly in defensive mode, but the song was really great for this.

Turleens returned, saw what was going on, landed, and started fighting. Only they didn't have the song in their ears or me right next to them to watch. Heard the music go louder somehow, and suddenly the other Turleens seemed to catch on. Risked a look into my purse—yep, my iPod was going and the speakers were on high. Lou Bega's only hit was working its magic once again, and my phone and iPod were, thankfully, synced so the beats didn't change for me.

The other Turleens got into it in a big way and were working in groups of two, three, and four. Time for team synchronized dance-fighting! Sincerely hoped for two things—that we'd manage to stop all these Lizzie-Bots and that no one would see us.

Some of these Lizzie-Bots tried for leaping up onto the walls and climbing, but the Turleens beat them down by landing on the Bots' shoulders and then hopping in time to the song's beat. Then, once those Bots were on the ground, the Turleens kept on dancing on their backs. It seemed to work. At least, those Bots didn't get up again.

Muddy landed on my other side from Mossy. "Interesting choice," he said as we all did the steps that got us out of harm's way and then were able to hit our opponents.

"Dude, I live my life by one code and one code only— whatever works."

"I thought it was going with the crazy," Mossy said, as we all did the roll your hands over each other while bending down and stepping forward move that meant the Lizzie-Bots' hits went over our heads but we were able to hit their torsos with our shoulders.

"Not my fault the crazy is what always seems to work." Did rising elbows when Bega sang the word "trumpet." Knocked two Lizzie-Bots back. This song was great. Realized it had been far too long since Jeff and I had gotten to go dancing. Then again, it was rare for the President and First Lady to get to get down and boogie. Decided to do my best to enjoy this.

More Bots came around the two corners. Well, presumed that's where they'd come from. The building was so huge it was hard to be sure. But they seemed to be on the run. Not a problem, Kitty and the Turleens were showing off their smooth moves. We just added in the new Bots to the program without a lot of issue.

My phone rang. Was truly thankful that the iPod was going. "What? Kind of busy here."

"Where are you?" William asked, thankfully foregoing titles.

"Our agents can't get through these Bots to get to the school. We're taking a lot of hits. We've managed to keep them from getting inside the Science Center, but that's about it."

There was nothing for it. "Um, put Lou Bega's "Mambo Number Five" on the sound system and blast that sucker as loudly as you can. If you can pipe it into or at least around the school, do so."

There was silence while I did a sweep in time to the music. Anything worked, as long as I could keep to the beat. "Excuse me? Kitty, are you alright?"

"Yes, I am, and the Turleens and I are kind of winning our particular fight. William, just do it, that's a FLOTUS order and all that jazz. And do it fast. I know you have the music, I programmed my iPod to update into the Science Center." Because I never wanted to be without tunes and we had the capability to do this. I might not know how the gates really worked, but if it related to the ability to have music with me at all times, I was the go-to girl. And right now, the go-go girl, too.

"Yes, ma'am." Heard the music come blaring out what sounded like all over, meaning William had managed to get the song to play at the school as well. And since I knew Algar had taken the wheel, the song started up perfectly with what was coming out of my purse.

"Now, tell the agents to move to the beat. If they can possibly *not* move to this beat."

Heard William share that order. "It's working!" He sounded totally shocked. Not that I could blame him.

"Don't film this."

"I'd imagine that's too late, since you have press at the school."

"Super. Then don't allow anyone to share the film. Gotta concentrate," Bega had just told me to put my hand on the ground and I didn't want to miss my cues. "Call if you need me, otherwise, make sure that if anyone finds a Kitty in either building that they get rid of her as fast as possible. I'm outside, in case you weren't sure."

"Got it and on it." William disconnected. My music started up again.

The Turleens were really quite good at the mambo. Wondered if I could send a tape of us to Kenny Ortega for consideration in his next musical production but figured that I didn't need any more impetus for anyone to think Code Name: First

Lady was a good idea. Though the Mambo Turtles had a cute ring to it.

Bots were down and staying down. Sure, we had lots more, but any down was a good thing. And still we mamboed on.

A thought occurred. Probably should have occurred to me sooner, but hey, I was busy dancing to save the world. "Muddy, we need to be sure that these Bots aren't making it over the glass walls."

"They aren't. I checked before I came to assist you. Most of them diverted when people came out of the Science Center. Though I don't understand why."

"I do. They have a Kitty-Bot inside the school. This is all distraction."

"It's effective. Why aren't you inside?"

"I delegated."

"You're capable of that?" He sounded like he was about to tell me to pull the other one.

Was about to give him a snide reply when the doors opened, shoving the three of us to the sides. Jumped back to stop whoever from doing whatever, but, happily, it wasn't a Kitty- or Lizzie-Bot that had opened the doors.

It was Jeff.

Jeff grabbed my hand and swung me out of the way of a Bot hit. To the beat. "I see we're doing things a little differently today." He grinned and spun me, which moved me out of the way and his free hand into the face of an attacking Bot.

We mamboed together side-by-side. "Where are the kids?"

"They're locked in with Paul, Naveed, Jenkins, and Dion. I know you suggested Naveed go help hunt down infiltrating Bots, but he refused to leave Wasim and, under the circumstances, I had to admit he was right. The others have orders to kill anything that appears to be you or Lizzie and they're on the hunt."

"Richard isn't with the kids?"

"No, Missus Martini, because I, too, enjoy dancing." White came out mamboing all the way and took out two Bots at once.

"Mister White, it's good to be boogying with you." Now we all did the hand roll, bend, and hit with the shoulder thing. "I'm amazed you guys know these moves."

"We watched you," White said. "The school and the Science Center both have perimeter cameras."

"Ah." What else, really, was there to say? Presumably William hadn't mentioned it because he was planning to sell the footage or something. Or else realized it didn't matter. Had to vote for the latter on that one.

"You're getting results, baby, and that's what matters. I don't even want to know how you thought of it, but it was inspired. It was interesting to see Christopher, Buchanan, and Siler doing this. Kevin and Wruck are naturals, though."

"Good to know. I wish James was here. He'd be awesome at this. Tim, too. Though you two are really representing."

"Thanks for that. And don't worry. The flyboys never got off the ground, and all five of them are making you proud around the front of the school."

"How did they get there?"

"Christopher took time out from his learning of this new dance craze to get them over to where they were requested," White said as we all put a hand on the ground and sent rising kicks up into Bot stomachs.

"What about the others?"

As I asked this, Adam, Raj, and the Kristie-Bot appeared, moving immediately into their team mambo routine.

"What are Adam and Kristie doing here?"

"Helping," the Kristie-Bot said. "And, this is going to be a great scene when the movie series gets to it!" Had to give her this—she was enthused, and that was indeed something.

The reinforcements helped a lot. The Lizzie-Bots were leaping for the walls, but the Turleens knocked them down and the rest of us mamboed them into submission. In less time than I'd have thought we had the last Lizzie-Bot trampled on the ground.

"Where are Len, Kyle, Joseph, Rob, Manfred, Mister Joel Oliver, and Gadhavi?"

"Hopefully destroying whatever infiltrated," Jeff replied.

The song ended and the music stopped. "I guess we stopped all the Bots." Or someone had stopped the music because it was helping us. Was about to suggest we get inside and start searching pronto, when something rolled out through the doorway.

A severed head.

CHAPTER 57

EVERYONE JUMPED as the head rolled quickly, bounced twice, and came to a stop at my feet. It was my head.

Or, rather, my robotic head. The neck had wires hanging out of it and the eyes were definitely glassy, as in made of glass or some other silica that resembled human eyes.

"And that is how we deal with those who oppose us," Gadhavi roared as he barreled out, robes flying, waving a crowbar around like it was a sword.

Len and Kyle were right behind him. They each had a Bot arm and leg. He tucked the crowbar into the belt around his waist as the boys tossed the Bot limbs onto the ground, then high-fived both of them at the same time. Joseph and Rob came out carrying the rest of the Bot body. They tossed it onto one of the many Bot piles. Then they, too, got high fives from Gadhavi.

Manfred and Oliver arrived now. "The rest of the facility is secured," Manfred shared, which earned him his Gadhavi High-Five.

"And press is contained as well," Oliver added, presumably to ensure he didn't miss out on his high-five, which he did not. "As are the visiting dignitaries."

"Well done everyone," Gadhavi roared. He was clearly having a great time. So were the other guys with him. Obviously this had been a much needed and happy team-building experience for all. Actively chose not to notice that they'd team-built by destroying my effigy.

"Um, go you guys and all that. But where did you find this Kitty-Bot and how are you sure all's secured inside?"

"We're secured because William sent all the Field agents in the school to guard all the outer doors," Manfred shared. "Even though the doors open out, we have other ways of locking and barricading the doors so that they won't open no matter what. The Field teams got those locks and barricades in place, then stayed there, to ensure that nothing could get in. Several teams were just in time, but there were no breaches other than this door."

"Great news. Is that how you found this particular Kitty-Bot?"

"We found her exactly where Mister Joel Oliver expected her to be," Gadhavi shared. He looked to Oliver expectantly.

Oliver gave Gadhavi a little bow. "Once Mister Gadhavi made the good point that the many Bots were likely there as a distraction, I assumed that the goal would relate to some form of sabotage and takeover versus destruction. President Martini shared that you'd found an opened door that led to the Operations area. And Mister Parker shared that you hadn't found the infiltrator. Meaning she was looking for something and it wasn't in the Operations Section."

"Makes sense. So where was she?"

"With the press and the rest of the visiting alien and human dignitaries," Oliver said, as if this was obvious. "Nothing says 'don't trust anyone from Earth' like the First Lady murdering important people in front of the press corps at the Intergalactic School on the first day of school, when all the offspring of every alien who's come to Earth are hundreds to thousands of miles away from their parents and others from their race."

"Wow. So, she was there?"

"Yes, and just about to start mayhem when we arrived. Mister Gadhavi was quite impressive."

"I'll bet. Where did you find that crowbar?" I asked him.

Gadhavi shrugged. "Each section has a small Operations and Maintenance area. We checked the one nearest to the stairway we used to get down from the roof. There weren't a lot of options for weapons, but crowbars are effective in many ways."

"True enough. So, did you beat her to death, so to speak, in front of the press?"

"No," Len said. "She ran. Mister Joel Oliver and Manfred stayed to explain what was really going on. The rest of us took off after her."

"The Bots don't have hyperspeed, which has always been a freaking blessing. But they're fast."

Kyle gave me the "really?" look. "We're agents, Kitty. All of us. And Mister Gadhavi keeps in shape, trust us. Len's the fastest of us, he got to her first and did a great tackle. Especially for a quarterback."

Len grinned. "Kyle's a lot faster than he looks, too."

"Then it was a matter of all of us getting her contained," Gadhavi said.

"We each grabbed a limb and pulled," Joseph said.

"That's the approved Bot Destruction Method I believe Wruck, Nightcrawler, and I perfected during Operation Madhouse, yes."

"Then Mister Gadhavi beheaded her with the crowbar," Rob added.

"Well played. So, she was running for the exit she knew about?" They all nodded. "Why? Why not try to blend in?"

"Because she's a robot," Oliver said. "You're thinking of a human response."

"An android would have tried to blend, too." Yet more circumstantial evidence that suggested that the Christopher-Bots, both First and Second, were not actually sentient but had been programmed to do exactly what they'd done and said. And yet, the Kristie-Bot was doing things that indicated total free will, meaning that the Rattoppare Cyborg Method might honestly be as advertised.

"True enough," Oliver said. "But that's why Manfred and I were here so shortly after the others—we took another educated guess for where to go."

"Works for me. Let's gather up all her parts. I think we need to get her next door so they can see what's going on inside. She's in pretty good shape despite all that's happened."

Jeff took Manfred's phone and made some calls. Then he had Manfred zip off with Len and Kyle in tow. They returned driving two large bulldozers. Chose not to ask where those had come from—gates could move big things as well as small ones.

While Len and Kyle started scooping up Lizzie-Bot remains, agents from Dulce assisted by tossing in Bots and Bot parts. Meanwhile, Manfred gathered the Kitty-Bot's remains.

"Be sure we keep them somewhere extremely secured," I told him. "Not just the Kitty-Bot but all of them, on the off chance this was an even more bizarre and baroque plan than normal and they're all just playing possum until we're not paying attention."

"I'll make sure it happens," Manfred said.

"Yes, ma'am," any agents nearby who'd heard me confirmed, most of them in unison. Yes, so much better than the robotic version.

Manfred and a couple other agents who were helping him carry the Kitty-Bot's parts zipped off as Christopher joined us. "I understand you had a casualty." He tossed Jeff a new phone.

Jeff caught it and grinned. "Thanks."

"Oh, we can't have our President be without the means to be contacted. You and Kitty would just spend the entire time having sex."

"You don't know us."

Christopher snorted at me. "Right. The flyboys are doing the same with the remains at the other side of the school and around the Science Center." He indicated the bulldozers.

"Did we open a John Deere dealership or something?"

He managed a chuckle. "No, we just made an arrangement with that dealership in Arizona that we could borrow their rigs as needed. We pay them well for the last-minute rentals."

"That's the way to get another win out of good ol' Operation Defection Election. So, now what?"

"Now," Jeff said, "we get those who are locked up for their own safety, verify that no one in the school is hurt or panicked, and ensure that the press isn't going to crucify us over this."

"You can stop worrying about anyone in the school reacting," Oliver said. "Manfred and I checked the entire complex. We couldn't find proof that anyone had noticed what was happening."

"How could they miss the explosions? Mossy and I heard them from over here."

"You two were outside at the time," White said. "The building is extremely soundproofed. Our kind of soundproofing. And the shields were up."

"So is the Science Center and their shields were up, too and everyone felt and heard those missiles."

"Well, the school campus is so large that there are no classes or personnel in the section where we were yet," Oliver explained. "And the shockwaves would have a challenge carrying as far as they'd need to, especially with the shielding up."

"It's why we had Jeff do his presentation there," Raj said. "That way we wouldn't interfere with any classes or students."

"The shield went down due to the missile strikes."

"The shielding on that portion, yes," Raj said. "We have separate shielding for each section within each side. It's a fail-safe. The shielding only came down where the missiles hit. The rest of the shielding held."

Looked at Christopher. "I think we want to verify that this rosy belief is still true."

He nodded and zipped off. For Christopher's speed level he was gone quite a while—five full minutes. We spent them forming a plan for the press, which was basically Jeff sharing that they couldn't report on this due to it being a matter of national security and then confiscating all film and digital cards.

We were discussing what to do with the remains of the busses and whether or not we wanted to try to see if we could salvage enough to determine what they'd been using that had caused our missiles to bounce back when Christopher returned. He had Gower, Lizzie, Wasim, Naveed, Jenkins, and Dion in tow.

"I'm amazed, but Raj is right. Things in this section that took the strikes are shaken up but there's no one in it, not even maintenance, and the only security are those guarding the emergency exit doors, and none of them were in the section when the attack started, so they only noticed once William had them go there. Well, no one but the people you guys locked up for their own protection."

"We wanted out once Uncle Christopher checked on us," Lizzie said. "I wanted to kill all these things, but you guys totes already took care of it." She sounded angry, disappointed, and relieved, all in one, and still seemed shaken, not that I could blame her.

Put my arm around her and hugged her. She hugged me back. "No problem, you just saved us the trip to go get you guys and make sure you're okay."

"And I insisted," Gower said. "Pontifex ruling and all that."

Christopher shrugged. "No reason to leave you guys there anymore, so why do it? Otherwise, no one else seems to have noticed anything. A few students spotted the missile that blew up in the desert, but since the Turleens were seen going after it and then coming back seemingly unscathed and in full force, it was presumed to be a training exercise."

"Wow. Who's in charge of the school? Because they're

amazingly trusting. Or amazingly calm in the face of seeing missiles fly by."

"Troidl," Jeff replied.

"Who?"

"She's one of the top Themnir and was in charge of education on their planet," Christopher said, giving me a nice shot of Patented Glare #5. "As in, she ran education for every school on their planet from preschool up to advanced degrees, as we'd understand it, and they aren't what you'd call automatons. So, we have the individual with the most experience running a large educational system as the principal of the Intergalactic School." He shot me a look I was familiar with. Not a glare, but one I'd gotten from a lot of people during my Centaurion career.

"I was supposed to already know this fact, wasn't I?"

"You were," Jeff said. "But you've had other things to deal with. Speaking of which, Adam, Kristie, let's get your camera crew and the rest of the press and make sure they aren't doing things we don't want."

Adam nodded. "Our cameraman especially."

"We have his equipment and all press are with Field agents," Oliver said soothingly. "Don't worry, he's controlled right now."

"Yeah, I checked on them," Christopher said. "All seems well. They have food and drinks, and it honestly seemed kind of like they'd turned it into a party. The press are getting really good face time with the dignitaries and vice versa. Seems like it's working out."

"Speaking of, we need to get out of here as soon as we can so, you know, we can get ready for Marcia's fundraiser party tonight."

"Good point," Jeff said. He looked at Raj.

Who shrugged. "We can take the press back to the White House with us. As for the other dignitaries, we can invite them to the fundraiser. They may see it as an honor."

"They will," Jenkins said. "But I think we might want to stress that there could be, ah, action."

"It's a fundraiser at a senator's home," Raj pointed out.

"Kitty's going to be there," Christopher countered.

"Oh, yes, good point."

"Thanks for the support, guys. So who's betting on it actually going smoothly, show of hands?" No hands raised. "Haters. Likely accurate and all, but still."

"I cannot speak for those who are currently off doing other

tasks," Gadhavi said, "but my impression is that nothing goes smoothly for any of you. I look forward to the party. It should prove entertaining."

"Or deadly," Christopher said.

Gadhavi shrugged. "What is life without a little risk?"

Gower laughed. "Or, as we call it, routine."

CHAPTER 58

SURE ENOUGH, press and dignitaries were handled easily. Everyone was happy to move their impromptu party over to the White House and then to the Kramer's party. Let Vance know he needed to advise Marcia that she was getting a lot of foreign dignitaries attending. At least the day would go well for one person. Hopefully.

The little damage the school took was fixed before we left, and the shields were reported regenerated and back up. The Turleens allowed the other aerial support aliens to take to the once-again friendly skies, and everyone went back onto patrol.

The bus remains were gated over to Home Base so they'd have the fun of figuring out if there was anything salvageable. All Bot remains were confirmed secure, and the reverse engineering team was enjoying Christmas in September because these Bots were in pretty good shape. Apparently being trampled to "death" left the Bots in better condition than they normally arrived in.

Lizzie was still furious, but I felt anger in this situation was wise, so didn't do a lot to try to calm her down.

The person who was focused on the calming her down part was Wasim. He seemed to be doing a reasonable job of it, too. She, in turn, was doing her best to reassure him that every day wasn't like these past two. Wasn't sure if he believed her—Naveed's expression said that he certainly didn't—but Wasim insisted that he wasn't ready to run home to Bahrain, so chose to look at that as one for the win column.

Christopher, all of our team who'd been outside, and Team Tough Guys joined us for the return, and Lizzie was definitely glad to see Siler, who kept his arm around her once they were together. He also spent quality time shooting the Keep Your Paws Off My Daughter look at Wasim. After all we'd been though so far, it was kind of refreshingly normal.

Took five minutes and met Troidl. I was still having issues telling one Themnir from the other, but Troidl seemed competent. As it turned out, she had noticed what was going on, had verified that nothing was happening near any of the children and that the shields were up, and had been on the line with one of William's team the entire time, in case she had to evacuate. She was quite clear that evacuation on the first day wasn't what anyone wanted, but she'd been ready to do it if necessary. She also felt that the evacuation plan was sound, but agreed that security needed to be assigned on a permanent, 24/7 basis on all the emergency exit doors.

Felt tremendously better, gave Troidl a hug, which was getting less icky the more Themnir I hugged, and we took off.

The security system worked pretty much as it had coming in. We handed over our badges, verified we were still who we said we were, verified that those without badges were who they said they were, went through the metal detector again, and then it was straight on through the Nausea Machines.

Had refused to take my earbuds out all this time just in case Algar had any more hints or warnings for me. He hadn't, but I chose to go through the gate alone, in part because I needed to be the example for Lizzie right now. Turned my iPod on and, since "Mambo No. 5" was still up, mamboed my way through the gate. Was possibly the best gate transfer of my life.

Took out my earbuds and put them and my phone into my purse as my team joined us at the Secret Service Offices. Wondered if we were going to need to make this area larger, since we seemed to be using it a lot for personnel transfers. A problem for Algar and another day, though.

Amazingly enough, we'd gotten home at the same time as the kids who were still at Sidwell and their escorts. Timing was everything. Not that I could see the kids, not with all the people who were currently in here, but I could hear them, and they sounded like they'd had a good day.

The Secret Service escorted all the visiting dignitaries and press out of here and across the Center Hall into the Diplomatic Reception Room, where they now became Antoinette's problem. Jenkins, Oliver, and Dion went with them, some for the party atmosphere, some to keep an eye on their brethren, though Mrs.

Maurer did give Bellie back to Oliver first, and in a way where the bird didn't see Jeff and Jeff didn't see the bird. Mrs. Maurer had earned herself a raise.

"Mommy, Daddy, we had the *best* time!" Jamie shouted when she could finally see us. "Miss Lisa is so much fun and Louise is so smart!"

Louise, who was holding Jamie's hand, blushed. "The kids were great. They didn't want to stop school after lunchtime, so we didn't. Missus Paster says that if we're all in agreement and amenable to it, we can have Early-Starters Kindergarten go for a full day."

"The Embassy kids are all used to being at school for hours, and they like it, so I'm good with it."

"I checked with the other parents already, including the ones with kids in the class that aren't ours," Louise said. "They all said what you did. So I'll advise Missus Paster of the change. I think it alters the school's fees, though."

"Whatever it is, it's not a problem," Jeff said as he picked Jamie up. "Now, let's all go upstairs and you can tell us all about your day and then we'll have an early dinner together before Mommy and I have to go to a grown-up party."

"Can't I go too?" Jamie asked. The other kids echoed her request with enthusiasm.

"No," I said firmly. "You'll need to be in bed so you can get a good night's sleep for school tomorrow. All of you."

"Wasim and I are going," Lizzie said. "But I agree that the younger kids need to stay home." We all looked at her. "What? We're going. Wasim is a prince. We're both enrolled in the school you're fundraising for. The Kramer kids will be there. Why not us?"

"She has a point," Vance said. "But no one younger than Lizzie." This earned disappointed noises from the little kids that all the adults chose to ignore. "Louise should attend, though, if at all possible."

"I can, but I don't have anything to wear. It's supposed to be black tie."

Groaned. "Another bit of information I didn't have. Can't wait."

"We'll handle it," Jeff said.

"Great, then let's get the last bit of the afternoon rolling. Anyone who wants to nap, take it. And I mean that seriously, for little kids, big kids, and adults. If you feel even kind of tired or are crashing from all that's gone on, nap. We need everyone fresh and alert."

Louise nodded. "I could use a nap, honestly."

"If Louise is napping, then we should, too," Jamie said cheerfully. She looked at Lizzie. "What do you think?" Nice to know that Lizzie was still Jamie's go-to for older girl worship.

"I think that's a great idea, honestly," Lizzie said. "As long as we get woken up for dinner." Assurances were given that no one would be ditched. "Cool, then Louise, do you need to crash in my room?"

"I don't want to be a bother," Louise said, looking as if she had no idea what the proper response to Lizzie's suggestion really was.

"That's a good idea, so why don't you plan to stay with us at the White House or the Embassy, at least for tonight?" Jeff suggested. "And, if you want, you could just stay during the school year. If you wanted." Said very casually, but I knew how much he missed being around his nieces and nephews. Wondered what Louise was going to say and noted her siblings paying close attention.

"The Embassy has room," Christopher added. Yeah, he missed the kids, too. "You could just move in. If you wanted to."

Louise looked surprised and pleased. "You're sure? My parents suggested it but I wasn't sure if it would be okay or not."

Noted that everyone was looking at me, either surreptitiously or obviously. "Yes, I think that would be great. All the now-former Embassy Daycare kids go to Miss Denise first and then gate over here. So that way, you can help wrangle over there and then come over here and ensure the kids are ready and prepped for school in the mornings. As in, welcome to more work."

Louise hugged me. "Thank you, Aunt Kitty!"

Hugged her back while noting that I'd earned a lot more Aunt honorifics from the Valentino kids than I had in the past. Hoped this was TCC's influence, not them trying to shine me on while secretly working with their older sister against us. Chose to believe that Serene's intel was correct and did my best not to worry about it.

Vance called Akiko and shared that we had more women who were going to need to be dressed for an event. Akiko now staffed A-Cs who enjoyed the exciting world of fashion so that she could accommodate our ridiculous timeframes. She seemed okay with it, so there was that.

We broke up, everyone scattering to their various locations in order to get ready in whatever ways they wanted for tonight. Adam was allowed to go home with a Secret Service and Field team guard, but we kept the Kristie-Bot with us. Like Adam, the rest of the *Good Day USA!* crew were heading home for a change of clothes because they'd planned to follow me all day anyway and, after the day with me they'd had, their producer refused to even consider passing on the fundraiser.

The Kristie-Bot was fine with sticking around, though, because Jürgen Cologne was still on premises and also going to the fundraiser. Somehow, in her mind, he was her date. Chose to let Cologne fight that battle on his own.

Gadhavi was bunking over at Blair House, since Wasim had our only available guest bedroom taken. Gadhavi didn't seem to mind or be offended, which was nice. He was assigned his own set of Secret Service and a Field team as well before he headed off to rest and freshen up and, presumably, high-five someone along the way.

Security of all kinds were told to follow in Gadhavi's footsteps and go rest, eat, and dress for the party. No one argued. Heard Joseph and Rob telling Evalyne and Phoebe about our afternoon. They were making it sound far cooler than I felt it had been, but at least they sounded cheerful.

The other parents took their kids off for naps and such before they all came back again later, either to go with us to the fundraiser or to be with Nadine, who was going to be babysitting everyone at the White House, since Denise was required to hit the fundraiser, too.

Kevin and his kids stuck with us, though, since Denise was here, and went up with the rest of us to the Presidential suite where Denise and Nadine were watching Charlie and Becky.

Zipped through the door first, picked Charlie up, and gave him lots of hugs and snuggles. Shifted him to my hip and managed to deftly snatch Becky with my other arm before Christopher got to her, but only managed one kiss and snuggle before he rudely took his daughter away from me and hogged her to himself. At least until White used grandparental authority and took her from his son. Charlie found this hilarious, then demanded to go to Jeff, leaving me bereft of small children to love on. Always the way.

The rest of the Valentino kids, who were still hanging about for some reason instead of having already gone home to their mother as I'd expected them to do, insisted on attending the party as well, and since Vance had said no one younger than Lizzie and all of them were her age or older, we kind of lost that battle. Texted Vance to advise him to share these latest additions with Akiko.

"You have to be prepared for your sister to be there," I said finally, after Sylvia and TCC had been called and had approved that their kids could spend the night and stay out late, on a school night, no less. What was the A-C world coming to? Then again, perhaps they were enjoying alone time. Someone should be scoring it, and it wasn't going to be me for the foreseeable future. "And if she's there, she's not necessarily going to go easy on you guys with whatever she has planned."

"If she's there, then we'll deal," Claire said.

"We get it, she's a traitor," Sidney added. "We still love her, but she's pretty much cut ties with us."

"Really? I thought she was sneaking by for visits when no one was looking."

"She was," Louise said. "But our father told her she needed to stop and come back and ask to be forgiven. She won't do it, said he wasn't really our father, and tried to force our mother to choose between him and her. Our mother chose our father."

"So, Stephanie's not welcome anymore," Anthony added. "Our mother told her that until she's willing to stop working against our family and people, she can't come home again. We haven't seen Stephanie since."

Sort of felt bad for Stephanie. TCC was a clone of Clarence and Stephanie was right—he wasn't really her father, just a copy of him. A far nicer copy, but still, not the same. And yet, the rest of her family had happily chosen to believe a lie they knew was a lie. Wasn't sure what I'd do in Stephanie's place, but had a feeling it would be what she'd done.

"So we'll be ready for her," Claire said before I could come up with any response. "Don't worry, Aunt Kitty. We aren't like our sister. We won't let you down." The other kids nodded, Louise most emphatically.

A few other issues—like no one drinking anything they didn't know for sure was alcohol-free—were discussed. Wasim and Naveed both seemed to buy our "against our religion" line. We did our best to not share with the world that A-Cs were deathly allergic to alcohol. That no one had slipped vodka into Jeff's drink yet was truly a miracle, and one I wanted to ensure continued.

Then Siler, Christopher, Becky, White, and all the Valentino kids went back to the Embassy for naps and party prep, while Nadine zipped off to take the nap she'd probably need most of any of us. The Lewises decided to rest and prep at the Embassy as well, so they took off for now, while Wasim and Naveed followed Nadine's lead and went down the hall.

Gower was still with us, but he chose to go back to the Pontifex's Residence. "I haven't heard from Alpha Team," he said before he left. "I'm hoping that doesn't mean they're in trouble."

"They'll be fine," Jeff said. "We'll know if they need us." He gave Gower a hug, then escorted him to the gate in our bathroom.

This left me, Jeff, and our three kids. "Family nap time," I suggested. "Who's in?"

Jamie ran for our bed and jumped on it. "Me!"

Lizzie lifted into the air, sailed slowly over to the bed, and was deposited on it. "I think Charlie says I'm in."

Hugged him. "Little man, that's not necessarily the right way to ask."

He grinned at me, but didn't talk. Maybe the telekinesis took so much energy that he just didn't bother with speaking. Now that I knew that he could, and could speak as well as Jamie had at his age, it was less worrisome and more interesting.

Kids and adults kicked off their shoes and I dumped my purse on the floor, then we all lay down fully clothed on the bed, Lizzie on one side of me, Charlie on the other, Jamie next to him, and Jeff next to her. Jamie told us all about her day, and as she did so, just allowed myself to relax and cuddle with my family and enjoy this nice, peaceful, loving moment in a day that had been far too insane.

Lizzie fell asleep first, then Charlie. Jamie lowered her voice, but kept on sharing. Jeff was the next one out. "Mommy?" Jamie whispered.

"Yes, sweetie?" I whispered back.

"You can go to sleep now."

"Not until you do."

"But you don't sleep when everyone else is sleeping."

This was true when it wasn't officially bedtime. Wondered how she knew it. "But I don't want you awake while all of us are asleep."

"I'm going to nap as soon as you fall asleep, Mommy. Promise."

I could argue, or I could let her win this one. Decided to trust her. "Okay, Jamie-Kat."

"I'll sing you a song." With that, she sang the songs we sang to her and her brother at night to me. I was asleep by the second one, my last coherent thought being that I really hoped falling asleep while my not-yet-five-year-old daughter was awake didn't earn me the Worst Mother of the Year Lifetime Achievement in Stupidity award.

CHAPTER 59

I WAS DREAMING AND I KNEW IT. Well, really hoped I was dreaming, because I was sitting in an empty theater, front row center, looking at an empty stage. A huge empty stage. As real life went, that would be creepy beyond belief. As my dreams went, this was just another in a long line of weirdness. Waited to see what my subconscious was going to barf up for me.

Music started. It was faint, as if it was coming out of an old radio that was far away from me, but was pretty sure the music was The Kinks' "Dedicated Follower of Fashion."

The curtain fell. "Introduction," the first song from Panic! At the Disco's first album, *A Fever You Can't Sweat Out* came on. About the only lyrics were "ladies and gentlemen, we proudly present" and the rest was a lot of static. I mean, the song was less than forty seconds. However, as an attention-getter for me, it was working, so who was I to complain? Really wondered what was going on.

The curtains opened and the music changed to blink-182's "First Date."

Someone walked onto the stage. Not the first person I went on my first date with. Thought it was me at first, having the fun dream experience where you're both watching the dream and in the dream as your own character at the same time. Realized it was the Kitty-Bot, however, when I noted she was in the pink linen suit. She walked to center stage, stood there for a moment, then slowly turned in a circle. Once that was done, she rocked out for a few bars of music doing the hands at shoulder level, torso going side to side and hips going back and forth, kind of dancing, where the feet don't really move. She didn't look bad, but sincerely hoped I danced better.

She stepped back and to the side, stage left, as "The Other Way" by Weezer came on. Clearly I was getting a floor show.

Jeff, Christopher, and Chuckie walked out. Well, really, shambled out. Totally naked, too, so I could see the neat stitching. Why they were all here in the dream flesh, so to speak, was a question I couldn't answer. Just lucky, I guess. And while Dream Flesh would be a great name for a death metal band, so far this dream really was all that and a big bag of stale chips.

They came to the front of the stage then hit the iconic *Saturday Night Fever* pose. Yep, just as I remembered them from Gaultier's Room of Hot Zombies—one hundred percent anatomically correct, though only Amy could give it the full confirmation for the Christopher Zombie. Of course, it would be far more titillating if I wasn't aware they were zombies made from dead A-C parts, which I very much was.

The three naked zombies did the full turnaround, presumably so I could also check out their butts—as fine a group of butts as any group of zombies could ever hope to have—then they shuffled to the back of the stage, in the center. Got the impression they were trying to move to the beat. Unsuccessfully.

The music changed to "Alternative Girlfriend" by the Barenaked Ladies and two others stepped out—Bryce Taylor and Leslie Manning, aka the android children of Antony Marling. These two didn't walk—they danced out together, doing a version of the tango. They reached the center of the stage, did a full 360 while dancing, then tangoed their way to stage right. Mercifully, neither one of them spoke. There was a part of me that still wanted to punch them both right in their android faces.

As Cory Morrow singing "Second Chance" came on, a supersoldier stepped out and daintily skipped forward. Got the full spin, and it really spun, too, as if it was modeling the latest in Paris fashions. Resisted the urge to applaud, but appreciated its attempt to keep it sassy. The supersoldier skipped back to stand between the zombies and the Kitty-Bot, but ahead of them, forming a new line. It curtseyed then went still.

The music changed to Joe Jackson's "Be My Number Two" and Col. John Butler and Cameron Maurer came out. Doing a soft-shoe routine. I tried to speak, to ask why I was getting this particular dance revue, but couldn't.

They came to front center, did their turn around, and went to their place onstage, dancing the whole way. Only they stood between and in front of the zombies and Bryce and Leslie, and they weren't quite on the line with the supersoldier but were forward of it just a bit.

The music changed to "The Third Hoorah" by Jethro Tull. A set of Fem-Bots sashayed out, arm in arm, just like they were walking the runway, including tossing their heads from side to side. A Kitty-Bot, a Janelle-Bot, a Lizzie-Bot, and the heretofore unseen Amy-Bot. Wondered not for the first time why Janelle had gone to the trouble to make a Fem-Bot of herself.

"Haven't you ever wanted to be two places at once?" the Janelle-Bot asked as they reached the front of the stage. "Especially if someone else could do the boring things?" I certainly had, so someone actually doing so didn't seem all that crazy now.

The Fem-Bots began dancing a jig to the tune, doing a fair impersonation of a segment of *Riverdance*. My dream was really going all out for the entertainment factor. They danced in their circle, then jigged it back, positioned directly in front of the original Kitty-Bot, though their line was in front of the supersoldier and, as I judged it, they were in front of Butler and Maurer, too.

"Better Luck Next Time" by Lifehouse came on now. And what came out were the clones of Reid and LaRue. Knew it was the clones because they were the young versions I'd met during Operation Infiltration. Them smirking at me was also a real clue.

Instead of dancing or twirling they slouched up to center stage and flipped me off. Even in my dream these two sucked. Then they slouched over to their place on the stage, which was in front of the zombies, in line even with the Fem-Bot Rockettes, who were doing the Rockettes' kick, which was hard to do to this particular song. I was grateful to the clones for the first time ever, though—they were blocking the total nakedness of the zombies, who were still attempting to dance and still failing utterly.

Another musical cue, this time Three Dog Night's "Mama Told Me (Not To Come)," and the Christopher-Bot appeared, kind of lounge singer-ing his way out, the cool-dude bob dancing, complete with finger snaps. Waved to me. Then, instead of turning or dancing, he divided into two Christopher Bots. Both of them waved to me now, in unison, then kept on cool-dude bobbing to the song. Still in unison. Oh yeah, regular people unison was so much better.

This was weird and I had no idea how it was done, but it

would explain why both Christopher-Bots had said exactly the same things and the one we examined only had about half the gray matter. Wanted to ask how the hell this was done, but the reality of a substance that could change into something else wasn't exactly all that new. And cells duplicated all the time. Though, since the brain seemed to be shared, this wasn't a method anyone should want to continue, since after just a few divisions you'd have almost no gray matter per Bot.

Had the feeling of someone being behind me, but couldn't turn around. Wasn't a threatening presence. Felt more protective than anything else. Noted the Christopher-Bots were looking just up and over my right shoulder. Wanted to ask who was behind me but figured it wasn't too much of a leap to guess that the other observer was Terry. Would have asked why we weren't speaking, but I still couldn't make my mouth work.

The Christopher-Bots cool-dude bobbed to stage left, directly in front of the supersoldier, but also in front of the line that had the Fem-Bot Rockettes and the nasty teenaged clones, so that it was ahead of and between the Fem-Bots and the clones. The Fem-Bots were still high-kicking up a storm.

The music changed to "Friends Forever" by Puffy Amiyumi, so I was totally prepared for Joe and Randy to join the party. They mamboed because of course they did. Center stage and then in line with the Christopher-Bots but between Butler and Maurer and the clones.

Still felt the presence behind me, still couldn't turn around, still couldn't talk. Wondered why—most of my weird dreams allowed me to chat a lot.

"Because you need to pay attention," Joe said.

"The big number's coming up," Randy added.

He wasn't wrong. The song was now the live version of Bette Midler's "Big Noise From Winnetka," and I was really being treated to a show.

The Kristie-Bot came out, tap dancing and spinning all the way. She danced around and with all those in the back row, including the zombies, boogied with the supersoldier, let Butler and Maurer each spin her, high-kicked with the Fem-Bot Rockettes, did the Charleston with the clones, mamboed with Joe and Randy, then shoved in between the Christopher-Bots in that Old Hollywood Musical way that sent each Christopher-Bot staggering to the side.

They got into the act now, though, and spun back. Each took

one of the Kristie-Bot's hands and helped her do a triple flip. Then she spun them away from her, did a flip all on her own, then landed in a scissors split, jazz hands up in the air, eyes wide, with a toothy grin in perfect time with the end of the song. She was in front of everyone, not in the center of the stage, but directly in front of Joe and Randy.

Applauded, since it seemed expected and I actually could. Plus, I didn't want to seem negative.

"Well?" the Kristie-Bot asked holding the pose and her expression. "Don't you think I'm ready for my galactic close-up?"

I did not, though I was still unable to share this vocally. Frankly, seeing all of this before me made me terrified of what the galaxy was going to do with all the shenanigans we seemed to always have going on here on Earth.

"Oh, they have lots going on, too, never you fear," the Kristie-Bot said cheerfully.

"And you'll find out," Bryce said.

"But not right now," Leslie added.

"Because you've got to solve the mess you've already started right now," the clones said in nasty teenaged unison. Tried to get up to go beat their faces in but couldn't. Also wanted to share that whatever was going on wasn't my fault, but couldn't. This dream was testing my patience—I didn't like not talking or moving for this long.

No one said anything else, no one on the stage moved or spoke—the Kristie-Bot's hands were still up, the Fem-Bots had their legs held up in the high kick, the zombies were back to channeling John Travolta but sadly without the white suit, everyone seemed frozen—and there was no music. Still couldn't look to my right or left, but the presence behind me hadn't gone.

Wanted to ask Terry what I was learning from all of this, but assumed this episode of Dancing With Your Nightmares: Special Victims Unit hadn't been put on just so I'd never want to nap again. Therefore, time to figure out what the hell I was supposed to figure out.

Studied the stage. I was better with chessboards. But this dream wasn't a game of chess. It was a lot more like *A Chorus Line* without the talent and fun. Not helping myself.

Was I supposed to figure out who'd made what? If so, why weren't those creators on the stage? No, who made what didn't matter as much as what was being made right now.

There was still room onstage, should someone clse want to

dance out from the back. Not that I wanted anything or anyone else, and not that anyone or anything else seemed to be about to dazzle us. Waited. Nope. Neither Naomi or any other Dazzler came out. We were dealing only with fabricated people or those who'd had that fabrication forced upon them.

It didn't take a lot to guess that everyone had come out in order of, if not creation, then use. The back row were the three starter projects, none of them perfect, though experience said that the Bryce and Leslie androids had been damned good enough to almost kill me.

The ones to stage right were all sentient with free will, at least once they were "fixed." The ones to stage left were all programmed, meaning the Christopher-Bot wasn't sentient, he'd just been programmed to think he was, which was cruel, really. Not that it was a surprise that the people behind this didn't care who they hurt.

The supersoldiers and the androids had been going at the same time. But based on stage placement, my gut said that the supersoldiers were perfected, to use the term loosely, by combining the Kitty-Bot and the Hot Zombies, at least their technology or how they were zapped into existence or something.

Taking that theory as fact, because I had no better ideas, this meant that Butler and Maurer had been created using android and zombie methods. The Fem-Bots were probably just the next phase of the Kitty-Bot, but that would mean the clones were the next phase of the zombies. Not really out of the question.

The Christopher-Bots were a blend of Fem-Bot and clone. Fem-Bots were made to blow up, though, and the Christopher-Bot clearly was not. Joe and Randy, though, were a blend of android and cloning. Why not? None of us knew what all those wires inside them actually did, other than make them better, faster, stronger, and the co-presidents of the Lee Majors Fan Club.

Based on stage position, the Christopher-Bots were potentially equal to Joe and Randy. Only Joe and Randy had free will and I was now pretty sure the Christopher-Bots didn't. So that couldn't be where they were equal. Could be strength and agility, though nothing was stronger than the supersoldier.

Or maybe it was technique, as in the creators of this level were, just like their creations, more advanced, or had the assistance of more advanced tech. Probably the tech option, and alien tech at that. The alien help that wasn't from LaRue or someone originally from Alpha Four likely started with the Fem-Bots and clones, but was more dedicated for the next generations. Cliff had had someone on speed dial, for certain. Why not the others?

Which brought me to the Kristie-Bot. She was the culmination of the android-zombie combo and she had no peer. Realistically, cyborgs were also the next inevitable phase when you'd already tried all the other forms of making human-looking robots. So, really, the Kristie-Bot should have been in center stage. Only she wasn't, and there was room on the other side of the stage for her to have an equal. Which boded.

The Smash Cast recording of "Big Finish" started. Had no idea if this meant that I'd figured out whatever confused thing I was supposed to, or if the time for this extravaganza was up and someone else needed the stage. But the cast of this show was definitely back in action.

The Hot Zombies were the first to leave the stage, backing up, sort of dancing still. The clones remained useful in blocking most of this—it was already kind of a nightmare and I didn't need nightmares *from* my nightmare.

Next the supersoldier danced and pirouetted off stage behind the zombies, followed by Bryce and Leslie, who did a reprise of their tango and exited stage right.

No one else moved. Butler got the "why me?" look on his face, walked up, and shoved the clones. "Oh, we're going," the LaRue clone said nastily. She looked at me. "But not forgotten."

"By at least one person," the Reid clone added, as Butler shoved them off backstage.

"You always forget about the loose ends," the LaRue clone yelled as she disappeared behind the backstage curtain.

Okay, this was clearly a clue. While one of the Christopher-Bots did the lounge singer strut off the stage, thought hard. The only loose string regarding the clones I could think of was Casey Jones, who remained at large. She'd been on a mission for Cliff. But we didn't know what that mission was or where in the world she was. No one had spotted her at the True Believer rally, but that didn't mean she wasn't there. Besides, no one had mentioned that they'd looked for her specifically.

The Kristie Bot waved at me now and gave me a very big, obvious wink.

Another clue. My brain chose to do me a solid and mention that while Casey might have been mad at Stephanie for letting Casey rot in the supermax prison under the Pentagon, the adage of any port in a storm was a really apt one. Casey liked benefactors and was good at serving two masters, either with or without said masters' knowledge.

"Good," Joe said. He looked at the Kristie-Bot. "But that's for later."

Randy nodded and looked at the Christopher-Bot. "You have to fix today, first."

But before I could ponder this, the rest of the cast went into action. The Kitty-Bot ran over to Butler and Maurer, did a rather graceful leap, and landed in their arms. They all spun around, put her down, then backed offstage, bowing and waving to me. Meanwhile, the Fem-Bots grabbed the remaining Christopher-Bot and Joe and Randy and they all did the Rockettes kick in a line behind the Kristie-Bot, backing up at the same time.

Meanwhile, the Kristie-Bot pulled up from the splits using only her legs, which was as hella impressive as the moving Rockettes kick line. Then she did an Ann Miller spin-and-tap thing across the stage, followed up by three backflips. She jazz-handed her way to center stage.

"We're here until you stop us or save us," she said perkily. "And don't forget to tip your servers!" With that she backed up, tapping and jazz-handing, as the curtain closed. The word "Applause" was now printed on it.

Applauded and realized I could finally talk. "Why this, why me, and what now?"

The curtain opened again and the entire "cast" was there, hand in hand, taking their Broadway bows. Kept on clapping because it really seemed expected.

"Because we needed your full attention," the cast said in unison. "Because you're the one who figures out how the unconnected connect. And now you go save the day over and over again."

The curtain dropped again. Kept clapping just in case. Wisely, as the curtain rose again and I got more bowing. "Is there any way for me to prevent whatever bad that's going to happen next from happening?"

"No," Terry said from behind me. "Because things still have to happen in order for other things to happen. Just as they always have."

Music again and another selection from Three Dog Night. The auditorium, stage, and everyone on it faded to the accompaniment of "The Show Must Go On."

CHAPTER 60

WOKE UP TO NO music but someone nudging me. "Where's Jamie?" Jeff asked.

"Crap." Sat up and looked around. "For that matter, where are Charlie and Lizzie?"

"In the living room, you ridiculous worrywarts," Lizzie shouted to us from, presumably, the living room. She came in holding Charlie in one arm, with Jamie next to her, hand in hers. "I woke up first, got up, went to the bathroom, then Charlie woke up, so I handled him. Jamie woke up then, and we decided to let the old folks sleep a little more. I was totes going to wake you up in fifteen minutes."

Lay back down on the bed. Felt physically rested and mentally exhausted. My dreams really worked overtime to ensure I didn't get the kind of sleep doctors tended to recommend. "Great. Wake me then."

"No way, you're up now. Get up. Pierre's texted me like a million times to let him know when he can come over and do your makeup and stuff. He's going to do mine, too!"

Sat up again. "Um, excuse me?"

"Something light, 'cause I'm just a teenager. I get a cool dress, too. Akiko's already on her way, so you might want to shower." With that, she turned and took the kids back out of our room.

We were silent for a few moments. "I'm not ready for a teenaged girl," Jeff said finally.

"I'm not either, but we have one, and at least she's the most awesome teenager we could hope to land."

"True enough. With the kids awake and obviously more alert than us, I think it would be smart if we shower separately."

"There go any hopes I had for the evening going well."

Jeff leaned over and kissed me deeply. "I'll make it up to you later," he purred. "Promise."

"Mmmm, I'm going to hold you to that." With that, got up and took my third shower of the day. I was, if nothing else, sparkling clean. I used the slow hyperspeed instead of luxuriating, mostly because I'd heard Lizzie talking to Pierre and he was heading over.

Jeff showered, using full hyperspeed, while I blow-dried my hair. We were done at the same time, so I only got to admire his wet, naked body and rippling muscles with just the right amount of hair in all the right places for far too short a time.

He grinned as he put his robe on. "I love your laser focus on the priorities, baby."

Would have said more, but heard Pierre. "Yoo-hoo! I'm here to make my darlings even more gorgeous and perfect than they are naturally."

Had a few moments to get into underwear while the kids piled onto Pierre and shared that they missed living in the same building with him. Akiko had long ago given up the notion that I'd wear a slip, ever, for any reason, and Pierre was not thrown by a woman in a bra and panties, but in order to not be the worst role model ever for the kids, I tended to wear a robe when I was heading over for the Let's Make Kitty Presentable Hour.

Of course, I'd left said robe in the closet, so, once I was in my underwear, I used hyperspeed to get into the closet and some semblance of propriety.

Jeff was already dressed in the tuxedo that Akiko had had Armani make for him specially—because you separated an A-C from their Armani about as easily as from their own head—when I got there, so he gave me a quick kiss and headed out.

Took the opportunity to talk to my hamper. "Thanks for all the help today, I really needed it."

Nothing.

"I will again not be able to hear music, though. I have to leave my regular purse at home for things like this and will only have a small clutch. Well, small for me. It'll have Jeff's adrenaline and my phone and my Glock, but otherwise, not a lot else. And if anyone hears music coming out of my purse, I'll be told to turn it off."

Nada.

"I don't understand my dream. I mean, I get it, but I don't

know why Terry wasn't allowed near me before but then got to spend what felt like an hour hanging next to me."

Silence.

Didn't heave the sigh I wanted to. It wasn't like I had a ton of time to chat with Algar right now anyway. "Just wanted to say thanks again for helping us survive."

Algar appeared. "My pleasure."

"Nice to see you. Since you're here, any tips?"

"Look for the unexpected."

Waited. "That's it?"

"That's it. As in, your expectations may not be accurate, so look for things that might contradict them."

"Are all my expectations wrong?"

"Hardly. But some are."

"Um, okay. Any tips about my dream?"

"Sometimes dreams bring clarity."

Waited. That appeared to be it. "And sometimes they don't?"

"Sometimes the clarity needs to be discovered."

"So, why didn't ACE let me talk to Terry before?"

"Terry isn't as strong a presence as the others in that collective due to only a small part of her consciousness being included. She has to work harder, therefore. It was nice of her to try to bring you clarity, wasn't it?"

"Yes, it was. Um, did you help her to do that?"

Algar shot me a totally innocent look. "Why would I interfere?"

Managed to keep the Inner Hyena and my sarcasm knob both under control. "Gotcha."

"It's not as if your understanding the progression of how these various replicants and simulacrums came to be is going to help you fight your enemies."

That was definitely a clue, because simulacrum meant an image or a representation, something insubstantial, and all of these things were very solidly real, and replicant was presumably referring to *Blade Runner*. "Um, yes, right, got it." I didn't have it, but like everything else, hoped clarity would appear when I actually needed it. "Anything else?"

He shrugged. "Just be yourself. That's always the best advice I or anyone else can ever give you." And with that he snapped his fingers and disappeared.

"Um, thanks. Again. For all the help and obscure clues and such." Looked around. Sometimes Algar left weird things that were somehow helpful. Saw nothing of interest, though as I looked back at the hamper a sparkly silver clutch appeared on its top.

Picked it up. It had everything in it I'd mentioned, as well as my earbuds, ID, credit cards, and some cash. Decided not to question, just took it with me out of the closet.

Pierre swooped me up immediately. "Let's get you all ready, shall we, dearest?"

"Of course we shall." I'd given up fighting this ages ago.

"Love your choice of clutch, it's perfect for your gown."

"Yay, I win the good guessing prize." My phone rang. Had to give it to the clutch, it was easy to dig that out. Sent another thank you to Algar. "Yeah, Vance?"

"Wanted to give you the heads-up—the party's moved locations."

"Really? Why?"

"Marcia's house can't actually handle all the people we're dragging along with us. She's thrilled, but doesn't have the capacity because, since she said you were coming and since you've had a lot of, ah, noteworthy press coverage today, everyone's RSVP'd in the affirmative."

"Well, I guess that's good. Where are we going?"

"Sidwell."

Let that one sit on the air for a long moment. "Excuse me?"

"The school has a huge ballroom over by the lower school. They were more than happy to accommodate at the last minute, unlike pretty much any hotel in town. And that way all proceeds really go to the school."

"Um, good, I guess?"

"It's good. Press is invited, of course, and I sent some A-Cs over to help get things set up."

"You sent Field agents to do party prep?"

"No, I sent who Raj said could be spared."

Meaning Raj had sent over some of the A-C CIA, meaning we'd have a ton of troubadours on-site to keep things calm if need be and to help me spot the unexpected. This was acceptable. "Great."

"Thanks as ever for approving my doing my job. Also, Sidwell's new faculty-parent liaison will be helping set things up."

"Is her name Camilla?"

"It is! So relax."

"Doing my best. Are we gating or driving?"

"Driving. This requires the big show. I've already arranged limos for the dignitaries who are drinking all our nonalcoholic beverages and eating all our food in the Diplomatic Reception Room."

"So bitter. I'm just happy they're all happy."

"I know. They'll be heading over first. You and Jeff need to arrive last."

"I'm not Cinderella."

"No, but you lose your shoes at least as much as she did." And with that he hung up.

Had Pierre relay the latest to Jeff while Akiko got me into my new dress, which was a sparkly silver that matched the clutch. As per every dress she made for me, it looked tight but was made of a fabric I could move in and, since this was black tie and I was therefore required to be in a floor-length gown, not only was there a long slit on the side, but it also had a lower portion I could tear off when I'd have to run. That I'd have to run was a given by now, and Akiko didn't even bother to mention the tear-away portions of the dress, she merely pointed to them once I had it on and continued about her business.

"I'm glad you had a clutch already," she said while rummaging around in her bag. "With this late notice I didn't have enough fabric for shoes and clutch both, so I went for the shoes."

She found what she was looking for, which was the shoes, which she handed to me with a flourish. They were extremely Cinderella-like, silver and sparkly. And, because Akiko was a genius, fit perfectly and felt great. "Shoes was the right way to go. They're awesome."

She beamed, then got me into my hair and makeup chair and put the giant bib on me that ensured that no makeup would get onto my dress. In order to keep me from fidgeting or talking too much during these sessions, Pierre had put a small TV in the room. It was turned to *ESPN*, where we were watching a preseason hockey game. I approved, especially since it was my team versus the Blackhawks.

Actually relaxed for a bit as Akiko and Pierre fussed over me and the announcers rambled over the game. "The Pueblo Caliente Chupacabras are looking forward to a good season," one announcer shared. "It's too bad their last preseason game is at the Capitals."

"Even though they're expected to be competitive, the Capitals are looking a little weak, Johnny, and their preseason isn't getting the fans out," the other announcer said, in a Canadian accent, meaning he was likely a former player and doing the color commentary. Didn't get a lot of time to watch sports anymore, so I didn't know who was who these days. "And the Chupacabras don't have a lot of fans back east. It's too bad. They're going to miss a hell of a game."

"They have one huge fan right here."

"Stop speaking," Akiko said.

"Well, Mitch," Johnny said, ignoring Akiko's order, "maybe it's because Capitals fans are putting all their hopes on their season opener against the Chupacabras the next day. That one's sold out. So, if you're in the D.C. area and you want to see the best team the Chupacabras have put forth in years and you can't get opening night tickets, head out for the final preseason match the night before."

"God, I would so love to go to that."

"Hush, Kitty, and we mean it," Pierre said sternly.

Sighed and shut up. Managed not to cheer when the Chups scored and only had to be told to sit still twice while a good fight was going on. Thanks to the hockey game, though, made it through the hell that was this portion of my life.

Primped half to death and declared ready for my close-up, I was dragged away from the game before the middle of the second period. My whining was ignored, which wasn't a surprise.

Lizzie was up next, and she took far less time than I had. She was in a modest but lovely light gray dress that made her look sweet and innocent and blooming at the same time. Jeff grunted. "She's too young for a dress like that," he muttered to me. "And why does she need makeup on?"

"She looks great and get ready, because she's only going to get older. Just like Jamie and Charlie will."

He heaved a sigh. "I'm not ready."

Took his hand and squeezed it. "No parent is."

There was a knock at the door. Jamie ran to open it to show my parents standing there. "You're not ready to go yet?" Mom asked as she scooped Jamie up in her arms. Dad was in a tux and she was in a black dress that looked great on her.

"Close to," Jeff said. "Just waiting for Raj and Vance to give us the go-ahead for when we're allowed to leave."

Mom hugged and kissed Jamie, then handed her to Dad as I trotted over. Got a big hug from Mom, which did a lot to make me feel better about everything. "No kissing!" Pierre shouted.

Mom rolled her eyes. "Got it. You look beautiful, kitten."

"Thanks, Mom, you do, too. I'm so glad you and Dad are coming with us."

"After the day you've had, it just seemed wise." Mom let me go, gave Jeff a quick hug, went to Lizzie, hugged her, then did the put your hands on the other's shoulders and do the critical examination thing. "All grown up already. You look wonderful."

Lizzie beamed. "Think my dad is going to like it?"

"No," Jeff said as he hugged Dad and took Jamie from him, so Dad could grab Charlie, who he brought over to Mom so she could get a hug and kiss, too.

"No father's ever ready for his little girl to grow up," Dad said. "But when she turns into a lovely, wonderful young woman, it's worth it."

"Your father's already there, along with the rest of security," Mom told Lizzie. "We've sent everyone else ahead, including your new Hollywood friends."

"Was that wise?" Jeff asked.

"They're surrounded by a variety of security personnel," Mom said, sarcasm knob easily at eight and rising, "including seasoned A-Cs, so yes. The ones still here are Ansom Somerall and Talia Lee. Serene cleared them, but I'm not wild about you bringing them to this. Especially based on the request I got earlier today."

"What request was that?"

Mom heaved a sigh. "Janelle Gardiner and Amos Tobin both want to attend."

CHAPTER 61

"WHAT DID YOU SAY?" Jeff asked.

"I hope it was yes." This got me the full room's attention.

"It was, because we have to walk a fine line with them," Mom said. "They aren't prisoners, they're in protective custody."

"I for sure want Ansom and Talia there, then."

Jeff ran his hand through his hair. "I have to ask, because I'm just funny that way. But why do you want all of them at the fundraiser?"

"Because Mom just said it—tons of security. I want to see these people interacting."

"It'll be cool," Lizzie said. "Kitty's right, what are they going to do at a big party?"

"The mind boggles," Mom said. "I'd like to remind all of you of the President's Ball from not so very long ago."

"Angela has a point," Jeff said.

"Whatever. As long as Gardiner and Tobin cough up donations to the school, they can come."

"You know that will reflect positively on Marcia, not you, right?" Jeff asked.

"Yes, but I don't care. Doctor Rattoppare is going to be there, and I'm pretty sure that Gardiner and Tobin want to go because of that. Whether it's to exchange information, trade cutting insults, or try to kill each other, I want to find out and, if at all possible, have our people eavesdrop. And by 'our people' I mean all the covert ops people who will be attending and by 'eavesdrop' I mean take recordings and pictures and all that good spy jazz."

Mom heaved a sigh. "Fine." She pulled her phone out of her clutch and dialed. "Yes, as you suspected, we're letting them out. No, not with you or with us. Separate vehicle, with the nastiest, most suspicious, and most trigger-happy agents we have." She laughed. "True, but he has a job already. Yes, good idea. See you down at the Carpet shortly." She hung up.

"Who were you talking to?"

"Kevin, who knows you very well."

"So he suggested Malcolm be with Ansom and Talia?"

Mom laughed. "Yes, good guess."

"I'm all about the good guessing tonight. But you said no, so who drew the short straw?"

"Airborne. Joe and Randy have the extra strength, all of them have been with you long enough to be suspicious fast, and they were going to be part of your escort anyway."

"Go team."

The others going over with us started arriving now, mostly so that Nadine could get a head start on this month's Babysitting Challenge. Cameron Maurer came with his mother and kids to do their drop-off, and he pulled me and Jeff aside. "I received information from Alpha Team."

"Are they alright?" Jeff asked.

Maurer nodded. "Butler is with them. They've started adding him onto the team anytime they're going into a dangerous area. He and I can communicate on a different level from all of you, and both of us can connect with Chernobog and her team at almost any time."

"You're both Wi-Fi and Bluetooth equipped? And you use that ability to hang out with Hacker International from a distance?"

He smiled at me. "In a way, only better. At any rate, I've run a great number of background checks today, as have, ah, Hacker International. Soon, we'll be able to verify where all the former human agents who used to work for Centaurion Division but left, disappeared, or retired are now living, what they're doing both for work and for fun, and if they have any connections to companies or individuals who are our enemies. By soon, I don't mean tonight or even this week. However, what Alpha Team was able to find will speed the work up."

"So nothing that helps us out for tonight?" Hey, a girl could dream.

"A little something. Hacker International has been following

up on the Rattoppare clue. They believe they've found the quite
hidden records of those who have had the special surgery. Most
of that is encrypted, but we've gotten some names to start digging into, and one was a name that we all believe matters—
Kramer."

"As in, Marcia's had the surgery?" Felt disappointed in her.
Not that we were pals, even if we both had that common enemy,
but it just seemed so desperate and sad in some ways. She'd end
up looking younger than her kids. My parents looked great for
their ages, but they also didn't look as young as Jeff and I did.
Which was right and normal. Maurer would be younger than his
kids soon enough, really, but that hadn't been his active choice—
it had been done *to* him.

"We don't know, and Kramer is a common name. But everyone figured you should be advised, just in case."

"Better forewarned and all that jazz, yeah."

Jeff had left the door opened once the Maurers had arrived,
so Joe and Randy came in without knocking, Ross and Sean in
tow. Denise and her kids were right behind them, and Doreen
and Irving with Ezra brought up the rear. "Christopher said
they'll be here in a minute," Doreen said, as she gave Ezra a
goodbye kiss.

All the men were in tuxes other than Joe and Randy, who
were in their Navy dress whites, and all looked great. All the
women looked stunning because Akiko was just that level of
talented where she could dress anyone perfectly at any time.
Plus, she'd been dressing most of us for several years now, so
she kind of had our individual colors and styles down.

"Colette is already at the venue," Mrs. Maurer said. "She
went over with Abner and his wife and Vance's husband. Vance
is on-site, has been in touch, and he says that we can all get going
as soon as we're ready. Which is his way of saying hurry up."

The Whites and the Valentinos arrived now, men and boys in
tuxes, of course, Amy in a green silk gown that looked amazing
on her, Louise in lavender and Claire in light yellow, all of them
looking beautiful.

"Where's Magdalena?" I asked White. Nurse Carter was conspicuously absent.

"She didn't feel right leaving the Embassy." Nurse Carter
was both White's main squeeze and had taken over the medical
at the Embassy when Tito had come to the White House with us.
"She and Doctor Hernandez discussed it. They both agreed that

it was wiser for her to be available for both the Embassy and the White House, and he should go with all of us to the fundraiser."

"She literally has all the luck."

White chuckled. "She said you'd say that. And she agrees. Mahin and Abigail are already at the venue with Paul."

"Is anyone left in the Embassy?"

"Oh, a few people. Everyone at the Zoo, and Melissa." We'd taken Melissa from Sydney Base and had her running security at the Embassy these days. "Magdalena is going to spend the evening playing cards with her. Apparently they're both disappointed that Denise and Irving are going along, since the four of them enjoy playing bridge."

"I may not even want to know, but as long as Missy's there, I won't worry about Magdalena being bored by herself." Boredom was something I envied and really enjoyed whenever I lucked into it, which wasn't nearly often enough.

"Are we ready to go yet, kitten?" Dad asked me. "The room seems more than full."

"Yeah, it does, but I thought Chuckie was meeting us here."

"I sent him over to the venue the moment Vance advised me there'd been a change," Mom said. "Nathalie is already with him."

"Okay, but where's Gadhavi? And we're missing Wasim and Naveed, too."

No sooner mentioned than all three of them were in the doorway, and the kids' Secret Service detail, led by Keith, their P.T.C.U. detail, led by Devon, and their Field teams, led by Melanie and Emily of all people, were right behind them.

"We figured we were good at protecting kids, and that way, medical's right here," Melanie said.

"And also that way, Nadine doesn't get to have fun with the kids all by herself," Emily added, as the various security personnel spread out in the room.

Wasim and Naveed were both in tuxedos, and while Wasim hadn't looked comfortable in the clothes he'd been in before other than in his Sidwell uniform, he looked fine in his tux. In the tux, I could see him as a prince with a car and a cool bachelor pad.

He looked around nervously, kind of ruining his Cool Tux Look. "I'm sorry we're late in getting ready. Naveed felt that we should ensure that Mister Gadhavi was able to join us."

Gadhavi was in new robes and a red and white checkered kufiyah. "I appreciate the great courtesy of the Royal Family of my adopted country of Bahrain," he said formally. "And the hospitality of the United States and the King and Queen Regent as well."

Wasim was going to say something else, but he stopped because Lizzie came into view. Gadhavi did him a solid and gently closed Wasim's open mouth. "You look beautiful," Wasim managed after a couple of moments.

Lizzie blushed. "You look great, too."

Jeff grunted quietly. "I've never realized how your father *really* felt when he met me, and I say that as an empath, mind you, until just this moment."

"And he got to run into you coming out of my room in the morning. So, you know, ponder that for a mo. Okay, everyone," I said in a louder voice, "let's let the kids do their sleepover and get ourselves to the fanciest impromptu fundraiser ever."

One last round of kisses and hugs for all the kids, then we headed out and down to the garage. On the way, Mom divided us up into various cars so that everyone would have security. We picked up Tito, Rahmi, and Rhee along the way, upping our royalty quotient. Tito was in the standard Armani tuxedo all the menfolk were in, and the princesses had both gussied up quite a bit, but even so, knew they had their battle staffs with them somehow, and that made me feel a whole lot better.

Agents had gotten clothes and such for Ansom and Talia, so those two were dressed appropriately and let out once Joe and Randy were back with the rest of the flyboys. Insisted on Manfred going with them, just in case. Otherwise, didn't pay a lot of attention to who was in what car. Mom had that under control.

Checked on the Christopher-Bot the Second. He was lying down but came over to the window. "Be careful."

"Of what?"

"Of them," he nodded toward Somerall and Lee. "They want to kill you, remember."

"I think you've been programmed to tell me that," I said gently. Considered asking him if he realized that the Bot he'd blown up was half of himself. But it wouldn't give me any intel and besides, I wasn't cruel like our enemies, so I refrained.

"Maybe I have been. That doesn't mean that I'm wrong. Or that who programmed me is wrong."

Pondered this while others got into vehicles behind me. "Was it you who met the Bahrainis at the airport?"

"No, that was him." Which might mean this half of the original Christopher-Bot was indeed on our side. Or not.

"Of course, you could be lying."

"But if I'm programmed, according to you, I can't lie." And this was one of those chicken or the egg conundrums that you thought about until your brain hurt.

"Kitty, come on," Jeff said as my brain shared that lying could also be programmed. He joined us and took my hand. "Play with the robot later."

"Be careful," the Christopher-Bot the Second said. Then he went and lay down on his medical cot again.

"Stop encouraging those things," Jeff said.

"I wasn't. I just . . . what if he's sentient and what if he's right, regardless of sentience?" My dream made this seem unlikely, but then again, there was no guarantee I'd interpreted said dream correctly. Or that all of it wasn't just my subconscious freaking out, Broadway style.

"I think the best thing for us to assume is that everyone's out to kill us. That way, we're always prepared or pleasantly surprised."

"Cannot argue with that logic."

Len and Kyle were also in tuxes and waiting for us with the rest of Jeff's and my Secret Service details and a whole lot more, all the better to drive us all around. A-Cs had reflexes that were actually too good to operate human machinery, though Stephanie and Serene both had proved that this "handicap" could be overcome with enough willpower. But for the most part, A-Cs passengered and humans drove.

Jeff and I were stuck in the Beast, which was the President's super-reinforced limo that the A-Cs had looked at, sighed at, and then improved by adding all the security bells and whistles their vehicles had as standard issue. It was a big, well, beast, and that meant that Jeff and I, Lizzie, Wasim, Naveed, Gadhavi, and my parents could all fit into it, with Len driving and Kyle handling shotgun as always. Just barely, because it wasn't as roomy as one of Centaurion Division's stretch limos, but it'd do in a pinch.

"Director Reynolds is already on-site," Len said as he and Kyle helped us into the Beast. "He says that not all the guests are there yet, specifically the one we're all the most interested in, at least as far as he's seen."

"It might not be Stephanie coming. The Tinkerer could be making the appearance tonight."

"We'll find out," Mom said, as the last of us got in, Len and Kyle closed the doors and took their positions, and we all started off on the fifteen-minute drive to Sidwell. Mercifully, Kyle turned on tunes. "I Think I'm Paranoid" by Garbage came on. Wasn't sure if this was an Algar clue or just random chance. Decided not to care at the moment.

Was about to ask if we had any idea of what the guest list looked like now when my phone rang. Got it out and looked at the number. Blocked. "Not this again. Hello?"

"Is this the First Lady?" Man's voice, not one I recognized. Sounded like he was gasping or wheezing or else had a really bad head cold.

"It is and aren't you surprised? Who are you and why are you calling?"

"Don't go to the fundraiser."

"Why not, pray tell?"

"The robots are going to try to kill you."

And with that, my phone went dead.

CHAPTER 62

"CURIOUSER AND CURIOUSER."

"Who was that?" Jeff asked.

Shared the contents of one of my briefer Opening Gambit calls. "So, no idea who it was, too short to have traced even if I'd thought to ask for a tracer thingy, and giving no information other than that robots might be out to get me."

"I point to the two you put into a secured SUV as options one and two," Mom said.

"Yes, but they're not robots." However, even though they hadn't been onstage in my dream, they would count in the same category as Joe and Randy. Or would they? Wondered why they hadn't appeared in my dream. Maybe that was the question I was really supposed to have asked Terry or Algar, but it was too late to do so now.

"To you," Gadhavi said. "Perhaps to those who are your enemies, they are."

"And perhaps there are robots we're not aware of yet," Mom pointed out. There had been a significant gap on my dream stage, so Mom was probably right. As per usual.

This gave us all something to ponder while the song changed to Garbage's "The Trick Is to Keep Breathing." Okay, seemed like we were on random on Garbage's *2.0* album. Stopped worrying and just allowed the music to keep me calm.

"Wicked Ways" was next, then "Push It" was on as we arrived at Sidwell. Wondered again if these were clues or not as we lined up with all the rest of our big, black SUVs and limos in order to get parked. Had to say this for doing an event at a big hotel—the exit from the cars tended to be easier.

We ended up going into the parking garage because there

was no parking available for us outside. "Is this normal?" Wasim asked.

"Kind of. For us." I mean, why would anyone save a spot for the President, right?

Mom was on her phone. "Charles would prefer all of us in the garage. He has agents, CIA and Field, assigned to it, so feels it's safer than parking in the regular lots, though they have security, too."

Siler was waiting for us at our assigned parking place. He smiled at me, but when he spotted Lizzie, he got a look on his face I'd seen on my dad's—wistful pride. Then he looked at Wasim and was instantly channeling Jeff. Once we were all out of the car, he offered Lizzie his arm, which she took. "You look amazing, Elizabeth. You'll be the prettiest girl there, without even trying."

I'd never heard him use her full name before, but it made Lizzie stand up a little straighter and look proud, though she blushed, too. "Thanks . . . Dad." He smiled and kissed her forehead, careful not to disturb her hairdo or muss her makeup.

Wasim looked disappointed that Siler was escorting Lizzie, but Gadhavi nudged him and he wiped the look off of his face. Apparently Gadhavi had chosen to take the role of surrogate parent, or at least adult pal from the same region, for Wasim while he was in town. Hoped this didn't mean that Wasim learned how to run an illegal operation and kill people, but then again, we were probably a master class in the killing of bad guys, so perhaps Gadhavi just wanted to ensure the kid got some game romantically.

Took Jeff's arm as Mom took Dad's, then we headed off, Kyle and Naveed in front, Siler and Lizzie between them and us, Mom and Dad behind us, and Len, Daniel, and Joshua at the rear, with Marcus and Lucas on either flank.

Thankfully the parking garage had an elevator. We had to split up for the ride, but we all made it down without issue or loss of personnel. Put that firmly into the win column. Sure, it was a tiny win, but it was a win nonetheless and the day had not been chock-full of them.

Secret Service lined the path to the ballroom, which was great, because it was dark and I had only been here once. Was greeted by Camilla at the door. She was dressed like someone who worked on a small salary would be—her outfit was clearly store-bought and not from an overly expensive store, her hair and makeup were normal person good, and she looked thrilled to be here. In other words, she was dressed exactly how I would have been before I'd run into the gang from Alpha Four, and she matched the expressions of most of the people I could see behind her.

"We're so thrilled to have you here, Mister President," she said to Jeff, looking and sounding as if she'd never met him or the rest of us in her life. Had to admit it, she was damned good at infiltration.

Jeff gave her his Charming the In-Laws Smile, which worked on everyone, everywhere. Not on Camilla normally, however, that I'd ever seen. But she was in character and she visibly melted. Realized just how she'd been able to get in so well in so many places. If I didn't know her well, I would have thought she just resembled the woman I knew.

"Thank you," Jeff said. "We're happy to do whatever we can to support this fine institution and all the hardworking people who make it a safe place of learning for our children."

Had no idea if Raj had written that for Jeff or if Jeff had come up with it on his own, but Mrs. Paster was headed for us and near enough to hear, and she beamed.

Which was my cue. After all, the FLOTUS wasn't supposed to hang out with the girl checking everyone in at the door. The FLOTUS was supposed to be gracious and take the POTUS in to meet the big cheeses she knew.

Smiled at Camilla in the way I would at anyone I didn't really know and didn't have anything much to say to, then headed us straight for my intended target. "Jeff, this is Missus Paster, the principal of the school. She's amazing. Missus Paster, my husband, Jeff."

I let go of Jeff's arm and he shook Mrs. Paster's hand while giving her the Charming Smile as well. "Kitty's told me so much about the school and how well she feels you're running it. It's a pleasure to meet you, and so soon."

Mrs. Paster gave the feminine laugh that was between a giggle and a real laugh. Yeah, Jeff had that effect. "It's so wonderful to meet you, Mister President."

"Oh, please, call me Jeff. Kitty and I don't stand on a lot of formality."

Raj came over now. "Excuse me, Mister President, there are

some people here who'd like to meet you. Missus Paster, if you could come with us and perhaps give the President the heads-up on who he's meeting?"

"Of course," she said. "I'd be more than happy to."

With that, Jeff gave me a kiss on the cheek, offered his arm to Mrs. Paster, which she took with what seemed to be great joy, and they all headed off.

Which was fine with me because I wanted to get the lay of the land and see who was where. Though I had no idea where to start, really. It was a big room, and it reminded me a lot of the ballroom we'd been in for the President's Ball—lots of food and beverage stations, lots of little tables, a dance floor, a stage, and a tonnage of people. If everyone only gave $100 each, Marcia's event would be a success.

Someone came up and put his arm around my waist. "What's a beautiful girl like you doing alone in a place like this?"

CHAPTER 63

MANAGED NOT TO JUMP, but only because I recognized the voice. "James! When did you get here?"

He gave me a shot of the cover boy grin. "Gates are amazing things." He kissed my cheek. "We need to walk and talk so we're not obvious." Then he wrapped my arm in his and we started to wander.

"So, you scored the Kitty Wrangling?"

"Nope. Your replacement for me is busy, so I'm taking it retro."

"Oh, my God, you and Vance need to stop your Jealousy Wars. He's him, you're you, I need you both. And you're still my best friend, you know that."

"True enough. He's busy getting intel, which is why he passed me the signal to take care of you. We can't have the FLOTUS standing alone like she's been dumped."

"Did I look that pathetic?"

He chuckled. "Honestly? No. You look like I wish I could manage to go straight or at least bi."

"Awww. I'd still leave it all behind for you."

"That's what keeps me going. No one's seen Stephanie yet. We have Richard looking for Trevor, however it's been decades since he's seen the man, so Jeff might get introduced to him before we find him, if Trevor's the Doctor Rattoppare who's here. Meaning we probably have a little time, so tell me what all I missed. I've heard it from others, but I want your impressions. Loved your dance moves, by the way."

"I'm hoping they play that song tonight so I can see yours." Tossed on my good ol' Recap Girl cape and brought him up to speed on all he'd missed, including what the Christopher-Bot the Second had shared and my short and not sweet phone call.

"So, it's the same crap, different hour of the day." Would have loved to tell Reader about my dream and conversation with Algar, but that wasn't possible and was definitely against The Rules. "What did you guys find?"

"Things I can't tell you about here. Suffice to say that I think we have a huge issue brewing with the True Believers and their best friends, bigger even than what Gadhavi thought. But we can't do anything about it right now." He looked back at the doorway then turned back to me. "We're going to need our best infiltrator on it. And even then, I don't know if we can move."

"We'll cross that bridge when it falls on us. So, thoughts about the Bots?"

"No one at Dulce nor any of the Hackers are convinced that the Christopher-Bot is sentient, some gray matter or not. However, I had a long chat with Butler, and he and Maurer make a good case for the Kitty-Bot having become sentient even without gray matter. Reverse engineering a sentient being is likely to kill it, which is why they're so adamant about not letting us touch her. So, we're leaving her alone for the time being. But that still leaves the Christopher-Bot questions open. As in, is it sentient and how many more of them are there?"

Now was the time for all good Kittys to figure out how to share what they thought they knew without sounding insane. Wished the Kitty-Bot and her sentience were here for a moment, but soldiered on alone. "Um, you know, I had a kind of weird thought."

"Yeah? Normal weird or Kitty Weird?"

"Oh, I'm betting on Kitty Weird. So brace yourself. What if there's more to the Christopher-Bots than we realize?"

"I'm sure there is, but that hardly seemed brace-worthy. What are you getting at?"

"The Christopher-Bot the First morphed into something else entirely, twice, and both of those things could fly. What if . . . what if the Christopher-Bot was made with some kind of polymer that's not really from Earth? Or is, but is a superpolymer?"

"Okay. And?"

"And what if that polymer can not only morph, but can divide? It would explain why the brain is half the size we'd expect and why both of them said and appeared to think the same things—because they're really the same robot, or whatever it really is, divided in half. I mean, I would think this tech is alien, and by alien I mean from far outside our or the Alpha Centauri system."

"Seems a little like a reach. Wruck hasn't said that the Anciannas have anything like that, and if the Z'porrah did, then I'd think we'd have seen a lot more of this and a lot sooner."

"Dude, Cliff had the freaking Killer Octopus, and Drax confirmed there was no way that puppy was made with things a hundred percent from Earth. We keep on thinking that the only evil aliens out to affect Earth are the Z'porrah, but I'm really sure that, in a galaxy with billions of stars in it, there are plenty of others who've noted what a cool little out-of-the-way vacation or experimental hot spot we are and are meddling accordingly. Drax is merely a benevolent example, and let's be honest—if we hadn't gotten to him when we did, he could easily be a member of the Cackling Megalomaniacs League right now."

Waited. Could see the wheels in Reader's head turning. "Fair, and accurate, points. I think this is something we need to run by Chuck, honestly. But in a way your theory would fit. So, when would the Christopher-Bot division have happened? Before or after the Bot visited the Bahrainis at the airport?"

The music started up. "Open the Gate" by No Doubt. Had doubts that the school had chosen this for their swanky soundtrack, but was happy to be on the Algar Channel once again. "What if the polymer can't handle gate technology and the division happened then?"

"The gates handle everything."

"*Au contraire, mon ami.* Your husband told me only this afternoon that the gates had to be altered to ensure that all the new aliens here and that they knew about could safely use them, indicating that gates were originally only made to handle Alpha Centauri and Solaris systems matter."

"Yeah, you're right, and it's nice to see you going fancy with the French and all that. So what you're saying is what if whatever the Christopher-Bot is made of is something that can't handle the gate transfer?"

"Yeah, I'm willing to bet they are. The living beings that are shapeshifters are organic. Maybe the gates aren't created to handle an inorganic substance that can also morph. Or if they are, those substances would be from our two systems. If the polymer is from elsewhere, or has something extra in it from elsewhere, and either isn't from a planet represented on Earth now in some way, or is from a planet we don't know about, then it's very possible that it was affected by the gate transfer. I mean, they always make me sick and I'm organic. And, while I realize I don't pay attention all that often to things of this nature, I've never considered that a substance might not get through the gates. Worrying about electronics was different. I swear."

"I'm letting all the comments pass, girlfriend. But yeah, I think you're onto something. So you think the split happened after the visit with the Bahrainis at the airport?"

"Right after, yes, because, as far as we know, that's the only time the Christopher-Bot used a gate. And the timing would work out for both of them—one heads for the mission, the other sees his duplicate, and determines that said dupe is up to no good."

"That would also explain why there aren't any others around. There was one, probably the prototype, like the Kitty-Bot was a prototype. At least, let's hope there was only one, but we'll attempt optimism for a change and say only one. It was sent on a mission, and that mission created something no one was prepared for. Unless you think this was planned, which I don't."

"I don't, either, because it seems more random than even the most baroque of our supervillains has managed prior. As we know, anything's possible, but I call knowing the gate would divide your snazzy new creation highly improbable."

"As long as whoever's behind that is from Earth," Reader said.

The music changed to Pink's "One Foot Wrong" which was even more unlikely to be on Sidwell's or Marcia's party playlist. Took this to be Algar explaining that Reader's last statement was incorrect. I agreed, so that was nice, too. The song was a slower one, at least, as far as rock songs went. Reader led me onto the dance floor. We started doing a quickstep.

"No, they wouldn't have to be, because even if you were from far away, you'd see what looks like literally everyone using the gates and you might not consider that you have some element in your special morphing substance that wouldn't get through a gate safely. Not everyone plays chess eight moves ahead."

"Yeah, you and Reynolds do, though. So did Cliff."

"And he's dead. So they could be from anywhere and just not have given this enough thought. And let's hope that we can contain the information so that they never find out."

"Agreed. But answer this—how did they calibrate the gate?"

"Really? They have A-C vision, they have an A-C helping them, Clarence and/or Stephanie wrote a manual and passed it out to all our enemies, cough up another idea, they're all possible. It's not hard to do it if you're taught how and can see the dial."

"That might be why the division of the Christopher-Bot hap-

pened, too, then. Slightly off calculations that caused the split."
Reader was a great dancer, as good as Jeff, and we were gathering an audience, since we were the only ones on the dance floor.

"That's for all the Dazzlers and Hacker International to enjoy determining. I'm the big picture girl."

"Well, it might also explain how the busses arrived to attack the Intergalactic School. Unless you have another answer for that."

"Um, their wheels go 'round and 'round and all that nursery song jazz." My brain nudged. No idea why. Forged on. "And we must assume said busses were driven by underage Lizzie-Bots because we found no one else, Bots or people."

Reader dipped me. "That's for the highway patrol to worry about, I'm the big picture guy."

"You're the research dude and you know it."

He grinned as he pulled me back up. "I can multitask, too, you know. No, I mean how did the busses get all the way out there in the middle of the nowhere that Dulce and the Intergalactic School are in without anyone spotting them before you all did visually?"

"Ah. I have no idea. When did the Science Center spot them?"

"Based on what William said, about the same time you did."

"Our enemies are using a big gate, then."

"But the only one left who can create an impromptu gate is locked up tight in the Zoo." Reader pointed out. "Barring Kozlow and Gadhavi running all this."

"I don't buy that. I could be wrong, mind you, but it doesn't fit their characters at all."

"So, again, that means someone has access to a large gate," Reader said as the music changed to "Come Dancing" by The Kinks, and he swung us into a cha-cha. Other people started to get onto the dance floor, too. About time and I figured this one was just a song, versus a clue. Though I stayed alert, just in case.

"Who doesn't? I mean that literally. There are large gates at the Dome and Home Base, but over time we've put a lot of big ones in due to Jeff's moving up in the political ranks. All it requires is a traitor or someone who needs some extra cash who can calibrate the gate and Bob's your uncle, seven busses roll into the desert."

Reader shook his head. "It would have to be from a site we don't monitor."

"Well, I'm pretty certain I know which site, then."

CHAPTER 64

"I'M ALL EARS, GIRLFRIEND," Reader said, as he danced us away from the few other couples who'd chosen to actually try to have fun.

"Dude, how quickly you forget. The NSA is involved with the Fem-Bot Factory. Meaning the NSA has a gate."

"Well, yes, they do, just like all the other Alphabet Agencies. Not big enough to send busses through, though."

"Really? I point to the NSA black site no one knew existed that was really close to home. If there's one NSA black site out there, then who's to say there aren't a dozen? It seems to me that half of the covert ops in this country are focused on hiding themselves and what they're doing from Mom and Chuckie as if their lives depended upon it."

Reader swirled me out, then swirled me back. "Which they do, in that sense. And Goodman could have put in a lot of things we don't know about, too."

"I agree, and I think it's safe to call it a fact. He could have gotten a gate installed that no one told us about simply by using his various connections." Maybe Z'porrah power cubes could do more than just move someone via thought, too. Sure, we had the one Cliff had used, but the Z'porrah had been back since then. Of course this was, like so much else, currently unprovable. We could test it, but only if Algar and the Poofs allowed it, which I wasn't betting on.

"It's hard to argue with the fact that we found that factory on the NSA's turf," Reader admitted. "I'll give you that. But we have no proof and less than no idea of who at the NSA would be the big cheese. As you said, they're hiding well from Angela and Chuck."

The music changed to "Rhyme Stealer" by Sugar Ray—a song I was a hundred percent positive no one other than Algar could have possibly programmed into the fundraiser's playlist—and my memory did me a solid and shared stuff I'd heard, seen, or thought in the past couple of days as it related to this, as Reader and I moved into hip-hop moves. Everyone else scurried off the dance floor. Algar was harshing the party's buzz, big-time, but it was helping the cause. "The nursery rhymes."

"Excuse me?" Reader sounded lost.

"Whoever's created the Christopher-Bot is into nursery rhymes. I don't know that I've run across anyone who's dropped a rhyme like the Christopher-Bots that wasn't teaching pre-school in some way. Meaning it was programmed in. If Antony Marling was still alive it would mean nothing. But he's dead and I don't think the Christopher-Bots have been around as long as they insinuated. They're too advanced." My dream had definitely confirmed this. "But they were told or programmed to believe they'd been around for a good long while."

"Why do that?"

"To throw us off if we ever got our hands on it. The First was going to tell us who was in charge."

"Per what Alpha Team was told, right before the Second blew him to bits."

"Yep. Morphing bits that ended up forming into a capture net just like my teams dealt with at the NSA black site. Meaning that whoever's in charge, they're for sure NSA. My bet is that they've been around for ages, well-hidden and even better protected, and none of us have noticed them, because they've kept the lowest profile of any of our other nemeses."

"So, anyone we've never heard of is a suspect? That won't take us long to hunt down. Only about a century or so." Like all the rest of my circle, Reader possessed a sarcasm knob.

"Maybe not. Mom's been hunting in a very determined fashion, and while she hasn't found who at the NSA authorized that black site where we found the Fem-Bot Factory, that does mean she's eliminated a lot of suspects. They could be a man or a woman, a human or an alien in hiding, but I guarantee we're going to discover that they were the person working first with either Madeleine Cartwright or Monica Strauss, or both, and now with Janelle Gardiner. And whoever they are, they're into nursery rhymes."

"Well, it might help us spot them, but only if we're interacting with this person. I sincerely doubt that Angela's going to be able to start asking suspects about their love of nursery rhymes unless she wants to be put on psychiatric leave."

"We have a little more than that. I'm sure they knew Yates, they probably know the Tinkerer—and this person could *be* the Tinkerer, because no one even suspected Trevor existed until Operation Madhouse, though I kind of doubt it. And they were likely a friend of the late Quinton Cross, too, since Cross was Janelle's protector and benefactor prior to Operation Epidemic."

Reader sighed as the music changed to "Private Eyes" by Hall & Oates and moved us back into a foxtrot. "The bottom line is that we're unlikely to figure out who this mysterious NSA honcho is at this party. But we have a far more urgent and pressing issue—someone called to tell you that robots were going to try to kill you here tonight. I think that has to be our priority, regardless of the fact that we have half of a full Christopher-Bot in custody. As today proved, they seem to have plenty of Fem-Bots to spare."

"We might have one here already, or one more like the Kristie-Bot. As I know you already know, Hacker International found the name Kramer during their otherwise fruitless and/or slow searches. Let's see if Marcia's the robot that's going to give assassination a try."

CHAPTER 65

READER TWIRLED ME OFF the dance floor and we got some polite applause. Noted a lot of faces I recognized—those applauding had been helpers at the Bake Sale Catastrophe. Those not applauding had been in Charmaine's Entourage.

Quietly pointed this out to Reader as I waved to the applauders and ignored the others. Spotted the kids—they were hanging out near a food table. Lizzie had been right, not only was the eldest Kramer boy here, but the Cordell twins were as well. Spotted some other teenagers, all of whom looked vaguely familiar. Clearly we weren't the only parents that had caved to the demands and let the kids dress up and come out on the first night of school. Bad parenting trophies for all!

As far as I could tell, the Valentino kids were doing what we'd asked them to and chatting up the Cordell twins, though Louise wasn't with them. Looked around for her as well as we wandered the hall looking for Marcia. There were too many people around us now for us to discuss what we had been, so I changed the topic. "Think you're going to get press as my new squeeze?"

"Only if I'm lucky. Chuck normally scores that honor."

"He's dating Nathalie now." Shared what Jeff had told me and Lizzie as Reader snagged some drinks for us from a tray marked as nonalcoholic being passed by a waiter.

Took a close look—Chuckie and I had almost died during Operation Drug Addict because we hadn't paid attention to the dude serving our drinks. There was nothing remarkable about the waiter, but did my best to log what he looked like, just in case. Sipped my drink. Cherry 7-Up wasn't my fave, but it did look like pink champagne, so could understand why it'd been chosen.

"Yeah? Good for them! It's about time."

"Excuse me?"

"While I'd never sell you short, girlfriend—because if you'd said yes he'd have never looked at another woman again—and I know how much Chuck and Naomi loved each other, Nathalie's a catch for anyone. And I knew her when we were both younger, remember, and what she wants really hasn't changed as an adult."

"What does she want?" The music was now instrumental and nothing I recognized. Apparently the Algar Channel was taking a commercial break.

"What she's always wanted—someone like Chuck. Smart, tall, handsome, successful, driven without being blinded by it, gentle, kind, caring, loyal. He's literally the guy she described to me as her perfect man when we were both seventeen."

"Wow. And yet she cheated on Edmund with Eugene. I can see some similarities to Chuckie in Edmund. Not so with Eugene."

"I'm guessing Chuck has what both of them had—Edmund's brains and drive and Eugene's abilities in bed."

"My husband will not like my confirming that latter point. Especially since I never slept with Eugene. However, yeah, I can't argue."

Reader grinned at me. "Jeff can get mad at me, then. He hasn't had a good jealousy rage for ages. Anyway, I'd have tried to fix them up but neither one seemed emotionally ready."

"You're just an old softy. But yeah, glad Elaine arranged it."

"You and she can fight over who gets to be the matron of honor at the wedding."

"You really think they'll make it?" I hoped so, because, as Jeff had said, they both deserved to be happy.

"I do. However, I don't see our hostess anywhere, do you?"

"No. But I don't see Vance, either. It's likely he's with Marcia." Spotted Charmaine. She was in a white dress and was near the stage, chatting up several people, Zachary Kramer included. Decided I could miss dropping by that group for a while.

Finally found Louise. She was sticking near to Jeff, who had a huge group of women around him. Actively chose not to be jealous—he went home with me, and one of his nieces was right there. Presumably he wasn't going to be cheating on me in the middle of the fundraiser, though several of the women looked more than ready to go for it.

"Vance wasn't with her when I spoke to him. He was with some others, though."

"Well, I guess we chat up whoever on our Hunt For Marcia Kramer so it doesn't look suspicious, and that way we can say we're asking people to donate to the school."

"Well then, let's check in with your Chief of Staff." Reader steered us toward a portable bar where Vance, Culver, Abner, Colette, and Gadoire were hanging out with a lot of people I didn't know.

Vance broke away and kissed my cheek. "Get ready to shout bingo," he whispered.

So, these were the other Dealers of Death. And it was time for my close-up.

Because Vance was my Chief of Staff, gave Gadoire a hug first and allowed him to slobber on me, or what he called being courtly, and kiss the back of my hand. That was me, always taking one for the team. "Ah, my dove, you're radiant as always."

"And you're still a wild flatterer, Guy."

Extracted my hand, gave Abner a hug, then ensured I gave Culver a bigger one and an almost-touching air kiss. "Lillian, it feels like ages since I've seen you and it was only yesterday. You're looking amazing as always. No one wears red like you."

She beamed at me. "And no one can carry off a dress of any color like you, Kitty. I don't believe you know everyone here?"

"No, I don't believe we've had the pleasure, either James or myself."

Culver did her best, but I stopped trying to remember who was who within five seconds. Some I'd recall and I'd be able to spot all their faces again, and Vance and Reader would just have to do the rest. However, there was someone conspicuously absent.

"Where's Thomas?" I asked Culver, midway through the intros.

"Oh, he's with Charles and Nathalie," Culver shared breezily. "They're discussing sports, and you know how quickly that gets dull if it's not your passion."

Chuckie had no sports passions other than Australian ones that didn't involve suffering through a game with me, Nathalie was into fashion, not football, and I'd yet to hear Kendrick mention a team or a sport, let alone a passion for one. Meaning they were snooping and that was just fine.

"Well, we'll leave them to it." Back to more meeting of people I instinctively knew I wouldn't care for. Profiling for the win.

Somerall and Lee joined us, trailed by a lot of our security forces, as I finished shaking the last paw, which belonged to Niles Berkowitz, while deciding that he was never getting invited for Passover, despite him going for the "we're both Jews, isn't that great?" opening gambit. Berkowitz was Big Oil's lobbyist and Somerall's bestie. Those two shook paws while I ostensibly looked around for Kendrick and watched this group out of the corners of my eyes.

All these people reminded me of two groups—the Cabal of Evil and the Land Sharks. Somerall and Gardiner were both in the Land Sharks and Kendrick had been. Of course, Culver, Abner, Gadoire, and Vance had all been in the Cabal. So had Nathalie. Things changed.

"Lillian, do you have any idea where's Marcia is? I spotted Zachary with the President of the Sidwell Friends School Parent Teacher Association, but I haven't been able to find our hostess. We were looking for her when we spotted you."

"They were here earlier," shared Simon "Homophobe" Hopkins, the Alcohol lobby's go-to man. He was standing as far from Gadoire as possible. Gadoire wasn't my favorite person, but he'd proven his loyalty, and besides, Hopkins disliked him for who he loved. Confirmed that I hated Hopkins, which came as no surprise. "But Marcia wasn't with them. How are you getting on with Charmaine?"

So, he knew her. Not a surprise. Had to come up with something positive to say. "She's quite the powerhouse."

Hopkins nodded. "Impressive woman. You'll like her husband, Bob, too. He's a venture capitalist." Loved the assumption that I liked Charmaine, but didn't contradict it.

"How wonderful." Wasn't totally sure what a venture capitalist did, other than make lots of money. Didn't care, either.

Berkowitz shoved back in. "Bob's a go-getter. He's on the board of several prominent corporations, too." Wondered if Cordell was as awful as his wife or if he worked hard to spend less time around her. My vote, without meeting him, was for the latter, but there was no accounting for taste.

"Really?" Reader asked, sounding just this side of bored. "Which ones?"

"YatesCorp, Gaultier Enterprises, Titan Security," Berkowitz ticked off without missing a beat. He kept on listing company names but my ears chose to share that the other names weren't relevant to my interests. "So you can see," Berkowitz concluded, "he's quite well-connected."

"Sounds like it." Now Reader sounded totally bored. He was good, and I was keeping my mouth shut. Spent the time looking around as if what I really wanted to do was find Marcia and stop all this boring business talk.

Interestingly enough, no one used this moment to try to sell me on anything. So they weren't all that much like the Cabal of Evil or the Land Sharks had been—they had no interest in playing nicely with our particular brand of others. Which still seemed odd and stupid. In less time than it had taken me to swallow a sip of tea, the Land Sharks had been at me. And the less said about how quickly the Cabal of Evil had pounced the better.

But the other Dealers of Death had no interest in swaying me, or even broaching the subject. Truly doubted they felt I was wily and someone to avoid, since everyone liked to sell me really short. Was about to create a reason to move on when I saw Hopkins' gaze move behind me. His eyes narrowed. Noted other Death Dealer gazes were also focused and angry.

"Seriously, has Marcia been kidnapped?" Turned around to "search" for her and saw who Hopkins had spotted—Lizzie. She was laughing at something one of the other kids had said, and she looked like a normal teenager at a fancy affair, not like someone worthy of the wrath of a dozen adults.

However, my ward having taught their kids a strong anti-bullying message—by kicking their butts—at her former school, which was possibly even more prestigious than Sidwell and was also in Portugal, was not the reason they hadn't spoken to us pretty much ever. It was why she was living with us now, but it wasn't why the Dealers of Death weren't interested in what American Centaurion and the Office of the President could offer them. Which bore more investigation, but not tonight.

Turned back. "I see her nowhere. James, we need to hunt her down, I need to find out how she wants to handle donations." Smiled at all the Dealers of Death. "And thank you all again for coming to support Sidwell. I realize most of your children don't school here, so it's doubly gracious of you to help out."

Eyes widened or narrowed, depending. But before anyone else could respond, Somerall spoke up. "Oh, look, there's Janelle and Amos."

Sure enough, Gardiner and Tobin had arrived, along with more security. Lee waved them over. Managed not to ask her if she wasn't worried about being called a traitor for having dropped by the White House the other day, but had a feeling that wouldn't get a useful response. Really wished I'd asked if Somerall and Lee were the robots who were going to try to kill me.

Gardiner was in her mid- to late-forties, trim, attractive, with long dark hair she always had in some sort of up-do. Her Washington color was green, possibly to match her eyes—I'd never asked, but she was in green tonight as per usual.

Tobin was a nice-looking, later-middle-aged black man, with only a little paunch around the middle. Tobin lived for a folksy look, so while he was usually in a suit and tie, the tie was a bolo, his shoes were expensive cowboy boots, and he always wore a Stetson. He had a lot of Stetsons, since his accessories always matched whatever he was wearing, though black was his favorite color, in part because he also lived to always say that good guys wore black.

They said hello to everyone, getting handshakes or hugs, depending. Had to fake it with Gardiner, since I didn't want her realizing that we'd figured out that she wasn't a victim. Gave her a brief hug because more effusiveness would be just as suspicious as avoiding her. "How are you doing?" Seemed like the safest form of hello.

She gave me a brave little smile. "As well as I can be," her eyes darted to Somerall and Lee then back to me, "under the circumstances."

Tobin, wearing his usual Man In Black attire, ten-gallon Stetson included, went in for a hug. I could let him do it or knee him in the balls. Took yet another one for the team and allowed the hug. "Madam First Lady, you're a sight for sore eyes."

"You're looking well yourself, Mister Tobin." Was glad he'd remembered that he wasn't on my list of those who got to be informal with me. The Formal Only list was far shorter, but felt that most of those I was standing with were firmly on it, at least for the time being.

Felt surrounded, because we were. In fact, Tobin had moved himself between me and Reader. Did not like this particular situation, because there were a lot more of them than there were of us. However, I didn't allow it to throw me. Instead, I smiled and nodded while they talked about absolutely nothing. Possibly they were passing coded messages, but if they were, the deciphering would have to be done by someone else, preferably Chuckie.

The music went from whatever instrumental selections I'd been ignoring to "Move Along" by The All-American Rejects. The Algar Channel was back from its commercial break and the hint could not be clearer. It was a direction I was all too eager to follow, too.

"James," I said, interrupting some boring story about the olden days of corporate mergers that Myron Van Dyke, the head lobbyist for Big Pharma, was droning on about, "I'm sorry, but we really need to find Marcia."

"Do you have to leave just now?" Berkowitz asked. "We were just getting to know you."

How they were doing that by not talking to me was anyone's guess. Maybe they were all robots and were filming us. Who knew? Figured I'd find out somewhere along the line. However, not right now.

Gave everyone a big smile. "So sorry, we'll try to join up with you again, but duty really does call." Mouths opened, but I was the FLOTUS and I had The Power Of The Paw. Put up my hand. The mouths all closed. "I appreciate your enthusiasm, but I promised Marcia I'd find her first thing, and we've spent all this time having fun. James? Let's move on, please."

Reader nodded to everyone, moved between me and Van Dyke, offered his arm which I took, and we left the Death Trap in our dust.

CHAPTER 66

"**G**OD, I THOUGHT we'd never get away," Reader said, as we started looking for Marcia in earnest again.

"Dude, truer words and all that."

Still didn't see Marcia, but spotted the corner where Chuckie, Nathalie, and Kendrick were standing and joined them, in no small part because they were hidden from the Dealers of Death Huddle. Hugged everyone, but noted that Kendrick looked worried. Chuckie too, though he was hiding it. "What's wrong?"

"I discovered that someone's stolen Titan tech," Kendrick said. "We aren't sure if it's domestic or international thieves, but all the information on our Miniaturization line has been taken."

"Taken or copied?" Reader asked.

"Taken, then replaced with schematics that look right but are wrong. It was discovered yesterday. We've torn the building and all our data apart, but it's gone."

"That line, that's the one with the metal tarantulas and other bugs, right?"

"Yes," Chuckie answered. "As in, someone's stolen the tech that was used against us and also taken the information that would allow us to combat it."

"My bet is Gaultier Enterprises and/or YatesCorp. Conveniently, Janelle Gardiner and Amos Tobin are here with a whole slew of other noxious people. Enjoy questioning them."

"We can't," Kendrick said. "There's literally no evidence that connects them to this at all."

We all heaved a group sigh. "I suppose I should go over and support Vance," Nathalie said. "Perhaps they'll say something that would give us a clue to who stole the tech."

"Only if you're thinking the tech was stolen before all of us

were born. Myron Van Dyke is possibly the most boring person
I've met in a long time, and he's telling the longest story in the
world. I'm sure it's not over. It may not be over until we all go
home."

"They won't tell you anything," Reader added. "I'm sure
they know you and Chuck are dating by now, even though it's
not common knowledge."

Kendrick looked surprised. "Really? That's great, congratu-
lations!"

Chuckie looked a little embarrassed, but Nathalie just
laughed and hugged him. "We were trying to be discreet."

"Sorry, I'm the one who told James. I was kind of excited to
share the news."

Chuckie smiled at me. "It's okay, Kitty. I'm glad you approve."

"I do. But since we're supposed to be all stealth about your
romantic life—and I assume that's just so Chuckie can continue
to dominate the tabloids as my not-so-secret lover because he
just digs the spotlight—have you guys seen Marcia?"

They all laughed. "Oh yes," Nathalie said. "And I want to be
on record as having an affair with Jeff, just so that we keep it in
the family."

"Let's just say you're all swingers now," Reader suggested
with a wicked grin.

"I think that would mean getting more attention from Guy
than I want." I wanted none, so any extra wasn't what I was
hoping for. "So no." The music changed to "In the Next Room"
by the Neon Trees. Considered this. "I realize this ballroom is
huge, but James and I have been what seems like all over. Is
there another room she might be in?"

"Bathroom," Nathalie suggested. "I know she's here, we
spoke with her when we arrived."

"Only if she's got a gastrointestinal issue. We literally hav-
en't seen her since we got here."

"The kitchen is all I can think of," Chuckie said.

"Worth a shot."

He told us where the kitchens were and Reader and I headed
that way. Jeff was now up on the stage, talking to Kramer and
Charmaine and whoever they were with. Would have worried
but he was loaded with security. Speaking of which, I hadn't
seen mine anywhere. Mentioned this to Reader, who sighed.

"Kitty, we're here to work. Everyone's aware that you work
better without the Secret Service shadowing you."

"I'm just shocked that everyone's finally accepted reality."

"They're literally lining the walls. They just aren't hanging out with us. You're still stuck with only me."

"I'll try to find the will to go on."

We reached the kitchen's swinging door, which Reader opened carefully since staff were bustling in and out and he didn't want to hit anyone or be hit. Entered a short hallway and came to another swinging door. Made it inside unscathed, but only just. To see utter bedlam.

People were running back and forth, others were shouting at each other or everyone, and it was hot. "What the hell?"

Reader chuckled. "Welcome to what a real kitchen looks like." He put his arm around my waist and moved us deftly through and around.

"Nothing's on fire, therefore, it's nothing like what I consider a real kitchen." Hey, I wasn't what anyone would consider good in the kitchen. I could make omelets normally without burning the house down. Otherwise? Jeff had done all the cooking when we'd felt unsociable and hadn't wanted to eat in the Base commissary or with the others at the Embassy, and the Elves had always delivered when Jeff didn't want to cook. Now Chef and P-Chef managed this part of my life, and I was droolingly grateful for it.

"Good point." Reader zipped us around a clutch of servers, backtracked us to avoid something spilling, stopped to point out a spice to a prep cook who was searching for it, and spotted Marcia, all in the space of about thirty seconds.

"How is it you're so comfy in here?"

"I'm from Vegas, remember? One of my uncles runs a restaurant in Caesar's. I used to help out when I wanted a break from modeling, especially when I was a teenager."

"Wow. You saw this kind of chaos as a *break* from being the world's top male fashion model?"

He grinned. "Yep. You can learn a lot about managing people and situations working in a big kitchen."

"Wow again. You learned major life skills, I learned about how to use the fire extinguisher. One of these things is not like the other."

Reader laughed. "Oh, you learned what you needed, girl-friend, never doubt it."

We reached Marcia, who was in animated conversation with the man I figured was the head chef. They weren't screaming or hitting each other, but both seemed just a moment or two away. They were fighting about supplies, as near as I could make out. And neither one of them noticed that we were there.

"Marcia, there you are." Said more to ensure she and the chef didn't come to blows than anything else.

It worked. They both stopped and turned toward us. The chef looked like he wanted to tell us to get out, Marcia looked ready to burst into tears. "Oh, Madam First Lady, I'm so sorry you had to come searching for me."

The chef jerked at my title, stood up straighter, and instantly put a pleasant expression onto his face. Wasn't surprised he hadn't recognized me—I wasn't with Jeff, I wasn't in my FLO-TUS colors, and the world wasn't blowing up around me. Totally understood his confusion.

"Marcia, it's fine, and we've known each other long enough that you shouldn't be calling me anything other than Kitty. But everything in here doesn't seem to be going well. Is there anything we can do to help?"

"I'm sorry, Kitty, I'm just so frazzled right now."

"So, tell me what we do to unfrazzle you."

She eyed Reader. "Ah, is your husband here?"

Knew what she was insinuating. Marcia had already thought I was having an affair with White, the tabloids lived to insist Chuckie and I were zooming each other, why not think I was parading my latest boyfriend around at the Sidwell fundraiser? At least it meant Marcia felt that I had great taste in men.

"Yes, he's currently talking to your husband and Charmaine Cordell. This is James Reader, the Commander of all of American Centaurion's military forces. He's my babysitter for tonight. Back to you. What's going on?"

"We're missing half of our food supply," the chef said, voice clipped. "As in, we're going to run out of hors d'oeuvres within half an hour. This would be bad enough at a regular event, but for this to happen when the President and First Lady are here, along with the foreign dignitaries they've graciously brought with them, is, frankly, going to ruin me."

"It's true," Marcia said, sounding close to tears. "And I'm so sorry. Things seemed so prepared earlier."

"Seriously? One event without enough snacks and you don't work in this town again?" They all looked at me. Could feel all three of them thinking "duh" at me in a very loud way. And, they were right. There was always someone right behind you, ready to leap when you made the smallest mistake. Screwing up the food—which would be considered the chef's fault, regardless of reality—was indeed career death. He'd have to pray Reader's uncle needed an assistant in order to keep working at the level he was at. "Um, yeah, okay, having given that another moment's thought, yeah, I get it."

"What happened?" Reader asked briskly. "And what do you need?"

"Three of our food delivery trucks haven't arrived," the chef said. "We have no idea where they or their drivers have gone. As for what we need, things we can't find at this hour in the quantities we need."

"We can," I said calmly. "Just tell James what it is you want. We'll get it for you."

The chef looked like he didn't believe me, but he gave Reader a list anyway. Or, rather, he gave Pierre the list via speakerphone.

Marcia shook her head. "Bob went off to try to gather things, and we haven't heard from him, either."

"Bob?"

"Cordell, Charmaine's husband."

"So, she's aware that we're having a food crisis?"

"She is." Marcia grimaced. "She didn't offer to help out, Bob did. He's a lovely man."

"What's he doing married to Charmaine?" Whoops. My mouth was speaking without my brain's permission. Hated when that happened.

Marcia rolled her eyes. "Who knows? I mean, she's attractive, and driven, and she's done wonders for the school. But she's so . . . mean."

"Yeah, and this is coming from two women who survived the Washington Wife class."

She managed to laugh. "Exactly."

"I was searching for you to figure out how we wanted to do the donations. I brought a lot of people who have told me they're going to give money, but I have no idea how they're supposed to do that."

"Charmaine was supposed to tell me what to do. But instead she and my husband spotted a mutual friend and went off to talk to him."

"Really? Who?"

"Doctor Rattoppare."

CHAPTER 67

HOPED I'D MANAGED TO get my poker face on. "Who's that?"

Marcia shrugged. "Someone they both revere. Zachary met him when he was on Senate business in France."

Realized that we'd assumed the Kramer on Stryker's list was Marcia. But, as I thought about it, Marcia was Kramer's third wife. Apparently when one wore out, he just dumped her and got a new one. So, the person aging was him, in that sense. But right now, he was at the Perfect Politician age and had Perfect Politician looks. Knew he wanted to be President, and looks had mattered in the Presidential elections since the Kennedy-Nixon debates. Why not stay just as he was now? He had a slew of kids, so wife number four could either come with her own or just need to not want any. Maybe he'd stored his sperm, for that matter. Either way, he didn't need more children. What he felt he needed was Jeff's job.

Time to find out if Marcia had done the Treatment, too, though. "So, you haven't met the good doctor?"

She grimaced. "No. Zachary feels that we wouldn't have anything in common. Which is insulting to me, but you put up with your husband's quirks, right?"

Jeff's quirks basically consisted of him being jealous and needing adrenaline if he'd overdone it in terms of saving the world and using his empathic talents. Other than that, I didn't consider perfection to be quirky. "Ah, right."

"Handled," Reader said to us, saving me from having to make any more comments about the state of Marcia's marriage, as a stream of agents flowed into the kitchens, carrying a lot of foodstuffs. "You have the number now, so if you need anything else, just call Pierre and he'll ensure that you have whatever you need."

The chef grinned and shook Reader's hand. "Thank you. I owe you, so if your chef ever needs a vacation," he looked me, "and I include the White House in this, just call me and I'll fill in, free of charge." He handed Reader his card, then went back to shouting at his staff. Decided that my not being comfortable in kitchens was A-okay.

"May I?" Reader asked Marcia, as he put his arm back around my waist.

She giggled. "It's hard to say no to the handsomest man around."

"Isn't it though? I almost never say no to James."

"Oh, that's because I'm always right." Reader put his other arm around Marcia's waist and escorted us out, once again moving us through the kitchen like a pro.

"Oh, and before I forget, thank you so much for bringing along the *Good Day USA!* anchors and that delicious Jürgen Cologne." Marcia giggled again. "He truly is a charming, talented man."

"He is. But I haven't seen him, Kristie, or Adam since we've been here."

"Oh, they set up with the *Good Day USA!* crew on the back patio of the ballroom. They're doing interviews with Jürgen and various guests. It's going to be wonderful publicity."

"I sincerely hope so. What are the odds Charmaine takes all the credit for it?"

"I wouldn't bet against it," Marcia said.

"I wouldn't either," Reader said as we rejoined the party. It seemed extremely calm in comparison to the kitchens. Reader spotted White. "Ladies, will you excuse me a moment? I need to speak with Richard about American Centaurion's donation."

"Sure, and whatever he thinks, ensure that the dignitaries that came along are giving at least as much."

Reader nodded. "Absolutely." He headed off for White, presumably to share that it was Trevor who was here and to help with the search. Hoped he'd also figured out that Kramer was the new cyborg, but it was Reader so he probably had.

This, though, left me with Marcia and not a lot to talk about. Went for the lame but obvious as we wandered through the ballroom, thankfully not on the side where the Dealers of Death were hanging out. "Sidwell has a nice setup."

"It does," Marcia agreed. "Since the lower schools have been able to join this campus, the amenities the school can provide have increased immeasurably. They've even added dormitories for out-of-state and out-of-country students."

"Impressive." It was. It was like this was a mini-college in some ways. The tuition, for starters. "Why does the PTA need so much money, though?"

"Oh, well, it's because we raise the funds for things like those dormitories, this ballroom, the kitchens, and so on. We ensure that whatever school supplies—be it books, tutors, professional guests and outside experts, and so on—are available for all of the faculty. As well as providing the ability for the teachers to take the children on trips to more than the zoo."

"Hey, I like the zoo."

"Oh, I do, too. And we have a treasure trove of museums and such here. But still, there's something special about being able to go to the place where the history happened."

"Wait, you do foreign field trips?"

"Well, we support them, yes, and the children get to go, within reason for their ages and what their parents will allow. We also cover the costs for the parental chaperones. As the President of the PTA, Charmaine is normally the one who gets to go, and she chooses the parents who are also allowed to go as chaperones. Needless to say, I've never been included." She tried to make the last sentence sound light, but didn't manage it.

Felt bad for Marcia. Her first set of friends had kind of dumped her to hang out with me—a state of affairs no one who'd known us in the Washington Wife class could have ever predicted, Buchanan included—and now Charmaine kept her out of Sidwell's PTA in-crowd. And, frankly, her husband had also backed the wrong horse and created enemies out of the people currently in power. The woman couldn't win.

"Well, I'm sure you and your friends here still manage to do fun things with the kids."

She looked at me with a combination of shame and pity on her face. "No. There's only two camps here for parents—those who've earned Charmaine's favor and those who haven't. I haven't. And, despite all you've done to help me make this fundraiser a success, I don't think I ever will."

"But that doesn't mean you don't have friends here." I sincerely hoped.

She shrugged. "In a way. But everyone's cowed by Charmaine. I am, too, so I can't pass judgment."

"So, she really is the head of the Mean Girls here, isn't she?"

"Yes. She gives you opportunities to get into her favor but . . ."

"Well, I'm about a hundred percent certain she set both of us up to fail."

"She might have," Marcia said sadly. "I just feel badly for Clinton."

"Clinton?"

"My stepson. He's the youngest of Zachary's children with his second wife, but he lives with us and he's our eldest here. He's a senior, but that's too close to Charmaine's children's year. They've made things . . . difficult for him. Especially because he didn't go to Sidwell all the way through, so he didn't have an established base of friends before Charmaine arrived."

"So, they've chosen to bully the kid of a senator? My God, what are they doing to your younger kids?"

"Oh, Mason and Maverick are fine. They're far enough away from Charmaine's children that they haven't been affected. All your younger children should be good." She glanced to where her stepson was, with Lizzie and the other kids. "Maybe your ward will change things."

"Like she did at her last school?" This time, my mouth wasn't writing a check my brain hadn't wanted to cash. I wanted to see Marcia's reaction.

She nodded. "Yes, hopefully just like that."

The music, which had once again been instrumental, changed to "Temptation Waits" by Garbage. Algar wanted my attention, or else he was just really on a Garbage kick, but I didn't know why. Considering who we had in the room, this clue could relate to anyone and anything.

Looked around, just in case. Jeff was still on the stage with Charmaine and Kramer and a few other people. Had no idea where Louise was, though. Maybe she was off canoodling with someone and Algar didn't approve? But she was a big girl and an A-C, so it was doubtful any human was going to mess with Louise unless Louise wanted to be messed with.

"Well, I'm not sure how well Clinton's gotten to know the kids that fall under the category of 'mine,' but they're all together, so maybe that's a good thing."

"Maybe." She sighed. "I just worry about him. He's a sweet boy. He deserves better than I think he's getting. Not in terms of academics," she added quickly. "The school is excellent in that way. And also in terms of opportunities and the wealth of universities who want Sidwell graduates."

"But socially. Yeah, it's hard to be the outcast." Chuckie could write volumes about that. "Then again, if a group of outcasts get together, they can overcome the mean kids."

"Somewhat, I suppose." She looked away. Not at anything that I could tell. "We made you an outcast in our class."

"We never really leave high school, I guess. Besides, I survived."

"Because of who you are. As a person, not your position." She turned back to me. "I wasn't kind, and yet you've done nothing but be supportive and gracious."

Shrugged. "I'm willing to give most people a second chance."

She cocked her head at me. "Why?"

"Because there's more to everyone than we see. And not everyone can stand up to bullies. I'm just good at it."

"You protected Eugene."

"Yeah, don't remind me."

She nodded. "He fooled everyone, in more ways than one."

"True enough." The music changed to Fall Out Boy's "The Kids Aren't Alright." Decided it was time to drop by and get down verbally with the young folks. "You know, speaking of the kids, I'm going to go over and see how they're doing."

"They don't like that."

"Yeah, I know. Which is why I'm going to do it and you're going to go make sure that Charmaine's not boring my husband to death."

She grimaced. "Okay, I'll do my best."

"Meet you over there. Remember—this is your event, you're the one who gets to make the decisions and announcements and so forth. We need to stop letting her give everyone blame while she takes all the credit." With that, I headed off for the kids.

Was coming up behind them, since they were still clustered around a food table, and a table with beverages that I hadn't spotted earlier. It had several punch bowls and cups on it with a large sign noting that these punches were all nonalcoholic and therefore what all the underage guests were expected to drink.

One of the waiters came by with an empty tray, filled and loaded a bunch of cups onto it, and headed off into the crowd, toward the stage it looked like, nodding to the other waiters he passed.

Examined him. Was pretty sure it was the same waiter who'd

served me and Reader earlier, but the waitstaff were all dressed
alike, and this man was average height and build just like the
other had been. He was about White's age, but so were many
others on staff, and though he was attractive, there was nothing
all that remarkable about him. He didn't seem interested in what
was going on, just doing his job, which was pretty much what
waitstaff did when they were working a party like this one.

Looked around. All the waitstaff nodded to each other as they
passed. Presumably it was a policy, possibly to be polite, possibly to indicate that someone needed assistance if they didn't
nod. Several waiters had the punch cups on trays, but they
weren't doing a brisk business in getting rid of them. The Cherry
7-Up was definitely moving better in the nonalcoholic department.

Apparently knowing that the President's religion forbade alcohol meant that they'd gone wild with the punch options, because there were six different choices, all of them in neon-looking
colors of red, white, and blue, which made sense, and green,
yellow, and pink, which didn't. Decided not to care.

Found Louise, though. Whether Charmaine had made her
leave or rubbed her the wrong way, or Jeff had suggested she try
to have some fun, she'd gravitated back to her siblings. She and
Clinton were chatting, and he had the look I was familiar with
whenever straight males or lesbian chicks were near a Dazzler—
wide-eyed interest.

Louise seemed interested back, so either she was faking it for
the cause or Clinton was smart, because brains were the Dazzler
weakness, and when they made that sapiosexual connection,
they tended to not let go.

Wondered if Algar didn't want them hooking up. Then again,
the temptation clue could be about so many other things. I had
a room full of options to choose from.

The kids all pretended they didn't see me, which was fine.
All the better to hear what they were saying without them realizing it. A-C hearing was quite good, after all, and, as always,
couldn't remember if the Valentino kids knew I was enhanced or
not. But they weren't talking about anything much. The Cordell
twins were sharing how lame they felt school was, the other kids
were either agreeing or disagreeing, but nothing seemed out of
control.

Was about to say hi and move on when I noted there were
trash cans under the punch table. This in and of itself wasn't a

big deal—there were tasteful trash receptacles all over the place. However, these were the rectangular rubber cans you'd find in places where no one was worried about impressing anyone with the beauty of their garbage catchers. And, in this setting, these cans were out of place.

Took a closer look. Not that I was into trash, but something like this could indicate a bomb of some kind. Didn't see anything that indicated bomb—the cans weren't that full, so it was easy to see the bottom of all but one of them.

That one wasn't full so much as someone had draped a napkin over part of it. Did pause for a moment, because I could see tomorrow's headlines screaming that the FLOTUS had spent her time at the fundraiser digging in the trash cans. But the music changed to "Cigarettes and Alcohol" by Oasis. Maybe the kids were smoking. Sniffed. Didn't smell smoke. Then again, maybe they'd Febreezed themselves after or something. Lifted up the napkin.

To find something far worse than cigarette ash.

CHAPTER 68

I **WASN'T STARING AT A BOMB**, so there was that. I was, however, staring at something just as deadly to every A-C here—a large, empty bottle of vodka.

Spun around. "If you're holding a cup of punch, put it down right now!" All the kids froze. Those with punch cups put them down. Other than the Cordell twins. "Who put that bottle in there?"

The kids stared at me. "What bottle?" Lizzie asked.

Pulled the can over and pointed. "This one. This supersized bottle of cheap vodka. Who put it in here?"

The kids all feigned ignorance, but the Cordell twins still had hold of their cups.

Decided it was time to take the gloves off. "Understand me," I said in a low voice I ensured was growly, "I will find out. If you don't tell me who put this bottle in the trash, right now, I can ensure that the Secret Service follows each and every one of you for the rest of your lives, so that you will never have a moment of fun, a moment of rebellion, or a moment of freedom ever again, and that if you do, you'll be arrested and pay the maximum penalty for whatever your charge is and then some. Or, you can tell me who put this bottle into this trashcan. Your choice. Choose wisely. I'm more than willing to have the D.C.P.D. dust it for prints and arrest anyone on the charge of underage drinking and contributing to the delinquency of a minor. And I'll ensure the charge sticks."

"I didn't see anyone throw anything in there," Lizzie said. The rest of the kids echoed her. Other than the Cordell twins.

Looked at them. "Tell me. Right now. Or there's going to be nothing your mother can do to protect you from my wrath. Not one damn thing."

The twins tried to stare me down. Hilarious, really. They weren't Chuckie or Mom, they had no chance. They both stared and I stared at both of them. I won. Quickly, too. Shelby dropped her eyes and heaved a sigh. "It wasn't any of us. It was some old man. He spiked the punch." She showed me her cup—she had the red punch. "We just wanted to have some fun."

"Lizzie, is this true?"

"Well, I totes don't know, but honestly, we've been talking the whole time, no one's gone to the bathroom or anything, and I've had my back to the punch table, so I think Shelby's telling the truth."

"I saw an old man throw away something," Clinton said. "I didn't see anything else, though, which is why I didn't speak up."

"I think we were the only ones paying attention," Seth said. "He winked at us when he did it. I kind of thought he was being cool."

"So, some stranger spiked the punch and you, what, think it's cool to not only drink it but let others, people who you know shouldn't be drinking alcohol, also have some? Without telling them? You're with people whose religion forbids drinking alcohol, but you thought it was cool and funny?" I was furious and my voice shared that. "And you were also too damn stupid, selfish, and thoughtless to consider that maybe it's not vodka but could be something else, like poison?"

The twins put their cups down fast. Seth shook his head. "We didn't think of that. At all."

"How dare you?" Wasim asked. He sounded as angry as I was. "How *dare* you not say something? We," he indicated himself and all the other A-C kids, "are forbidden. We *choose* to follow our religions. How *dare* you risk our faiths on your meaningless quest to 'party'?"

The Valentino kids had all gone pale. "We drank punch," Claire whispered.

"What bowls did he spike?" I snarled at Seth.

"The red, white, and blue ones," he replied quickly. "He ran out before he could do the other three."

Or else he knew what colors the President would be handed. "Kids? In order, who had what?"

They all quickly sounded off. Only Shelby and Seth had taken any from the spiked bowls, and they'd had a cup each and were on their seconds. The others had chosen the other colors due to flavor preferences. Lizzie was the last one to share. "I totes got a Coke. From a can. The bartender poured it into the glass for me and everything."

"Good. You now have orders. No one touches this trashcan and no one, and I mean no one, takes any of that punch, not just you guys, but anyone. It's evidence, and it also could be deadly." And it certainly would be death to any A-C. "Guard this table, because if you don't, all the things I said will happen to you will, and then some."

"We're not in trouble?" Shelby asked, sounding as if that could not possibly be the case.

"No. You broke down and told the truth. You have a freaking job to do now. Don't do that? *Then* you're in trouble. Kids, pay attention to Shelby and Seth. If it seems like anything is even slightly wrong with them, Lizzie, you call Nurse Carter at the Embassy. Doctor Hernandez is here but Nurse Carter can get them to Dulce fastest and if they're having any reactions, then it's poison, not vodka, and time will be of the essence."

The Cordell twins now blanched. Ignored them—they could freak out with their peers. Had to get to help. For the first time ever I missed my Secret Service detail shadowing me. The one time I needed them, they'd obeyed my wishes. Always the way. The music changed to Steely Dan's "Hey Nineteen." Worked for me. "Louise, come with me."

She scurried over and we took off. "What do we do, Aunt Kitty?"

"We assume that any punch that's red, white, or blue is poisoned. I have to focus on your Uncle Jeff. You need to use hyperspeed and get to every A-C, Field agents included, and tell them what's going on. We need to have Dulce standing by—if anyone drinks any of that, they're going to go into convulsions, if we're lucky."

"Uncle Jeff almost died from one shot," she said, voice filled with dread.

"And he was twenty and under far less stress than he is now. Yeah. Get to your Uncle Christopher as fast as you can. He's the fastest. Get the Flash going. Now." Just prayed the Flash hadn't drunk any punch.

She disappeared and I headed for the stage. I could use hyperspeed, but there were too many witnesses, and I still wasn't sure who knew I had A-C abilities and who didn't. Plus, the First Lady appearing out of nowhere onstage when a lot of people were watching was considered to be bad form because it gave far too many people reasons to hate us, and while they loved hyperspeed when they needed it, they weren't so thrilled with it when we used it otherwise. But, most importantly, I felt far too stressed to ensure I had control. If I'd been enraged, no worries. However, stressed and scared meant that all the skills I'd learned to monitor and utilize to their fullest disappeared. I could over-shoot Jeff and crash through the wall if I wasn't careful, and that wouldn't make anything better.

Was about halfway there when I saw the waiter I'd spotted earlier bring his tray of punch to the stage. Either no one had taken any while he made his way to the stage, or he'd been told to serve it only to those onstage. One way or the other, he had plenty of choices on that tray, but as I remembered, he'd taken punch from only the red, white, and blue bowls. Didn't mean he was doing anything other than his job—red, white, and blue were what you'd serve the President.

Only Kramer, Marcia, Charmaine and Jeff were onstage now, but everyone took some punch. Sped up. The waiter left the stage but no one had taken a drink—yet.

They were talking, then it was clear from the way Kramer now held his cup that he was saying a toast, meaning that very shortly Jeff was going to drink vodka and, most likely, die on-stage.

Well, the hell with that.

CHAPTER 69

HAD NO IDEA what to do other than scream, and that might not work. Then the music changed to "The Way" by Fastball, and I knew what I had to do.

There was a person next to me who had a plate with a roll on it, since among other things, there were little sandwich stations. The rolls were the round, hard kind that I, personally, hated because I always felt like I was eating a baseball when I tried to ingest one. But a baseball was just what I needed right now.

Grabbed the roll, ignored the complaints of the man whose food I'd taken, used my clutch like a baseball mitt, and went into the windup. I was a jock—sure I'd been a track hound, but we'd played other sports in the off-season, just to keep in shape, and in addition to the most sadistic track coaches in the history of the sport, the other coaches at my high school had made sure we all graduated knowing how to throw a baseball or softball, make a basket, volley a tennis ball, and so forth. And, as with shooting, I'd been good at hitting what I was aiming for naturally.

They were clinking cups, so to speak, and I threw. My fastball wasn't up to Christopher's standards, but it made do. The roll hit the cup in Jeff's hand and sent it flying. So far, so good.

Of course, the roll hit the other cups, too. The one in Jeff's hand flew all over Charmaine, Marcia's and Charmaine's went all over Kramer, and his also hit Charmaine, because my life didn't work any other way.

Happily, none of the punch had hit Jeff or Marcia, so that was one for the win column. Didn't get to enjoy the win column long, though, since the Secret Service erupted from where they'd been lurking. Joseph and Rob had Jeff down within a second, the rest of the agents nearby had the others onstage covered right after.

The entire room turned to look at whoever had thrown that killer roll. Didn't stop to wave for the cameras, just ran to the stage as fast as the dress and my shoes would allow, which wasn't as fast as I'd have liked.

"The punch is spiked!" I shouted to Jeff as I got closer.

Assumed he'd heard me, because Joseph and Rob let him up. Evalyne and Phoebe caught up to me. "Oh my God, we literally cannot leave you alone for a second," Evalyne said.

"The punch is spiked. As in, it's loaded with vodka."

Once those on our details had passed our tests of trustworthiness, they'd been filled in on what alcohol could do to an A-C. Phoebe cursed. "Who? The kids?"

"No, an old man. My money's on Doctor Rattoppare, but I'm open to suggestions. You guys need to get all the trash cans searched. The one the kids are guarding has a bottle that will hopefully have fingerprints on it."

"We're on our way," Evalyne said as those two took off, Evalyne barking orders into her wristcom.

Rob came and helped me up onto the stage. "I'd ask for an explanation, but I heard you, and Evalyne's shouting the same thing in my ear. The President hasn't had anything but water, which I got for him, before just now, and you stopped him in time."

Felt relief wash over me. "Go team."

The relief was, of course, short-lived because—the Secret Service having confirmed that the First Lady was the roll shooter—everyone was back on their feet. Charmaine's white dress was covered in red and blue punch, and Kramer's tux was drenched with white. Tried to feel bad. Failed.

As the music changed to "The Girl in the Dirty Shirt" by Oasis—which was Algar forcing me to control the Inner Hyena—Charmaine turned on me, of course. "You lunatic! What was that all about? Do you just feel the need to have a food fight wherever you go?"

"No. Someone spiked the punch with alcohol. Be happy it wasn't your children, because I'd have them arrested and charged with anything and everything the D.C.P.D. could come up with."

She sniffed. "My children would never do something like that."

"Yeah? Not from lack of desire, since they had over a cup each the moment they knew there was vodka in it. Which isn't awesome, but it's worse since we're not sure that what was poured in isn't poison in a vodka bottle."

"If anything happens to my children . . ." She sniffed again, this time clearly insinuating that she was going to sniff me to death. As if.

"It'll be your fault, yes."

She stared at me. "What?"

"Your fault. You're delaying me, right now, from getting medical to them to verify that they're not poisoned. So, you know, you do you and all that." Turned to Jeff. "Are you okay?"

He nodded, but Charmaine shoved in between us. "Listen, you," she snarled. "You and your horrible brats don't belong in this school, and everything you've done shows that. You've ruined my dress!"

"Yeah. Um, did I mention that we know there's vodka in the punch and it could be poison? And that your children drank it? Because, if it were me, I'd be freaked out about them, not about a tacky dress you got at a department store aimed at teenagers."

Charmaine wasn't used to someone else being the Mean Girl. Her eyes widened. "How dare you? This is a designer original!"

"The hell it is." I didn't really care about what I was wearing all that much, but I'd always had an interest in designers and what they were offering. And with Reader as my BFF and Pierre, Vance, and Akiko around, I knew what was what. "That's from Forever Twenty-One."

She blanched. There was a lot of that going on. And she sniffed because, hey, it was Charmaine and that was her thing. "How dare you insinuate—"

"No insinuation. Flat-out saying. You got that at a clothing chain store aimed at your daughter. Her dress is nicer than yours, by the way."

"How dare you speak to Charmaine that way?" Kramer said, inserting himself into our argument. He put his arm around Charmaine in a similar way to how Reader had with me and Marcia. "You're the most classless First Lady this country has ever had."

The music changed to "Tempted" by Squeeze. The chorus of which was "tempted by the fruit of another" which I presume was a big clue. Well, one easy way to find out. "Yeah? I care about your opinion like I care about who you're sleeping with. Which is not at all."

He jerked. "What are you insinuating? I'm not having an affair with anyone!" He yanked his arm away from Charmaine.

Marcia stepped up. "I think it's really interesting that you're defending an accusation Kitty didn't make. And that the first thing you did was take your arm away from Charmaine." She looked back and forth between the two of them. "So, that's it." She sounded angry and sad. "Your other wives told me this day would come. I didn't believe them. I should have."

"You don't know what you're talking about," Kramer said.

Clinton joined us. "Missus Martini," he said quietly, "Lizzie wanted me to let you know that the bottle and punch have been taken into Secret Service custody. And Seth and Shelby seem fine. We found Doctor Hernandez and he said they show no signs of poison, but do have a blood alcohol of zero-point-four."

"So it was vodka, not poison. Well, thank God for that." And thank Algar for everything else. Because that was a lot of alcohol in their systems from just a cup and a half of punch. Well, it had been a big bottle.

"When were you going to dump me?" Marcia asked her husband. "Before or after Charmaine made me do another fundraiser?"

"I'm not dumping you," Kramer protested. "Charmaine is a good friend, you know that."

"She's not *my* friend," Marcia said. "Maybe you didn't want me to meet that doctor friend you two have in common because he thinks Charmaine is your wife."

Not a bad theory. Mine, however, now included Charmaine in the Cyborg Lifestyle. The music changed to Fall Out Boy's "American Beauty/American Psycho," which made me wonder who was counting as the beauty and the psycho in this particular scenario. The song just fit so many people I knew and situations I was in so often that it wasn't a clue so much as something that could work as our theme song.

"What are you talking about?" Clinton asked. He was standing between me and Marcia.

"Your stepmother's being crazy again," Kramer said.

Clinton stepped nearer to Marcia. "She's not crazy that I've ever seen, Dad."

"You don't know her like I do, son."

"I know you." Clinton put his arm around Marcia's shoulders. "It'll be okay."

She shook her head. "No, it won't." She was trying not to cry. "So, this is how it ends. I wish Kitty had dumped a whole bowl of punch over both of you. For starters."

"Don't push it, Marcia," Kramer said. "You don't want to test me."

She laughed bitterly. "Oh, you mean our prenup that you insisted I sign? I'm aware that we're just under ten years, and that the prenup says nothing about your infidelity, only mine."

"And are you aware that you'll get nothing?"

She nodded. "I am. Very aware."

"Then you'll apologize right now, to me and to Charmaine, for these baseless accusations."

There was no microphone onstage that I'd seen, but due to what I'd done we had the room's full attention, and most of said room had moved to be close to the stage. So, as near as I could tell, most were hearing this, because no one up here on the stage was actually speaking all that quietly.

"Or what?" Marcia asked.

"Or you get out of the house I own, leaving the car I own, and all the other things I own in my house. That I own, that you do not own. And you do it tonight."

And the room waited to hear what Marcia was going to say.

CHAPTER 70

SOMETIMES PEOPLE disappoint you. And sometimes they surprise you.

"I will not."

Marcia pulled herself up to her full height as DJ Algar spun Helen Reddy's "I Am Woman" making my Inner Hyena of Hilarity fight with my Proud Peacock of Feminist Solidarity. Maybe I was the psycho right now.

"It's clear that it's true that you're having an affair with Charmaine," Marcia went on. "You wouldn't be tossing the threat of the prenup around if you didn't fully intend to use it. You're willing to throw me and our children into the street because you're guilty. If you weren't, you wouldn't have spent all evening with her. You'd have been with me, helping, supporting. Not with your mistress."

Kramer shrugged. "So be it." He turned to the audience. "You heard her, folks. She's made her decision based on a crazy idea."

The room didn't seem to be on Kramer's side, which said a lot for the room. Or for the fact that "I Am Woman" really remained *the* feminist anthem. Hopefully both.

He turned back to Marcia. "You're not taking the children, however."

Marcia didn't reply. Clinton did. "The hell she's not." He stepped away from Marcia and nearer to Kramer. His fists were balled and he was shaking he was so angry. "You did this to my mother. I watched you make her stay, make her suffer, while you cheated on her. She put up with it to protect me, because she felt I was too young to be forced into the poverty you're trying to shove Marcia and my little brothers into. Well, they're not staying with you. And neither am I."

"You want to stay at this school?" Kramer asked. "You want to go to a good college like all your brothers and sisters? You want a good career? Then you'll shut your mouth and behave."

Clinton stepped in front of Marcia. "The hell with that. My mother told me to take care of Marcia, because she knew what you'd do to her somewhere down the road. And she asked me to do that because Marcia's been the best stepmother anyone could have asked for. She never treated any of us as anything less than hers, she was always kind to my mother and your first wife, and we all know she loves us. Which is more than I can say for you, Dad. And I'm not deserting her just because you're still the same asshole you've always been."

"Then enjoy living in the streets," Kramer snapped.

The room was silent. I mean, good theater like this was hard to come by in a live setting. Normally one had to go to New York and catch a Broadway play for this level of family drama and intensity.

A throat cleared. Heads turned to look at said clearer, who turned out to be Wasim. Who, for the first time, truly looked royal. He was standing ramrod straight, eyes flashing, and he looked imperious, as if he'd been ruling a country all his life. Algar clearly agreed—we were now hearing Adam Ant's "Prince Charming."

"That will not be happening." He sounded imperious, too. "Missus Kramer, we own an apartment that we don't feel we will be using in the near term, thanks to the generosity of the King and Queen Regent. There is room in that apartment for all of you. You and your family are more than welcome to reside at the Cairo, courtesy of the Bahraini Royal Family. We will send a car and driver as well as others to assist you in gathering your things and your children in safety and without being rushed."

"Th-thank you, Your Highness," Marcia managed to stammer out. Tears were running down her face, but she wasn't sobbing, which was her totally holding it in, I was sure. "We're grateful to you for your kind generosity."

"It is what decent people do." Wasim now looked at Kramer. "You, sir, are a disgrace. To act as you have toward your wife and your children is disgusting. We will be telling our grandfather, the King of Bahrain, about your actions. He will not be impressed."

"And yet he's impressed by *her*?" Kramer pointed at me. "The woman who throws food to make a point?"

"The woman who preserved her husband's grace with his God," Wasim countered angrily. "It is forbidden in our religions to drink alcohol, knowingly or unknowingly. That you see nothing wrong with that shows how weak your character truly is. We will speak no more to you, as you are beneath us." With that, Wasim turned on his heel and stalked off to where Naveed was standing, which happened to be with Mona and the rest of the Middle Eastern Contingent, though Gadhavi wasn't with them Hadn't realized they'd arrived, but then, I'd been a little busy.

Mona bowed her head to Wasim. Saw her speak to him and was pretty sure she was telling him how proud his grandfather would be. Wasn't sure if Wasim had had a Royals class similar to the Washington Wife, but if he had, he'd channeled it at totally the right time.

Noted that Cologne and all the *Good Day USA!* folks had come to join the party. Sadly, could not blame them. They were getting at least a month's worth of great footage from hanging out with me for the equivalent of two days. Wondered when they'd send a contract over for exclusive rights to follow me daily. Had a horrible feeling that contract would show up tomorrow, if not later tonight.

"Let's go," Clinton said gently to Marcia, as he put his arm around her shoulders again.

"You're throwing away your life," Kramer told him.

"No, Dad," Clinton said sadly. "I'm throwing away yours." He helped Marcia offstage, where the Middle Eastern Contingent was now waiting for her. Caught Mona's eye and she nodded to me. Good, they'd be the ones covering, so I didn't have to worry.

Jeff signaled to someone. Vance, as it turned out, who zipped up onto the stage. "We'll cover the tuition," Jeff said softly. "They stay in the school, Clinton and the two youngsters. Go help Marcia—we'll be fine here and she needs someone she can cry in front of. Take some Field teams with you, as well, for help and protection."

"And remind her that anything bought for her is a gift," I added. "That includes clothing, jewelry, shoes, and, very possibly, her car, if it's in her name or if her name is included on the title. Artwork, if it was gifted to her from him. And anything given to her by someone else is also hers. All the children's things are unlikely to be considered under a prenup, so take all their stuff, clothes and bedding and toys and anything else that you think is theirs. We also need to ensure that we have witnesses that can share that Marcia was forced out of the house under duress, because we'll want a divorce attorney to take a careful look at their prenup and how it affects them in D.C."

Vance nodded. "On it." He joined up with the others and went to Marcia's other side.

"Who did you help get divorced?" Jeff asked me.

"I believe you've met my Aunt Carla? The several-times-divorced attorney? She was big on drilling what to do 'when the inevitable' happens. Though, in her defense, she's not wrong." And the Aunt Carla I'd met in Bizarro World had been pretty great. So the one I had in this world had good qualities, too.

Jeff grunted. "Say no more, baby."

"I hope you're pleased with yourself," Charmaine said, as I turned back her way.

"Really? You're the one who just home-wrecked two families."

"Two?" She honestly didn't seem to have done the math.

"Um, you're telling me your husband's okay with you cheating on him with Zachary Kramer? I haven't met the man, but I'm just going to go out on a limb and bet that he isn't."

She sniffed. "Bob has nothing to do with this."

"Really? What does Bob say about that?"

"I don't know." Another sniff. She was on a sniffing roll. Maybe that meant that if there was a fire she'd smell it first and sound a warning. Though, from the little I knew of her, the warning part was unlikely. "He isn't here right now."

"Right, because you sent him off to help Marcia instead of doing it yourself, or having her husband help. Because that way the two of you could have some canoodling time."

"We don't canoodle!" The music was now "Dirty Work" by Steely Dan, so Algar begged to differ.

"You call it banging? Macking? Doing the dirty deed? The romance that is one for the ages that will never die?" Heard some titters in the audience. So we were definitely being heard.

"We don't call it anything, you horrible woman!"

"Oh, so it's just business as usual. Got it."

Charmaine looked around. "Well, this is certainly business as usual for *you*."

"And that is?"

"Another event ruined."

"If you call it that. Me, personally, I call it another last-minute event you forced someone to have that, all things considered, is somehow managing to still be going well."

"This isn't 'well.' The donations haven't begun and half the party is leaving. Another fundraiser not raising the needed funds. Because of you."

This was true. Apparently Marcia's departure had signaled that it was time to go. This was likely more of a result of those leaving having realized that they could escape without donating if they left now, rather than any real negative effect from what had just gone on. Frankly, I was shocked we weren't holding on to more of the audience—if it were me, I'd wait around to see what else was going to happen.

"Well, if you didn't shove people into things without even asking them if they had time or ability to handle them, your events might go better."

"We haven't had any issues until you showed up."

"Ha. I doubt it. I think you're great at telling everyone how hard you're working while at the same time belittling everyone else's achievements. You set me and Marcia both up to fail. You get to look aggrieved that we just 'can't handle it' and somehow will take all the credit for any funds raised."

"That is not true! I've spent years determining which fund-raisers work and why! And how much each one should raise."

"So you can go on the all-expenses paid trips but not let the parent who actually ran the fundraisers go? Unless they're one of your cronies, that is."

She sniffed. "The parents who chaperone have proven themselves capable of handling more than just their own children and navigating tricky situations."

"Sure they have. And they're all the people who kiss your butt, too."

"As if you could do this job!"

"As if I want to? I'm all for helping the school, but you went out of your way to make things difficult. Who asks anyone to plan and host either a bake sale or a swanky party the day before the event? No one other than you. You had weeks to let me know about the bake sale, but you waited until less than twenty-four hours prior to let me know about it, let alone that I was running it, and you ordered me around without taking any of my concerns or schedule conflicts into account. You did the same to Marcia. We offered to switch who did what, and you refused to allow it. In the business world that's called a planned failure. In the real person world, it's called a setup."

"Everyone else who's run these has done so without having food fights."

"I'm sure they have. Because they weren't the freaking First Lady who has to have a tonnage of security around her. Security that reacts immediately and asks questions later."

"That stupid parrot wasn't security!"

"Floaty" by the Foo Fighters came on. "Yes, she was." Took the song to be Algar indicating that Bellie had indeed felt she was protecting me. From Charmaine. "She felt you were going to try to attack me."

Charmaine sniffed. "You still ruined that event. Just like this one."

Found it fascinating that Charmaine hadn't said that Bellie was wrong. Needed to get that parrot some extra bird treats, pronto. "Well, you know, God forbid that you'd take anyone else's circumstances, strengths, and weaknesses into account. That might actually indicate that you understood how to manage people properly."

"You couldn't run a successful lemonade stand, let alone a real fundraiser."

"I could if it was something I actually wanted to do and had prep time for."

"Prove it!"

"Right."

"I mean it! Prove you can do what you're claiming. You've been involved with two fundraisers today that have both been ruined, where we've made less than half of what we expected. Prove you can do better," she leaned forward, so her kangaroo nose was right next to mine, "or take all of your children and get out of this school. Forever."

"Fine. You're on."

"Great. The first thing is to come up with the idea. Which I doubt that you have. And it had better be a good one, because we need to make up for both of the fundraisers you ruined."

Naturally, I had no ideas, because I'd been focused on everything else going on and my chick fight with Charmaine. But if I didn't say something fast, she was going to win this battle, and that might allow her to win the war, too.

The music changed to Billy Joel's "Running on Ice." Thought fast and remembered what I'd heard while getting ready for this party. "We'll do a charity hockey game."

Charmaine stared at me. "What?"

"A charity hockey game. The last preseason game for the Capitals is in three weeks, against the Arizona Chupacabras, and it's not sold out or anywhere close to sold out. My office will contact the NHL and both teams and get it set up."

She sniffed, but this time the sniff sounded almost impressed.

"It's an interesting idea. We'll plan on that, then. Confirm the date, time, ticket prices, number of available seats, and what percentage will come to the school. And get that all confirmed in the next two days."

"Or what?"

"Or we don't have enough lead time and your third event in a row will fail. Of course, I don't believe hockey is played well if a food fight is going on, so I'm expecting this to be truly embarrassing for everyone. I just hope no one gets injured. And we'll ensure that everyone dresses in jeans, lest you throw a hockey puck at them while they're drinking an Icee."

"While I'm impressed that you actually know what an Icee is, I'm not going to apologize for ensuring that my husband didn't break a very important commandment in his religion. That you're not more interested in finding out who spiked the punch your underage children drank and, therefore, caused me to have to get creative, is what amazes me." I was certainly interested in finding him.

She shrugged. "You said it was an old man. There are plenty around. Your people should start questioning them. So they don't donate, either." Charmaine definitely had a sarcasm knob.

"Well, while we're doing that, they should question Zachary. And probably your friend, Doctor Rattoppare, too."

Charmaine stiffened, just a bit. Kramer did, too. "What would he have to do with anything?" she asked with a sniff, because she apparently had to sniff every couple of sentences or die.

"He's an old man, isn't he?"

"He's in the prime of life," Charmaine said primly. "Just as Zachary is."

"And you are, too?"

She stared at me, then her eyes narrowed. "What are you insinuating?"

Decided it was time to once again toss on my Megalomaniac Girl cape and make the leaps that kept me in tight with the League of Crazed Super-Geniuses. "I'm insinuating that Zachary's had the Treatment. And that you have, too."

Both of their eyes opened a little wider. Didn't get a verbal response from Charmaine, or Kramer, for that matter, but that was because we were interrupted.

By the police.

CHAPTER 71

THE OFFICERS WEREN'T any I knew, and neither were the detectives with them. Clearly they weren't here on a drunk and disorderly or partying too loud charge.

The music changed to "Watching the Detectives" by Elvis Costello. So I did.

Didn't see all that much, since Chuckie was here and he intercepted the police before they were too far through the door, keeping them far away from those of us on the stage. Couldn't hear what they were saying, but they talked for more than two minutes, which seemed a lot longer under the circumstances. Saw Chuckie's head rear back a bit, then he looked at me. I recognized the look—I was in trouble and Chuckie might not be able to cover.

The policemen spread out in the room, but the detectives went with Chuckie. As he led them to us, saw him scratch his ear. Mom appeared out of nowhere, as did Kevin, trailed by Amy and Gadhavi. Apparently Amy had learned the Chuckie Code for Backup Now and Gadhavi probably knew every code ever used.

"Mister President, Madam First Lady," Chuckie said as he reached us, "these are Detectives Sawyer and Beckett." Sawyer was a big guy in an ill-fitting suit. Beckett was a smaller guy in a slightly better fitting suit. They were both unremarkable otherwise, so what I was supposed to be watching was unclear. Maybe Algar was just in Soundtrack vs. Clue Mode.

"Ma'am," Sawyer said, "I'd like you to explain your relationship with Robert Cordell."

"Um, absolutely zero." Pointed to Charmaine. "He's her husband. I only found out what her husband's name was tonight.

But he's been off running errands, as I've been told, so I haven't met him yet."

"Can you explain why he called you tonight?" Beckett asked.

"He didn't call me tonight. I've never spoken to him."

"That she knows of," Mom said. "Explain why you're questioning the First Lady or leave." She had her P.T.C.U. badge out and handed it to Sawyer.

The music changed to "One More Murder" by Better Than Ezra. That boded.

Sawyer glanced at Mom's badge, nodded, and didn't touch it. This was the first time I'd ever seen anyone unimpressed by Mom's badge. Mom had the best badge around, and, to date, this one police detective was the only guy who wasn't awed by it. Had no idea what this meant, but had to figure it wasn't good. "We know who the First Lady's mother is, ma'am. That doesn't protect her from a murder charge."

We all stared at him. "Um, excuse me?"

Amy stepped up and put her arm around me, similarly to how Clinton had held Marcia. "All A-Cs confirmed as safe," she murmured as she put her head next to mine in a way that looked merely like she was comforting me. "They all went with water or sodas from the bar. Caroline and Vander were here, but they've left, taking any politicians they felt might be at risk with them. Everyone gone is cleared. Caro said she'll get donations out of them, so not to worry about that."

Felt relieved. Punch wasn't really an A-C thing, as I thought of it. I'd rarely if ever seen it served. Clearly Algar didn't approve of punch and, after this evening, could tell why. And it was also a relief that whatever was going on wasn't going to be witnessed by everyone Jeff had to work with.

"Murder," Beckett said, reminding me that my relief needed to be short-lived. "As in, Robert Cordell was found murdered, and the last call he made was to you."

Looked at Charmaine and Kramer out of the corner of my eye. They didn't look surprised or shocked. Turned to them. As soon as they realized eyes were on them, they both looked horrified. But they looked wrong—too horrified, no shock, like they were acting but weren't very good at it. So that was why Charmaine had been confused—she'd only home-wrecked one family because her husband was already dead by the time her affair had been exposed.

This was neat, very neat. Whether that was because that was

how Charmaine worked, or because they were following a plan of someone else's—and, if so, my money was on the Tinkerer—it was well laid out. Wasn't sure if the plan had included Cordell calling me or not, though.

"What are you saying?" Charmaine gasped out. "That she murdered my husband?" She pointed to me dramatically.

"No, because I didn't. I wouldn't know your husband from Adam." Turned back to the detectives. "I did get a call on the way here, from someone who didn't identify themselves and whose voice I didn't recognize. He called to warn me that someone was going to try to kill me at the party tonight."

"Can you prove that?" Beckett asked.

"Why would she have to?" Gadhavi asked before I could reply.

"Because we only have her word," Beckett said.

"She's the First Lady and the Queen Regent," Gadhavi countered.

Sawyer shrugged. "And that means exactly dick in this situation."

"There are children here," Jeff said in a tone that said Sawyer was one word away from Jeff having the Secret Service dispose of him. "You'll watch your language."

Sawyer looked around. "They're teenagers. They've heard all the words and then some."

"That doesn't mean you get a free pass to say those words around them in a school setting," I pointed out.

"You need to answer my questions, instead of trying to lecture me," Sawyer replied snidely. "Now, tell us the truth—how long have you known Robert Cordell?"

While I contemplated just how much I already didn't like Detective Sawyer, realized that Cordell had probably been gasping during our brief call because he was dying. Felt bad for not having realized it and not having been able to help him. Like Karl Smith during Operation Drug Addict, Cordell had died trying to warn me of danger.

"Again, I've never met the man." Dug out my phone and handed it to Beckett. "I can't prove anything about the short conversation warning me that I was a target for murder—I didn't record the call because it was too brief. But I'm betting now that the call came from Cordell."

Beckett pulled out a plastic baggy and had me drop my phone into it. Then he did the search on recent calls. "The time matches and the number called matches. You were definitely the last person Robert Cordell spoke to before he died."

"Great. I was in a limo with the President, the Head of the Presidential Terrorism Control Unit, my father, my ward, one of the many Princes of Bahrain, and a visiting dignitary." Wasn't sure what title I should toss at Gadhavi, particularly under the circumstances. "Oh, and our driver and bodyguard. So, unless you think all of us swung by wherever and killed some poor man we didn't know, I believe this is you barking and this is me being the wrong tree."

"How is it that the victim had your direct line?" Beckett asked.

"How did his wife get it? We're all parents of kids at Sidwell, and she's the President of the Sidwell Friends School Parent Teacher Association. For all I know, she programs every parent's number into both of their phones. I have no idea. I don't know these people. I've 'known' Charmaine for a day, and I've never met her husband. For all I know, they're both drug dealers and this is a gangland murder. Or they're both dull and the man died in a car accident. I have no idea, because I didn't do anything and whatever it is, I'm not actually involved."

"I'm curious as to why you're completely uninterested in the fact that the First Lady just said she received a call warning her that she was a target for assassination from a man who's just been murdered," Chuckie said. "Very curious."

"Because we don't believe her," Sawyer said. "She's a politician's wife—that means she knows how to lie."

"You know, what does my husband's position have to do with this?"

"Not one damn thing, which is why we'll need to take you to the station, ma'am," Sawyer said smugly, as Reader and Gower joined us. The stage wasn't that big and it was getting really crowded. "To test for gunshot residue." He was playing with his handcuffs in a way that indicated he wanted to use them.

Tried not to freak out. This wasn't the way the FLOTUS should leave any party, particularly not this one. And was pretty sure that if I protested at all, Sawyer was going to slap those cuffs on me.

Saw Charmaine smirking. Neither she nor Kramer looked worried about gunshot residue. Then again, they had people for that. Wondered if Evan the Limo Driver had added assassin to his resume, and figured he had.

"The hell you will," Jeff said calmly, but his Commander Voice was on Full. "You just want to embarrass people you see as above you in terms of wealth and class. You're fully aware that my wife couldn't possibly have killed this man, since you know where she was in relation to where he was, she's been surrounded by witnesses, and you suspect several others, including a possible random mugger, more than you suspect her."

Sawyer eyed him. "Don't think your voodoo magic affects me."

"Search him," Mom barked, her Commander Voice on More Than Full. "Both of them."

Buchanan appeared out of nowhere, and Kevin was already here. They had the two detectives in an upper arm hold where neither could go for their guns and neither could get out of the hold, either.

The uniformed officers started to get interested. The Secret Service ensured that the interest was quickly contained. All of a sudden, was really grateful for all of the security we dragged with us all the time.

Chuckie did the searching, Beckett first, since he was nearest. "Beckett's clean." He searched Sawyer and grunted as he was going through Sawyer's wallet. "Well, what a surprise. Guess who's a card-carrying member of the Club Fifty-One True Believers?"

CHAPTER 72

BUCHANAN, WHO HAD Sawyer, slapped handcuffs on him. Definitely preferred this version to the one I'd been contemplating seconds earlier.

"What in the hell do you think you're pulling?" Sawyer snarled.

"You're under arrest," Buchanan said calmly. "Suspicion of domestic terrorism. Oh, and that's part of what the P.T.C.U.'s job is. We appreciate your self-identifying."

Beckett's jaw dropped. "You . . . you can't arrest a police detective!"

"Can, will, and am," Mom said. "You appear clean. Now, you want to run this investigation according to police procedure, or do we assume that you left your True Believers card at home tonight?"

Beckett turned to Sawyer. "Did he plant that card on you?"

Sawyer gave him a look I was familiar with—I'd seen it on the face of every Club 51 member before their schism, and on the faces of all those who were now Club 51 True Believers—unadulterated hatred, with a crazy twitch in the eyes. Sawyer must have really been holding himself in prior to this, because normally this level of crazy wasn't allowed through the doors. "You think aliens are here to help us. I know they're here to destroy us."

Beckett, who was still held by Kevin, backed up. Didn't think he'd done it intentionally. "We've been partners for five years. Have I ever known you?"

"No." Sawyer turned back to Mom. "Do your worst."

She rolled her eyes. "They're always so dramatic. Get him in a car, get him to the holding area, send teams to search the entire school grounds for bombs, and verify that Robert Cordell is actually dead, how he died, and so forth. I want all that done in five minutes."

Reader was giving orders to Field, since they'd do the bomb search the fastest. Kevin handed Beckett off to Gower, meaning Beckett was going less than nowhere, and Kevin and Buchanan took Sawyer off. Sawyer, for his part, walked out with his head held high, a Hero For The Cause, captured but not contained. Jerk.

Gadhavi took Sawyer's picture with his phone.

"Why did you do that?" I asked. We'd moved a bit away from Kramer and Charmaine, at least as much as the small stage allowed, and all of us were turned so they couldn't hear what we were saying or, hopefully, read our lips.

Gadhavi was texting. "In case we can spot him at the 'seminar' or can place him with those who are or were at that rally."

"Oh. Um, good thinking." I should have thought of it, but almost being arrested in front of a ton of people for the murder of a man I'd never met had shaken me up a bit, go figure.

"It was," Chuckie agreed. "Thank you. But how did you miss him coming in?" he asked Jeff quietly.

"I didn't," Jeff replied. "But he's had some training—he was focused on the murder investigation more than his hatred. And he was concentrating on Kitty, and how he wanted to embarrass her. Somewhere in there, he also wanted to solve the murder, but it wasn't his main goal. Hence why we're all glad Mister Gadhavi had the presence of mind to take Sawyer's picture. And, let's all remember that my blocks are up."

"No one's complaining," I said. "I'm just curious if he was chosen specifically to come here, or if us getting Detective True Believer was a coinkydink."

"We were assigned the case," Beckett said, sounding shaken. "We didn't ask for it."

Chuckie grunted. "I don't believe in coincidences. They happen, but rarely."

"Call our captain," Beckett suggested. "To my knowledge we were assigned the case because of where the victim was found."

"Finding out the right territory specific detectives cover isn't all that hard to do," I said. "If you happen to know there's an anti-alien or anti-President and First Lady homicide detective that will get the case if you kill someone in a specific area, then that's where you at least dump the body, even if you did the deed elsewhere."

"That's a good theory," Beckett said. "Because we're pretty sure that the murder was done in a different location from where we found the body."

"Does this mean I can let him go?" Gower asked Jeff, indicating Beckett.

Jeff nodded. "He's horrified, confused, and freaked out, but he wasn't here to try to damage human-alien relations like his partner was." Gower nodded and let go.

"Thank you," Beckett said, as he rubbed his upper arms. "And no, I'm not here to do anything but find out who murdered Robert Cordell."

"Fine," Jeff said, speaking so that everyone nearby could hear. "Now, I echo my mother-in-law—tell us what's actually going on and get some real police work going, or I'm calling in the unit we know actually does that sort of thing and we'll let the K-9 squad handle it."

"Not those damn dogs again!" Charmaine said.

Beckett looked at her and, for the first time, I saw him look like a detective. "Mister President, I think the dogs might be an excellent idea." Beckett stepped over to Charmaine and Kramer. "Your reactions, Missus Cordell, seem remarkably calm for someone who's just found out her husband's been murdered."

"That's because she's having an affair with Zachary Kramer here," Amy said, as she let go of me and went next to Beckett. He pulled out a notebook and scribbled while she gave him the whole story as viewed by the audience. It had been even more lurid from the cheap seats, apparently.

While that was going on, Gadhavi faced the remaining people. "We came here to raise funds for a school. All education is important. I would like to suggest that you not be like those who took the opportunity to leave early with their checkbooks full. I will begin the donations. I, Ali Baba Gadhavi, who have no children in this school, will donate ten thousand dollars."

The audience gasped as "Rockin' the Suburbs" by Ben Folds came on. "Do the damn follow-up," Charmaine hissed at me. "Keep it rolling!" While being interviewed by a police detective about her husband's murder. She might be an Evil Kangaroo, and her priorities sure seemed out of whack, but you had to hand it to her for PTA dedication.

Stepped up next to Gadhavi. "I'd like to ask Rajnish Singh, my husband's Chief of Staff, and Colette Alexis, my Press Secretary, to please assist the Honorable Mister Gadhavi in handling the rest of the donations. Please give as generously as you can—we'd like to cover scholarships for the Kramer children, since we've all heard that their father is leaving them penniless."

Hey, Charmaine hadn't said *how* to keep it rolling.

Raj and Colette zipped up to the stage and they brought along a celebrity guest—Cologne was with them. They'd also all found microphones. "Who's next?" Raj asked, Troubadour Tones set to Generous Donations.

"Ten thousand," Jeff said. Managed not to have a heart attack—whether the A-Cs printed their own money or the patents that Alfred and the others had were so lucrative or the government paid them to continue to be awesome for truth, justice, and the American Way—or all of the above—we were always loaded with cash.

"Ten thousand from our President," Colette shared, Troubadour Tones set on Don't Be A Slacker.

"Ten thousand," Chuckie said. Then he and the rest of us got off the stage, Beckett and his suspects, too, though with Secret Service assistance.

"Ten thousand from my production company," Cologne said. "The company that's going to be making the Code Name: First Lady series." This earned wild applause. Joy. "Now, come on, folks. Let's get this really rolling. We want to support those poor kids whose dad just dumped them in front of all of us, and we want to support this school community as well. So, who's giving next?"

Others started calling out sums. Nathalie got busy gathering names, pledged amounts, contact information, and, where she could, checks. Abner, Mrs. Maurer, the Kristie-Bot, Adam, Lizzie, and the Valentino kids started helping her. Pretty soon we had a full on function going again, with lots of money being raised.

DJ Algar kept the tunes rolling with "You Never Give Me Your Money" by the Beatles, "Mind on My Money" by Flo Rida, "Lay Your Money Down" by the Exies, "Easy Money" by Billy Joel, "Money Honey" by Lady Gaga, and "All That Money Wants" by the Psychedelic Furs. Then we got The Black Crowes' complete "Shake Your Money Maker" album including bonus tracks. Algar really liked to stick with a theme, and I couldn't argue with the commitment.

Mom got information back while we were waiting. No bombs around the school that any Field agents could find, and they'd brought in the full K-9 squad to sniff, just in case. The dogs were all now used to taking Tito's Hyperspeed Dramamine, so they'd sniffed at hyperspeed. And I was assured that all of them had gotten extra dog treats for it, too.

Buchanan and Kevin had done the Sawyer handoff and were on their way back. Since they were both awesome and good at multitasking, they'd confirmed that Robert Cordell had been shot three times in the gut, had all the money taken from his wallet, and also had his watch and wedding ring stolen.

Clearly Cordell's murder was supposed to have looked like a wrong place, wrong time mugging since the police only had suspects because of the call he'd made to me. Meaning him calling me was probably not in the plan. Which made sense, since that call had brought the police to me, and therefore to Charmaine and Kramer.

However, Sawyer getting the case seemed to have been what whoever killed Cordell wanted, but why? Was it truly a coincidence, or did Chuckie remain correct in believing real coincidences didn't happen all that often? If I took the assumption that Sawyer coming here to try to arrest me was what was wanted, then whoever killed Cordell had to have known he'd try to call me. Again, why and how? How did you set up a murder victim in that way? Or, rather, who would go to that level of intricacy? And, again, why?

Thought about the uncles. The Dingo had been a little bit like my own Sherlock Holmes. So, what would Uncle Dingo have said if I'd asked him about this? Came up with two things—who stands to gain by the detectives coming to this party and what, exactly, do they gain? Figure that out and I'd know who orchestrated Cordell's murder.

The Tinkerer was my number one suspect in all of this, but whoever was running robotic things at the NSA could also have wanted this. Maybe they'd worked together. Or maybe they hadn't and whoever had killed Cordell hadn't been who'd put him where the police found him.

While all this was going on and I was pondering the situation, Detective Beckett was actually doing his job. Charmaine and Kramer had airtight alibies for the time of Cordell's death, but since they'd literally admitted to an affair in front of hundreds of witnesses and had both acted shady when the news of the murder was shared, they were both now suspects. Sadly, they were not suspects in handcuffs, but you couldn't have everything.

Beckett questioned Mrs. Paster, who was trying to take care of the Cordell twins, both of whom looked stunned and confused since they'd just discovered their father was dead and their mother was a cheating ho who hadn't even bothered to come over and comfort them. Couldn't hear everything, but basically, the kids appeared to have no idea what was going on and Mrs. Paster had even less information.

Of course Beckett questioned those who'd been in the limo with me—including Jeff, who I could tell was really controlling himself from either bellowing, punching someone, or just demanding that Chuckie, Mom, or Reader take over the investigation—but ultimately gave me my phone back.

"Did you find the old man who spiked the punch?" Hadn't seen anyone looking for our mystery man all that hard, but then again, I'd been focused on what the detective was doing. On cue the music changed to "My Old Pals" by Kim Carnes.

"Not so far," Beckett said. "We got good prints on the bottle, though."

"Which only matters if the person is in the system, right?" Which I knew Trevor would not be, and I was about ninety-nine percent sure that Trevor was the punch spiker. Wasn't sure what the musical clue was supposed to tell me, just, as always, hoped I'd figure it out in time.

"Right."

"Did you interview a Doctor Rattoppare?"

He looked at his notes. "No. Uniforms handled most of the guests and, again, some booze in punch, while an issue for you religiously, doesn't matter to the police as much as a murder."

Managed not to say that if the President and every A-C here had died it would matter. We'd managed to stop that, so I could pretend that Beckett was correct. "Um, right. What about if it was a hate crime, though? It's well known that it's against our religion to imbibe alcohol at all. I mean, it's not like someone putting a swastika on a synagogue, but still."

"It's not in homicide's bailiwick. It's up to you if you want a different crime unit to come out. If so, your friends in the K-9 squad are already here, and they float into whatever department, so I'd suggest them."

"Super," I lied. "I'll take that up with Officer Melville." Who knew that alcohol was a murder attempt in our case, not a hate crime. So much for focusing Beckett where I needed him focused.

"So no, we don't expect to discover whoever did that—that's for the school to determine and punish the offending kids, because in my experience, kids lie about stuff like this, and they're the likely punch-spiking culprits. My focus is and will remain on the murder. Where I now have no leads at all, since you're cleared, and even though I have suspects, I have nothing on them that would make a judge want to give me a search warrant."

Gave up and didn't share, again, that we knew the kids didn't do it, because they were the witnesses for the fact that we were looking for an old man. Prejudices were hard to combat, regardless of who or what they were against.

"Senator Kramer has a limo driver named Evan," I said quietly. "I sincerely doubt either Zachary or Charmaine pulled the trigger, but Evan might have. If she's around, we've confirmed that Marion Villanova is working with Kramer on things I can promise you are shady, so she could be involved as well. Also, three delivery trucks with food supplies for the kitchen didn't show up tonight, which was why Mister Cordell left the fundraiser to try to help out and gather replacements. The chef probably knows what company or companies they were with. To me, that seems extremely convenient, because he was sent out after Kramer and Charmaine had their alibis established, and while it could have really been a mugging, I think it's too coincidental."

Plus, Cordell had told me the robots were going to try to kill me. Possibly because he felt that robots had been who'd killed him. The question was—who were the robots Cordell was warning me about? My money was still on Kramer and Charmaine— they were cyborgs, but I only knew to call them that because of Marling telling me so in my dream. Of course, Somerall and Lee were possibilities, too. One way or the other, if you'd found out that people had a bunch of wires in them, you might call them a robot, too. Or a nightmare. Maybe both.

Beckett nodded. "Thank you for the tips. I'm sorry this started off so unpleasantly for you. Sawyer was convinced you were guilty, and until this evening I didn't know he was anti-alien. I just thought he was following a detective's hunch."

"Well, the tips are good, but I have to warn you, I'm already betting that whoever pulled the trigger has washed their hands and clothes really well. Just know that they're out there, and if you need help, we'll be glad to do what we can. And, hopefully, you'll find a lead based on the missing food deliveries."

He smiled. "Thank you."

"What happens now?"

"I've told the Senator and Missus Cordell not to leave town. They're not likely to be a flight risk and I don't have enough to bring them in."

"Figures."

He shrugged. "It is what it is. Uh . . . could I ask a favor?"

"Um, sure?"

He pulled out his cellphone. "Could I get a selfie with you? My wife will literally kill me if I don't get a picture with Code Name: First Lady."

CHAPTER 73

THE POLICE FINALLY LEFT. The moment they were gone, Charmaine tried to get Mrs. Paster to give her the funds raised. Mrs. Paster declined, citing the fact that the donations were made to Sidwell for the Kramer kids' scholarship fund, not the PTA.

This, of course, didn't sit well with the Evil Kangaroo. "Don't look so pleased with yourself," she said to me as she finally gathered up her children, who still looked shell-shocked, understandably. "You've raised funds for scholarships, not for the PTA. So your hockey game had better be a success or you're still a failure."

"And a pleasant night to you, too."

Kramer came and put his arm around Charmaine's waist. "I'll take you and your children home." They left to the vocal stylings of Donald Fagen's "The Goodbye Look," Kramer and Charmaine giving me a death glare, the kids just looking dazed.

Under the circumstances, we started closing the party up. Reader arranged for a floater gate that was stationed near to the main entrance, where he and Chuckie stood guard to ensure that whoever went through wasn't Dr. Rattoppare.

Meanwhile Jeff, Mrs. Paster, and I were standing a little ahead of them so we could shake paws and thank everyone for their support. Christopher and Amy lurked nearby, just in case we needed the Flash or Mean Girl Support, depending. We were back on instrumentals, too. Hoped that meant things had finally calmed down.

The *Good Day USA!* team was back outside, doing final interviews and letting people get their pictures taken with Cologne, Adam, and the Kristie-Bot. They were a far bigger draw

with this crowd than Jeff and I were, which was fine with both
of us.

"Where're Richard and Camilla?" I asked Jeff quietly while
there was a lull in people leaving and Mrs. Paster was in conversation with a group of parents.

"Searching for Trevor. Camilla's with Richard to protect him,
under the guise of showing him around, per Mrs. Paster's request."

Mrs. Paster's group headed for us before I could ask anything
else, and we were once again shaking paws and such. No one was
mean, no one was nasty, though some of these people were for
sure in Charmaine's entourage. Wasn't sure if they were faking
us out or if they were normal and nice when she wasn't around.

Finally, everyone in the ballroom was gone, other than those
who were a part of our gigantic entourage, were associated with
the school, or were working as waitstaff. "Do you need to stay
or do you get to go home now?" I asked Mrs. Paster.

She heaved a sigh as the assistant principal joined us. "I'd
love to say we're going home, but we do have to be certain all's
well here."

"The President's security forces were kind enough to double-
check the school grounds," Yamaguchi shared. "We have no loi-
terers, all buildings are locked, and all the cars are gone from the
lots, other than those of staff or the President and his many
guests."

He and Mrs. Paster both looked tired. Could relate. "Then
let's hurry things up so you two can get out of here."

Mrs. Paster nodded. "Thank you. By the way, I heard what
Missus Cordell made you agree to. Please know that we who
actually run Sidwell don't want your children leaving."

"Not to worry. I expect the hockey game to be a big hit." Said
with far more confidence than I felt. But that was why I had staff
of my own.

She smiled. "I'm sure it will be." The music went back to
rock—"The Last DJ" by Tom Petty & The Heartbreakers. She
made a little grimace. "We also need to make sure whoever you
have doing the music leaves the building before we lock up, too.
I don't know that I approve of their choices, but who am I do
question the First Lady?"

"Um, I will definitely get on that." Had no idea who Mrs.
Paster thought she'd met. Algar's influence meant she'd seen
whoever he'd wanted her to see. Had no idea where the DJ

actually was, or if it was just Algar making people *think* someone was there, but in case someone actually was, made a note to
find them before we all left.

Reader shut down the floater gate, and we headed for the
others who were hanging around the door I assumed led to the
patio. Chuckie gave a signal, and Amy came over and started up
a conversation with the administrators. She also moved them
just a little bit away, so the rest of us could talk without them
overhearing. Clearly Amy had joined the CIA in her spare time.

"Wasim says that everything's totes going smoothly with
moving Clinton and his family," Lizzie shared as we joined them.

"We're just waiting for the *Good Day USA!* team to finish
up," Louise added. Noted that there were no windows that
showed the patio area. Frankly, if I hadn't been told there was a
patio, I'd never have assumed the door we were near led to anything other than dumpsters.

Tim joined us as well, the rest of Alpha Team following him.
"Kitchens are secured and staff is home."

"It's only all of us," Lorraine said.

"And whoever's outside," Claudia added.

"Who *is* outside?"

"Not sure," Lizzie replied. "People can leave from out there,
and a lot of them have. Get their photo op, take off."

"Where's Richard?" Serene asked, as I opened the door to
check who was delaying our getting out of here.

"I haven't seen him since I told him what was going on,"
Reader said, sounding worried. "He got Camilla to help him
hunt for Trevor."

"Um . . ." White was outside, with the flyboys and all the K-9
squad, dogs included. They were getting interviewed, and White
and the flyboys were apparently helping with the dogs. The music piped out here, too, and I knew this because we were now
treated to David Bowie's "Diamond Dogs."

"Find anyone?" I asked White as I waved to the humans and
petted all the dogs. Considering my dress wasn't wrecked—for
possibly the first time ever—getting dog fur on it wouldn't be a
big deal. Chose to count it in the win column, even. That was
me, crazed with optimism.

"No. I believe I looked at every man here, Missus Martini. If
Trevor was here, I couldn't recognize him. I also heard no one
that sounded like the voice from the recording."

We'd figured out who the Tinkerer was based on a video

message that showed me being maimed and tortured. Only it was a Kitty-Bot and therefore fake. But White had recognized the speech patterns of the man who was doing that video's voiceover. However, the last time he'd seen or even thought of Trevor had been decades ago, and he'd presumed the man dead for that long. That he couldn't spot this guy wasn't all that shocking.

"Bummer."

White sighed. "And we couldn't find Doctor Rattoppare, though others said they'd seen or met him."

"So he was avoiding you?" Certainly felt like he'd been avoiding me.

"Who knows? He may not be giving it a second thought. There were a great number of people, the majority of which I've never met before, and I even missed your trying out for a pitching position with the Nationals."

"My heart belongs to the Diamondbacks, as would my baseball skills."

"As you wish. What did you discover and what else did I miss?"

"Not much." Filled him in fast on what had gone down. "Where's Camilla?" I asked as I wrapped up.

"Following a lead. She felt that the Dealers of Death were interesting."

"That makes one of us."

White chuckled. "Since she and I had no luck discovering who Doctor Rattoppare is, I agreed it was a better use of her time."

"Live and Let Die" by Paul McCartney & Wings came on. So we still had someone doing the music, and Algar wanted me paying attention.

The K-9 squad was done with their close-up, but before we could escape, the Kristie-Bot suggested that it was time for Jeff to do an interview. She included Mrs. Paster and Yamaguchi in this, meaning that Jeff didn't have a good way to get out of it.

Now might be the time to search for the DJ, since I definitely wanted to be able to say whether he or she was with us or had left—and if I wasn't around, then *Good Day USA!* couldn't interview me again.

Knew I needed to go with someone else, and that meant White or Gower, because who we were actually looking for was Algar or whomever he'd put into place. Gower was nearer to Jeff, and White was right here. Besides, he was my partner in butt-kicking.

Tugged on White's sleeve as he handed the dogs back and took Prince's lead from Melville. "Borrowing my best protector for a moment." Melville rolled his eyes but didn't protest, and I headed back inside, White with me.

"Where are you going?" Phoebe asked as we stepped through the doorway.

Managed not to jump or scream, but it took effort. "To give the person handling music the heads-up that we're about to leave."

She sighed. "I'm going with you."

Waved the leash. "I have Prince, and Mister White. Stay here in case of anything."

"Before you argue," White said, "let me say one word—hyperspeed."

Phoebe heaved a sigh. "If I didn't like you all so much, I'd really hate this job. Don't be gone long, and scream or call for help. Please."

"Will do." White offered me his arm, which I took. "So, Mister White, where to?"

"The one place no one's gone, Missus Martini. Upstairs."

"There's an upstairs?"

"Yes, for specialized lighting, music, and such. One additional story, low ceilings, limited roof access. Charles had it searched before you arrived and there were guards at the door. Anyone up there was approved to be there, and only those approved could go in or out."

"Approved by whom? Because Mrs. Paster didn't sound like she'd ordered someone to spin the tunes, because if she had, she'd have fired them, from what I can tell. And it's not like the lights have gone up or down in the entire time we've been here."

"I don't know. Camilla seemed to feel that all was well."

As we reached the door, which was between the bathrooms, the music changed to the Don Henley version of "New York Minute." Was pretty sure this was a warning, since the song dealt with how fast things could change. "Where are the guards?"

"Perhaps they went with the others. Everyone is out with Jeffrey on the patio."

"Huh."

"I know that tone. Is it catsuit time, Missus Martini?"

"I believe that it is, Mister White. I truly believe that it is."

Let go of his arm and handed him Prince's leash. Got my Glock out of my clutch and tucked said clutch under my arm.

With that, I nodded and White opened the door.

CHAPTER 74

"WELL, THAT WAS ANTICLIMACTIC."
The door led us into a short hallway with stairs at the end. There was no one and nothing else.

Prince took the lead, sniffing up a storm. Took his leash from White, who produced a gun from inside his suit jacket and indicated he'd bring up the rear.

"I am so proud," I whispered as we started off, half of the Scooby-Doo team in action. Wasn't sure if that made me Velma or Daphne, but White was clearly Freddy, because I could totally picture him in an ascot and he didn't have the eat-everything stoner vibe Shaggy did.

"I prefer to learn from experience, unlike Jeffrey and Christopher who like to repeat their mistakes for fun."

"You rock as always, Mister White." Thusly amusing ourselves, we headed up the stairs as quietly as possible.

The bathrooms were near to the kitchen area, but couldn't smell anything in here, good or bad, and it didn't feel hot, so the insulation was spot on. Couldn't hear the music in the hallway or on the stairs, either. However, as we reached the top and exited into what looked like a big room with an open floor plan, could just hear the last strains of "New York Minute" ending. Only there was also applause. Meaning Algar had played The Eagles' version of the song, too.

That was a different form of repeat than he normally used. Wasn't sure why, but it made me extra alert. Maybe because this version of the song was from their *Hell Freezes Over* live album, recorded during the reunion tour they'd vowed would never happen. Wrapped Prince's leash around my hand several times—didn't want him getting too far ahead of me.

It was dark—lit but with very low wattage bulbs and not that many of them. Since the little hallway and the stairs had been decently lighted, this, like the rest of what was going on, boded.

"Hello Kitty" by Avril Lavigne blasted out. The three of us jumped, it was so startling. Would have lost my hold on Prince if I hadn't had the leash so well wrapped. As we landed, a man appeared out of the darkness. He was wearing a waiter's uniform.

As he got closer, realized it was the waiter I'd noted before, the one who'd taken the spiked punch to Jeff and the others onstage. He stopped walking a few feet away from us.

"Excuse me, but we're looking for the DJ." Hey, had to say something. "And, um, the party's over. You can go home now."

"Oh, I can never truly go home."

Due to how we'd all jumped and landed, White was standing next to me, and I felt him stiffen. "It's been a very long time," he said calmly.

"Oh, Richard, Richard, Richard. It honestly hasn't been long enough." The waiter stepped closer to us. "Hello, Kitty, Kitty. You're so pretty, pretty."

"Trevor Rattoppare, I presume?" Knew White was ready to run. I was, too, but saw no weapons on Trevor, and White and I were both holding guns. So perhaps running wasn't necessary. Yet. "You like this song enough to repeat the lyrics?"

He shrugged. "It was effective."

"Nothing else you did tonight was."

He chuckled and stepped closer. Prince growled. Trevor did not smell right. He smelled like Kristie Bot. Not a surprise. "No, I suppose not. But it was instructive. And I've been waiting to meet you. I thought the song was quite a nice touch."

"How so?" It was time for my time-honored technique of Keeping The Bad Guys Monologuing For Fun, Profit, and Longevity. "On any of that, nice touches and instructions and all that jazz."

"I enjoyed watching you work. A little roll. Who would think to throw that?"

"Um, you mean, besides me? I'm sure many people."

"I'm not."

"I was looking for you all night," White said. "How did I miss you? I examined the waitstaff because some of us try to only make a mistake once." So, White remembered Operation Drug Addict, too. Not that I thought anyone had forgotten, but it was good to know he paid attention to all my recaps.

"I know." Trevor took his waiter's jacket off, while both White and I pointed our guns at him. He chuckled. "Oh, you two can relax. I don't do the violence."

"I'll bet you have people for that. People who enjoy doing 'the violence' and would like to perpetrate it on us."

Trevor turned his jacket inside out and put it back on. He was suddenly an average man in a nice tuxedo. "It was simple. Any time you were too near to me, I went into the kitchen or a restroom, reversed my jacket, and came back out. No one noticed, and I avoided you and that school employee easily."

Good to know that Camilla had fooled him. Another one for the win column was always nice. Rare, too.

"That doesn't mean you don't have accomplices lurking about, waiting to strike," White pointed out.

"What Mister White said. To the tenth degree. At least."

"Such worrying. No one is up here other than the three of us." Prince growled. "Excuse me. The four of us."

"There's a DJ up here," I said. "Somewhere. That's why we came upstairs—to find him or her and tell them it was time to go home."

Trevor chuckled again, only longer and with a lot more emphasis. "Oh, that's charming. You are certainly a hands-on First Lady. No, there's no one else here. The music is being controlled from elsewhere."

"It is? By whom? And where?"

"I have no idea. But there's no one else here. I checked." Avril stopped singing and no other music came on. If I strained, I could just make out what sounded like instrumental music playing in the ballroom below us. "The music ceased after the last song, so I assume your elusive DJ has discovered that it's closing time."

"Then who played the "Hello Kitty" song?"

Trevor held out his phone and the song started up again. It was still hella loud. He stopped it. "I did."

Meaning Algar had put the music on hold or the DJ was dead. It was possible Trevor was telling the truth, of course. Only one way to find out. "Mister White, if you would? Just to be sure and all."

"It would be my pleasure, Missus Martini." He zipped off. Leaving me to wonder just where Algar had set up musical shop and who with, and why, despite all of this and the current situation, Trevor didn't seem remotely threatening.

"Richard's aged quite well."

Music started again, at the normal volume it had been all evening, "Live Forever" by Oasis. Wondered who or what White was going to find. Or had already found.

"So have you. I mean, you should look as old as the Crypt Keeper, and yet you actually look younger than Mister White does."

He shrugged. "I never had children. They age you."

"Wow, that's your story and you're planning to stick with it? Dude, we know about the Treatment. And I'm pretty damn sure you've done the Treatment on yourself."

"Of course I have. You'll do it, too. Eventually."

"I doubt it."

"I don't. The opportunity to live forever, to protect and serve forever? You and Jeffrey won't be able to resist the lure."

"I'll bet that we will. But then again, are you so certain because you plan to force us into it? All of us?"

White returned. "Trevor is correct—I didn't see anyone else up here. Meaning we'll still have to find the DJ, though obviously at another time."

"Huh. Trevor was just saying that we'll give in and do the Treatment."

"And Kitty—may I call you Kitty?"

"Go for it."

"Kitty and I were discussing her understandable concern that I would try to force the Treatment upon you all."

"We saw the wire boards and the plans," White said, sarcasm knob easily at nine on the scale. "We rescued several of our people just in time. We're all fairly certain you plan to murder us and put robots of some kind in our places. You've already set that precedent."

"Cyborgs," Trevor said in that Schoolteacher Nicely Correcting A Student way.

"Excuse me?" White asked politely.

"Cyborgs. That's what Kristie has become. And, as you rightly guessed, Zachary and Charmaine." Trevor smiled at me. "I realized you'd figured it out when I saw you on *Good Day USA!* yesterday morning. Kristie was quite out of turn with her little act."

"Awesome. I'd figured out that something was wrong with Kristie. Cyborgs is a new one, but it makes sense." Yay! I could call them cyborgs to everyone now. It was the little things you cherished, after all. "We don't want to be cyborgs, thank you very much, despite Kristie swearing by the Cyborg Lifestyle and your particular genius with the wiring."

"That's very sweet of her. Perhaps I won't have her meet with an unfortunate accident."

"You'd better not." Said as calmly as I could manage.

"Well, we shall see. Again, I believe you'll change your minds about the Treatment. Eventually. Richard might as well. When age catches up, as it appears to be doing."

White shrugged. "Aging isn't the worst thing in the world."

"You know, your father said the very same thing to me, when he refused the Treatment. Of course, it was still experimental and, frankly, with that superbeing inside of him, the Treatment probably wouldn't have worked. He didn't fear dying, your father. He feared not getting to complete his plans, but not dying."

"Oh, bullshit."

Trevor's turn to look shocked, as the music changed to "She's Electric," meaning Algar was potentially now on an Oasis kick. Or that he was sharing that all the cyborgs had to plug in like they were Priuses to recharge. Really, either option seemed sound.

"Excuse me?" He sounded shocked.

"You heard me. Ronald Yates wanted to live forever. He had his whole Yates Gene crap going and then some. I mean, seriously, name someone in the League of Extraordinary Genius Monkeys who doesn't?"

Trevor stared at me. Then he started to laugh. "Oh, if only he'd lived to meet you."

"He did. I killed him. Well, really, Mephistopheles killed him. I killed Mephistopheles."

"I know. I meant meet you in this way. As a peer. As someone to get to know."

White and I let this remark sit on the air a bit. "Um . . . did you just call me your peer?"

"I did, yes. And Ronald's peer. Richard's improved greatly under your tutelage as well."

"Dude, I don't mean to be rude, but are you high?"

He laughed again. "No, but oh how I wish she'd understood that you would have made the best ally."

"She. You mean Stephanie, your new 'granddaughter' Stephanie, the real heir to the Ronald Yates Throne Stephanie?" Then again, maybe the musical clue was that Stephanie had had the

Treatment already. Or Algar was giving me an Atta Girl. Decided not to care and just enjoy the song.

"I do indeed. She's a headstrong girl, and sometimes she doesn't listen. Her great-grandfather was the same."

"She's a wacked-out bitch with severe Daddy Issues who's all about blaming everyone else for the things that have gone wrong in her life while simultaneously using and being used by every man she meets. So, just to be clear, we're talking about the same person?"

"We are and, I must confess, you have outlined her weaknesses rather well. And his."

"Go me, I feel all tingly. Look, what's your game? It's late and I have little kids to get home to and a bigger kid to put to bed." Several bigger kids. All of Stephanie's siblings. Really hoped this wasn't an elaborate ruse to snatch them out from under our noses. Or that they'd been setting us up. Or both. Really wanted it to not be both.

Trevor didn't reply, and he looked just slightly disappointed.

"Oh, my God, not this crap again. Okay, fine, I got your totally broad hint. I just didn't need to exclaim, 'Oh, say it ain't so, Steph's just like her great-granddaddy, y'all,' because we already know that. I mean, *we know it*. We figured it out at least two Operations ago. Maybe more. They're all distinct but the details all sort of blend together for me after a while. Crazed lunatic makes bizarre opening move, things get dicey, plot is foiled, world is saved, usually at the last second, blah, blah, blah."

Trevor blinked. "Ah . . ."

"And Stephanie's told you I'm a moron, as has anyone else from the League of Genius Lunatics up to and definitely including LaRue Demorte Gaultier, and so you wanted to see if I was stupid and lucky or smart and lucky or just lucky and lucky. Particularly because if I'm stupid and lucky there's a chance you can bring me over to your side of things."

"True and I believe—"

Cut him off. "I, frankly, don't care what your determination was. Let me make it simple for you—I'm not stupid. The only person on your side who's ever 'gotten' me was Madeleine Cartwright and I'm betting that she never told you she thought I was smarter than the average bear. Could have hung with her if she hadn't wanted to, you know, kill everyone and take all the power for herself. Otherwise? As far as I'm concerned, you're all a bunch of moles in the Whack-A-Mole game, and I'm the freaking hammer."

Trevor stared at me. Then he looked at White. "How did you recruit her?"

"The same way we did anyone else," White replied calmly. "By telling her the truth."

"We-ell, you know, as much of it as they were telling everybody else. I figured out a lot of it." Because most A-Cs sucked at lying. Wondered if Trevor was one of them. Figured I'd find out, one way or the other. "So, what's your play here, Trevor? Cackling at us while telling us you're about to blow up the city? Snarling about how we've ruined all your plans right before you try to kill us? Frothing at the mouth while telling us new, bigger, badder, scarier aliens are coming to get us? Trying to steal my children?"

"No. I'd like to have Stephanie learn from you."

"Seriously? God help me, if this was all to try to arrange a playdate for me and Stephanie, I have only two words for you: Epic Fail."

"No, that's not what I mean. I mean, I want to propose a truce."

CHAPTER 75

WHITE AND I BOTH STARED. Prince shared that, while Trevor smelled hella wrong, he also didn't smell like he was lying. Algar, meanwhile, shared "Truth Be Told" by Megadeth.

"Come again?" I asked finally.

"A truce."

"Why?" White asked flatly. "You're here. Missus Martini and I, with the assistance of Prince, should be more than able to stop you, even if you are a, ah, cyborg."

"You might," Trevor allowed. "But if you do, then Stephanie will stop behaving and go on a rampage. And we know we don't like that."

"We might be willing to take our chances."

"Don't be," Trevor said, and finally there was a knife in his tone. Just a flash, but it was there.

"Better give me a reason better than 'because I said so,' then, because I'm ready to whack your mole head right now."

"I want to deescalate. *Detente*, if you will."

"I echo Missus Martini. Why?"

Trevor heaved a sigh. "Because we're not winning."

Waited. That seemed to be Trevor's entire statement. "Um, so? I mean, that never stopped anyone else."

"And yet, it should have. They'd all still be alive, for one thing, if they'd stopped and truly assessed their enemy. I have. You're formidable. LaRue felt that it was all luck. However, I watched you tonight. I set in motion something simple, but something that should have killed at least one A-C. No one was harmed. No one. Because of you."

"Look, spiking the punch is a nasty idea, true, but if that was your entire plan . . ."

"Why would I have needed more? Simple is always better. Always." He sighed at our expressions. "Normal people don't pay attention to what's inside a trash can. Normal people don't grab a dinner roll and throw it like a baseball. Normal people don't spot terrorists based on one sentence."

"That last one was my mom." Hey, she deserved the credit.

"Yes. She *raised* you. Of course she's not normal, either. Your family is filled with the abnormal."

"Humans tend to find that to be an insult. Just sayin'. And all that." The music changed to "We Are the Normal" by The Goo Goo Dolls. Perhaps Algar didn't feel it was an insult.

"I don't mean it that way. I'm abnormal. Richard is as well. And so is Stephanie."

"So are a lot of people." Jeff and Christopher and Chuckie for starters, followed closely by Reader and Gower and Tim and everyone else we worked with. Siler maybe should top the list, but it was a hella long list.

"I just saw you mentally tally off people you feel are abnormal in the way I mean," Trevor said. "And I know all of them work with you or are related to you, or both. That's my point. Because of you, the abnormal people were pulled together, making all of you stronger. You forgive your enemies and the abnormal ones accept that and they join you and you all become stronger."

"It's called seeing the best in people, and some of you could freaking try it."

"No. It's the abnormality calling. It's what pulled you into this world you live in now."

"That's true," White said quietly. "Human agents were rare, and females rarer."

"Go me. Go being nice. Go whatevs. Look, I'm not going to forgive Stephanie. I realize that that's what half the A-C population wants. But I know her. I know her in the bone. She will never be anything but our enemy. And, since you're with her and protecting her, you'll never be anything but our enemy, too."

"The United States has many enemies. And yet, they work together or leave each other alone."

"Not always."

"No, not always. The stronger, the craftier, the more willing to die for the cause, they win. That doesn't mean they were the best, or right, or even good, or that they had the superior numbers or firepower. It just means they were better when it mattered most. You're consistently better when it matters most and we are not. And I want to call for a truce, so that Stephanie can actually have a life."

"Explain this truce," White said, before I could reply. "Because I don't know that we believe it."

"I, for one, don't believe it, so right on, there, Mister White."

Trevor shrugged. "We stop bothering you, you stop hounding us. We continue our practice in France, you stay away from us and don't try to stop us."

Thought fast. There had to be a reason he wanted this, and it wasn't the reason he was stating. He'd compared Stephanie to Yates more than once, and we already knew that he saw her as the true heir. So, what was it he wanted her doing to be more like Yates?

"Your practice is turning people into machines," White said.

"They know that. It's their own choice. Their eager, willing choice. We have a waiting list in the hundreds right now, and that's without any form of advertising. Imagine the possibilities when we do advertise. And they all pay us well for our work."

And sometimes, I didn't even need a song cue. Though hearing Oingo Boingo right now would be nice. "That's it!"

"What's it?" White asked.

"What Trevor really wants. Because there's nothing wrong with capitalism." On cue, the song changed to, sure enough, Boingo's "Capitalism." Nice to know that Algar was paying attention.

Trevor's eyes narrowed. "Hardly."

"Dude, stop trying to lie, you're not that great at it. You want Stephanie to be the next Ronald Yates. While she has all his drive and his mania, and she has talent, and she has an inferiority complex that manifests itself in being a bully, just like he did, and she has his voracious taste in the opposite sex that she constantly screws up, what she doesn't have is a modicum of business sense. Ronaldo Al Dejahl did, but Stephanie doesn't."

"So . . . what?" White asked.

"So, that's how you get true power in this world. You own things. You create wealth and you buy things. Not yachts and mansions, but companies. Media conglomerates, utilities, oil, stocks, the list goes on. And once you're hella rich, the kind of rich most people in this country can't even conceive of, then you buy things. Like countries, and politicians, and high public office. And the more money you have, the more media you control, the more lobbyists working for your cause, the more powerful you are and the more people believe your lies, because your many businesses focus on your lies and call them truth."

"Yes," Trevor said. "Exactly. The others truly didn't understand that you're someone they should have cultivated. And they still don't."

Filed that last sentence away for later. "I wouldn't have said yes."

"Oh, you never know. But yes, that's what I want. To have Stephanie grow in power, wealth, and experience. So that she becomes a titan of industry, just as her great-grandfather did." He sounded proud. He looked proud. Prince took a few deep sniffs and shared that he smelled proud, too.

"You really do love her as your own, don't you?"

He nodded. "I do. As I said, I had no children and I never married. Ronald was my world."

"Were you in love with him?"

Trevor rolled his eyes. "No. I don't waste my time on that kind of thing, on either side of the fence. My one true love is possibility and all it holds for us. No, I loved him for who he was, but I was not 'in love' with him. Any more than I am 'in love' with the girl I do think of as my granddaughter, lest you make another disgusting assumption."

"Geez, sorry. I don't think men being in love with each other is disgusting."

"I find all of that disgusting, frankly."

"He's asexual," White said quietly. "Just in case you weren't picking that up. Seeing as how I know you don't roll that way."

"Mister White, while I love it when you go all 'street' on me, don't make me hurt you. I got it, I got it. Everyone's a critic. Okay, so, we call a truce and, what, let you perpetrate your evil on Europe while allowing someone who is probably our most formidable enemy still alive to become more powerful? I'm not seeing the upside for us. I *am* seeing the take Trevor into custody and see what happens side as being the way to go."

"As I said, if you do that, then Stephanie will counterattack, and this time I won't be there to temper her."

"I shudder to discover what you call 'tempering,' but fine. So does that mean you've already put wires in her brain so you can control her?"

He looked aghast. "Absolutely not!"

"Dude, you're the Tinkerer, and I want to be on record that

that's what I've been calling you even before I learned your alias."

He smiled. "I'm impressed. But not surprised."

"But you are someone who tinkers." In Bizarro World, Alfred tinkered and came up with a million and one new things. There was no way Trevor wasn't doing the same here. "So, why wouldn't you tinker with Stephanie's brain to make her all docile and crap?"

"Because that would be wrong." He sounded sincere. "I want her to become all that she truly can be. On her own. As herself. Not as some machine of mine. I never tinkered with Ronald—I could have done something about his cancer, but then he joined with the parasite and I didn't need to. But I would never have altered his magnificent brain. And I won't alter Stephanie's either. Besides, the wiring helps the brains work better, it doesn't control them. But until such time as Stephanie is ready—and that won't be for quite some time—she remains fully organic."

"Okay. Let's say I believe you. I kind of do and I kind of don't. But let's pretend that I'm with you all the way. What the hell do *we* get out of the deal? Because if we don't get something good, why would we agree?"

"Well, I've offered the Treatment. You've said no. For now."

"Yeah, you're not selling me, Mister Captain Of Industry. You want us to give you a free pass. Right now, you're the best bargaining chip we have. I see no reason to let you go. Stephanie might turn herself in to save you."

"She won't."

"She might," White said. "And I agree with Missus Martini. We want far more than what you've offered if we're to broker any kind of deal with you."

"What is it you want, then?"

"In order to leave you alone and give you time to get stronger? We want a lot. We want all nefarious activities stopped. No more making Bots or androids or illegal cyborgs. If someone chooses the Robotic Lifestyle, fine. But you'll be sending us copies of every contract and, if you don't, we come in and kill you."

"You don't know where we are, and you can't find us or catch us."

Siler appeared behind Trevor, grabbed him, and had a gigantic knife at his throat in a matter of a moment. "Yeah? Think again. 'Uncle' Trevor."

CHAPTER 76

THE SONG CHANGED to Joshua Kadison's "Invisible Man" and, for the first time, Trevor seemed freaked out. "What? Benjamin? How are you here?" He struggled, but Siler was strong and clearly prepared. Cyborg or not, Trevor went nowhere.

"I'm everywhere," Siler replied, sounding like the most bad-ass assassin the world had ever known. If Cologne could hear this, he'd dump the Code Name: First Lady crap in a heartbeat in order to do the Sexy Alien Assassin series, and he'd for sure take the starring role. "I know where your precious Stephanie is. I have no love for any of you. In fact, the sooner you all die for good, the better. Kitty's the only reason you're not all dead right now. So, if the First Lady says she wants something, you give it to her, or you and Stephanie both die. And yes, I know how to kill a cyborg."

"What? How?" Trevor seemed honestly shocked.

"Really? We have, like, the best reverse engineers in the world working for and with us. You guys made Ben the most dangerous weapon you could at the time, he escaped, and he's his own dude. And, as he said, he doesn't like you. I don't like you, either."

"I'm with Benjamin and Missus Martini. In case you weren't sure."

The music changed to "My List" by The Killers. Back in full sync with Algar, always a plus. "We all don't like you, Trevor. Sorry. I'm sure you'll just hurt someone to get over it. So, let's get back to the nitty and the gritty before Ben's arm gets tired and he accidentally slices your head off. I'm ready to share my List of Demands." Wasn't ready to share what I called Siler, though. That was a nickname the Tinkerer didn't get to hear.

Trevor nodded carefully. "They are?"

"I wasn't being funny—we want the list of everyone who wants to have the Treatment, and we want the list of everyone who's had the Treatment, and we'll want the list of those who get the treatment, ad infinitum, and we want to see all their contracts. I want all the ones you've done already, and then I want to receive applications and contracts as you receive them."

"We promise our clients anonymity."

"And Hoover promised a chicken in every pot. Sometimes you lie for the greater good or because someone with a gigantic knife at your throat makes you promise to do so. This is one of those times."

"That makes you like your enemies," Trevor said.

"Does it? Let me see if I can find the will to go on. Gimme a mo . . . well, it's a shocker, but I can indeed manage. Here's how I'm different from our enemies—I'm not taking this list because of who they are but because of what they're actively choosing to become, I don't want to coerce these people into doing anything against their will, I don't want to take them and force them to do terrible things to themselves or others, and I don't want to hurt them. I do want to know who and where they are, so when the zombie switch I'm sure you have installed in all their brains is flipped we know who we have to stop and why."

"We don't have that, but I understand why you think we do. That was standard on all androids."

"And it's standard on the Bots, too."

"Yes, as far as I know, it is. But it's not in the cyborgs." Well, we certainly hadn't been able to find bombs or kill switches, in anyone, so he might be telling the truth. "What else?"

"Stop all the crap. No more evil, either straight up or on the side. You want us to leave you and Stephanie alone? Then you give us no reason to go after you."

"Agreed."

"That was easy," White said.

"I wasn't lying. I want to give Stephanie a chance to become a real person of power. She can't do that if she's focused on ridiculous vendettas against people who, if she just leaves them alone, will willingly leave her alone."

This was true enough. Jeff would welcome the opportunity to keep everyone away from his niece, and he certainly wouldn't be the only one. Anyone related to Alfred would want that, and since all the A-Cs were related somewhere back there, most of them were going to side with the live and let live policy if they possibly could.

"And if we discover you're up to something, I'll be watching you, and so will others. Then I kill you," Siler said silkily. "Without asking permission of anyone other than Kitty. What do you think she'll tell me to do?"

"Kill 'em all, Ben, that's our motto when it comes to the Tinkerer and his Protégée. Kill 'em all and take along your friends so they can help kill 'em all, too."

"I love working with you," Siler said.

"The feeling is very mutual."

"If you're done with the lovefest?" Trevor asked snippily. "Really, get a room."

"The First Lady's taken," Siler said, with a wink for me. "Despite your best efforts tonight."

"Which brings me to Part B of this particular entry—the 'stop all your crap' directive includes plans currently in the works."

"We have none. Other than my attempt tonight."

"Really? Then why were you invited to tonight's party and who the hell sent those Bots to the Intergalactic School? And that's just a for-starters two-part question."

"Part one—Zachary is my client. He invited me because we assumed I could recruit new clients here, though I did promise not to recruit anyone who might have a political edge against him. I have a list of names of interested parties, and yes, yes, I'll give that to you. I added on tonight's attempt to see what a simple yet wholly effective plan would reap. It reaped your stopping it without a single casualty, which, to me, proved that my initial choice to force Stephanie to stop her vendetta was the right one."

"Go team."

"Yes, truly. Part two—you have more enemies than us. We are not involved with the Bots, as you call them, so I have no idea what went on or why or what the goal was, other than scattered news reports and what was being discussed by those who were at the school tonight, none of whom appear to have the information you seek."

"Ah, but you were involved at one point. Which leads me to my next demand. I want to know who's running things against us in the NSA, and by that, I mean, who's managing the Bots and such with Janelle Gardiner and, presumably, Amos Tobin. You know, the initiatives that have been causing us problems that you claim aren't being run by you?"

"I don't know."

"Oh, Trevor, Trevor, Trevor. And it was all going so well. And now? Now I have to tell Ben to kill you. Just don't get any blood or oil or whatever's in their veins onto my dress, Ben, please and thank you."

Really wasn't sure if Siler planned to kill Trevor or had just taken the Baddest Cop role. He'd worked well with me during Operation Immigration when we were flipping Kozlow, so chances were he was just acting. Didn't want to bet against him, though. Assassins could be touchy, after all, and he appeared to have decades worth of anger to work out.

"Wait!" Trevor sounded freaked. Siler had probably twitched or something.

But the music changed to "Even Better Than the Real Thing" by U2. The lyrics dealt with second chances and so forth, so hopefully this meant Trevor had more for us.

"I'm listening."

"And I'm serious. I don't know who's behind the Bots. That was Madeleine's project initially, and it was she who I assisted. As we took casualties and plans were being foiled, I turned toward the cyborg project, she brought in Monica Strauss. Who then brought in Janelle Gardiner once Madeleine was dead. But Monica and I were not close, and she had someone she took into her confidence long before Janelle. She was quite cagey about it and I never met them. I don't even know if they're a man or a woman. Whoever they are, they're expert at hiding in the shadows, and this is coming from someone who's been hidden in the shadows on this planet longer than two of you have been alive."

"Why haven't you bothered to find out this person's identity?" White asked. "Having been alive longer than you've been hiding, that seems remarkably unlike you."

"I had no need. They didn't interfere with my plans, they didn't try to do anything to me, and if they were trying to discover who I was, they weren't successful."

"As far as you know," I felt compelled to point out. "I mean, you didn't think we knew who you were and all that when we already did."

"True. As far as I know. But I don't know who they are. If they know who I am, they haven't bothered me or interfered with me, either."

"And yet, Stephanie's lair was right by the NSA black site, and she was siphoning off their power. Now, try again."

"I know *of* the Bot projects," he said peevishly. "I don't know who was working with Monica and is now working with Janelle. Whoever they are, they're the brains behind the Bots, however, because Monica was no Madeleine, and Janelle is no Monica. And Stephanie created her lair all by herself," he added proudly.

Wasn't sure that Trevor should be selling either Strauss or Gardiner short. Cartwright had been an expert at doing the woman thing of pretending the men around her were smarter so that she could get what she wanted, and I doubted she'd brought in someone who was less able with that technique than she was. Trevor might be asexual, but he was still male and still very impressed with himself. However, that line of questioning seemed tapped out.

"So, when did Stephanie find out about her new grandfather?" Wanted to see if what I'd been assuming—that Trevor found her after she'd stolen Drax's helicarrier—was correct.

"Once she'd proven that she had what it took. She'd taken that ridiculous Gustav Drax's machine along with hostages, and she'd created her own androids. I knew it was time, and I reached out."

"You make it sound so Hallmark and homespun, I could shed a tear." Always nice to be right. "Okay, so, what do you know about the other Shadow Person hanging around? Are they alien or human?"

"Honestly, again, I don't know. But I lean toward human. Monica was not a fan of aliens and Janelle was less so. They both despised LaRue."

"Wow, a mark in both their favors. But they all loved Ronald Yates."

The music changed to "You Can't Always Get What You Want" by the Rolling Stones. Interesting choice. Hoped I'd get what I needed, then.

"True enough. However, Ronald had something that LaRue lacked—charisma. LaRue was attractive to men, and that was how she worked her way in where she wanted to. But Ronald's charisma affected everyone."

"Yes, yes, he was a great man, blah, blah, blah. Great at evil. At any rate, what do they call them, the Bots?"

"Ah, they call them Bots. Why are you asking that?"

"Missus Martini, again I'm impressed with your ability to mind meld with our enemies."

"Me, too," Siler added. "So, can I kill him yet? I spent several hours sharpening this blade. It'll slice through steel. I'd love to see how fast it slices through flesh, bone, and wiring."

Trevor went pale, or at least he looked more pasty in the low light. "Ben, did you lower the lights or were they always this creepy?"

"That was me. I liked this ambiance better."

"No argument. It definitely says 'someone is dying here to-night,' and I just wanted to make sure whose side the lights were on, so to speak."

"I can give you something better than whoever's working with Janelle now," Trevor said.

Yawned, because Charmaine had really helped me channel my Inner Mean Girl. "And what might that be?"

"The name of the person behind the Club Fifty-One True Believers."

CHAPTER 77

YAWNED AGAIN. "We know who's running the True Believers. Harvey Gutermuth with a big assist from Farley Pecker."

"They're the titular heads, yes. But they have a backer, someone who's funding them worldwide."

Perhaps they did. The first Club 51 leader, Howard Taft, had had Reid backing him, after all. Why assume that Gutermuth wasn't just another puppet? "I'm listening."

"Myron Van Dyke."

"The most boring dude on the planet? Pull the other one and all that."

"No, it's true. He's their silent partner."

"In alien hating?"

Trevor looked at White. "Does this shock *you*?"

"Not really," White admitted. "Not in that sense. Hatred is an odd thing, and it manifests in many ways. I wonder, though, if you're being truthful, Trevor. I mean, I, for one, find it difficult to believe that any A-C, no matter who but especially you, would not build in a fail-safe. You're telling us that the cyborgs have no self-destruct mechanisms or kill switches. I find that hard to believe."

"We aren't doing this to create an army."

Snorted. Couldn't help myself. Siler laughed softly. "Yeah, I'm with the First Lady on that one 'Uncle' Trevor."

"Yes, Stephanie was," Trevor said patiently. "However, since you took all of her test subjects—easily, I might add—you helped me to show her that my way is the better way. No one receiving the Treatment has anything to fear from us in terms of becoming a zombie."

"So, you're saying once a cyborg, someone's untouchable?"

Knew he was trying to distract us, but the information was necessary, so I'd let him think he was getting away with it. The music changed to "Show Me What I'm Looking For" by Carolina Liar. Wasn't sure if that meant it was time to question Trevor about everything, mistrust anything he said, or both. Decided to bet on both.

"Oh, no. Not at all. As Benjamin is aptly proving, the removal of the head is quite a permanent measure. Diseases are unlikely, though possible. However, stress is the biggest factor. Aneurisms are a great risk—should one form and burst, the wiring will be negatively affected, just like the rest of the area where the aneurism is. And due to the wiring, medical aid will be hampered if not impossible."

"So . . . what? You and Stephanie are the only doctors who can cure these sorta people and cyborgs need to keep their cool?"

"In essence, yes, at least in terms of staying relaxed. Just as it was a wise way to avoid being targeted by a parasite. Being calm is usually the best course of action."

My experience said that rage was my friend, but everyone was different. "Gotcha. So, as long as the cyborgs keep cool and don't force someone to decapitate them, they'll live forever?"

"In a sense. Everything wears out. The Treatment just ensures that the minds and bodies will wear out much more slowly. The wiring enhances many things, including keeping bones strong and skin supple."

"Amazing. And yet, again, you two are their only choice for medical help?"

"At the moment. If all goes according to plan, however, there will be a Rattoppare hospital, and then many."

"Oh my God. You want to franchise this!"

He beamed at me. "Yes, I do. Imagine the possibilities when anyone can live three times longer, or more! Think of what could be accomplished, if the fear of death and the ravages of disease, age, and time were removed."

He clearly believed in this—it showed in his voice and expression. He was practically quivering with excitement. He also had a point. "Yeah, I can see it. I'm just waiting for the other shoe to drop onto someone's head, though."

"Benjamin is a good example of what extra longevity can do."

"I don't have wiring," Siler growled.

"No, you do not. However, you have far more potential than you've realized."

"Like what?" Siler asked, still sounding ready to cut off Trevor's head and live with the mystery of whatever was being insinuated.

"You'll find out, I'm sure. If you try and expand your mind."

"Speaking of minds," said more to keep Siler from losing it than a lack of interest in all the wonders Trevor felt we hadn't discovered about Nightcrawler, "Ansom Somerall and Talia Lee claim to not know who put wires into their brains, or how they even got there. See, I'd be buying all you said a lot more if I didn't know they were working with Janelle, meaning that all of them are also working with you and Stephanie."

Trevor looked concerned. "I didn't do that to them. The Bots are in competition with us. We're not working together on anything and haven't been for quite some time."

"How are they competition?" White asked. "They don't seem the same."

"Creating a duplicate of yourself to do whatever dirty or boring work you want is fine if what you want to do is fool weaker minds." Trevor could not sound more derisive if he tried. "However, they don't *think*. They're programmed. Cyborgs, on the other hand, are autonomous. You, you yourself, could live forever, or you could have a facsimile of yourself that likely has a longer lifespan, to use the term loosely. What would an intelligent person choose?"

"Whatever's behind Door Number Three, only I'm betting that's cloning."

"Not anymore." Now Trevor sounded pleased.

"Beg pardon?"

"No more cloning. Not as was being done. You destroyed all of that. You people took all the research, and then you destroyed all the facilities. Androids, Bots, or cyborgs—those are your choices now."

Sincerely doubted that Trevor the Tinkerer had nothing up his sleeve in regards to this. Was super positive that the Rattoppare brand extension was going to be cloning. However, now wasn't the time to push it. I still had too many questions that needed some sort of answers.

"So, if we're to believe you about Ansom and Talia, then Stephanie's the one who wired their brains. Unless you're going to tell me that there's someone else with your extremely proprietary abilities out there."

"No, there is not." He looked and sounded just like my dad

had any time he'd caught me, Amy, or Sheila doing something he'd pointedly told us not to do. Chuckie had never received this tone from Dad, but the rest of us had, many times. "I will speak with her. That is not what we agreed to. At all."

"Uh huh. So, what else has Stephanie done that you supposedly didn't approve of? Stolen Titan's miniaturization tech for you so no one else could have it?"

Received a very derisive look. "Why would I need her to steal their tech for me when I can recreate it at any time if I want to?"

"You're saying you were a part of that?"

"Yes, of course. Antony did marvelous work, as did Herbert Gaultier. But still, I was involved. I can create that tech at any time and likely improve upon it. I haven't because we don't need weapons."

"Trying so hard to believe you, and yet it's just so difficult."

"You'll believe what you want. That's what people do." The music changed to "Stranger Things Have Happened" by the Foo Fighters, so apparently Algar agreed.

"Yes, I suppose it is. So, where is Stephanie, exactly?"

"Right now? I have no idea. In France, I assume."

"Uh huh. So where was she earlier in the week? Because I don't believe that Ansom and Talia have taken a recent trip to France wherein they were captured, wires were put into their brains, and they were released, all of which they now don't remember."

He sighed. "I assume that Stephanie disobeyed me and came to the States."

"We have every agency looking for her," White said. "She's one of America's Most Wanted."

"She may be, but, honestly Richard, why do you pretend that the humans are as bright as we are? They aren't."

Had about every Dazzler in existence to say that Trevor was wrong, since they were all about brains and brain capacity and most of them panted after humans, but whatever. Allowed him to enjoy his superiority.

"I disagree," White said calmly. "As always, I believe you sell humanity quite short."

"Well, they're easy enough to fool. Stephanie is well aware of how to disguise herself if she has to. I didn't want her to come here, mind you. I want her to remain in safety while we build up her skills and expertise. However, children will do what they will."

"And when the cat's away the mice will play. Yeah. Speaking of that . . . you know anyone who's hugely into nursery rhymes?"

CHAPTER 78

THIS QUESTION THREW TREVOR. Understandably. He gaped at me for a few moments. "I'm sorry," he said finally. "I truly don't believe I understood your question."

"Nursery rhymes. Do you know anyone who likes to use them a lot? The way you like to say 'imagine the possibilities' and the late and totally unlamented Cliff Goodman liked to say 'part to play' and so on."

He appeared to give this thought. "I don't know. However, I believe that Stephanie mentioned someone like this. When I return to her, I'll ask and advise you."

"I love the assumptive close there, but we haven't agreed to do a catch and release on you yet, Trevor, so cool your jets. I'd like to go back to how you know Myron Van Dyke is the one funding Club Fifty-One."

"Well, he's really funding the church they're associated with, but that church funnels the money to the True Believers."

"Super, good to know. What you're avoiding saying, though, is how *you*, you specifically, know this. And you tell me that, or we don't let you go. Ever."

"Fine. You'll find out anyway, per our agreement. He and I have been discussing him getting the Treatment. The Treatment is not inexpensive. Therefore, funds have to be confirmed. While he and I were so confirming, he received some texts from both Farley Pecker and Harvey Gutermuth, discussing funds and funding. It was quite clear that they were used to getting money from him."

"And they didn't code their messages?"

Trevor shot me a derisive look. "Of course they were coded. And of course I decoded them. They're not smart enough to use a code that someone with actual brainpower couldn't crack. I include the three of you and your Mister Reynolds in the group that is smart enough, by the way. So, should you want him to investigate, I'm sure the CIA can easily tap their phones or whatever."

"Gosh, we're flattered, and I'm sure we'll do that and then some." Time to get Hacker International working on money trails and all that jazz. The music changed to "Mr. Roboto" by Styx. "Since we're talking about codes and all that, you've reminded me of a little enigma I'm betting you can solve for us." Well, really, Algar had done the reminding, but whatever.

"Happy to."

"I'll bet. Eugene Montgomery was given robot schematics and told that robots were going to be created to impersonate high government officials. All my people feel that we could make working robots from those plans, but said plans don't match what's come out of the Bot Factory. There's some bizarre logo written in what might be the Anciannas language or might be Z'porrah or just might be humans and A-Cs being funky and imitating Hirschfeld's artwork. We've identified the Gaultier logo in it. Who else's logos and names are in there?"

"Everyone you'd expect. Those plans were from the old days, when we were all working as one. We'd planned to do exactly what he was told—replace high rankers with robots we would then control."

"What stopped that from moving forward?"

Got a shot of the "really?" look. "You did."

"Mind explaining?"

"The first robot created was fashioned to look like you." So the Kitty-Bot's schematics matched what we'd gotten from Eugene. No need to reverse engineer her now. Butler and Maurer could rest easy. "A test run that would allow us to get rid of someone who was causing us to waste a great deal of time hiding everything we were doing and everyone we were doing it with."

"My mother." Felt cold and enraged, even though we'd realized this was what the Kitty-Bot's initial job had been way back when during Operation Fugly. Just really didn't enjoy hearing someone casually discuss killing my parents, call me Sally Sensitive.

"Yes. It didn't work."

"It wasn't really given time to work."

"No, it wasn't, but at that time, we had so many options." He shrugged, at least as much as Siler would allow. "You were on international news. You stopped being no one and became someone. The idea of the test was that it wouldn't be noticed. You foiled that."

"Thankfully," White said.

Trevor shrugged again and winced. "Every war has winners and losers."

Another song. This one was "Her Diamonds" by Rob Thomas. Sent a thank you to Algar for the memory nudge.

"True enough. Related question. Marion Villanova had robot plans that she shredded and left in her apartment for her co-conspirators to find. We found them first. We put them back together. They, too, are factory worthy and factory ready, but they don't match up completely to what's coming out of the Bot Factory, either, other than in one way. Thoughts? As in, tell us what's going on with those."

"I'd assume they were modified versions of the first model. You must understand—we all tinkered. Fix a plan here, make a new one there, modify this, change that. Just because the plans you found aren't a complete match doesn't mean they weren't the basis for creation. It just means what you found was an upgraded model."

"Well, per what we've found, there are five levels of Bots, so this actually tracks."

"Of course it does. What's the similarity your people found?"

"These robots need diamonds in their brains. The Fem-Bot Factory has lots of diamonds. Well, had. They were confiscated."

"Really?" For the first time since I'd started this line of questioning he seemed interested.

"Yes. And I'm kind of surprised you seem surprised. Monica, Marion, and Marcia, aka the Three M's, all seemed to have donated their diamonds to the cause. And these robots were supposedly easy enough to build that literally anyone could make them."

His eyes narrowed. "You're certain?"

"Per those who verified the plans, I could make one without breaking a sweat. As long as I had enough diamonds."

"Those thieves!" This was a new one. Even Siler looked shocked.

"Um, come again?"

"They're using my plans for a revised supersoldier. I discarded it as too expensive to be functional. Diamonds aren't in endless supply, meaning the number of supersoldiers created would be limited."

"So, these were next-gen supersoldiers? Because the ones I've met were hella big, had an iron shell, and a squishy super-being center. No diamonds or anything else nice. And I opened many of their cans, so to speak."

"Yes. Madeleine was all-in on those. I, however, felt that the main issue with them was never resolved in a satisfactory manner."

"You mean that the moment the superbeing could get out of the shell it tried to kill everything, especially those who'd put it into the shell?"

"Exactly so. My work on the next-generation supersoldiers was, as I said, discarded. Since it had been something Madeleine had approached the government with, the plans were locked away. Monica asked to review the plans for the original robot and these as well, but I refused to allow it. She had plenty to work with without those."

"Well, they got them without your permission somehow. Possibly by Monica being the Secretary of State and all that. And they destroyed said plans." In a weird way, too, but that seemed to be Team Shadow's modus operandi.

"Lunatics," he muttered. Managed not to say that it totally took one to know one and only succeeded because "Neutron Wireless Crystal" by Swimming came on. Algar was really helping me with the memory banks.

"So, speaking of the Shadow and their team's playing dirty—"

"Excuse me, who?"

"The Shadow. That's his or her name now. It's easier than The Other Mastermind Who Is Not Cliff Goodman, don't you think?"

"Oh, I do. I'm sorry, I should have caught that. I, ah, believe that Benjamin may have nicked my neck, for the third time, I might add, which is why I've lost focus."

"Be glad that's all I've done," Siler said in the voice I now felt he should trademark or patent. Trevor went back to pasty white. Yeah, it was a *good* voice.

"So, back on track here, Trevor. About the Shadow—did you create or do you know of a polymer or similar that can divide and can also shapeshift?"

His eyes widened. "It doesn't sound familiar," he said eagerly, "but I'd need more to go on."

Why not? Either he'd helped create the Christopher-Bot or he might have some insight into what was going on there. Did a fast recap of that situation. "So, it's the same stuff that was being used at the NSA black site to keep our people contained. But those are the only places I've seen it. And it's definitely destroyed by fire."

"It's not Earth-created," he said firmly. "There are things on Earth that could do one or the other, but not to the level of autonomy that you've described and currently not both. And I doubt the technical acumen and expertise of whoever Janelle is working with—this sounds far above a robotics assembly line. This also isn't something that I had or that LaRue had because, believe me, we'd have both used it, so it's not from the Alpha Centauri system, nor from the Z'porrah, nor the Ancients."

"Anciannas," White said, returning the Teacher Politely Correcting A Student voice with a strong backhanded volley. Managed not to give him a high-five, but it took effort.

"Whatever," Trevor snapped as the ball bounced in front of him and out of his side of the court. "At any rate, it's not something that's been around too long. Beyond that, I have nothing, because you probably know more about the aliens from the other systems than I do."

Considering it was now one of my jobs, had to admit that I probably did, albeit unwillingly. "So, the Shadow has an alien benefactor from outside of the systems we'd expect."

"I'd have said to look to the Anciannas if I didn't know that there was no way LaRue would have or could have hidden a material with these properties," Trevor said. "Natural shapeshifters would have the edge, I'd think, on this creation."

"Beta Twelve?" White asked me.

"No way would anyone there be working with our enemies. Well, let me rephrase—it's not Renata, Rahmi, or Rhee. And here ends the number of Free Women who've been allowed to legally leave their planet. The last time any took off illegally, Renata was right behind them. And she'd have told us about this kind of scientific breakthrough and she has not. Meaning this isn't coming from Beta Twelve."

"I agree," Trevor said. "Without examining it, the substance doesn't sound like something we have in our systems, so it would require someone from elsewhere bringing in the materials. I strongly suggest you verify which of the new alien races that are here on Earth are able to shapeshift or similar, because

I'd be willing to bet that they're the ones who've helped the Shadow to use this substance."

"You think it is or isn't a polymer?" I asked.

"It doesn't matter. It's not from this planet. Call it whatever you like, but assume you don't know the extent of what it can do, including if it's sentient or not."

"Ick. But, good point." Had no idea what to do with the Christopher-Bot the Second.

"Keep the one you have under lock, key, and observation," Trevor said, apparently reading my mind. "Something like that shouldn't be allowed autonomy."

"This from the man making cyborgs?"

"Yes. Weapons should not have autonomy, and that thing is a weapon."

"Can't argue with you there."

"In terms of cyborg technology, I firmly believe in the idea that the merging of organic and inorganic is the wave of the future. Autonomy is, therefore, a requirement. Clifford and LaRue's cloning methods were impressive. However, once the data for how to build the brain storage and cloning chambers was lost, all else was lost. With the cyborgs we have the method working smoothly, and if you destroy one base, we can rebuild in another, because we haven't written the data down by hand and kept it in binders in an underground bunker." Trevor definitely had a sarcasm knob and his went *well* past eleven.

"Aren't you worried we'll hack into your system and steal it?"

"You could. But since I've patented it, you'll be hard-pressed to win the lawsuit."

Stared at him. "You've patented this?"

"I have. Stephanie is on the patent, too." He smiled at me. "The beginning of her journey has truly begun. Don't sell us short—very soon now you'll be signing our contracts, whether for yourselves or others."

"Such as the military," White said. Trevor nodded. Carefully.

"I feel all tingly. So, in that vein, you mentioned that others currently are selling me short. Which others? As in, name names."

"Everyone you were speaking with this evening, the ones who are friends with Janelle and her cronies."

"Death Dealers" by Discharge came on. Could hear Algar saying "duh." Loudly. Trevor's expression said "duh" as well, also loudly. Chose to forge on and refuse to be embarrassed about verifying suppositions. That was my story and I was sticking with it.

"The Dealers of Death? Yeah, okay, I was thinking that they seemed remarkably unwilling to try to use me as the weak link."

"They are. They don't feel that they need to curry your favor to succeed."

"They seem to be succeeding without us, yeah."

"It won't last. They should do what I'm doing, which is broker a truce. Otherwise, you'll beat them as you have everyone else. I expect you'll beat Myron and his noxious friends, too."

"You're not one with the whole purity of the race thing? I don't buy it."

"I don't care about it in the way that Ronald did. I understand why he felt as he did, but I believe that the possibilities are greater the more different options are available to us. That includes races and such. I may feel, correctly, that we from Alpha Four are far smarter than most other races, but you all still provide something into the mix. And that something is worthwhile."

"Gosh, you're like the King Of The Backhanded Compliments, aren't you? So, to circle back on things you expect us to simply take at face value, why would Stephanie wire Ansom and Talia? And, seriously, don't lie."

"I don't know."

"*Please* let me kill him," Siler begged.

"Benjamin, if I die, the information about yourself, all the things you don't know, dies with me."

"Wolverine found the will to go on, Ben, so don't let that stop you. However, I still have questions. And statements. Such as: Trevor—pull the other one. I don't believe that Stephanie's acting alone and is the only shooter. I'm just betting there are things going on up on that grassy knoll that you know about. So spill it or Ben spills your blood, oil, and wires."

"What have you found inside them?" Trevor asked.

"Nothing. Other than the wires. Nothing we can identify, at least."

"Hence, as I said, I don't know." But his eyes weren't meeting mine.

Prince growled low. Now Trevor smelled like lies. "Good boy. Extra biscuits for that dog. You're lying, Trevor. Truth, now. Or death now. You pick."

Heard a step behind me. "Oh, that's not something you need to worry about."

CHAPTER 79

SPUN AROUND TO SEE JEFF, followed by Chuckie, Christopher, Buchanan, Evalyne, Phoebe, Joseph, and Rob. Clearly the cavalry was here.

"Why not?"

"Because we know he's lying, baby." Jeff gave me a kiss on the cheek. "But knowing who did the work gives us plenty to go on."

"Does it? Good to know, I guess. How long have you guys been lurking back there?"

"Long enough. You can put the guns away. Siler can and will kill Trevor there faster than you can shoot." Jeff didn't sound like he disapproved of this at all.

"So, did you hear about the Van Dyke stuff?" I asked as White and I put our guns back and Prince demanded petting from Jeff.

"We did," Jeff confirmed as he squatted down and vigorous pets were given while Prince shared his love of all things Jeff.

"I sent the information to Stryker," Chuckie said. "We should know soon if there's a money trail." His phone beeped. He looked at it and grunted. "I love A-C systems. The money trail is hidden but clear enough. Trevor here is telling the truth. About that."

"Wow, I'm amazed. So, are we letting him go, then?"

"Not just no, but hell no," Jeff said pleasantly as he stood up. "We'll deal with whatever it is Stephanie thinks she's going to throw at us."

"Trevor did deal with us, and shared information with the idea that we'd call a truce." Felt compelled to point this out. He'd given us some good intel.

Saw Siler's eyebrow raise, just a bit. Moved my head

casually to see who he was signaling. Buchanan. Who nodded almost imperceptibly.

"No, baby," Jeff said patiently. "He dealt with you and Uncle Richard. Who are not in positions to grant clemency to terrorists. I am, Chuck is, and your mother is. We're agreed—it's not happening."

"Benjamin, if they lock me up, I won't tell you what you know you want to know," Trevor said urgently. "I won't help Kitty ever again, either. If I'm out, I can be an asset. You know this. She knows this. Richard even knows this."

"Stop insulting my uncle's intelligence," Jeff said. "It's not helping your cause."

"Benjamin . . . answers you seek, help you know you'll need. Or a war I don't want and, if you're honest, you don't want, either."

Siler looked directly at me. "He's right." Then they both disappeared from view.

"I can't see him!" Jeff shouted.

"Grab him!" Chuckie shouted. "That's an order!"

Buchanan lunged and was knocked into Joseph and Rob, who knocked into Phoebe and Evalyne.

Once everyone was on their feet, the room remained devoid of Siler or Trevor. "Um . . ."

Chuckie put up his hand. Closed my mouth and no one spoke. Instead, DJ Algar spun the Rolling Stones again, this time "Waiting On a Friend."

The song finished and "Everlasting Friend" by Blue October started before Siler returned. He still had his big knife. He nodded to everyone as Buchanan handed him a sheath that appeared to be made out of metal, not leather. "It's handled."

"Why the big show?" I asked as Siler put the big knife away. The sheath blinked red, then blue, then white. How patriotic. Confusing, but patriotic.

"What do you mean?" Chuckie asked.

"The whole Nightcrawler saves Trevor at the last minute crap. I don't get it. I mean, I'm sure I speak for Richard, too, when I say that the whole shtick was obvious. To us. Presumably not to Trevor. But Christopher didn't even move, so we're clear that it was all theater. I just don't know why anyone felt the need to do it."

"What Missus Martini said."

"Ah. The President can't make a deal like Trevor wanted. Not with a terrorist. The CIA can, but not the President."

"Um, Chuckie? Did you not realize we've made exactly that deal with Gadhavi?"

"But we haven't," Buchanan said. "Gadhavi came to us openly, taking the deal you offered of going straight, giving us information, and working with our government."

"Trevor offered pretty much the same thing. And, um, just in case you guys are mad at me for giving up any of what might be our proprietary intel, I wanted to get what I could from him while we had him, because who knows when we'll get another chance."

"It's okay," Chuckie said. "I agree that you got more than you gave."

Christopher shot Patented Glare #2 at the room. "Seriously, why are you not just telling her? Kitty, we figure we'll get more out of Trevor this way, and that's the excuse that you, my dad, and Siler can use whenever you're dealing with him—that you're not in positions to grant clemency of any kind."

"Um, huh? Sorry to seem dense, but Richard, Nightcrawler, and I were getting plenty."

Buchanan nodded. "Yes, you were. But the moment that man thinks he's got the upper hand, all the information will stop."

"We needed to be sure that he respected you and is terrified of me," Siler said.

"Dude, mission accomplished in terms of his terror. My respect I'm not so sure about."

"Oh, I am." Siler grinned. "We had a little chat. Trevor now believes that I care about whatever information he thinks he's holding back from me, and he's also clear that you're now the one and only person who can stop the rest of us from going after him and Stephanie. Therefore, he's going to want to give you what you want, when you want it, or we'll just capture them both."

And kill them both, but chose not to say that aloud, in part because I wasn't sure if Jeff had agreed to that portion of the overall plan. Knew without asking that Buchanan and Chuckie had. Mom probably had, too.

"Can we really find them if and when they move?"

"Well, we can now," Buchanan said. "Because Ben got the targeting parasite into him. So your worry about giving away too much is moot. If they try to take action on anything you told them, we'll know."

"Excuse me? Did you say parasite?"

"He did," Siler waved the sheathed knife at me. "The blade was drenched in it. I nicked him several times to ensure that the virus got into his bloodstream. Something they've been working on in Dulce at the P.T.C.U.'s request. It's a parasitic virus that will attach to his internal organs. Trevor can only get rid of it by taking the antidote."

"What's the antidote?"

Siler grinned. "Alcohol."

"Wow. We can all be really nasty when we want to be, can't we? I approve. If it works."

"It's working," Chuckie said, looking at his phone. "He's heading for the airport. In a car, as near as I can tell."

"He called for a cab," Siler said. "Conveniently, there was one really nearby. Melville would appreciate it if you'd take Prince home tonight, Kitty. You're getting Duke and Riley, too, because their owners are shadowing Melville, just in case."

"I have never complained, nor will I ever complain, about K-9 companionship. They can sleep on the bed with us tonight, since all the other animals will be with the kids, I'm sure." Like they always were.

"Oh good," Jeff said, though he patted Prince's head again. "Thank God it's a big bed. Oh, by the way, Thomas called while you were up here. They found one security tape that had an image on it. It was brief, but we were able to get a good image. Guess who broke into Titan?"

"Stephanie for the win."

"Got it in one," Buchanan said. "Though I never had a doubt."

"Yep." Jeff ran his hand through his hair. "So Trevor might not know."

"He knows," White said. "I paid attention to what he was saying, since Missus Martini has pointed out so often how we're able to lie by not telling the entire truth, or by using specific words that mean we're not speaking an untruth. I'm certain Stephanie stole those because they want them. And I'm equally certain that there's a kill switch in all the cyborgs."

"But he said there wasn't."

"No. He said there was no zombie switch. As in, they can't take control of the cyborgs. But they can flip the remote-destruct switch and destroy them."

"Why steal the miniaturization stuff if he already knows how to make it all, though?"

Chuckie jerked. "Because if we could look at them, someone—Serene, me, Thomas, any of the scientists at Dulce or NASA Base—might be able to determine how to make them even smaller. And, if that's the case, then the self-destructs are microscopic or smaller."

"Or he's telling the truth about it," Siler said. "It's possible, after all."

"Anything is," Jeff agreed. "Let's get going. I think we're done here."

"Actually, we still need to find the DJ."

Siler grinned. "That was me. The sound and lighting area is up here, and it has an excellent view of the entire ballroom, meaning it's an assassin's perfect spot." He looked right into my eyes. "I just played the tape that was there already. It should be done soon, I think."

Sure enough, the last song ended and there was silence. Siler and I clearly needed to have a chat, but not right now. "Ah . . . got it. Um, did Richard find you when he went looking? Because Trevor thought he was alone."

"I blended when I heard Trevor coming up here. Did it again when Richard came in, but talked to him."

"Oh, Mister White, you said you didn't see anyone. You didn't say that you didn't talk to anyone. You are a sly boots."

"I am, Missus Martini. Now, let's get these boots home."

Jeff offered me his arm, which I happily took. "I never got to dance with you."

Joseph held the door and Rob took point, then Evalyne, Jeff, and I walked out, and everyone else trailed behind us.

"James picked up your slack."

"So I saw. I'll be jealous about it later."

"Oh good, I'll schedule it in. So, how'd you know to come up?"

"I'm an empath. Try to keep up."

"I point to your blocks and say you haven't felt much recently."

He sighed. "Kitty, it was only our people left. I turned the blocking device off, meaning I can and did feel you. And even if I hadn't, you were gone too long."

"Plus Ben sent me the signal that he'd found Trevor," Buchanan added, as we reached the ballroom. "You know we can't stay away from you for too long, Missus Executive Chief."

"Idle flattery gets you nowhere, but keep it up, I love it. At least we learned a lot."

"We'll see how much of it is actionable," Chuckie said.

"Peace of mind, however rare and slight, is always welcome," White said.

"Truer words and all that. You know what we still don't know? Why did Robert Cordell call to tell me that robots were going to try to kill me?" Was going to say something else but my phone took this moment to ring. Stopped walking and got it out of my clutch. "Hello?"

"Madam First Lady? It's Detective Beckett."

"Hey there, Detective, it's been so long."

Buchanan passed some signals and suddenly a lot more people were with us, Mom included. But not the kids. Presumed Dad was riding herd on them somewhere.

"It has. I thought you'd be interested to know that your lead about the delivery trucks paid off."

"Great. Let me put you on speaker." Did so, and Buchanan shoved in his tracking device thingy. Actively chose not to ask why. "What did you find?"

"The place where Robert Cordell was actually murdered. Along with three other dead people. You were correct—he was moved to alter the jurisdiction. If the body had been found here, Sawyer and I wouldn't have been assigned the case."

"Good on the first, horrible on the second, go team on the third. So, are there other detectives there with you, then?"

"Yes. They're investigating the murders of the truck drivers. I followed a lead and wound up here."

"Really? What lead?" Hey, I liked cop shows just like the next girl, and as long as I wasn't being accused of the murders, this was kind of interesting.

"The chef at your party said that Missus Cordell had suggested that Mister Cordell 'backtrack' the drivers' route, to see if the trucks were in difficulty. From what we can tell, it appears he did just that."

"Well, that's interesting."

"Yes, it is. One of the drivers was an off-duty cop."

"Oh, wow, I'm so sorry. Was it someone you knew?"

"Not well. He was a uniformed officer. However, he was diligent and dedicated. Apparently, when he drove on the side he had his cell phone videotaping so that, in case of an altercation, he had proof of what had happened."

"So, did he do that tonight?"

"He did. Because of that, we have a confirmation of what happened and who killed everyone."

"That's wonderful! Who?"

"Well, it looks like you did."

CHAPTER 80

LET THAT ONE SIT on the air for a moment, while everyone stared at each other. "Okay, since you're not here trying to arrest me, you want to say that again?"

"I said, it looks like you're the one who killed Robert Cordell and the three drivers. However, we know it wasn't you."

"I know it wasn't me, too. How do *you* know?"

"There were two of you."

"I'm sorry. I'm getting confused. What the hell?"

"There were two of what appeared to be you at the scene. Here's the timeline as we know it. All six trucks left at the same time. Three of them went through a traffic light. The other three caught the red. Then a car accident happened in the intersection in front of them, a very minor fender bender. People claiming to be cops were there immediately, though, and held them up as witnesses."

"Only they weren't cops."

"Correct. We've found them. They were all actors hired to do one of those stupid impromptu performances. They were told that it was for a D.C.P.D. charity fundraiser. And they were paid in cash and have no description of who paid them because it was all done by phone and the number that called them was a burner."

"Weird. But effective." Meaning this was likely being orchestrated by the Shadow. Because Trevor and Stephanie wouldn't have wanted the cops at our event—he was there recruiting, and Kramer and Charmaine had not impressed as examples of the Fine Cyborg Lifestyle. Plus, he had to have been in on Cordell's murder, meaning he wanted the police at the event possibly less than Kramer and Charmaine did. The

Shadow, however, had cut ties with them, at least as far as we'd guessed during Operation Madhouse. Or, maybe not.

"Yes," Beckett went on. "So that accounts for the delay between the first three trucks and these three. Once they were able to take off again, they continued on. Part of their route here was through a business district that was closed down by the time they got there, so there weren't really any people around at the time. In this area, a woman stepped into the street in front of the trucks, signaling for help. They stopped, because, again, there wouldn't be anyone else to help her and the lead driver was the off-duty cop. The drivers got out to help, the woman was joined by another woman who looked just like her—enough to be twins—and those two women proceeded to break the necks of all three drivers, despite those drivers putting up a fight and the off-duty officer shooting both of them several times."

"Okay, I'm not a triplet, so those were likely Fem-Bots and we can explain that later. But, trust me, they aren't women as you and I know the term."

"Yes, I imagine you can, and I'll want that explanation. The, ah, Fem-Bots blocked off the street behind the trucks using the road hazard equipment the trucks carry standard. Cordell arrived soon after, and the Fem-Bots did it again—one hid, the other signaled for help. He got out to help, the one that had been hidden took the off-duty cop's gun and shot Cordell three times in the gut. She'd have shot him more, but the gun was out of ammunition."

"That's why he lived long enough to call me."

"Yes. They left immediately after killing him, though they took the gun with them. The video ended shortly thereafter. And not because it ran out of battery. Someone turned it off, but that person was never in view."

"Evan. I can almost promise it was Evan the Limo Driver." Who was smarter than a Fem-Bot. Which was likely a low bar, as I thought about it.

"Maybe. We'll see if he has an alibi."

"I'm sure he will, but he'd be number one on my suspects list. So, what now?"

"Now someone tells me what the hell these Fem-Bots are and what's going on."

"This is the Director of the CIA. I'll meet you at your precinct and fill you in. After I verify that you can meet the security requirements." Chuckie rubbed the back of his neck. "Anything else you haven't shared?"

"No," Beckett said. "But it certainly looks like whoever did this wanted the First Lady to be a suspect."

"Or those were the only Fem-Bots they had available." Everyone looked at me.

"Huh?" Beckett asked, speaking for everyone around me.

"It's part of the long story the Director of the CIA will tell you if you get the clearance. So, I can't tell you, but again, Evan, Kramer's limo driver, is where you need to start."

Beckett heaved a sigh. "Yes, got it. Mister Director, you'll meet me when?"

"Name the time," Chuckie replied. They set their fun date. Beckett promised to keep me apprised of all that they learned as they learned it, and we hung up. "Now, Kitty, tell us what you meant."

"How quickly we all forget. The Fem-Bots from the Factory use diamonds for their brains. Trevor was upset about that, remember? Because no one was supposed to have access to those plans anymore. However, during Operation Madhouse, Malcolm made the point that we all agreed with—that there's been a schism of some kind between Janelle Gardiner and Zachary Kramer."

"I did," Buchanan agreed. "And Missus Executive Chief felt that Evan and Marion Villanova now have two bosses, as in, they're supporting the Kramers and possibly Gardiner and her group, too."

"I can see it," Mom said slowly. "And this Shadow might be running both."

"I'm willing to bet on it, Mom. So, the Kramers and their small team scrounged enough diamonds to fuel, we figured, no more than two Fem-Bots. And if they were snagging Fem-Bots, let's be real—they were snagging Kitty-Bots for a whole variety of reasons."

"So, following that line of reasoning," Reader said, "the Kitty-Bots who murdered all these people were doing so on Zachary Kramer's order."

"Most likely on Charmaine Cordell's order. I'm betting she's the new brains of the Kramer Operation. Marcia seems clueless, but we need to question her in a nice but severe way."

"Already on it," Reader said. "I've been sending Vance questions, he's been asking them in a way that works with her, and we're getting answers. Right now, Marcia wants to be on Team Kitty more than, possibly, anyone else in this world."

"I'm touched. How dirty is she?"

"Not as bad as you'd think. She had to give up her diamonds because her husband told her they were making a special investment in his political prospects and she'd reap a much greater reward in the future. Mossad is with Vance, remember, and Leah's helping with the questioning. Nicely, she said to tell you. At any rate, Marcia appears to have been kept in the dark."

"Meaning that Kramer's been planning to dump her and move to Charmaine for at least as long as Jeff's been President. Which makes sense for those in the Megalomaniac League."

"And that means this murder was always planned," Tim added. "Meaning that's why Charmaine both sprang this fundraiser on Marcia when she did and why she wouldn't allow you to take it over."

"Confirmed that Kramer told Marcia who to order food from," Reader said, looking at his phone. "So I agree with Tim."

"Megalomaniac Lad is rarely wrong."

"Megalomaniac Lad would like to know what we do next."

"I think we all go home or, in my case, to the police precinct," Chuckie said. "It seems over for now. We'll keep eyes on Kramer and Charmaine, but only the truly stupid would try something right now."

"I'm having Van Dyke brought in for questioning," Mom said. "From what Charles was funneling to me while you were interrogating the Tinkerer, though, I'm betting the bastard is safe because he's going to merely claim that he was supporting his church and that he can't control what the church does with his money."

"The other Dealers of Death are up to things, too, but I'm with you, Mom, probably nothing we can prove yet."

"We and the FBI have these people under surveillance, so no. Frankly, I'm far more upset about the fact that Janelle Gardiner and Amos Tobin are running things using Christopher and Amy than whatever these others are up to."

"We'll handle it," Amy said confidently. "Now that we know, it's simple for us to run whatever we get by you and Chuck, Angela. We'll catch them at it sooner as opposed to later."

"So who attacked the Intergalactic School, then?" I asked. "Janelle's team, the True Believers, or the Shadow?"

"Assume the Shadow is playing the same Sith game as the Mastermind was," Chuckie said. "Chernobog feels that the Bots were ordered via the Dark Web. She's researching, but her preliminary is that Van Dyke sent the money, Pecker transferred it to Gutermuth, and he ordered his attacking forces from the Fem-Bot Factory but via the Dark Web, not face-to-face. They might not even know who's running the Factory."

"I'd like to know what they wanted to achieve," Joseph said. "Aside from chaos."

Considered this. "The True Believers decided to attack the school where all the alien kids are going to be most of every day. Away from their families and species. How fast would those aliens take off if, on the very first day of school, their children were harmed or worse? I'd have to think pretty fast."

"Makes sense," Jeff said. "Too much sense." He ran his hand through his hair. "Speaking of kids, can we get all of ours home?"

"Yes," Mom said. "Other than the cleanup, it all appears to be over for now."

We gathered up Dad, the kids, the flyboys and remainder of the K-9 squad who were with them and the *Good Day USA!* camera crew, figured out where anyone else still here was and got them, too, and headed back for the cars. Amazingly enough, the parking garage did not collapse on us, the cars did not explode, and the rides were uneventful.

Fortunately, Wasim and Naveed were with Marcia and that team, because the three German Shepherds were in the Beast with us, Prince and Duke in the back, Riley riding up front between Len and Kyle. Filled the boys, Dad, Lizzie, and Gadhavi in on all they'd missed during our ride home. Everyone expressed disappointment for not getting to meet the Tinkerer, dismay over the dead truck drivers, and otherwise all seemed normal. For us, anyway.

All the P.T.C.U. folks and Chuckie went to their various fun locations. The rest of us went to wherever we were sleeping. Another day of total insanity over.

We got all the kids into their various beds, ensured that Wasim and Naveed were safely back in the White House, and settled the K-9 dogs into our room. Jeff and I chose to shower and have sexy times there so that the dogs wouldn't make Jeff feel like we were being watched, since the dogs totally would do that, seeing as they felt it was their job to protect me from all things.

Got the rewards I felt I'd earned and then some, which was by far the nicest part of this day. Then we collapsed into bed.

"What do you think tomorrow's going to bring?" I asked Jeff as I snuggled up next to him and rubbed my face into the hair on his awesome chest.

"Hopefully nothing but boredom, baby. I'm really hoping for boredom."

"Me, too." Closed my eyes and was out like a light.

Had mostly dreamless sleep. The dreams I did have were fractured and odd, nothing concrete, other than I kept on hearing Gladys reassuring me that Joe and Randy were okay, which was nice. Heard someone else that might have been Mephistopheles or might have been Michael Gower or might have been someone else telling me to stay alert. But that was it.

Woke up to the sounds of Fall Out Boy's "Calm Before The Storm." Hoped that meant we'd get some breathing time.

Spent the whole day waiting for the next attack, but nothing happened. The kids got to school safely, I got my team onto the hockey charity game idea, normal political business was handled, things were the calmest I'd seen for a while. Did not argue with this outcome.

The hockey game was set up fast—apparently when the White House asked for a fundraiser for a preseason game that wasn't sold out, the NHL jumped. The game was the first weekend in October, and we got the word out immediately, right within Charmaine's time limit.

There were weekly PTA meetings and, God help me, I attended every one, and forced Marcia to go with me. Charmaine was her usual sniffing self, but since everyone knew about the scandal, Marcia was getting a lot of sympathetic support and Charmaine had to behave herself.

The kids were loving Sidwell, and Lizzie reported that the Cordell twins were doing okay and actually trying to be nice to her and the rest of "our" kids, which now included Clinton and the younger Kramer boys. Wasn't sure if they were faking it to learn things for their mother or if they were trying to separate themselves from her. Figured time would tell.

Mom's hunch about Van Dyke turned out to be true—he was able to fully hide behind freedom of religion, and there was nothing we could do about it. Presumably he was all tapped out financially, or was saving all his money for his Treatment, because no other attacks were perpetrated on the Intergalactic School and all was well there, too.

The police investigation into Robert Cordell's death was at a standstill. We all knew who'd done it, but proving it was another thing entirely. Even with CIA assistance, the case was going to end up in the cold case section, and we all knew it.

Due to all that had happened, we were getting wonderful coverage from *Good Day USA!*, and the Kristie-Bot didn't miss any chances to say how great I was and how fantastic Code Name: First Lady would be. Adam was managing to fake enthusiasm, and he sent me daily reports on how the Kristie-Bot was acting. Normal, so far.

Cologne and Gadhavi both chose to hang around until the hockey game, Gadhavi because he was working closely with Mom and Chuckie on a variety of things, Cologne because he was negotiating with Raj and Colette about what he was and wasn't going to get to represent in the movies. Actively chose to avoid those meetings as much as possible.

Basically, three wonderful weeks went by and the only things I had to worry about were learning more about my Galactic Representative role and my normal FLOTUS and mother duties. After the couple of days I'd had, this all seemed remarkably easy.

Got to meet the Chupacabras too, which was really exciting, and the Capitals, which was nice but slightly less exciting because they weren't "my" team. But they were all really nice, too.

Both teams signed a team picture for me, and I signed a stick and a puck for both of them. Then the Capitals gave me my own official puck and the Chupacabras gave me my own official stick, both of which I was going to get to use at the game, since I was going to get to slap the opening puck. Might not slap it right at Charmaine, but wasn't going to guarantee that.

The night of the game came almost too quickly, but I was so excited about it that the day prior seemed hella slow and was, thankfully, totally uneventful. Opening day was on Sunday, so our game was Saturday and, thanks to the fundraiser and Charmaine's rabid advertising of such, we were sold out and everyone had spent a damned pretty penny to be in the seats, too. Most of D.C.'s and a lot of Hollywood's movers and shakers were going to be there, so I expected to make a ton of money over and above what we already had on the tickets alone. Go me for fundraising done right!

Naturally, I couldn't convince Jeff to wear jeans to this event. The suit was going to adapt and make do or Jeff was going to die trying to make it work. I was decked out in full Chupacabras gear, including a team t-shirt, a team jersey, and a team cap, and I'd gotten said gear for all the kids, too. Every kid called out as "mine" got the gear, because if you were mine you were a Chups fan or you were dead to me. We looked like a giant Chupacabras rally being led by a museum docent, but chose not to share that with Jeff, because it would have hurt his feelings.

Thusly attired, we arrived at the arena early, so I could make sure that everything was going according to plan. Making me want to faint, it was. We had the best seats I'd ever had—center ice, first row, right on the glass. Security was all set, the teams were in readiness, the Chups assured me they were going to win, and I was ready to get this party started.

Game time wasn't for another hour and a half, however. So, we got snacks that Jeff didn't want to eat but all the kids did. Apparently, A-Cs weren't used to eating crappy hot dogs, cotton candy, nachos, and the like—most of the A-C adults seemed to be making do with sodas and, in some instances, peanuts. Jeff was happy with a Coke, but that was about it.

But he ate the food anyway, to show willing and so the kids would follow his lead and not cause me to have to pout and eat all the junk food myself. Not that there was a risk of that. All of them, Jamie and Charlie included, wolfed down this junk food like it was Nectar of the Gods, just like the rest of the human adults with us did. I was so proud.

Forty-five minutes to go, though, and my phone rang. Looked at it.

"Oh, fantastic."

"What?" Jeff asked, as I dug out the tracker thingy and put it in.

"Another call from an unknown number."

Jeff groaned while I answered. "Hello?"

"Get out of the arena right now," a voice I didn't recognize said. "Or everyone's going to die."

CHAPTER 81

"WHO IS THIS?" Wasn't Robert Cordell, unless he was calling me from beyond the grave.

"Someone who doesn't want to see the end of the world."

"Right. Seriously, who is this?"

"Who else is listening to this call?"

"Um, only me. So far. I mean, I could put you on speaker if you so desire."

"No, let's keep it just you and me." The voice sounded weird, not a like a real person's voice.

"Um, why should I? Just asking and all."

"Your tracking equipment can't trace this call, so stop trying to draw it out."

"Honestly wasn't." That was the tracker thingy's job, not mine. *Was* trying to get them to give away word or phrasing clues as to who they really were, however, and that did require a longer conversation. "Truly trying to figure out who you are. The last dude who called me like this was dying. Are you also dying?"

"Everyone's dying, some slower than others."

"As I always say, philosophy's nice. I'm not sure why you're calling to share your philosophy with me, let alone using a voice modulating system to do it, but carry on."

"Well done."

"Do people not figure out that you're using voice modulation? I mean that question seriously. You sound like *Arrow* on The CW when Oliver Queen is pretending to himself that no one can see his face 'cause it's kind of dark. How would anyone not realize you're using some kind of voice modulating software?"

"You'd be amazed. Or maybe you wouldn't."

"Apparently I wouldn't."

They laughed. "Good point."

Had a really strong feeling about who this was. "Hang on a mo, need to get to a more private place." Hit mute and turned to Jeff, who was holding Charlie and doing his best to distract him so our little boy didn't hear this call. Yeah, Jeff rarely had a Parenting Fail. If I made it through a day without one, I threw myself a party.

"Planning a tryst?" Jeff asked, sarcasm knob at only around five, while he pointed at the skaters warming up and Charlie clapped his little hands with glee.

"In a way. I *think* I'm talking to the Shadow, though I could be wrong. Going to leave the best seats and take this where little pitchers can't hear."

Jeff grunted. "I should go with you." He did the hold the baby's hand and wave thing as a couple of the Chupacabras skated over to wave at us. The rest of the kids waved too. I gave a thumbs-up. The players waved and did thumbs-up back, then skated off.

"Then who would buy the kids frozen lemonades and more cotton candy? No one. Stay with our children, sugar them up, I'll be right back."

"I wonder about your parenting skills. I know your parents didn't raise you on sugar."

"They did not. That was their one failing. Choosing not to make the same mistake. Now, hold down the fort. I have the Latest Lunatic Opening Gambit to deal with and I think I'll handle it better if I know that you're with the kids."

He squeezed my hand. "Keep me posted and be careful, baby. They could be in the arena for all we know."

"Exactly. And if they are, I want to find them." Gave Jamie, who was far more into the cotton candy than whatever I was about, a kiss on the head. Gave Mom and Dad, who were on the other end of our row, the "watch the kids for me signal," and gave Lizzie, who was behind me, the same. Moved out of the seats and headed up the stairs, waving to various people I knew—politicians, Sidwell parents, Hollywood people, various dignitaries domestic, foreign, and alien—as I did. Didn't want anyone wondering what I was doing beyond taking a call in the bathroom or going to get more snacks. Which I was definitely doing once my latest Call O' The Weird was done.

Wasn't sure where Team Tough Guys was but took it on faith they were either following me or watching me. Turned off mute. "I'm back."

"Have you reassured your husband that you're not going to go have sex with another man? Or woman?"

"Ha ha ha, are you in here with us, monitoring us, or do you just know Jeff really well?"

"It doesn't matter. I'm calling to warn you."

"Great. Is this the Shadow?"

"The who?" The voice might be computerized but shock made it through. "Come again?"

"The Shadow. Um, I tend to nickname our enemies. And friends. And other things."

"Oh. Yes. It's kind of a cute trait. So, you're calling me the Shadow?"

"Yes, if you're who I think you are—the shadowy figure that's manipulating Janelle Gardiner, Zachary Kramer, someone or someones at the NSA, and probably many other people. The person who learned a lot more than anyone else realized from Madeleine Cartwright."

The Shadow was quiet as I reached the top of the concourse and spotted Buchanan, presumably because he wanted me to so spot. Headed over to him. He took my arm and led me down the concourse. My Secret Service and Field team details appeared and surrounded us as we kept moving. Stopped paying attention to anything other than my call.

"Yes, I am. The Shadow. I like it."

"So pleased. So, you were calling to warn me supposedly?"

"Yes. There's going to be an attack. Focused on you."

"Why do you care as opposed to throwing a party and managing the pay-per-view? And why would that signal the end of the world? Was that just for dramatic effect?"

"Because I don't want you dead. At least, not yet. It's also not hyperbole to suggest that, if we lose the person who's been averting Armageddon, the world could end."

"Huh. Those are statements that really beg several questions. I'll bet you can guess them all, too."

The Shadow chuckled again. "I suppose I can."

"Suppose you share, just to make me feel all special."

"Suppose you guess, to prove you're as smart as I think you are."

This was different. Wasn't used to any of them actually giving me credit. The Tinkerer had felt he had to come meet me in person to confirm if I had two brains cells to rub together. And yet the Shadow seemed to be taking it for granted.

Therefore, had to think fast. Why wouldn't the Shadow want me dead yet? That they'd want me dead in the future was a given, but why not right now?

"Honestly? The only thing I can think of is that you're happy that we're taking out your competition."

"See? You are as smart as I'd thought."

"Okay, but I kind of thought all of you were in the same club."

"You were on the track team, in the chess club, and in a sorority. And those are just the first three organizations off the top of my head. Did you like everyone in those organizations?"

"In chess club, yeah." Hey, I'd been the only girl and the guys were all sweet and cool. Besides, I'd been BFFs with the president of the club for four years. Wondered if anyone had let Chuckie know I was on the phone. Had to figure Jeff had, if not Buchanan. "But in the others, no, I didn't. And yeah, if we use the PTA as an example, if someone got rid of Charmaine for me, I'd be cheering them on and probably send them a fruit basket."

"Most of those in my 'club' are more like her than not."

We reached an office. Evalyne opened the door, Manfred went in, did the Hyperspeed Sweep, then the rest of us went inside. Once in with the door shut, Buchanan showed me his phone. There was no evidence that my tracker was working, meaning the Shadow was right—we had no idea what he or she was.

"Ugh." Had nothing else to say. It worked on all the levels.

"Exactly."

"So . . . I honestly don't get it, though. You still have more in common with them than me."

The Shadow chuckled. "Okay, that's true. In a sense. But, oh . . . think of it as if we're each the head of a drug cartel. You're the law. And you're making really good inroads into dismantling my competition. You make my life easier, because I've realized that if I let you take care of business, I don't have to spend the effort to do so."

"And, using your example, your cartel sends the cops tips, and maybe even warnings, since the cops are, in essence, being treated like a branch of your business. Maybe you even help us to take revenge when we lose one of our own, because that bonds us more."

"Exactly. And until all the others are gone and I have a clear track, well, you're far more useful alive and well than not."

Chuckie arrived, looking worried. Waved, but kept my focus on the call.

"Huh. Well, it's a novel approach, I'll give you that." It was the same approach the Tinkerer was taking, in essence. Only he'd asked for a cease-fire, and the Shadow wanted me to keep on kicking in doors and raiding meth labs. "And, ultimately, maybe it'll work like Chicago in the nineteen-twenties. The cops make a deal with you, with 'you' standing in for Capone in this example, because they're happy doing business with you after all this time, and it keeps more cops alive."

"Yes. Though you don't need to tell me that you won't take that deal. I'm willing to wait, because I believe that, in time, you very well might." The Tinkerer thought we'd take his deal, too. Far more positive offers than we usually got. "After all, Mister Ali Baba Gadhavi is sitting behind your husband, cheerfully sharing cotton candy with Prince Wasim and your ward, who opted to sit next to him because he promised to buy even more treats than you did."

"Are you in here?"

"No. But some of those who are my eyes are."

"Ansom and Talia?"

"You'll have to wait to find out. Though I really suggest you evacuate immediately."

"You know I can't do that without a confirmation of a real threat." And if this wasn't a real threat, if the Shadow somehow wanted Charmaine to win this round, then me evacuating would be the end. My kids would have to leave Sidwell, regardless of whatever dare I'd taken, because they'd never live it down.

"All you're getting is what I've said."

"Yeah, got it, such as it is. Forgive me for not trusting your tip. Which is partly because I'm wondering how you know there's going to be an attack in the first place. Did you order it, and now you're trying to foil it because you're really one with the whole Sith Lord plan?"

"No. I know because certain deals were made on the Dark Web and I can put two and two together."

"More Fem-Bots?"

"The Mob never gave the cops tips that were all that specific, you know."

"They did, actually. When they wanted to be sure the cops got the other cartel."

"Maybe I don't want to be sure."

"You mean, maybe you enjoy the entertainment."

The Shadow laughed again. "Yes, I do."

"So glad I can help. Here's something you may actually be willing and able to answer, though. Why did Janelle's team make Bots that look like my ward, Lizzie, and why were those sent to attack the Intergalactic School?"

"That's what you want to know? Seriously?"

"Yes. It's been bugging me."

"Because many of your enemies hate her at least as much as they hate you. You've been a problem since you appeared on the scene—she hit the scene a good fifteen years before you did, age-wise. Think of what she'll be like when she reaches your age."

"She'll be totally awesome."

"Yes, she will. She also embarrassed the children, nieces, nephews, and grandchildren of many of those 'in the club' with me, and they didn't care for that. It's the same reason most of the Bots being created look like you—they hate you. Both of you."

"I'm going to refrain from comment, because it seems weird—and I'm talking weirder than your side of things normally manages, which is pretty-damned—that you'd make Bots of the people you hate, then hire them to do your dirty work. Wait. Now that I say that aloud, it totally makes sense. If you were nuts, and all these people are, present telephone company possibly not included."

"Oh, I'm not insane. It's why it's taken so long for you to even realize that I'm here. You're used to finding lunatics, and I'm not one."

Potentially very true. "How did you know I'd figured out you existed?"

"That's for me to know and you to find out."

"Nice to see you embracing the clichés." But the Shadow hadn't used a single nursery rhyme, meaning that whoever had programmed the Christopher-Bot was someone else. "You know I can't evacuate the building on the basis of an anonymous call made by someone I'm calling the Shadow that most rational people wouldn't even say exists."

"Well, it's up to you. Just stay alert. Things are going to get dicey and, as I said, I'd like to keep you around for a while."

And with that, the Shadow hung up.

Stared at my phone. "Well, that was different."

CHAPTER 82

"SO," CHUCKIE SAID. "Want to tell us about it?"

"Kind of." Donned my Recap Girl cape yet again and did the deed. "Basically, I don't know if the Shadow's warning me for real or just to see what we'll do, like we're her entertainment for the evening."

"Her?" Buchanan asked. "I thought you said the voice was disguised."

"It was. I just . . . some of the things she said, and how she said them . . . the willingness to be behind the scenes, the fact that there was no argument when I said the Shadow had learned from Cartwright . . . I just think it's a woman."

"I can buy it," Chuckie said slowly. "The Shadow seems less . . . grandiose than the Mastermind ever was."

"Less grandiose than most of them were, honestly. I think that those who are tightly adhering to the curriculum set forth by The Madeleine Cartwright School For How To Succeed In World Domination Without Appearing To Be Trying are all women. Strauss, Gardiner, whoever the Shadow is. It just says smart chick to me. Smart chick who's smart enough to check her ego, versus smart chick who wants the world to bow down to her like LaRue."

"But we still don't know what to do," Evalyne pointed out. "Protocol says a threat like this means we should get you, Jeff, and the kids out of here ASAP."

"Protocol also says that if the person putting on the fund raiser gets the bum's rush out of the building via the Secret Service, it's time for everyone else to do that old Blind Panic Mambo. So that option is out."

Wondered what to do about the kids. And not just mine.

There were a lot of kids in the audience tonight—many had brought their families along for the fun.

"It could be a ruse to see how we'd evacuate in this situation," Manfred suggested. "Especially since the Shadow has people inside observing."

"Or she's watching on television," Siler said as he appeared and everyone other than Chuckie jumped. "This is televised, after all, and the cameras are spending most of their time looking at the President and his entourage."

"Nice to see you, Nightcrawler. And, um, yeah, that makes sense. Why didn't you let us know you came in with Chuckie?"

"Because I wanted to make sure this room was secure before I showed myself. I've also been working to hold a blend longer. Double duty."

"Gotcha. So, okay, the Shadow's watching on TV. Why didn't she just say so?"

"She wants you to earn it," Siler replied. "I think she respects you, in a different way than Trevor does. And I agree that it's probably a woman—as you pointed out, my mother was good at background manipulation."

"But is the threat real?" Chuckie asked. "That's the relevant issue."

"The Romanians aren't here," Buchanan said. "They made a donation, but Adriana said that Olga wasn't feeling well and that, therefore, they weren't going to attend."

Meaning Buchanan and Adriana were not having a Security Date Night tonight. But it also might mean something else. "You think that's a hint that it's real? We normally get a heads-up from them. And many times Olga has Adriana go even when she can't."

"I'm not sure, Missus Executive Chief. Olga has MS. She can and does have bad days, and Adriana's first duty is to her grandmother."

Chuckie was texting. "Chernobog says that Olga hasn't told her to hunker down or similar, and that the Romanians are in their embassy, versus American Centaurion's."

"So no expectation of needing a shield," Phoebe said.

"Then, maybe there is no attack? I mean, Olga knows pretty much everything."

"No," Buchanan said slowly, "she doesn't. Because she's never once insinuated that we needed to find the Shadow."

"Someone smart enough to hide from the All-Seeing Oracle? That bodes."

"I can believe it," Siler said. "This person is even better at hiding themselves than my mother was. So that means they're leaving a very small footprint."

"Yeah, everyone else is doing their dirty work, or taking credit for it."

"Or it could be that there is no real threat." Chuckie rubbed the back of his neck. "I honestly don't know what to advise."

"One thing before we decide," Siler said. "I received a call from Trevor a little while ago. He wanted to share that Stephanie wasn't the one who put the wiring into Somerall and Lee's heads. He was emphatic about it, by the way, and this after I told him that you weren't going to come down on them for it, since it had happened prior to the truce that exists only between you and him."

"Well, if not her or Trevor, then who? He basically said they were the only ones with the ability and know-how."

"After a lot of hemming and hawing, he admitted that Stephanie might have taught the Kendrick android how to do the process." Siler shook his head. "That is one messed-up girl."

"So, the Kendroid did it? Why?"

"He went off to 'find himself,' Missus Executive Chief. Maybe what he found was the Fem-Bot Factory and decided to keep his hand in."

"I don't want him to be evil." Whoops, hadn't meant to say that out loud.

"He might not see it as evil," Chuckie pointed out. "He's a living machine. He might feel that he was helping."

"Helping who? Ansom and Talia claim to not know what happened to them."

"Maybe he's helping his new benefactor," Evalyne said. "As in, maybe he's met this Shadow and is now on her side."

"And maybe she's telling him that he's doing good," Phoebe added. "He might not realize that she's evil or against you or anything like that. If she's being kind to him, he also might not care."

"The question of the moment, however, is—does this new information impact what we do tonight?" Chuckie asked.

Considered all the options. "No. We keep the event going. We're alerted. Let's be honest—if it's bombs, our people can find them. I know the K-9 squad is standing by outside—have some Field agents and the dogs do what they did at Sidwell, the Hyperspeed Sniff 'N' Search."

"That's sound," Buchanan agreed.

"I agree, and I'm on it," Chuckie said, texting away.

"Beyond that, Missus Executive Chief, everyone was already searched and scanned coming in."

"Here's a question—did the scans show that the cyborgs are all wires?"

"No," Evalyne said. "And the androids mask as non-metallic, too. There's something in whatever was put into them that is able to fool any and all of our metal detectors."

"Wish I'd asked Trevor about that."

"You got what you got," Chuckie said. "That was more than we had. Siler just got more. Call it good and move on. I'm far more concerned about this call and the fact that this event could be compromised than understanding our enemies' ability to disguise their various nonorganic parts from anything other than an OVS."

"Which Congress still refuses to okay as the metal detector of the future."

"Jeff's working on it," Chuckie said with a wry smile. "So, you know, give him a couple more years."

"From what I've seen," Daniel said, "that will just mean Congress is still arguing about the ramifications while more of our enemies slip through."

"Easily," Joshua added. "They seem to prefer blocking and arguing to actually doing anything productive." Lucas and Marcus nodded their agreement.

"Politics is what it is," Manfred said, shooting my other Field agents the "not your place to say" look. Manfred rarely pointed out that he was the head man on my Field security team, but when he did, the others subsided, and it was the same tonight. Four attractive heads nodded so that the fifth attractive head was appeased.

Time to ensure there wasn't an awkward silence. "Well, then let's get back out there and try to keep the peace in whatever ways we have to."

We left the room, Siler blending before we did so, and headed back toward our seats. As we exited, a woman I recognized from earlier team meet and greets came rushing over. "There you are!" she exclaimed. "Madam First Lady, we need to get you down to the ice. It's time to prep you for the dropping of the ceremonial puck." Good thing I'd left my purse with Jeff—there was no way they were going to let me take it onto the ice, and that way it wasn't out of our control.

Managed to remember her name. "Cool! Hang on just a minute, please, Sandie." Sent Jeff, Mom, and Lizzie texts about where I was and where I was going, with admonitions to take a lot of pictures. Received varying degrees of sarcastic responses back. Felt the love. Sent the same text to Dad. Got a supportive, "I'm videotaping this" response. Knew Dad loved me best. Shoved my phone into the back pocket of my jeans. "Okay, good to go."

Chuckie bowed out of taking me down to the ice and headed back to our section. The rest of my security entourage came with.

Sandie led us down to the ice, chattering the whole way about how exciting this all was and how grateful the Capitals organization was that we'd chosen to do this. "I know the Chupacabras are your team, but we're willing to be your number two!"

"That's great, and I'm willing to say that you are." Hey, why not? They'd given me a special puck and everything.

My security teams did whatever fast fades they always seemed to manage. Had no idea where Siler was and figured that he was a big boy and could handle whatever without me. Scanned the crowd and the arena—saw nothing out of place. No one had a rifle I could spot, there were no Fem-Bots I could see, no one looked like anything other than a hockey fan or someone here to Support The Cause. Decided Manfred had been right— the Shadow had wanted to see how we'd evacuate so she could counter it. So, back to what mattered—the fundraiser and the game.

The *Good Day USA!* camera crew was down here, though I noted that the cameraman that Adam had had an issue with was gone, replaced by some other guy. The arena had its own camera crews, and the news channels were out in full force as well. The hockey revolution was indeed going to be televised.

Adam and the Kristie-Bot were getting last makeup touch-ups, as was Jürgen Cologne. Apparently we were going to be pushing Code Name: First Lady and I was going to have to grin and bear it. Oh well, anything for the cause, right?

No one tried to fix my makeup, possibly because I wasn't wearing much. Or else I was supposed to have dragged Pierre along and hadn't. It was gently suggested that I remove my Chupacabras jersey if I had a shirt on underneath, though. Apparently the jersey was going to make me look shapeless on camera.

Considered saying that I preferred to stay warm, but decided to err on the side of making those who did this stuff for a living happy. Took off my jersey. Phoebe came over, took it, and helped me fix my hair. Someone cared. She also took my phone. "I'll give it back to you the moment you're done."

"I'm bereft and without the means to go on."

Phoebe snorted at me and did the fast fade thing.

"We have a special guest singing the national anthem," Sandie informed me as soon as Phoebe left, sounding totally excited. Wondered if I'd share her emotion.

"Oh yeah? Who?" Hadn't spotted a singing sensation on my way down here.

"Jack Johnson! He donated his talents in support!"

CHAPTER 83

MANAGED TO SLAP AN excited expression onto my face. "Wow! So cool."

If Other Me from Bizarro World was here, she'd be jumping up and down. Actually, she'd be hanging out with said special guest, since she and her family were close friends with one of the artists I considered the most boring in the world. However, he was a nice guy and, for a preseason game and as a donation, not a problem. Wondered if he was here because he wanted to sing the Code Name: First Lady theme. Made a mental note to tell Raj that this was a deal breaker.

"Isn't it though?" Sandie beamed. "We've been playing one of his best albums to kind of warm up the crowd. We figured that, since you're a rock and roll aficionado, you'd really appreciate it."

Realized there was music playing and had been since at least when I'd gotten my call from the Shadow. It had been quiet and unremarkable and I'd ignored it completely. Focused on listening. Sure enough, it was Jack Johnson. How anyone could consider this man's sound to be rock and roll was beyond me. But who was I to argue with Sandie's clear Jack Johnson–positive bias? "Ah, yes. Which album is this again?"

"His *In Between Dreams* album. It's my absolute favorite of his." Yep, Sandie was a Jack Johnson fangirl.

Did my best to channel my Inner Other Me. "Oh, yeah, mine too! He's just so soothing and, um, meaningful."

"Isn't he?" She beamed again. "I'm so glad we could give you this wonderful surprise!"

"Oh, yeah, I'm totally surprised. Totally. Very wonderful

indeed." Hoped I'd sounded believable. Sandie seemed happy, so presumed I had.

Naturally, this meant that I had to Meet The Artist. He was very nice as we shook paws and exchanged meaningless pleasantries. Fortunately, Sandie was handling the fawning and fangirling portion, so I didn't have to.

Intros over, it was time to get this party started. Normally the anthem was the last thing before the game started. But since Jeff and I were here and this was my fundraiser and all that jazz, and *Good Day USA!* was here, too, *and* we had not one but two additional celebrity guests on the ice, we were mixing it up tonight, big-time.

First off, Adam and the Kristie-Bot did a variety of intros and crowd warm-ups, which included a reminder that this was a fundraiser and that there were raffles, normal and 50/50 and others, so the people who'd already shelled out big bucks to be here could give more. Mrs. Paster was brought down now, and she gave a short address about all the good that Sidwell's graduates went on to do. Even I was ready to donate more when she was done.

Next up, a short interview with Cologne wherein he did indeed push the Code Name: First Lady franchise—and he called it a franchise, too, making me cringe inside—and one with Johnson, where he merely said it was an honor and a thrill to be here, but did add that he was flattered he was one of my favorite artists, meaning that's what Sandie had told him. Really hoped my Happy Poker Face was firmly in place for all of this, since I knew if it wasn't I'd enjoy a lecture tomorrow.

Both hockey teams skated out and lined up. Since Johnson was now on the red carpet on the ice, he went into the national anthem, accompanied by a nice patriotic light show. He did an admirable job, hitting the high notes well, which kind of surprised me, and he received thunderous applause. So far, so very good.

Now it was my big moment. Adam came and escorted me onto the red carpet that held the *Good Day USA!* team. Did the little fundraiser chat with him and the Kristie-Bot, spoke about how we wouldn't let anti-alien forces break up the unity that was currently going on all over the world, and only had to say once that Code Name: First Lady would likely be fun.

The torture portion of the festivities over, it was time for the good stuff. I stayed where I was while the others, including the hockey teams—other than the new *Good Day USA!* cameraman who was filming the rest of the festivities—got off the ice. The cameraman had a big bag slung over his neck, kind of like how I secured my purse when I was in action mode, only his bag was behind him. He saw me looking and gave me a thumbs-up. Did the same back.

I was escorted off the carpet and onto the ice by the Chupacabras' goalie, team captain, and main enforcer, aka my favorite players. Fortunately, I was an athlete, knew how to ice skate and therefore how to keep my balance on ice, and Converse were great shoes for ice sliding. Didn't really have any issues, and if I did, the hunky hockey players were holding me in such a way that I wouldn't go down. Really hoped Dad was getting all of this on video and that others were actually taking stills.

Got a lot of applause and waved to the crowd in what was hopefully the approved manner as I was positioned in front of the Capitals' goalie and net.

The Chups' mascot, Killer the Chupacabra, skated out to wild applause, from me as well as others. It was a rarity that he was here, since mascots weren't normally at away games, but I'd requested him specifically. Sometimes being the FLOTUS was worth it.

I loved Killer, just like all the other fans did. He was ugly— since Chupacabras looked like hairless wild dogs with extra-large fangs and spines on their backs—but misunderstood. He didn't want to eat anyone's goats or cattle or pets, he merely wanted his hockey team, the best hockey team in the league, to win. He was Arizona's Champion of Desert Hockey and a total fan favorite. You had to sign up before the game to get your picture taken with Killer, he was that popular. Basically, you'd take Killer from us over our cold, frozen bodies.

He also had the puck and stick. But they weren't the ones I'd been told we'd be using. The stick wasn't signed and the puck looked more gray than black.

"These aren't your signed ones," Donovan, the Chups' captain, said, clearly reading my expression. "Team management didn't want them to get wrecked. You can keep this puck and stick, too, though."

"Cool!" Extra pucks and hockey sticks were not a problem. The Diamondbacks could take a lesson from the Chupacabras was my thought. Maybe I'd see about doing a fundraiser with them next. Clearly I was good at it when I was actually given more than a day's notice.

Killer gave me the puck and stick, while doing a bit where he pantomimed wanting to keep them and I had to try to take them away from him. Could hear peals of laughter, much of it sounding as if it came from the kids in the audience. Good, we were entertaining the crowd, which was great. Killer was totally kid-friendly and focused.

In the end, Killer gave me the puck and stick and a big hug, too. I was far more excited about getting to hang out with Killer than with Jack Johnson. Killer skated backward off the ice, blowing kisses to me the whole way, which I returned enthusiastically. So far, best night at a game ever.

The Capitals' goalie, Carcento, skated up. "Aim right between my kneepads."

"So you can block it?"

He laughed. "No. So I can miss it impressively. You're the First Lady. We're letting you get the puck into the net, if you have any aim at all."

"I do!"

"They gave us extra pucks," Donovan, said. "So we can do it a few more times."

"We have a dozen," Carcento added.

"So if I miss we can do it again?" Didn't like that I was being sold short and was expected to miss a dozen times, but more time on the ice was fine with me.

Donovan laughed. "No. They're doing a raffle where the crowd is taking bets on how many pucks you get into the net. They'll draw from the group that chooses the winning number. Winner gets a signed jersey from each team."

"Oh, awesome! I'm all for it!" Noted that the announcers were sharing this news as well. Realized they'd shared it before, I just hadn't paid attention. Also realized that it was Johnny and Mitch doing the announcing, making it all so much cooler. My Celebrities I Cared About Meeting quotient was going way up.

"You're lucky this is preseason," Carcento said. "We'd never get away with all of this in regular."

"Well, preseason is the most fun then!"

As Carcento went back to his net, the Chups' goalie, Bays, went behind me. "To cover your rear," he said with a grin I could see behind his mask.

"Everyone's a comedian." Not that I minded. Bays was an awesome goalie.

The enforcer, Pulley, helped me get into position. "Remember, for this, it'll be like putting in golf, not driving."

"I don't play golf."

"For this, it'll be like miniature golf."

"Got it! Softer hits, not harder, right?"

"Right!"

Donovan put the puck Killer had handed me down onto the ice, and he and Pulley helped me get into the right position.

Did as I was told, aiming right where Carcento had told me to, though might have done more of a slap shot than a soft nudge. The puck slid over the ice, going right between his knee-pads, as he closed his knees together far more slowly than normal.

The crowd cheered and the announcement for more betting went out, as Donovan put eleven more pucks onto the ice. "Go wild now. It doesn't matter how many you get in—the one you just did counts, so if you miss the rest, they can still pick a winner."

"And if you make them all, then those who wisely bet that you're good will get their chance to win," Pulley added.

"I love you guys. So, um, can I do a real slap shot, then?"

"You're the First Lady," Donovan said. "You can do anything you like."

"Even me," Bays called out.

We all laughed and I got down to business. Slapped the heck out of the pucks. Carcento blocked most of them, but I actually got a couple by him.

As I readied to hit the last puck, the music—which had heretofore been the typical arena electric organ stuff—changed. As I listened, recognized that it was Dean Martin, which seemed an odd choice. Singing "Mambo Italiano" which was an even odder choice.

Paid attention to the lyrics. They started slowly, but "something's wrong" was clearly called out.

So, when the puck in front of me raised up into the air, I was kind of prepared.

CHAPTER 84

KIND OF PREPARED wasn't the same as totally ready. So the puck had time to sprout little metallic legs, little metallic arms with pincers at the end, and pop up a rounded button-like protrusion from its top that then sprouted two tiny metallic antennae, while I watched, processing that no puck in the league worked like this.

"What the hell?" Bays skated nearer to us. "What's going on?"

"Um . . . this isn't something planned?"

"No," Donovan said, as the flying puck sort of hovered in front of us, moving in a weird, syncopated pattern that was vaguely familiar. "No one said anything about this."

"What is it?" Pulley asked.

Was about to say that I had no idea when I saw the other pucks on the ice also rise up and sprout all these special extras. Dawned on me that there was a high probability that whoever was in charge of the music here wasn't who'd put on the Dean Martin song.

"Um, you guys? Any of you know how to swing a baseball bat?"

"Sure," Pulley said. "But why would we need to?"

The music changed to "Mambo No. 5" and gave me all the confirmation I needed. Lou Bega was in the house, so to speak, and so was Algar. And the Shadow hadn't been a liar.

"Fight and swing to the beat!" So saying, slid forward so I wouldn't brain Bays, who was still behind me, swung my stick up, and took a shot at the flying puck.

Which dodged my strike and headed for Bays. But he was a goalie, and he slapped it away with his mitt. The flying puck careened toward Carcento. Who had several of these flying pucks around him.

Carcento slapped at one of the pucks. And it sent an electric charge out of its antennae.

The charge hit him where he had no padding, meaning it was able to aim precisely, because goalies wore a hell of a lot of padding. He shouted in pain, but didn't go down.

Didn't wait, just "skated" toward him as fast as I could. This would have been easier if I'd been on actual ice skates, but it wasn't as bad as it could have been. Besides, careening around was a good idea when you were fighting weird things like this.

Swung, slid, swung again, doing my best to keep to the beat, which helped avoid being hit by the antennae charge if nothing else. Even if I didn't hit one, I was able to keep them away from Carcento. "Hit or swing to the beat," I called to him as I did just that.

Managed to hit one of the flying pucks with my stick. It slammed into the glass, which afforded me a good look at those sitting behind the net, since I slid into the glass, too. They were all staring, open-mouthed, but no one was actually moving. Meaning they all thought this was part of the show.

The four players on the ice, however, were clear that we were under attack. Five of us against a dozen little flying things should be a battle we easily won. Donovan got one onto the ice and Pulley did what he did best—slammed his stick on it, which was what I was doing with the one I'd managed to stun against the glass. It took a couple of hits, but both of our adversaries were finished at the same time.

The cameraman was still on the ice. But he wasn't filming. His camera was down and, as I watched, he dropped his bag down onto the ice next to it and took off. No sooner was the bag down than more flying pucks burst out of it and headed for us.

So he'd been planted by our enemies, and Adam's fight with his regular cameraman had given them their opening. My brain shared that it wanted me to remember this point, but had to save it for later. Right now, I needed all my focus here.

As if this wasn't enough, as the music changed to "Hey Mambo" by Barry Manilow with an assist from Kid Creole and the Coconuts, looked up. To see that we didn't have just the ten pucks and however many were in the bag left to deal with. No, the ceiling was moving and, as I watched, what were several hundred flying pucks flew down toward the ice, sending out their electric shocks on what appeared to be a pattern.

Whether that meant the one that had hit Carcento had gotten

lucky or whether whoever was controlling these things just wanted to remind us that they hurt, I didn't know.

What I did know was that I'd been kind of freaked out before, but now, now I was mad. My kids were here, having an extremely rare fun family outing, and if anything happened to them, including something as mild as them spilling their Cokes or dropping their cotton candy due to fear, heads were going to roll. Flying pucks were going down one way or the other. Bottom line—it was now clobberin' time. Pity we didn't have The Thing with us, though. Could have used someone made of stone.

"Incoming!" I bellowed. Wasn't up to Jeff's standards, but made do. Looked around for Jeff and the kids. Their seats were empty. Sincerely hoped this meant the Secret Service had done what they were meant to do and gotten them to safety. If not, flying pucks weren't going to be all I was clobbering.

Donovan body checked me out of the way of several of the flying pucks that were all around me. This sent me sliding into Bays, who caught me, righted me, then headed off after some of the other flying pucks.

"Grab on," Pulley said as he skated over to me. Did as suggested and grabbed the back of his jersey. We sped along, him slapping at the flying pucks around us with power, me just holding my stick out to catch what I could. Managed to hit several in this way. Also managed to get zapped in the butt more than once.

"Ouch! That hurts!" I didn't have the same padding on as the players did. Plus, a couple of the flying pucks had grabbed me with their pincers, ripping my jeans and my skin.

The rest of the teams had figured out something was wrong and came onto the ice. So now there were a lot of us swinging sticks around like bats, but far more flying pucks to hit than there were players.

Most of us were getting zapped, too. So when the music changed to Perry Como's "Papa Loves Mambo" of all things, and I naturally altered how I was moving and avoided another couple of zaps, finally got the clue. "Always move and swing to the beat," I shouted to the players. "As the beat changes, you change, too! Swing at the flying pucks on the backbeat!"

Shouted this particular rallying cry several times as players skated past me and I slid past them. Dodged some flying pucks along the way—which I really wanted to rename, but the only nickname that came to mind probably wasn't appropriate for the First Lady to be shouting, though it was fitting, all things considered.

Donovan and Pulley got on either side of me and stayed there. "Work as a line," Donovan shouted.

"I can do that! Follow my lead on the way to move!"

"You're the center, you lead," Pulley said. "We'll follow."

We swayed our way around the ice while Como crooned, lifting feet or jumping over downed flying pucks, smoothly dodging the flying pucks that were coming at us, and hitting a lot of them, too. Other players saw what we were doing and formed up into lines as well.

With the guys on either side I had a little more protection so could risk a look around. Almost wished I hadn't. The flying pucks weren't limiting themselves to the arena—they were in the stands, too.

Naturally there was chaos because of course there was. Apparently my confidence in my abilities had shown up far too early—I was doomed to never throw a party or an event that didn't self-destruct in some way.

Could see Field agents trying to get these things, but they weren't in tune with me and the players and, hyperspeed or not, they were losing. So were all the Secret Service in the stands. So were all the others. Still couldn't spot my family and hoped this was a good thing.

As we swung around the curve of the rink and boogied back, heard Johnny and Mitch. The press box they were in was protected, so they were doing commentary on what was going on. Really hoped the Shadow was enjoying the floorshow.

"Oh!" Mitch said. "The First Lady just gave that thing a vicious hit. Where are the scouts? She's got a hell of a slap shot in the air and on the ice."

"She does indeed," Johnny replied. "This is amazing, folks. We're seeing what might be the first ever synchronized hockey fight in history."

"Love the musical selections, too. Johnny, this is amazing."

"And those flying things are changing their methods once again, Mitch. They appear to learn the song's beat and then adapt to it." Realized that Johnny was right and sent up a silent thank you. This was also likely why Algar was changing music instead of putting us onto a one-song repeat.

"Johnny, I'm just glad we're in here and not down there. Oh, look, more people are getting involved."

Sure enough, as the music changed to Big Bad Voodoo Daddy's "Mambo Swing"—and I therefore changed how I was moving, meaning the players did, too—saw some people run onto the ice. People in suits.

Jeff, White, and Reader had hockey sticks and somehow managed to slide-skate over to join my line. "What are you doing?" Jeff shouted.

"Trying to stay alive! Why are you here and not protecting our children?"

"They're already safe, all the kids are safe. We got them to shelter immediately. What kind of father do you think I am?"

"Um, a great one! Now, move to the beat, Jeff. It's dancing time again! And form your own line, guys. Three to a set!"

White was already boogieing like he'd spent his life on skates, even though he was in dress shoes, just like Jeff and Reader. He zoomed in front of us. Reader and Jeff took his flank, adjusted to what they were doing, and started really moving, slapping flying pucks out of the air and slamming them with their sticks once the pucks were on the ice as if they'd actually practiced before the big match.

Christopher, in the meantime, wasn't faring as well. Super hyperspeed was great, but he wasn't a great dancer, he hadn't brought a stick, and he also hadn't been prepared for how slick the ice still was around the boards.

He hit a really slick patch and slid around the outer part of the rink. Heard him shouting "Whoa!" as he passed us, which happened several times. He didn't appear to be slowing down at all and, in fact, was pretty sure he was speeding up. Seemed like he was trying to slow down by running faster, which was truly unlikely to work in this situation. Then again, Alpha Four was a desert planet, and that meant he probably had very little historical information on how to handle this. Would have stopped to help him, but had too much else to deal with, beating flying pucks down and destroying them being Job One. Not tripping on downed flying pucks being Job Two.

Synchronized skating/sliding seemed to be working. At least, we had a lot of metal on the ground. Which created its own challenges. We were all now having to spend more time avoiding rubble on the ice than hitting the still-active flying pucks.

Needed to do something, because we didn't have time for a Zamboni break. Had no other ideas, so tried something that had worked in the past.

"Poofs assemble!"

CHAPTER 85

POOFS APPEARED ON JEFF, White, and Reader's shoulders. Took a fast look around—all the players I could see had Poofs riding shotgun. So far, so good.

"Poofies, Kitty needs an assist! Can you figure out some way to clean the ice up so Kitty, Jeff, Richard, James, and all the nice players can concentrate on stopping the bad flying pucks instead of focusing on not falling?"

"Why are you talking to those animals and what can they possibly do—?" Donovan started to ask.

He was interrupted by Poofs zooming down to the ice, scooping up rubble in their mouths—which, since they were still small but their jaws expanded, was freaky as hell to watch—and left the ice nice and slick in their wake.

"How do I get me one of those?" Pulley asked.

"Get us out of this alive!"

"On it!"

"Good, because they're learning." Pointed up. The flying pucks were forming lines, with far more than three per line. They looked ready to dive-bomb us as the music changed to Don Henley's "All She Wants To Do Is Dance."

White's line broke formation. "Getting behind you," he called to me. "As instructed." That was an order to follow me? Well, okay. Who was I to argue with someone listening carefully to the Algar Channel?

Saw Reader wave in the "get over here" manner as Tim came out now, stick in hand, wearing skates. Well, nice to know why he'd arrived late—he'd taken the time to prep for the situation. Thank God one of us had.

Tim zoomed next to me and shoved me forward. "You lead, Kitty! I'll cover your spot on the line."

"Thanks for that." Changed my movements as the first wave of flying pucks dived toward us. Slide-skated low, bobbing to the beat, added in some spins, because that was dancing, and all of it seemed to help. We were avoiding most of the hits and were hitting flying pucks. So far so good.

"Mitch, it looks like the First Lady is leading the players in another dance routine."

"You're right, Johnny. The President's got some moves, too, doesn't he?"

"He does, Mitch, he does. Frankly, everyone on the ice is doing a great job. Oh, wow, look at those hits the two teams' enforcers are managing. Those flying things are going to be sorry they went up against two prime NHL teams."

"And the First Lady's holding her own, too, Johnny. Impressive since she's not on skates."

"Well, natural ability's a wonderful thing, Mitch. Not everyone has it, but those who do sure impress the heck out of me. Folks, if you're just tuning in, we're underway in what should have been the last preseason game between the Washington Capitals and the Arizona Chupacabras but what's turned into a gigantic free-for-all combining hockey, tennis, synchronized dancing, and more. Don't change that channel, we're going commercial-free right now and you don't want to miss a thing."

"Johnny, look! New arrivals."

As Mitch said this, heard a bird's angry scream and looked up again. More help was indeed on the way—the Peregrines had arrived. All of the males, as near as I could tell.

Bruno landed on my shoulder as I did another spin and heard Christopher whiz by, still shouting "Whoa!"

"Bruno, my bird, what kept you?"

Bruno cawed, warbled, leapt off my shoulder to avoid getting hit, grabbed the flying puck in his talons, ripped it to shreds, dropped it down, and landed back onto my shoulder to finish his sentence. The Peregrines had been protecting our kids and families until said kids and families were deemed safe, Peregrine safe. Lola and all the females were with our kids, and definitely had their Kill 'Em All and Let Kitty Sort 'Em Out mindsets on.

"You all rock above all other birds, now and forever."

Risked another look around while I did another spin. There were now various Lyssara honeycomb shelters all over the stands. Saw people being moved to them by Field agents, Secret Service, and arena security. Flying pucks were bouncing off the honeycombs and, once bounced, didn't try again. "Good thinking, those Honeybees."

Bruno cawed. He agreed that the Lyssara were excellent to have around and suggested we add a few onto our security teams.

"We'll revisit that great idea when we have some downtime, but I'm with you."

Assessed the current state of the situation. Positives were that the people in the stands were getting to safety and becoming harder to hit. Negatives were that security in the stands were having to focus most of their protection on the Lyssara, since there weren't that many of them here and we needed a lot of honeycombs made, and that those of us on the ice were once again getting the full brunt of the flying pucks' attack.

"Any ideas?" I asked Bruno. "I'm hella open."

He shared that he was confident I'd figure it out. Always the way.

The music changed to Gloria Estefan & Miami Sound Machine's "Conga" right as I heard Christopher's "whoa" getting closer. Considered options as he zoomed past. Spun around. "Dudes, conga line! Hold on tight! Pass it down!"

Turned back and readied myself, as Jeff somehow got ahead of Tim's line and grabbed the back of my jeans. "I hope you know what you're doing, baby."

"Oh, me too. Glad to see that you're focused on the priorities and not letting someone else grab my butt."

"Never have, never do, never will. The situation doesn't matter. Your butt is mine."

"No argument from me and right back atcha. Now probably isn't the time to share that some of the flying pucks have pinched me, is it?"

"No, it's the perfect time." He slammed his stick against two of them, destroying them both with one blow. "Jealousy helps my aim, as far as I can tell."

"I'll keep that in mind and won't comment about the fact that you're jealous of some metal disks of evil."

"Everyone needs one flaw, baby, or else they're boring."

"Oh, stick with that story, Jeff. It's working for you."

The sound of Christopher's inability to slide-skate came nearer again. Or maybe he was the best slide-skater around. Tough one to call. However, knew without asking that he'd like to slow down or, barring that, at least be more helpful in the fight. Planned to help him do both.

As the sound got louder, reached out with my left hand and grabbed for him. Managed to catch his suit jacket and held on tight. Go team. Literally.

We moved into the fastest spin I'd personally ever done. I could still hear the music, though, meaning I could still move to the beat. So I did. We were going clockwise around the rink. As I started bobbing, used my left foot to push us away from the boards while swinging the stick in my right hand around to the beat. Hit flying pucks by the droves this way.

Could see the others do the same since we were now the snake eating its own tail and the guys were still doing whatever I was, proving that hockey players were a lot smarter than they tended to be given credit for.

The Poofs, meanwhile, were slide-skating or whatever they called it right next to us, scooping up every flying puck we slammed to the ground, making little growly sounds that, as far as I could interpret, meant they were totally having fun. So far, so very good.

Christopher caught up to the player at the end of our conga line, just managing not to hit into him, but only because I yanked him back. "Christopher, grab hold of the hockey player in front of you!"

Apparently he'd had enough of his own personal version of the Spinner, because he didn't question, complain, or snark, he merely did as requested. Well, ordered. Clearly, spinning around like this had been good for him.

He got a hold on the player's jersey and, once I knew he had it, I let go of his jacket. Momentum and the slickness of the ice meant we still kept moving briskly, but no longer at the fastest hyperspeed imaginable. Heard some gagging, but these guys were all top athletes and everyone's adrenaline was running well past eleven, so no one barfed.

"Conga" was still playing. When I'd done this dance before—you know, at frat parties and the like, where there weren't flying metal puck things trying to kill us—moving in a circle over and over again wasn't fun. You had to move around, serpentine-like. Normally you went through rooms, but we'd have to make do with just the ice rink and the nets, which were, somehow, still mostly in place.

So, I did, because us going in a circle would make it really easy for the flying pucks, and this was more interesting for me. Began to slide-skate in earnest again, only this time I snaked us around, doing a big S shape, and then circled around the nets, just to keep the flying pucks guessing.

Had to lift up my right foot, then my left, then jump to avoid flying puck parts the Peregrines had created that the Poofs hadn't gotten to yet. The guys in the line did the same. Ducked and bobbed and got to see the line imitate this as well. Only managed to control the Inner Hyena because the situation was still serious. Plus, it was kind of cool.

We had a lot of debris still in front of us, because the Peregrines were doing their thing and they weren't following our conga line, so had to slow us down. Heard gunshots and looked around to see who was shooting—if we had a shooter then we also had someone who might be trying to shoot Jeff. This was truly a great opportunity for an assassination.

Had to look way up, but was relieved when I spotted the shooters—Mom, Kevin, Buchanan, and Chuckie were up in the cheap seats, all firing at the flying pucks that were above the Peregrines. Hitting and not missing, too, which was totally one for the win column.

More gunfire. Looked around to spot some people high up in the rigging—Siler and a Turleen I was pretty positive was Mossy. They were also shooting, but they were using sniper rifles. Where they'd gotten them I didn't know, but kind of figured Mossy had brought them along somehow, because he was cool that way.

There were far fewer flying pucks about, but we weren't out of the woods yet. There were still plenty in the areas where those with guns couldn't shoot without risking hitting those of us on the ice, those still in the stands, or the Peregrines. And either the flying pucks did learn, or whoever was controlling them did, because the remainder moved lower, out of safe firing range.

The Peregrines were flying where most of the pucks were congregating in order to prepare for more attacks on the ice, which was good, in that when they caught one they destroyed it. But it was bad because there were still more flying pucks than there were birds, and the birds were far bigger targets.

Three flying pucks surrounded a Peregrine, then they all zapped it at the same time. Heard the bird shriek, then it plummeted down and hit the ice with a thump.

And it didn't move.

CHAPTER 86

INSTANTLY SAW RED. I'd already been furious that whoever had launched this attack had done so when my children and other people's children were here. But now they'd hurt one of my pets, an innocent animal just trying to protect innocent people. An animal dedicating its life to protecting me and mine. They might have even killed it. And I knew they wanted to do the same to all my pets, and my children, my family and friends, our protectors, and everyone else, too, if they could.

Bruno flew off my shoulder, shrieking, and the other Peregrines joined him, attacking the flying pucks with even more ferocity.

"Son of bitch must pay!" It might not be the greatest war cry, but it was working for all the Peregrines, so it worked for me. "Break up, guys! Jeff, let go and pass it on!"

He let go of my pants and I headed for the Peregrine as fast as I could, which, considering I was now fully enraged, was pretty darned fast. Scooped him up into my arms right before a flying puck could hit him again. It was one of our younger Peregrines, Edgar, who'd attached to Lizzie, and he was still alive, but I wasn't sure for how long, or how badly he was hurt. "Hang in there, buddy."

"Oh no, Johnny, it looks like we have a man down. Bird down."

"The First Lady seems to be trying to get him to safety, Mitch. Folks, do we have any veterinarians in the audience? Any vets at all here tonight? If so, you're needed down at the ice."

Doubted we'd get any takers, but it was nice of Johnny to give it the old college try.

Cuddled Edgar to my chest and headed us for the nearest net, dodging flying pucks and shielding him with my body, because while I could take more hits, knew Edgar couldn't. Several flying pucks tried to surround us and I couldn't really swing the stick and hold onto Edgar.

Flipped us into a forward roll on the ice. Landed well and our momentum allowed me to slide the rest of the way to the net on the Butt That Belonged To Jeff.

Got to my feet with an assist from the net, put Edgar on top of it, where the goalies left their water bottles during games, put my stick next to him, and started shoving the net toward the area where the Zamboni came from, pausing to hit flying pucks with my stick as needed and kicking some, too, because the skills were working perfectly—when I had a live studio audience, no less—scooping up busted puck parts in the net along the way. That was me, getting at least a double out of everything.

"Our First Lady's a firecracker, isn't she Mitch?"

"She is. And, look, Johnny, there's someone hurrying toward her."

"Hope it's a veterinarian, not an attacker, Mitch." So did I, Johnny. So did I.

Thankfully, that someone was Tito, and he reached the opening at the same time I did. "You're a vet, too?"

"No, but I'm the best we've got for this."

"Dude, you're the best we've got period and you know it."

He grinned as he carefully took Edgar from the net. "Hang on, more reinforcements are coming."

"Who!"

The music changed to "Hips Don't Lie" by Shakira and Wyclef Jean. As it did, Rahmi and Rhee leaped over the glass, which was hella impressive considering how high it was, landed on the ice, and started spinning their battle staffs, with the glowing ends definitely activated. They sliced through several of the flying pucks before the little machines had time to react.

"They waited until all the civilians were safe, children and the elderly in particular," Tito said. "Now, go fight with your protégées. This is your kind of fight, Kitty, remember that."

He ran toward the nearest honeycomb, and I grabbed my by-now-rather-bedraggled stick and slide-skated toward the princesses. "Guys, get off the ice now," I shouted to the hockey players I passed. "I don't want you getting hit by friendly fire! You, too!" Shouted at Christopher, who wisely hadn't let go of his hockey player. He nodded to me and left with the others.

Several of the flying pucks surrounded me like they had Edgar. Well, screw that. Listened to the beat and moved to it, swinging my stick on the backbeat, using my hips to keep from getting hit. The princesses saw what I was doing and started imitating me, since they were surrounded, too. Back to synchronized dance-fighting for the win.

"The two new ladies seem to be as good on the ice as the First Lady," Johnny said.

"They do!" Mitch agreed. "I think the number of flying weapons has been reduced by quite a lot, too."

"Let's hope that this fight continues in this way, Mitch. Most of the hockey players are off the ice now."

"I think the First Lady told them to go, Johnny."

"She did, Mitch. Folks, now on the ice it's just the First Lady and her, ah, female honor guard, the President and three other men, those big birds that look like peacocks, and those weird little animals doing cleanup."

"Amazing how well they're all doing in street shoes, isn't it, Johnny?"

"That it is, Mitch, though one of them managed to grab some skates. Maybe he's trying out for one of the teams." Mitch and Johnny both chuckled at this as the song changed to "She Bangs," thankfully the version by Ricky Martin, not the cover by William Hung. "And apparently they all bang, too." Oh yeah, they were hilarious, but the song was great at helping us bang on the flying pucks.

"Pretty birds, aren't they, Johnny? Real fighters, too. More than a few teams could use a couple of those in enforcer roles."

"Ah . . . I suppose so, Mitch. Might have an issue putting them into skates, though."

Mitch laughed heartily while Johnny chuckled at his joke as well. Clearly Johnny was on a comedy roll. "And those fluffy little animals doing cleanup? Those things are damned adorable, Johnny."

"That they are, Mitch."

"I want one, Johnny."

"Take that up with the First Lady, Mitch."

"Great idea! What a show, folks! What a show! And the music—it's Latin Night here at the Capitals arena, folks! What. A. Show!" Mitch was really into it. He should get out of the safety of the press box and try it down on the ice and see how into it he was then. He might score a Poof that way.

The princesses and I were drawing most of the remaining flying pucks' attention, which made sense—the Shadow had said this attack was going to be centered on me.

The Peregrines were forcing the flying pucks lower and not allowing them to escape via the air. Jeff, White, Reader, and Tim were effectively herding or hitting the flying pucks toward us, depending. The princesses and I shook our hips and swung our sticks and made good progress.

As always, though, the remaining flying pucks regrouped and attacked in our rhythm. Fortunately, it was taking them about a full song to adjust, so as they landed zaps on me, Tim, and Rahmi, the music changed to Shaggy's "Chica Bonita."

New beat, new moves, more flying pucks shattered on the ice. This was the way to do it, though I kind of missed the hockey players. This song had a little more of a reggae beat, and while the backbeat remained constant, the main melody went from faster to slower, making it great for confusing nasty flying machines with more smooth dance-fight moves.

Took the full song, but by the time it was done, we were smashing the last of the flying pucks into the ice and the Poofs were finishing cleanup. The moment they were done, the Poofs disappeared. Bruno squawked at his flock and they all flew off, perching on the tops of the honeycomb shelters.

"Wow, folks," Johnny said, "looks like it's all over." The music changed to "Pause" by Pitbull. Had no idea if this was Algar telling Johnny and Mitch to shut up or if it was a hint that more was coming.

"Has the fat lady sung, though, Johnny?"

"Not that I've heard, Mitch. All the artists we've heard were or are in shape. Commercial break time, folks. Don't go away, though, because we'll have interviews with all the participants once we're back, and don't forget, the game hasn't even started yet!"

"Are those guys for real?" Tim asked as we regrouped.

"Hey, they want you to try out for the Capitals."

"I'm a Kings fan."

"You're dead to me."

"Hey, the Chups are my second team."

"You get to live again."

"If you two are done bantering," Jeff said, "is it safe to let people out of the shelters?"

Was about to reply in the affirmative, when I heard something, and it wasn't music.

Turned toward where I'd left the net. It was still there. But not for long.

A Zamboni was coming through, going as fast as a Zamboni could, which was about nine whole miles an hour. But it was going far faster than I'd seen most of them come out of the gate.

"What the literal hell?" Reader asked. "Do they seriously think the game's really still on?"

"Don't they normally wait for everyone to get off the ice before they begin cleaning it?" White asked.

"Normally." The Zamboni hit the net and kept on going. "They also normally don't wreck the nets, either."

"Did they not realize the net was there somehow?" Jeff asked.

Looked hard at who was driving. "Um, gang? Despite our hopes to the contrary, it's totally not over."

Charmaine was at the wheel.

CHAPTER 87

"WHY IS THAT horrible woman driving the machine?" Rhee asked.

The music changed to "Everyone Knows You're Crazy" by Royal Crown Review. Swing instead of Latin beats, but whatever worked. "Because she's totally cray. That's why."

"Let's handle her," Jeff said with a sigh.

"Not just no, but hell no." All the mouths opened. Put up the paw. All the jaws slammed shut. The One True FLOTUS Power worked its magic again. "This woman is *my* nemesis. I've known her less than a month and I hate her more than most of our other enemies. Put together. As such, I'm going to beat the crap out of her. The President of the United States is going to be taken to safety now, just in case the Zamboni Gambit is to distract us so that ninja cyborgs can attack us or something."

"But—" Reader started.

Put up the paw. He stopped speaking. Indicated we needed to move out of the way of the Zamboni, which we did. Once out of the path, put the paw down. "May I mention that my very young and talented children are somewhere supposedly safe but without either one of their parents nearby to reassure them that everything's okay?"

"Shouldn't that reassurance come from you?" Jeff asked hopefully.

Gave him a look I ensured was icy, pun totally intended. "Are you insinuating that a woman's role is only to cower and comfort, as opposed to kick butt and that, as a man, you're unwilling to comfort our children and take a less active role because, frankly, your job demands it?"

"Ah, no. Never. Because I'm not stupid."

"No partnering this time, Missus Martini?" White asked, sounding disappointed.

"I think it's better form for this to go girl-on-girl, rather than us ganging up on her. I can guarantee there are still cameras rolling." The others nodded. Nice of them to see reason. "Speaking of which, someone find that cameraman, the new one with *Good Day USA!* who's also a traitor."

"We caught him already," Reader said. "Because we were doing things other than watching you practice for the ice dancing event at the next Olympics. He claimed to not know what was in his bag. We don't believe him."

"Why so tense, James? Too much caffeine?"

"You're planning to fight a cyborg with a broken hockey stick?" Jeff asked, presumably to stop us from bantering. Sad when your husband joined the haters.

"Nope. Rhee, if you would?"

She handed me her battle staff with a little bow. "I am honored you chose my weapon." Rahmi looked disappointed. There was a lot of that going on right now.

Heaved an internal sigh. There was always time to take a moment to teach the big lessons. "Let's remember what true honor is in these situations, girls."

"To ensure that your opponent is really most sincerely dead," they chorused cheerfully.

"That's what I like to hear!" The princesses beamed while the men all tried to hide their shuddering. Looked around. The Zamboni was "barreling" toward us. Had us move out of its way again. Took almost no effort to do so.

"Does she really think she's going to run us down in that?" Tim asked.

"I think she does, yeah. Now, get Jeff out through the player's locker room. If I need assistance, we have all the Pissed-Off Peregrines here, and the Poofs are always ready to Assemble. I'll call for help if I need it, I promise. Rahmi, take point along with Mister White, and don't assume that all the enemies are down, but also don't randomly attack someone. Follow Richard's lead."

Jeff, Reader, and Tim all looked like they wanted to know why they hadn't scored taking the point position, but they were all smart enough to keep quiet. Leaned up and gave Jeff a quick kiss. "Take care of the kids and keep the home fires burning."

He heaved a sigh. "Be careful, baby."

"Always, as you know."

"Never that I've ever seen." With that, Rahmi and White headed for the player's exit while Rhee took Jeff's arm and led him off the ice, Reader and Tim flanking them. They all had to go more slowly on the cleaned ice, but managed it without anyone going down.

Waited until they were off the ice to face the Zamboni. Yeah, nine miles an hour wasn't all that fast and, to top it off, Zambonis weren't all that maneuverable. Charmaine hadn't watched a lot of hockey, or else she hadn't paid attention, because she wasn't giving the Zamboni enough room to turn and was very soon going to run into a wall.

Beta Twelve battle staffs were a lot like a javelin-light saber combo. They responded best to women, and by now I'd used one many times. But I waited. Might as well recharge the human batteries, though I wasn't enraged now, just kind of weirdly amused.

Checked the upper levels. Mom and the others weren't up there anymore, which was fine. Looked up at the rigging. Was pretty sure Siler and Mossy were still at their sniper posts.

The music changed to Saliva's "She Can Sure Hide Crazy." About time we got some rock. Definitely helped me start to get revved up. Found myself bobbing to the beat and getting ready to fight.

"And we're back, folks," Johnny announced. "Interesting developments while we were on commercial break. A blonde woman has taken control of the Zamboni and appears to be trying to run down the First Lady with it."

"Which is pretty hard to do if the First Lady's mobile, which she is," Mitch shared. "Also, this woman is a terrible Zamboni driver."

"She should have asked the professional operator for help, Mitch, I totally agree."

Was fast losing any desire to meet Mitch and Johnny in person. However, they had a point, and sincerely hoped the Zamboni's official operator was safely in a honeycomb shelter, not dead somewhere in the arena. I put nothing past people who would send a ton of flying pucks at us at a charity event for a school.

Charmaine was nearing the next turn and, sure enough, she couldn't make it. She managed to stop before she hit the boards and protective glass, but just barely. How she'd managed to actually clean some of the ice was beyond me. Maybe she'd hit some levers or pushed some buttons in an attempt to make the thing go faster and it had worked out. Sort of.

"You might want to back that puppy up," I called to her.

As she tried to do so, noticed movement in the stands. Mister Joel Oliver, Bellie on his shoulder, and Dion were both sneaking down toward the ice. Oliver had what looked like a boom mic and Dion had a video camera, though not the one the traitor cameraman had been using—that one had gotten trashed ages ago.

Memory nudged. There was a question I wanted answered, and now was a good time to ask it, so that she'd stay focused on me and not notice Oliver and Dion. Bellie was amazingly silent, for which I was sure we were all grateful. Chose not to question how the bird had gotten in—she'd probably charmed the male security guards and they were now part of her fan club.

"So, Charmaine, how did you get your flunky onto the *Good Day USA!* crew?"

"Some of us have pull. I had one of my friends contact the production company as soon as I realized that one of the anchors was going to have their cameraman fired."

Nice to be right again. "You spent a lot of money to launch this attack."

She glared at me. "And it would have been worth it." She was still struggling with the Zamboni and still going nowhere.

"You suck at this, Charmaine. At evil plotting and Zamboni operation both."

Apparently that was all it took or Charmaine gave up easily. She leaped off the Zamboni as the music changed to "Livin' la Vida Loca" by Ricky Martin. And just like that we were back to Latin beats. Worked for me. Started to spin the battle staff as I slide-skated slowly toward her on the portion of cleaned ice nearest to me. Maybe cyborgs also fought to a syncopated beat.

"Why aren't you dead?" Charmaine shrieked at me.

Oliver and Dion were both on the ice. Oliver made the "we're rolling" motion. Had figured they were—why else would they be risking being down here with a crazed woman badly driving a Zamboni on the loose?

"I'm good at surviving."

"Well, not after tonight!" With that, she launched herself at me.

Well, she tried. Only she'd had to walk onto the slick ice and she was wearing high heels. Clearly this woman had never been to a sporting event in her life. She fell forward, which was not the way you wanted to fall on the ice.

"You done?" Waited for another attack from someone competent.

Was still waiting when Charmaine managed to slip and slide her way to the choppier ice and regain her footing, so to speak. "I . . . will . . . end . . . you!"

"Why? I mean, why do you hate me so much? I don't get it. I'm clear that you've hated me from Day One, I just don't actually understand why."

"Because you ruined everything!"

"That is my specialty, I'll give you that. What things in particular did you care about?"

"Zachary was going to be the Vice President! Then Marcia would have an accident and I'd leave Robert! And then Zachary would be President and I'd be the First Lady. You don't deserve to be in the White House! You're nothing but a common . . . a common . . ."

"Street rat?" Hey, I could channel *Aladdin* with the best of them. It was interesting to discover that Charmaine and Kramer had been plotting for a lot longer than we'd figured. Wondered if they'd planned to kill Gideon Cleary once they were all in office together, then gave myself the duh on this one. Of course they had. The question was—who else was supporting them?

"Yes! You went to some meaningless university. You've done nothing to deserve your position. You're just . . . just . . . just lucky!"

"Arizona State is the largest university in the country, and it's a great school that didn't put me into fifty years of debt. My husband and I actually care about more than ourselves, and we're where we are not because we want to be but because we actually do the jobs, instead of gloat about the positions and power. And, yeah, you're right. I *am* lucky."

As the music changed to "Right Behind You" by Brandon Flowers, Bellie screamed and I spun around to see Ansom Somerall and Talia Lee both leap the glass like the princesses had. Their expressions were odd—eyes wide, expressions slack. Likely meaning that the Shadow had asked the Kendroid to install a zombie switch in their heads.

Now the situation was a little dicier. I had a confirmed cyborg on one side and two people who were under someone else's control on the other. Somerall and Lee might not be cyborgs, but if their brains were controlled then they probably weren't going to feel pain and were going to have more strength because their brains were telling them that it was so.

Really didn't want to decapitate these people if I could help it. Not only was that a big negative for Jeff's approval rating, but the Cordell twins had just lost their father—she might suck, but Charmaine was the only parent they had. And while I had no love for Somerall or Lee, they weren't under their own control.

Could call in the Peregrines and Poofs like I'd said I would, but that would mean that they'd shred or eat these people on national television. My animals—all of them, be they domestic or extremely foreign—would be quarantined at best or killed most likely under the idea that they'd murdered "innocent people." I owned a pit bull—it wasn't hard to extrapolate the outcome if the Peregrines attacked or the Poofs went large and in charge.

Sent out a mental brainwave telling the animals to stay put, no matter what. Bruno wasn't happy with the order, but he agreed to abide by it. The Poofs sent me warm fuzzies. Bellie said too damn bad—she was ready for her close-up and I wasn't taking it away from her. Decided I'd live with that.

Defensive fighting for the win, then. They and Jeff's approval rating were all lucky that I'd just deactivated the glowing end of the staff as the three of them attacked me at once.

I'd studied kung fu for many years, and I was trained in staff. Kung fu used a lot of forms, all of which were practiced at slow speeds, but they were designed to teach you how to fight multiple opponents with the expectation that you'd be moving a lot faster in an actual fight.

There were specialized staff forms, and I started doing one of them—Tiger Sleeps in the Grass. Which sounded sweet and snuggly, but was actually a really nasty form focused on taking out your opponents' knees, groins, and temples. You hit them in a lot of other areas, too, but those were where the most debilitating hits went.

The form worked well, and I was executing it flawlessly—leaping to avoid hits here, slamming the staff against a head while I kicked out a knee there, ramming the butt of the staff into a stomach now, hitting a back with the length of the staff then, all while sincerely hoping my instructors were all watching this particular rank test—but my opponents weren't normal. It was creepy as hell to take out Somerall's knee and watch him keep going, leg dragging funny, just like he was a zombie. Zombie switch was definitely the right term.

Had no idea how to get out of this, because, short of me or someone else killing them, I was going to tire out a lot quicker than my opponents.

The music changed to "Bleed Into Your Mind" by The All-American Rejects, and I realized that Trevor had told me what to go for. Had no idea how to do it, though, and I needed to figure it out fast.

Bellie cawed her new name for me. "Floaty! Floaty! Floaty!" Sounded like she was cheering for me. I'd take it—currently needed all the support I could get.

Charmaine grimaced. "What *is* it with you and that damn bird?"

Always enjoyed when inspiration chose to show up. "Bellie, come to Floaty!"

CHAPTER 88

BELLIE CAWED JOYFULLY and swooped right over, avoiding my opponents' attempts to hit or grab her. She landed on my shoulder. "Bellie loves Floaty!"

"And Floaty's found a whole new appreciation for you, too, Bellie. Do Floaty a big favor—spend quality time with Charmaine over there. Just be sure she can't hurt Bellie. Floaty doesn't want Bellie to lose a single feather."

Bellie cooed, rubbed her head against mine, and lifted off. Screaming a bird battle cry instead of a word. It was, however, the same battle cry the Peregrines had used, with a slight modification— Bellie was aware that Charmaine was no one's son.

Charmaine screamed as Bellie aimed her talons at Charmaine's face. Despite being a cyborg, she literally had no fighting skills when it came to the bird, and instead of doing anything smart, just flailed at the parrot, which was great. Bellie was going to take her battle easily.

Now that Charmaine was occupied, had to figure out how to cause Somerall and Lee to overload. Didn't have a lot of ideas, but before I could put even a weak plan into action, the Zamboni moved backward. Kramer was at the wheel.

Whether he'd paid attention or was just luckier than Charmaine, he got it backed up and headed for us. He didn't look zombie-brained, but he didn't look sane, either. Then again, Charmaine had shared their plots with me and, therefore, the media.

Distraction wasn't good. Somerall and Lee grabbed my arms. Thought they were going to pull, but they didn't. They didn't move at all, other than to yank the staff away from me. Somerall was the one to do this, which was a relief. The staff might respond to Lee, but Somerall was unlikely to be able to activate it.

Kramer had the Zamboni cleaning the ice, just as Charmaine had. This was great for the rink, not so hot for anyone else, since a Zamboni's blades were scary big and sharp. If they could cut through ice, cutting through people was a piece of cake.

Kramer aimed for Oliver and Dion, who had to scramble off the ice to get to safety, Dion filming the whole way, Oliver keeping him moving. They didn't leave but stayed in the stands, out of Zamboni range.

Once they were run off, Kramer curved the Zamboni in the tightest turn it could make, which wasn't all that tight. However, it was effective—realized we were now right in the path of the Zamboni. And, despite my best efforts, couldn't get away from Somerall and Lee.

Charmaine and Bellie were still swirling around each other, and Charmaine, who hadn't taken off her high heels, slipped and fell. Right in the Zamboni's path.

"Bellie, get away from her!"

Bellie squawked and flew toward me. At the last moment she changed course and landed on the top of Somerall's head. He didn't move or even react, and neither did Lee, which was totally creepy, and also indicated they were being controlled by someone who was likely watching. My money was on the Shadow.

Meanwhile, Charmaine was still on the ground and the Zamboni was headed straight for her. "Charmaine, you need to get up!" Tried to pull away again, but I wasn't enraged, just kind of horrified.

She tried, but she was slipping and she was on a slick part of the ice. Kramer had the Zamboni at top speed for sure. "Zachary, what the hell are you doing?" I shouted. Maybe he didn't realize his girlfriend was on the ice in front of him. "You're going to run over Charmaine!"

He smiled at me, and it was a really awful smile—the kind of smile someone gives when their mind's snapped. Apparently Kramer wasn't great at all this evil plotting stuff either, though he was far better at Zamboni operation than Charmaine.

She was clawing her way on the ice, but wasn't moving nearly fast enough. The music changed to "My Old School" by Steely Dan, and the chorus said how the Donald Fagen was never going back to his old school. Which, under these particular circumstances, boded in a big way. "Let me go, you mindless automatons! He's going to kill her!"

"And you'll be next!" Kramer shouted. He followed that up with a maniacal laugh. Yeah, he was definitely around the bend.

The Zamboni was almost on Charmaine when Somerall and Lee both jerked. "What's going on?" Lee asked.

"What's on my head?" was Somerall's question. "And why do I have this stick?" Then the pain of all I'd managed to do to him hit and he screamed. Lee started screaming, too.

Yanked my arms away as Somerall and Lee both fell and they let go. "That stick is mine." Grabbed it and ran toward Charmaine. "Hang on, I'm coming!"

But the Zamboni got to her first.

While Lee and Somerall screamed, now in horror as well as pain, and Kramer shared his maniacal laugh again, changed my trajectory fast, which caused me to slip, but at least I was slipping in a direction other than toward the Zamboni.

Bellie zoomed over and grabbed the end of the staff in her talons, which helped me stay upright. "All is forgiven, Bellie. You really are amazing."

"Bellie wants to leave," she said as she returned to my shoulder. "Floaty needs to get to Mister! Bellie wants Mister!"

"Good plan, that parrot." Heaved a sigh. "Only we have to save the two part-time zombies." Turned to go back, only Somerall and Lee were both silent. Not run over, thank God, but still, silent and unmoving.

Kramer remained at the Zamboni's controls, meaning he could still hurt people. He was sort of slumped over, and the machine wasn't moving, but that might only mean that he was going to try to back up over Charmaine's remains. There was a horrible stain of blood under the machine that was spreading out over the ice. Didn't want to get closer but felt that I had to.

Only someone grabbed my free hand and pulled me to him. "We're getting you out of here, baby," Jeff said, sounding as horrified as I felt. "It's over."

"Um, how is it over?" I asked while Bellie cawed out Jeff's name, but quietly. She was horrified, too. Took her off my shoulder and cuddled her while Jeff stroked her head. "And how did you get here? You were supposed to be staying safe."

"They're all dead. Kramer, too." Jeff got us off the ice as Mom, the K-9 squad, and a huge number of security personnel moved onto it. "I imagine we'll discover it was aneurisms. And I had Christopher help me. He really wanted to be useful and hadn't been, so he held off everyone else while I got out of the room they had me locked into for my supposed safety."

"I'm amazed anyone willingly stays on our security details for more than a day. Real aneurisms or ones triggered from afar?"

"Not sure."

Pondered this as we reached Oliver, and Bellie got her reunion, lots of treats, and even more petting. Even so, she wasn't preening so much as huddling. Could not blame her. "I think that Ansom and Talia were triggered, either via a switch or just because their zombie switch was turned off at the right time."

"What about Kramer?" Jeff asked. No one had to ask how Charmaine had died. Cyborgs couldn't survive a Zamboni, which was possibly good knowledge for the future.

"Could go either way. He was literally barking mad by the time he ran her over. A natural aneurism wouldn't be out of the question."

"We may never know," Oliver said. "But the world saw this, so you need to be prepared."

"Yeah, maybe they won't want to make Code Name: First Lady anymore."

"Don't sound so hopeful," Oliver said, "because you're sure to be disappointed. I meant that you need to be prepared for more movie pressure and then some."

"Ugh."

We were retrieved by Alpha Team and taken to the rest of our security forces, then to our children. The kids were happy to see us, but seemed reasonably okay and not horrified at all. Hoped this meant that they hadn't seen or figured out what had gone on, or that ACE had kept it from them.

Dad looked shaken. "The adults know some of what went on," he told us quietly as he gave me a big hug. "I'm relieved you're alright, kitten."

"Me, too, Dad."

Naturally the *Good Day USA!* team was with Oliver and Dion now and they were all interviewing people, including Cologne. As Oliver had predicted, he was talking about how great Code Name: First Lady was going to be.

"Can we go home? I have no idea what's happened to all the money and I just don't care."

"Mister Gadhavi handled it," Lorraine said. "None of this threw him."

"At all," Claudia added. "He's really kind of cool."

"And he's escorted Missus Paster and the money," Serene added. "Airborne went with them."

"As did Mossad," Tim said. "So, no worries."

"I wasn't worried. He's not a cyborg, an android, or a Bot. I'm all about the Mister Ali Baba Gadhavi Experience."

Because we weren't on Alpha Team or part of the P.T.C.U., CIA, FBI, or Homeland Security, we got to go home. Because we were tired as hell, we got to take a floater gate. Phoebe gave me my phone back and Lizzie handed me my purse, so I was able to put in my earbuds and listen to music on the way through the gate. Hit random play then picked Charlie up. Was treated to "Upside Down" by Jack Johnson.

I was still laughing on the way upstairs to our rooms.

CHAPTER 89

NATURALLY, WE DIDN'T get a lot of downtime after all of this, though Raj and Colette were able to deflect much of the press and Jeff was able to deflect my mother and Congress. For a full thirty-six hours, which was amazing, really.

The kids had indeed been sheltered from most of what had gone on. The older ones found out, of course, because the news was a wall of images from the event, and ESPN, who'd had the full footage feed thanks to Mitch and Johnny, was riding high. I was invited to do guest commentary any time I wanted, which was what I figured would be the only positive to come out of all of this.

So, the older kids, being teenagers, had spent Sunday "being totes horrified and grossed out" and hanging out, bonding with and comforting Clinton over his father's death. Considering what the man had just done, while he was upset, Clinton wasn't nearly as messed up as he might have been a month prior. I did get a shout-out as being parkour, so there was that for the win column, too.

The little kids were blithely clueless about what had really happened, and I sent a mental thank you to ACE for that, because there was no way Jamie could have or would have missed it all otherwise, and I had to figure the other hybrid kids wouldn't have missed it, either.

Thankfully, while Edgar was still in the Washington Zoo's hospital, he was doing great and would be home soon. The kids were looking forward to a zoo trip to visit him once any adult was up to it, which was not going to be in the next few days.

The adults were in various stages of collapse, so Sunday was spent trying to get some rest and keeping an eye on Marcia, who we'd had stay at the Embassy with her kids, just in case. She appeared to be vacillating between Mary Tyler Moore ready to take on the world and Kim Kardashian ugly crying. Couldn't blame her for it. It had been a tough time for everyone, but she'd had to deal with the most personal crap. And finding out your husband had been planning to kill you for years was also a reason for hysterics and Atta Girl Spunk at the same time.

Somehow American Centaurion had managed to get the Capitals rink back into shape before their season opener. We all watched the game on TV, so the kids did get to see some hockey. Both teams played great, and the Chupacabras won in overtime, which was also nice. Was relieved that all the crap that had gone on hadn't negatively affected all of them.

Now it was Monday, the kids were in school with lots of extra Field and Secret Service agents, and we were in the OSR with Alpha Team and some other key people, my mother included. But not the full Cabinet or other political allies. Just in case.

"I think this was all the Shadow's doing," I said as I finished my portion of the Fundraiser Fiasco Recap. Had my phone out and was paying attention to it, because I fully expected a call from the Shadow, from Trevor, or from Sidwell, asking us remove our dangerous presence from their heretofore-calm institution of learning.

"Why so?" Gower asked. "She called to warn you."

"I think Manfred was mostly right—I think she called to see what we'd do. I also think she was cleaning house. And that means we need to track down Evan the Limo Driver and Marion Villanova."

"Why?" Reader asked.

"Because they're loose ends. If the Shadow's getting rid of people who she feels are past their sell-by date, or who have information she doesn't want us getting, I think she's going to kill them or arrange for them to be killed like on game night. That means that Evan and Villanova are at risk. They haven't worked for us and I'm sure they've worked against us, but they don't deserve to be run over by a Zamboni, either."

Everyone grudgingly agreed that finding those two people was probably in all our best interests.

"What about Marcia?" Mom asked. "What do we think she does or doesn't know?"

"Frankly, though I sound like a Mean Girl for asking it, could Marcia be the Shadow?"

Nathalie and Vance both shook their heads. "She was sitting with us, between us, at the hockey game when Charles said you had your call with the Shadow," Nathalie said. "She never left her seat, and she only spoke to buy treats for her children and discuss how much money she hoped the game would raise."

"And how much she hoped you weren't playing her and actually liked her," Vance added.

"Really?"

"Really. I had a long talk with her after Zachary dumped her at their fundraiser," Vance said. "And I spent time with her yesterday as well. She's shocked that you're being nice to her and is afraid it's all an act. I know it isn't, and reassured her, but she may need to hear it from you."

"Noted. But then Mom's question is even more key."

"Right. She knows Evan, of course, and Marion. She hasn't seen Evan since she moved to the Cairo, and she said she hasn't seen Villanova since she was forced to give Zachary her diamonds in order to 'get a better present later' which, by the way, she never got. She seemed genuinely shocked that he was involved with Fem-Bots."

"We've done extensive background checks," Chuckie said. "Chernobog agrees with what Vance has said. I think we should still keep an eye on her, but that will be relatively easy, since she's on our floor."

"Which means we have to guard her, because she's probably also a loose end."

Vance nodded. "She is. Zachary's estate is in flux, so she's also looking for a job. Prince Wasim's generosity can only last so long."

"Oh, I imagine it can last as long as we request it to. And before I forget, we need to keep an eye out, because we could have two rogue Kitty-Bots on the loose." Or they were with the Kendroid. But now wasn't the time to figure that out. "But, going back to the matter at hand, I agree that Marcia needs to be a contributing member of society. Have no idea what job she's qualified for, though."

"Secretary of Education," Nathalie said. "And yes, I'm serious."

"Come again?" I was clearly asking for the room.

"She has a master's degree in early childhood education, she's a Senator's wife, so she understands how this town works, and after all that's happened, she's definitely pro-alien, pro-Jeff, and particularly pro-you, Kitty." Nathalie smiled. "Remember, I was her close friend when I first arrived in D.C. I've spent time with her since their split—she's told me more than once that she regretted following Abner's lead in class and then listening to her husband about hating all of you. As you know, people can change."

"Yeah, they can. And won't Missus Darcy Lockwood be all pleased that her graduates are all working in the government, even though we were all supposed to just hang out and look good."

Mom grunted. "I still can't stand that woman and yes, she's actually had the nerve to tell me that Jeff only made it into the White House because you were in her class."

"Can I kill her?"

"Just cut her dead again the next time you see her," Vance suggested. "That's a far more lingering injury to Darcy."

"I knew I hired you for good reasons."

"Back to Nathalie's suggestion," Jeff said, presumably to stop the bantering. "We already have a Secretary of Education."

"But he wants to be an Ambassador," Nathalie said. "He's tired of the grind of the Cabinet, he feels that anyone in your Cabinet is probably a target for your enemies, and he just wants to go to some little country and be the nice man who helps out."

"How do you know all this?" Jeff asked, sounding shocked and impressed.

She shrugged. "People tell me things."

Elaine Armstrong nodded. "I agree with Nathalie. Howie just wants to be moved in a way that doesn't feel like he's deserting you. He respects you, Jeff. He's just tired."

"I get it," Jeff said, running his hand through his hair. "I'm tired, too."

"And you've been at this for far shorter a time," Elaine pointed out gently. "Let him go, put Marcia in."

"She's actually qualified?" Jeff asked, sounding uncertain. "I'm all for putting in our friends when they're qualified, and I can stand behind that. But to give someone a Cabinet post just because we think they're our friend now and they need a job seems reckless at best."

Chuckie's turn to snort. He was looking at his phone. "Stop worrying. Chernobog just shared Marcia's full history with me. She lied to Nathalie."

"About what?" Nathalie sounded shocked and pissed.

"She doesn't have just a master's. She has a PhD in education. She met Kramer when she interviewed him for her thesis, since he was her state senator. He apparently felt that it would make her look better than him if she used the title of doctor, so she didn't, because he painted the big 'we're going to the White House, baby' picture and she bought it."

"Dude, seriously? Why the hell would she buy that line of crap?"

Chuckie looked up at me with a wry smile. "Not everyone was raised by your parents, Kitty, or has your sense of self and self-worth. Some people believe what they're told, even if, deep down, they know it's wrong or goes against their better interests."

"In that case," Elaine said briskly, "I believe the appointment would make sense."

"I agree," Chuckie said, "because her thesis was on how to improve the public school system to bring it up to private school standards."

Jeff heaved a sigh. "I'm sold. If she wants it."

"She'll have to have her kids in daycare of some kind," Nathalie pointed out. "And she's been an involved parent at their school—that's one thing I don't believe she'll want to give up."

"Let's call her in and see," Elaine suggested.

Nathalie sent a text. "She's gating over from the Embassy right now. Should be here momentarily."

My phone rang. Mrs. Paster's number. Heaved my own sigh. "Hang on. Our issues with the school may be solving themselves, even though we won't like the outcome." Got up and left the room as I answered—didn't feel like sharing this call with the others. "Hello, Missus Paster."

"Madam First Lady, I hope I didn't catch you at a bad time."

"Oh, no, this is fine. What can I do for you?"

"Well, I have you on speakerphone. The active members of our PTA are with me."

Fantastic. Well, better to get it over with now. "Hey everyone. What's up?"

Someone cleared their throat. "Ah, we've discussed it and taken a vote." Had no idea who the woman speaking was, but that she was taking Charmaine's spot was a good bet.

"Okay. On what?" Figured I knew. Marcia arrived. Grabbed her and held her up. We both might as well hear what was going to happen, since I had to assume her kids were now counting as "mine" and, therefore, if the school was booting us, they were booting the Kramer kids, too. "Hang on, Marcia Kramer is with me, putting this on speaker."

"What's going on?" Marcia asked softly.

"On with Missus Paster and the PTA," I whispered back.

Her shoulders slumped. "Oh."

"Yeah." Put the call on speaker and my arm around her shoulders. "Go ahead."

"In light of recent events," the person whose voice I didn't recognize said, "we have a request to make of you, Madam First Lady."

"Sure. What?" Wasn't going to fight it. The Intergalactic School was great and would be just fine. Other parents were sending their kids thousands of miles away daily, why not us?

"Before you say anything," Marcia interjected, "I just want to assure you that everything that went wrong at my fundraiser and at the hockey game were my or my late husband's fault. Kitty had nothing to do with the failures, that was all on me."

"Beg to differ. I'm more than willing to blame Charmaine, but that's neither here nor there." Hugged Marcia. "But I appreciate the effort," I said quietly.

"We agree with you, Madam First Lady," the same voice I didn't know said. "We'd like to ask you to become the President of the Sidwell Friends School Parent Teacher Association."

Had to let that sit on the air for a moment. "Um, excuse me?"

"Your fundraisers have brought in more money in less than a month than anything we've done for a full year," a different voice shared. "Yours and Missus Kramer's events were, from a financial standpoint, raging successes."

Marcia perked up. "You should say yes," she whispered. "You'll be great at it, and your children will truly benefit."

"So, you're all in agreement with this idea?" I asked.

"Yes," Missus Paster said. "What went on at the three fundraisers you and Missus Kramer handled wasn't your fault. As you said, clearly Charmaine was around the bend and trying to discredit both of you. That you both held up so admirably was impressive."

Considered this. "You know, that's all great. But I'm too busy to do the job. The person I'm going to suggest is about to be too busy also, but I think that, if you ask her really nicely, she might say yes. Marcia Kramer is far more appropriate to be the President of the PTA than I am. She's had children in your school for several years, and she put together a swanky fundraising party in a day without anyone's help. I realize that getting the FLO-TUS as the President of the PTA sounds grand, but getting the likely next Secretary of Education to head it up has to be a feather in the school's cap, too, doesn't it?"

Marcia stared at me. "What?"

Hit the mute button. "Surprise. That's why you're being called into the meeting I just stepped out of. We've discovered that you put your hopes and dreams by the wayside for a man who didn't deserve you or the sacrifices you made for his career. So, want the career you might have had already back?"

She continued to stare at me. Then she burst into tears, flung her arms around my neck, and sobbed. Meanwhile, the people on the phone were excitedly sharing that the Secretary of Education would be more than super as the new PTA Prez and asking if Marcia would be willing.

"Nathalie's the one who suggested it. The rest of us just agreed. Pull it together and remember this rule—never, ever let this group see you sweat."

Marcia let go, took a couple of deep, gasping breaths, and nodded. Took my phone off mute. "I'll be happy to consider it," she said, sounding fairly collected. "However, I do have to say that my children, the President, and the running of this country will come first."

"As it should," Mrs. Paster said. "Madam First Lady, can we convince you to at least remain active in the PTA?"

"Well, you know, since one of my BFFs is going to be the President of the organization, I'm sure I'll be happy to help out as I can." Marcia's mouth dropped. Closed it gently. "Will that be all? We're about to make several positional changes, including a Cabinet appointment. Spoiler alert. Also, please don't share this with the press. You can say you were there after the official announcements go out. And, trust me, I have people watching."

"Yes, we'll be the souls of discretion and thank you for your time and assistance," Mrs. Paster said. "We look forward to a new era of the PTA."

"So do we. Believe me, so do we. And we guarantee that the new era begins now."

CHAPTER 90

HUNG UP AND MARCIA SPOKE. "I'm one of your BFFs?"

"Babe, look. I've forgiven literally everyone I interacted with from the Washington Wife class who's still alive. You were the last holdout. Having gotten to know you and seen what your stepson was willing to give up when he chose you over his father, I think it's safe to say that you're going to fit in with our new world order. So, yeah, welcome to the team and welcome to no longer having to hide that you're smart."

She heaved a huge sigh. "Oh, God, that will feel so . . . good."

"Yeah, it will. Get all the crying done now, though—there are a lot of men in that room and you know how us crying makes them feel all uncomfortable and crap."

She laughed and we headed for the nearest bathroom. Marcia cleaned herself up, then we headed back to the OSR. Was glad I'd given her the heads-up, because she managed to be pretty professional and only got teary a couple of times. Hey, it had been a hard month for her.

Jeff had taken care of the Ambassador stuff—Howie was heading to Bahrain, which was a cushy post thanks to our relationship with King Raheem—and they were onto other things I was only mildly interested in when I got a text. Not from the Shadow or the Tinkerer, but from Siler.

Excused myself and left the room again, this time going to the Rose Garden, where no one happened to be. Well, no one other than Siler. He was sniffing roses when I got there. "What's up?"

He shot me a smile, then went back to the roses. "I figured we should talk. About music."

"Can you? I mean that seriously. The only two people I know for sure who know—the three of us can barely discuss it with each other, let alone others."

"I can, as long as we're talking about it as music."

"So, when were you able to, um, learn to DJ?"

"Always. Someone was always there."

"That's ACE. I mean, most likely. A voice guiding you?"

"Yes."

"ACE helped all the supertalented A-Cs. I guess it never occurred to me to ask him if you were his first. And he never mentioned you."

"He . . . understands why I needed to hide. He knows I'm not hiding anymore. At least, not from you." Siler chuckled. "You're his favorite. He was so pleased when I started working with you. I just felt this massive . . . relief. It's not the only reason why I'll always be with you and on your side, but it's a big one."

"Good to know. I'll always be on your side and with you, too. But . . ."

"But, yes, I know that ACE is not the same . . . entity as the DJ. I noticed him after I joined up with you."

"How so?"

"You mean besides the Poofs, that you've dealt with super-consciousnesses from across the galaxy, and so forth?"

"Yeah." So he'd noted that the Poofs were extra-special. Well, he did have three of them, these days, since he'd inherited the Dingo's and Surly Vic's. Assassins had to be observant, after all, and Siler had that whole invisibility thing going.

He stopped looking at the roses and turned to me with a grin. "There isn't any actual Operations Team. Everyone seems to think there is, but there isn't. You were yanked into another universe, dragged off to another planet, and it just occurred to me that simply because we're told something is so, doesn't mean that it is."

"There are other things, too."

"Like the fact that when you're in a danger situation you're always listening to music via your phone or your iPod, and when you're not able to do that, somehow every song is something that can spark you into figuring out what's going on? That music shows up in places it shouldn't, but always when you need it?"

"Um yeah, like that."

"And the secret entrance in the desert outside of Dulce which should take you to the second floor but actually takes you to the fifteenth? Yeah, noticed that, too, the first time Buchanan trusted me enough to show me all of Dulce's weaknesses."

"Does Malcolm know, too?"

He shook his head. "He's human. They're easier to fool. And I think the DJ has more . . . trouble hiding from me than most."

"Because of the things Trevor says he knows about you?"

"Yeah. That's my guess."

"Well, don't sell Malcolm short. I mean, I'm human and I figured it out. Well, not right away, but eventually."

"You're special, Kitty. I know you don't really see it, not like others do. But you're special. It's why you've saved my people and this world so many times."

"So you're calling the A-Cs yours now? Fully?"

"Yeah." He laughed again. "They've protected me, they've protected Lizzie. There's no people she'll be safer with than you and Jeff. She was introduced at the fundraiser by the Valentino kids as a second cousin twice removed."

"I have no idea how all that stuff works, and it's been explained to me more than once."

"Yeah, and the intricacies don't matter. It's the acceptance. She's in. She's part of your family, part of the A-C community. She's taken care of now."

"She still needs you. You're her father and have been for years now. Quick Girl doesn't want Mister Dash to go away."

"Good. Because it's because of Quick Girl and Megalomaniac Girl that I'm staying. Mister Dash has found where he belongs."

Didn't think about it, just hugged him. He hugged me back. "I'm really glad I didn't let Prince eat you. Or let you bleed out."

He laughed. "I'm really glad your husband isn't seeing this."

"He's feeling it, I'm sure. Besides, he hasn't had a good jealousy rampage in forever." We ended our hug and Siler nodded his head toward the path around the roses. We wandered. "You know, I never get to spend time in this garden. This could be the first relaxed minute I've had in it."

"Relaxation is good. But vigilance is better."

"You think another attack is coming?"

"Honestly? Yes. But maybe not for a while."

"How so? They've been nonstop for what seems like months."

"True. And you've wiped out everyone who's been coming at you. The ones left—the Shadow and the Tinkerer—they're smarter, more willing to wait and play the quiet game."

"Cliff played the long game."

"Cliff was insane. I don't think either the Shadow or the Tinkerer are. I'll be watching Marcia Kramer—she could be the Shadow."

Told him what I'd learned from Nathalie and Vance. "So it doesn't seem like she could be the Shadow or even really knows who the Shadow is."

"Maybe she's not. Maybe they're all in it together. Maybe Elaine Armstrong is the Shadow."

"Um, I can't live my life by suspecting everyone of being out to get us."

"I know. But I can. I've spent my entire existence that way. So let me, and Wruck, and Buchanan all handle that. We're not trusting at all, so you get to be."

"Chuckie doesn't trust anyone, either."

"Reynolds trusts far more people than he wants to admit. Far more than the three of us do, possibly combined."

"Really?"

"We all trust you. Buchanan trusts your mother. I trust Lizzie. Wruck trusts, well, really only you. We all trust each other. And that's it. Period. End of trust story. Anyone else we all trusted fully is dead and gone."

"Wow. Team Tough Guys keepin' it suspicious?"

Siler laughed. "Exactly. So, you can relax, because we'll be doing the digging and the hunting."

"The Hunt for Red Shadow?"

"Something like that, yeah."

"Works for me."

We finished our stroll and Siler escorted me back inside. Then he went back to the Embassy to have a meeting with Christopher and Doreen about staffing and room assignments.

I headed back to the OSR, but was intercepted by Jeff. "We're on a lunch break and I figured, why not actually go out for lunch with my wife?" He handed me my purse. "You left this in the conference room."

"Sounds good on lunch, and thanks on my purse, I guess I didn't expect an attack for the first time in weeks. Who else is coming with?"

"No one. Not any of our friends, family, colleagues, or security. Not even the kids."

"Wow, where are we going? Our bedroom?"

Jeff's eyes smoldered and he got the Jungle Cat About To Eat

Me look on his face. "After we eat, yes." He pulled me to him and kissed me. I was ready to skip lunch by the time we were done.

"Seriously," I asked as he ended our kiss. "Where are we going? Do I have to dress up?" I was in jeans, an Aerosmith shirt, and Converse. In other words, I was comfy.

He grinned. "Hell no. We're going to your favorite chicken and waffles place in Pueblo Caliente. It's breakfast time there, but they serve the same things for lunch, and we haven't been there in a really long time. And yes, you can bring back as much takeout as you want and yes, we can have it with the kids for dinner, regardless of whatever Chef's planned."

My stomach growled happily. "You really are the most romantic man in the world, aren't you?"

"I have to live up to my wife, baby." Then he put his arm around my shoulders and I put mine around his waist and we headed off to a delicious little hole-in-the-wall restaurant like normal people.

It's the little things you cherish, after all.

Read on for a sneak preview of
the sixteenth novel in the *Alien* series
from Gini Koch:

ALIENS ABROAD

"HELP ME."

"Huh?" I'd been having a really great dream, where
my husband and I were in Cabo San Lucas without our kids, our
family or friends, anyone political, any press, any aliens from
any planet, or any paparazzi. We were having sex on the beach,
and it was great, and no one was bothering us. At least until
someone asked for help.

"Help me. I'm an alien and need your assistance."

Well, that left a wide-open field. My husband was an alien—
an A-C from Alpha Four in the Alpha Centaurion system. His
entire huge extended family had been exiled to Earth before Jeff
was born and they'd been here for decades. All of them were
American citizens, though A-Cs were all over the world. But the
voice didn't sound like any of them.

Recent events had brought more aliens to Earth, though. We
had representatives from every inhabited world in the Alpha
Centauri system—and there were a lot of those—here, as well
as residents from other solar systems both nearby, galactically
speaking, or as far away as the Galactic Core.

They, too, were scattered all over Earth and the Solaris
system—alien relocation for immigrating aliens having been
going smoothly, as had terraforming of some of the planets and
various-races-forming of the others—because we had all those

extra planets and moons we weren't using and most of these aliens were refugees from some really horrible galactic wars. So Earth was no longer a lonely inhabited planet of one with a single race of aliens living on it in secret, but part of a bustling, expanding planetary system with many different types of aliens hanging out. And more coming by to visit or apply to move in every day. Though not, normally, via my dreams. And the voice didn't sound like any of them, either.

That all of this New Age of Intergalactic Harmony stuff had happened in less than a year and a half since Operation Fundraiser had ended in a truly dramatic Zamboni drag race, so to speak, had much more to do with all the aliens from various solar systems helping out than that Earth had suddenly leapt into the far *Star Trek* future on our own. We were still number one with a bullet when it came to being nasty and warlike, but we were definitely reaping the benefits of having made some swell new friends. I just wasn't in the dream mood to make another new one.

"I really can't help you. We have an office of Intergalactic Immigration you might want to apply to. I'm sure they'll be as excited to talk to you in their dreams as I am."

"No. I'm an alien to you but like you."

Nice, but the speaker wasn't saying anything exciting because I'd discovered that people—be they the best-looking humanoids around who happened to have two hearts, super-strength, and hyperspeed, or be they giant humanoid slugs or honeybees, or be they ethereal cloud-like manta rays or gigantic Cthulhu Monsters from Space, or be they anything and everything in between— were basically people, no matter where they were from, what they looked like, what planet they called home, or who or what they considered God.

"I doubt it. And I don't care." My dream was getting hazy. Did my best to concentrate on Jeff and the beach and the sex.

"Help me. You're my only hope." The voice sounded female, maybe, and alien, most likely. Most humans couldn't get that kind of reverberation going without the use of electronic equipment. And, just like the voice, the reverberation wasn't familiar so, again, not an alien race I'd already met, at least, unlikely. My dreams, they were really the best.

"Um, I wasn't really trying to add Princess Leia or Obi-Wan Kenobi into this dream. If that's okay and all that. Especially not Old Obi-Wan. Young Obi-Wan, yeah, maybe."

I could, quite frankly, find it in my libido to add Ewan Mc-Gregor into many things. Then again, Jeff was the strongest empath in, most likely, the galaxy—because A-Cs also had a variety of psychic talents that showed up pretty often—and he was also easily the most jealous man in it, too, under the right circumstances. Me fantasizing about Ewan McGregor was likely to spark some jealousy, especially since I'd seen *The Pillow Book*. Twice. And the second time was not for the story.

Not that Jeff had anything to worry about. He was the classic—tall, with dark brown wavy hair, dreamy light brown eyes, built like a brick house, and definitely the handsomest man in the universe. And that wasn't me being biased. Well, maybe biased, but only a little. The A-Cs were, to human eyes, the most beautiful things around. They came in all shapes, sizes, colors, and builds, just like humans did, as long as you included "hard-body" in their definition.

Humans lucked out, though. In addition to the fact that A-Cs and humans could and did create healthy hybrid offspring—with the external favoring the human parent and the internal favoring the A-C—the A-Cs thought humans were great. Well, most of them thought that.

The female A-Cs, whom I called the Dazzlers, at least to myself, were sapiosexual, didn't care what someone looked like, and they felt that humans had more brains and brain capacity than their own people did. I didn't necessarily agree with this theory, though I got where it came from—I'd never met a dumb Dazzler because even those considered idiots by their peers were genius level for humans, but I had hit a couple of not-so-bright male A-Cs, though they were few and far between.

The male A-Cs just liked people who made them feel smarter than the female A-Cs did, meaning humans were really scoring the excellent mating opportunities. And I wasn't going to argue with the situation either, since, by now, we had a lot of really happy humans married to equally happy A-Cs and I was all for couples' harmony. Particularly my own.

"I need the greatest warrior in the galaxy." Despite my focus on Jeff's hotness, the beach was starting to fade away. Did my best to hold onto the dream and, if not the dream, at least Jeff's naked body.

"And you're talking to me why?"

"Because your reputation precedes you."

Things had been relatively quiet on the Political Crap front, even quieter on the Evil Megalomaniac front, and the Marauding Aliens front had been blissfully silent. Apparently this last one was silent no longer, though.

Visions of Jeff's naked body washed fully away. I was now officially bitter. "Super. As dreams go, this one stinks. Just sayin'."

"My mind has traveled through the DreamScape in order to find you."

"Whee. I think you got lost somewhere along the way."

Really wondered if I'd eaten something that was causing this kind of bizarreness. But we hadn't had a State Dinner, I hadn't snuck in a huge amount of junk food, and the White House chef wasn't prone to making anything bad. Chef was far healthier in what he prepared than I'd ever been. And I'd only had two of his chocolate mousses for dessert, so it couldn't be that.

"No, I've worked my way through the DreamScape to find you. I need your help."

This dream wasn't going away. Tried to wake up. Failed. "So you said. And I ask again—why me? And what the heck is the DreamScape, anyway? That sounds like an old Dennis Quaid movie." I could find it in my libido to add in Dennis Quaid too. Dennis Quaid, Ewan McGregor, and Jeff would be a combination I could enjoy for a really long time. In another dream. One not being constantly interrupted by an alien I didn't know and didn't want to know. Had to wonder if other people had dreams like this. Probably not. I was "lucky" this way.

"Why you is because you always manage to win. The DreamScape is the realm that connects us all. And I have no idea who Dennis Quaid is or what a movie is, either."

"Uh huh, right, pull the other one. It has not interested bells on and all that jazz."

"The fate of my world depends upon you."

"Doubt it. Sincerely doubt it. I officially want to tell myself that this kind of dream is not on my particular Netflix queue and I don't want anything similar to it suggested, either."

"I don't understand you."

"So few ever do. Look, good luck with whatever you've got going on wherever in my subconscious you happen to be. But I'm not your girl."

"I'm not in your subconscious."

"But that's what my wily subconscious would say, now, wouldn't it?"

"I don't know." The voice sounded desperate. "My name is Ixtha. Please help me."

"Well, that's different. What's my name, then?" I mean, my subconscious certainly knew my name.

"I only know you as the Warrior Queen."

"Right. Not as the First Lady of the United States, not as the Queen Regent of Earth for the Annocusal Royal Family of Alpha Four, and not as Earth's Galactic Representative to the Galactic Council. But as the Warrior Queen. Gotcha. I think you were looking for Queen Renata of the Free Women of Beta Twelve."

"I have no idea who those people are or what those titles mean." Ixtha sounded serious. Which was odd, because my subconscious certainly knew all the various and current roles I was stuck doing whether I liked them or not.

Figured I'd try one last title. "What about Shealla? Do you know her?" That was my God Name on Beta Eight.

"Yes! Shealla is the Warrior Queen. You are Shealla?"

"If you already knew, why'd you ask?"

"I don't . . . what? What do you mean? I don't understand you."

"I thought you said you didn't know my name." Well, my Beta Eight name, but still it was a name I answered to. Though Shealla was supposed to be the Queen of the Gods and the Giver of Names, not the Warrior Queen. "Then again, my wily subconscious also knows that name."

"I am not in your subconscious! I am in your dream, via the DreamScape. I have searched for you for so long, Shealla. I need your help, my people need your help. You who have saved so many, why will you not hear my plea?"

"Because I think you're a figment of my vivid and overworked imagination. Though Ixtha is a cool name I haven't heard before, so go team in terms of my creativity."

"I am real, Shealla. As real as you are."

"Yeah? Figure out what my real name is, and then visit me again. Or don't. Really, you disturbed a great dream and I'm still bitter about it."

"The longer we speak the better my connection is to you and I can search your mind for clues. Please give me that time, Shealla. I will do as you ask, discover your true name, and then you will help me and my people, yes?"

"Sure, I guess. Why not, right?" Was going to add a really witty and sarcastic comment, but the sounds of the Red Hot Chili

Peppers' "Universally Speaking" came on and thankfully dragged me into consciousness and away from the "DreamScape".

The little joys of greeting the dawn, especially after this Dream O' Weirdness, were without number.

Normally I hated dragging up as early as we now had to since Jeff had become the President, but never had I been so happy to wake up. Let the music play and rolled over to see if Jeff was still in bed.

He was not and I was displeased. Chose to blame my weird dream and got up. Checked for him in the bathroom. Not there. Trotted back and checked Mr. Clock in case I'd somehow slept through hours' worth of musical alarm. I had not.

Went to the living room. Nada. Was about to just give up and take a shower when the main door of our Presidential Suite opened and Jeff came in with a big breakfast tray. He grinned at my expression. "I didn't mean to worry you, Kitty. I just thought it would be nice to have breakfast in bed today."

Ran through the potential reasons. Jeff was far more romantic than I was, and there might be something important I was missing. All our family birthdays were past—mine was the last one for several months, and it had been yesterday and we'd celebrated by going to Paris as a family—and I couldn't come up with anything else.

"Um, great!"

Jeff laughed. "I'm giving the State of the Union address today while we christen the *Distant Voyager* and I just want to be alone with my wife before I have to do that."

"Oh! Right you are." Felt bad. Jeff was in the middle of his accidental term as President and he took the job seriously. He'd been working with his team for weeks on his speech, meaning I should have remembered. Then again, turning thirty-five had felt very milestone-ish for me and Paris was awesome, and generally forgetting stuff like this was very par for my course.

"Not a problem, baby, and don't feel bad. Just eat with me and be my wife."

"That I can do!"

We snuggled back into bed and had a lovely breakfast of eggs scrambled with lox, croissants, excellent coffee with cream, and fresh fruit. We talked about Paris and how great it had been to be there. We weren't jet-lagged because we'd used gates—A-C technology that looked like airport metal detectors but were capable of moving you across the street or across the world in one step. They could move you to other planets, too, but we didn't use them for that a lot and, now, we might not have to use them for that ever again.

"I'm glad we were able to celebrate your birthday before the address," Jeff said as we finished up.

"Me too. And I'm sorry I forgot. Earth's first manned, long-distance spaceship with true warp capability is a huge deal. I'm so glad it's happened during your Presidency."

Jeff smiled. "Me, too, baby. It's one of the few truly good things that's happened that didn't have something horrible attached to it."

"Well, I think that most of the aliens now living in our solar system would disagree with you, but I know what you mean."

Considered telling Jeff about my weird dream, but didn't want to spoil his mood or slip up and mention my fantasizing about Ewan and Dennis. Besides, he'd just tell me that two chocolate mousses were too many and since I knew he was wrong and I was going to eat two, minimum, any time Chef made his mousse, what was the point of fighting?

We showered together, which was one of my favorite things to do, ever, because we had great sexytimes in the shower and today was no exception. Once climaxed to the max, we got dried off, clothed, and ready.

Our first stop was to check in on our children, Jamie, who had just turned six, Charlie, who was just over two, and our ward, Lizzie, who was now sixteen. They were all up and breakfasting in the family dining room on this floor of the White House Residence. They were with our live-in nanny, Nadine Alexis, her middle sister, Francine, who had the job of being my far-hotter FLOTUS double, and their youngest sister, Colette, who was my press secretary. All three sisters were A-Cs and lived in the White House with us, and they liked to breakfast together with the kids whenever they could.

"Raj asked me to let him know as soon as you were up, dressed, and had eaten," Francine said. "Both of you. Should I advise him now?"

"Sure," Jeff said as he sat down between Jamie and Lizzie and pulled Charlie onto his lap.

Wanted to ask if this was about White House business or something else. Rajnish Singh was an A-C who'd been bored out of his mind at New Delhi Base but had been ignored because he had troubadour talent. Troubadours affected people by modulating their voices, expressions, body language, and so forth. Meaning they were great actors and politicians, and both professions had been looked down up on by the residents of Alpha Four.

Here, however, I'd found them and started giving them jobs to do, like impersonating people, handling our press and PR, and similar. But I wasn't the only one who'd felt that the troubadours were being unfairly pushed aside and that they could do so much more for their people and their country and, now, their planet, if they were merely organized and focused.

Like Raj, Francine and Colette were also troubadours. And they were part of the very clandestine but also very cool A-C CIA, which was made up of mostly troubadours, with some empaths, imageers, regular A-Cs, and even a few humans thrown in. I was considered an honorary member.

Raj was the number two guy in that organization and he was also the number two guy in this one, because he'd been made Jeff's Chief of Staff. So, him wanting to talk to us could be about the State of the Union address or it could be about something far less threatening. Or even something more threatening.

We didn't have to wait long to find out. Being an A-C, Raj used hyperspeed to get to us from wherever in the complex he'd been—the lower dining room, if I was going to take a guess, since that's where all the White House staff, both ours and those who came with the building, so to speak, ate when they weren't with us in the family dining room, the State dining room, or some other dining area. There were a lot of places to meet and eat in this complex, especially a lot most regular people didn't know about, because the complex went down several floors, most of which weren't talked about much.

But, wherever he'd been, Raj was with us in about ten seconds. "We need to talk, just the three of us," he said as he entered the room.

Jeff's eyes narrowed. "What is it? And why can't I feel what it is?"

"I'm testing the newest empathic blocker. You should be able to circumvent it, but I'm not allowed to tell you how. However, you need to do that circumventing elsewhere."

Jeff sighed. "The things we do to overcome our enemies."

Raj shrugged. "It's a living."

Jeff and I gave the kids kisses. "We'll be back soon," I

reassured. Not that I was positive that would be the case, but the kids were coming with us to the State of the Union address, so we'd have time together at least in the car.

We went right back over to our rooms. "What's going on?" Jeff asked as he closed the doors behind us. "And why the hell are you using a new piece of tech today of all days? I think I have enough stress going today."

"Sorry, but you're about to have more." Raj turned on the television to a major station.

"We have reports coming in that the location for today's State of the Union address," the Serious Newscaster said, "Cape Canaveral, will be the focus of a terrorist attack."

The camera feed switched and we were looking at an elderly, apple-cheeked man with white hair and long, muttonchops sideburns. He looked kindly. He wasn't. He was the religious leader of the most hateful, intolerant people in, these days, the world. Farley Pecker, Pastor to the Haters, Leader of the Club 51 True Believers.

"The one true God will strike down these demons, these blasphemers, these *aliens*," he spat the last word. "God will destroy their ship, the ship that they created to go find *more* of these aliens to bring back to Earth. To *our* world. The world that belongs only to humanity! Those who help to destroy this evil will be commended to the highest ranks of heaven, for they alone do God's work!"

During the thunderous applause, the feed went back to the Serious Newscaster. "Intelligence reports confirm that the Club Fifty-One True Believers organization is planning a massive attack on Earth's first long-range spacecraft, the *Distant Voyager.* We go live to the Pentagon, right after these commercial messages."

"Why the hell was I not told about this?" Jeff asked.

"No idea," Raj said. "Director Reynolds and Director Curran have both received intelligence reports, but nothing to indicate an attack of this nature and at this time. They've spoken with the rest of those involved in counterterrorism and defense, as well as the heads of the other Alphabet Agencies, and no one has any intel that would indicated an attack of this magnitude." Charles Reynolds was the Director of the CIA and my best guy friend since ninth grade. Tom Curran was the Director of the FBI. Normally, a terrorist threat of this magnitude would have gotten them out of bed early.

"What about Mister Joel Oliver?" I asked. Oliver was truly the top investigative reporter on the planet. He'd been a laughingstock because he'd been insisting that the A-Cs had been here as long as they had and were doing the things they were doing. Once we were outed, during Operation Destruction, Oliver was given a lot more respect. But he was still the top man in his field.

"He has the same intel as Directors Reynolds and Curran. Nothing of this magnitude, nothing happening here, nothing happening today."

The commercials ended and the news came back, showing us a female reporter standing outside the Pentagon. "I'm here reporting on the latest terrorist threat focused on the President's State of the Union address. We can't get anyone at the Pentagon to give us any answers," the Investigative Newsgal said. "We're not sure if they're stonewalling us or just working frantically to stop this threat."

"What the hell?" Jeff asked, as she started repeating what the Serious Newscaster had said earlier. "What is going on?"

A suspicion formed. "Raj, take off the emotional whatever you have on or turn it off. I think we've missed something."

"Like a viable terrorist threat," Raj muttered, as he fiddled with something in his breast pocket.

Jeff jerked. "Ah. I see why you wore that. Sorry. And, turn it back on, please."

Raj managed a chuckle. "Yes, I'm really upset. This has blindsided us, and I have nothing for you—we had today planned out and now . . . this." He looked at me. "The other agency has nothing like this, either." Meaning the A-C CIA was also blindsided.

"I'm sure we don't. But, again, I think we're missing something, and it's not good intelligence gatherers. What I think we've forgotten is the fact that this station is owned by Yates-Corp. What are the other stations saying?"

"Well, they're all running this story now," Raj replied. "But this is the station that broke the story."

"Uh huh. And the ways the news is today, when one outlet makes a bold statement, the others just pick it up and run with it, they don't investigate first."

"What, are you saying we don't have a terrorist attack to worry about?" Jeff asked.

"No, we do. But what I'm saying is that this is the terrorist attack."

Both men stared at me. "What?" Raj asked finally.

"Dude, you must be really stressed out of your mind, because you're usually faster than this. Jeff, too. I'm saying that this news story—this *fake* news story, I see I'm forced to add—*is* the terrorist attack. And it's working, too."

Gini Koch lives in Hell's Orientation Area (aka Phoenix, Arizona), works her butt off (sadly, not literally) by day, and writes by night with the rest of the beautiful people. She lives with her awesome husband, three dogs (aka The Canine Death Squad), and two cats (aka The Killer Kitties). She has one very wonderful and spoiled daughter, who will still tell you she's not as spoiled as the pets (and she'd be right), and a fun son-in-law who doesn't seem to mind that his mother-in-law is just this side of crazy.

When she's not writing, Gini spends her time cracking wise, staring at pictures of good looking leading men for "inspiration," teaching her pets to "bring it," and driving her husband insane asking, "Have I told you about this story idea yet?" She listens to every kind of music 24/7 (from Lifehouse to Pitbull and everything in between, particularly Aerosmith and Smash Mouth) and is a proud comics geek-girl willing to discuss at any time why Wolverine is the best superhero ever (even if Deadpool does get all the best lines).

You can reach Gini via her website (www.ginikoch.com), email (gini@ginikoch.com), Facebook (facebook.com/Gini.Koch), Facebook Fan Page: Hairspray & Rock 'n' Roll (www.facebook.com/GiniKochAuthor), Pinterest (www.pinterest.com/ginikoch), Twitter (@GiniKoch), or her Official Fan Site, the Alien Collective Virtual HQ (thealiencollectivevirtualhq.blogspot.com/).